DECEMBER

Also by Phil Rickman

CRYBBE
CANDLENIGHT
THE MAN IN THE MOSS

PHIL RICKMAN

DECEMBER

PAN BOOKS

First published 1994 by Macmillan

This edition published 1995 by Pan Books
an imprint of Macmillan General Books
25 Eccleston Place, London SW1W 9NF
and Basingstoke

Associated companies throughout the world

ISBN 0 330 33677 0

1 3 5 7 9 8 6 4 2

A CIP catalogue record for this book is available from
the British Library

Typeset by CentraCet Limited, Cambridge
Printed and bound in Great Britain by
Cox & Wyman Ltd, Reading, Berkshire

Author's Note

The Abbey may prove difficult to find; other locations are not. The Holy Mountain, Ysgyryd Fawr – the Skirrid – noses out of the lushly mysterious area where Gwent (South Wales) blends with Herefordshire (England) beyond the friendly market town of Abergavenny, scene of the notorious massacre of December 1175. Well worth a visit.

Although events and characters from both *The Man in the Moss* and *Crybbe* are referred to in *December*, this novel is not a sequel to either. In the Unseen world, many strange connections may be formed . . .

Prologue

Prologue

I

Cemented in Blood

DECEMBER 8, 1980

By the time he makes the doorman's office, his glasses have come off, and blood and tissue and stuff are emptying urgently from his mouth.

He falls.

He lies in the blood on the office floor, and he doesn't move. A short while later, two cops are turning him over, real careful, and seeing the blood around the holes – four holes, maybe five. And then they're carrying him, bloody face up, out to the patrol car, leaving behind these puddles and blotches on the doorman's floor.

Normal way of things, these cops wouldn't move a man in such poor condition. The state of this one, it's clear there's going to be no premium in hanging around for an ambulance.

'This guy is dying,' one cop says.

When they raised him up, the doorman thought he heard a sound like the snapping of bones.

It's just after eleven p.m.

Somewhere out there in the night, Dave hears what he thinks is the snapping of twigs. And the twigs are talking, crackling out words.

death oak,

Say the twigs.

Dave's under the swollen branches of some old tree. *Not* an oak tree. But twigs in the copse are crackling the words, and they come as this weird rasp on the night wind, and he hears the echo of a barn owl across the valley, and the owl – he'd swear – is screeching,

death oak.

*

3

Between the shadowy mesh of bare branches and broken stone arches, Dave can see the lights inside the Abbey.

The Abbey is old and ruinous. A glowering heap of twelfth-century stone, which by day is the raw, wind-soured pink of an old farmer's skin. By night – like now – it's mainly black, a jagged and knobbly rearing thing among the wooded border hills flanking the Skirrid, the holy mountain of Gwent. Legend says the Skirrid was pulled apart by a massive seismic shudder at the very moment of Christ's crucifixion.

The shudders inside Dave tonight are not exactly seismic. But he wouldn't deny, standing trembling under the dripping tree, that he's coming apart.

In a corner of the ruins, incongruous as a heart inside a skeleton, is a stone tower built over the vaults where the monks stored wine imported from France. The studio's down here now, built into the vaults. A romantic, evocative place to record music. In the daytime. In summer. Maybe.

At night, in winter, forget it.

Tonight, nervy lights were wobbling behind pimply, leaded glass as Dave spun away from the Abbey, hurling himself, sobbing, at the trees, his canvas shoes skidding on the winter-wet lawn. Clamping his hands over his ears, vibrating them as if he could somehow shake the phrase – *death oak* – out of his skull.

I can handle it, I can direct it, I can . . .

Ah, but you know you really can't.

See, the problem is, if you're in some way . . . *sensitive*, then people – the ones who don't think you're a phoney, or misguided or totally out of your tree – have this curious idea that you must be spiritually advanced. Serene. In control.

This means *not* running away.

Well, it's fine for *them* to talk, the ones who think it's a beautiful gift. They should be here tonight in this *holy* place.

And *we*, Dave thinks, should have listened to Tom Storey.

*

'What the fuck is *this*?'

Big Tom from Bermondsey, lead guitar, fearless on the frets, was wedged into the narrow, arched doorway at the top of the steps, roaring at everybody. Some of it was outrage. Most of it, Dave could tell, was panic.

In the studio, the churchy light, wavering.

About a dozen lighted candles in metal holders, brass and wooden candlesticks and saucers were spread out, apparently at random, around the whitewashed vault.

In the recording booths, candles burned. Little white snowdrop lights glimmered from ledges and amps. Melted wax was oozing down Lee Gibson's middle cymbal.

No other light than this. Looked quite cosy, Dave thought irrationally. A touch Christmassy.

And then he thought, No, it *could* be cosy. Somewhere else. Almost anywhere else. Anywhere but the Abbey of Ystrad Ddu, where it was said that every stone in the walls had been cemented with blood.

He'd followed Lee, Moira and Simon into the studio, and Moira had stopped at the bottom of the steps and said quietly, 'I don't like *this*.' And now Tom wouldn't come through the door.

Dave looked at Moira and mouthed a word: joke?

'Well, I'm no' laughing,' Moira said out of the side of her mouth.

She was young and moon-pale, wearing a long dark velvet dress and a lustrous silver headband and glowing far brighter, for Dave, than the candles.

'OK.' Simon St John strolled languidly into the centre of the studio. 'If whoever did this is listening from anywhere, we're all suitably terrified, aren't we, Dave?'

'Er . . . yeh. Right. Crapping ourselves.' Dave looked at Simon and Simon raised an eyebrow, probably signalling that Dave should remember tonight's motto, which was, Don't Worry Tom.

Dave nodded.

'Come on down, Tom. Come on.' Simon sounding as if he

5

was calling a dog. 'Nothing to worry about, squire. Nothing sinister. Somebody taking the piss, that's all.'

Simon, smooth and willowy, had credibility. While it was acknowledged that Tom was the best musician, he was still a *rock* musician. Whereas Simon was, er, classically trained, actually. Plus, he was public-school educated, a laid-back, well-spoken guy, a calming influence. Serene? Did a good impression, anyway.

Tom looked nervously from side to side, like he was on the edge of a fast road, and then came down, making straight for the metal stand where his solid-bodied Telecaster guitar sat. He snatched up the Telecaster and strapped it on, like armour. He was tense as hell.

'Joke, right?' The brash young session drummer, Lee Gibson, had followed Tom down the steps. Lee was not a full member of the band, lacking the essential qualifications – i.e. he was too close to normal.

Dave began to count the candles, becoming aware of this rich, fatty smell. The candles had been burning a while and dripping. Christmas was wrong; the studio looked like a chapel of rest awaiting a body. Except in a chapel of rest, the candles wouldn't be . . .

'Black!' Tom let out this hoarse yelp, flattening himself instinctively against a wall. 'Fucking things are *black*! You call that a bleeding joke?'

Dave finished counting. Thirteen. Oh *hell*.

'Hey, come on, candles can be protective, too,' Moira said uncertainly.

'Bullshit.' The wavy light was kinder to Moira than to Tom. His eyes were puffy, heavy moustache spread across his mouth like a squashed hedgehog. 'Bull*shit*!' Clamping his Telecaster to his gut, its neck angled on a couple of candles like a rifle.

The flames of the two candles, dripping on to adjacent amps, seemed to flare mockingly.

'Brown,' Lee Gibson said. 'They're only dark brown, see?'

Dave peered at one. It looked black enough to him, and it smelled like a butcher's shop in August. Also – and this wasn't

6

obvious because several were concealed by the partitions around individual booths – if you stood in the centre of the studio floor, you could see the candles had been arranged in almost a perfect circle. If this was a wind-up, somebody had gone to a lot of trouble.

Be totally pointless organizing a witch-hunt. This was a residential recording studio, people coming and going, silent, discreet, like the medieval monks who'd built the Abbey.

'Fuck's sake, man, they only *look* black.' Lee had on leather trousers and a moleskin waistcoat over his bare chest, a guy already shaping his own legend. Clearly anxious to get started; this session would be crucial to his career-projection.

Tom regarded him with contempt. 'Thank you, son.' A warning rumble Dave had heard before; he tensed. 'That makes me feel so much better,' Tom said. And then spasmed.

'Hey, man . . .' Lee reeling back '. . . fuck's *sake*!' as Tom swung round, his guitar neck sweeping a candle from an amplifier stack. It spun in the air before dropping into a heap of lyric sheets on the floor. Cold flames spurted.

Nobody spoke. Simon walked over and calmly stamped on the papers. Meanwhile Russell Hornby, the producer, had slid noiselessly into the studio.

'OK, guys. Let's become calm, shall we?' Russell was slight and bald. He wore dark glasses, even at night.

'Russell,' Tom snarled, 'this is the end of the line, my son. We are packing up. You are getting us out. We have taken enough of this shit.'

'Excuse me,' Russell said blandly, 'but surely this "shit" is part of the object of the exercise, isn't it?'

'Hang on.' Dave picked up one of the candles. It felt nasty, greasy, like a fatty bone. 'Are you saying *you* did this, Russell? These are your candles?'

'Dave, you think I'd cut my own throat? Nor, before you ask, do I know who's responsible for the blasted *lightbulbs* bursting last night. Nor the apparent *blood* on the *dinner plates*. Nor even your inability, Dave, to keep a guitar tuned for five minutes.'

He snatched the candle from Dave and blew at it. The candle stayed alight. Russell threw it to the stone floor and crushed it with his heel. 'Now, what I suggest is we get rid of them before we're in breach of fire regulations, yeah? And then let's go to work.'

This guy was well chosen, Dave thought. If you were putting four musicians with *special qualities* – one of Russell's slightly sneering phrases – into a *situation* as potentially *volatile* as this, you needed a producer who was calm, efficient, businesslike and about as sensitive as a shower-attendant at Auschwitz.

'Look,' Russell said reasonably. 'Let's not overreact. It's been a difficult week . . .'

'"Difficult",' Dave said. 'That's a good word, Russell.'

'. . . But I take it none of us wants to have to start all over again, yeah? So I suggest we bolt the doors against any marauding ghouls, restless spirits and whatever the word is for those things alleged to move the furniture around . . . and give me something I can mix.'

'*I'll* give you something you can fucking mix . . .' Tom advanced on Russell, his face pulsing electrically in the unsteady candlelight.

'Stop it!' Moira had marched between them and stamped her foot. 'Tom, you're taking this far too seriously. And Russell, you're not taking *us* seriously enough. Nobody's asking you to believe in the paranormal, just don't be so damn superior and contemptuous of people who do, OK?'

Oh God, Dave thought, I love her.

Everybody had gone quiet. 'Yeah, well, that's all I've got to say,' Moira said. She came and stood by Dave. He felt her warm breath on his ear, essence of heathery moors sloping down to long white beaches and a grey, grey sea, and he thought he was going to pass out with the longing.

'Come on then.' Snapping out of it, slapping his thighs with both hands. 'Let's get rid of the buggers.' Dave padded around the studio, blowing out the remaining candles, collecting them up. Afterwards his hands felt like he was wearing slimy rubber gloves. Yuk, horrible! He piled the candles into a corner, feeling slightly sick.

Someone put on the electric lights, and Russell Hornby took Tom into another corner and talked placatingly at him until, at last, the big guy shambled to his feet, his brass-studded guitar strap still over his shoulder like the bridle on a shire horse.

'Right, then. Four hours.' Tom jabbed a big, hard finger at Russell. 'And then I'm out of here, no arguments.' Tom was the only one of them staying in a hotel, to be with his wife.

He stared balefully at the rest of them before stumping off to the payphone in the passage. They heard him bawling down the phone, telling the long-suffering Deborah when to pick him up. 'Yeah, main gate, say 'bout half four, quarter to five . . . Yeah, yeah . . . Too right.'

'Guy's got no consideration whatsoever,' Moira said. 'Eight months gone, Jesus, she needs all the sleep she can get. I mean, how's he know what the roads are gonna be like by then?'

Dave was wishing *he* was driving back to a hotel ten miles away. There to lie with Moira, warm and naked in his arms and smelling of heather and salt-spray and . . .

He stifled a moan. It was only these little Moira fantasies that kept him sane. He watched her pick up her guitar, one of the new Ovations with a curving fibreglass body. She began to sing softly.

. . . the doors are all barred, the candles are smothered . . .

Her tune, his lyric. He loved watching her soft lips shape his words, eyes downcast over the guitar, the black hair swaying like velvet curtains drawn across an open window.

. . . and nobody wants to hear Aelwyn . . .

Moira's lips had touched his own just once, in greeting – Hi, Dave, mmmmph – but a man could hope.

When Tom slouched back into the studio and grumpily shouldered his guitar, they all wandered into their booths and pushed on with it, prisoners of the small print on their contract.

. . . this album shall be recorded exclusively and entirely at the Abbey Studios, North Gwent, between midnight and dawn.

The great experiment initiated and financed by Max Goff, founder and managing director of Epidemic Independent Records UK Ltd and student of the Unexplained, the man who maintained that: *Music is the only art form that's also a spiritual force.*

Outside, the wind might have been moaning a little, although you wouldn't know it in the sealed capsule of the studio, but it was really quite a mild night. For December.

But it was cold out on the hills, and there was snow, and he had no cloak; he could feel neither his fingers nor his toes in his worn-out boots, and the sweat froze on his face as he ran towards the distant light, a candle in a window slit.

At least the killing wind was with him. The wind blew at his back and speeded his footsteps, though he stumbled many times and knew his hands and face had been opened and the blood frozen in the wounds.

His ears always straining for the sound of other footsteps on the icy track, the clamour of men and horses . . . knowing the wind which speeded his flight would also speed their pursuit, these murdering, damned ewe-fuckers . . .

Final track, side-one, live take: 'The Ballad of Aelwyn Breadwinner.' In which, absorbing the subtle emanations, we retell the tragic tale of the famous medieval Celtic martyr in the very place where he was so brutally cut down by Norman soliders in the year 1175.

Let's get this over.

In his personal booth, hugging his Martin guitar, eyes closed, Dave *was* Aelwyn. But Aelwyn was alone, while Dave could hear Simon on safe, plodding bass, Tom's low, undulating guitar. And there was Moira's voice in his cans, soft and low and dark as Guinness. He could feel the closeness of her, closer than sex; she was in his head, she was with him on the frozen hills, as he ran from the soldiers and mercenaries, wondering if he would even feel it as they cut him down with their blades of ice. The cold from the song, the all-shrouding inevitability of imminent death, the end of everything, was around him in the booth, his bare arms tingling as he played.

When the cans went funny, Moira was playing soft, gliding, rhythm guitar and singing counterpoint – an ethereal voice, distant on the winter wind. The voice from the holy mountain guiding Aelwyn to safety.

Aelwyn had been very tired, tramping through the snow towards the Abbey. Had known they were coming for him, but simply hadn't the strength to run any more. But he also knew that when he reached the Abbey he'd be OK. Even these bastards were not going to smash their way into the house of God, especially not *this* house of God, founded upon the site of a famous Holy Vision.

This was where the cans went funny. Where other voices came in, as though, as sometimes happened, a radio signal had got into the system.

She couldn't hear what the voices were saying. She carried on playing and singing but looked out of the glass panel in the partition around the booth. Nobody came out on to the studio floor waving his hands. In the booth opposite, Dave played on. Maybe – she didn't understand too much technical stuff – Russell and Barney, the engineer, were not picking up the extraneous voices on their tape.

So Moira played on, too.

The band had rehearsed the song several times today. She figured she was pretty much immune to the ending by now, but she'd still been feeling tension on Dave's behalf. Dave was not what you'd call a great singer but he sure could get himself into a role. For now, for the duration of this song, Dave was Aelwyn and Aelwyn was Dave, and the last sound she'd heard before

11

the voices intruded was his breath coming harder, and she'd felt the fatigue and the creeping sense of cold despair as Aelwyn realized he wasn't going to make it.

But surely . . . he *could* have made it.

This strange thought came to Moira just as the lights dimmed outside the booth.

She leaned forward on her stool, still playing, and peered out through the glass. All was indistinct: tumbling shadows, the snaking flex and rubber leads were like roots and vines, the amplifier stacks like black rocks. As she watched there were three small explosions in the sky, lightbulbs blowing silently in the ceiling, like the dying of distant worlds.

Under her fingers, the guitar strings felt cold and sharp like the edges of blades. As the bulbs went out, several small, blue-white spearpoint flames flared in the middle distance.

This would be the corner where Dave had laid the candles, some still upright in trays and holders. All of them snuffed.

All of them snuffed.

Oh *no* . . .

II

Electric Grief

He saw . . .
. . . a fortress: massive, dark, forbidding, ungiving – a *Bastille* of a place. It rose in billows, a towering mushroom of smoke, lighted windows appearing, and peaks and gables forming out of the smog. Overpowering. Dizzying. And warped, like through a fisheye lens. Like it was swaying before it toppled on to him. Or somebody.

He heard a roaring, shot through with vivid screams, like thunderclouds speared by lightning forks.

And more.

Through the glass side of his booth, he'd seen the dead candles flickering, triumphant.

Heard the voices hissing,
deathoak

Still hearing, from somewhere, Moira's voice against the elements, but the words were inaudible, the only words he could make out were *death oak* suspended in the tight studio acoustic, and he was sure that if he looked hard enough, he would see the words light up, blinking in the smoky space like neon, like the cold fingernails of fire at the tips of the candles.

And he was so cold.

And then an explosion of lights and he was looking up at the fortress. Monster of a building. Bit like one of those French whatsits, châteaux. But too big to be an original and not so delicate. Overwhelming. Forbidding – kind of Victorian Gothic.

And then blackness. Deep, throbbing blackness.
And someone saying,
this guy is dying.

Outside now, clinging to the tree, Dave vaguely remembers unslinging the Martin, letting it fall, bolting out of his booth.

Still hearing it, *death oak*, as he rushed at the rear door, seeing Russell and his engineer, Barney, on their feet in the control room, behind the glass panel, mouths moving, no sound. Passing the booth containing Tom, hunched, red-faced, doubled up over the Telecaster, as if his appendix was bursting or something, the guitar bansheeing from the amp.

Plunging through the rear door into the stone passage, his legs weak and cold, like poor bloody Aelwyn's. Dashing across the lawn towards the trees, for shelter.

Sanctuary.

Realizing now how perishing cold he is, slumped under the dripping tree in his T-shirt, canvas shoes soaked through. But not cold like Aelwyn and not cold like . . . who?

Now, out here on the edge of the wood, comes another voice, the only voice he ever wants to hear.

'Tell me about it. Davey, for God's sake . . .'

He mumbles, 'I love you.'

'Davey . . .!'

He opens his eyes, sees concern furrowing her forehead. She's edged with gold from the lights in the house, and he's starting to cry, just wanting to hold her and lose himself in the dark wildwood of her hair. Drunk with relief, he's burbling through the tears, 'Oh God, I love you, Moira, I really love you.'

'Davey, listen, something awful bad's going down.'

'Can we go away together? I really do love you, Moira. Can we . . .?'

'Sure. Oh, Davey, please, you have to tell me what you saw.'

'If I tell you, can we go away?'

14

'Oh Jesus, Davey,' Moira says ruefully. 'I think we'll all be going away soon.'

Ten minutes later, she's saying, 'Where? Where was this?'

'I couldn't tell you. I'm sorry. How long have I been out here?'

'An hour. Maybe more. We couldny find you. Davey, think yourself back. Come on now.'

Moira is standing on the edge of the lawn, shivering in her stupid black velvet frock, the kind of frock fortune tellers wear at the village fête. The session broken up into chaos and recriminations, Russell throwing up his hands, Lee hurling his drumsticks at the wall. Not everybody wanting even to look for Dave.

Dave says, 'What about you?'

'I . . . I can't remember, Davey,' Moira lies. 'Like a bad dream after you wake up, and, like, all you recall is the atmosphere.'

Oh God, she's thinking, why'd we agree to come here?

It was really wonderful, at first, this band. Communal therapy, sitting in a circle like an encounter group, exchanging wild tales over gallons of tea and coffee. Incredibly reassuring to know there are other people like you: Simon, kind and diffident and mixed up sexually. Tom, like so many of these guitar virtuosos, a touch unbalanced (OK, *very unbalanced*) but with this grumpy charm. And Davey. Soft-centred and funny, and he fancies you madly . . .

We were a good band. We were getting along, we really cooked musically. Because we have problems in common, *a* problem. Some people would say it's a gift; some people would say a club foot's a gift. But, as the old saying goes, a problem shared is a problem halved.

So why, in the *sanctified* atmosphere of the Abbey – forgetting for the moment about all this steeped in blood stuff – is a problem shared turning out to be a problem enhanced and multiplied?

Dave's shaking his head. 'Traffic? Lights?'

'Traffic-lights, Davey?'

'No, traffic – and lights. People . . . People shouting. Wailing. Somebody hurt, maybe.'

'Man or a woman?'

'Or dead. Dead, I think. I don't know.'

'What about the wailing? Why are they wailing? This is no' Aelwyn, is it? I mean, this is nothing to do with . . .'

'Shock.' Shaking his head. 'Shock and grief . . . kind of an – electric grief. Hundreds of people. Not wailing. Singing? But not happy. Not happy singing, y' know?'

Moira's eyes, adjusted to the lack of light, can see him clearly now. He's looking awful cold, still in just his white T-shirt, sweat and mud stains on the chest. Gonna catch his death.

'Come back to the house, Davey.'

'Nnnn.' Shaking his head. Assuming that whatever brought this on is back there, waiting for him, and he might not be wrong. Mumbling again, eyes squeezed shut.

'OK, then,' Moira says calmly. 'Take me there.'

And he does.

'I'm looking down on it now . . . down *into* it . . . it's on all these different levels, and packed with, like, jutting, thrusting masonry . . . turrets, chimneys, spikes . . . like, if you fell into it, you'd impale yourself. You know what I . . .?'

Gently, she pulls his arms away from the tree, holds them, one in each hand. She can feel the goosebumps.

Dave says, 'A cupola kind of thing, glass sides. And below me, on the ground, a black . . . a rigid thing with black . . .'

'Petals,' Moira says suddenly, not thinking about it. 'It's a flower, right?'

'Yes. It's a black flower.'

'Metal?'

'A metal flower, right. And noise, rising up. Black noise. Lights that crash. Lights that scream. Heavy lights shattering. Christ, there's no *sequence* to this, it's . . .'

'I can't hear it, Davey.' Holding tight to his arms, the

16

coldness coming through, but nothing else. 'Let me in, Davey, let me help.'

But he's pulling away from her, as if he's been hit. Clutching at the tree, starting to slide slowly down its damp, knobbly trunk.

'Eyes.' Whimpering now. 'Me eyes are full of blood.'

Moira sees a torchbeam waving back and forth across the lawn. 'Simon? Tom? Help me, please. It's Dave, he's . . .'

This guy . . .

somebody says,

this guy is dying . . .

Really clearly. Saying it very simply, like it isn't something you can easily believe. A man says,

do you know who you are?

For a moment he's not sure. Darkness enfolding him, the metal petals of the black flower closing over his head. He tries to say something; his voice has gone. He tries to focus; his vision has grown grey and dim. Tries to move, but the petals are holding him. Tries to breathe. But there's no air.

this guy is dy—

The black flower has a waxy perfume.

Do you know who you are?

And, somewhere else, very softly, 'Davey . . .'

Crags and moorland and long white beaches. Grey seas and long white beaches, rocks wet

'Davey!'

with a splash of spray. Desperately, he throws himself into the spray.

'Dave Reilly.' Whispering. 'I'm Dave Reilly.' Gripping an overhanging branch.

'Simon, quick! Over here . . .'

He starts to breathe in the night, blinks. Feels the breeze. Blinks. Open his eyes as wide as they'll go.

Blinks again, frantic now. 'I can't see.' Brings a hand to his eyes in panic, keeps opening and shutting and rubbing them. 'Me glasses. Where's me glasses?' Looking blindly from side to side, up towards the branches, down towards the grass, starting to sob. 'Where's me bloody glasses?'

Bloody glasses. An unremarkable pair of tinted glasses, misted and opaque. Rimmed with blood.

In the car, the cop says, 'Do you know who you are?'

He can't talk. Just moans and nods. Of course he fucking knows.

Moira says gently, 'Davey, you don't *wear* glasses.'

'No.' Dave, calm again, opens his eyes very, very slowly and becomes aware of a very still winter night in the Black Mountains of Gwent. A night in December, two, three weeks off Christmas. A night with no visible moon, only lights from the Abbey fifty yards away, behind huge, black, stone arches like the ribcage of a dinosaur skeleton.

The Abbey: twelfth-century stone, a crackling log fire in the panelled hall, mulled wine in pewter mugs. And in a long, black velvet dress . . .

'Moira?'

'I'm here.'

He sees her face, touches her hair. Slowly shakes his head and begins to cry. 'I blew it. Moira, I buggered it up.'

Psychics cry more than most people, he's learned this.

Simon says, 'Dave?'

'He's OK now,' Moira says. 'I think he's OK. Tom?'

'Pretty much what you'd expect. Left him in the courtyard, marching round and round.'

'Go find him, huh? We'll all go.' Moira turning back towards the Abbey, the bastard place looking so benign with the glimmering lights in its downstairs windows.

At this point, the session drummer, Lee Gibson, joins them. He's carrying a long, black torch and grinning. 'What the fuck was all *that* about?'

'I cocked it up,' Dave says to Moira.

'Come on, Davey.' She doesn't want him talking about this in front of Lee.

'I screwed up.' Shaking his head from side to side. 'You know that. You were there.'

'Not really, Davey. I only caught the flower.'

'What have I done, Moira?'

'Leave it, Davey.'

'What have I fucking *done*?' Keeps rubbing his eyes as if he's expecting to lose his vision again.

Moira snaps, 'Stop it.'

Lee's shaking his head in disbelief, still grinning. 'You guys really kill me.'

Then, as they enter the courtyard, there's a bellowing scream. 'Poor bugger,' Dave mutters. 'We should've listened to him. Could you make out the circle? Did you see how many candles there were? Did you see what *kind* of candles?'

'Davey.' Moira's hissing through her teeth. 'Will you just *shut the fuck up*!'

Lee Gibson snorts with laughter. Can't blame him. We're all terminally neurotic bastards, far as he's concerned. He's a normal guy.

The tower house sprouts from a corner of the Abbey. There's a courtyard with a high stone wall, the fourth side open to the trackway, rough lawns either side of it. Three shadowy vehicles standing in the courtyard. Moira watches poor, frazzled Tom Storey stagger out from behind one of them, the mad bull looking for somebody to gore.

'Monks!' Tom's face is bulging in the beam of Lee's flashlight. 'Either side the gate. I'm telling you . . . two fucking *monks*.' And Moira shivers at this.

Russell, the producer, is watching from the doorway. What has he done to deserve this? From Russell's side of the fence it must be clear enough that whatever's scaring Tom would hold few fears for a halfway-decent clinical psychiatrist.

'Candles.' Tom shuddering and shaking like an old refrigerator. 'They was holding candles. Bastards.'

'Come on, squire.' Simon claps him on the back. 'We'll talk about it inside.'

'No *way*.' Tom snatching at Simon's arm. 'Time is it?'

'Half four-ish,' Moira says. 'Let's go down to the kitchen, make some tea, huh?'

Tom scowls. 'I'm getting out. Russell, keys.'

The big guy's feverish, incandescent – an unhealthy glow, like radium. 'Tom, listen . . .' Moira reckons that if all the lights suddenly went out they'd still be able to see him. 'You're no' fit to drive, believe me.'

Tom's face is truly ghastly in Lee's torchbeam, a Hallowe'en pumpkin. 'Russell, you don't gimme the keys to that Land Rover, I'll tear your fucking head off.'

Moira said, 'I think we should stop him, Russell.' But Russell only shrugs helplessly, goes back into the Abbey, shaking his shaven head at the futility of trying to reason with loonies. Just another normal guy.

Tom's already climbed into the Land Rover, now cranking down the window and shouting out gleefully, 'S'all right, keys are in.' There's a sudden, ludicrous blast of big band music over the courtyard, the Syd Lawrence Orchestra.

'. . . this shit?' Tom stabbing at the radio buttons, searching for the comfort of hard rock music. Then the scrapyard rattle of the engine. 'Debs shows up in the Lotus, tell her I already split, yeah?'

Moira says, 'Jesus, can she get into that thing in her condition? Tom, why don't you come down from there, call her?'

The Land Rover's headlights have bleared into life, under cakes of red mud; its wheels are spinning, flinging gravel at them. The radio, volume as high as it will go, says,

'. . . *believed to have been returning home to their apartment near Central Park when the gunman struck.*'

'Listen, my friends.' Simon guides them into a corner of the courtyard. 'I hope I'm not speaking out of turn here, but I think we should put the arm on Russell to wipe tonight's stuff.'

For a moment, Moira thinks she can see a ghastly white light at one of the tower windows, as if the Abbey is registering mild annoyance. The Land Rover clatters across the courtyard towards the main gate.

She sighs gratefully. 'Took the words out of my head. Will you tell him or will I?'

'Hey now . . .' Lee Gibson is not happy. 'Let's not be so friggin' hasty.' He's wearing an ankle-length army greatcoat now, over his moleskin waistcoat. 'Correct me if I got this wrong' – echoing Russell – 'but the whole point of the exercise is that something should get, you know, *stirred up*, right?'

'No, look.' Dave Reilly wanders shakily into Lee's torch-beam. 'Better idea. Let's scrap the lot. Wipe everything.'

'Wipe . . .?' Lee hurls his torch at the ground. The light doesn't go out; it plays on Dave's soaked trainers.

'We don't need this,' Dave says. 'Any of us.'

'Speak for your fucking self!' Lee ramming his hands into the pockets of his greatcoat. 'Wipe the tapes?' Flapping the skirts of his greatcoat. 'You can wipe my arse.'

Tail-lights wobble as the Land Rover hits the dirt track. Moira says softly, 'Lee, this is no' your problem, OK? You'll have the full fee, whatever happens.'

'I don't believe this.' Lee turns away in disgust. 'You bastards need putting away.'

Simon waits until the studio door has slammed behind Lee. 'Right. We're obviously not going on with this. I don't think we need a vote on it, do we?'

'I think we can safely speak for Tom.' Dave picks up Lee's torch. 'He won't be back. He's had it with invoking ghosts.'

'We all have, Dave. But if we walk away, we have to accept that's it for the band. Irreconcilable musical difference is, I think, the usual term. We'll have to say that.'

'Hang on,' Dave said, 'I don't think I understand.'

'It's simple. If we're still together as a band, Max Goff will sue us for breach of contract. He'll nail us to the wall. He'll know we can't afford the action – except for Tom, maybe, so he'll try and force us to come back.'

'Sod that,' says Dave.

'But if we've split up, he'll know there's no prospect of that. He may decide to write us off. What I thought . . . I'll . . . I'll go and see him myself. Come to an understanding.'

Simon's face, half-lit, is entirely without expression. Moira knows how much he hates Goff. She also knows that Goff does *not* hate genteel, willowy Simon. 'We'll all go,' she says carefully.

'No.' Simon's smile is sad, rueful. 'That wouldn't be appropriate. I'll do it.'

Moira watches the Land Rover's red tail-lights fading into the night mist. She looks up at the Abbey. As usual, it seems to be gazing down on her with an ancient knowledge and a frightening edge of derision. The part housing the studio has a single sawn-off tower, with windows where once, presumably, there were only slits. She looks to Dave, who shakes his head.

'Too small, too old. This was in a city, I think. Doesn't matter now, though, does it?'

Moira shakes her head too, knowing that neither of them believes it doesn't matter, and then she says what she ought to have said hours ago.

Dave, who just a minute ago thought he couldn't get any colder, cries out, 'No!'

'Listen.' Moira's is a lonely voice, but calm, all *too* calm. 'This has to be the real end. I mean, we're no' gonny work together again, are we?'

Adding, as if she can feel him reaching out for her, 'Davey, love, we're no' *safe* together. We're too much.'

'We need each other,' he protests hopelessly. Knowing she's shaking her head. He needs her; she doesn't need him. Or she wouldn't be saying this.

'You could've . . . come to some harm tonight, Davey. We've become unlucky. Simon knows that, don't you, Si?'

Simon doesn't reply. Moira says, more harshly, 'We're the band that should never've been, a bloody toxic cocktail. We *daren't* see each other again.'

Dave turns away, clenching his fists. Wanting to sob. He

doesn't, it would be despicable. How can he possibly walk away, and just forget about her? He's thinking, wish I'd died, like . . . like *who*?

He's looking towards the east, where there's no suggestion of a dawn. Around them, there's an unnatural silence, as if all three know what's coming next. As if they're all waiting for the sound which will prove how right Moira is and will snap the spine of the night.

In the long, heartsick days to come, Dave Reilly, approaching his twenty-seventh birthday, is going to drive himself half-crazy playing it all back. Always ending in tears. And flames.

It's as if time's mechanisms have gone haywire, all the shattering moments of the night occurring simultaneously in one endlessly distressing present-moment. The dark fortress and the broken glasses and a prolonged rending and mangling of metal. And Moira breathing, 'Jesus . . . no?' – an appeal for divine intercession in the split second *before* it happens.

Before they turn as one and run out of the entrance onto the slippery track leading into an oblivion of hills and forestry and starless sky, and it begins to rain.

Maybe two hundred yards along the dirt track, they see a lone, steamy headlight beam, pointing vaguely into the sky like a dying prayer and then dissipating into mist. A single, faraway scream is cruelly amplified by the valley, beneath it the distant, almost musical tinkle of collapsing glass, before the night gets sheared into streamers of orange and white.

Twenty yards away, the old blue Land Rover driven by Tom Storey has brought down a low, sleek Lotus Elan, like a lion with a gazelle. The Land Rover has torn into the Lotus and savaged it and its guts are out and still heaving, and Dave can see flames leaping into the vertical rain. A voice is talking crisply from the Land Rover's radio, but he can't hear what it's saying for Simon's wounded cry,

'Oh, Jesus, look . . .'

On the fringe of the burning tableau, surreal in the remote

rural night, a large, shadowy, lumbering, crumbling thing is half carrying, half dragging a lumpy, sagging bundle and babbling to it,

'Debs, Debs, Debsie, Debs, s'gonna be OK, Debsie, s'OK . . .'

guy's got no consideration . . . Eight months gone . . . Jesus, can she get into that thing, her condition . . .?

There's a blast of hard, golden heat from the wreckage; Tom is thrust forward as if he's been kicked in the small of the back and drops his awful, pitiful burden. Both sleeves of his jacket burst spectacularly into flames, shoulders to cuffs.

As Dave runs towards the heat, a smut floats into his left eye, forcing him to close both of them. He feels like he's entering hell, hearing Tom bellowing, the hiss of flames and rain and then – like the voice of the Old Testament God from the burning bush – the Land Rover's radio voice, heavy with history.

'*. . . and to recap, if you've just joined us, it's now been confirmed that the former Beatle, John Lennon, has died after a shooting incident outside the Dakota apartment block in New York where he and his wife . . .*'

Part One

November 1994

I

Darkness at the Break of . . .

Maybe you read in the papers about what happened in Liverpool on the 13th of December 1993. Well, anyway, I was there. In the middle of it. Scared me a lot. Not so much at the time – it happened in full daylight. In fact it's taken me nearly a year to get a perspective on it, but it still . . .

Crap. Crap, crap, crap.

Scrub it.

Wasn't what he wanted to write, anyway. Really, he wanted to pour it all out about Jan and the tragic black bonnet business and what it had done to them. But where would that get him? And also . . . it would be *pathetic*.

Nearly as bad as his usual *please contact me* letters, which, getting no replies, had been followed up – weeks, months, years going by – with the *please, please, please . . . just get in touch, write, phone, carrier pigeon, anything . . .*

Talk about pathetic . . .

Start again.

Dear Moira,

Liverpool. December 13, 1993. I know it was nearly a year ago, but bear with me. Even if you read about it in the papers, the significance would probably pass you by. For everybody here, it was like an act of God. Picture the scene. God's at a loose end one afternoon. Spots Liverpool out of the corner of an all-seeing eye and He thinks, Yeah, why not . . .

Or – what about this? – He notices one of His less successful creations strolling along Whitechapel towards the

29

guitar shop and He thinks . . . that's bloody Dave Reilly, let's see if he gets the message this time.

And then He glances at His watch (one of those fancy ones, tells you when it's teatime in Paraguay), does a little countdown, points His finger and He says, out the corner of His mouth, 'OK . . . LET THERE BE DARKNESS!'

Too whimsical. You've probaby lost her already, pal. If it even reaches her.

This was the other problem. He could never be sure the letters and postcards and Christmas cards and birthday cards were even getting through.

No replies. Could be she thought even communications by post could reawaken things better left comatose, but Dave was buggered if *he* could see it. Whenever he was locked out in the night, he wrote to Moira. This amounted to a lot of letters.

He'd tried ringing this feller in Glasgow, Malcolm Kaufmann, the agent, but he was always 'in a meeting', according to his secretary.

Could Mr Kaufmann perhaps call back?

Aw, the secretary said, between you and me, you'll be waiting for ever for Mr Kaufmann to call back. My advice would be to write . . .

And write. And write.

Maybe Moira had directed that all the envelopes addressed in Dave Reilly's handwriting should go directly into the bin. Dave had thought of this some while back and had one typed, but no reaction to that either; maybe she thought it was a bill.

And yet, even though he'd never seen her since the morning of the 9th of December 1980, she was always there for him. Kind of. For instance, there was the time, after the humiliating failure of his solo album in 1987, when, facing the prospect of having to get a Proper Job and no qualifications, he'd sat down at the piano in Ma's front room, started plonking the keys, putting on his poshest McCartney voice.

Moira My Dear,
I am reaching out in desperation
Please . . .

And thought, out of the blue, You know, you could survive on this for a bit. If you can't be original, why not take
the piss out of people who can? And while you might not be
technically as good at it as some, there are ways you can make
up for that. Like going into the quiet place, absorbing the
essences . . .

Look, the only way I can handle this thing, he'd once said
to Moira, is to try and channel it into creativity. To make
something lasting and positive out of it. Isn't that what art is?

Ah, the idealism of youth. Maturity tells you that if all that
comes back in your face, if you can't make anything lasting and
positive out of it, don't mess around . . . put it into something
negative and transient.

Yes. Well. No wonder Moira had looked distinctly dubious.

Anyway, I was in town that day, Monday, December 13, for a little
gig (I'm not going to tell you where it was, I do have some pride).

I'd gone to buy a few sets of strings at this little music shop which
sells me them in bulk. The guy there was trying to flog me a
secondhand acoustic guitar, a Takamine – Japanese, brilliant built-
in pick-up with sound-balancing, everybody's using them, ultra-
reliable – you know the way they go on.

But I was in a relatively good mood. For the time of year. It's
always a relief when the 8th of December goes past and nothing
destroys me. So, anyway, I was giving it a go, this guitar, and for
some reason I started playing 'Julia', the Lennon song off the White
Album, the one introducing Yoko to his dead mother. The one I
never could rewrite for laughs.

Well, I must have been feeling wistful, you know how it is. I
was doing the voice, which is John at his most ethereal. I always
like the opening of that one – about half of what he says being
meaningless, but he says it just to reach you, Julia . . . It's so

31

personal and spiritual, much more so than the self-indulgent primal scream stuff on the Plastic Ono Band album.

Anyway, it was just after one o'clock, everybody buggering off for lunch, the pubs filling up, and I'm perching on an amplifier, droning out 'Julia', feeling unusually . . . wistful (I can't get away from this bloody word 'wistful', but you know what I mean, kind of coasting on memory, but nothing more complicated than that . . . or so I thought) and I remember looking down and seeing something glistening on the curve of the guitar, just above the pick-up, a blob of liquid, and then another one landed next to it.

Plop.

Well, of course, it was a bloody tear, wasn't it?

I was really embarrassed. But at least it was Liverpool, where more tears have been shed into more pints over that bastard . . .

Anyway, the feller who runs the shop comes over – he'd been watching me, not saying a word. So when he sees I've finally noticed him, he wanders across, big grin. 'Got to buy it now, matey, you've christened the bugger. That'll be nine hundred and thirty five quid, including discount.'

I'm thinking, You dickhead. Not him, me.

Then the lights go out.

Bang.

You're never going to send this, pal. Might as well admit it. You're just tormenting yourself.

Dave was writing it on the card table in his old bedroom at Ma's bungalow in Hoylake, on the Wirral, where the seagulls cruised past the window and crapped on the glass.

Always used to stay here when he was working clubs and pubs in Liverpool and the North West, even though it depressed the hell out of him. Now, with the Jan thing on the blink, he was killing time, gearing up for a final rescue bid.

In a situation like this, he always wrote to Moira, which was as much use as writing to Santa Claus and sending it up the chimney, but must be therapeutic because he was unloading it, like – presumably – spilling it all to an analyst.

On the wall, directly facing him, was a reproachful picture of the matryred John Lennon, going yellow now, like the adjacent poster from inside the Beatles' White Album, which, twenty years ago he'd – presciently, no doubt – had framed in black.

In fact, apart from his own artwork for the first Philosopher's Stone album, the room was still the way it had been when he was a student, back when the world was innocent. 'When you're famous,' his ma used to say, 'I'll open it to the public at a fiver a time.'

Even she must be realizing the prospect of Dave becoming famous was about as likely now as the seagulls flying off to crap somewhere else.

The old girl had a man friend these days and went off on regular 'dates' in this feller's ancient Morris Oxford, sometimes staying out all night. She was seventy.

Before Jan, Dave had lived for brief periods with four women, all of whom had known about him or learned very quickly. (The sudden coldness of the bedroom sometimes in the early hours, the way owls would always find them, even in the city.) Initially they'd been excited by it. It was his bit of 'charisma'. (Moira used to talk, quite cynically, about her 'glamour'.) But it faded fast.

If he was ever to trap some happiness, it could only be with a woman he couldn't frighten, and he'd only ever met one, and among her last words to him had been the endlessly echoing

we're no gonny see each other again, ever.

And she'd never replied to his letters.

I mean all the lights went out. Everywhere.

Remember Dylan's line about darkness at the break of noon. This one was just over an hour after noon, but I'll get to that.

Well, obviously, we thought it was just the shop, at first. I said, 'You shouldn't keep waiting for the red bill, Percy, sometimes they forget.' Then we go out into the street and everybody's lights have gone, and I can hear this terrible screeching of brakes from the main road around the corner – I mean, not just one screech but a whole chorus of screeches, and it's obvious what's happened – the bloody traffic lights have all gone out.

Well, I couldn't have bought Percy's Takamine even if I'd had the money – the bloody till wouldn't work. So I walk out into the centre of town, and it's like the end of the world's been announced. Some people are really panicking – I mean, everybody's had a power cut at home, maybe even the whole street's been off . . . but an entire city? Customers and office workers trapped in lifts? Streets clogged with cars and buses and taxis? Trains frozen in coal-black under-ground stations?

This is not natural.

And it's dead eerie, somehow. Although far from quiet, what with the streets full of police trying to get the traffic flowing again, shops being locked in customers' faces because of the looting threat.

I remember this feller banging on the door of a newsagent's shouting, Hey, come on, gissa packet a ciggies, will yer? Just one packet, yer bastards!

And there's a woman rushing out of a hairdresser's with half a perm and her face all smudged clutching a towel and grabbing hold of people, screaming, You've gorra help me! He's taking me out tonight, it's me anniversary!

Which might have been funny if she hadn't been wearing (oh God, oh Jesus Christ) the black bonnet.

Half an hour later, the rumours are spreading. Some people are saying it's the IRA, and a woman at a burger stall with its own generator is doing fantastic business and telling one customer after another, 'It's not just Liverpool, you know, luv, it's the whole country that's been blacked out! You've had it for hot meals now. Gerrit while you can!'

It wasn't, of course. It was just Liverpool, as if that wasn't bad enough and totally unprecedented – a hundred thousand electricity users cut off for the best part of two hours, shops and businesses losing millions of pounds.

According to next day's Daily Post, a spokesman for the National Grid said it had been caused by 'an outside body'. It was eventually traced to the valves on two transformers in the Lister

Drive power station at Tuebrook. This is one of the places which passes on the juice from the National Grid to the local lecky company, MANWEB.

In the DP the following day, a MANWEB official was quoted as saying it was 'extraordinary' two transformers going down at once. A 'million to one chance', an 'untimely coincidence'.

And then another unnamed spokesman actually said, 'The fates came together on this one.'

Interesting, isn't it, that when official bodies can't explain something, they still revert to expressions like 'the fates'.

Was it ever actually love all those years ago? Or just a subconscious plea for empathy?

If it didn't come back to John Lennon, it always came back to Moira. In the spring of 1981, he'd decided he couldn't stand this any more and set out to find her.

This meant Scotland. He'd rung all the people he knew up there – about five of them, mainly musicians. One guy said, yeah, she was certainly gigging, done some support for Clannad, he was sure she had. Another said, hang on a mo, there was a line or two in the local rag – Aberdeen University – the 20th, was it?

So Dave had loaded up his van with all the clean clothes he could gather together, thrown an old mattress in the back in case he ran out of cash. And the Martin guitar, in case he had to sell it, perish the thought.

Well, actually, the guitar was also there because of this little fantasy he had. A darkened folk club somewhere picturesque and atmospheric, and she'd be doing her act with everybody sitting around quietly, revering her. And then she'd get on, solo, to a song which really could have used a second guitar, a few harmonies. She'd be in a long black dress, and when she reached the chorus she'd sound so alone you could die.

At which point . . .

. . . another guitar, the incomparable Martin, would join in from the back of the hall, getting louder as the figure from the past weaved between the bodies towards her, looking as handsome as ever but maybe a little weary; he'd travelled a long way, after all . . .

Dave still cringed over this.

Spring had been late that year. Especially in Scotland. Snowdrifts in March, the travelling hard, especially in a nine-year-old Ford Thames. And when he got to Aberdeen University, there was no concert on the 20th involving Moira Cairns.

Moira who? She wasn't even that well known. She'd made one album of her own songs – including The Comb Song – and then gone back to the traditional folk stuff. She was not famous; she had a *following*. He didn't know about Malcolm Kaufmann in those days; maybe the agent hadn't yet come on the scene.

It was hopeless. She didn't seem to work to any kind of pattern. Or she knew somehow that he was around.

Example. He'd turn up at some pub in, say, a fishing village in Fife, having spent most of a week on the trail and just enough money left for a night's B and B, and he'd find it was *last* night, she'd already been on, fixture altered by request of the artist.

This would keep happening, in different ways. Town halls, theatres, arts centres, students' unions . . . always *last* night, or it had been postponed, or it was the wrong town, or it was the right town and the bloody van broke down and he arrived too late.

All of this happening in a kind of haze, like in those infuriating dreams where you're trying your damnedest to do something dead simple, like make a phone call, and your fingers keep hitting the wrong numbers. Each day he'd set out with the certainty that *this* time . . . And each night he'd wind up confused and knackered, getting pissed and weeping off the quay at Oban or somewhere.

She was always ahead of him, always the next town along the line, and an impenetrable mist between them.

Some days he'd climb a hill and stand with his hands spread and his eyes closed. *Where are you? Just give me a direction*. Like the way he'd reach out for her mind on stage or during a session when a song took off on its own. *We going into the chorus again, or wind it up?*

Nothing.

And then he'd got ill, running a temperature. Couldn't even drive home. Lay sweating on the mattress in the back of the van until he must have passed out or something and the next thing he remembers he's in an ambulance and then a hospital and someone is saying, Nothing obvious, looks like plain old nervous exhaustion to me.

Next thing, he's sitting up in a cold sweat, throwing off the blankets, screaming, the Martin!

Who is this Martin, Mr Reilly? Is he a friend?

The bloody Martin's still in the bloody van!

It wasn't, naturally. Fifteen hundred quid's worth of customized, hand-tooled acoustic guitar. They hadn't taken the van; even thieves have standards.

He'd never been back to Scotland.

OK, read this carefully. Read it twice.

The official time of the Liverpool blackout was 1.13 p.m.

It was the thirteenth minute of the thirteenth hour of the thirteenth day of December.

Fact.

Another one of those untimely coincidences the electricity company was on about.

It spooked me, kid. I couldn't keep a limb still when I read that. I don't like December, how could I? What about you? Do things happen to you in December? Do you start to get nervous when the nights are growing longer?

It's November now, coming up to a year since the big Liverpool blackout. Worried? Me?

Bloody right I am.

Here's another untimely coincidence that never made the papers – they probably thought it was too bloody stupid to mention.

Nineteen ninety-three. Thirteen years since December 1980, when

*people were crying in the streets of Liverpool, everybody gathering in
Mathew Street, where the Cavern used to be. Do you remember that
woman on the radio? 'He was still one of ours, was John. He'd
never really left. It's a death in the family.'*

*The lights went out in Liverpool in the thirteenth minute of the
thirteenth hour of the thirteenth day of the month in the thirteenth
year since the murder of the city's most famous son.*

And that happened on a Monday too.

Moira, what can I do?

I'm heading for the loony bin.

Which was still better – or was it? – than being dead.

Maybe not.

'I'm the same age as you now, pal,' Dave told the picture of
John Lennon. It was the one from the front of the *Imagine*
album, Lennon hazy in the sky. Lennon the seer, Lennon the
sage.

Mark Chapman, the killer, in his spurious role as crusading
Holden Caulfield from Salinger's *The Catcher in the Rye*, had
claimed Lennon was the ultimate phoney. Self-justifying shit.

'In a year's time,' Dave told the picture, 'I'm gonna be older
than you were. That can't be right.'

John observed him sardonically through glasses like the
bottoms of school milk bottles.

yeah, well, you shoulda thought of that at the time.

A white cloud blossomed like ectoplasm from the centre of
John's forehead.

'I was scared, pal, I keep explaining.'

*that's nothing to do with it, Dave, if you don't mind me saying
so. we all get fuckin' scared. when you're scared, that's the time to
act, man.*

'Look . . . I didn't know. I didn't know it was gonna be
you, did I? I've explained that. Loads of times.'

*so what you're saying – let me get this right – is that it'd've been
OK if it was some other poor fuck. You wouldn't be agonizing . . .*

'No, that's not . . .'

38

you're sooooooo full of shit, Dave. you hated me, man.

John's thin lips were slightly parted; a small puff of white smoke drifted from his mouth into the clouds.

Dave lowered his face into his hands.

If you die tonight/who has the last laugh?

Far above the bungalow, a seagull keened.

He often had the idea that wherever Moira was, there were also seagulls, maybe the same ones flying back and forth.

He gathered up the letter. It was almost unreadable. He wondered if his ma still had her little Olivetti. One way or other he'd have to get this one typed.

Meanwhile, Jan. He couldn't put this off. It was just over an hour and a half's drive to Jan's place. He would make it before nightfall. There was no point in considering what he was going to say to her. It all depended on how far she'd been able to come to terms with what he was. And on what the doctors had said about Sara.

Out of his hands. It was always out of his hands.

Bloody Lennon was sneering benignly from behind his cloud.

fuckin' useless, Dave, you know that?

'Now listen, you smug bastard,' said Dave, rallying. 'You were becoming a sanctimonious sod, and just because you're bloody dead doesn't give you the right . . .'

There was a small thump on the window. He turned in time to watch coffee-coloured seagull shit sliding slowly down the glass.

II

The Next Big Thing

'That guy, what was his name – found Tutankhamun's tomb . . .' Prof Levin was fumbling with a penknife. 'Howard somebody . . .'

The elegant, if frayed, Stephen Case, greying hair in a pony-tail, was keeping his distance, not wanting dust on his clothes. Plonker.

'Anyway,' Prof grunted, putting down the knife to wipe condensation off his rimless glasses. 'I feel like him.'

Somebody apparently had said to Steve Case that he ought to take a close look at the junk in Epidemic's attic. As a result of which – *what* a surprise – they'd discovered this box, like a long, wooden cashbox, under Goff's bed.

'He was cursed, though, wasn't he, this bloke?' Prof replaced his specs, slid a blade under the lock. 'Didn't they *all* get cursed? Didn't they all die horribly?'

'Yes, well, we're not archaeologists, and this isn't a tomb.' Stephen Case smiled thinly. 'It just feels like one.'

They'd clambered up the linoleum stairs by torchlight, their echoing footsteps making it sound like there was at least fifteen of them, and the beam had been suddenly flashed back by the darkly glittering eyes of Jim Morrison, of the Doors, twenty-odd years dead.

Jim was stripped to the waist, a floor-to-ceiling, black-framed photo blow-up, full of scorching menace. *1943–1971. Singer, poet, shaman* – this on a tarnished brass plate.

Prof had remembered how Morrison had had a major drink problem. He knew everybody famous who'd ever had a major drink problem. Not that his own problem had ever been *major* . . .

They'd moved up two more flights of stairs and found similar figures looming over the landings: Jimi Hendrix and then John Lennon, both in black frames the size of coffins, leaning out at you over the stairs. A memorial gallery of dead rock stars; was this natural?

'Tell you one thing,' Prof said, feeling the lock of the wooden box begin to loosen. 'If there's tapes in here, they . . . see that?'

'Mould? Can't have got inside though, can it?'

'Want to bet, son?'

Prof was still suspicious, because Steve had known exactly where to look: not in the actual attic, if there was one, but in mad Max Goff's private apartment, this once-luxurious penthouse, now stripped of everything but the giant bed and these godawful, black and purple funeral-parlour drapes framing the 'rural' side of Luton.

The building used to be a shoe factory before it was the headquarters of Epidemic Independent Records, with the founder sometimes living over the shop. Now the founder was dead and Epidemic, leaderless and crunched by the recession, belonged to TMM, Steve's faceless, multinational employer.

Place had been closed only two or three months, but already these top windows were the only ones not boarded against vandals. There were security men and dogs in the grounds, and Steve'd had to produce verifiable ID before they'd been let in.

'What's A and R mean?' The chief security guy had demanded, studying Steve's card.

Arrogant and ruthless, Prof Levin had thought, having known Stephen Case since before he'd sold his soul to TMM, back when he was just another hustler, and having no basic reason to think he'd changed.

Steve had sighed in annoyance, his shoulders thrusting under the imitation Armani jacket he wore with creamish, stonewashed jeans. 'Artists and Repertoire. Means I get to decide who we're going to record. My colleague here is one of the people who push the buttons. That's what "recording engineer" means.'

The security man's face had read, *I'll remember you, pal*, but, for now, he'd just nodded. 'OK, you can go in, but we have to keep a record of anything you may remove from the premises.'

'Jesus, we *own* this place now,' Steve had moaned, then had thrown up his hands wearily. 'All right, all right.'

Finally, they levered up the lid of the box, the edge of it splitting.

'Careful now, Prof, we don't want to . . . Is that an envelope on top?'

'Yep.' A thick A4-size one, made of heavy parchmenty stuff, adding to the feeling of phoney antiquity coming off the black-painted wood of the box with its greenish brass shoulders – built for doubloons, Prof thought, rather than sensitive recording tape. This was going to be messy.

Steve was snapping his fingers impatiently. Prof handed him the envelope over his shoulder, thinking, Why me? Why not one of the smart-arsed, hi-tech boy wonders always hanging around his office, *please, please, Mr Case, Steve, just gimme a break* . . .? What's he want with a sixty-four-year-old alcoholic with a long-established attitude problem?

Except, of course, that the boy wonders maybe wouldn't know where to start with the kind of tape that might have been stored for years in a wooden box under the late Max Goff's well-used kingsize bed. Whereas Ken Levin was known as Prof not only because of his glasses, his pointed beard and his encyclopedic knowledge of the British music scene since 1955, but on account of an expertise with recording tape which some distinguished producers considered was verging on the extra-sensory.

Also, another point – Steve Case had obtained work for Prof at a time when his drinking was causing some consternation (this in an industry fuelled by dope!) and therefore was aware that Prof owed him one.

There was a certain type of bloke, especially in this business, who was never quite as good as his reputation. Who only survived at the top by doing people carefully-judged favours at the right time and recouping later.

'What you were expecting, Steve?'

Steve looked at Prof furtively, down his nose – not many people could do this.

Prof said, 'You'll let me know then, will you? One day?'

The box had actually been in a cupboard set into the panelling in the base of the bed, this enormous four-poster – repro of course but starkly impressive all the same, even though stripped of its curtains, sheets and pillowcases.

Which would all have been black, of course. Best not to even imagine what the founder of Epidemic Records had got up to here with various girls and boys. And sheep and donkeys and Alsatian dogs, probably.

Max Goff must have been dead a couple of years now, knifed by some little glue-sniffing teenager deluded into thinking the great man was going to turn him into a rock star, allegedly driven into a homicidal frenzy when he found out the truth. Well, obviously, there was more to *that*, wasn't there always?

It hadn't happened here, of course. But this was still a murdered man's bed, wasn't it?

Aw, leave off . . . Prof shook himself.

Didn't seem to bother *him* – straw-haired, fortyish Steve standing in the shadow of the four-poster, prising away at the parchment; you could almost see his long, bony nose twitching. Stephen Case: twenty years in the business, cynical, manipulative . . . but still prepared to be romanced, if not fully seduced, by the Next Big Thing.

He was going to be disappointed, however – Prof extracting the first tape-carton from the box, blowing off the mould – when he saw this lot.

Grimacing, Prof slid the tape back and counted up. A dozen cartons of two-inch tape in ten-and-a-half-inch reels. Masters, obviously.

Steve was fondling the stiff paper like it was an erotic love letter oozing scent.

'What you got then, Steve? Gonna trust old Prof, are we?'

Which he knew he could or they wouldn't be here together. Prof Levin's discretion was legendary. Even pissed, Prof stayed shtumm. Even his ex-wife would accept this.

'It's an album,' Steve said guardedly. 'Or part of an album.' He folded the papers, leaned over the box. 'How many in there?'

'Twelve.'

'Super. It's probably all here then.'

'In a manner of speaking,' Prof said.

Problem was, even if Elvis himself, in his undeniably cranky final years, had secretly signed to Epidemic to record his farewell opus, it quite possibly wasn't going to matter a flying fart any more.

Prof held up one of the reels, unrolled a couple of inches of tape. 'Steve, this tape is knackered, mate.'

He dropped it back into the carton.

'Unplayable,' he said. 'Kaput.'

This boudoir was the size of a modest dance hall. Its walls were all white. *Had* been white; there was a coating of dust now, except for the etiolated rectangles where pictures had hung. Prof didn't like to think what kind of pictures these had been.

He brushed some mould from his cuff. If Steve was expecting some help here, he could be a little more forthcoming.

'I'm only guessing,' he said, 'but from what we know Max Goff used to get up to, the atmosphere in here would have been pretty humid much of the time. And then cold as the grave again, when he went away.'

Steve Case was staring at him, his hands hanging limply by his sides. A thin vein meandering along his left nostril seemed to throb.

'Look . . .' Prof held up a reel between thumb and forefinger, going into his Sotheby's routine. 'This is late seventies, early eighties, right. What you had then were manufacturers experimenting with new synthetic materials. With unfortunate results. You got a class of tape which, if left for too long in unsuitable conditions, could turn out worse than the BBC museum pieces, you know what I'm saying? Look . . . feel it.'

Steve drew back.

'These conditions,' Prof said. 'Hot and cold and bucketsful of evaporating sweat and other bodily secretions . . .'

Steve had let the papers from the envelope fall to the mattress. The papers looked quite crisp and fresh. There was typing or print of some sort on them. Prof made out one word, in capitals.

DEATH.

He blew out his lips. Terrific.

'What you're saying,' Steve said tensely, 'is that the oxide . . .'

'Oxide, right. There's like a binder. Which holds the oxide on to the base film of the tape – stop me if I'm being oversimplistic for a man of your experience . . .'

'Don't piss about.'

Prof grinned. 'So you get humidity in the tape, it causes the binder to kind of exude on to the surface. When you play it, the tape glues itself to the heads, the machine stalls, everything gets very, very gooey.'

He took out four cartons one by one, each grey-green with mould.

'Look at the state. How long you say this lot's been stored? Fourteen, fifteen years?' Prof shook his head, enjoying himself. 'You could be screwed then, mate. Be like black treacle on the heads, chocolate fudge . . .'

'Shit.' Steve Case looked about to kick the box across the room. 'Shit, shit, *shit*!'

'This a disaster then, Steve?'

Steve looked about to kick Prof Levin across the room.

'So what was it then, mate? What we looking at?'

Steve turned away and walked over to the window, sighed. 'The Stone.'

'The Stones? When? How? You're kidding.'

'No, Prof. The *Stone*. Singular.'

Prof looked blank. He was freelance, wasn't getting paid for this, had agreed to tag along because he owed Steve and also because Steve had implied there was a big project on the cards if they struck oil. This was it? This was the big one, the contents of the Ark of the bloody Covenant?

Steve was gazing out of the window across a grey field with a shed in it. 'You don't remember this?'

'Should I?'

'A band put together for Epidemic in seventy-nine?' Steve turned back into the room. 'Tom Storey?'

'I *see*.' The old wheels turning. 'Recorded nineteen-eighty, you say. December eighty, would that be?'

Steve said, 'Full title was the Philosopher's Stone.'

'That's a mouthful, Steve.'

'This was the item medieval alchemists believed would turn base metals into gold. Metaphorical, apparently.'

'Didn't do a lot for Tom Storey, though, did it? Not in December eighty. Are you saying then . . .' Prof unearthed another reel of tape, scraped at the mould with a fingernail '. . . that this is the actual album Storey was working on when he had his fabled accident?'

'The Black Album. Recorded at the Abbey at Ystrad Ddu – *ddu* being Welsh for black. In the Black Mountains of South Wales. And black also because of . . . what happened.'

'Piece of history,' Prof said. 'Who else was in it?'

Steve took the papers from the mattress. 'Disappointingly, except for one of the session men, nobody who counts for shit any more. There was a folk singer, Moira Cairns, and a refugee from some string quartet called Simon St John . . .'

'I remember Cairns. Nice voice. Smoky.'

'And someone called Dave Reilly.'

'Dave?'

'You know him?'

'Well, I . . .' Prof decided to cool it a little, until he knew where this was headed. 'I *did* know him. I worked on his solo album. Eighty-six, eighty-seven.'

'You know where he is now?'

Prof shook his head.

'Was he any good?'

Prof shrugged.

'All nobodies, you see,' said Steve. 'Except for Tom Storey.'

'Who's also a nobody now. Reclusive, they say. And a session man, you said? Someone who *does* count for shit?'

'Drummer. And some backing vocals, possibly. In effect, the fifth member of the band.' Steve paused for effect. 'Lee Gibson.'

Last Sunday Prof had read a feature in the *Independent* about Lee Gibson, who'd left Britain over a decade ago and was now monster in the States. These things happened.

'Really? Well, well.' Prof pinched his beard. Storey's swan-song and the launching of Lee, all in one album. 'Pity about the tape.'

'Come on, Prof, stop fooling about.' Steve sat down on the bed which Prof suspected would be cold and damp. 'There are, at the end of the day, things you can do with this tape, are there not?'

Prof raised an eyebrow, saying nothing.

'What I mean is you can bring this stuff back from the dead. And discreetly.'

Prof hefted the box, stood up. 'Tell me something. How did you know about this? How did you know these tapes even existed? How did you know where to find them?'

'Prof . . .' Stephen Case touched the vein on his nose. 'You simply don't need to know.'

He opened the door and waved an arm, as if to waft Prof and the box out of the room, but Prof stood his ground.

'Hang on, let me get this right – this is the stuff laid down on the night of the Storey calamity. Why did Goff sit on the tapes? Lie on them, in fact. Shit, the fat bastard must've been *bonking* on them for bloody years.'

'Let's go, Prof.'

'And am I correct in thinking that while these tapes, strictly speaking, now belong to TMM, nobody there, apart from you, actually knows they exist? Talking private enterprise, are we?'

Steve Case didn't reply. Everything inside Prof Levin screamed, *leave this alone*, but he was curious, now.

'OK, I'll talk to a man I know.'

'Super,' Steve said. 'And I'll talk to a man *I* know in connection with the reclusive Tom. Who won't even talk on the phone, did you know that?'

Going down the stairs, the box in his arms, Prof said, 'You got any idea why Max Goff should keep this under his bed?'

They moved around the picture of John Lennon, who was standing in a doorway, looking sardonic. He was the least spooky; the other dead rock stars loomed out at you like dummies in a ghost train.

Prof said, 'Suppose they don't want this stuff released. Suppose it's too painful. Storey, I'm thinking about.'

Footsteps clack-clacking on the stairs of the deserted building, the torchbeam waving. Tutankhamun's tomb; the pillaging of grave goods.

'Too bad,' Steve said coldly.

In Prof's arms, the box felt like the coffin of a child.

III

The Hideous Bonnet

S omeone was approaching.

   She arose to look out of the window. No one in sight. No one among the flaking autumn trees which lined the track. The three other houses between her and the shore were all holiday homes, empty now until the spring, when she'd be gone.

She listened, and heard only the sound of November on the Isle of Skye: scrabbling wind and seabirds.

But someone was approaching, and with an awful heavy burden.

She sat down again on the couch, pulling the guitar on to her knees. She plucked three harsh chords . . . *I do not . . . need . . . this.*

She stood up, flung the guitar on the couch. It rolled on to the floor, kind of bounced, the way Ovations did, durable instruments. Maybe she should write some more songs. Write it all out of her.

Dangerously restless, she ran up the uncarpeted stairs, to the smallest bedroom, an untidy cell, where she slumped down angrily at the dresser, sleeves rolled up and roughened elbows in the mess of hairbrushes and make-up, aspirins and chewing-gum wrappers.

She gazed into the mirror – oval, like her face – and with the fingers of both hands she pushed the heavy hair back from the cold, white skin. Her hands could no longer smooth out the frown fluting her forehead; the frown lived here now.

And it would soon be December again.

In the mirror, as her hair fell back into place, she saw the silver-grey ripple re-emerging in what once had been a torrent of black. By the end of the year it maybe would reach her shoulders again.

Return of the Witchy Woman.

Malcolm, her agent, used to call her this. She didn't like it any more. What she should do was discard all her ankle-length black dresses and her drab cloaks and replace them with – dear God – bright fluffy things in soft pastel shades or crisp, efficient blouses and suits, as worn by female executives.

Moira laughed.

And then stopped, biting her lip. Hold on there, hen, that was no' a *bitter* laugh, was it?

She watched her eyes. She was thirty-eight, some way along the steepening road from maiden to hag.

And someone was coming with bad news.

Jan's face was very much like marble: white, shiny with tears and hard as stone.

No, he thought. No. No. No. Never had he prayed so hard that it had been wrong, a delusion.

Red-haired Jan was sitting at the work table, a drained coffee cup at her elbow. She was looking out of the window into the street where, in the November twilight, two kids were crashing a football at a metal garage door. When Dave had come in, Jan hadn't looked at him.

It was a reconditioned eighty-year-old end-of-terrace house in an old South Lancashire pit village, now commutersville. It had an open coal fire. They used to make love in front of it. Dave remembered saying, *I bet you lie around and fantasize about the generations of miners who sat here in zinc baths.* And Jan, naked, had said, *Pass me that bar of soap again, would you?*

Now the fire was out.

The room was very tidy. Had been completely tidied. He imagined her hoovering viciously, slamming books back on shelves – books on history, sociology, humanist philosophy and political theory. Ramming the CD unit flat to the wall, clacking together the piles of discs – modern classics, some jazz, very little rock.

Jan said, very precisely, the icy schoolteacher voice, 'I believe that I told you not to come back.'

He stood in the doorway, fingering the ends of his scarf. Everything he could have said at this point would have sounded trite.

Can't we talk about this?

Could I at least try and explain?

Will you just listen to me for ten minutes without jumping down my throat?

Yeah, well, pleading would only sicken her. Even sickened him. So he stood in the doorway, playing with his scarf.

Shit.

The really heavy, unspoken question related to the results of Sara's latest tests and he was scared to ask.

Bitterly, she answered it for him. Her voice was also like marble now, gravestone-cold and glassy.

'She's to have an immediate programme of chemotherapy. Three months. At least. But I didn't need to tell you that, did I?'

'Oh God.' He'd seen Sara precisely once and couldn't really remember her face, only the thickening black and purple haze around it like a luminous bruise, a hideous bonnet. 'I'm so sorry. You don't . . .'

'Are you? Are you really?'

'Jesus, Jan . . .'

'Because you'd have looked pretty stupid if it *hadn't* been inoperable, wouldn't you, Dave? You'd have looked like A, a phoney or B, a serious psychiatric case.'

'Look,' he said, 'we can't talk here, the atmosphere's like . . . Can we go for a drive?'

'I don't want to talk here,' Jan said. 'Or in the car. Or anywhere. With you.'

Dave clenched his fists on the woollen scarf, pulling it down tight against the back of his neck. He closed his eyes, felt furious and hopeless and ashamed. Sensitive? You could keep it.

Once – three months ago, in bed – it had been incomprehension, then nervous giggles, then . . .

She's not ill. What makes you think she's ill?

Just a . . . a feeling.

Well, thank you very much, Doctor Reilly, for that considered diagnosis.

Then she'd sat up in bed, pulled on the light. *Look, what is this?*

I just think she should go and get herself checked over, that's all.

You're serious, aren't you? What the hell's got into you, Dave?

The problem was that a grown man who saw fuzzy colours around people's heads went totally against Jan's cheerfully rigid world-view, her cast-iron concept of what was real and acceptable.

Jan, twice divorced at thirty-four, was a very determined unbeliever. A roving supply-teacher who refused to work at any school where old-style religious instruction was on the menu. Who saw everything in that area, from organized worship to New Age farting about, as not so much the opium as the *heroin* of the people: addictive and destructive, something that should be fought in the streets and seized at the ports.

Which was wonderful. She was lovely and carefree and laughed a lot and liked to help people. In fact, the best reason he'd ever found for concluding that, OK, there were more things in heaven and earth, but who gives a shit?

The Dave–Jan thing had been nearly four glorious months old when she'd dragged him over to Southport and introduced him to her sister. Sara was twenty-eight, the high-flyer of the family, just back from a year's guest-lecturing at the University of Illinois.

Nice girl.

Nice, but clearly and horribly sick.

Was he supposed to keep quiet about it?

Coincidence! Jan had shrieked at him five weeks later, when Sara had been to her doctor complaining of listlessness and the upshot of that was some consultant ordering a biopsy. *An appalling, ghastly coincidence!*

Sure, he'd said, to get them through the night without eyes being torn out. *You're right. It's probably a complete coincidence.*

Jan had sat up in a distant corner of the bed, duvet clutched around her chin. *But you don't believe that, do you? You don't believe it was a coincidence at all.*

Looked at Dave as if she'd just learned he had a string of convictions for indecent exposure.

A look which was to become unbearably familiar. His one chance had been for Sara's condition to prove eminently treatable, so that the whole business might, given a respite, turn into something they could laugh about.

Until the next time.

For it had been clear enough, after this, that he'd never again be able to tell himself with any confidence that there'd be no more next times.

Jesus, what *was* this? Moira was shaking. She went back out to the landing, to the top of the stairs, stared down into the lower room, where the guitar lay supine, a dead guitar.

The room was like a tiny stone chapel, with a plain hardwood table under the small window. There was also a big brass oil lamp on it, for reading.

On account of there being no electricity. She'd had the converted croft house *un*converted, getting the power disconnected. Don't know why I did that, she'd say. But, of course, she did know. When she'd first arrived – nine . . . *ten* years ago, Jesus, is it as long as that? – she'd been rather less than one hundred per cent rational.

Now I'm slightly more than fifty per cent *ir*rational.

And something's coming.

Without warning, for there was no phone either. The only person she would accept being disturbed by was her mother, and her mother had no need of phones.

If it was lonely sometimes, she could handle that. If she was lonely, she was safe.

There was an open fireplace, with buckets of coal standing by; in front of the hearth, a bright orange fleecy rug on which you could sit cross-legged at night in the oil-lamp's placid light, reading or maybe just singing softly to yourself, the guitar in your lap, rearranging traditional songs.

Idyllic, huh? Renewal. The recharging of the spiritual batteries.

What a lot of crap. The island's a demanding lover; you *don't* get to relax, not often. Especially just lately, with the dreams. All those images which your conscious thoughts suppress keep emerging, red-haloed, in your dreams.

Aw, hey, go make yourself some tea, huh?

She walked slowly down the stairs, straightening this ludicrously jolly woollen sweater, bright sea-blue with happy seals jumping up for the boobs.

At the bottom of the stairs, facing the window, a movement in the trees made her stiffen, heart leaping like one of the seals.

She peered out, to where the mist began.

One time, not long after she'd bought the place, she'd lain awake in her bed – this was December, always December – and heard a seagull. A seagull in the night. The gull's lonely cry was agony to hear, made her weep.

Davey?

It had been a mild night – the worst kind, in December – and she'd done a stupid thing; she'd allowed herself to respond. Had risen, as if sleepwalking. Had opened the window and gone back to her bed.

She hadn't seen it come in, but she'd known it was here, she could feel its cry, deep in her breast now. She'd opened her arms to it.

Davey . . .

No sooner had the breath left her lips than she knew it was all wrong, and she leapt up, flapping her arms, shouting, *out! out!* and slamming the window shut so hard the glass cracked.

Following morning she'd come down the stairs and out of this same window, the sea mist heavy all around, she'd seen them coming, watched them form out of the dense air, a terrible bedraggled procession: Simon in a monk's robe, barefoot, his feet torn by the stones, blood seeping up between his toes. Behind him lumbered Tom, a hairy caveman in rags, eyes full of fear and bewilderment. And Davey . . . was this wee Davey? He kept fading and changing colour, like he didn't know where or who he was. Then came a blast of confusion, sheer cold bewilderment that knocked her back so hard she'd lived with the headache for two days, then started running a temperature, and it had turned into flu, and oh God, never again.

Hey . . . come on. Get your act together. She headed for the kitchen.

And then screamed a fractured scream as the pounding began on the front door of the croft house.

She stared for a long time at the little old man in the bright muffler and the beat-up trilby hat.

'Are y' OK, Moira?'

They were not there, Tom and Simon and the hazy thing which might have been Dave. Why should she think that? She was a mad woman.

Moments passed. The image of the wee elderly guy did not waver: brown-faced, in a trilby with a greasy golden cord around the crown.

It was the long wet tongues on her cheeks which brought her out of it. Both dogs, one either side, their front paws on her shoulders. Shivering now in the barbed air from the sea, she hugged the Dobermanns and blinked at the wee man.

'Donald?'

He smiled. 'Ah widny ha' come, hen . . . Ah widny bother ye . . .'

A hundred wrinkles had become channels for his tears. His smile started to swim for it.

She said breathily, unbelieving, 'Hey, Donald . . . no?'

He was nodding gravely. The dogs had moved away and were sitting either side of him, watchful and sorrowful.

'Hey, come on, will you, Donald,' Moira said, smothering the solemnity of the moment with her anger. 'It's no' possible. I would have known. *I would have fucking known!*'

'Wis sudden,' Donald said.

Moira marched out of the doorway and went and stood in the middle of the little, rough lawn, by the broken sundial. 'Ah, Jesus,' she murmured. 'This is no' real.'

Behind her, one of the dogs whined gently.

'This morning, hen. Wis a stroke, they reckon. Nae warning. Ah've been on the road since nine.'

Moira, turning back to the door, said emptily, 'I'm sorry. Please . . . come away in.'

'The dogs?'

'Sure.'

Donald put himself shyly on the edge of the sofa. He picked up the guitar and sat it on the cushion next to him, as if it was a holy relic, the Dobermanns like temple dogs at his feet.

Moira crept numbly into the kitchen to make tea, moving crockery, milk, sugar, spoons, oatmeal biscuits on to a tray without thinking, like setting up the piecies on a chessboard, slow and precise and deliberate, laying it down for herself: a not-yet-elderly woman, known, a little irreverently, as the Duchess because of her authority and her wisdom and her grace, this woman had died, suddenly, in her palace on wheels, on a run-down local-authority gypsy caravan site near the west coast.

And yet this simply was not possible. It was not possible the Duchess would die without telling her. It was not possible the Duchess could die *suddenly*.

She carried the tray into the living-room, set it down on the deep window ledge. 'And did no one,' she said grimly, 'think to call the poliss?'

'Hey, now, come on, hen. We had the doctor. Wis natural. She wis always frail.'

'Was *not at all* frail, Donald, you know that . . .' Moira dropped a cup, felt her face collapse, the grief finally overcoming the disbelief. 'A damn *stroke*? My mother spent half her life learning . . . learning how to die, you know what I'm saying?'

'Aye,' Donald said, sighing, knowing there could be no argument. 'Wid ye let me drive you doon tae the site?'

Moira shook her head. He knew more than he could say. 'Was good of you to come.'

'Nae choice in the matter, hen. It wis laid down. If she wis ever . . .'

'But I have to go down alone,' Moira said. 'You know?'

She bent down to pick up the pieces of broken cup. 'I'll fetch some water,' she said. 'For the dogs.'

When Dave came down after packing his things, Jan was still in the same position, only it was near-dark outside and the kids with the football had gone home.

The room was cold, but he knew she wouldn't light the fire until he'd left.

'Put the light on,' Jan said. 'You'll break something with those cases.'

He had two suitcases and his guitar case. He put on the wall lights with their Tiffany shades, a soft ambience.

'The main light,' Jan said sharply.

The main light was hardly ever used. In its hard, white glare he searched her face for anything salvageable. She held his gaze, with all the insolence of grief, for more than long enough to convince him. Her thick red hair was tied back. She wore no make-up. She'd never looked as beautiful.

But that was always the case, wasn't it, when you were getting the elbow?

'Can I call you? I'd like to know. How it works out.'

'You've done enough,' Jan said. 'We don't need you to know.'

He started to feel angry. 'I didn't *make* it happen to her, Jan. I just saw that it *had* happened. I mean, shit . . .'

Jan took a long breath. She was a professional teacher; she made it all sound very reasonable.

'Dave, I know very well you didn't make it happen. I know you *couldn't* make it happen. Of course I don't believe you did anything. I also don't actually believe you saw anything. But it's the thought that *you* believe you saw something . . . Can you understand that?'

'To a point, but . . .'

Jan held up both hands, warding him off.

'But more than that,' she said, 'it's the thought that one day you might be convinced you saw something around *me*. Or my parents. Or one of our friends. Now I know there has to be a sound psychological explanation for your appalling behaviour, but it's not my field of study. You've put yourself outside my parameters, Dave, and I want you out of my life. That plain enough for you?'

All he could think to do was nod. The bright light made him blink. It was completely plain. Jan despised him. Fear and ignorance could be overcome, given time. Contempt – forget it.

Silently, he picked up his suitcases, carried them to the door, went back for the guitar.

'Dave, haven't you forgotten something?'

Like she was asking for a goodbye kiss.

He stopped and thought, bitch. He laid the guitar case down, found his key ring in a hip pocket of his jeans. From it he detached her front door key.

He laid the key, almost ceremoniously, on the table in front of her. Feeling like a small boy required to turn out his pockets and surrender his bag of toffees. The humiliation somehow made it easier.

He thought, fuck you, Jan.

'Thank you,' she said.

*

Climbing into his peeling Fiat, he looked over his shoulder once and saw the curtains had been drawn in Jan's living-room and the hard light had given way to the soft light. All very homely. He used to love arriving here after midnight, and these lights would still be on. Or, better still, there'd be a rosy light in the bedroom.

It was cold in the car and wouldn't warm up; the heater was clapped. It occurred to him that he had nowhere to go, ought to have had something worked out. Wasn't as if he hadn't known this was coming. There should be a telephone help-line organization, Self-Pitying Bastards Anonymous, which you could dial on such occasions as this, it was . . .

somebody call?

Glancing up warily, Dave saw two tiny orbs of white light in the misted rear-view mirror.

some ineffectual little twat seeking a spot of advice?

'Piss off, John.'

now what kind of attitude's that? listen, take it from someone who's been there, you're well out of that one. nice girl and everything, but you start suppressing one side of you for a quiet life, you're inviting grief, pal.

Dave drove away.

tie a knot in it, that's my advice, son. just for a while.

Dave considered his options. Muthah Mirth had offered him a few gigs coming up to Christmas. Fees weren't monster, but the availability of Bart's bedsit round the corner was a plus.

cos you've got problems coming.

'What?'

fax it.

Moira? You reckon?

fax it, dickhead.

It was fully dark now. The link road to the bypass curved back over a new viaduct overlooking Jan's terrace. The last he saw of the end house was a curl of new white smoke from its chimney.

IV

Profanity from a Man
of the Cloth

Two men and a sheepdog strolled down the valley from Ystrad Ddu, thickly conifered hills either side and the grey sky flat and low like a lid on a box.

'Why do you say "brave"?' the new vicar asked.

'Ah well,' said Mr Eddie Edwards, who was built like a pillar-box, 'perhaps ill-chosen, that was, I don't know. It depends on what kind of a man you are.'

He looked up at the vicar from under the brim of his crimson cap, pulled down to prevent the wind stealing it and thus enhancing the illusion that you could post letters in him.

'A challenge, it was, for some of your recent predecessors, see. The old biblical stony ground. Could they persuade from it a harvest?' Mr Edwards laughed. 'Could they hell.'

'But in trying . . .'

'Aye. In trying, they produced their own harvest. Or not. As the case was usually.'

'You sound disillusioned,' the vicar said.

'An old cynic I am. Not from these parts, see, originally, as you might have guessed, but from a, shall we say, less *agricultural* part of Wales. Another refugee, Vicar, like yourself. Early retirement, ten years ago. But, still, we nosy retired people, we have our uses. And we talk. We talk to the locals, and we also talk to the strangers. And this way we find *out*.' Mr Edwards beamed. 'Sooner or later, we find out everything.'

This was true. The vicar had served at two previous parishes, one as a curate, one his own living. And each of them had had its Mr Edwards: bright, retired, time on his hands. Anxious to show the new vicar around, put him wise on local issues.

'I knew a lot about this place, mind, before we came. Zap, come yere, boy, it's only an old dead sheep. Typical, this is. Bloody farmers are supposed to bury them. Hydatid disease, heard of that? Tapeworm. Breeds in the sheep, gets picked up by dogs from carcasses and passed on to the owner. No time at all, bloody cyst the size of a grapefruit in your liver or somewhere. Dangerous place, the countryside, Vicar, got to learn the rules.'

'Yes,' the vicar said, 'that's true.' Several clergymen had expressed an interest in having this parish. He suspected he'd been chosen because the others had been simply too enthusiastic about the delights of rural life. And also, perhaps, because he'd hoped so desperately that he *wouldn't* be chosen.

'And also, see, Vicar, it's a funny place as regards the church. Ecclesiastical history lies deep on the ground – all these ancient abbeys and priories: Abbey Dore, Craswall, Llanthony. And of course our own, which we shall come to soon.'

Mr Edwards paused to take in the sharp November air.

'When we lived in Aberdare, we'd spend weekends out by Raglan, so we always knew we'd retire this way, get ourselves a bit of ground. But the prices! The motorways done it, see, M4, M50. But this is a bit out of the way, so the prices come down accordingly.'

The home Mr Edwards and his wife had finally acquired was the former vicarage, now replaced by a smaller, less characterful modern dwelling in Ystrad hamlet. For which the vicar, who lived alone, was grateful.

The track followed the path of the river, not much more than a rocky stream. They came to a vague fork, marked by a wind-bent thorn-bush. The main path went with the river, but Mr Edwards took the other one, not much more than a sheep track.

'Zap! This way, boy. Bloody silly name for a dog, eh? My grandson, Jason, his mam and dad brought him up to see the puppy; he says, Grandad, you got to call a sheepdog something simple, so's he can hear you when you gives him a command. What would you call him then? I says. Daft thing to say to a ten-year-old. Now he's Zap.'

The dog grinned at the vicar, the way sheepdogs did. The vicar gave him a sympathetic pat.

'Slowly now,' Mr Edwards said. 'Don't let him know you're coming. Have to try to catch him unawares, see.'

'The dog?'

'No, no, man, the Abbey.'

The vicar said sharply, 'Why do you say that?'

'I don't know really. Daft to talk about catching a building unawares. But the Abbey . . . all alone down here, the Abbey's got his thoughts, it always seems to me. And his moods. Well, how would you feel, Vicar? For centuries you're this important place, this great centre of worship, everything revolving round you, and then you're nothing and falling down a bit more each year. I can sympathize with the Abbey, being retired, like. Now . . . prepare yourself.'

They were half-way to the summit of a green hump when Mr Edwards stopped and seized the vicar's arm. A row of stones like brown and rotten teeth had arisen from the grass.

'Here he comes, see.'

The sight of the rising stones had taken the vicar's breath away. Literally. He stopped.

'Out of condition, you are, Vicar. You townies.' Mr Edwards chuckled and pulled the vicar towards the top of the hump.

As they climbed, the teeth began to lengthen and then holes appeared in them. And then a huge hole, which became an archway, and then a series of ruined arches, like worn, pink-brown ribs, and suddenly they were looking down on all of it.

'Bit like that old dead sheep, isn't he?' Mr Edwards said. 'On a grand scale. Come along now, there's a path winds down. And I was right, though, wasn't I?'

'I'm sorry?'

'You can't do it. Can't sneak up on him.'

The Abbey seemed to be stretching, almost languorously, rising up around and beyond them.

The other times, the vicar had come to it by the more direct route, the narrow, twisting road, like a tunnel in summer. And never before on foot.

'I've tried it from every angle,' Mr Edwards said. 'Stroll down the valley, the normal way and, of course, he spots you from a distance, that's easy. Come through the wood, and he explodes on you all at once – well, too much to take, that is. But even this way, sneaking in from behind, he knows you're approaching and before you know it, he's got you surrounded.'

The vicar looked nervously behind him and there was this jagged stone wall he didn't even remember passing. A lump of rubble was lying by his shoe like a brown skull. When he turned again, the great archway was rearing over him, the holes in the wall above it like cold, white eyes.

'Come on, then, Vicar, I'll show you the layout.'

'Perhaps another day,' the vicar said, adding faintly, 'There'll be lots of other days.'

At the far end, the Abbey ceased to be a ruin. There was a square tower with a chimney, its stone the same weathered pink-brown but not so rough-hewn, its windows opaque.

A wind had arisen. Backing off, the vicar felt the Abbey somehow swirling around him, a dusty mist which might get into his lungs.

Zap began to whine.

'Bloody dog,' Mr Edwards said. 'No feeling for the glories of the past. Never likes to come this way.'

'Let's go.' The vicar was shocked at the weakness of his voice, no projection, so much for the sermon-training at college. Perhaps it *was* in his lungs.

Mr Edwards had started down the slope. 'Won't take ten minutes, Vicar. We can take a quick stroll around the ruins and then return along the valley bottom, more direct, see.'

The vicar said, 'Let's just get the fuck out of here.'

If Mr Edwards had heard this sudden, surprising profanity

from a man of the cloth, he didn't react. He began to climb back to the top of the hump. Perhaps he actually wants to get this over, the vicar thought. Then we wouldn't have to return to the Abbey.

Mr Edwards arrived next to him, panting a little. 'Aye, he's a funny old bugger, the Abbey. The tourists and the backpackers come and go, but local people ignore the place, no appreciation. No feeling for the past. Have it demolished, they would, the farmers, to make more grazing land.'

'Who owns it now?'

Mr Edwards explained that it was in the *care* of the Government. The ancient monuments people, they maintained it, although it remained in private ownership. Had been a hunting lodge, an inn, an outward-bound centre for bad boys. And then a recording studio – 'more bad boys, rock and rollers, see. Not seemly for a holy ruin, you ask me'. He smiled slyly. 'You have views on this, Vicar? Sacrilege? 'Course, being an Anglican . . . All left-footers, we were, when the Abbey was last in use.'

'We're still all Christians, Mr Edwards.'

'That's the modern view, is it? Ecumenical. Well, I have no quarrel with that, though I know some that would. But as a ruin, is this still a holy place, would you say?'

The vicar pondered what he should reply to this.

Eventually, he said, 'Some people say, fancifully perhaps, that the stones retain things. All that worship. All that veneration.'

'All that rock and roll?' said Mr Edwards. 'And what would old Abbot Richard have said to *that*?'

'What *could* he say, Mr Edwards, with his own personal history?'

The story of Abbot Richard, who founded the first abbey at Ystrad Ddu, was set down in the Department of the Environment official handbook which the vicar had found on his shelves when he arrived, along with local Ordnance Survey maps.

'I never thought about it like that,' said Mr Edwards. 'Gives hope to us all, I suppose, old Richard.'

It was an apocryphal story: the maverick monk who'd

founded the Abbey in the eleventh century had been dismissed from a religious house at Hereford for alleged thieving and fornication and had finally found salvation through a holy vision in this beautiful valley, falling to his knees, vowing to establish a new religious community on this very spot.

'I suppose Richard would have been quite sympathetic towards rock and roll,' the vicar said. 'At least it was an attempt to put new life into the place. What happened to it, do you know?'

It had closed down some years back, Mr Edwards said, shaking his head. The boss of the record company that owned it had died suddenly, leaving problems over the estate. Rumours were that it had been resold. Rumours suggested the people who'd recently bought the old Abbey farm across the valley were interested in acquiring it. But there were always rumours in a place like this, and meanwhile the tower house lay silent and derelict. Shame.

'And people in Ystrad, see, they are always a touch restive when the place is derelict.'

'I thought you said they'd all rather see it flattened.'

'Aye, but as long as it's *there* they like to have someone in residence. They've never forgotten the tragedy, must be twenty years ago, when it was abandoned for a year or so and two young people, boy and a girl – in search of a spot of privacy as you might say – climbed the spiral staircase to the south-west tower and half the bloody wall collapsed and they tumbled thirty feet to the ground, with a ton or so of masonry on top of them.'

'God,' said the vicar. 'What happened to them?'

'Lay there all night, at the foot of the tower. Young chap was dead by the time one of the farmers found them next morning. And the girl . . . the girl's still paralysed from the waist down. Your Mrs Pugh, your housekeeping woman . . . her daughter, you know?'

'God almighty. Isabel Pugh? That's how it happened?'

Mr Edwards beamed at having imparted to the new minister another essential piece of local knowledge. 'As I said, Vicar, the countryside is a dangerous place.'

As if to amplify his point, the slated roofs of the hamlet that was Ystrad Ddu slipped into view, and the little community did indeed look vulnerable, the black and viridian forestry swooping down on it from either side, the bare, pink, clefted rock partly overhanging it in a huge shelf. The old church, which at some stage had lost its tower, was so small and insignificant that it might have been just another of the hillside cottages which lay haphazardly, like old books fallen from the shelf.

It was late afternoon now and hesitant wisps of smoke curled from the squat chimneys. One smudgy plume had drifted up into the cleft of the overhanging rock, making it look like a smoking volcano. Beyond it was the lump of a semi-distant mountain top.

'That the Skirrid, Mr Edwards?'

'It is indeed. Notice how, from here, the peak seems to be rising from the gap in our own rock? Perhaps it is on the very same fault line. Perhaps they were both cloven at the same time.'

'What, during the Crucifixion?'

One of the guidebooks left behind for the vicar had dutifully related the local legend explaining how the Skirrid, the mal-formed mountain beyond Abergavenny, had acquired its pecu-liar shape, having been split by an earthquake at the very moment of Christ's death on the cross. The event was also graphically depicted on the sign outside the Skirrid Inn – an arrow of lightning piercing the peak.

Mr Edwards donned his sly expression again. 'You believe that, Vicar?'

'Now, what am I supposed to say to that? I'm sure there are sound geological reasons why I should dismiss it as superstitious bollocks. On the other hand . . .'

'Yes!' The little man quivered with delight. 'Exactly what I meant when I said the modern church was a bit uncomfortable in this area. So much history, so much legend – and most of it distinctly ecclesiastical in nature. The vision of Richard, the martyrdom of Aelwyn. And the holy mountain of Gwent.'

Mr Edwards extended an arm towards the horizon. 'For

many years . . .' his voice deepened, went suitably sonorous and sepulchral '. . . people would take helpings of soil from the summit of the Skirrid. Farmers scattered it on their fields for fertility and whole churches, it's said, were built on mounds of earth brought from up by the site of the old chapel of St Michael, close to the great cleft – the spear wound in the side of the saviour. Am I embarrassing you, Vicar?'

'Just a little.'

'Your predecessor, now, he wouldn't hear a word of it. Oh, no place for this old nonsense in the modern Church! Got to move on from superstition! Even wanted to start a fund for electric lights and heating in the church. Didn't get very far, I'm afraid.'

They came to the new vicarage, built of brick, faced and whitewashed, on the edge of the sloping village. It was just out of the shadow of the cloven rock, open to the fields and the valley.

'And where do you stand, Mr Edwards? Do you think we should all be up the Skirrid with our shovels?'

'Well . . .' Mr Edwards took off his cap, scratched the centre of a full head of pewter-coloured hair. 'Before I retired I was, as you know, a history adviser for schools in Mid Glam. So my feeling is that we should continue to be aware of these matters, but not to the point of – how can I put this? – getting obsessed.'

'No,' said the vicar, who knew all about the power of obsession. 'And you really don't like the Abbey, do you, Mr Edwards?'

'What do you mean?'

'The Abbey. The atmosphere there.'

'It's a piece of history,' Mr Edwards said, as if this was all that mattered. 'Isn't a question of not *liking* a place. If we all stopped visiting ancient sites because we found the atmosphere oppressive, what would happen to them then? Go to rack and ruin.'

'Which it has,' the vicar pointed out, lifting the latch on his garden gate. 'And how do you mean, "oppressive", exactly?'

'Oh, the wife, I think it was, used that word, the first and last time she walked there with me. The wife, God help us, likes old places to be . . . *pretty*.'

The vicar thought, his wife won't go with him, his dog only goes on sufferance. 'I bet,' he said carefully, 'that you don't really like going on your own.'

'Now, that's ridiculous,' said Mr Edwards, putting his cap back on, tugging it over his ears. 'Stuff and nonsense, that is.'

V

A Sighing of Satin

'**Y**our daddy wis here last night,' Donald said. 'Still wearin' the big horn-rims. When he came out they wis good an' misted.'

Donald stepped back and waved her up the steps of the huge caravan, a mobile mansion, and into the china cave which had been the Duchess's parlour.

Amid all the china plates on the walls, there was a gilt-framed board with about twenty photos under glass. A young man in a suit and horn-rimmed glasses smiled worriedly in black and white out of the bottom left-hand corner.

'Who told him?' Moira asked.

'She left instructions, hen. Him tae be told. And yourself, of course. Afterwards.'

'And when did *she* know?'

'Now there's a question. Maybe two days. Maybe two weeks.'

'Or maybe,' Moira said bitterly, 'it was written in her teacup years ago. Donald, what did I do to her? Why could she no' tell me?'

She looked out of the end bay window, from which the Duchess would sit and observe. The caravan was on a mound at the top of the site with all the lesser caravans laid out below it, like a village around a castle. The Firth of Clyde was a grey pencil line along the horizon; the hint of shading was the Isle of Arran.

Donald wasn't looking at her. He had his disgusting old trilby hat in his hands, a brown finger poking through the hole in the crown.

How much was he keeping to himself, this cousin who'd

guarded the Duchess for more than half a century, whose task it had been, as if laid down in the stars, to watch over the Duchess since she was a wee girl and him not that much older?

Who, thirty-eight years ago, had seen her through the awful scandal of giving birth to the daughter of a young council official in horn-rimmed glasses – the very man ordered to clear the gypsies from their summer site overlooking the Clyde, the bureaucratic busybody so bewitched by her beauty, it was said, that he couldn't hold his clipboard steady.

'She wis worried about you. I'll tell ye that much.'

'She'd no cause,' Moira said.

'Wisny easy for her, y'understand. You bein' away so much.'

Thirty-eight years ago, mysteriously, the gypsies had been allowed to keep their autumn site overlooking the Clyde. Her father – and his indomitable mother – had received the child. 'Rescued the child,' as her gran had phrased it. A deal. The wee girl, abandoned to a starchy Presbyterian upbringing in a genteel Glasgow suburb, abandoned to a weak and diffident father, a powerfully narrow grandmother.

'Will ye go in now?'

Donald nodding at the sliding door to the wee hallway and, beyond it, the bedroom where the Duchess was.

'I can't,' Moira said. 'I can't see her dead.'

Donald finally lifted his gaze to her, the lines deepening around his mouth. 'She'll be offended. The nieces ha' been with her all the morning. Until you came. It was assumed . . .'

'I'll have no one make assumptions about me.' Moira shook her black, nearly-shoulder-length hair, turned sharply and walked out of the caravan door.

The old man followed her, clenching and unclenching his fists around his hat, very agitated.

'Listen . . . stop.' Clattering down the steps after her. 'Wait.' Pulling out an envelope. 'You wis to have this – when you saw her.'

'What is it?'

'Take it now,' Donald said, and she nodded.

But still walked away, pushing the envelope into a side pocket of her tweed jacket.

The Duchess's death lay over the site like low cloud, the colours of the caravans dulled.

There was nobody much about as she wandered among the caravans on this drab autumn morning, as she had a quarter of a century ago; a twelve-year-old girl on her way home from the high school, a girl who'd been warned, since she could toddle, to stay away from the old railway where the gypsies camped in the autumn.

The woman in her early thirties with the long dark hair and fingers of fire had been waiting, unsmiling, on the steps of the caravan. Had flicked disdainfully at the clipped hair of the plain, quiet child. *How is your father? Does he speak of me often?*

He never speaks of you. Defiant.

But he thinks of me, I reckon, as he shuffles his papers in his wee office. And he dreams.

A dozen rings on her hands: rubies and emeralds and sapphires, glittering hypnotically. Moira had been so confused and her stomach churning; she'd been having headaches on and off all day, had not wanted to get up, her gran giving her the stern eye, *'Don't you go telling your fibs, you're looking perfectly fit and well, did you no' complete your homework, is that it?'*

The woman with the rings had said, *Don't you worry yourself, you're not sick, you're just changing.* And had given her only child a present. An old comb of dull, grey metal, like a dog's comb with teeth missing.

Take it. It's yours. For a time.

What do I . . .?

What would you expect to do with it? You comb your hair. And remember today, 'cause you'll never be a wee girl again.

Twelve years old. Bewilderment. The excitement of the unknown. Headaches and tummy pains. Blood on white cotton sheets. *Hush, now, you're no' dying, it's only the curse.*

The curse? The gypsy curse?
Don't talk such nonsense, Moira, go back to your bed.

The comb, gliding through her lengthening hair in the darkness, making static electricity, blue sparks.

The hair grew. And the rows began. *You look like a damned gypsy, get it cut, get it cut at once.*

Never.

Moira walked off the site now, past piled-up black rubbish sacks awaiting collection, one already plundered by the crows. Well, she'd known, of course, as a kid, that her mother was with the travellers. Except that the way the story had been told to her was, like: Your mother didn't want you. Your mother abandoned you and ran off with the dirty gypsies. The words, *that whore*, passing from grandparent to parent in times of stress.

It was a scrappy place. There'd been an industrial estate here in the old days; now there were breezeblock walls and girders.

When she was rich, when she'd signed the contract with Epidemic and got an incredible amount up front, she'd come here to see her exotic mother and very foolishly offered to buy her a house of her own or at least a nice place to put her caravan.

She remembered sitting in the china cave, so full of herself. *I've been asked to join a band on a two-album contract, Mammy; the money's amazing.* So excited at being able to do something for the Duchess. Hard to believe now that she'd ever been quite that dense.

Even the jewels on the Duchess's hands had seemed to sparkle with a cold rage.

I would not take your money (the Duchess with magnificent severity, a strong, cultured accent by then) *even if it was good money. Don't you dare insult me, girl. You were directed towards a spiritual path, and you've forsaken it. You're dabbling. Deviating. You've taken the devil's currency. You're a stupid, stupid girl. I cannot* believe *what you're doing.*

She hadn't seen her mother for close on four years after that.

Moira wandered up the rubbly lane which led to where the factories might once have been. The sky had gone white, the sea had disappeared and the Isle of Arran was no more than an impression on a tablecloth.

She sat on an upturned oil drum and took out the envelope Donald had given her and stared at it for a long time.

There was nothing on the front except for one letter, in the Duchess's familiar baroque scrawl.

M

She stared for several minutes at the envelope.

Four years on, after the Abbey, she'd returned to the site wearing dark, dowdy clothes and no make-up. Amid the tumble of her long, black hair there was now a single, slender vein of white. A souvenir from the Abbey.

She'd walked boldly up to the door of the palace on wheels, looking the Duchess in the eye.

And *then* she'd broken down.

Just like now.

She slipped a hand inside her jacket, unzipped the breast pocket and took out the cloth bundle. Slowly, sitting on the oil drum, she unwrapped the comb; metal, grey-brown like stone. A thousand, two thousand years old. Undistinguished, utility, like a doggy's comb.

Moira wept, sliding the envelope with *M* on the front back into her pocket.

It was very dim in the little hallway with all the doors closed.

She knocked on the plywood panel. The door slid back, and there was Donald in his blue suit with his hat in his hands, the bobbing light of candles at his back.

He said, very softly, 'The Duchess'll receive you now, hen.'

Used to put pennies on dead people's eyes, didn't they, to keep the lids down?

Oh, Christ.

She looked around for Donald, to ask him why . . . *why?*

But Donald had slipped away and closed the sliding door behind him. She was alone in here with the curtains closed and candles, four of them, at the head and the foot of the long, wide bed.

No china in here; the walls were clean white. Where Donald had stood, behind her, his back to the wall beyond the bottom of the bed, shadows reared in the dancing light. She stood watching these shadows, her back to the bed, afraid to turn around again.

She closed her eyes and tried to steady her breathing. The air had a scent of violets. She tried to speak, to pray, but it was as if there was a film of wax over her lips.

You are not supposed to do this to me, Mammy.

Slowly she turned around to face the deathbed and started to open her eyes, but she was too afraid and closed them tighter. And she could still see the little candle flames, reddened through the eyelids, giving off heat like the flames which, all those years ago, had engorged two mangled vehicles in a country lane.

Remembering how the flames had risen through the hissing rain, two columns of fire joining above the wreckage, forming a shape like a giant blazing harp, its strings the gilded arrows of the rain.

Why? Why this, now? Get me out of this.

She took a breath and opened her eyes.

The Duchess wore a satin nightdress of grey, edged with silver, like cold sun behind rainclouds.

White pillows behind her shoulders, white pillows behind her head, a bank of pillows. Her river of long white hair spread into a delta, her lips slightly parted over grey-white, pearly teeth.

Moira's heart hung like a stone in her breast and beneath her jacket and the sleeves of her silk blouse, she felt the goosebumps rise.

The Duchess was sitting bolt upright in her bed and her eyes were wide open, still as glass and fixed coldly upon her only daughter.

You are dead. You are supposed to be quiescent, on your back, with that marble, sculpted look so that people can say, Doesn't she seem so peaceful? You are not supposed to challenge me, Mammy. I'm too old to be afraid of a corpse.

There was electricity in the violet-scented air. Candlelight flickered in the gems of the rings on the hands of the Duchess, a proud, vain woman, a mother before twenty, dead now before sixty.

Dead? Was this thing dead? Was this how she'd been when Daddy had come? Was this why, for Christ's sake, his glasses were misted?

No. This was for her.

The long, thin hands were rigidly clasped upon the sheets, one little finger curled slightly outwards as if pointing at Moira.

You have some damage to repair.

The Duchess had said this once. Now, as if the body on the bed had opened its lips, she heard it whispered, with studio clarity, in her head.

Damage.

You set me up, Donald, you auld bastard, you set me up for this.

She took out the envelope, pale blue Basildon Bond, and the Duchess watched from her pillows as she slit the top with the thumbnail of her right hand.

One sheet of paper, folded in two.

The Duchess watched her read the words, two of them, printed in capitals, each followed by a large question mark.

BREADWINNER?
and
DEATHOAK?

Moira said, voice as dry as woodash, 'You can't do this. You're a sham, a phoney. You can't con me with your wee tricks . . . you hear me?'

She tried to tighten her lips in defiance, but her mouth had gone to rubber, like after anaesthetic at the dentist's.

Instead, she struggled to get both hands together around the paper, gripping her right hand with her left to make it close. She crumpled the paper in her hands. It crackled as if it was on fire, so loud that she barely heard the other sound, the silken slithering.

As two pillows slid to the floor and the Duchess, with a sighing of satin, subsided into the sheets.

Part Two

I

A Sob You Could See

Sir Wilfrid, striding stiffly in his gardening tweeds, led the way to the end of his terrace to offer up the full horror of the eyesore on the hill.

'And the trees – the few that there were – they *chopped them down*. Can you imagine doing that? This is the Cotswolds, heaven's sake. Do they *know* who lives over the valley?'

'You mean the Prince of Wales?'

Sir Wilfrid snorted. 'Do you think *he* should have to see *that* every time he drives up the lane?'

Martin Broadbank, for his sins, chairman of the district council's environmental health committee, said, 'I'm sure that, on his scale of monstrous architectural carbuncles, that place wouldn't be terribly noteworthy. But I see your point.'

The house on the hill was the size of a moderate Victorian mansion. It had been built, in what, loosely, could be described as the approved Cotswold style, employing the kind of reconstituted ochre stone used for council houses, to make them blend in with the traditional village architecture.

It blended in like a cheeseburger at a vicarage tea. Sir Wilfrid was right: not a tree of any substance, nor even a trickle of ivy up the walls. All the other newish houses in the hamlet had been neatly stitched into the tapestry of the landscape. This one was sliced off from it by a fence six feet high, slats damn near as thick as railway sleepers.

'Twenty-two years at the D of E.' Sir Wilfrid brushed a dead leaf from his gardening trousers. 'And one ends up with *that* on one's skyline. And at night . . .'

Martin Broadbank noted the lawns sloping up to the yellow house, flanking its gravel drive, the grass shaven billiard-table smooth. He counted six tightly clipped dwarf conifers, of the kind you found in your suburban handkerchief patch. So much for landscaping.

He said carefully, 'I believe he was quite a well-known musician at one time.'

'Hmph,' said Sir Wilfrid. 'Nobody I've ever heard of. Nobody the *granddaughter* has even heard of. Besides, thought all these pop chaps were supposed to be members of the damned Green Party. Fellow wants to keep nature at bay, hell doesn't he go and live in Battersea?'

'Er . . . quite.' Martin Broadbank always felt a trifle uncomfortable in discussions of this nature; three of his supermarkets had been built in the face of impassioned protest from local environmentalists. 'But your main problem is . . .'

'The horrific noises. My wife feels threatened.'

'How so, Sir Wilfrid?'

'I mean, *she* seems normal enough, the woman. Runs some sort of healthfood business in Stroud. Him, we simply never see. *Nobody* ever sees him. There's an evil-looking little hippie type, lives in a caravan in the grounds – that's *another* scandalous breach of planning regs. But, you see, we *hear* the beggar, at night.'

'The hippie?'

'No, no . . . Storey. Presumably. The most frightful howling and wailing . . . dreadful shrill mournful whining, like a sick fox in the woods. And lights on, all night. *All* night. They say the man's disturbed, of course. And so, obviously, my wife . . .'

Martin himself would probably have popped round and invited them for supper, check these people out. *Not* Sir Wilfrid's style; only way he'd communicate, if it ever became unavoidable, was by solicitor's letter.

'And there's the daughter. Don't get me wrong, I'm not saying they should be in *homes* necessarily. But the way they have her dressed you'd swear they think she's normal.'

'Normal, Sir Wilfrid?'

Sir Wilfrid sniffed. 'Anyway,' he said, 'what does your council propose to do about them?'

OK. Maybe there was a rational explanation. Fair enough. No hassle.

The Weasel set off from his caravan, stepping over tree stumps.

Rational? Nah. Rational, bollocks. As Tom would say.

It was cold, the air gnawing at his sunken cheeks. He pulled down his woollen hat and buttoned his old US Army combat jacket. Wedged under his left arm was an LP record, *Goat's Head Soup* by the Rolling Stones.

The yellow back wall of the big, boring house loomed over him like a prison block. It was an ugly fucking house. They could've done better, Tom and Shelley; you could get yourself a terrific old drum hereabouts for half what this pile cost. Yeah, yeah, Shelley needed somewhere big, with the office and the computers and that. And, yeah, the local council had been good with the grants and stuff, dead keen to promote all this tele-village, home-business shit.

But it still didn't figure, any more than a lot of things.

And – Weasel sniffed the damp-bonfire smell of autumn – there was still too much *pain* in the air. Left over from last night, maybe, when the great rainbow of purified pain had arched, throbbing, over the house.

The Weasel had worshipped the electric guitar since the days when the Stratocaster was just a gleam in Mr Fender's eye. The guitar dragged out of you what you couldn't otherwise express: pulled the rage out of your head, the fear out of your guts, the hard longing out of your . . . groin.

Turned all this into music. Wielding your axe like Tom Storey could was like sprouting a new vital organ.

It was a beautiful thing.

But last night the Weasel had been almost cowering in his caravan, fifty yards behind the house, where it sounded like

Tom Storey had cut open his belly and was slowly unravelling his guts.

It'd started normally enough, with Tom playing along with old Cream and Yardbirds albums, nostalgia time. But then Tom's playing had kind of reeled away and you didn't hear the records any more, only these slippery ribbons of pain.

And when you looked out, you'd swear you could see it, hazy around the rooftop: what Weasel called the rainbow.

Except a rainbow was a pretty thing, and this was all dark colours, purples and greys: like a sob you could see.

He stopped. He was about six yards from the house. He could hear voices, not from the house. He looked down across long lawns the size of three bowling greens and saw the titled geezer that lived in this quaint old cottage on the edge of the village. He was talking to another, taller guy and pointing up this way.

Which made the Weasel suspicious, and legitimately so: part of his job was to look out for Tom and Shelley and the kid, Vanessa, and anybody that might give them hassle.

He watched the two geezers for a minute or so and then turned back to the house and saw a figure, very still, in the kitchen window, heavy blonde hair on the shoulders.

Shelley. Standing there, looking out, but not in his direction. There was a mug of coffee steaming in her hand. She had no expression on her face. Only tears.

The Weasel thought: That bastard. Don't he realize what he's *doing* to her?

Not the time.

The Weasel wasn't stupid, knew when to back off. He slid away before Shelley could turn and spot him and went round the side of the house to spy on the two geezers.

She was a really wonderful woman, was Shelley. The Weasel had long ago given up wondering what hidden qualities Tom possessed that he could've pulled a chick of this quality and –

more amazing still – kept her for so many years. 'Cause it wasn't the money; if it wasn't for Shelley Tom wouldn't *have* no money.

But how much more of this – of Tom – was she going to be able to take?

See, Tom was getting worse, not better – all too obvious to a mate who'd known him since they was kids in Bermondsey, back before Tom's old man died.

OK, it was true, right from the old days, that Tom was the first to blow his stack. Temperamental, like any great artist. But not like he was now. Not like some hunted bear, and if you went too close, he'd have your throat. Not so hung-up he couldn't even confide in the faithful little guy who'd carried his amps out of the Transit van and into the halls, hunting for power points, changing plugs by torchlight, procuring dodgy susbtances or clean chicks or whatever else was required at any particular time to satisfy whatever needed satisfying.

The Weasel stood on the edge of the circular drive and looked down, across the lawns. The two geezers, old Sir Wilf and the younger, taller one, had pushed off.

He thought: Time I done a bit more nosing around. Go down the pub tonight, clobber the yokels at pool, find out what the score is with this Sir Wilf.

But first things first.

Making his meal, before work, the Weasel had come to a decision. 'Go down the house,' he'd told his half-pounder. 'Soon's as I get finished. Get some answers, find out what's going down. And no bullshit off the big guy. Not this time.' In the frying pan, the big burger had sizzled its approval.

Wouldn't normally chance his arm like this, prejudice his position in the Love-Storey set-up. Next to being a temporary roadie for the Brain Police this was actually the best job he'd ever had, which still surprised him; he hadn't expected to be able to stick it more than a few weeks, all this fresh air shit. He might *look* like a shrivelled hippie – little round shades and grey hair half-way down his back (despite there not being much on top these days) – but he'd never been able to grasp the attraction of living in the sticks, communing with nature, getting your balls frozen off.

But here in his caravan, all connected to the juice, with an electric heater, a good little sound system with a stack of vintage vinyl, plus a microwave and a hotplate so's you could make yourself a couple of greasy half-pounders after a day out delivering healthy shit to wholefood shops and vegetarian restaurants, well, this was OK, this wasn't half bad, to be quite honest, feet up in your 'van, good old stuff on the deck, Cream, Doors, Hendrix.

In fact, it was the late Jimi Hendrix, Weasel's all-time fave axeman, that had started him thinking.

Weasel stood at the edge of the lawn, lit a fag.

How it happened was like this.

Week or two ago he'd noticed that his fourth copy of Hendrix's *Electric Ladyland* LP (the one with all the naked chicks on the sleeve) was beginning to show serious signs of becoming unplayable. So Weasel, still resisting CD – crackles is *life*, man – had wandered down the big house to ask Tom if he could borrow his copy to transfer to cassette, which would mean he could also play it in the van as he drove around delivering his consignments of soya sausages and wholenut goulash.

Now, when it came down to sounds, Tom was generosity itself, recognizing that to a guy like Weasel, sounds was lifeblood, right? As a rule Tom said: Yeah, sure, man, words to that effect.

But this day, on this question of *Electric Ladyland*, Tom had come over distinctly weird, gone all confused, said nah, nah, he hadn't got that one no more, you take this one instead, palming Weasel off with this crappy old Jefferson Airplane LP. But not before Weasel had seen what'd happened to Tom's once-magnificent collection of rock albums, stretching over three whole walls of the big guy's ballroom-size den.

Had seen that there was not one single Hendrix disc on the shelves.

Along with other notable absences.

A week later, just to test this theory of his, he'd presented himself at the back door with a view to borrowing the Rolling Stones' *Beggar's Banquet*, and Tom had come over all weird again and told him he'd lent it to someone and never had it back, what a drag. And sent Weasel off instead with *Goat's Head Soup*, a particularly creepy-looking Stones album from the seventies with references to the devil and stuff that Weasel figured Tom, considering his past, would want nothing to do with.

For some reason, *Goat's Head Soup* was all right but *Beggar's Banquet* was not.

Weasel had dithered around a bit to get another quick scan of the rows of album spines on the shelves and, sure enough, he'd spotted a few more significant gaps: the Doors. Joplin.

Which proved his theory, no question.

He dropped his fag on the grass, stamped on it. Too late now. They didn't like – *Tom* didn't like – to be disturbed after dark. He'd give it another day or two. Then he'd definitely go back, face up the big guy.

Making sure, however, before he said a word, that he was the one closest to the door.

'You were quite right,' Martin Broadbank said into the phone. 'It's *most* peculiar.'

'You seen him, then?'

'You're joking. Even his nearest neighbour hasn't seen him. He's *heard* him . . . playing his instrument.'

'More than I have, Martin. He won't even come to the bastard phone.'

'What about the wife?' Broadbank asked.

'She quizzes you. If you're anything to do with the music business, it's "I'm sorry, Tom isn't working at the moment." Naturally, I didn't tell her what it was about, I want to spring it on him, I want to hear *his* reaction.'

Martin Broadbank sighed in mild annoyance. He didn't know why he was getting involved in this, except perhaps out of boredom – you inherited your father's business, expanded it during the acquisitive eighties into areas the old man didn't even know existed; that didn't mean you had to find it interesting or regard it, God forbid, as your life's work. Boredom: he was spending an increasing amount of time fending it off.

'It's all pointless, though, isn't it, Steve, if the tapes aren't worth it?'

'The tapes will be . . .' Stephen Case sounded a little nervous '. . . fine. That's my feeling.'

'God save us from feelings.' Martin Broadbank's own feelings had told him to have nothing to do with it when his old university chum had called a couple of nights ago to ask if he knew he was residing not ten miles away from a living legend. But he'd been bored and slightly intrigued, and remembered the environmental health officer telling him about Sir Wilfrid Tulley getting ratty over some insane pop star at the bottom of his garden.

'Anyway, it seems your friend Storey's taken to playing his guitar, none too tunefully, in the early hours of the morning. His neighbour wants it stopped.'

Stephen Case said urgently, 'How can I get to see him, Martin?'

'Buy yourself a powerful pair of binoculars is all I can advise. Man's a total recluse, as you say.'

'No, come on – you could help me. You've got contacts.'

'Steve, you know how much I hate to say "What's in it for me?", but . . .'

'I was your best man!'

'Were you really? I must have forgotten that particular marriage.'

'*And* you're a TMM shareholder. A substantial one.'

'Lord, haven't I got rid of those yet? Must be losing my financial acumen. Look, OK, you want to meet Storey . . . give me a day or two.'

Why *was* he doing this? Possibly for the same reason he'd got himself elected to the tedious bloody council. Because he just had to be at the centre. Because he saw life – and business

– as a huge railway system. A matter of being at the right terminus at the right time. Sometimes you could even switch the points, and when two trains collided, capitalize on the salvage.

'I might have a chat with the wife,' he said. 'I tend to like wives.'

'As long as they aren't yours,' said Stephen Case, 'presumably.'

'Quite,' said Broadbank.

II

Baking

Unearthly in the dusk, wreathed in white silk, the head glided silently past the vicarage window.

The vicar looked up from his desk, disoriented.

His study was at the side of the house facing the village, across the steep lane from the church under its protective rock of ages.

The vicar, in jeans and sweater, moved to the window, leaving open on his desk an ugly old book, a Victorian account, with engravings, of the ecclesiastical buildings of Gwent.

Isabel Pugh was in one of those electric wheelchairs – quite sophisticated, but not designed for Ystrad Ddu, struggling a little now, gliding less evenly, as it moved up the hill. A couple of feet behind it walked Mrs May Pugh, the vicar's part-time housekeeper, hands out ready to grab the chair if it stalled and slipped back.

The vicar saw Isabel turn her head violently, tearing off the silk scarf. Behind his double-glazing, he lip-read, 'For God's sake, Mother!'

Mrs Pugh's arms dropped to her sides and then folded in exasperation across her quilted chest as the wheelchair laboured away up the hill in the failing light.

'What a bloody life,' the vicar mumbled, returning to his desk. If she'd been a post-pubescent schoolgirl when she fell from the Abbey, Isabel Pugh must be in her mid-thirties by now. How could she go on living here, half a mile up the valley from where she'd spent a night of agony, lying under rubble, next to the corpse of her young lover?

People were unbelievably stoical in Ystrad Ddu, its foundations perhaps, like the Abbey's, cemented in blood.

The vicar sat down and switched on his green-shaded desk lamp. The battered book before him was opened to an engraving showing a bearded man in a torn and ragged monk's habit, on his knees, hands together in prayer. On the opposite page, the text read:

> Richard Walden, his back bent and twisted under the burden of his sins, descended from the Black Mountains by the old road and found himself in a most wondrous place, a deep valley with a trickling stream and lush green hills all around, the air of this paradise being as rich as the wine he had tended in the great cellars at Hereford. All his senses swollen with joy, he fell upon his knees and drank from the stream, and then, lifting his eyes humbly to Heaven, gave thanks. And it was at just this moment that the light fell around him like golden rain and Richard had his Holy Vision and the Revelation that this was the place where he must spend the rest of his days in the service of the Lord and gather around him those of a like disposition, repentent sinners in search of redemption.
>
> And so Richard built for himself a rude wooden hut by the stream and lived there, and from that day onwards, others came to the place in search of sanctuary and the message was carried far and wide. Indeed, such was the reputation of the community at Ystrad Ddu for piety and humility that gifts were bestowed upon Richard Walden by lords and barons anxious to atone for their own misdeeds, and he was soon able to fulfil what had been foretold in the Revelation, the raising of a great Abbey to the glory of the Lord, from whose towers could be glimpsed the Holy Mountain Ysgyryd Fawr, the Skirrid . . .

The vicar thought of poor Isabel Pugh, angrily urging her electric wheelchair up the hill. How could Richard Walden's earthly paradise have shrivelled into that grim, mean, stunted place which bestowed only misery and death?

He looked out of the window, lights coming on in the cottages which seemed to hang from the hillside.

No use putting it off, mate, the vicar told himself. This is what the job's about. This is the sharp end.

I can't.

Oh, yes, you bloody can. Can't expect to be able to cast out other people's demons until you confront your own.

Maurice, of Audico, said, 'OK, we'll bake them for you. We'll bake them at fifty-five centigrade for three days. No guarantees, of course; they may come out like crusty French bread, who knows?'

'Don't worry about it,' Prof Levin said. 'I won't.'

Because he took things as they came these days, didn't he? Stayed cool, avoided aggro, drank only coffee and Pepsi. Sure.

He lifted the wooden box on to Maurice's desk.

'My,' Maurice said. 'Some container.'

'Yeah.' He was glad to leave the box at the factory to-night. Every time he looked at the thing, he found his body crying out for a proper drink – this being his regular barometer these days, how badly any particular situation made him long for a drink.

With this box, the barometer read: *Stormy. Stay in. Close windows, lock all doors.*

Of course, he'd known all along there was a fair chance of rescuing the tape, but with Steve Case it was always better to play your cards close to your chest. And in this case he was rather hoping that in three days' time Maurice would throw up his hands and say: Sorry, mate, it's just too far gone.

This private enterprise bit: worrying. Prof was planning to semi-retire in a couple of years, pick and choose his jobs. If he had a choice of committing what was left of his future and his reputation to either Stephen Case or the entire TMM organization, well, not much of a contest, was it?

'Look,' Steve had said, the little vein under his nose twitching, 'do what you can. If it costs, it costs.'

Well, it wouldn't actually cost that much, considering. Not when you had a mate in the recording-tape manufacturing industry and this mate owed you a favour or two for recommending his product to people who mattered. This was a business cemented by favours.

'So here's the situation,' Maurice said. 'The baking should harden the binder, glue it all together again. But you know that without repeat bakings it won't last? What I'm saying, you need to dub off a copy, PDQ.'

'Yeah, yeah. Can you ring me the minute it's out of the oven?' They actually had special ovens at Audico for this; a lot of duff tape was produced in the seventies.

'You want me to have a listen afterwards, see how it's come out, put you out of your misery?'

'Don't bother. I'll collect. PDQ.'

He knew there'd be no unauthorized copies run off, not with Maurice handling this personally. He was simply covering himself. He didn't know where this was going.

It was near closing time, almost dark outside, no other customers in the store. An assistant was wiping the counters with a damp cloth.

He took to the main cash register a bilious-looking item clingfilmed into a foil pastry case.

'What exactly is this?'

She was a largish blonde in a blue and white butcher's apron, which, in a vegetarian foodstore, was probably something of a gesture.

'It's a savoury flan, sir,' she said crisply. 'With onions and chives and a rather interesting soya-based cheese-substitute.'

Martin Broadbank, Cotswold councillor, owner of supermarkets, said, 'Interesting, how?'

He put her age at about the same as his, mid-forties. Earthmother type, he supposed, but very attractive with the wide mouth and the heavy blonde hair like a big brass bell. And, of course, those wonderfully generous breasts. She looked slightly harassed but very capable.

He remembered Sir Wilfrid . . . *I mean* she *seems normal enough, the woman. Runs some sort of health food business in Stroud . . .*

'We think it's probably the closest anyone's yet come to developing something which actually tastes like cheese rather than sour yoghurt,' said Mrs Shelley Storey.

'I see,' Martin said. 'But surely at least twice as expensive as what we traditionalists like to think of as *real* cheese.'

She said, 'If you're talking about bulk Cheddar, mass-produced, that's one thing . . .'

Martin Broadbank felt the lever controlling life's railway points begin to tremble significantly under his hand. A remarkable number of interesting trains were now converging on his part of Gloucestershire.

'. . . but if you look at specialist cheeses,' Mrs Storey said, 'you'll find this is actually not incomparable in price to some of the locally produced goat and sheep cheese, and when you consider . . .'

Who was he doing this for? For Stephen Case, who'd been his emergency best man when they were at university together (studying law, which neither of them had turned into a career)? Or for Sir Wilfrid, who was set on a collision course with the reclusive Tom Storey, whom Martin Broadbank wished no harm at all, and why should he?

No reason at all, except that Sir Wilfrid was clearly a vindictive man and, what was worse, a vindictive man with some residual influence at the Department of the Environment, which had sometimes been less than enthusiastic about plans for large supermarkets like Martin Broadbank's on the fringes of country towns.

Well, I'm doing it for me, of course, Martin Broadbank acknowledged, accepting a sample of cheese substitute. And for the general good of mankind, which has to be more or less the same thing.

'Interesting aftertaste,' he said. 'Good seller, is it?'

The business was called Love-Storey (rather cute, the woman's maiden name had been Love), with specialist retail outlets in Cheltenham, Stroud and Cirencester and a wholesale warehouse supplying a range of home-made vegetarian gourmet delights of the nut-and-beanburger variety to sundry village stores.

A couple of swift telephone calls had revealed Love-Storey to be in some financial difficulty stemming, apparently, from over-expansion in the late eighties. *Most* opportune.

'I mean, how many of these, er, flans do you manage to unload in a week?'

Never before had Martin Broadbank attempted to ingest anything in the soya-substitute line and he was not terribly impressed, to be honest. But vegetarianism was no passing fad; supermarkets back-shelved it at their peril.

She was looking at him curiously. He met her eyes.

'How many would you say?'

Mrs Storey bridled. 'I . . .' Then she closed her luscious lips, smiled wryly and called to an assistant. 'Jan, the savoury flans – what would you say? Fifteen, this week?'

'Fifteen?' said Martin Broadbank with no hint of a sneer. 'Suppose you had an order for, say, five hundred? What would your price be then?'

'All right,' Mrs Shelley Storey said, hands on hips, glorious chest out. 'Who *are* you?'

Martin Broadbank had the not-so-absurd desire to lean across the counter of yacht-varnished pine and bury his face in those wonderfully *friendly* knockers.

Instead, he told her his name. On the offchance she really didn't know, he told her what his line of business was. He told her they appeared to be living in neighbouring villages. He invited her to discuss the possibilities of wider marketing of cheese-substitute flans and similar items. Over dinner.

'And your husband, of course,' he added regretfully.

'Oh,' she said.

'Problems?'

'No, I . . . it could be a little difficult, that is . . .'

She was silent for a moment, then she smiled. Behind the smile he could see a whole computer-game of criss-crossing emotions: a ray of hope zapped by dark apprehension, a trace of fear even.

'Of course,' she said. 'We'd love to.'

After his supper of cheese and water-biscuits, the vicar wandered across to his church.

It was a smaller building even than the vicarage, probably never much more than a chapel, an outpost of the Abbey. And quite intimate, especially at night, soft, white moonlight washing through high windows, making pools on the stone floor around the altar.

The vicar knelt in the silence before the altar and prayed for strength.

'How are you going to get me out of this one, eh?' he said forlornly. 'I didn't want to come, but you – and he – put the arm on me and so here I am, and look at me. Shit-scared. I need help.'

He waited, hands clasped, elbows on the altar. A wooden cross in its centre had an aureole of moonlight.

The vicar listened to his heart.

Half an hour passed. The only image he received was one of Isabel Pugh, poor cow, in her electric wheelchair.

Eventually he sighed and got to his feet.

'Not time yet, then? That what you're saying? A few things to work out?'

Well, what had he expected? A golden light around him, a vision like Richard Walden's, accompanied by an overwhelming sense of joy encased in strength?

He stood in silence and raised his eyes to the small Gothic window above the altar. The moon chose that moment to vanish into cloud, and it became very dark in the church. When the vicar opened the door, there was a quick push of wind, as if the night was elbowing him aside in its hurry to enter the church. The vicar felt empty, lightweight, ineffectual and stupid.

It was going to be hard.

*

That night, in bed, Martin Broadbank mused to his house-keeper, Meryl, 'Could be rather fun, don't you think? I do love surprises, confrontations, human friction. I'm almost inclined to invite old Sir Wilfrid, too. In fact, I think I bloody well will.'

His housekeeper said, 'You think that's wise? He's not what you'd call a sociable old man.'

'What's wise got to do with it?' Martin was feeling good. Five minutes ago, at the critical moment, his mind had seized an image of Mrs Shelley Storey with earth-shaking results. He didn't think Meryl would mind, this once.

Meryl said, 'I know one thing. The Lady Bluefoot wouldn't care for him. I reckon she'd find him rather common, for a Sir.'

'Mmmn,' Martin said. 'Well . . .' This was Meryl's way of voicing her own dislike.

'And she's been very sweet lately, haven't you smelled it, in the drawing-room?'

'I'm really quite intrigued, you know,' he said, dismissing their house-ghost with his usual non-committal tolerance. 'What will Storey be *like*? How will the humourless Case actually handle him? Hey, you do know *why* he's a recluse, don't you?'

'You're not God, you know, Martin,' his housekeeper reminded him. 'To arrange people like chess pieces.'

'Because he actually killed his wife; it's quite a story. God? Who wants to be God anyway? God never has any fun.'

Her third night at the Glasgow airport hotel and Moira Cairns, in a baggy, knee-length Bart Simpson T-shirt, was lying rest-lessly between a couple of pillows as hard as flour bags. And nurturing a low anger, maybe to keep the fear away.

Three anonymous nights here were the kind of luxury – if you could call these pillows luxury – which, hardly having worked at all the past year, she'd have to start learning to do without.

On the slippery side of midnight, she lay all alone in the double bed and held in both hands the single page of paper:

plain blue Basildon Bond, not a whiff of perfume, nor even a hint of deathbed violets.

Was this it? Was this the old witch's principal bequest – a sheet of folded chainstore notepaper with hex-words scrawled upon it?

She glared at the two bland plant pictures on the wall, especially chosen for people who hated art. Yet she'd come here precisely *because* it was so damn bland, every room alike. Well removed from both a croft house on Skye and the one palatial mobile home among the jumble of patched-up caravans on a scruffy, statutory gypsy site an hour's drive from here.

Round about now, Donald and the nieces would be arranging the Duchess neatly in her coffin – her big day tomorrow – and praying to God the old besom would not sit up suddenly in the night and rebuke them for doing it all wrong.

And tomorrow Moira would drive back to the site, for maybe the last time, and would have to react to her mammy's final challenge.

How?

Twenty-five years ago, she gave me the glamour on a plate, handed princess-potential to a dowdy kid. Twenty-five years ago, she touched me with her glitzy music-hall magic and while all that glitters may not be gold, it sure as hell still glitters.

So where's the damn glitter in this?

All she leaves for me is a bleak reminder of the worst of times, two words she surely got out of my own head when I was not taking care. And scrawled in pencil on a sheet of . . . not even her usual gilt-headed parchment but the stuff you can buy pads of at any newsagent's.

This was not the Duchess's style. Had the letter been given to her by anyone but Donald, she would have been suspicious of its origins. But, hell . . . even in a scrawl, the character of the hand was plainly the Duchess's.

Written in pain? Written in anger? Frustration?

Moira tensed, went as hard inside as the pillows.

The bedside lights seemed to dim in acknowledgement and, around her, the sheets on the bed suddenly felt deathbed-stiff.

She scrambled out in a hurry, fumbling for the dressing-table lights.

Sitting at the dressing-table, breathing rapidly, she spread out the paper, held her head in her hands, her elbows on the linen mat, and she stared hard at the words: *Breadwinner, deathoak.*

This was the point: no glitz.

The note said to Moira: *Listen. I am a woman. I am frightened. I make no pretence of being able to deal with this. There is no crest on this paper, no perfume, because against this thing the glamour is no defence. I am on my own with a stub of pencil, one sheet of blue Basildon Bond and my terrible, terrible fear.*

This humble, scrawled message, without grace, without elegance, was therefore the heaviest warning the Duchess could give her.

There was a small noise from behind her. Like an affirmation. Like *yes.*

Moira spun in time to see one of the bland Trust House Forte plant pictures tumble the final few inches to the carpet. When she picked it up she found the glass had split from corner to corner.

III

All Dead

S helley had her back to the window this time, talking to somebody. Probably the man himself.

Be dark soon. They didn't like the Weasel coming round in the dark, but the days getting shorter reduced his options.

Lights were blinking on in the village. It looked like a much bigger place at night; you could see all the lights from up here, the pub and the church hall and that.

Previously there'd been trees, mostly saplings and half-grown conifers planted by the developers, this specialist firm that built the house around the shell of a ruined barn in '92. In a couple of years the new trees would have been blocking out the village lights, giving Tom and Shelley more privacy.

Except Tom didn't want that. Privacy, sure; this had to be important, he never came *out*. But he couldn't be shut in by nature, needed to see the lights at night.

Also, for some reason, he didn't like big trees.

So the trees had gone, the young ones dug up and given away, the others chopped, a big fence put in. Shelley hadn't been happy about all this, and some local conservation type had also kicked up, raising, at the same time, the issue of Weasel's mobile home. To cool the protests, they'd agreed to conceal the caravan with bushes and larch-lap, but they were still getting hostile looks from the green-anorak brigade.

Tom didn't care. He never had to see any of them, on account of never going out. He'd found his place and he wasn't moving.

The Weasel saw Tom's hulking shadow blocking out the kitchen light, waving its arms about like King Kong.

He remembered standing on this very spot about a year ago when the house was only half-built, watching the dowsers, two serious geezers gliding around the site with their forked twigs and their, whatdoyoucallems, on strings – pendulums. Seeing if it was safe for Tom to live here, with no ancient vibes and stuff.

Poor paranoid bastard.

'No bleeding way,' Tom Storey said. 'And this, darlin' . . . this is my last word. OK?'

She didn't reply. Tom's tone turned threatening. '*I said . . . is that OK?*' Spittle at a corner of his mouth.

He looked away, shut his lips tight, clearly regretting it. He was like a big, stupid dog, growled at you then wagged his tail apologetically.

She watched him glaring over her shoulder out of the wide kitchen window at the lights in the village houses which might have been a hundred miles away across what she always thought of as his moat. It was after five and going rapidly dark. Shelley knew she was going to hate the long nights.

Tom said, more quietly, 'Toffee-nosed gits in monkey suits?' He sniffed hard. '*You* go.'

'Honey . . .' Shelley sighed, wiping her hands on her butcher's apron. 'I think – I really think you're living in the past. Dinner parties are – I mean, nobody's going to turn a hair if you show up as you are now. Obviously, I'd *prefer* you in a suit, you know? Just for once?'

'Oh.' Tom faced her now, unsteadily, across the heavy pine kitchen table. 'You would prefer me in a *suit*.' His big hands flat on the tabletop, but quivering. 'I ain't *got* a bleeding suit, have I? In fact, I ain't never . . .'

'I'll buy you one,' Shelley, steeling herself for the inevitable response, took a tin from the Welsh dresser, began spooning out decaff.

'Like fuck you will!'

'Tom.' Shelley swallowed. 'It's not been a wonderful year, all right? If things don't show a clear improvement by the end of January, Cirencester's got to go, and it's a good shop, potentially.'

'So you close it down. How you gonna sell it? Nuffink moving, nowhere.'

'No, look . . . what I'm saying is, Tom, I need this. It's on a plate. I'll probably never get a chance like this again. I need Broadbank. He owns seventeen supermarkets and he's expanding. He's a gift.'

'So go, doll, just *go*. What's your problem?'

You are my problem, she wanted to scream at him. You have been my problem for much of my adult life. She turned away, but could still see him reflected in the shiny hotplate covers on the Aga, his yellow-white hair sprouting in harsh tufts and his mouth vanishing into his moustache. The face was distended by a big scratch he'd once made with a saucepan, in anger.

He tried to smash Agas with stainless steel saucepans. He'd never laid a finger on her. He was forty-seven years old. He was a child.

Shelley said calmly, 'He rang again, Tom. He suggested Tuesday. He said he was particularly looking forward to seeing *you*. He said a friend of his was coming who's . . .' Oh God '. . . who's a long-standing fan of yours.'

'Oh well,' Tom said. 'That's different, innit?' She saw the table starting to rock under the pressure of his great hands. 'You know how I love to meet my old fans. Autograph an album or two. Talk about the classic gigs, how I used to know the actual Lee Gibson.'

'Tom, please . . .'

'No more congenial way to spend an evening, sweetheart. Analyse the techniques of Clapton and Knopfler, discuss the merits of the Telecaster against the Les Paul. Explain in detail why I ain't done a gig in ten years. Oh, what jolly fun, what . . .'

'Stop it!'

'Anyway.' Tom's mouth smiled. 'Let me make it simple for you. What you do is, you ring him back, tonight, and you say, Mr Broadarse, you say, my husband has asked me to convey his best wishes to you and his express desire for you to go and stuff yourself right up . . .'

'You f—' Shelley slammed the coffee tin on the dresser. Bit her lip, stared at the floor. 'Oaf.'

Tom was swaying, fish-eyed. Shelley said, 'You know what this *is*, don't you? This is clinical agoraphobia. You're a very sick man, Tom, you know that?'

'You just don't . . .'

'Understand. I know, I know. It's all you ever say.'

She turned away from him. In the Aga's covers, she saw him start to shake and splutter, a big vein burrowing under his forehead like a sand-worm.

'And one day,' she said softly into the stove, 'you will *have* to leave.'

'The men in white coats? That what you're saying? Gonna get me committed, are we?'

'Tom,' she said through clenched teeth. 'You *are ill*.'

'Piss off. Day after day I get this shit. Night after bleeding night.' He was trembling badly; sometimes she wondered if there *was* something seriously, physically wrong coming on. Parkinson's or something.

'Tom . . .'

'Shut it! I don't have to take this . . . bleeding sixth-form psychology. You don't know nuffink. You ain't been frew *nuffink*.'

Ain't been frew nuffink. How many thousand times had he thrown this at her? Never spelling it out. Never saying, *you don't see the things I can see*. Certainly never itemizing the things he could see and she couldn't.

'No.' Shelley crushed three fingers of her left hand in her right fist. 'You don't have to take it, this is true. And neither do I. I . . .'

She looked up. Tom had gone quiet.

Shelley saw that his daughter was watching them solemnly from the doorway.

'Dad,' Vanessa said. 'Weasel's here.'

'Just what we needed,' Shelley said. 'Get rid of him.'

Through the kitchen window she saw him at the door, a sinewy little man with a smile which somebody, Dave Reilly probably, used to compare to a vandalized cemetery. Except at weekends or when invited, Weasel never came up to the house after work. He sat in his caravan and played music and probably smoked dope; it was an understanding and a good one.

So this was not Weasel's time, and he knew it, but here he was, leering grotesquely through the window, an LP record under his arm.

The anger fell away, and Shelley – big, busty, bustling Shelley Love – felt suddenly rather fearful.

Vanessa.

The kid opened the door for Weasel, gave him a grin, not quite so wide as usual.

Triffic little girl, nearly fourteen years old now. Beautiful kid. Not in the usual sense, but because of what she was.

This was the reason Shelley stayed with Tom, despite all the shit. Vanessa was everything to Shelley.

Everything but her own child.

'How are ya, Princess?'

'All right, thank you, Weasel.' Vanessa was wearing tight black jeans and a big white sweater with a black cat motif. Her brown hair was cut short and curly and she wore plastic rainbow hoop earrings that matched her big glasses.

'Dad and Shelley have had another row,' Vanessa said solemnly.

The Weasel smiled. These kids, their minds were less subtle. Operated on less wavelengths, not the same range, something like that. Anything bothering them, they came right out with it, hearts on their sleeves.

'Come in, then, Weasel,' she said impatiently.

The Weasel was as careful about Vanessa as Tom was, both of them blaming themselves. Obviously the big crash would never have happened if Tom hadn't been left without his personal roadie that night. If Weasel hadn't been in hospital (hepatitis; occupational hazard). And if . . .

'Fanks, Princess.'

. . . What the hell; she was all right, was Vanessa. Everybody liked her; how many people could say that?

He followed her inside and stood outside the kitchen door while she went in. 'Tell your old man,' he said.

When the doctors told Tom that the baby they'd pulled out of Debs before she died was Down's Syndrome, the big guy had gone on this six-day bender, hoping to drown himself. The chick in Publicity at Epidemic Records had pulled him out and into a private clinic Max Goff paid for – guilt money, Max feeling responsible too, poor dead megalomaniac.

Everybody felt responsible for Vanessa; the kid would've grown up some kind of icon in a glass case, but for the chick in Publicity, who threw in some love on top of everybody else's money. The chick was *called* Love, very apt.

Had a cool head, too, over those enormous bristols, enough common sense to unscramble Tom's finances and nail Epidemic to the wall for compensation. And then – having negotiated herself out of a job and realizing Tom wasn't going to be earning rock star's money for a good long time, if ever again – she'd invested the loot in a health food shop in Cheltenham, where she was born, and they'd lived over the shop for a while and tried not to look back.

The Weasel, meanwhile, coming out of hospital to find himself skint and jobless, had drifted back into what he'd been doing before, which, basically, amounted to rescuing wealthy and overprivileged people from the soul-destroying consequences of their own acquisitiveness – this was how Dave Reilly had described it when they were pissed up one night, the Weasel, delighted, getting him to write it down.

But the Old Bill was still calling it burglary. When he was finally nicked, after a good run, around the end of '87, he was looking at eighteen months.

Served twelve. Time for a new start. When they let him out of Wandsworth, he'd figured his best bet would be a small shop, nothing too ambitious.

So he's jemmying away round the back of a little tobacconist's when the alarm goes off, right? Suddenly, a great light is shining down on him – this super-powerful wall-mounted security spot. But it has the same effect as if this was the Damascus bypass . . . hey, man, what the fuck am I *doing* here?

And the Weasel, a changed man, is off on his toes, empty-handed, never to offend from that day to this, instead to embark on a search for Tom Storey that has – as Dave Reilly puts it – the epic quality of Lassie's journey home.

It was Dave pointed him in the right direction. Dave gives him the name of Tom's business – Love-Storey, get it? Two weeks later, he's – you ready for this? – E. L. Beasley, Transport Manager, Wholesale Division.

With certain additional duties, which become apparent when Tom and Shelley and the kid, Vanessa, move into the new house.

The Weasel sometimes wondered about Dave Reilly, who knew where Tom lived yet never came round to visit. He wondered about Simon St John and Moira Cairns. (It was no surprise they never heard from Lee Gibson; Lee was on a monster earner in the States now, no cause to look back.)

But most of all, Weasel wondered what *really* happened that night in December 1980 when he was in the hospital and Tom drove a Land Rover all the way to hell.

The kitchen door opened. No lights were on inside.

'You really know how to choose your bleeding moments, Weasel,' Tom said, from the shadows. 'Come up.'

As long as the Weasel had known him, way back before his old man was killed, Tom had been a big-time record collector. Blues, mostly, in those days: John Lee Hooker and Muddy Waters and, the pride of his collection, some old Robert Johnson at 78 r.p.m.

Johnson – who died half a century ago at, what was it, twenty-seven? – was just about the best, Weasel always figured. It used to be said he'd sold his soul to the devil on account of all the devil-bits in his songs and the fact that he was just so good so young and that he died so mysteriously – murdered, wasn't it?

And where was Robert Johnson now? Not in Tom Storey's record collection any more, this was for sure. Neither was Muddy Waters. Although, as Weasel could see even from here, old John Lee was certainly still on the shelf.

The music-room was at the top of the house. The way it was arranged now, you came in through the door at one end and all the records were stacked at the other, a good twenty feet away. Between you and them were a beat-up pub table, a sprawly old easy chair, two fifty-watt practice amps arranged like a barrier, and the clutter of all Tom's guitars, about fifteen of them.

So, what with the beams and trusses and that, getting across to the records was like some kind of commando training-exercise.

Weasel took the Stones' *Goat's Head Soup* from under his arm.

'Not a bad album,' Tom said gruffly. 'Coulda been worse, considering.'

Weasel moved towards the shelves to put the album back.

'Leave it,' Tom growled. 'Leave it on the table.'

'Yeah,' Weasel said. 'Right. I, er . . . I fought I could maybe have a lend of one of the earlier ones.'

'Slung 'em out,' Tom said straight off. 'They was knackered.'

The room was stifling. Tom had this pot-bellied stove on a flagstone plinth on the boarded floor, with an iron flue going up through the roof. There were a couple of buckets of coal. Most mornings, Weasel awoke in his 'van to the sound of Hilda, the cleaner, filling the buckets and clattering off with them to the house and up all the bleeding stairs, poor cow.

'So,' Tom said. 'What's the beef, Weasel? Ain't we paying you enough or summink?'

Tom's eyes burned with challenge. He was still a scary sight sometimes, despite Shelley keeping his tough white hair trimmed and his moustache blunt.

'Yeah, well.' The Weasel shuffled about near the doorway, pushing some of his long grey hair behind his ears. 'Fing is . . . you and Shelley, you done all right by me, ain'tcher? Pulled me out the shit.'

Tom sat down on one of his amps. 'So put a word in for me for the New Year's Honours. Count for a lot, that, coming from you, Weasel.'

Good guy, Tom, generosity itself, if you could take the verbal abuse.

'What I mean . . .' Weasel pushed on, as best he could. 'You know I'll watch out for yer – you and Shelley and the Princess. You know that.'

'What we pay you for,' Tom said, all heart.

'So, like, if there was someone after you. Or Shelley. Or the kid. Then you'd tell me, wouldn'tcher?'

'Maybe.' Tom's eyes had gone dull. 'If it was summink you could fix. If it wasn't, then I wouldn't. Some fings, you talk about it, it don't help. Makes it worse.'

Weasel nodded at the pot-bellied stove. 'That safe, is it? Up here in the roof space, all this wood, joists and all?'

Tom shrugged.

'Only I figured maybe an electric heater'd save a lot of, you know . . .'

'Useless,' Tom said. 'Wouldn't . . .'

'Wouldn't burn vinyl,' Weasel said, easing back into the doorway. 'Am I right?'

Tom was at the door before him. Tom had moved faster than you'd reckon he could, given his size and his gut, and he'd cut off Weasel's escape route with one crunch of a Doc Marten on the door panel. The door shuddered and the latch went *clack* and Tom turned, his back and shoulders flat to the door.

And Weasel feeling like he was locked in with a monster.

*

They'd been up there too long in silence. Shelley was worried. The times Weasel came round, Tom would put albums on or maybe play a little, Weasel fumbling along on bass. What they didn't do was talk.

Tom, it was fair to say, was not what you'd call a great conversationalist.

Shelley finished her coffee. Decaffeinated was something Tom accepted now. Accepted that caffeine was a drug, just like tobacco, alcohol and cocaine and the other stuff. None of which Tom had gone near since their marriage, although her attempts to turn him into a vegetarian had been abandoned some years ago when Tom had pointed out – and he was right – that a no-meat diet lightened his senses, made him more receptive.

No *way*. Just what he *didn't* need.

Shelley washed her coffee mug. Vanessa was in the TV-room watching a video. She watched the same ones three and four times, Eddie Murphy usually.

Shelley sighed over the sink. What a long, debilitating journey marriage to Tom Storey was. A woman taking on Tom loaded herself up with an incredible amount of sheer craziness, was obliged to acquaint herself with a body of knowledge uncatered for in the smaller branches of W. H. Smith.

No question of bringing the books home. ('Whassis shit?' – Tom hurling Colin Wilson and Brian Inglis into the Jetmaster in a kind of furious terror.)

In the end, what she'd done had been to install little carousels of New Age-type paperbacks in the shops on the basis that many vegetarians were into this kind of thing as well.

And she'd read them all herself, in the shops, of course, never again bringing any home. And ordered others, more specialized. Indeed, for someone with no psychic ability at all (would Tom have gone near her if she'd had any?), she was becoming quite an authority on aspects of the Unexplained.

Or, in this house, the Unmentionable.

*

'Explain,' Tom said.

His voice had gone hard and dry. He looked ready to pick up the Weasel and snap him in half.

The Weasel stood in the middle of the room, sweating. There was a glass panel in the front of the iron stove and he could see deep red coals. The stove shimmered in its own heat.

Weasel looked away, half afraid the face of Robert Johnson, the bluesman, would materialize smiling in the coals and the white-hot ash.

'*Goat's Head Soup*,' Weasel said. 'Heavy stuff, innit? Goats' heads, the devil, right?'

'Devil, bollocks,' Tom said. 'It's a try-on. Creepy picture. Means nuffink.'

'You said you ain't got *Beggar's Banquet*.'

'Maybe that *is* a nasty one,' Tom said reflectively. '*Sympathy for the Devil*. That festival in the States where the poor bleeder got murdered in the crowd when they were doing *Sympathy*. Maybe a bad vibe running frew it.'

'You ain't got no Stones albums *before* that, though, either, right?' The Weasel standing his ground. 'No Doors. No Hendrix. No Bolan. No Elvis. And no Beatles. Wassat telling me, eh?'

There was a long silence. It was nearly dark and the windows were narrow and high in the walls, so you could only see the sky, no village lights, and the only light in the long room was coming out of the stove.

'All dead,' Weasel said. 'All dead 'uns. You got rid of all the old Stones albums wiv Brian Jones on 'em, 'cause he's dead, drowned, whatever. And the Doors, 'cause of Morrison, snuffed in a bath. And the Beatles – this is down to Lennon. Soon as somebody dies, you dump their albums. They comes off the shelf and into the stove. Up the chimney. Gorn.'

Red lights gleaming in the silvered machine heads of an acoustic guitar on a stand. Red lights in Tom's eyes like distant aircraft at night.

Weasel's eyes started roaming the junk, the guitars and the

amps and stuff, wondering what he could pick up to defend himself. Then he saw the monster was crying quietly.

He sat down on one of the practice amps, looking down at his hands in his lap. Couldn't look at Tom, couldn't watch this.

'I been in Paris wiv Morrison,' Tom was whispering. 'Dead in the bath. Bloated.'

Weasel went cold.

'I've heard the crash of Marc Bolan's motor going into that tree. Time and time again.'

Weasel wanted to be out of here but couldn't move.

'I can't take the sound of a car crash, Weasel. Why I can't live in a city, no more. Always brakes squealing somewhere. I can't stand that.'

'Yeah,' Weasel said faintly. 'I can understand that.'

'Most of 'em was twenty-seven when they snuffed it. You know that? Hendrix, Morrison, Jones, Joplin?'

'And Robert Johnson.'

'Yeah. Free times free times free? Wossat mean? I dunno, I don't read those books. Who needs fucking books like that?'

Weasel said, 'You're saying you play the records and you see them, how they died.'

'Dead,' Tom said baldly. 'I see 'em dead.'

IV

Protection of the Ancestors

Standing by the ragged hole, dug out of bitterly resistant stone and clay and already waterlogged, the vicar had intoned the usual.

Man born of a woman hath but a short time to live and is full of misery. He cometh up and is cut down like a flower . . .

It was, he thought, a depressingly long-winded way of expressing a fairly simple truth: Life's a bitch and then you die.

And then what?

He wished he knew.

It was his first funeral here. A farmer of eighty-six, who'd died in the same house he'd been born in, raised hundreds of thousands of lambs in the same scrubby fields, protected them against the climate, the crows and the foxes and then sent them off to market and to die.

The farmer, one Emlyn Roberts, had apparently gone out cursing. Life at Ystrad Ddu seemed to be all about cursing – cursing your neighbours, the council, the tourists, the foxes, the crows, the weather. Until the day you claimed your reserved chunk of the churchyard.

As the mourners trooped away in apathetic silence, the vicar's surpliced arm was clutched by Mr Eddie Edwards.

'Did you see it?'

'No,' the vicar said. 'The family were merciful enough to keep the lid on.'

'No, no, no . . . the van, man. The big, white van.'

'Van?'

Mr Edwards said that shortly after the service he had seen

the van coming up the valley road, having a hell of a job getting past all the Land Rovers.

Too fast, far too fast, it had ploughed through the lane, past the church and the village and the cottages and the new bungalow, the way some vehicles often did before the drivers realized their mistake and turned round, the lane being a dead end leading only to a certain ruined, twelfth-century abbey.

But this van did not return.

'So,' Mr Edwards said, with his customary drama. 'To the Abbey, it went. And at the Abbey it stayed, for quite some time. Four men, at least. Went into the tower block, they did, and there was knocking and hammering, I am told.'

'You are told,' said the vicar.

'Oh, all right, I cannot lie to the clergy, I went to see for myself. I couldn't get close enough, mind, to make out what they were doing exactly. That building, well, the windows are so high, you can't see a thing from the outside. But is it changing hands again, I wonder? Is it being converted into something else? Have you heard anything?'

'Now, why should anyone tell me, Eddie? The Abbey's got no connection with the church. It's just an ancient monument.'

'Apart, that is, from the tower house. Which has been locked and derelict for years, and nobody knows who owns it.'

The vicar stared at him. The late November mist hung drably over the grey settlement like dust-sheets over old furniture.

'And another thing,' Mr Edwards said. He paused, his glasses misting. 'Lights!'

'Lights?'

'In the Abbey, man. At night.'

'You've seen the lights in the Abbey?'

'Not me! I don't go out there at night, got to be careful at my age. But the farmers have seen them.'

'What kind of lights?'

'They would hardly go close enough to find out, now, would they?'

'Look, Eddie,' the vicar said hastily, 'funerals being major social occasions in these parts, I need to do some mingling. Why don't you pop round to my gaff in an hour or so, have some coffee.'

'Good idea,' said Mr Edwards happily. 'I never refuse a warm drink. Gets to you, this damp, when you're retired.'

After the burial of her mother, Moira concluded it was not wise to go back to the croft house on Skye. Too powerful, too much natural magic. The island didn't compromise; it made you confront your own weaknesses.

'And there's things,' she said to Donald in the Duchess's caravan – no more character, now, than a china shop – 'that I don't even *dare* to think about.'

'Get yourself some sleep,' Donald said.

Moira rubbed her tired eyes. 'Big circles, huh?'

'Aye,' said Donald, 'big circles.'

The Duchess had made no formal will. Moira, as the nearest relative, had found herself presiding over an informal meeting of the Elders, assuring them she wanted nothing. The china and the brass were to be divided among the nieces, the palace to be sold and the proceeds to go, despite his protests, to Donald. There was no obvious successor, and the Duchess, she figured, was not in the market for a shrine.

'Donald, before I go . . .' Moira fumbled in her bag. 'I want you to read this.'

She showed him the paper, with the two words on it.

BREADWINNER

and

DEATHOAK

'This wis it?' Donald scratched his head through the hole in his hat. 'What she wrote for you?'

'Mean anything to you, Donald?' Watching his eyes.

He shook his head slowly, baffled. No, it meant nothing to

him; wasn't supposed to. It meant nothing to anybody but her. Donald looked at her inquiringly, waiting. He would have sat there, silently waiting, for an hour or more until she was ready.

This was his first visit. They'd always spoken at the church, or the village hall or during one of Mr Edwards's personal guided tours of the surrounding countryside.

His first time inside the vicarage, and the little man was clearly making a mental inventory of the contents of the living-room.

The vicar was glad to note that he seemed disappointed, the room being utterly anonymous, the furniture tidy and modern, the books on the shelves ecclesiastically anodyne. Only the view from the double-glazed, aluminium-framed window was at all distinctive, an expanse of wild hill-country probably unchanged for a thousand years.

'Are we alone?' asked Mr Edwards.

Mrs Pugh, who came in for half a day to clean and wash and to prepare the vicar's lunch, had departed. The vicar nodded, trying not to smile.

'Then,' said Mr Edwards, 'it's time I confessed that I have been studying you.'

Mr Edwards was squashed into a wicker chair with his cap on his knees. He wore a collar and tie, suit and waistcoat. This was how he dressed even when there was no funeral. As well as an education adviser, he had been a churchwarden and a member of the local history society. The vicar had learned that he was, beneath his garrulous manner, a disturbingly shrewd man.

'My conclusion, see, is that you are unlike most clergymen. Certainly the least reverent reverend I've encountered on my travels.'

'That a compliment?'

'For the life of me,' Mr Edwards said thoughtfully, 'I do not know. Most of the time you act as if you just don't care. Your eulogy to old Emlyn this morning, tongue quite patently in the cheek. And – I have to say this – your language, for a man of your calling, is often quite appalling.'

'Jesus Christ,' the vicar said. 'So it's true what they say about you Welsh being natural poets.'

'See . . .' Mr Edwards threw an exasperated fist at the air. 'And yet – I cannot help feeling in my gut that it is all a façade. Tell you what I think, shall I?'

'Go ahead.'

'Well, first, a man with your disregard of convention and protocol would surely feel happier in a rough area of Cardiff or Manchester or London, among the delinquent youngsters, the joy-riders, the ram-raiders, the racial problems. The people here, your irony is wasted on them. They are working farmers. All they want is someone to marry them, bury them and dunk their offspring in the font.'

'Oh, I don't know. It's an interesting area, really,' said the vicar inadequately. 'I've four churches to manage, scattered over fifty or so square miles of the Black Mountains. I keep busy.'

'Pah,' said Mr Edwards. 'You know what I think? A man with a past. You've come here to hide away. What was it, a woman?'

The vicar laughed.

'And then,' said Mr Edwards, 'there is the Abbey. Why are you afraid of the Abbey?'

'OK,' Moira said, 'a long time ago I was at a recording session down in Gwent, South Wales.'

She broke off, thought about what she was going to say, then started again, at the beginning this time.

Starting with when she'd left Scotland to go to university in Manchester and left there on a whim, mid-term, to join a professional folk group led by a man who played the pipes. Saying no more about that; it was part of a different story.

'It'd all really started with the awakening to the glamour,

you know? Meeting my mother again on the very edge of adolescence, rediscovering the bizarre family heritage, all this stuff. Discovering there were certain things I could . . . do.'

She laughed lightly, but Donald stayed sober-faced.

'I was no' very discreet,' Moira said. 'It went to ma head in a big way, the glamour.'

'Aye, well . . . The Duchess herself when she was young wis a wild and wanton creature, as your daddy . . .'

'No' what I'm saying, Donald. Wasny a question of promiscuity so much as, hey, look at me, I've got the Power, I can read your palm, your future in the tealeaves. And the exotic black dresses and stuff . . . You parade around like that, you've got yourself a reputation in the music business almost overnight.'

She told him about Max Goff, the independent record company boss who followed mysticism the way people followed Celtic and Rangers and was just as blinkered. How Max Goff had been told of Moira Cairns, the witchy woman.

'He called me up. He said, "Would you like to realize your full potential? I can help you."'

She laughed. 'I thought, aw, hey . . . Then he started talking money and nationwide tours and two-album contracts. I was just a kid, twenty, twenty-one. I started thinking – the way you do – I may never get an offer like this again. I mean, I was flattered. He liked the voice, the whole Celtic bit – this was before Clannad and Enya and all this ethereal, breathy stuff was hot. And then he hit me with the clincher.'

Moira thought, The folly of youth, eh?

'Which was working with Tom Storey, who was like, *the* guitarist. A musician's musician. Not the fastest or the loudest in the business; what they said about Tom – and it was true – was that it was the *spaces*, the spaces between the notes that sang the sweetest.'

Donald nodded, maybe knowing where this was headed.

'What it came down to was Tom had my own problem – except I didn't know it was a problem then and he did. And Dave had it too, and Simon. We'd been set up.' Moira smiled. 'Stupid, huh?'

115

'We're all of us stupid,' Donald said, 'when we're young.'

'Aye. Anyway, we made the one album together and it was fine. We understood each other, we meshed musically. Yeah, it was fine. Built up our confidence no end. And Goff was very fair; there was none of this "All-psychic Rock Band" stuff on the cover. Nobody knew about that, ostensibly, apart from Goff and us. Then he said he wanted to try something special. An experiment. There was this studio in a place he said was . . . resonant. But nothing to worry about, this was an abbey, a holy place. Seen a lot of violence over the centuries, sure, but it'd survived, was therefore a strong place, full of . . . *potent spirituality*. Jesus, I can't believe we swallowed that shit.'

'You wis . . .'

'Wis young. Yeah. No excuse, Donald. No . . . excuse . . . at . . . all. So, the idea was we'd talk to the Abbey and let it kind of talk to us, and come out with an album that told the story of the Abbey and maybe said something about us, too. This is where Breadwinner comes in.'

Donald opened out the paper again and read the name. He looked up at Moira.

'His name was Aelwyn,' she said. 'Known as Aelwyn Breadwinner, and he died at the Abbey many years ago. When did the Duchess write this, Donald?'

The old guy shook his head.

'When did she give it to you, then?'

'Wid be a couple of days before she died, hen.'

'Yes. And what did she say when she gave it to you?'

'Well . . . she . . . she had it in the wee box she kept by her bed, y'know? And she said, Donald, y'see where I'm putting this – it's for Moira. She said, if I see her I'll gie it her myself. If I dinna see her before I'm dead and buried . . .'

He took off his hat. Tears had formed in his eyes like marbles.

'Right,' Moira said. 'I know the box. Where she used to keep the stuff she'd written down from dreams. Donald, I've asked you this before: she really had no feeling she was gonna die?'

'If she knew . . .' Donald rolled his head from side to side in anguish. 'If she knew, she didny tell me.'

This hurt.

'Nor me,' Moira said softly. 'And yet, from time to time, since the day she gave me the comb, she's been . . . *there. And it's been bugging the hell out of me, Donald. If she knew inside that she was gonna die, why did she no' send for me?*'

Donald was staring down at the paper, mouthing the words *BREADWINNER* and *DEATHOAK* over and over again.

'Do *you* know why?'

He looked up at her. His mouth stopped moving. Moira tried not to get riled but her next question came out in a low growl.

'Why'd you have her rigged up wi' her eyes wide like something out the chamber of horrors?'

Donald stared at her mournfully, lips stitched up like a badly darned sock.

The vicar wondered how far he could trust Eddie Edwards. The old chap wasn't exactly a gossip, more a *collector* of gossip, who probably acquired much more than he gave out. The vicar decided he would take a small step towards him.

'Well,' he said tentatively. 'How do *you* feel about the Abbey?'

'Drab,' said Mr Edwards. 'Neglected. And full of an old sorrow.'

'Why sorrow?'

'Perhaps it goes back to Aelwyn. You know of him.'

'A little. Welsh harpist who witnessed the Abergavenny massacre in eleven . . . er, eleven-something.'

'Seventy-five. And fled the scene pursued by Norman soldiers. Came for sanctuary to the Abbey, and his pursuers caught up with him on the steps and cut him to pieces.'

'Making him a kind of instant martyr. Every great ecclesiastical building should have one.'

117

'So cynical, you are,' Mr Edwards said.

'Aelwyn Breadwinner, they called him, didn't they? I often wondered why.'

'Corruption of the Welsh, that is. The language hasn't been spoken much in this area, to its shame, for a couple of centuries at least. So, what happens, when they come across a difficult Welsh name, bit of a mouthful, turn it into an English word, they do, that sounds the same. Aelwyn Breadwinner indeed! If he ever existed.'

The vicar blinked. 'I thought it was fully documented.'

'Oh, the massacre is. Little doubt what happened there. But Aelwyn may be no more than a legend, one of those romantic tales that no one ever bothers to go into, except for retired folk with time on their hands. There are a number of anomalies, see. Things that don't add up. I tell you what . . . if you're interested – don't want to bore you, see, us old retired folk can get carried away – if you're interested, I can take you through it some time.'

'Yes,' the vicar said warily. 'I suppose I am interested.'

'But still, you're a busy man with your fifty square miles and your five churches to look after and your music . . .'

Mr Edwards paused.

The vicar said nothing.

'A shame, it is, that we don't have a Christmas concert in Ystrad any more. Could have given us a tune . . .'

The vicar said nothing.

Mr Edwards beamed. 'I wondered if that was why you were interested in Aelwyn, see . . .'

'Did I say I was particularly interested?'

'You being a fellow musician. What is it now, the cello? And the electric guitar?'

'Bass.' The vicar sighed, gave up. 'The electric bass. But I don't play any more.'

The vicar had carefully concealed his instruments in the loft – the old bastard must have been chatting up Mrs Pugh.

'Shame.' The wicker chair was wobbling with Mr Edwards's

delight at having got the vicar with his back to the wall at last. 'Were you in one of these pop groups, ever?'

'I was, er, classically trained,' the vicar said. 'But I've never really done much with it.'

'Oh,' said Mr Edwards. 'There's sad. A good name, it is, for a musician, Simon St John.'

'Sometimes . . . Sometimes, Moira . . .' Donald's voice slurred and broadened by his discomfort '. . . sometimes, the dead, they just willnae lie doon. Sometimes they'll no close up their eyes, y'ken?'

Moira said, 'She lay down again, when she'd seen me. As if she'd said her piece.'

'Aye,' Donald said.

'Proving your point, huh?'

Donald was silent for a moment, then he said, 'She wid always do things for you.'

Meaning the times when the Duchess had altered the course of human nature. Like when Moira had been defying her gran over the length of her hair and it was getting to a crisis point, complaining to the headmaster or some such. And something would happen to divert the old girl's attention, some minor ailment, or Gran's attitude would simply soften inexplicably.

'See, this song, Donald – "The Ballad of Aelwyn" – no record was ever released, nor ever could've been. The recording was . . . never finished. And I've never sung it since. What I'm saying, this song has never existed outside of that recording studio. *The Duchess could never've heard it.*'

Donald remained expressionless. He wasn't at all surprised. Eventually, he looked down at the paper and then looked up at her again.

'Deathoak? It's just a nonsense word,' Moira said uncertainly. 'It's all nons—'

She felt her throat constrict.

In a much smaller voice, she said, 'If this . . . this shit was coming through to her . . . if it was, like, coming for me and she intercepted it, you know? Something coming out of the past, and she caught it? Was that why she wouldn't have me come to her? Thinking she could deal with it on her own, just like she sorted out Gran, way back? That how it was, Donald?'

Moira sighed.

'It's me should be dead, not her. Everybody here knows that, you can see it in their faces.'

'Ach,' Donald said, 'she had a stroke. She wisny expecting it. There is no evidence otherwise.'

'Yeah. Time I grew up.' She stood up, folded the paper, stuffed it in her bag. 'I realize that. Maybe that's why I gave her the comb back.'

He rose at once to his feet. 'The comb?'

Moira said, 'Don't get mad at me. She needed it more. I figured if she'd put herself in the way of this shit, she needed the protection of the ancestors more than me. OK?'

'What?' She saw the flicker of fear in his old eyes, quickly doused, like a poacher's light in the woods. 'What have you *done*?'

'Aw,' Moira said uncomfortably, 'I just put the comb in the coffin with her. Between her hands.'

'*What?*' Now sorrow swam openly with naked terror in the bottomless pools of his eyes. 'You buried the comb?'

'Made sense, Donald.'

'Sense? You stupid wee bitch, what wid you know about sense? You're as bloody green now as when you took that fat man's gold. By *Christ* . . .!'

He snatched his hat off, clutched it to his chest, inserted the forefingers of each hand into the hole and tore the hat the length of its crown. 'By Christ, hen, you're on your own now, all right. And naked.'

It was the third day. Time for the tapes to rise from the grave. Prof Levin had been hanging around his flat all morning, waiting

120

for the call. Steve Case had rung him twice, the first time before nine a.m., demanding to know if they had a result.

Prof had called Audico at nine. No, Maurice was not in yet. Things sounded confused. He'd left a message. Tried again at eleven; no answer. No answer? This was a bloody factory!

When the phone finally rang, mid-afternoon, Prof was at the bathroom mirror, idly trimming his beard, mostly white nowadays; did that look distinguished or decrepit?

Maurice said, 'Your tapes, Prof.' He sounded upset, regretful, weary as hell. Bad news, then.

'Oh well,' Prof said, for some reason relieved. 'It was worth a try.'

There was a long pause.

'You've been busy today,' Prof said. 'I rang several times.'

The silence in the phone was cavernous.

'You could very well say that,' Maurice said after a while, and there was another silence and then he said, very precisely, 'Mr Levin, would you like to do me one great big favour? Do you think' – a tremor under his voice – 'that before I lose control of myself and throw the bastard things into the furnace, there is any chance of you getting these tapes out of my factory, and soonest?'

V

A Moth in Winter

First there was no light and no sound.

He waited.

After a few seconds, he thought he'd break the silence with a light laugh, just to show he wasn't taking this at all seriously, wasn't letting it *get* to him. But he was on his own in the dark, so who was he trying to convince?

Maurice, of Audico, had said,

'You think I'm joking? You think I'm having you on? I'm not. Listen, there was nearly a walk-out. I've had a deputation in here. I've had the police. You think this is funny?'

Prof Levin had put the wooden box on the back seat of his car but kept seeing it in his mirror and thinking about what Maurice had said. It was just a black wooden box, brass corners, broken brass lock. Just a wooden box.

He'd pulled over on to the hard shoulder of the M25, coming back into London – and he'd stowed it away in the boot before setting off again.

Which was a completely ridiculous thing to do.

Also, he hadn't taken it into his flat last night, but left it in the car boot in the lock-up garage he rented.

Which was crazy; he'd had his car nicked twice from this garage.

*

*'They're probably laughing about it now, Prof, the ones who know.
Well, you do, don't you, when it's all over? There are things you
don't want to believe. Well, I'm still not laughing.'*

Prof had arrived shortly before ten a.m. at this tiny commercial
studio under a scruffy South London record shop. It had been
discreetly hired by Steve Case, who was to meet him here at
twelve, not before, OK?

Recording engineers were just technicians who put the gilt
on other people's creativity; not their job to *question* anything.
Well, sod that. The bloke in the shop was a dozy bastard; Prof
had bluffed his way into the studio, no great problem.

He unpacked the box. The tape looked very clean; despite
everything, Maurice's people had done a proficient job,
obviously. He wound the first reel into the machine, around half
a dozen metal capstans, on to the take-up spool. There were
twin speakers, on a tilt, just above his head.

He hit the 'play' button and – as he usually did – removed
his glasses and switched off the lights.

A mistake, although he didn't realize it at first.

*'This factory is – what? – four years old? It's on a business park, for
God's sake. It's surrounded by other factories, all air-conditioned,
dust-free, hi-tech units. Before they turned it into a business park, it
was a football pitch, a school playing field. You know what I'm
saying, Prof? I'm saying it wasn't an old battlefield or an overgrown
graveyard or anything like that. Shit, I can't believe I'm saying this
to you at all . . .'*

On the first half-dozen reels, he found four songs, unmixed,
several takes of each. Scraps of conversation, musicians talking
to each other – a handful of men and one woman. The producer,
whose voice came in occasionally, sounded like Russell Hornby.

One of the musicians had a bit of Merseyside in his voice and could well have been Dave Reilly.

Who would the sound engineer have been? Someone he knew?

The songs were good, although they didn't make a lot of sense, especially a hard blues piece, gruffly sung by Storey, about a man with . . . two mouths, was that? A man with two mouths? He wished he'd seen those papers Steve had taken away, probably a track list.

But there was one song he could get the measure of. This was a live take, the whole band playing together, instead of the usual jigsaw.

This number was over seven minutes long, about a prophet of some kind with a Welsh-sounding name, who

> . . . *came down from the mountains*
> *with a harp on his shoulder*
> *and dreams of the future* . . .

It was one of those songs like Led Zeppelin's 'Stairway to Heaven' which got bigger and more complicated, more *violent*, a male and a female singing alternative verses. No mistaking the voices; Dave Reilly and the Cairns woman.

Prof changed the reel, found another version of the same song, even longer. But this was a quieter version; he could hear all the words. There was this very gruelling episode in the middle where this prophet bloke witnesses what seems to be a multiple murder in a stone-walled banqueting hall during a meal, swords and knives and axes coming out, people getting stabbed and hacked to death over the table, dishes running with fresh blood.

Not too pleasant.

Also, the woman was singing in a very curious way, as if she wasn't thinking about the words or the tune or the rhymes or the timing. It was as if she was *watching* the dreadful scene, happening in front of her eyes as it were, and describing what she could see in words which just seemed to fall into place.

Like improvising, but it couldn't be.

Afterwards, the prophet guy was running away, accompanied by lots of pounding bass, chips of acoustic rhythm guitar,
streamers of lead guitar like bird calls.

And then, after a long, tense silence, it all started to get *very*
peculiar.

*'We ran a few feet of tape first – don't worry, we weren't trying to
listen to it. There was a lot of wow, as you'd expect and one awful
smell, like overcooked liver or something. So we gave up and put the
reels in the ovens, divided them up between all three ovens, turned
on the heat, locked the room. As normal. You don't want anybody
going in there messing up your settings, turning up your levels . . .
this could be disastrous, right?'*

The quality of the silence altered. It had become like . . . like a
vastness. As if he was standing not in a tiny studio but in a huge
ballroom with all the lights out.

There was a hollow resonance. The hollow resonance of
death, Prof thought suddenly.

What the bloody hell did that mean?

He'd seen the word

DEATH

in capitals on the paper Steve
had taken out of the envelope they'd found inside the box.

Now, obviously, some of this was his imagination, due to
the location of the grotty little studio, this tatty, plastic room
buried in the earth or whatever passed for earth in South
London, no windows, no slit of light beneath the door – not
even a tiny red pilot on the tape machine, which was the cast-
off he'd asked for to test the gunged-up tape, and its pilot light
was broken.

So the darkness in the cellar was absolute.

And the music was darker still, if you could call it music.

Listen. Work it out.

OK, several people are breathing, hollow yawning breaths,

like *haaaaaaaaaaaw*, a cavernous sound; you feel yourself drifting into it, like slipping backwards into a pool; closing your eyes, throwing your arms back over your head.

Then one of the breathers' pitch alters, constructing uneven, fitful notes, notes like small boats on a dark sea.

Slowly a tune begins to form in the background, a cold, brittle, repetitive tune played on an acoustic guitar, plucked by the fingernails, plucked close to the bridge, where the strings are tight.

An image that came out of this music in a kind of vapour, drifting into Prof's mind, was of a woman's waxen face, dwindling tendrils of breath from parted lips, eyelids fluttering as feebly as a moth in winter.

His own lips felt dry. He licked them; his tongue was even drier.

The music softened into mush.

Out of this reared a discordant cello followed by a sonorous bass, sounding as if they'd been recorded in a vault or a church crypt.

Prof felt the studio floor tilt beneath his feet, felt he was falling through a series of echoing passages of sound. Would there be light down there?

No. Only a deeper darkness.

So put on the light, you stupid bugger!

I can't do that. It would be wrong. It would not be professional. I have to stay with this.

Prof found himself shuddering with a very unprofessional dread. And wanting a drink, badly.

'So, I'm at home, Prof, in bed. This is the third night, the tapes should be baking nicely, ready to come out like fresh buns in the morning. So. It's about half-eleven, we'd just watched Newsnight on the bedroom set, and the phone rings. Angela gets it. "It's the factory," she says. "The night watchman." Well, if I've told the guy once . . . don't ring me, ring the police, ring the fire brigade, don't disturb me unless . . . Anyway, he says, "You know that room with

126

*the metal door?" "The bakery" – this is what we call it, obviously.
He says, "The one I haven't got a key to?" I say, "Yeah," he says,
"Well, is there supposed to be somebody in there at this time of
night?"'*

'Help me,' a woman's voice sang distantly and then, off key,
'Help me . . . please . . .?'

He was shocked. It sounded as if something had disrupted
the session, like she was being attacked, like when she cried
out, *help me*, it was for real.

And then her voice trailed off into an achingly melodic
whimper.

A hand seemed to close inside Prof's chest. His eyes felt
hot. He was glad he hadn't chickened out and put on the
lights, suddenly grateful for the darkness, discovering he wasn't
frightened any more, simply . . . quite profoundly moved.

He thought, she's dying. This woman is dying.

He could at once sense the pitiful desolation of something
small and vulnerable being absorbed into something massive
and indifferent. He held his breath.

Years since he'd responded emotionally to any kind of music.
Music was *product*, a commodity.

Realizing he was clenching his fists, he opened them out; his
palms were wet.

Also, his eyes were moist, which was ridic—

There was a stuttering of strings, viola maybe, a fragmenta-
tion and then a frozen second or two of . . . well, no identifiable
sound, just a kind of vibration, dancing waves of electricity in
still air.

'She's going.'

He realized he'd said this aloud.

For almost a second there was complete, hollow silence. The
studio had become a ballroom again or a giant indoor stadium.

Prof felt cold, he felt bereft. He needed a . . . Oh God . . .

*

'So I come in . . . after midnight by the time I get here. The night watchman is rushing to meet me, oldish guy, I mean, seasoned, you know? Come on, come on, we have to get her out. Her? Her? What the bloody hell . . .? I get the keys from my office, we go down there. I unlock the metal door . . .'

When the music resumed there was a subtle difference, a change of key, an acoustic rhythm guitar chugging patiently along, a slow horse-and-cart rhythm, the woman's voice reaching out. A hesitant remission? Some hope in here?

A second of silence, the ballroom ambience again, and then suddenly she's getting battered about, tossed from one speaker to the other in a dark wind of sound.

The sense of build-up, of *foreboding*, is suffocating.

Prof made himself take a couple of long breaths, but he couldn't seem to fill his lungs. He clutched at the tape machine. This wasn't the music, this was him. He was ill, he was a sick man. Music alone could not do this to you.

What he should do now was very carefully switch off this machine, put on the lights, clear his head, go back upstairs – taking it very slowly – go and find a café, get a mug of nice sweet, milky tea.

Only, to do this he would need to breathe.

Oh, Jesus. He felt the floor tilt again beneath his shoes. He stumbled to his knees. Breath . . . Breath and . . . alcohol . . .

When it happened, he was down on the floor, his heart banging away like a jack-hammer, his sweating face upturned towards the invisible speakers.

What happened was a hiss of power heralding a cruel, jagged electric chord sequence – Tom Storey, in full rage – which ripped from one side of the black void to the other.

The breath exploded into Prof Levin.

And then

'God al*mighty*,' he croaked,

as it chewed her up.

128

The electric music chewed her up, the dying woman, with all the dispassionate fury of a chainsaw.

'Of course, there was nobody there. The night watchman, you could tell he was torn between terror and acute embarrassment. I gave him a good rollocking. Getting me out of bed. What was up with him? Had he been drinking? This kind of stuff. I'm shouting at the poor old git for a good two minutes, rollocking him while I'm surreptitiously checking out the bakery, checking the levels on the ovens, making sure everything is as left. Which it is, all set to fifty-five centigrade, nothing tampered with. Nothing.

'And why am I doing this?

'I'll tell you why. It's not a big room – I'll take you down, Prof, give me a couple of minutes – it's not a big room, as I say, and with three substantial ovens in there it's always what you might call nicely warm, or in summer, bloody suffocating.

'So why – you explain this to me – is it freezing cold in there, with three ovens still going at fifty-five C? Why is it cold enough to freeze the whatsits off a brass thingy?

'And why am I still shouting at the night watchman? Because suddenly I believe him. The thing is, he's never been in there, he doesn't know it should be warm. Now, me, I know there is no scientific reason at all why it should be freezing cold. With three ovens on, over three days and nights? Prof, I'm a religious man, an Orthodox Jew – I'm telling you this, background information. I do believe in certain things, although I am not gullible. OK, I take the night watchman up to my office, I apologize for losing my cool, I give him a whisky, I ask him what he heard, he says, "A woman, I swear there was a woman in there, gasping, suffocating, although at first," he says, "at first I thought it was, you know, sexual." I say, listen, maybe you fell asleep, it was a bad dream. Maybe it's better we say it was a bad dream, keep it between ourselves, yes? He gets the message, finally, and we drink to it. Uncomfortably. This is an end of it.

'I should be so fortunate. I arrive this morning for work – late,

*I'm afraid, I make no excuses for that – and I walk into bloody
uproar. People outside my door, admin people, technical staff,
secretaries. Who's been in here, messing things about, turning out
drawers, kicking chairs over and . . . and tangling everything in
tape? Miles and miles and fucking miles of high-quality Audico
recording tape worth thousands of pounds, binding the place . . .
there are whole offices strangled in tape! It seems like there is not a
single reel in the building left unrolled! What the insurance people
are going to make of this is quite beyond me. Not a single reel left
unrolled!*

'*Except, of course, for one batch.*

'*I go to take them out myself – in broad daylight, being very
careful to leave doors open, bright sunlight coming in everywhere.
The temperature in the bakery is back to normal. Very pleasant. I
open the first oven. Usually we wear gloves for this; after three days
at this temperature the tapes are not so comfortable to hold. I take
out the first tape.*

'*I drop it immediately. Crash! My hand's on fire! I go charging
out to the toilets to hold it under cold water. Only when I get in there
do I realize it's an illusion. You know how extreme cold can feel just
like extreme heat?*

'*Prof, explain this to me. Explain how this tape can absorb all
that heat – oh, it's baked all right, it's baked perfectly, everything
fused together again – so explain, before you take the bloody things
out of my life for ever, how this otherwise unexceptional recording
tape, can take all that heat and remain as chilled as one of those
cans of lager you forget about at the back of the fridge? This frightens
me, Prof, I would like you to explain what it is about that tape?*'

The sound was like the inside of a foundry, confused clangour,
the spell broken.

Prof clawed at the lights.

It was illusion, he thought, blinking wildly in the glare.
Illusion and coincidence. The insurance company would pay
for the damage at Audico, the poor sodding night watchman
would be sacked and Maurice's long-standing favour owed to

Kenneth Levin would be considered repaid in triple triplicate, for ever.

Russell Hornby's voice cried out, 'What's going—?' And was overwhelmed.

Prof didn't know how to handle this. Was he going to calmly hand over these tapes to Stephen Case? Was this stuff going to be released for mass display in Virgin Records and Our Price and airings on the more sophisticated late-night radio shows? Would it even affect other listeners as it had him, or was it some weird individual response? Was he, in fact, going insane? This business with Audico; he was beginning to think already that he'd dreamed the whole thing.

Russell said, '. . . it, Barney, I don't know . . .'

The sound died.

Prof went still.

. . . it, Barney, I don't know. . .

He staggered up the stairs to the record shop, carrying the black box at chest level. Always, it reminded him of a kid's coffin.

'All right, squire?' The dozy bloke glancing up from his copy of *Viz*. 'You bring that box in wiv you?'

Prof said, 'Gonna be sick,' and lunged for the door.

The dozy bloke said, ''Ere, mind the . . .'

The door opened.

'Ah. Prof.' Stephen Case, looking slim and dapper and hungry. 'Why did I just know you'd come early?'

He held out his hands. Prof stared at him, feeling old and grizzled and frazzled, throat full of bile. Steve didn't smile.

Prof thrust the black box at him, and Steve wrapped his arms around it. Prof managed to say, 'I wish you well with it, mate,' and pushed past him into the street.

He threw up in the gutter. A woman crossed the road to avoid walking past him.

His beard wet and disgusting, he looked up into the clouds and gobbled some air, the carbon monoxide tasting like wine, but not *enough* like wine for him at this moment.

Steve looked down on him with distaste. The vein at the end of his nose was very prominent. Prof knew this was a man who could cause him some trouble, maybe finish him in the business. He should be afraid of this bloke, but he was far more afraid of what he'd heard on the tape.

. . . *it, Barney, I don't know* . . .

'Steve, did you know Barney Gwilliam was the engineer on that session?'

Steve said, 'Was he? Dead now, isn't he?'

'Yeah,' Prof said.

'You've been drinking,' Stephen Case said with contempt.

'No.' Prof began to walk away. 'Not yet.'

VI

Dead Sea Scroll

Malcolm gave her a very severe look indeed. 'Another six months of this,' he said, 'and I'm afraid you will have entirely ceased to exist.'

His features were small and precise, his hair a very strange colour of light brown, a bit like that terrible teak furniture everybody seemed to acquire back in the seventies.

'Between April and July . . .' Malcolm consulted his desk diary, 'I received fourteen inquiries about your availability.'

Actually, Moira thought emptily, this is probably the only guy I ever saw whose hair looks more like a toupee than a toupee does.

'And between July and September, precisely five.'

He closed the diary with a meaningful snap.

'Aye well,' Moira said. 'I've been kind of resting.'

'As you are perfectly entitled to do. However, it is my job, as your professional adviser, to warn you that in order to maintain any sort of career as a popular singer . . .'

'You are my agent, Malcolm, not my professional adviser.'

Malcolm leaned back in his chair. His office door was open a chink, and she knew that young Fiona, the secretary, was close to the other side, antennae attuned for details of whoever might presently be sharing Moira's sheets.

'Well then . . .' Malcolm Kaufmann spread his hands.

'One day maybe I'll explain everything,' she said.

They had dealt with the condolences, the psychological impact of the death of a parent of the same sex, with the implication that this was always a valid short-term risk for those the wrong side of their thirty-eighth birthday.

'Have you sufficient money?' Malcolm asked. Meaning had there been . . .?

'An inheritance? No. Not to speak of. I've enough to get by.'

'Are we talking then – please excuse the cliché, Moira – of a mid-life crisis?'

Moira started to laugh.

'A mid-life crisis is rarely funny,' Malcolm said with feeling.

'I'm sorry,' Moira said. 'No. This is not what you would describe as a mid-life crisis.'

She was wearing a fluffy lemon sweater and light blue stonewashed denims. The new, ordinary, totally unsinister Moira Cairns. She felt a touch ridiculous.

'Anyway,' Malcolm said. 'I'm glad you dropped in. You really do need to do something about this man Reilly. It's gone far enough.'

From a drawer in his desk he took a roll of white paper and held down one end with his metal telephone index.

'Endless letters and postcards I can cope with.'

When he'd unrolled the paper, weighting the other end with his in-tray, it stretched almost the length of the desk, nearly five feet.

'But fax ribbon,' he said, 'is expensive stuff.'

'Jesus, he faxed all that?' After five years she still couldn't work out whether or not Malcolm's fabled meanness was real or a pose.

'Thus demonstrating his frustration, Moira, at never getting replies to his letters and his postcards. He's taking it out on me and my fax machine.'

'Well, it's not gonna get him anywhere,' Moira said, nervous at what this might have to say for all to read . . . like, for Malcolm to read and obviously Fiona, his secretary. 'It's been nearly fifteen years. I can hardly remember what he looks like.'

'Moira. Time for plain speaking.' Malcolm made a steeple out of his dapper hands. Dapper hands? It was true, she thought, even his damned hands are dapper.

'You're not concentrating,' he said. 'You've got that dreamy look, meaning you intend to avoid my questions.'

She blinked. 'Mmm?'

'Don't think I haven't often wondered,' he said, 'why a young woman of your abilities should have chosen to operate within such a confined area – i.e. Scotland – and to sign up with an agency on the top floor of a scruffy tenement, dealing largely in freelance pipers, dance bands and second-rate nightclub comics.'

'Mustn't undervalue yourself, Malcolm. You have many special qualities.'

'Gullibility, however, is not among them. I've never questioned you too deeply, Moira, but I have, as you might say . . . heard things.'

'Fiona, too, probably.' Moira glanced at the almost-closed door.

'And . . . *and* . . . as I may have remarked before . . . you are – let's not be coy about this – you are a rather strange, witchy woman.'

'Aw, come on.' Moira pinched her fluffy jumper. 'Do I look like a witchy woman?'

'No more than would Lucrezia Borgia in a shell-suit.' Malcolm shuddered. 'Perhaps you should revert to the black apparel, at least we know where we are. Now . . .' From a tray he pulled out a sheet of stiff paper with a letterhead. 'Let me deal with another pressing item. The Music Machine.'

'What's that?'

'TMM, these days, my dear.'

'I've never recorded for TMM, Malcolm.'

'TMM now owns Epidemic,' Malcolm said patiently. 'Go on. Read it. It sounds like money.'

'Oh.' She unfolded the letter as she would a police summons and looked immediately at the signature. Max Goff's used to be an inch high and often rolled off the page. This one was concise and pointed, and you could read the words.

Stephen Case, Recordings Executive.

The letter was similarly concise. It stated that the under-signed would like to speak with her in connection with the masters for an unreleased album recorded for Epidemic in December 1980 at the Abbey Studio, Gwent.

Moira went very still.

There was a horrible drumming inside her brain.

She thought of the last letter she'd unfolded and the words on it in her mother's lucid scrawl. *BREADWINNER*. And *DEATHOAK*.

She looked at the date. It had been posted nearly a week ago.

'Good news?' asked Malcolm.

She didn't reply.

It was not possible.

After the ambulance had pulled away, shrieking, with Tom and the dying Deborah inside, after the police statements, after their own short and meaningless inquest, she and Dave and Simon and their producer, Russell Hornby, had walked out into the damp morning with the reels of tape and a can of paraffin. They had climbed to the top of a hillock at the end of the ruined nave of the old abbey and unspooled the tape from the metal reels and poured on the paraffin, with Lee Gibson watching aghast from a distance. A breeze had blown up; Simon had had to strike about fifteen matches before he managed to bring one in cupped hands to the trail of paraffin-soaked tape, and the flames had emerged at last, a mean and feeble conflagration compared with the savage inferno of the Land Rover and the Lotus. But the tapes had been destroyed, and when the others had left she'd gone alone to the summit of the hillock and trampled the ashes into the wet ground.

And so it was impossible.

'Are you going to tell me about this, Moira?'

'Huh? Oh . . . it's nothing, Malcolm.'

'There's certainly no percentage in it for me, if that's what bothers you,' Malcolm said huffily. 'Before my time. I act purely as intermediary.'

'You know me better than that,' Moira said. 'And it's still nothing.'

'I'm sure. Which is obviously why it's left you looking so shattered.'

'Leave it, Malcolm.'

'Will you contact this man?'

'No.'

And she meant no, by Christ she did.

'Then . . .' Malcolm lifted his telephone index and sent the five-foot-long fax billowing into the air, 'what about *this* man?'

She pushed her chair back from the desk as the fax tumbled over her knees, straightening her legs and letting it fall to the thin carpet. She felt truly exhausted. What she really wanted was to leave the paper where it lay and scurry to the furthest corner and burrow there like a mouse, with her arms over her face.

Malcolm had on his magistrate's face. 'You have led me to believe, Moira, that this Reilly is a rejected suitor who would not accept no for an answer and to whom your whereabouts must never be divulged.'

'Please, I *have* asked you to leave this.' She was looking across at his filing cabinet, remembering the day she'd made all the drawers come shooting out, from approximately six feet away. But she'd been younger then and full of fury.

Wouldn't work with Malcolm again, even if she could cut it.

'And I was willing to accept that, why not?' he said. 'What business is it of mine? He sends his letters to this office, I pass them on or destroy them unopened, according to your instructions.'

'For his own good,' she mumbled. 'Believe this.'

'But a fax, you see, is essentially a public document. Plus, it arrived with a personal note to me saying please to give her this – very, *very* important. Read it if you like. And then a lot of spiel about an enormous power cut in Liverpool and John Lennon. It doesn't make a great deal of sense, indeed it suggests a condition bordering on dementia.'

'Aye.' Moira sighed.

'But it does have an urgency about it I find hard to ignore, so don't ask me to destroy it this time. You may shred it yourself, Moira, if you wish, but not in my office please. This time you take it with you.'

He glared down at her as she bent and gathered up the fax. 'Must've been shorter Dead Sea Scrolls than this, Malcolm.'

'And none more portentous, I don't doubt,' Malcolm said. 'Look, there's another point . . .'

From entering the office, she'd known what was coming.

'If you *do* communicate with Mr Reilly, perhaps you'd give him another address to write to. Nothing personal, Moira, but I . . . Well, I don't think I'm prepared any longer to be a clearing house for the Nostradamus-like outpourings of your strange friends.'

Moira nodded. There was nothing to be said about this. She did have strange friends.

They looked at each other in silence for a few seconds and then he looked down at his desk and she said, 'Malcolm, are you saying you'd rather not represent me any more?'

'Look . . .' He sighed. 'Moira. With all the goodwill in the world, I can't truly see that there is very much left to represent.'

'No,' she said. 'I understand that. Besides, the witchy woman aspect . . .'

'It's not *that*.'

'No. Of course not.' She shouldered her bag. 'Well.' Gathered up armfuls of fax paper. 'Bye, then, Malcolm. Thanks for everything.'

'Come back, won't you,' he said, 'when your affairs are . . . unravelled.'

But she left the office doubting it. Feeling red raw inside, embarrassed as hell, and all the more ridiculous for being swathed in fax.

On your own now, Donald the gypsy had said. *On your own now and naked.*

*

Another day, another dusk. The afternoon was seeping away when they brought the vicar to the church.

He'd been asleep in his living-room, in an easy-chair with its back to the window, the Bible on his knees, for the weight of it and that fact that the Bible – *this* Bible, old, brass-bound – seemed to prevent dreams. In bed, he sometimes slept with the Bible across his legs, but occasionally it rolled away and the dark mirror of the night splintered into images.

The feeling of security the old Bible brought had evaporated in seconds when he'd found Eddie Edwards at the door with a wispy little woman called Helen Harris, who cleaned the church every third week. *Trouble, Vicar. Something very strange.* And they'd brought him to the church, practically pulling him up the few steps into the churchyard, cold dusk setting in around the mottled gravestones, bringing with it a spattering of rain, the vicar still shaky with sleep.

And then the candles.

There were ancient cowsheds grander than Ystrad Church. Which was fine by Eddie Edwards.

Not that he was particularly Low Church or a Puritan or any of that Noncomformist nonsense. Just that a church like this one, you didn't need to lock it up between services, which was how a church should be – open, available. The place was like a block of stone, rock of ages; all that you could prise off and take away were slates from the roof.

And, from inside, candles.

A necessity, for the church had no electricity and no gas. Also candles were cheap and Ystrad folk thrifty. For as long as anybody local could remember there'd been two candles in tin dishes on the altar, big fat, white candles.

Never anything like this. Mr Edwards had never seen – or smelled – *anything* like this in his life before.

He pulled a pencil from his breast pocket and tapped at the wax . . . not wax, tallow, anybody could sense that. Congealed, nauseous, like something out of an old chip pan abandoned for many weeks.

And brown-black, like ancient earwax.

'It makes no sense,' Mr Edwards kept repeating. 'What kind of sense does this make?'

And yet he'd never imagined that the vicar, the irreverent reverend, would have appeared quite as disturbed as this. Not his style at all.

Simon St John had sunk back into a front pew, the greying light from the dusty window over the altar shining on the outbreak of sweat across his forehead. Only once before had Mr Edwards seen him like this – the other day, in the shadow of the Abbey, when he'd turned away, used the F-word.

'Thank you, Helen,' Mr Edwards said. 'No need for you to hang around.'

And the poor woman went gratefully, and Mr Edwards said, 'I do not like this, Vicar.'

'Mrs Harris found them?' It was as if the vicar was trying out his voice, seeing if he could still speak. The teatime light flashed pink on the whitewashed walls.

'All of a dither, she was,' Mr Edwards said, 'because they were new candles, new this morning – they'd had to replace the old ones, see, not wanting to, they were hoping they'd last out until Christmastime.'

Was it conceivable that these *were* the new candles, that something was wrong with them, that when exposed to cold air they could kind of . . . decay?

It was not possible.

A full twelve inches high, these candles had to be. But . . . emaciated. Shrivelled and twisted, full of holes and notches, like sweating, putrid cheese, withered to a thickness of no more than half an inch in places.

And yet hard. Hard as old bones.

'Have you ever seen the like?'

The vicar didn't reply. He came to his feet and stumbled to the door and stood in the arched doorway, which opened directly to the churchyard, breathing in the darkening air, exposing his face to the rain.

Without turning round, he asked Mr Edwards, 'Were they alight when she found them?'

Mr Edwards was saying, 'Is this a joke, do you think? And if it is, why? And who? Who would want to come in here and replace our new candles with these raddled old things?'

'Eddie, were they *alight*?'

'Nonsensical, this is. Well . . . she told me . . . poor woman, the shock of it . . . that when she came into the church the candles were not alight and she did not notice them, but when she was getting on with the dusting – that back pew there, presumably, where the mat has been removed – suddenly there was a hissing in the air, *spssss!* And then a flaring from the altar. Wild, white flames on the end of both candles! Oh, hell, I do not know what she really saw, Simon, I'm just telling you what she told me. A state of terror she was in, certainly, when she arrived at my door. When we returned, all I can say is the candles were out. Only the smell in the air. You tell me, is this some kind of a joke?'

Fucking things are black. You call that a bleeding joke?

There was one tiny gleam of white between the closing clouds, like a mocking candle in the sky. Simon felt cold in his thin cassock. He was shaking with it and with fatigue and also revulsion.

Fourteen years ago he could handle this, no problem. He remembered Tom Storey knocking one of the old, brown candles to the floor with the neck of his guitar and the flames igniting a pile of Dave's lyrics sheets. How he'd *so* casually stamped out the flames, thinking, *got to stay calm, can't have Storey throwing another wobbly*.

The difference then was he felt in control, thought he was beginning to understand. Felt that, within himself, he was already a priest, possessed of the essential priestly calm which allowed him to wander across and coolly stamp out burgeoning hellfire.

But the sudden shock of it penetrating his world again, after all these years. For God's sake, these could be the very same candles. Candles from the Abbey. Candles from the time of Aelwyn.

He began to mumble a prayer, conscious that Eddie Edwards was watching him, but he couldn't help that.

'Oh, Father . . . Please. Don't let me fuck up. Let me get it right this time.'

Mr Edwards wandered across, patted him on the shoulder. 'Go home, Simon. I'll deal with them.'

'Deal?'

'I'll throw them away.'

'Of course,' Simon said. 'Thank you. But I'll stay until it's done, if you don't mind.'

He watched Mr Edwards pick up a large duster Helen Harris had left behind and fold it over his hand to prise the candles out of their holders. They were surprisingly stiff.

'Bugger,' said Mr Edwards. 'How long have they been here, for heaven's sake? It's as though they've been burning for hours and the wax has expanded.'

He wrapped the stinking, brown candles carefully in the duster and they both took them around to the dustbin at the rear of the church.

'Bloody kids,' said Mr Edwards. 'Though where they got them from I cannot imagine. Do you want to lock up the church tonight?'

'I don't think so,' Simon said wearily, lifting the dustbin lid. 'I don't think it would help.'

Mr Edwards glanced at him with curiosity. The candles did not land softly in the bin but clanged as if in protest.

When they were walking away, there was another resounding clang from the bin.

'Bloody things,' Mr Edwards said.

*

When he and the vicar had gone their separate ways, Mr Edwards took Helen's big duster from his pocket and returned to the dustbin.

It was dark now. Too dark to see inside the bin. He had to put his whole arm inside, reaching down to the very bottom before one of the discarded candles slid greasily into his palm.

He brought it out – just one would do – and wrapped it in the duster.

Something very strange here, and he had to know.

VII

Delphinium Blue

Everything was the same. And yet nothing was.

There was this small, cheap, private hotel outside Greenock where she stayed when the finances were wobbly. A good Presbyterian house, with no bar and therefore no commercial travellers. But always a room – with a *single* bed – to spare for a *respectable* woman on her own.

Mrs Coffey, the widowed proprietor, would have noticed that this time the dark-haired, dark-eyed woman didn't have a guitar case with her. Would be gratified to think that the woman had at last found a respectable job.

Would never know how alone Moira was this time. How the guitar had been like a sister, and her moulded leatherette case had also enclosed, in a concealed velvet pocket, the famous family heirloom, one comb.

What you see, Mrs Coffey, is a very confused woman entering middle age with no mother, no job and no past that bears contemplation.

It was nearly seven p.m. when she arrived; she didn't feel like one of Mrs C's traditional home-cooked dinners. She went to the window of her room and found that a new building had gone up across the street. Although the hotel was still called the Clydeview, this development would effectively block out what used to be Moira's morning glimpse of the glum, grey sea.

Everything the same; nothing the same.

She drew the curtains and fell down fully dressed on the bed, under the dingy, brown-framed picture of a sad-looking Saviour on the Mount.

Within a minute or two, she was unhappily asleep and

dreaming of poor Dave Reilly, reams of fax paper around him from nose to feet, like a winding sheet.

What was he supposed to do after this? Go home to his bland, clean, modern vicarage, light the fire, make a sandwich, watch TV?

Simon went, instead, head first into the night, pushing through a hardening rain, eyes open wide.

Reverberating in his head, as he walked, was the sound of the disgusting candles when Eddie Edwards had tossed them into the dustbin behind the church, the mocking, cackling clang.

And as he walked swiftly along the slanting, hillside lane into Ystrad Ddu, the twisted, skeletal candles went on clanging, as though they were inside Simon's skull, bone on bone. He kept rubbing the rain into his face and hair, as if this could stop it.

A dozen or so lights showed in the houses and in the bar of the Dragon, which was able to survive because the licensee was also the local newsagent and fuel-merchant. Out there, along the valley where the Abbey crouched, there was nothing but darkness and falling water.

Simon reached the village hall, a feeble, tin-hatted bulb over the door, as two women lowered their umbrellas and went in. 'Good evening, ladies,' he called in his cheery vicar's voice. They both nodded, and then the door slammed.

Good. It *was* Women's Institute night. Simon waited a while in the darkness until he could be sure all the women had gone in. Then he ran to a cottage set back from the road and knocked lightly on its front door.

'Who is it?'

'It's Simon St John. The vicar.'

'Mother's out.'

'I know,' Simon shouted through the rain and the door-panels. 'I wanted to talk to *you*, Isabel.'

After a moment, the cottage door opened smoothly, and

Isabel Pugh looked up at Simon from her firelit world. It was raining much harder now; his cassock was soaked through, water dripping down his clerical collar.

The front door opened directly into the living-room. There must have been a small hallway once, but the dividing wall had been knocked down, perhaps because it would have been impossible to manoeuvre a wheelchair around the corner to the door.

The stairs were in the enlarged room and there was also a square hole in the ceiling for a chairlift like a fireman's pole. A coalfire burned in a big black stove, blasting heat out of the door, out to the path where Simon stood and dripped.

'If this is an excuse to come in and take all your clothes off,' Isabel Pugh said, 'be my guest.'

Moira awoke suddenly, after no more than half an hour. She was feeling awfully cold. On her own now, and worse than naked, her first thought was, *It doesn't have to be like this.*

Did it not?

She arose stiffly and put on the light, a forty-watt bulb in a faded shade with burn-marks like black bruises. She went and stood by the lukewarm radiator under the drawn curtains. It was a grumbling old accordion of a thing; shivering, she pressed her thighs against it, but the heat was dying on her. She was probably the only guest; Mrs Coffey wasn't going to waste any warmth on her.

She filled the kettle at the basin, plugged it in on the unit, dumped a couple of teabags in the pot. She knew this kettle of old; getting it to boil was going to be like climbing Ben Nevis in a wheelchair. She plucked the rolled-up fax from her bag and took it back to the cooling radiator.

Dear Moira, Maybe you read about it in the papers . . . what happened in Liverpool on December 13th, 1993.

I don't think so. Maybe I read the wrong papers.

It was like an Act of God . . .

Aye, well, everything happening to Davey was either an act of God or the Other Guy. Or due to the malfunctioning of something less reliably good or evil out there on the supernatural shop floor.

The fax told her about an entire city losing its electricity after the million-to-one failure of a couple of transformers. About this happening in the thirteenth minute of the thirteenth hour, of the thirteenth day of the dreadful month of December, and more or less exactly thirteen years since . . .

See, the other problem with Davey was, it always came back to John Lennon, everything funnelling down to this one disaster, Dave's personal vortex. Dave saying, OK, Lennon may not actually have been shot on the *thirteenth*, but it happened on a Monday and sure enough, in 1993, the thirteenth was the first Monday after the anniversary of the murder. And the thirteenth is, after all, the *thirteenth*.

Davey, listen . . . She wanted to reach out and grab him by the psychic lapels, give him a good shaking . . . you can do anything with dates, times, synchronicity, all this shit. Damn it, you should have learned that by now.

She tossed the fax on to the bed, turned back to the vanity unit, pulling out a kind of piano stool to sit in front of the mirror. Reaching down unthinking for the guitar case, where an ancient Celtic comb with many missing teeth had lived in a velvet-lined pocket. How many times, weary in this very room, had she drawn out the comb, let it glide through her hair, drawing blue sparks in the dark. Bringing the place alive.

The comb lay in the Duchess's coffin. No redemption. On your own, hen. You gave it back.

On the unit, the kettle was making a noise like a death-rattle. She sat and watched the slow steam softening her face into a peachy fuzz.

Poor Davey.

Who would, this year, be exactly the same age as John Lennon when a fruitcake had flown in from Hawaii to blow him away.

Poor Davey, who'd believed in love and peace, etc., and that you could aspire to rearrange areas of your psyche that didn't conform to the natural, the reasonable, the acceptable, the *known*.

Who'd talked of taking the unwelcome, the burdensome aspects of himself and channelling them into *creativity*.

Who had, therefore, bought it, the whole Epidemic scam, accepting without question that the fusion of maverick minds would produce some great, immortal music.

And didn't you believe it just the teeniest bit yourself?

Aw, hell . . . at that age you still think this is something you could learn to control, something you're *bound* to be able to discipline, given time.

And Jesus, this room was colder than the frozen food alley at Safeway.

Half of him was pitying her; the other half was increasingly in awe.

Papers were spread all over a trestle table, under an Anglepoise lamp. Bills and invoices and bank statements. A new-looking IBM computer.

'Do you do *everyone's* accounts round here?'

'Mostly,' Isabel Pugh said. 'The farmers like it if they don't have to go into Abergavenny or Hereford. And they trust you, when you're a cripple. They think you can't do a bunk.'

She was rather a pretty woman, a little overweight, as you'd expect with her disability. She wore gold-rimmed glasses on a chain. Her hair was brown, with gold highlights. 'I've got all the qualifications,' she said, as if he'd challenged her. 'Correspondence course.'

There was a tartan rug over her knees. She flung it aside, revealing a hand holding a carving knife.

'Jesus Christ.' Simon backed into the doorway.

Isabel Pugh tossed the knife on to a settee. 'Can never be too sure nowadays, can you? It *sounded* a bit like your voice, but . . . I like to be in control.'

'Right.' He breathed out. 'Actually, I wasn't sure you'd be in. Thought you might have gone to the WI with your mother.'

She looked disgusted. 'Sorry,' Simon said. He moved into the room and closed the door behind him. It had a Yale lock and a double bolt half-way up, so they could be reached from a wheelchair.

'I'm thinking of having an electronic device put in, with a little two-way speaker thing,' she said. 'Why not? I can afford it. Going to take those sodden clothes off now, are you? I haven't seen a dick this close in twenty years.'

'No.' Simon smiled. 'But I'll sit by the stove and let them dry on me, if that's all right.'

'Soft bugger. Can't rape you, can I? And I don't think you'd want to touch *me*.'

'I'm a man of the cloth,' he said solemnly.

'And gay, too, isn't it?'

'You don't mess about, do you?' Simon said. Disabled people tended to be aggressive, he'd found, especially with vicars; they often blamed God. Part of a clergyman's job was taking the shit for all the things God allowed to happen.

'Good-looking man like you,' Isabel said. 'It's obvious. All alone and at your age. How old are you, forty-two, forty-three? Where do you do your cottaging, Abergavenny?'

'It's no bloody fun, either, on nights like this,' Simon said, no hint of a smile. 'I've been trying to persuade the council to build a public convenience at the top of the churchyard.'

Isabel laughed. It made her look younger. She couldn't have been more than fifteen when she fell from the south-west tower of the Abbey with her legs around a boy called Gareth Smith.

'Like a coffee, would you, Vicar?'

'Simon. You wouldn't have any Scotch in the house, would you? I'm perished.'

'Bottom cupboard, side of the fireplace. Glasses in the kitchen, ice in the fridge.'

He found an impressive selection of good single malts. The home-based accountancy business paid, then. 'You?'

'Why not. Southern Comfort. Neat. No ice.'

He went to look for glasses. The light oak-fitted kitchen had been extended into a conservatory with double-glazing. The rain was very loud in here.

'What've you come for then, Simon?' Isabel called out. 'Not the usual time for sympathy calls.'

'I came because your mother was out.'

'Ooo-er.'

Simon brought whisky glasses back. Poured Southern Comfort into hers until she nodded.

'To come straight to the point,' he said. 'I wanted to talk about the Abbey.'

Isabel lifted her glass, frowned. 'You really will have to get me pissed then.'

Moira flexed her shoulders. The kettle raised its tarnished lid and let out a thin whine, turning the mirror into mist, all white, white enough to write on. And because she couldn't see her face in it any more, her mind projected upon the mirror an image of what she'd been shoving to the back of her thoughts for some hours.

> *Dear Ms Cairns,*
>
> *Keeping this brief – I should very much like to speak to you in connection with the masters, which have come into my possession, of album tracks recorded at the Abbey studio, Gwent, in the early days of December 1980. Perhaps you would contact me as soon as possible.*
> *Yours sincerely,*
> *Stephen Case*
> *Recordings Executive*

The short message – *ultimatum?* – was already burnt into her mind, word for word, like a ghost image stencilled into a computer screen.

which have come into my possession.

OK. Let's work this one out. The decision to destroy the album was unanimous. That is, taken by Dave and Simon and me, in the absence only of Tom – who would hardly have objected and has never, to my knowledge, raised the issue since. And in the aftermath of Deborah's death, Russell Hornby, who *might* have resisted, just shrugged and handed over the reels.

But – this is the question – were these the actual masters? One reel of tape being just like another until you play it. Which, just wanting to forget, we never did.

So, did you double-cross us, Russell? Maybe thinking we were acting in haste, under stress, and would come around when the heat was off?

Are those tapes really still in existence? The sound – among other sounds – of the young, wildly over-confident, fucking stupid Moira Cairns allowing herself to be led like a lamb over Death's dark threshold?

There was no need to get her pissed. Isabel Pugh leaned back in her wheelchair, took off her glasses, let them fall to her breast on the chain.

'This may surprise you,' she said. 'But you're the first person who's ever asked me about the Abbey.'

Simon sat quietly, sipping his whisky, his cassock drying stiffly around him.

'When they got me out of the rubble it was the following morning and I was semi-conscious. Delirious, they said. They took me to hospital. A couple of days later the police took a statement to read at the inquest on Gareth. They kept it very discreet. We'd been . . . "exploring". I was in various hospitals for about six months. Nobody mentioned the circumstances again, not when I was in hospital, not when I came home.'

'When was this? What year?'

'Nineteen seventy-three. I was sixteen. Just old enough. I'd lost my virginity – just – when it happened.' Isabel laughed without humour. 'When the earth moved. For the first time. And the last. How about that for bitter irony? How about that for the wrath of God?'

'It wasn't God.'

'Well, pardon me, Vicar, but you would say that, wouldn't you?'

'Yes,' he said. 'I suppose I would. However . . .'

He wanted to tell her now. All about the session inside the walls cemented with blood and the dark brown candles and the centuries of evil and the reason he'd come back. He said, 'You haven't even asked me why I wanted to know.'

'Because I don't care.' Isabel held out her glass for more Southern Comfort. 'Thanks. When I got out of hospital, see, people were quite nice to me. People have *always* been quite nice. But there's no basic respect. I've always been the little whore who lured the Smith boy to the top of the tower and got him killed in the act. "Oh, she didn't deserve *this*" ' – slapping her unresponsive denimed legs – ' "but, well, it only goes to show, doesn't it?" '

Simon said, 'I'm . . .'

'Yeah, terribly, terribly sorry. So am I. Hardly thought to be spending the rest of my life in Ystrad Ddu, with my mother, so chuffed to be collecting her official carer's allowance. Still, I'm doing all right, biggest earner in the village now. And nothing to spend it on except luxury domestic aids for Mother and fancy mail-order clothes for the top half of me.'

'Damn,' Simon said. 'And I could've brought my violin.'

At first she looked furious. Then she grinned, the firelight making little red coals in her brown eyes. 'Are you really queer?'

'Let's just call me celibate.'

'Oh God, that's even worse.'

'We all have our cross to bear,' Simon said.

Isabel's eyebrows rose. 'And you really *are* a clergyman, aren't you? You wouldn't be having us all on?'

Simon spread his hands. 'And I really have got a violin. Isabel . . .' He leaned forward, hesitated.

'Go on,' she said. 'Ask me. Whatever it is, you've earned it. You've made me laugh, loosened me up a bit. That's worth a lot.'

Outside, the rain seemed to have stopped. A trail of singing reached them. 'The WI choir,' Isabel said. 'They're a good crowd, really. Keep themselves entertained.'

Simon said, 'You've skipped over a few things: what really happened at the Abbey, and what happened afterwards. You said you were delirious.'

'No. I didn't say that. They said I was delirious.'

How could she stand this life? What advantage was there in living in the country if you couldn't stride out on the hills, seeing the Skirrid rising in the east like a giant's nose, lie in the grass and watch buzzards swoop?

Isabel stared into the bright embers behind the glass doors of the stove. 'Simon, it's been fun tonight. Don't spoil it.'

'I don't understand,' he said. But of course, he did.

'This isn't what I wanted to go into.'

'Listen,' he said. 'Whatever they said about what happened that night being . . . delirium, I'm not going to think that.'

'No?'

'No, and I'll tell you why. I'll tell you what nobody else here knows, though Eddie Edwards possibly suspects.'

And he told her about the Philosopher's Stone and the Black Album.

'My God,' Isabel said. 'The vicar's a rock star? I'm sorry – go on.'

And he told her – not in any great detail – about the last night at the Abbey. The end of which, of course, she knew.

'Tom Storey's wife. I remember being woken up by the ambulance racing through the village. Everyone was out in the lane, you could see the flames, I got them to push me . . .'

She stopped. He couldn't tell whether her face was flushed by remembered excitement or by the deepening glow from the

153

stove. Or by embarrassment because she and the other villagers had been animated by someone else's tragedy.

'Keep it to yourself,' he said. 'For the present.'

Isabel put both hands to her cheeks, knowing they were red. 'Why?' she said. 'I mean, what the hell are you doing here, Simon?'

'Good question. Never wanted to see the fucking place again.' Simon paused. 'But what's the point of being a clergyman if you're aware of something deeply spiritually amiss in a remote part of South Wales and you just shrug your shoulders and bugger off to organize vicarage garden parties in Buckinghamshire?'

He stood up. 'Look, it'll be chucking out time at the WI in a few minutes. I'll be back. I'll call in some time while your mum's Hoovering my bedroom. Just one last question, OK?'

Isabel picked up her tartan rug and arranged it across her knees to see him to the door.

'Have there been other . . . accidents, like yours? At the Abbey? I mean, over the years?'

'We don't keep records of that kind of thing,' Isabel said, suddenly guarded, and Simon knew he was going too far, too fast. He pulled open the door. The night was calm enough now for him to hear a barn owl's screech from across the valley.

'Goodnight,' he said.

'Simon . . .'

He turned to look at her at the door of her prison: Isabel Pugh, thirty-seven, accountant, spinster of this parish, but not a virgin – just.

'One thing. I'll tell you one thing. When Deborah Storey died in that crash, everybody here was very sorry, for her and for her husband and the poor baby.'

'They're compassionate people,' Simon said. 'Thrifty, as Eddie Edwards put it. But no less compassionate for that.'

'They were sorry, yes. And yet they were also glad. In some awful way that they would never admit even to each other, they were glad.'

He was still standing there, his lips slightly parted, when it began to rain again and the door closed gently in his face.

The kettle's whine had been squeezed into a thin scream. Moira hit the red and black switch to cut it off.

And are they proposing to *release* this horror, the album that we used to call, in our innocence, the Black Album, because of the name of the Abbey?

Well, they couldn't, surely; insufficient material – five tracks? Six?

Whatever, of course, we have to stop this. All those Gothic heavy-metal albums made by brain-dead fascists in leather-studded wristbands, those albums the tabloids are always claiming drive fans to suicide, they're kidstuff.

So it has to be stopped, no question about that.

Who? Who's gonna stop it?

Maybe I'll call up this Case and say: Look, I think you should consider the ethics of what you have in mind.

Ethics? A record company?

Damage to repair, the Duchess said one time. You have damage to repair. Never making it clear what she meant . . . 'What the hell is *wrong* with this antique?'

The kettle carrying on screeching and wobbling on the dresser, bubbles fizzing around the lid. She hit the red knob again; damn thing was stuck. She reached through the hot vapour – *ow, Jesus!* – to switch it off at the plug, and remembered there wasn't a switch; it was so old even the plug was round-pin. 'Fuck you!' She grabbed hold of the cracked, brown, Bakelite plug and let go at once, gasping at the heat in it.

We're the band that should never've been. A toxic cocktail. We can't even see each other again. Ever.

Did I say that?

The kettle was just about going berserk, the whole room filling up now with grey steam. In its midst, the mirror was a luminous grey screen, like when you switched off the room lights and the TV was still radiating a dead glow.

Above her the ceiling bulb sputtered in its drab shade.

You too. Huh?

Moira went still inside. Even around the kettle, the room was unpleasantly cold, *especially* around the kettle, and that was wrong. That was *wrong*.

She thought, I'm not gonna run from this. I'm gonna sit here and wait it out. Wait until the kettle boils dry.

She saw her own face in the mirror and as she watched, the lips of this face – *not me, not my face, this doesn't scare me any more, it doesn't, no way* – stretched quite perceptibly into a rictus, revealing teeth and gums. The eyes were widening in helpless terror.

She was aware that the ceiling light had gone out and behind her, in the darkness of the faded bedroom, the steam was playing games; it had made its own pallid light and within this light it wreathed and spun like skeins of grey wool.

Please, she thought, but could not speak, forced into accepting ownership of the stricken face in the glass. *Please, no*.

And even as the thought escaped, the swirling steam became, as she knew it would, the dead face of the Duchess, long white hair uncoiling, eyelids sprung back . . . the Duchess rising in the greyness of her shroud, thin fingers splayed above the shoulders of the reflected image of her daughter in the mirror.

And in the condensation on the mirror, in a stricken, spidery hand, the Duchess's thin forefinger began to inscribe

Death

In the glass, Moira saw her own mouth form into an O of explicit revulsion, and she threw herself around, hauling on the damp flex so hard that the wires were jerked out of the plug and she and the Duchess were suddenly wrapped together inside a wildly crackling electric sheet of glorious delphinium blue.

VIII

Predator

'**O**pen up, please, sir.'

'Who is it?'

'It's the police, sir. We've had reports of a disturbance, if you wouldn't mind . . .'

He struggled with the top bolt, jammed it back, which sounded like a car-crash in his head. One of the coppers was right up against the door; he was in the flat faster than the hard night air.

'Dunno what this is about, officer, but I think you got the wrong place.'

'Won't mind if we take a look around then, sir.'

'Why the f—? No. No, sure. Go ahead.'

The two of them were in by now, young blokes, dead keen. One stayed between him and the door, the other searched the flat; took about a minute, came back, quickly shook his head. What were they expecting, bodies?

'You had the TV on, sir?'

'I was in *bed*, son. Asleep. And . . . and dreaming.' Yeah.

This time the first one stayed with him while the other had a nose around.

'According to our information, Mr—'

'Levin.'

'According to our information, Mr Levin, someone was screaming and yelling in here shortly before five a.m. You're saying you've been here alone for . . .'

'Several years, officer.'

'Tonight, sir.'

'Since about eleven.'

'Where were you before that?'

'I . . . went for a drink.'

'Which pub?'

'A couple. The Sheridan, that was the last.'

'A couple. I see. Did you hear anything suspicious in the last hour?'

'I was asleep. No. I didn't. Only you two trying to batter my bloody door down.'

'You live alone here?'

'I live alone. I'm happily divorced.'

'You don't look very well, sir.'

'Yeah, I lied about being happy too.'

'You're covered with sweat, if you don't mind me commenting.'

'Course I mind, you cheeky bastard. Maybe you made me nervous. It ever occurred to you you might make somebody nervous beating the crap out of their door at five in the morning?'

'Have a *lot* to drink, did we, sir?'

'And that's a crime in itself now, is it?'

'You're sure nobody came back with you, spent the night here?'

'If only.'

'I should put something on, sir, the way you're shivering. Harry?'

'Nothing.'

'Right then, sir. Let's hope we don't have to come back. I'd start having a little more consideration for the neighbours if I were you. Never know when you might need them, neighbours.'

'Yes. No. Sorry you were dragged out, son.'

'Goodnight, sir. What's left of it.'

Too much, Prof thought. Too much darkness.

When they'd gone, he poured himself three inches of Scotch and swallowed half of it. He sat in the living-room in his dressing-gown. He didn't even try to go back to bed. When he felt himself falling asleep he got up and went to the kitchen tap and splashed cold water on his face.

158

He stood there, water streaming down his face, the way the blood had run down Barney Gwilliam's face when Barney had slapped both dripping hands on his cheeks in his agony.

God help me, that I should ever have a night of dreams like this again.

Prof plunged his face into a tea-towel and scrubbed until it hurt. He went back into his living-room, dug out a copy of *Time Out*. Ran his fingernail repeatedly down the folk/rock/jazz pages but couldn't find what he was after. Could have sworn he'd seen a poster somewhere . . . Dave Kite, he was calling himself, as in *For the Benefit of* . . .

Kite, Kite . . . nothing.

Just before dawn, he started to weep with fatigue and sought strength once again in the sodding bottle. Yeah, yeah, bad idea, but the drink was a safer option.

Thus emboldened, Prof lurched to the window and screamed over the rooftops, at the sky, 'Get light, you bastard!'

Darkness left you prey.

Prey to what? To a recording? Was this realistic?

Yeah. Even the cheapest kind of pop music was like chewing-gum for the mind. You'd be doing a session, committing to tape some really innocuous piece of crap and next morning you'd wake up and your mind was singing it over and over, and wouldn't let go. You'd be in the bathroom, shaving, or on the bog, and you couldn't flush it out of your head.

Music was a predator.

Prof tried to read a feature in *Time Out* about Joanna Lumley, whom he'd fancied for more years than she'd care to have it known. It seemed irrelevant to where he was now.

Had that been him screaming? It was the young woman, surely, rushing through the ruins until her lungs were bursting, reaching for the night sky, the arches above and around her like dinosaur bones framing the cold, white moon. The young woman desperate to fly.

And the derisive singing, Gregorian chant gone sour.

And over all this, the death agony of poor, bloody Barney Gwilliam.

Prof had awoken maybe five times in the night, rolling in his solitary bed, the sheet sweating to his back like clingfilm on cheese.

He needed somebody to talk to. A woman. Every time since the divorce he'd had a woman here for more than two nights, he'd told himself, this is it, last time, never again, don't ever get tempted, Kenny boy. Because two nights was enough to demonstrate the way women liked to place you into a bloody *structure*, and he was too old for that.

Yet structures, however flimsy, stopped your life breaking up into anarchy and chaos, and he hadn't realized before how close at hand it was, the bloody chasm. Just as close as sleep. You spent a third of your life sleeping, out of control, and when chaos started to take over your sleep . . .

Hold it . . .

By accident, he'd found what he was looking for. Dave Kite. It was listed under 'comedy'. Two pages, now, of bloody comedy clubs, everybody suddenly wanting to escape into laughter.

The relevant gig was tomorrow night. No, shit . . . tonight, this *was* tomorrow.

The sky acquired light. Soon after seven. Prof lit the gas fire, opened the curtains wide to the dawn and bedded down on the sofa, knowing he'd awake unrefreshed but, if his subconscious had any mercy, without music in his mind.

The kind of music that could swallow your sanity.

First thing, Eddie Edwards was ready with his parcel, a shoebox begged from Mrs Edwards, with straw inside . . . and a candle.

He took it to the shop at the Dragon, which was not an actual post office but sold stamps and had mail picked up there by special arrangement.

The parcel was addressed to an old friend of his, Ivor Speed, a chemist at the University of Wales, Swansea. When he arrived home he telephoned Ivor, told him about it.

'A candle? What am I supposed to do with a candle?'

'A candle such as you have never seen before, I'll bet,' Mr Edwards said. 'Playing detectives, I am. I want an analysis.'

'Even if I can arrange to do it here, it'll take time. Couple of days, maybe more.'

'Quick as you can, Ivor, quick as you can.'

'And what do you expect me to find?'

'Probably nothing. Just a feeling I have.'

And that ought to have been that, until Ivor got back to him. But he couldn't get it out of his mind.

He took Zap for his walk, along the path curving up into the cleft of the rock. The path was steep; it occurred to him he might be too old for it before the dog was, which was a depressing thought.

It was a cold, colourless morning with a haze on the horizon, over which the Skirrid was printed like a patch of damp on a napkin.

From the other side, it was nothing to speak of, just another hill with a rocky bump, like a scab, near the summit. Even from here, it was not, in truth, so remarkable, its main peak like the keel of an upturned boat. It was inspiring, mystical, *because* it was the Skirrid, because you never looked at it without being aware of the most significant, terrible moment in the history of mankind. The power of legend. Which made the little Skirrid, in its way, more dramatic than the Matterhorn, or the Taj Mahal. And touched this undulating border landscape, and its ruins of abbeys and castles, with magic.

And this made Mr Edwards think of *black* magic. They had not been black candles, not quite, but there was about them . . .

'An evil,' Mr Edwards whispered aloud to the Skirrid, seven miles away.

There. He'd said it.

How strange to be using that word in a place like this, where there was no malice in the people, only an occasional – how could he put this? – *leadenness* of spirit.

But he had seen dread on the face of the vicar when he'd been shown those candles. The vicar knew what it meant, all

161

right. And if he would not tell, Mr Edwards was honour-bound, in this place, to find out for himself.

Four p.m.

Hunched over the gas fire, Prof had three attempts at tapping out the TMM main number on the cordless before he got it right. Nerves? Fatigue? The booze?

'Steve?'

'Hello, Prof. I wondered when you'd call.'

'Did you?'

Something wrong.

In a sham-breezy offhand tone, Steve Case told him he'd be getting a cheque, plus remittance note detailing two weeks' session work, plus exes. More than he deserved was the inference.

'So you've finished with me. That's what you're saying?'

'I thought you'd be glad.'

'You sound happy, Steve. Buoyant.'

'I'm a buoyant sort of guy.'

'I'm not. I'm feeling bloody awful. You want to know why that is?'

Steve said he was sorry about this, in a tone implying he was not sorry. 'Prof, you need to go back to AA, mate. Sorry to be so blunt, but word gets round. You want to work again, you should be sensible.'

A pause.

'You shit,' Prof said. 'I've never been an AA member.'

'I'm trying to help you.'

'You want to help me, tell me something. You listened to it yet?'

'Prof, nice to talk to you, as always, but I've got a meeting at four thirty . . .'

'*The tape*.'

Stephen Case's voice went high and airy. 'It needs remixing, but, yes, I think we can make something of it, with a little padding.'

'Did nothing *happen?* When you listened to it? Afterwards?'

'I'm sorry, I have to . . .'

'Don't you fucking hang up on me, Steve, else I'll be round there . . . I'll make trouble, embarrassment. You tell me . . . what did you *feel?*'

'I don't know *what* you're talking about. You've been paid. Let's leave it there, shall we?'

'Thanks for services rendered and goodnight. Great. Listen, I'll take your money. I'll take your money, and I'll give you some advice. You get *rid* of those tapes, you don't even *contemplate* putting out an album.'

'Mr Levin, let me get this right – you're telling *me* what we can and can't release?'

'I'm telling you it would be . . . irresponsible. Don't laugh. Don't you *dare* fucking laugh at me! Steve . . .' Lowering his voice. 'That music messes people up.'

'Other alcoholics, you mean?'

'Christ . . .' Prof bit off a breath. 'Steve, I'm swallowing what's left of my pride. I'm telling you this thing is not healthy.'

'It's just an album.'

'The fuck it is! Listen to me. Barney Gwilliam. Did you know Barney Gwilliam engineered this session?'

'Does it matter?'

'Barney . . . Barney *died*.'

'People do die, Prof. People die all the time.'

'No. People don't die all the time like this man died. Listen, I trained Gwilliam, OK? In the mid-seventies. Very quiet guy, very unassuming, but a bloody whizz. Full of ideas. Any kind of new technology, Barney'd have it in his head soon as it was available. The goods, was Barney Gwilliam. Could've been making five times what I was turning over, no question.'

But then, suddenly, aged twenty-eight, Barney had given up the music business, gone to work for the BBC as a radio engineer in Cardiff. Prof, amazed, had given him a bell, asking what the hell was he *doing?* Barney had said uncomfortably that he needed a break. Prof said, listen, we should meet some time. Barney said, yeah, sure.

But it never happened, and three months later . . .

He heard Stephen Case's bored sigh.

'Jesus, the more I think about this . . . Listen, radio editing at the BBC, it's razor blades. Editing block and a blade. Primitive but efficient. So in Studio Nine, eighth of December 1981, Barney Gwilliam – you telling me you never heard this?'

'Nor do I particularly want to, by the sound of things.'

Barney Gwilliam, all alone, twenty-eight years old, had put himself in a comfy swivel chair in Studio Nine – now closed down, Prof gathered – and swiped one of these keen little blades, as used for cutting tape, hard across his throat, five, six times.

'How very distasteful,' Stephen Case said.

He knows, Prof thought. This bastard knows.

He said, 'The best, most promising young engineer ever worked under me, gives up a potentially brilliant career and bleeds to a lonely death in a radio studio, and all you can say is "*How very distasteful*"?'

'These things happen,' Steve said. 'I suppose people at one time used to talk about a promising young-ish sound engineer who turned to drink.'

'Bastard,' Prof said; they seemed to hang up simultaneously.

The rest of the afternoon went by in a fever, Prof bumping up his phone bill like someone else was paying it. He drank one or two whiskies and he made call after call until it was dark outside and for some reason his fingers weren't hitting the right numbers any more.

He wanted to know about TMM: who was inside the company that he might be acquainted with, that might listen to him telling them: do not on any account make this album available to the impressionable public.

Sile Copesake, now, the old bluesman, ringmaster of the sixties R and B circuit. Sile was a big-wheel in TMM these days. And old bluesmen, by the nature of their calling, were always superstitious. Maybe Sile would give him a hearing. He called TMM, got nowhere. Sile Copesake, they said, came in infrequently. Prof could leave a message. No, they were not able to release Sile's home number.

The Abbey then. What had happened to the Abbey? Years since he'd heard of anybody recording there.

Prof looked up some music journalists he used to know. When he called the numbers, two of them turned out to have been dead over a year. God almighty, the way time went by, rock music journalists dying of old age!

Around five-thirty, a freelance hack called Peter Marriott said, 'The Abbey? An unlucky studio that, Prof. Had it in mind to do a piece once, but it'd closed down, nobody cared any more.'

'This was when? After 1980? After the Storey tragedy?'

'No, no, this would be eighty-five, eighty-six. After the Soup Kitchen business.'

'After the what?'

Peter Marriott said they – meaning this Soup Kitchen – were not big enough to make much of a splash in the Press, even the music papers. They weren't even a *little* name. Peter Marriott said that if Prof was on to something, he would like to know about it, and Prof said, 'Yeah, yeah, you'll be the first, Pete, I promise.'

'Sure I will. If you even remember making this call.'

'I'm clean these days. Dry. Trust me.'

'OK,' said Peter Marriott. 'I may have a couple of cuttings in the files. I'll photocopy them, put them in the post. Where you living now?'

'Tonight? You'll post them tonight?' He was sounding too keen. 'What I mean is, I'm going away, I'd like to see it before I go.'

'Sure. Tonight. But you remember who sent them, Prof, OK?'

'I'm writing it down in my diary.'

Prof put the phone down and went to lie on the sofa. He was too old for this.

But when he felt himself dropping off to sleep, he sat up in panic, snatched up the phone again and summoned a minicab.

Dave Kite, he thought. What kind of stupid name is that?

Where do you actually go to when you are dead to find redemption for all your sins?

Do you indeed go anywhere? Or are you distilled in a bottle and uncorked now and then as a reminder to the living? A scented breath of love. A gasp of pain. A rancid stench of hatred?

Where do you go to find redemption?

Simon St John had written this in his journal before lying back in his chair and closing his eyes, the Bible on his knees.

The journal was an old cashbook from his father's estate office. His father had been a prosperous land agent in Kent, with pretensions, who had disowned Simon when, at twenty-eight, his son had left the string quartet to become violinist/cellist/bass-player in a damned pop group.

He would undoubtedly have thrown him out sooner had he known what Simon was up to with Jeremy, the quartet's angular, bearded viola player. Might have *welcomed* his switch to an otherwise heterosexual folk-rock band.

And the church? His father didn't know about that. His father had died by then. It made no difference; whenever Simon sought to justify his apparently-drastic career-change, it was his father to whom he would try to explain it.

Do you remember when they brought me home from Sunday school, Dad? In hysterics, aged six? Palm Sunday, 1955. I can still remember it in detail.

You see, kids can be very callous. It's usually the stupid, theatrical things that frighten them – witches and evil stepmothers. Little boys, you tell them about the Crucifixion, they're scrabbling for their drawing books. Giant nails and splatters of red. Me, I could feel the agony. Not just the physical pain, but the passion, and because I couldn't understand what that was about, I went into hysterics.

I remember the bandages on my hands. The Sunday school

teacher telling you and Mum I must have shoved a sharpened pencil into each palm. Oh, the disgrace, get him into the car quick.

The passion. I think it must be like this for a lot of priests. They love Christ, and it's a physical thing as well. They're so deeply moved by His image in all those Renaissance paintings and statues, His beautiful, slender body dangling there.

So that first Palm Sunday, when I was six, that's when the spark was kindled. And then going into churches, the energy in those places. All the other kids bored out of their minds or just getting into the singing. I couldn't understand why I was the only child in the pews who felt the energy. It wasn't like, let's all be hushed and subdued until we're called upon to raise the rafters with the ghastly rhyming couplets of a bunch of pompous Victorian gits, for we are on Holy Ground. It was . . . wow. And I still can't explain it, except that it can be better than sex, which is how many of us have been able to put up with celibacy – or even get an exquisite satisfaction from it.

You see . . . the essence of it is very close to what we're taught is blasphemy. Dangerously close.

And I don't mind admitting I still can't make any bloody sense of the metaphysics, particularly the concept of heaven and hell. Even though I've seen the dead walk, I still don't know where they go.

The phone rang.

Simon lifted the Bible from his knees, placed it on the chair arm, went over to take the call at his desk.

'Simon?'

'Yes.'

'It's me, Isabel.'

'Oh. Hello.'

'You sound different.'

'Do I?'

'Look, Mother's going to a choral concert in Abergavenny. Why don't you come round?'

She sounded excited. A tone of voice he recognized from other places, other parishes.

'Simon? Are you still there?'

'Yes.'

'So, what time?'

'I'm sorry,' he said. 'I can't. I'm sorry.'

His mind had broken the connection long before his hand put the phone down.

'Sorry,' he said.

IX

Allergy Syndrome

'Shelley!' The Weasel hovered anxiously in his caravan doorway. 'You all right?'

Tuesday, five p.m. Just back from delivering this cargo of Quorn and spinach pasties and stuff to Banbury. A good run, traffic unexpectedly light and with the short cuts he'd been sussing out, here he was, home before dark, just.

And here *she* was, running across the yard from the house, bristols jogging like turnips in a Tesco carrier bag. Must've been *waiting* for him.

'Weasel, thank heavens.' She was panting, blonde hair all over the place. 'Look, I need your help.' Her voice higher pitched, maybe on account of running.

He looked beyond her to the house, two or three lights on, but not in Tom's attic. No sounds from up there, none last night either. Bit worrying, that, the way Tom was coming unspooled.

'It's Vanessa,' she said.

The Weasel went rigid. Most of the worst things he imagined happening if Tom finally threw the big one involved the kid, Vanessa.

He jumped down all three steps to the slippery grass and stumbled to his knees. Action-hippie. Jeez.

'Oh gosh, no panic, Weasel. I was simply wondering if . . . Look, what are you doing tonight? I mean, you know, I'm sorry to drop this on you, but Tom and I are sort of . . . going out.'

'You what?' Weasel straightened up, relief giving way to astonishment. 'You're going out? *Wiv Tom?*'

'Yes, yes, all right.' Shelley shrugged awkwardly. 'Let's call it my personal coup of the year. It's a client, you see. Potential client, anyway. For the business. He's invited us to dinner.'

'Us? Tom?'

'Tom too, yes. Tom was . . . resistant, at first. As he would be. This was last week. You probably . . .'

'Oh. Yeah.'

'The night you came to see him. Which didn't exactly improve the situation either, at first.'

'No. Sorry 'bout that.'

'Well . . .' Shelley was struggling a bit; personal stuff. 'No need to be, as it happens. It did, you know, take the wind out of his sails, somehow. He was very quiet all night. Been fairly quiet since, actually.'

'Yeah. Sir Wilf'll fink it's his birthday.'

'I'm sorry?'

'Your neighbour. Been bitching about the riffs in the night, 'parently.'

'I didn't know that,' Shelley said. 'You should have told me.'

'Nah,' Weasel said. 'No probs. Down the pub they don't reckon much to Sir Wilf.'

Shelley was silent for a moment, filing this away for future smoothing-out. And then she said, 'I don't *know* what you were discussing . . . not my business.'

She wouldn't ask Weasel outright, 'cause that'd be disloyal, wouldn't it? However bad things got, Shelley was always loyal. Sometimes Weasel admired her above all other women, the shit she'd taken and still stayed loyal.

'It's complicated,' Weasel said. 'About the music.'

'Oh,' she said. The music was an issue not relevant to right now, obviously. 'It . . . Weasel, I . . .' She took a serious breath. 'What I think is, he's made a decision to try and pull things together. You know what I'm talking about? Maybe you don't. I mean, with Tom, you have to . . .' Gabbling a bit now; nerves.

Nerves? Shelley Love?

'I mean, he *knows* we've got problems with cash-flow and we might have to lay people off – *and* before Christmas, God help us.'

She folded her arms across her chest; she had on this bulky Arran sweater. Weasel wouldn't have minded folding his arms across there either.

'So I held on as long as I reasonably could, just vainly hoping and then this morning I picked up the phone to tell Broadbank I'd got flu or something and couldn't make it, playing for time, you know? Tom just took the receiver off me and put it back and said, "OK." Just like that. Very calmly. "OK."'

'Stone me,' Weasel said.

'Don't say it like that, Weasel. He's not that bad.'

'He is, Shel,' Weasel said soberly.

'Yes, all right. Has been. But it's . . . it's not that you could say he's coming out of it, as such. It's that . . . I think finally he *wants* to come out of it. You know?'

Weasel was very dubious. He said nothing.

'So what I was wondering,' Shelley said. 'As this has never arisen before . . . was if you could come up to the house tonight and sit with Vanessa. I mean I'm sure she'd be all right on her own – be absolutely furious if I said otherwise. But it *is* the first time we've had to leave her.'

'What, in fourteen years?'

'Sounds terrible, doesn't it?'

'Nah, nah . . . it's just . . .'

Realizing now why she'd come racing across the yard, why her voice had risen about half an octave. Why she was so nervous. This was, like, the crucial period. Any time between now and actually getting the car on the road with Tom inside it, there was an 80–20 chance of him spinning round and making a dash for his attic, and that'd be it for another ten years.

Weasel said, 'Never been on holiday?'

'Are you kidding?'

'What about . . . like . . . a honeymoon?'

Shelley said deliberately, as if she was working it out, these indelible details, 'We lived together for two years. One afternoon, the seventh of July, a Tuesday, we went out to the register office with a couple of my friends. And then they went home and we came back. To the flat.'

Shelley sighed. 'Vanessa's actually seen more of the world than we have, what with going to school . . .'

Weasel remembered how Shelley had had a major bust-up with the education bods to get Vanessa into an ordinary state school, with, like, normal kids . . . then there was the convent.

Shelley tossed back her hair. She was a gorgeous woman, and she'd never spoken to him like this before. Not at such length. Never even stood as close to him when they was alone, always suspicious of him, what he might be after.

But Weasel feeling honoured was only the half of it. This was an opportunity that could not be missed.

'Shel,' he hesitated. 'I'd be proud to sit in wiv the kid. But . . .'

'Go on, Weasel, you're holding the cards.'

'All right . . .' Pushing his luck a lot lately. 'Whatever's, like, wrong wiv Tom, it ain't improving, right? I mean, I accept he's making a big effort tonight, but . . .'

'No,' said Shelley heavily, 'things haven't been improving. Maybe tonight's just another false dawn. I have to take that chance.'

'Maybe I could help. Not just staying wiv the kid, in other ways. If you was to fill me in . . . on how . . . Jeez, I wouldn't know where to start describing his condition.'

'There is a name for it,' Shelley said.

There were suddenly so many comedy clubs in London that people were saying humour was taking over from rock and roll.

Was this likely? After thirty years of youngsters posing in front of the bathroom mirror holding a tennis racket like an electric guitar, would they be practising deadpan expressions and working on their timing, collecting jokes instead of records?

It certainly didn't bode well for the industry which had supported Prof Levin since the days when the Beatles were in suits.

At least comedy clubs *looked* like rock and roll clubs: a scruffy doorway and steps. This joint was still hedging its bets, singers and bands sharing the bill with stand-up comics. And tonight, a bloke who had a foot either side of the great divide.

The place was called Muthah Mirth.

Ha bloody ha, Prof thought, paying dearly for the gig he'd seen billed in *Time Out* and an extortionate membership fee on top.

Inside, a three-piece blues band was doing GBH to an old Elmore James number while about twenty people sat around at tables, some of them eating nasty-looking bar-meals.

A dump. Poor sod couldn't be doing that well, reduced to this level.

It was eight p.m.

Prof went over to the bar. 'What time's Dave Kite on?'

'Be a couple of hours yet, squire. Have a drink while you're waiting?'

'Yeah,' Prof said. 'Gimme a Pepsi. Non-diet.'

The barman was a thirtyish bloke in a pink T-shirt with a Muthah Mirth logo involving a voluptuous solid guitar with one pick-up turned into a mouth so the guitar looked like it was grinning. He poured the Pepsi without comment.

'What's his act like?' Prof said.

'Who, Kite? Spooky. A bit spooky.'

All I bloody need.

'Spooky? What's that supposed to mean? I thought this was supposed to be a comedy club.'

'Yeah, well,' the barman said. 'Sometimes he's funny, sometimes he ain't. How the mood takes him. I reckon he's got a problem, but they say that about all the best ones, don't they? All the best comics, there's a tragedy going on behind the scenes.'

Prof glanced down into his full-strength Pepsi. In this light it looked like blood.

Sod it.

'Do me a favour, son. Take this away and fetch me a large Bells.'

The barman grinned. 'You one too?'

'A comic? Meaning you can sense a powerful air of tragedy about me?'

Prof put a tenner on the bar and grabbed his double Scotch with both hands, like a mother reclaiming a lost child.

'You might be right, son.' Taking a deep swallow. 'You might be right at that.'

Shelley did some thinking, her Arran sweater and her hair the same colour in the dusk. She was possibly doing a bit of lip-pursing too, which he couldn't see in this light.

Shelley said eventually, 'Have you heard of a thing called Total Allergy Syndrome?'

'Er . . .' Everything was a bleeding syndrome nowadays.

'It's where . . . Look, lots of people are allergic to different things, like the smell of paint or floor polish or diesel fumes or whatever . . . They come out in rashes or get asthma attacks.'

'I'm wiv you. Cats. Some people is allergic to cats.'

'And with some it just runs riot, and they're allergic to a whole lot of different things. There've been people who've had to live in sort of sterile bubbles. I mean, it can be life-threatening.'

'Sometimes freaten other people's lives,' Weasel said darkly.

'And Tom . . . God, it all sounds so ridiculous. Look – you must know this, you've known him a lot longer than me – Tom's always been very . . . *sensitive*, OK?'

'If you mean the second sight, yeah we all knew that. Scary stuff. We all had a few frights, being around Tom. And Tom hisself . . .'

'Was probably more scared than any of you, I'd guess.'

'I fink it just made him mad,' Weasel said. 'Angry.'

'Same thing,' Shelley said.

'And then he went frew this stage where he'd make, like, a joke of it. 'Cept it wasn't that funny. Like . . . OK, when he was wiv the Brain Police, in about '72, we had this manager for a while, real money-grabbing, slave-driving bleeder, he'd have the band gigging eight till midnight, seven nights a week. Anyhow, one night, everybody's well knackered and Tom just points at this manager, Carlos, and he goes, "You wanna take a night off, tomorrer, mate, gonna do yourself a mischief." And then he turns his back and just slopes off, the way he does, you know? We don't fink nuffink of it. And then next night, same time – same time *exackly*, I reckon – the geezer goes and falls downstairs at his gaff and breaks his bleeding back. Stoke Mandeville job, we never seen him since. We said, bleeding hell, Tom . . . He says, "Nah, nah, piss off, I didn't *do* it, I just seen it coming, all right." And we didn't say nuffink else, seeing he was about to get . . . annoyed.'

'Coincidence,' Shelley said unsteadily, hugging herself.

'Sure,' Weasel said. 'You call him sensitive, Jesus, sometimes I reckon he's the most *un*sensitive bastard I ever met. Look, Shel, it's getting parky, we could go in the van, make a cuppa . . .'

'I haven't got time, Weasel. Besides I've said too much already.'

'No you ain't. It needs to come out, this does. Go back to what you was saying. This syndrome bit.'

'Oh, Christ . . .' Shelley glanced behind her towards the house, began talking low and quick. 'Look, after . . . after Deborah died, as you must've gathered, he was very bad. He saw Vanessa being Down's Syndrome as a kind of retribution. I mean, I *don't* know what happened that night, I convinced myself I didn't *want* to know. I really thought it was just a *phase*. And I thought – arrogantly, I realize that now – that I could pull him out of it. But it got worse and worse, as you know, he withdrew . . . You know about this house, why we had to come here?'

Weasel said carefully, 'I seen these geezers, the dowsers?'

'Checking out the spot, yes. Making sure it wasn't on a ley-line or something. Had to be a site nobody had lived on before – hence the barn conversion. And using new materials, no old stones. And no old trees – I still don't understand that one.'

'You got real problems, Shel. You oughter've told me before,

175

not been so self, self . . . proud. I fink a lot about the big stupid bleeder, you know that.'

'I've coined my own phrase for it,' Shelley said. 'The problem. My own clinical term.'

There was a familiar roar from the house. 'Shelley!' A sash window shot up with a crash. 'Where are you, darlin'?'

'I'm out here, Tom.'

'Shelley, do I own a fucking *tie*?'

Shelley gave the Weasel a really hopeless smile and turned back towards the house. 'We'll be leaving at eight-fifteen, OK?' she said hopefully.

'Sure. Don't worry 'bout a fing. Shel . . .'

She stopped. He could only see the white sweater, grey from this distance, and the paleness of her hair.

'Wossa term?' Weasel said. 'This problem? Wossit called?'

Shelley carried on walking until she was just a smudge. Then she stopped and called back, over her shoulder.

'Total *Psychic* Allergy Syndrome. Work it out.'

And she disappeared into Tom Storey's ugly, yellow, sterile house.

'This is Meryl,' Martin Broadbank said. 'She does for me.'

She was tall, an inch or so taller than Martin and maybe a year or two older. Black hair coiled up into something exotic. A long, tight black dress with a little apron over it.

Fantasy figure, Stephen Case thought. Miss Whiplash meets Mrs Danvers.

'How do you do,' Meryl said, and she had a deep, fairly cultured voice, a voice you'd expect from the mistress of the house, as distinct from the mistress of its owner.

Mistress. Archaic words came easily to mind in this setting, the baronial hall with the Jacobean panelling and the big, central staircase and that musty, fruity smell, like old, stored apples.

'Interesing place,' Stephen observed, trying not to appear over-impressed. 'How old?'

'Mainly seventeenth.' Martin Broadbank was casual-formal,

black suit over a white polo shirt. 'With some sixteenth-century bits, or is it fifteenth, I forget.'

Meryl said, with authority, 'There's a core of a smaller house, at least fifteenth century, possibly earlier. Are you interested in old buildings, Stephen?'

Letting him know with that 'Stephen' that she'd transcended the paid-retainer stage.

'I'm interested in all kinds of old things,' he said, meeting her eyes, as dark and tranquil as rock pools. He looked away, suddenly uneasy about her.

'Which reminds me,' Broadbank beamed. 'I've invited a couple of other neighbours, Sir Wilfrid and Lady Tulley. They, too, have a certain interest in your mate Storey.'

Stephen Case wondered what he was getting into here, in this essentially Addams family setting, the Jacobean farmhouse and the awesome Meryl. Martin seemed to have developed a disturbing taste for costume drama.

'They're not exactly fans, though,' Broadbank said. 'Not of his music, at least. Come through to the drawing-room, Steve.'

Meryl said, 'Excuse me,' and glided away to the side of the staircase.

'Dinner to prepare,' Broadbank explained. 'She's an absolute treasure, that woman. Used to be one of my store managers. Now she manages me.'

'I bet she does,' Stephen said, following him into more oak panelling, wing chairs around a deepset log fire, burgundy velvet curtains, drawn. Thinking of his open-plan flat in Islington: white walls and black ceilings, three sofas and a bed angled around a £30,000 hi-fi system. Wondering where he'd gone wrong.

'I've always liked older women,' Broadbank said. 'Meryl understands me. Knows when to be around and when to make herself scarce. Awfully perceptive. I think this house would be a bit too much for me without her. They can be quite oppressive, these old places. What is it you chaps drink, tequila?'

'Sherry will be fine, thank you, Martin,' Stephen said resentfully. He *did* prefer tequila, actually, fuck it.

177

'Sit down, Steve. We've probably got a few minutes before anyone shows. Let's plan this thing out. Tell me, what precise result are you looking for this evening?'

Broadbank opened a previously invisible door in the panelling. Lamplight glinted on bottles. 'Now – sweet, dry, Bristol Cream?'

'Dry.' Stephen slipped into a deep, fireside chair. 'It's difficult. You see, I've acquired some tapes, back from when Storey was a force to be reckoned with, when people were still talking about the great guitarists of our time as Hendrix, Clapton, Beck and Storey. After this stuff was recorded – *immediately* after, according to some sources – Storey started to go downhill.'

'Drink? Drugs?'

'That's the curious thing, I don't think so. His wife died, as I mentioned, in difficult circumstances, but when did tragedy stifle creativity? Look at Clapton, when his child was killed – writes a song which becomes a kind of anthem for the bereaved.'

Stephen stretched his legs, making furrows in the deep, soft rug. 'No, there's more to it, Plus, there are other people we believe were on this album. Lee Gibson?'

'Even I've heard of him,' Broadbank said, handing him sherry in a crystal schooner. 'And his women. Piece in the *Mail*, I think, the other week.'

'Yeah, yeah.'

'So there's money in this material, is there?'

Stephen Case shrugged. 'You can never tell.'

'Oh, come on, you wouldn't be going to all this trouble . . .'

'Well, it's possible, yeah. You discover a missing album connecting Lee Gibson, even if he *was* only a drummer in those days, with the fallen idol, Tom Storey, plus whoever else. Sometimes a mystique forms.'

'And if there isn't one already, you'll manufacture one. Don't look at me like that, I'm a businessman. CDs, tins of soup, what's the difference? And savoury flans with vegetarian cheese-substitute.'

'What?'

'Doesn't matter. Why do you need Storey? Why not just do what you like with the stuff? You don't need his permission, do you?'

'No. The band have no rights. They took money up front. It's our album – we could even sue them for not finishing it. But that's all in the past. Right now, his co-operation wouldn't go amiss.'

'And you're curious, aren't you?'

'Just a little,' Stephen said.

'Steve, it's burning you up.'

'Yeah. Sure.' Better he think that than get the idea Stephen Case might need a recording coup to save his career, to keep his head above all the other younger heads with thicker hair.

A sudden draught, like a lorry going past, made him glance up; one of the curtains was quivering.

Martin Broadbank smiled. 'You feel that?'

'Feel what?'

'This is my drawing-room. I went to considerable expense to ensure it's totally draught-proof.'

'What are you saying?'

Martin Broadbank was sitting on the opposite side of the fire, drinking something pale in a brandy balloon. He gave it a swirl.

'An old house just doesn't seem like the real thing *at all* without a ghost or two, don't you think?'

Stephen Case smirked. 'That's rather pathetic, Martin.'

'We country dwellers keep an open mind on such matters,' said Broadbank. 'And if I were you I'd keep my scepticism to myself when Meryl's around. She attends a spiritualist church in Gloucester, every Friday evening.'

'Jesus Christ. She *must* be good in bed.'

'The Lady Bluefoot. That's our ghost. Lost her husband in a hunting accident in eighteen-something. Couldn't come to terms with it, apparently, and used to have a place laid for him at the dinner table every night. Now Meryl likes to set out a place for *her*, extra knives and forks and things. Keeps her sweet, she says.'

'If this is what living in the country does to you,' Case said, 'I think I'll put up with the M25.'

Martin Broadbank stood up. 'I do hope the Storeys aren't going to be late. Meryl's putting you next to the living legend himself, by the way. I shall be next to *Mrs* Storey. Or rather, next to Mrs Storey's sublime left breast.'

'Won't, er, Meryl be jealous?'

'Oh no,' said Broadbank. 'Meryl isn't like that at all.'

They heard a car approaching along the gravel drive.

X

The Man With Two Mouths

It was a fifteen-minute journey, no more than ten, eleven miles beyond the village. Past the pub and the village hall, which were all lights. Past the post office, in darkness. Past the pretty Cotswold stone church, floodlit.

In the first three-quarters of a mile, Tom Storey made three attempts to get out of the Volvo.

'You bloody idiot,' Shelley yelled, as they crested the last hill, the one with the sign which had Larkfield St Mary on the other side.

She put on the headlights, shoved her foot down on the accelerator. If he jumped now he'd break his bloody neck and serve him right.

Safe in the knowledge that Tom was not a brave man in that sense, she listened to him pulling the passenger door shut. She could also hear his breath, like a distant train.

'Oh, honey, it'll be all right, trust me. People. You have to rediscover *people*.'

'You don't understand,' Tom mumbled sourly. 'You will *never* understand.'

'I think I do, Tom,' she said, knowing all the same that, in a sense, he was right.

He *had* tried, though, digging out a quite respectable green cord jacket and a pair of brushed denim trousers which were almost not jeans. No, he didn't have a tie, but she did, a black one from when they were in fashion for women a couple of years back, so he was wearing that; with all the three jacket buttons fastened you almost couldn't tell the tie ended half-way down his chest. Or, if you could, it looked like a fashion statement that hadn't quite come off.

Tom was a silent, tense presence for about eight dark, rural miles, Shelley drove into Broadbank's village. It looked more intimate than Larkfield, cottages squashed together.

'Looks awfully cosy. Don't you think?'

'No.'

Broadbank had said,

About two hundred yards past the church, you'll see a phone box on your left, in a layby. Almost opposite that there's a little signpost with Bisley 4 on it. You turn up there . . .

'Where the fuck we going?'

'Only another half mile Tom.'

'I hate these little country lanes.'

'I know you do, Honey, I know you do.'

Deborah.

'Wish I'd never fucking . . . Gawd, whassat?'

'Only a rabbit. It's gone now. Through the hedge.'

Talking to him like you'd talk to a child. Soothing. Oh God, how long could this go on?

After about half a mile, you'll come to a hairpin bend, and right on the bend you'll see an opening dead ahead of you. There's no sign, but this is it. Hall Farm.

'It's OK, Tom, we're here now.'

Changing down to second, hitting the gravel, headlights full on.

An avenue of trees, almost leafless now, and at the end of it was a cluster of lights, warm and mellow. They drove between gateposts with some sort of birds on them, eagles or owls.

'I don't like the look of this,' Tom said. 'You said he'd *built* hisself a place.'

'I thought he had,' Shelley lied, glad he couldn't see her face. 'It doesn't matter, though, does it?'

Conspicuously ancient stone in the headlights.

'It's old.' Tom began to bounce on the seat like a huge child. 'It's fucking old.'

Whirling on her as she applied the handbrake. 'It's *old*, you lying bitch!'

'Tom, it'll be OK. It'll be fine.' Reaching over the back seat for her coat.

'Turn the car. Turn the fucker round. You get me *away* from here.'

'No. You're not running away this time.'

'The hell I'm not.'

Tom threw himself at the door like a gorilla in a metal cage.

Vanessa had made Weasel an omelette, with tomatoes and soya-based cheese-substitute. There was too much pepper and it was overdone. Weasel liked his omelettes runny and made with mature Cheddar.

Tucking in at the kitchen table, he told her it was, no question, the most brilliant omelette he'd ever had in all his life.

Vanessa beamed pinkly and asked him would he like to watch a video.

'What you got?'

'Eddie Murphy,' Vanessa said. 'I've got to wind it back, though.'

'Yeah, great,' Weasel said. 'You like Murphy?'

'He's cool,' Vanessa said. She thought about it some more. 'Seriously cool.'

She was wearing a blue frock, instead of the jeans and sweater. This was obviously on the basis that you had to dress up if you were entertaining a guest. She had make-up on: eyeshadow behind the thick-lensed designer glasses and scarlet lipstick.

You wouldn't know, you really wouldn't, Weasel thought admiringly. He wondered if she'd ever get around to having boyfriends, and if they'd be, you know, like her, or, well, normal.

Aw, Jeez, she *was* normal. She'd never had cause to think otherwise. OK, probably she knew she wasn't like the other kids at school, but not on account of being *handicapped* or *challenged* or however they put it these days. But because she was *Vanessa*. Special.

'Princess,' Weasel wondered, 'was you named after that actress, Vanessa Wossername?'

She didn't seem to understand.

'Your name. Vanessa.'

Vanessa considered this seriously for a few seconds, then she said, 'Daddy gave it me.'

'Redgrave!' Weasel remembered. 'Vanessa Redgrave, right?' He pushed back his plate with a sigh. 'Triffic, Princess.' Blew her an appreciative kiss. 'Knockout.'

Vanessa was looking at him through her big glasses like he was very thick indeed. 'Van Morrison, silly,' she said. 'I was named after Van Morrison.'

'Oh. Right.' Weasel nodded slowly. 'Obvious when you fink about it.'

'It was a com-plim-ent,' Vanessa said. 'He's a big, fat, *rude* man, but Daddy says he's the best. Weasel, would you like coffee, or lager?'

'There you are then. Clever Daddy.'

'Or Ribena?'

'Oh . . . er, lager, please, Princess, if you got it. That'd be great.'

She brought a can from the fridge, set it down on the kitchen table for him with a tumbler. It was this low-alcohol stuff the Scotch geezer plugged on the box.

'It's Shelley's lager,' Vanessa said. 'Daddy doesn't drink any more.'

'Very wise.' Weasel was remembering when Daddy had been through a period of drinking a great deal and also injecting funny stuff into his arm. Daddy had done the lot in his time. Daddy was well out of it. (Although, actually, not well at all, and it depended on how you interpreted 'out of it'.)

'He didn't want to go out tonight.' Vanessa sat down at the table opposite Weasel with a can of diet Tango. 'Shelley had to Put The Arm On Him.'

'Likes a quiet life nowadays, your dad.'

'He's not quiet at all! He's very noisy!'

'Yeah. Course he is.' You had to say exactly what you meant to Vanessa. You had to think about how to put it.

'He'll be all right, though,' she said.

'Course he will, Princess.'

'Because . . .' Vanessa leaned across the table and whispered it '. . . the Man with Two Mouths will be looking after him.'

Weasel stiffened. 'Say that again?'

Shelley was out of the car before Tom and dashing round to his side. If she could pull him into the trees perhaps they could talk this out without making a public scene of it.

She'd been really very stupid. Why hadn't she used the childproof lock? The truth was she'd never bothered to find out how to work it. Vanessa, even as a kid, would sit there for hours watching the world through the windows.

He was out now, standing swaying like a drunk on the gravel path in the headlights, his jacket straining over his stomach. Oh God, God, God, was there no end to this?

She approached him warily. In this mood he was quite likely to lash out, forgetting who she was in his panic.

'Tom,' she whispered. 'Come on, Tom. Over here.' Like calling a frightened puppy.

He said hoarsely, 'Gimme.' And advanced out of the headlights towards her.

'Please, Tom. You're a grown man. You're a *big* man. Nobody's going to harm you.'

'Shelley, darlin', I'm ain't going in there. No way. You wanna stay, you stay, it's your party. Just . . . Just gimme the keys.'

Something walked over her grave, the way he said that.

And then more light suddenly gushed out from the house, followed by quick footsteps on the gravel, and a man was in the headlights, a sleek man with crinkly hair and a plump, genial face.

'Shelley. Hi. You found us. Wonderful.'

185

'Oh,' Shelley said. 'Mr Broadbank. We . . . We were just wondering if we'd come to the right . . .'

Urgently looking around for Tom; he'd gone, vanished. *Oh, please . . .*

'Martin, for heaven's sake,' Broadbank said heartily. 'Now. Where's your old man?'

Well, actually, Martin, he was here a moment ago but then he panicked and now he's going to walk all the way home, unless I follow you into the house and happen to leave the keys in the car, in which case . . .

And then Tom was towering over Broadbank in the lurid area where the headlights and the houselights met. *Oh, Christ, he's going to hit him.* Shelley gripped the handle of the driver's door, regretting everything. Wishing that Broadbank had never come into the shop that day. Wishing above all that a big bluff guitarist had never stumbled into the Epidemic press office on a winter's day fifteen years ago. ('. . . that bloody Goff and his Earl Grey and his Lapsang wotsit. Got any PG Tips?') Wishing . . .

Tom's right hand came down. Shelley's eyes closed.

When she opened them, Tom was gripping Broadbank by the upper arm, as if for support.

'Tom . . . Tom Storey,' he said gruffly. 'How are . . . how are ya, mate?'

He was trying very, very hard.

Shelley wanted to cry. Oh God, Tom.

Tom didn't look at her once while the faintly bemused Broadbank was ushering them into the house.

Her husband was walking rigidly in the tight jacket, hands by his sides, the left one trembling.

Vanessa was arranging chocolate biscuits on a plate.

'The Man wiv Two Mouths,' Weasel said. 'You said the Man wiv Two Mouths.'

Vanessa said, 'I like these ones best. They've got orange cream in the centre.'

'Princess, who is the Man wiv Two Mouths?'

Weasel was thinking, *I should be there with them. I shouldn't have let them go on their own. Not with somebody after them.*

Somebody after them. He didn't know how he knew this, he just did. Maybe being near Tom made you a bit extra-sensory too. Maybe it rubbed off.

Vanessa said, 'Daddy doesn't like him.'

'He ever come round, Princess? He come round here when I'm out wiv the van?'

'Oh,' said Vanessa. 'He's *always* around.'

'Why don't your daddy like him?'

Vanessa thought about this. 'He likes him a bit,' she said. 'But he's frightened of him. He doesn't like to see him. Have a biscuit, Weasel.'

'Princess, have *you* seen him? Have you seen this geezer?'

Vanessa nodded, turned away from him, scrambled down from her stool and ran out of the kitchen. He heard her stomping up the stairs. *Shit, she's taken offence. What'd I say?*

Weasel went to the door. 'Princess! I'm sorry. Didn't mean to put the squeeze on yer. Come down, all right?'

Silence.

'Vanessa! I fought we was gonna watch Eddie Murphy!'

No reply.

This was difficult. What was he gonna do now? It'd been a big act of faith on Shelley's part, leaving the kid with Weasel. What was this gonna look like?

Weasel went over to the sink, dunked his glass. What a situation, eh? With Tom's brains turning to pot-noodle, Shelley had to be on the verge of booking a cheap-day return to Valium Valley. So what was all this doing to the kid? Screwing her up good, that was what. If any kid didn't deserve this . . .

Weasel splashed cold water in his face.

Total Psychic Allergy Syndrome. Jeez.

Couldn't help thinking back to last week when he'd faced up Tom with the mystery of the missing albums. Tom finally breaking down, admitting it: soon as somebody snuffed it their albums went straight in the stove. The implication being that

Tom was so thin-skinned – on the psychic level – that all it took was being exposed to the music of some geezer what had passed over, hearing it at just the right time . . . the *wrong* time . . . and he'd be off into something.

Jimi Hendrix, Janis Joplin, Mama Cass Eliot, Brian Jones . . .

'And Jim Morrison. I been in Paris, wiv Jim Morrison. Dead in the bath, all bloated.'

Weasel had got the hell out. Couldn't stand it no more. Run back to his caravan and blasted his brains out with ZZ Top.

He wiped his face on a piece of kitchen towel and blinked.

The kid was back. Weasel breathed out a throatful of tension.

She was standing in the doorway, big hoop earrings still swinging from running down the stairs. Her arms were full of this huge brown book.

'Sorry it took me so long, Weasel.' Dumping the giant tome on the kitchen table. 'I had to go to the attic for it.'

'Bleedin' hell, Princess, in the dark? Whyn't you get me to go up for yer?'

Vanessa looked sly, which was a rarity. 'Because it was hidden.' A cobweb snapping as she opened up the book. 'Daddy chucked it out for the dustman 'cause it wouldn't fit in the stove. I brought it back and hid it.'

Weasel moved over to the table, interested. Was there gonna be more albums in here?

'Look,' Vanessa said, peering down through her thick lenses.

'Oh,' Weasel said, disappointed. It was just photos, ancient pix, mostly black and white – people at weddings, people with babies, studio portraits of kids with their hair combed straight.

'Er . . . yeah,' Weasel said. 'Very nice.'

Vanessa, very solemn, started turning pages over slowly, creasing each one flat.

'There,' she said.

It was a faded photo of a couple either side of a small boy. The bloke was very tall and gangly, wearing an open shirt that looked kind of ex-army, and you could see his string vest underneath. He was grinning down at the small boy, had a big hand on the kid's shoulder.

'There you are,' Vanessa said.

'Yeah.' He hadn't seen the picture before but he recognized the people all right. 'That's an old one, innit, Princess?'

'That's *him*.'

'Yeah, it's . . .'

'*The Man with Two Mouths!*'

'What?'

Weasel started to feel a little queasy. He said hesitantly, 'He's . . . he's only got the one, Princess.'

'Not now.' Vanessa shook her head. 'He's got one here.' Putting a finger on the bloke's lips. 'And another one . . .' Moving the finger just slightly '. . . here.'

'Oh jeez.' Weasel felt almost faint.

'Only bigger,' Vanessa said.

Bloody Glasses

When the lights went down, there was just the piano – a grand piano, but not *that* grand, even by nightclub standards: battered, legs chipped, rainbow grease marks on the lid.

The piano sat just left of centre stage, only half in spotlight, so that Prof never saw the figure emerge from the shadows and slide on to the stool, only noticing that people around him in the club had gone quieter.

Not that there were people exactly *around* him . . . *around* him was a conspicuous circle of vacated chairs; he'd knocked a couple of drinks over earlier on, other people's, a little clumsy tonight. Not pissed, you understand, if only because he couldn't seem to get pissed any more, not in the old sense of enjoying it. And *needing* it, well, that was a sad situation, when it came down to needing it. Which he didn't; this was a conscious decision or, at worst, a temporary abrasion . . . aberration.

He didn't realize he'd spoken aloud until this big, bearded git in a creased tuxedo leaned over and whispered, 'If you'd like to pop outside, sir, I'd be happy to assist.'

The bloke had hard eyes. Prof held up his glass of scotch. 'Diet Pepsi,' he said, and he chuckled.

The man took the glass out of his hand and set it down on the table. 'You're spilling it, sir.'

'Why don't you just piss off, eh, son?' Prof turned his chair away.

And then the piano began, those famous, sublime opening chords, and he didn't see the bouncer any more.

Light came down on the pianist. It was like a heavenly light, like you saw illuminating angels in those naff, sentimental Victorian pictures in your granny's sitting-room. But Prof stared with this fuddled kind of awe, the same way he'd stared at those pictures as a kid.

The pianist was white and luminous in some kind of loose T-shirt which somehow made his body hazy, seem to shimmer in the air with those beautiful chords, da da da da-da . . .

The pianist turned his head. He looked directly at Prof, and Prof's hand tightened in the dark around his slippery glass.

For the man's eyes were white and waxen circles, like two communion wafers. When his head bent over the keys, the light glimmered from small, round, wire-rimmed glasses.

Everyone was very quiet. The playing softened. The pianist looked up, almost drowsily drawing breath, and began to sing into his microphone, this calm, human, painfully familiar, flat-vowelled nasal drone.

Imagine . . .

A shivery glow lit Prof up inside, like old malt whisky used to, once.

. . . *Imagine there's no audience* . . .

The singer looked up, peered over his little round glasses into the sparseness, continued in sardonic Liverpudlian.

. . . *that's not so fuckin' hard* . . .

Everybody laughed. Except for Prof. All around him, outside the toxic circle, all the other people laughing, the stupid crass bastards, as he threw down the rest of his whisky and tried to blank out the heresy – that the guy should come down to *this* – by amplifying the white noise in his head into a black roaring, screwing up his face to close his ears.

He closed his eyes too, but he could still see the man at the scuffed and battered grand piano, his cold, white eyes, his blank, pale face and small mouth spewing its cheap parody.

191

'Scumbag,' he muttered. Then saw the bearded man starting to advance, and shut up.

There probably hadn't been as tense a meal as this, Shelley thought, since the Last Supper.

Seven of them at the long dining-table in the panelled hall. Sometimes she thought there were eight and counted them again: herself and Tom, their neighbours Sir Wilfrid and Lady Tulley (call me Angela, my dear), the thin man with the pony-tail, Stephen Case – Tom's fan, allegedly – and Broadbank and the startling Meryl.

And although only she and Tom appeared on edge, that was enough tension to go round, twice.

Meryl, in black, part waitress, part hostess, was in motion much of the time; perhaps this was why she kept thinking an extra person was present. This and the empty chair.

Shelley was having difficulty finding sufficient saliva to savour the meal. 'Wonderful,' she remarked periodically, smiling stiffly at Meryl.

The dinner was meatless. A melon and cherry starter, followed by vegetable soup. Then an expertly conceived risotto-type thing with a marinated meat substitute. It clearly fooled Lady Tulley, who twice commented on the succulence of the pork.

Actually, Shelley – in whose honour the dish had obviously been prepared by Meryl – would, for Tom's sake, have far preferred it to be real meat. Something to weigh him down, make him tired and lugubrious.

Instead, his jaw remained rigid and his face shone with sweat in the light from half a dozen silver candlesticks, arranged in a straight line down the old oak table. He hated candles.

In fact, Shelley would have preferred them to be dining from a table with a vinyl top and metal legs inside some fluorescent-lit chromium conservatory with glass walls – preferably assembled in a factory less than six months ago.

'More wine, Shelley?' Broadbank offered.

'Not for the moment.' She covered her glass.

'More, er, orange juice, Tom?'

'Cheers,' said Tom, without enthusiasm.

He was at the top of the table, his back to the reconstituted Jacobean panelling. He was looking isolated and his expression was frozen. Shelley, next to him, kept squeezing his cold and flaccid hand and getting no response, because Tom was very angry with her for deceiving him about this place and how old it was. Stephen Case, on his other side, opposite Shelley, kept trying to engage him in conversation, to which overtures Tom replied monosyllabically without even glancing at the guy.

Case was 'a record company executive'. Well, he would be, wouldn't he. Hmmm, Shelley thought. Bloody hmmm.

Next to her was Martin Broadbank himself, opposite the dramatic Meryl in her black dress and her diamanté choker. Sir Wilfrid and Lady Tulley (Angela) were down at the bottom end, furthest from Tom, which perhaps was as well. The seat opposite Tom, at the bottom of the table, was the one that was empty.

'You know, TMM,' Case was murmuring to Tom, 'is not the philistine, profit-oriented monolith you might imagine. Our directors are all *enthusiasts*, and if I mention the name Silas Copesake . . .'

Tom turned and observed his neighbour for the first time. 'Sile Copesake?'

'The man they call the Godfather of British Blues,' Case said proudly, spelling it out for everyone to whom the name would mean nothing – i.e. everyone here except for the Storeys – 'has been a non-executive director of TMM for some years. It's about musical integrity, Tom. Recognizing our roots. You were in his band once, of course.'

'Yeah. When I was a kid,' Tom said and turned back to his meal.

And Shelley knew for certain now that this dinner was about Tom rather than her. Tom and Stephen Case. Seated together at the top of the table, with Broadbank himself centrally placed to deflect conversation away from them if necessary.

I've been bloody well set up, Shelley thought, outraged.

'Tried your cheese-substitute,' Broadbank said, as if he'd picked up on this. 'Been right through the range. Preferred the smoked, actually, is that terribly naff of me? Angela, what about you, have you and Sir Wilfrid been carried along at all by the healthfood revolution?'

'Well, you know,' said Angela, Lady Tulley, 'I do have to say that when in Stroud now one does find oneself drawn *increasingly* towards Love-Storey. Such an *appealing* little shop in itself.'

Shelley had seen her in the shop twice, buying fruit mostly, certainly nothing that might be construed as cranky. She was solid, square and red-cheeked. A walker – or rather, a strider, and clearly more at home in the Cotswolds than Sir Wilfrid, who was looking rather shrivelled tonight.

'Indeed,' he kept saying, in a non-committal kind of way. 'Indeed.' Perhaps he always looked shrivelled. Previously, Shelley had only seen him from a distance, pottering aimlessly in his acre of cottage garden, on one occasion prodding about with a dangerously new-looking shotgun. He was supposed to have been an environmentalist – although she supposed being a Senior Something at the Department of the Environment was not quite the same thing.

'If you'd like to *meet* Sile again,' Case was saying to Tom, 'we could arrange something, no problem . . .'

Not the way, Case, Shelley thought, hostile now. She'd known too many record company execs to trust any, particularly specimens like Stephen Case with his Armani suit and his greying pony-tail. Anybody who'd survived to grow grey hairs in this business had to have his poisonous side.

'Got nuffink in common wiv Sile no more,' Tom said. 'Must be due a bus-pass by now, anyway. If not a bleeding bypass.'

'He keeps himself fit,' Case said. 'He's working with a number of young musicians.'

'Figures.' Tom shovelled in the last of his risotto.

'Tom's a hopeless carnivore,' Shelley found herself saying,

almost shrilly, as a way of hauling him into their own chat. 'Aren't you, love?'

Sir Wilfrid looked up with grudging approval.

'Nothing wrong with that,' Broadbank said. 'Besides, a chap needs a bit of muscle in Tom's profession. Must burn up a terrific amount of energy in one of these two-hour rock concerts. Saw that chap Springsteen on the box the other week, didn't we, Meryl, absolutely drenched in perspiration.'

An unfortunate comment, Shelley thought. Although a good few miles from his Telecaster and wielding nothing more demanding than a knife and fork, Tom, at dinner, wore the surface moisture of a musician at the end of a very heavy gig.

Shelley sneaked a glance at her watch: not yet nine-thirty, and the sweat was already rolling down his cheeks like lava from Vesuvius. If she could just get him through another hour without an eruption, then perhaps they could make an excuse to leave.

'I don't know why we're talking about boring old rock and roll,' she said with a light laugh. 'Tom hasn't done a concert in years.'

'Gets plenty of practice, though,' Sir Wilfrid said grimly from the end of the table. 'Round the clock, sometimes, if I'm any judge. Sounds like a damned horse having a tooth pulled.'

Shelley dropped her fork. 'I'll prepare the pudding,' Meryl said.

It was less offensive for a while.

After that one song as John Lennon, the singer abandoned the piano and took up an acoustic, a working guitarist's Takamine with the built-in pick-up and a little Trace amp.

He did Paul Simon, clipped and clear, comically overplaying the Noo Yawk vowels. Then he gave himself messed-up hair, an amiable shamble and a wonky grin: Neil Young to the life.

The bloke was actually good, even better between numbers, staying in character, fumbling at his machine-heads, mumbling at his audience or giving them the phoney history of some song: dates, times, women. Sometimes you could even forget it was an act. When, during his Leonard Cohen spot, he politely invited a lady from the audience to sweeten his night, the woman actually looked charmed, and flushed, silly bitch.

No real harm in this. Prof relaxed for the first time since he'd rolled off his sofa around mid-afternoon. The man on stage was screwing a harmonica around his neck, putting on dark glasses: Bob Dylan.

Prof caught a waiter's eye, pointed at his glass. He still couldn't see anything about the man himself that he recognized. He was in hiding, deep cover – Bob Dylan being as good a place as any if you wanted to confuse the issue.

Prof leaned over the table and closed his eyes, head in his hands, a five-pound note trapped under one elbow.

The Dylan opened with what you'd call an affectionate pastiche, the young, rasping, incisive folk-rocker of *Highway 61* days, mid-sixties.

Prof heard a clinking, lifted an elbow. The voice from the speakers had loosened, deepening and warming up before your very ears, into the phoney, countrified, down-home, big-brass-bed Dylan in a cowboy hat.

A big whisky had materialized at Prof's elbow in exchange for the fiver. He was wondering how this act would sound on record. Probably less effective; you closed your eyes and the actual impersonation was not all that hot; what made it work was the guy's obvious understanding of his subjects, where they were coming from emotionally, psychologically. Like he'd been there too.

Like he was there now, in fact.

Dylan was into this one-to-one dialogue with his ole buddy God. After which, in a scruffy little Tombstone hat, he got progressively frayed – you could hear this happening, the artist growing slovenly and decrepit like the lyrics – so that in the end you couldn't tell whether these were Dylan's own duff words or substitutes. Clever, very cruel: the transition from freewheeling hero to a kind of embarrassing vagrant, in ten minutes.

Prof laughed, the booze making it easier. He'd a pretty good impression by now of who this bloke approved of, who made him suspicious and which one – just the one – was causing him some personal pain. With a few songs he changed all the lyrics, with others none at all, bringing out the irony through emphasis, or sometimes he'd alter a single line or maybe just one word and it reflected back on the composer. In some way he was telling you more than you'd learn if you saw the guys themselves in concert.

And then at the end he dropped the satire. It just fell away; the whole atmosphere changed. He strolled around a couple of times, looked up at the ceiling. Sat down to present again the man who caused him pain. And for real this time.

The communion-wafer glasses again. Could the bastard see through those glasses, or had they been sprayed white, so that when he was wearing them all he could see was light?

And what else? What else can he see?

He sat on a stool, up front, with his guitar. He said, by way of introduction, Lennon's voice – his speaking voice, which was different, deeper. 'This is one for me old mates.'

It went as quiet as these clubs ever did.

In my Life. Tissues out, folks, Prof thought cynically. People and things that went before. Tears in the whisky: poor bastard, this was his personal epitaph five years before the event.

He had a drink, closed his eyes. Rooms didn't even swim any more when he did that, lead in his boots nowadays.

Places he remembered. Some had gone, some remained.

Prof thought about when he had lived in a real house. Fulham. Wife and kids. Cherry had been remarried two years now – an estate agent, what could you say? Saw his kids, occasionally, two at university, the eldest girl, Carla, in what she called 'a serious long-term relationship', which meant he was going to be a bloody *grandad* by Christmas. *This is your grandad, he once re-mixed an album by Marc Bolan, dead now but he was famous for a few years.*

People he'd known. Some deceased and some still living – just about. In his life he'd loved them all.

Prof took off his glasses, rolled the sticky whisky glass across his forehead.

Had he ever really loved anybody when he was totally sober?

He pushed the base of the glass into an eyelid, bringing up a night sky full of pulsing nebulae, like he used to do as a kid, a swirling orange-coloured blob coming at him, expanding and then dissolving into many scattered fragments of light, like lights in windows, rows and rows of windows in a great, wide tower block, bigger than any tower block he'd ever seen, bigger than . . .

places I remember

This was one he *didn't* remember. He just felt this overwhelming loneliness, damp and gassy, heavy in the air. Something had happened to make everybody lonely.

And all the people were singing, *Hey Jude*.

Something wrong. How could you be listening to one song and yet hearing another sung by many voices, mostly out of tune?

Prof, floating above it all in the miasma of loneliness, thought suddenly, *I'm looking through his glasses, I'm seeing this through the wrong bloody glasses*.

Out, he thought, get out of this. This is nothing to do with you, Kenneth, don't get involved.

But he *was* involved. He'd been involved since he conned his way into a cramped listening studio under a tatty South London record shop and ran some tape that should have been left to bake to a crisp.

When he managed to open his eyes, the room seemed bigger than he recalled. He was looking up at the ceiling, so far above him it disappeared into shadows. The atmosphere was dense and smoky, too many bloody cigarettes.

It was all a blur. He patted the table, trying to find his glasses. The table was damp.

He peered at the bleary people at the tables, men and women, mostly men. He wished he was with them, just part of the crowd, normal, invisible. And yet they were all idiots, they knew nothing.

places I remember . . .

He was still alone in his little circle – what am I, radioactive? In his own atmosphere, a different sphere, not part of their world, thanks very much . . . please let me in . . .

. . . though some have changed.

Glasses, glasses, where the hell . . .

A white hand beckoning. Prof took a tentative step up a long passageway into a white place. There were people in there. White people. People like gas.

. . . some forever . . .

Stop it!

The whisky glass exploded in Prof's hands as he cranked himself to his feet, his limbs unfolding stiffly like a rusty crane.

'Stop it. *Stop it! Get me out!*'

He was closing his fists, forcing the spearpoint shards of glass into his flesh, urging the fresh blood to run. He knew he was screaming again, just like last night, his whole body wracked with painful shivers.

In the tumult, he couldn't hear *what* he was screaming until the bouncers, two of them now, were escorting him, feet off the ground, towards the exit and he could hear the echo of it and see the singer's eyes flaring up behind the glasses and the hands freezing on the strings.

XII

Reassurance for the Living

'If this turns out a disaster,' Meryl said, 'it'll be no more than his own fault. I did *warn* him not to invite the Tulleys. Sir Wilfrid is not a pleasant man, I said. My old uncle, that's Geoff Thornton, from Shackleys' old cottage, up by the church – were they there in your day, the Shackleys? – he once did some gardening for the Tulleys, my uncle Geoff. Never again, he said. Never again.'

She was chatting to the Lady Bluefoot. The ghost, a sensitive soul who did not like upset of any kind, had been the first to leave the dining-room, gliding ahead of Meryl across the back hall and into the long, low-ceilinged kitchen.

Meryl could hear the swish of taffeta as the Lady Bluefoot passed through the wall.

'But he'll likely smooth things over. He usually does. Be a challenge for him. He's bored, you see, is Martin. Could have twice, three times as many supermarkets. Not interested.'

Meryl, who prided herself on her discretion, became unusually garrulous when talking to the Lady Bluefoot – who, after all, knew everything that went on under this roof, so where was the harm?

'A challenge for him. Which his work isn't any more, that's the problem. So he sets up these situations – confrontations, people who he knows'll be rubbing each other up the wrong way – almost as entertainment. Which he shouldn't do, m'lady, and he knows that, too.'

Meryl held up a cut-glass sundae cup to the soft, concealed lighting. 'There now – what do you think?'

A former domestic science teacher at a high school near

Cheltenham, she herself had found it an interesting challenge to prepare a sophisticated dinner involving no animal products whatsoever. She'd used soya cream for the raspberry mousse and was pleased with how it had turned out.

'Rather like the old syllabub,' she explained, still trying to calm the ruffled spirit. 'You used to have those in your day, m'lady. I'll bet you did.'

To her abiding sorrow, Meryl had never actually seen the Lady Bluefoot, nor even the tiny blue shoes after which she was named and which, it was said, could be observed sometimes padding from the hall to the dining-room, where Lord Rendall's body with its broken neck had been laid when the servants carried him into the farmhouse.

How, then, people would ask, did she know that the spirit so sensitive to any form of domestic upset was indeed the Lady Bluefoot?

Well . . . because it had a perceptible air of femininity, the shade, and would sometimes leave a distinctive scent behind, slightly musty like *pot-pourri*. And when she broke a plate – an expression of her distress at, say, Martin losing his temper over a business hiccup – she'd delicately drop the thing from the dresser, not fling it with any violence. Sometimes this was accompanied by a sharp tap on the floor, as if Her Ladyship was petulantly stamping her foot.

Tonight, Meryl had made a point of seating Sir Wilfrid and Lady Tulley at the foot of the table, either side of the place laid for Lady Bluefoot. For while he was hardly aristocracy – no more, indeed, than a snivelling little civil servant collecting his expected reward – they were likely to be less disruptive than Tom Storey, if what Meryl had heard had any truth in it.

And she'd heard quite a bit because her brother played darts at the Swan with that scruffy little chap Beasley, who, according to Ted, told you more about life with the Storeys with all the things he *didn't* say.

She positioned the last mousse on the large oak trolley and stood back.

'Now then, m'lady. Will it do, do you think?'

Nothing fell off. Meryl smiled in delight. 'Well, *good*! Thank you so much.'

She gave a gracious semi-curtsey and strode briskly across to the half-length mirror next to the larder door to inspect herself before taking in the sweets.

The mirror was in a wide frame of American oak to match the fitted kitchen which Martin had allowed her to install – she couldn't abide the dingy Victoriana it had replaced.

Meryl patted her lustrous hair, liking what she saw: a tall woman who was forty-eight and probably, she would admit, looked it. But her age would be expressed chiefly by the wisdom lines around her eyes, which was no bad thing, not so long as her carriage was still good, her waist still slim, her breasts still proud, her neck long and unlined. She was looking, in fact, every bit a lady and rather more of one than Angela Tulley.

'Right,' Meryl said to the *other* lady. 'Let's see if Martin's managed to soothe the ruffled feelings.'

As soon as the dreadful Sir Wilfrid had made his thoughtlessly insulting remark about Tom Storey's night-time guitar playing reminding him of a horse having a tooth pulled, Meryl had seen a gleam spring into Martin's eyes and his fingers begin to make little twiddling movements on the table, a sure sign of rising adrenalin.

He was much admired for his charm and aplomb, was Martin, especially in the village, where Meryl's appointment as his cook/housekeeper had, she knew, aroused gossip only of the most envious kind – while Martin was well aware that the role of cook/housekeeper, as it were, suited Meryl as well as it suited him (and who was she to object if he was lusting after Mrs Storey's spectacular bosom?).

Their arrangement was one giving, you might say, satisfaction to both parties.

Meryl smiled at herself in the mirror. She'd leave the sweet-trolley in the hall and take in the smaller one for the dirty dishes.

As she turned, two hands gripped her waist.

*

It was the way he was staring, and the way his breathing had become harder and faster. She'd seen it before, and Shelley had had a mental preview of Tom thrusting back his chair and shambling gorilla-like to the bottom of the table, there to snatch Sir Wilfrid out of his seat and throw the old man through the leaded casement.

The straight line of candle flames had leaned towards Sir Wilfrid's end of the table, as if propelled by Tom's staccato breath.

And then, like a thoroughbred engine slipping into higher gear, Martin Broadbank had gone smoothly into diplomatic action.

'. . . ever want to sell your place, Sir Wilfrid, you'll find a few hundred wealthy rock fans happy to pay *well* over the odds just for the sheer privilege of being awoken in the night by the golden er . . . licks . . . of the great Tom Storey, wouldn't you agree, Steve?'

God bless you, Martin, Shelley thought.

Stephen Case was nodding expertly. 'What was it we used to say? Hendrix, Clapton, Beck and Storey.'

'But not necessarily in that order, eh?' said Broadbank. 'If I were you, Sir Wilfrid, I'd be out in my garden with a tape recorder. Make a fortune. Bootleg tapes. Isn't that what they call them?'

'Steady on, Martin.' Stephen Case flashed his host a warning glance.

But Shelley saw that Tom hadn't even heard. He was staring down along the line of candles towards the other end of the long table.

'Get out,' Tom was whispering with each rapid breath. 'Get out.'

And she realized he wasn't looking at Sir Wilfrid at all but at the empty place where a chair had been pulled out and where, she noticed for the first time, a full place-setting of cutlery had been laid for no one.

Oh *no*.

'But talking of tapes,' Case said, turning casually to Tom.

'Some old ones of yours have sort of come into our possession. Really terrific stuff, Tom, which you recorded for Epidemic some years ago and . . .'

Oh!

Shelley became aware that Martin Broadbank had placed his warm hand between her shoulder-blades. She was wearing a cream dress which was high at the front but backless, and Broadbank's touch was not entirely unpleasant.

'Shelley,' he said warmly.

'I'm sorry?'

'My dear, we were going to talk about your wholesale business. As Angela's already pointed out, much of the appeal lies in the presentation. Am I right?'

'*Lovely* shop.' Lady Tulley's enthusiasm was doubtless more fulsome in the uncomfortable aftermath of Sir Wilfrid's regrettable outburst. The moving candlelight rippled across her large and too-perfect teeth.

'Precisely,' Broadbank said. Shelley thought, damn the man. He's trying to draw my attention away from Tom, leaving him exposed to this bloody Case.

'. . . conscientious,' Case was saying. 'We're a company which likes to do the right thing. And as it's obviously incomplete, we'd love it if you could listen to it again, see if there's any changes you feel you'd like to make.'

Tom was still staring at the empty place; his left hand was trembling – Shelley could see his gold ring vibrating in the shivery light. She felt a slow thickening of the air, and if nobody was smoking, why was there a blue haze?

'I make no bones about it,' Broadbank said. 'I think my outlets could benefit enormously from your input.'

Some of the candles had melted down into gnarled and curly stubs and were issuing more smoke than you'd expect.

Tom spoke. 'I don't know nuffink about no tapes.'

He didn't move his head. Shelley wanted to bury hers somewhere.

'Tom,' Case said caringly, 'nineteen-eighty, as we all know, was a bloody awful year for you, and it's hardly surprising if

204

anything you recorded around the *end* of the year, especially at
the Abbey, was . . . disregarded . . . abandoned . . . forgotten
about . . .'

'But I think we have to do *more* than simply stock the
products on the shelves, Shelley . . . What I'd really *like* to
see . . .'

'I never done no album.' Tom was talking tonelessly to the
air ahead of him. 'Anybody says otherwise is a bleeding liar.'

'. . . an entire display unit set apart in each of the stores,
arranged with a distinctive . . .'

'Tom, we *have* those tapes.'

'. . . in the inimitable Love-Storey fashion, perhaps with an
attendant to explain . . .'

To Shelley, the room seemed much larger but the table
smaller and further away, the voices too, as if she was watching
it all on a cinema screen from the back circle. As if she was not
involved. Drink could do this, but she'd had less than a glass of
wine, and with food.

Tom said, 'You ain't got shit, mister.' His left hand closed
around a sharp little knife provided for cutting into bread
rolls.

The air, to Shelley, was suddenly almost black with tension.
She began to cough.

'. . . and with perhaps a market-stall effect or continental
blinds in the famous blue and white Love-Storey livery, it would
all look really quite terrific – what do you think, Shelley?'

'I . . .' Shelley watched – as though from fifty yards away,
seeing the table as if from above so that it was like a runway
with the twisted candles as landing lights for something coming
down – as her husband rose to his feet, gripping the little bread
knife like a dagger.

'That would be wonderful,' she said faintly.

Angela, Lady Tulley screamed as, one by one, the candles
went out.

There was a rush of movement.

*

'Oooh!'

Martin did this occasionally, so Meryl was not unduly perturbed – until she saw that the door was still closed and there was no one else in the long kitchen.

She gasped in genuine shock. 'Oh, my lady!'

This was not like *her* at all. The Lady Bluefoot did not *touch*.

Meryl's hips tingled where the hard, lascivious hands had slid. A strong smell wafted across the kitchen, and it was not raspberry mousse and not *pot-pourri*.

'Who's there?' she called out sharply, wrinkling her nose in distaste, her fingertips moving to her velvet choker.

The smell was oil, engine oil, reminding her immediately of the decrepit cabin cruiser her ex-husband used to keep at Minehead. It certainly wasn't a smell you wanted in your kitchen.

'Oh, m'lady,' Meryl called out in dismay. The stench would offend her terribly.

Meryl was concerning herself with the Lady Bluefoot and how such an intrusion might offend *her*, because she was not prepared even to contemplate anything else in here. Lady Bluefoot was *the* ghost of Hall Farm; she was fragrant, sad, graceful and considerate, and Meryl loved her.

And believed in her.

Yes.

And knew the truth of her.

Knew that she was not 'condemned for all eternity' to walk this house, as it said in the flimsy Cotswold guidebooks, a shoddy misinterpretation of the role of the earthbound spirit.

The truth was that a spiritual aspect of the Lady Bluefoot, fine as a veil of muslin, lingered in the atmosphere of this place as evidence of the survival beyond the grave of a loving and beautiful grief.

She was not here to *frighten* people but to offer comfort . . . just as comfort should be extended to *her*. Which was why Meryl (who had accepted many years ago that she would never experience a great and profound love with another human being) attended the spiritualist church in Gloucester every other week: to learn how she might help.

And so she spoke regularly to the Lady Bluefoot, with sympathy and humility and respect . . . and the hope that one day she would be granted a *manifestation*.

Now the air had gone stiff and somehow gritty around her, the concealed lights grown dim and greenish, draining the kitchen of its glamour, reducing the opulent sheen of American oak to the stained drabness of the old Victorian fittings which had been here before but were still too recent to be a part of Lady Bluefoot's world.

'Go away!' Meryl snapped, not yet afraid. 'This is not *your* house. You don't belong here.'

It had not touched her again, but it was spreading over the room, an aura of damp and dust, a dreary atmosphere reeking of low-life depression.

And then, for a frigid instant, she saw it, over by the door, haloed in dusty sepia, like an old photograph. And – almost – just like a real person, except that she could still make out the door panels behind it and it was so tall that it would have had to bend its head to get under the great oak cross-beam.

Its head! She could see the cross-beam through its gaseous head!

Meryl – who had once prayed to see a ghost, who attended the spiritualist church every other Friday to commune in comfort with the dead, who chatted gaily to the spectral Lady Bluefoot – felt her lungs fill up with dread.

No one, none of the genial mediums in Gloucester, none of the authors in her Theosophical library, had *ever* said it would be like this.

She saw it for barely a second and then it was gone, leaving the smell of engine oil stronger, darker, corrosive on her nostrils.

Meryl couldn't move and she couldn't dismiss the dirty, swarthy face from her mind, a face which, she knew, would always be with her, wherever there was darkness. When had hope last burned in those sunken, black, pebble-eyes? When had the mouth ever known a normal smile? When had it been *able* to smile?

'M'lady . . . Oh . . .' Meryl sank to her knees, fighting for breath, tearing the velvet diamanté choker from her throat. 'Help me!'

The face – and she could see its image still, vibrating in the dust-motes of a dingy kitchen she didn't know – had been deformed into a perpetually twisted, grinning thing, the skin dragged up at one corner until it almost met the hole where there ought to have been a cheek.

The ragged hole, with puckered skin and scabs of black blood. The hole like a second mouth.

Meryl was flinging herself around the room, throwing herself at the walls. She didn't scream, she wasn't a screaming woman; she made little whimpering, buzzing noises like a fly in a jam-jar. She was desperate for a way out, suffocating, and she couldn't find the door.

He was here, still. She couldn't see him, but she knew he was here. Every time she thrust herself back from a wall or a cupboard she expected to arrive in his sorrowful, life-draining embrace.

Meryl prayed silently to Lady Bluefoot and to God, one to send him away, whoever he was, the other to accept his soul, oh Lord . . .

Then she saw him again.

This time only a shadow, a shadow on the wall, a shadow receding *into* the wall, a light burning dully beyond him and it was a light she recognized – the pineapple-shaped wrought iron lantern in the inner hall.

The kitchen door had opened.

Oh, thank you, thank you, Lady Bluefoot.

Her instinct was to go down on her knees, but when Meryl put out her hands to balance herself she found familiar warm wood, the handles of the serving-trolley. She took a breath, made herself expel it slowly. Then she steadied herself, held her head high and walked quickly through the doorway, leaving the door open behind her, not looking back. Pushing the trolley before her with its cargo of raspberry mousse.

In the hall, in the pineapple light, it was very still and quiet, not even a buzz of conversation from the dining-room – as if everyone had gone silent on hearing her footsteps approaching.

Meryl tried to compose herself.

You have seen a ghost. Many people have seen ghosts. You always wanted to. Ghosts cannot harm you. Ghosts are here for a purpose . . . reassurance for the living.

She took two long breaths and pushed open the dining-room door. 'Sorry I've been so . . .'

Meryl entered the dining room to find not candlelight, but the same greenish glow as in the old kitchen, the *spirit* kitchen.

Too late to turn back now; the trolley was already in the dining-room.

And what she saw here was far worse than anything she could have imagined.

There was a deep, yawning silence like when you pushed open a door and found you had unexpectedly entered a theatre or a concert hall.

There was a slow, throbbing stillness.

And there was a smell.

It was a warm smell, a smell from Meryl's childhood on the farm, from the top shed where the pigs went one by one, usually on a Friday morning, and did not return to the sties.

Meryl said, 'Martin?'

All the candles on the table were dead, except for the one closest to her at the bottom of the table which was greenly, greasily alight, dark smoke spiralling from its frizzling wick.

This candle's sallow glow lit the face of Sir Wilfrid Tulley. He was sitting in his chair, his head thrown back. As if laughing.

Laughing fit to burst, Meryl thought.

Like cheese straws dipped in tomato ketchup, yellowish tubes poked out of Sir Wilfrid's throat. There was a glint of white bone, a bib of blood on his shirt-front. The head of Angela, Lady Tulley, hair still frizzed and formal, lay amid the shards of a broken side-plate. Lady Tulley's body was humped across the table, its neck still bubbling black blood.

Another candle came to life, this one near the top of the table, under the Jacobean panelling. Stephen Case lay across the table in an attitude of sleep, except that one eye was wide open and looking across at Meryl in surprise and the other was hanging out on a blood-licked sliver of membrane . . .

Meryl did not move.

She heard her own echo. 'Martin?'

Two more candles sprouted flames.

Martin was also in his seat, midway along the table.

Meryl began to laugh shrilly. Hadn't exactly talked his way out of this one, had he?

Martin's face was buried in an exposed and bloodied breast. The blood river, in spate, had its source either in her chest or his face. Or both.

Neither of them moved.

Meryl felt light-headed. The rich, acrid aroma of spilled blood was strangely intoxicating.

She felt her legs turning to liquid and closed her eyes before she fell.

When she opened them, no more than a few seconds later, she saw the brown beams of the ceiling and felt the boarded floor beneath her head. Her mind refused to remember.

But the smell remained.

Supplemented by sweat.

Between two ceiling beams, the big, red face of the rock musician, Tom Storey, swam into view. Raw meat shrink-wrapped in sweat.

Meryl tried to speak. Tom's legs in black jeans were astride her body. His arms were by his sides, at the end of one a steely gleaming.

'Don't mind me, darlin',' Tom said hoarsely.

XIII

Dakota Blues

The coffee swirling round, the cream making pretty circles in Prof's cup. He wished he could dive into it, go round and round with the cream, not thinking about anything. He'd be warm and safe in the coffee, the round walls of the cup protecting him.

He looked up at the bloke sitting opposite. The wafer glasses gone, the blue eyes sparkling. But Prof could tell it was anxiety, not merriment.

'I looked you up in *Time Out*.' Prof poured in more sugar. 'Wasn't what I expected.'

'It pays,' Dave Reilly, who called himself Dave Kite, said. 'It's cheap, it's naff, but . . .'

'It's not cheap and it's not naff, and it's too late for bullshit, Reilly, and I'm too old for it, so get serious.'

They were in some all-night coffee shop a couple of streets away from Muthah Mirth. Prof had prowled the pavement outside, sobering in minutes and feeling no better for it. Figuring Dave wouldn't hang around afterwards, not surprised to see him emerge within five minutes, winding a long white scarf around his neck, glancing worriedly from side to side, one screwed-up individual.

Prof peered down the side of Dave's stool. 'Where's your guitar?'

'Back at Muthah's. I stay in a room round the corner, pick it up the following day. They've got it off to a fine art.'

'Got what off?'

'The muggers. They'll have it off you between the taxi and the kerb, and resold before midnight. I've never been lucky with guitars.'

'Bastards.'

'Yeh. It's a hard life, Prof.'

If it was, it didn't show, not until you got close. Dave was ageing like Paul Simon: from a distance you'd swear his clock had stopped at twenty-four and he still wasn't shaving much more than twice a week. How old was he now? Thirty-nine? Forty?

Prof said, 'It's a good routine you got there, son. Psychologically acute, as they say.'

Dave shrugged it off. 'All it is, instead of just learning the chords and intonation, you start thinking about the person, where they were at when they wrote the song – I mean, not every song will do. You know instinctively which are the ones.'

Dave was drinking apple juice, slowly, like it was brandy. 'Thing is, these guys – travelling around, hotels, all this – have more spare hours to worry about life. And death. They die for the first time at thirty, and then it's borrowed time. So I just think about that and . . . it comes.'

'Out of thin air,' said Prof.

'Yeh.' Dave was glancing over his shoulder, like someone about to put out a line of cocaine. 'Thin air.'

Bollocks, Prof thought. 'Takes a lot out of you, I imagine.'

'Not really.' Lying again, Prof thought. What am I gonna do with this bugger?

A psychiatrist would say Dave was retreating into all these other personalities because he was scared of his own. They'd first met when Prof was engineering Dave's solo album, back in eighty-seven, Dave having to be himself then, and finding it hard. Result: not a very good album, only a few hundred copies sold; the single, 'Dakota Blues', had some airplay – strictly novelty value, it probably embarrassed people.

'Well.' Dave smiled, stupidly. 'Here we are again, then.'

He paused. 'Prof, you going to tell me why you went berserk in there? You back on the cough mixture?'

'What the fuck's that got to . . . ?' Prof snarled, the way he always snarled at anyone who raised the booze issue.

'You were sober when you were screaming at me?'

'I wasn't screaming at you,' Prof said through clenched teeth. 'I was just bloody screaming.'

'Where'd it come from?'

'What?'

'*Deathoak*,' Dave said softly. 'Or maybe I misheard.' He still wore the white scarf, like a neck-brace.

Lifting his coffee cup, Prof's hand shook. Two raving neurotics together. 'Sod it,' he said and put the cup down. 'Not got anything I can put in here, have you?'

'I don't drink.'

'Aren't *you* the little Cliff Richard.'

Dave shook his head. 'That's Simon.'

'Simon who?'

Dave sipped his apple juice, cautiously. 'You said you looked me up in *Time Out*? What for? Why'd you do that?'

Now he'd come this far, Prof was almost scared to talk about it. A lighted bus went past the coffee shop window. He wished he was on it.

'Maybe you didn't say it at all.'

'Say what?'

'*Deathoak*. Maybe you didn't say that at all. Sometimes I just kind of hear it, you know.'

'What's it mean, anyway?'

'Bugger all. Well . . . it's an anagram of The Dakota. With a T to spare. Maybe I made it up myself subconsciously and got it slightly wrong. You get a signal about something, your mind converts it into a currency you can deal in. That make any sense? No, shit, it doesn't. Sorry.'

It did make sense, in a way Prof didn't care to fathom. He started to sing, in a tuneless wheeze, '*Seven long years since I heard the news . . .* '

'*I'm still wakin' in the night with the Dakota Blues*. Still true, Prof.' Dave screwed up his face, drained his glass. An old couple looked over from a nearby table and the woman smiled; middle-aged drunks obviously didn't worry her.

Dave said, 'Only it's nearly fourteen long years now.'

Prof said, 'We all felt upset about Lennon. We didn't all get obsessed.'

Dave said, 'You didn't all feel responsible.'

'I need a drink,' Prof said. 'Let's find somewhere.'

'I'm not drinking with you, Prof.'

'Sanctimonious little shit. What d'you mean, responsible?'

Dave's eyes clouded. 'Maybe I killed him.' His face made the tablecloth look grey in comparison. 'Maybe I killed John Lennon.'

Weasel said, 'How'd you know this geezer's looking out for your old man?'

Vanessa didn't reply. She was curled into a giant armchair. She'd made herself some hot chocolate in a mug with the Manhattan skyline silhouetted around it.

On the TV, Eddie Murphy said, 'Hey, man, what the fuck is goin' down here?'

You might well ask, Weasel thought.

'You ain't going like him, Princess?' he whispered, more to himself than her. 'Tell me you ain't going like him.'

Could they? If their brains was tuned into less circuits than – got to say it – *normal* people, you wouldn't think they'd run to an *extra* circuit, would you?

'Princess. Do you know who he is?'

Vanessa took a sip of her chocolate. 'Who?' She didn't seem very interested any more.

'The geezer wiv . . . wiv two mouths.'

'He's my grandad,' Vanessa said to Eddie Murphy. 'My daddy's daddy.'

'Your daddy tell you that?'

Vanessa shrugged.

'He tell you about him at all?'

'He's dead,' Vanessa said. 'Let's watch the film, Weasel.'

She knows, Weasel thought. Whether Tom told her or not, she knows.

Weasel remembered. It wasn't a memory he liked. It had coloured his childhood. Coloured it red.

Weasel leaned back in his chair, closed his eyes. What the fuck *was* goin' down here?

'Listen . . .' Prof Levin had gone red in the face. It made his white beard look pink. 'Don't you start telling me what's impossible, Reilly, I know what I bloody heard.'

Dave said, 'Here, have some more coffee.' Catching the eye of the guy behind the counter. 'Get's another pot, would you, pal?'

Thinking how much he liked Prof, a straight guy, one of the few. But the old man had to have been misled. Hadn't been too hard to convince himself that, when he thought he'd heard Prof screaming *deathoak* in the club, it had been no such thing . . . just like the owls in the night, the train whistles, the screech of brakes, the crackle of twigs underfoot . . .

And now Prof was talking tapes: music from a dark place, music to pollute your dreams, bring on the night-sweats. And sliding from his stool mumbling about knowing a better place than this.

'I'm sure you do, but we're staying here.' Dave's mind full of flames. A dismal winter morning, sickly fire and a stench of paraffin. His memory had it all mixed up with the other fire, the Lotus and the Land Rover. Looking back, it was as if they'd been cremating Debbie . . . and the baby, because nobody who'd been there could have imagined a live baby coming out of the scorched mess that was Tom's wife.

Keeping it casual, he asked Prof where these tapes had come from. Prof talked of a man called Stephen Case, and a box under a bed. 'Thing is, David, he knew where to look. Steve Case. He knew exactly where to look. This made me suspicious straight off.'

Dave's stomach had turned to frozen meat. *Fourteen years since I heard the news/Still wakin' in the night with the Dakota Blues*. Fourteen years in a half-light of doubt and guilt.

'How many tracks, Prof?'

'Five or six. I only played half of it. That was enough, believe me. *Nobody understands "Aelwyn the Dreamer"*. What was that about?'

'Prof, I . . .' The stifling heat in the coffee bar was not enough. His lips felt cool and raw and cracked as he tried to speak. 'Don't remember too much of what we *did*, only what we planned to do, which might not be the same thing.'

'Why, what were you on?'

'Not that simple. Well, yeh, it was. For me.' Dave looked down into his empty apple-juice. 'A woman. I was high on a woman.'

'Yeah,' said Prof. 'I saw her once. Very gorgeous, Moira Cairns. Where's she now?'

'I don't know.'

'I mean, she's . . . alive and everything?'

'What's that mean?'

Prof came over anguished. 'I dunno, mate. Some stuff on this album . . . these tapes. Distressing.'

Dave, shivering, pulled his white scarf tight. 'Did you hear a number called "On a Bad Day"?'

Prof shook his head. 'A woman,' he said. 'A woman dying.'

'I don't know what you're on about.'

'The woman *dying*. On the tape. She's fading – the voice, the whole *quality* of the voice getting sort of brittle. And then – yeah – she's saying, very feebly, *Help me, help me*.'

Dave said, 'I don't remember it.'

'Come *on*, son, you were there.'

'Prof, I don't remember it, I swear to God.'

'And then . . . She's on the very point of death . . . don't ask me how I know this, it's in the music . . . when . . .'

'This didn't happen . . .'

'. . . when Tom Storey's inimitable guitar comes roaring in, very offensive. *Savage* . . . Come on, David!' Prof thumped a fist on the counter, his white beard harsh, like a nylon hairbrush. 'Talk to me. I've heard the music. It's living in my dreams. Tell me all the things you think I won't believe!'

'Shut up, you'll get us thrown out.'

'And tell me . . . ' Prof shouted, '. . . tell me what it is about you and Lennon.'

There was obsession here. Obsession of a kind Prof Levin had never encountered before. Obsession so intense and vivid you couldn't help but get pulled in. Like in the club, Muthah Mirth. Like in the nightmares. And the music. Especially that.

Years ago, Prof had been on this one-day seminar for record producers and engineers, conducted by some university professor whose theory was that certain music could open up your subconscious. The guy said that babies in the womb, used to the same old sounds – the mother's breathing, the mother's heartbeat – could be kind of traumatized by some sudden vibrating sound from outside, like a door slamming.

So here we are, Prof had been thinking, safe in our material world full of traffic and horn-sections, pneumatic drills and drums machines, and then we're exposed to sounds from . . . from *somewhere else* . . . And we say, so glibly, *this music is really haunting.*

Dave kept moving his glass around on the counter, like a glass on a seance table. The walls of the coffee bar dissolved for Prof, projecting his own visions from Muthah Mirth as Dave talked of a soaring building, like a castle, at night, pinnacles and cupolas. Blenheim Palace or somewhere, only taller, and obviously in a city.

A vision seen on the eighth of December 1980 during a recording session at the Abbey studio. People singing and wailing; somebody dying, somebody dead.

And the same building photographed for a thousand newspapers, filmed for a thousand TV reports, beamed across the world on the ninth of December, 1980.

The Dakota building near Central Park in New York, where John Lennon had lived and died. The Dakota building, the most forbidding edifice in New York, with gargoyles and a metal fountain like a big, black flower.

Prof said, 'You're telling me you saw all this? You saw him . . . ?'

Dave nodding and then shaking his head. Not telling him the whole truth, obviously. Maybe not knowing what the truth was. The only constant was this monstrous building, the core of the obsession, so much a part of Dave that he'd been throwing it out like smoke as he sang, and Prof had choked on the smoke.

Prof was off his stool. 'David, I'm not a psychic, I'm a bloody technician. I mix sounds. I'm a simple man who just wants a night's sleep and maybe a drink or two.'

He waved an arm at the guy behind the counter. 'OK, OK, I'm making an exhibition, I'll behave myself.'

Climbing back on his stool, mumbling at Dave. 'All right, so you have this vision. You're outside the Dakota and bang, bang . . . only three Beatles left.'

'Five bangs,' Dave said. 'I think there were five. Were there five?'

'How the hell should I know? You were there. Go on. Five shots. You see him go down?'

'No, you're not getting this. *I* went down. I couldn't see what was happening. Glasses had gone. I didn't realize his eyes were that bad.'

'Oh Jesus,' Prof said. 'This is not what I want to hear. This is frightening, David. Also tasteless, very tasteless.'

'They put me in a car. I was in the back of a car. "This guy is dying." Somebody said that.'

'I know somebody said that. It's a very famous line. It was in all the papers, which is where I prefer to think you got it from.'

'Sure.' Dave shrugged. 'You prefer to think that, it's fine. Really.'

'Finish it,' Prof said. 'What's the punchline? There's always a punchline. What was it like being shot? Did you suffer much? Did you die in the car or on the operating table, I forget?'

This was not what he'd been expecting. He was *not* going to take it seriously. He'd been fucked up enough. This was where it ended. This was where he came out.

'I chickened out.' Dave had gone pale again. 'I didn't stay with it. It was ugly, incredibly distressing. And also . . . shit, it was irrelevant to what we were doing at the Abbey. I wanted nothing to do with it. That's the crunch – if I'd stayed with it, all the clues were there. I could've heard his voice, and it's not a voice you'd mistake. If I'd had the nerve. If I'd been interested enough. If I hadn't made the Godlike judgement that *this was irrelevant*. Moira sensed it was important, tried to make sense of it, but I lost it. I wasn't trying hard enough.'

'You're saying you saw this thing, you were a part of this scene, but you didn't know who it was?' Prof felt a touch of impatience. He welcomed it. He wanted to walk out of this in anger, not make a timid retreat. 'What difference would that have made? You'd been shot – *he'd* been shot by then. All over. End of story. How does that make you responsible? Jesus, you're so full of shit sometimes, Dave . . .'

Dave Reilly reeled back, like he'd been hit. Like somebody had walked over his grave in Doc Martens and kicked his headstone over.

'I'm sorry.' Prof moved unsteadily towards the door. 'I've had enough.'

'Take it out of that.' Dave had stuck a ten-pound note on the counter. 'Sorry for the fuss.' He held open a door for Prof.

'Come back any time,' the guy behind the counter said. 'I'll get you a bigger audience.'

Prof shook Dave off. 'No, leave me alone, there's a good boy.'

'I'm putting you in a taxi.'

'Florence fucking Nightingale, now, are we?'

As it happened, there was a minicab right outside, on the double yellows under a streetlamp. 'Take him home.' Dave was producing more money, a twenty and another ten. 'He lives off the Edgware Road. Don't stop at any clubs.'

Prof started to get in the back. 'What about you?'

'Bedsit. Walking distance. I've got a key.'

Half inside the minicab, Prof struggled out again. 'Sod you, David,' he said. 'Finish it.'

'I'll call you.' Dave turned and walked away, his white scarf a ribbon of light.

'*Bloody well finish it!*' Prof roared. 'Why d'you feel responsible?'

Dave stopped. He turned back.

'Time zones. It happened around eleven p.m., New York time, right? Is that a four-hour gap, or five hours, in winter?'

'You relived it? After it happened? Shit, I can't think straight, what . . . ?'

'No. Wrong way round. I *pre*-lived it. It hadn't happened yet. Work it out. I'd have had at least four hours to warn him.'

'Look, I ain't got all night,' the cab-driver said irritably.

'This is a load of balls,' Prof said, 'this is . . . fantasy land.'

'I could've reached him through Yoko. Yoko was very open to this kind of stuff at the time, and there was a woman I knew, a psychic, who was living in New York. I could've . . .'

Prof clung to the flaking door of the cab like it was a log keeping him afloat in his sea of bad dreams.

'David, you told anybody John Lennon was gonna be shot, they'd have thought you were a nutter and you know it. I'm going to sleep on this one, son. Correction, try to sleep.'

'You'll be sleeping on the fucking pavement if you don't get in.' The cabbie revved his engine.

'And that's it, you see,' Dave said sadly. 'That's the "Dakota Blues".'

XIV

Keys

Tom Storey was swaying almost rhythmically above her. His eyes bulged and glittered in a face the colour of boiled ham. The knife hung limply from his right hand. His jacket was undone revealing the bottom of his tie – a ludicrous thing ending half-way down his chest.

Silly little details you noticed when you were terrified out of your senses.

Could be rather fun, don't you think? I do love surprises, confrontations, human friction . . .

Oh, Martin, Martin, poor Martin, your stupid schemes, all your little psychological games . . . what have you brought down on us?

I'm really quite intrigued, you know . . . what will Storey be like?

Meryl rolled her head on the floor in a fever of terror. Above Tom Storey's left shoulder there came a swift, brown blur and she was drawn again to the deep, dead eyes of the dreadful entity from the kitchen, the man with a hole in his face. He was mouthing something at her over Storey's shoulder, seemed to have no teeth, just another puckered hole.

Please God, please Lady Bluefoot . . .

When she tried to pray, her mind wouldn't form a prayer, only presented her with a trite image of her spiritualist church, a simpering medium in butterfly glasses with a message from the Other Side about the important letter in Aunt Daisy's linen cupboard, and father is so happy now in the heavenly garden, and the Lady Bluefoot . . .

is another world.

She tried to turn her head away. She could feel her eyes

widening. Her throat closed a couple of times when she tried to speak.

And then the entity crumbled into a brown dust which settled upon the air and then clouded like a swarm of midges drawn to the candles. It made her want to cough, but her throat was locked.

Tom Storey hadn't dissolved. Storey, looming over her, was an apparition of flesh and blood and sweat.

Meryl's foot caught against one of the table legs. In desperation, she kicked off her shoe and used the foot to push herself backwards across the polished floorboards, away from the table.

Away from *that* table. She could smell the blood in a foetid haze above her, could see in her mind the ruins of Sir Wilfrid's neck, slashed tubes protruding.

'Here.'

A big, red hand.

Tom Storey offering to help her up. In his other hand the knife.

She shrank back, trembling, snaking away on her bottom across the polished floor, feeling her tight black dress beginning to come apart.

Managing, at last, to croak. 'What have you done?'

At which, to her horror, Tom Storey giggled. 'Stone me. What have *I* done? Jeez.'

'Look,' she whispered. 'I . . . I didn't . . . didn't see anything.'

Thinking, *I'm the only witness. He's got to kill me.*

'Don't give me that shit, lady, it's in your eyes. You seen everyfink.'

'Please. Please don't . . .'

'The old man,' Tom said, watching her squirm. 'You even seen the old man, yeah? You seen him just now, right?'

'Please . . . I didn't see anything.'

Glancing quickly sideways to where the door was hanging open behind her. There was a good six yards between them now. If she could only reach the door . . .

Tom Storey was staring around the room in bewilderment. He beat the palm of his left hand against his forehead.

Meryl had managed to slide another couple of feet before he looked at her again. Not much use; he knew what she was doing. He didn't come after her, but he was only a few strides away, only a pounce away.

'I don't believe you,' he said. 'You seen the old man, dincher?'

He half-turned. The knife dropped from his fingers.

'Fuck you, lady,' he said. 'Fuck the lot of you.'

Before the knife hit the floor, Meryl was up and stumbling for the doorway, her back to Tom Storey and the bodies at the dinner-table, knowing that when she started running she'd keep on running out of the main door, through the grounds and into the trees where he would never find her.

In the doorway hands seized her from behind.

Simon St John turned over in bed, and his companion slid softly to the carpet.

For some time, his conscious mind blinking on and off, he'd been half-aware of a shifting of weight, a part of him wanting to lose it, needing the freedom to move.

He'd been in and out of sleep, his throat vaguely sore, perhaps a cold coming on; each time he moved towards wakefulness it seemed more constricting than sleep and he burrowed back into the dark.

Sleeping with the Bible.

Sometimes with his arm around it; sometimes on his chest, across his legs, over his groin. Because it stopped dreams, *those* dreams.

But not necessarily *all* dreams, and tonight, in his half-fever, he'd dreamt repeatedly of Isabel Pugh, whose life was lightless and whose company he'd spurned because he'd heard that tone of voice before from other lonely women in other parishes.

In penance, he was pulling Isabel in her wheelchair to the top of the south-west tower, which had been rebuilt to match the one where the studio used to be. Gripping the chair, he was struggling backwards up the spiral staircase, sixty of them, he knew, but when he reached fifty and could see the sky above him he would immediately find himself at the bottom again, and Isabel was looking back over her shoulder at him, anxious and impatient. *Come on, Simon, he's expecting us.*

God knew he was doing his best, but it took all his strength and demanded more. His arms hurt and his stomach hurt and the cumbersome chair was barely wide enough for the spiral – the metal scraping along the stone, with a horrible rending sound, causing red sparks to fly up, or was it flecks of blood from Isabel's arms, torn on the rough stones projecting from the wall?

Twice Simon awoke in the middle of all this and struggled back into the dream because he knew that if he let go of it, the wheelchair would crash and tumble down the spiral stairs, a helter-skelter of death.

Turning once more to his task, pain in his throat, turning over in bed, something sliding to the floor, and they were coming out, at the top of the tower, into the night, hands from above helping him with his burden.

'I'll get you a drink.'

'I don't *want* a drink.'

'*I'll* get it. Where . . . ?'

'It'll calm you. Brandy, I think. Top shelf.'

'Oh God. Oh God. Oh God.'

'Stop it, Meryl.'

She just couldn't stop shivering. Enclosed in the plushest of the chairs, pushed close to the built-up drawing-room fire, and she couldn't feel any of her limbs, as if they'd all shivered away.

'Come on, take a sip, the old remedies are the best, as you're always saying yourself.'

Even the brandy felt cold. It lodged in her throat; she started to cough, doubled up.

'I can't understand it. This is not her at all. This is just not Meryl. I'm really terribly sorry, this . . .'

'No, *I'm* sorry. This is all my fault. We should never have come. Tom has a . . . condition.'

'Well, whatever it is, it can hardly be contagious, Shelley.'

Through watering eyes, Meryl saw Shelley Storey shimmering in the haze around the fire. 'Oh, it can,' Shelley said. 'Believe me.'

'The whole world's gone completely mad,' Martin said. His polo shirt was as white as when she'd ironed it. Not a bloodstain on him.

Martin.

Martin in his drawing-room with his books and his panelled walls and his long curtains and the mellowness, the soft, buttery lamplight. She thought, Tom Storey's killed me, too, we're all here in spirit.

A piece of ectoplasm floated towards her. She stared at it.

'Take it,' Shelley said. 'It's a clean one.'

Meryl accepted the tissue from Shelley to wipe her eyes. Shelley, too, was unstained, and her cream high-necked dress was untorn.

'You're all here,' Meryl said in wonder.

'Except Sir Wilfrid and his lady,' said Martin. 'But let's not talk about him, cantankerous old sod.'

Sir Wilfrid. Meryl sat up. 'Martin, but he's . . . he's . . . Where is he?'

Someone laughed. 'He made an excuse and left.' It was Stephen Case, his pony-tail coming apart a little, but both his eyes tightly in his head. 'I think he thought Tom was going to murder him.'

'To hell with Tulley.' Martin came over and knelt by Meryl's chair. 'It's *you* we're worried about. How do you feel?'

'Strange,' Meryl said. 'A little bit strange.'

'We should get a doctor. Which one's your doctor, Meryl, Perkins or Lefevre?'

'No need for that, I'm not ill.'

'Have you had any kind of . . . I don't know how to describe it . . . fit? Anything like that before?'

Shelley said, 'Martin, I've seen . . . things like this before. She'll be all right. She's right, no need for a doctor. Really.'

Martin got to his feet looking, for the first time in Meryl's experience, entirely out of his depth. 'I think *I* need a drink.'

'Lord above,' Meryl said. 'What happened here? What did I *do*? Mrs Storey, would you tell me, please?'

Shelley said gently, 'You . . . We heard you screaming before you came in. Do you remember that?'

Meryl said nothing. She remembered too much.

'You came in, you were pushing the trolley, and you just sort of froze. You kept staring at us – particularly at Sir Wilfrid, that was when he started getting annoyed. He seemed to think he'd been brought here to be made a fool of. You went a little . . . hysterical. And then you had your blackout. Fainted.'

Meryl became aware of Tom Storey standing behind his wife, hands plunged into his pockets, where she knew they were trembling. His face was still red and hot-looking. His bloodshot eyes came to rest on her.

'Tell 'em, darlin'.'

He didn't look dangerous any more, his eyes weren't bulging. He just looked unwell.

'Go on . . . Tell 'em. Tell 'em what you saw.'

The eyes sorrowful now, bruised like a bloodhound's. He knew what she'd seen. How did he know? Only one way he *could* know: because he'd seen it too, including the grisly creature with the hole in his face whose manifestation had started the whole terrible cycle. Had Tom Storey killed them all in his imagination; was that what she'd seen?

It was clear that none of the others had seen anything, except for her – and Storey, obviously – behaving very strangely. And whatever Tom had done, nobody was commenting on it, perhaps because, for him, this kind of behaviour wasn't so unusual.

And, oh Lord, it wouldn't go away. She only had to look at Stephen Case to see him again with his mouth open and an eye hanging out. She was never going to be able to sleep again. She'd keep waking up in the night and feeling for Martin's blood on the pillow.

And the Lady Bluefoot, the dear, gentle, eternally grieving Lady Bluefoot, her sanctum invaded by another presence which was dark and gross and oppressive and . . .

And brought in here by *him*.

Tom Storey was still looking at her, mute appeal in his eyes, but no hope there. Whatever it was he had, it had clearly brought him nothing but anguish.

'I really think,' said Martin, who knew about her and the Lady Bluefoot, who would smile wryly but never quite patronizingly, 'that if you thought you saw something, Meryl, you ought to enlighten us.'

Meryl panicked and fought to conceal it, staring at the carpet, and then into the fire, not wanting to see any of them, especially Tom Storey, whose gaze she could feel like steady heat.

I can't.

'Please . . . I didn't see anything. I just fainted. It was probably the cold in the hall after the warmth of the kitchen. I'm sorry to have put you all to any trouble or worry. I shall be fine now. Just fine. Really.'

There was an unsatisfied silence. What was she supposed to say? I saw you all dead, butchered where you sat? Case's eye out? Lady Tulley's head lying casually on the table like some sort of novelty cruet?

I can't. God help me, I just can't.

The silence went on and on, Meryl slumped, staring into the fire, Martin watching her baffled. The silence went on until Tom Storey broke it.

Tom said, leaden fatigue in his voice, 'You stupid, selfish bitch.'

'Tom!' Outrage from Shelley, but it wasn't awfully convincing.

'And you . . .' His wife was still kneeling by Meryl's chair, Tom towering over her like some flaking tenement block. 'You betrayed me, darlin'. You set me up. You brung me out here so this . . .' jabbing a contemptuous thumb towards Case. '. . . this streak of piss . . .'

'Hang on . . .' Case said.

'Stay outa this, dickface . . .'

Tom turned slowly towards Meryl, looked her in the eyes, then back to Case, saying very deliberately,

'. . . else I'll have your bleeding eyes out, won't I?'

Meryl gasped.

'Fought I could trust you,' Tom said to Shelley. 'You was the only person I fought I could truly trust. And you set me up. All this . . .'

He waved a hand towards the table. Meryl thought, nobody but me understands what he means. They all just think he's mentally unbalanced.

'. . . is your fault. You said you understood. You *never* understood.'

Shelley reached up for him. 'Tom, believe me . . .'

'Believe you,' Tom said, with sadness and contempt, 'is what I ain't never gonna do again, darlin'.'

Martin said, 'Tom, listen to me for a moment. Shelley knew nothing . . .'

'And you,' said Tom. 'I been observing you. I been finking, what's this smarmy git after? He don't want more money. A seat on the board at TMM, maybe? Nah, I couldn't fathom it. I'm looking at you, I'm finking, what . . . ? And all I seen in your eyes . . .'

Martin started to say something.

'. . . is a big pair of tits,' Tom said.

Martin stood there, mouth open. Probably, Meryl thought, the first time since childhood he's looked ridiculous and known it.

'That it, mister?' Tom grinned savagely. 'That really it? Everyfink? My missus's tits?' He turned away. 'Pathetic, innit? Jeez.'

He held out a hand to Shelley. 'Bag. Where's your bag?'

'Tom, no . . .'

Tom said, 'I'm outa here.'

'Please . . .'

'You can stay. Don't let this spoil your glittering evening, darlin'. Stay as long as you want. This geezer'll put you up for the night, won'tcher, mate? Show him your jugs or summink. See, he's drooling already, the poor sod.'

'Tom,' Shelley said, still on her knees. 'We have to talk about this.'

She's actually a good woman, Meryl thought. She's been through a lot of grief. But he's right. She doesn't understand and she never will.

Tom held out a hand to Shelley as if to help her up.

Shelley didn't move.

'Car keys,' Tom said, palm open, fingers stiff.

Simon stood panting at the top of the spiral, where it came out on to a square stone platform, no more than fifteen feet in diameter, a wall around it, broken down in places, missing altogether in others, stepping off points into the shaft of the night.

A waning moon silvered the cold, wet land and the arcades of archways and the clumps of fallen masonry on the ground, fifty feet below. It was very still.

Simon.

He looked up. Two black-robed monks were there. One spoke in a guttural whisper, in a language he felt he ought to understand but didn't. French? Latin? It didn't matter, the message was clear.

Welcome back.

Simon felt a crown of cold air around his head. Knew it had been shaven. Knew he, too, was wearing a monk's habit, rough and hairy.

The other monks were looking down at the woman in the wheelchair. 'I brought her,' Simon said.

Isabel said, 'No, you didn't. Helped me up the steps was all you did. I came because I wanted to. I came to be healed.'

She had on a white towelling bathrobe, large silver earrings and a silver necklace with a locket. 'Don't worry,' she said to Simon. 'You won't need to help me down. I'll be able to walk, won't I?'

Or fly. One of the monks giggled.

Simon stepped away from the wheelchair. Isabel sat alone in the centre of the platform. 'When you're ready.'

Do it.

Simon said, 'Please, no.'

The monk smiled. Simon didn't know how he knew this, because the monk had no face. But the monk smiled and pulled on the loose cord of hemp around his waist.

Simon drew breath.

The cord fell to the stone around the monk's leather boots. The robe parted, and the monk's dark penis reared glistening into the cold moonlight.

Simon shivered.

Isabel turned her head and looked into his face. He felt his eyes glaze and harden. He took hold of the handles of the wheelchair.

Isabel said, 'Simon?'

Her voice was distant, a little croaky, a voice on the end of a telephone. He had heard voices like this before, the lonely voices of other women in other parishes.

Her eyes widened. She gave a little sob.

'I'm sorry,' he said coldly.

He pushed the wheelchair easily to the gap at the edge of the tower, where the perimeter wall had been. Glancing back at the naked, grinning monk, he gave it a final little prod and watched it vanish. Stood on the edge and waited until he heard it smashing into the rubble fifty feet below with a noise like a cutlery drawer being emptied.

And then he took off his robe, went down on his knees and began to crawl across the stone towards the monk.

*

Shelley *couldn't* move. Her bag was on a Queen Anne sort of coffee table under the window where she'd put it down to bring a chair close to the fire for Meryl.

She didn't dare look at it, so she carried on looking at Tom, right into his creased-up eyes, heavy with a sense of betrayal.

Please, honey, please.

Sometimes he would hear her silent appeals clearer than if she'd spoken. Sometimes, like tonight, he could transmit his unease to her, and her perception of atmosphere would be heightened and change and she would know something was happening . . . and believe that she was somehow sharing his burden.

'Keys,' Tom said.

He looked old. Stricken and ravaged. His moustache was almost white now. He was only forty-seven, barely middle-aged these days.

Shelley said, 'Let me drive you home, Tom.'

'Keys. I'll spell it out. I ain't going nowhere wiv you. And I ain't walking.'

She remembered him saying, on the way here, *I hate these little country lanes*. All country lanes, for Tom, were haunted by the clash of metal and the roar of flames. Shelley knew exactly what it had been like; she'd made Dave Reilly tell her about it, every horrifying detail.

Including the bit about Tom demanding car keys from Russell Hornby, the producer, before driving off in the old Land Rover which would destroy Deborah.

What time was it now? A long time after midnight, that was certain. Nearly *that* time. They should have been home by now, safe in bed.

Shelley rallied. 'You're not having the keys, Tom.'

'Don't make me angry,' Tom said.

Shelley didn't move.

But someone else did.

'Look.' The awful Stephen Case had wandered over. 'Perhaps I can resolve this. Tom and I need to do some talking about one thing and another. Tom, why don't you come over to my hotel in Stroud? Be very quiet. We can talk, and I can book you a room for the night, what's left of it. No problem. I've got a bottle of Chivas Regal in the car . . .'

Oh God. Shelley closed her eyes on Tom's disbelief.

'Why you fink I should wanna talk to you?'

'Because, Tom, to be blunt,' Case said, 'I've got the Abbey tapes. I'd like to know more about them and you'd probably like to know how I got hold of them.'

'I don't give a shit.'

'I think you do.'

'Yeah? Keys, Shelley.'

'You should come and talk to Sile Copesake. He's listened to the tapes. He says he . . .'

Shelley opened her eyes at precisely the moment that Tom hit Stephen Case open-handed in the face, tipping him backwards like a bottle from a shelf. She saw Martin Broadbank step hurriedly out of the way as Case crashed into a coffee table, bouncing a black patent-leather shoulderbag into the air.

Tom caught the bag.

He turned it upside down, and Case, struggling to sit up, was showered with sundry items of make-up. Also, a comb, a hairbrush, a notebook, a pocket calculator and a bunch of car keys.

Tom snatched the keys from Case's left armpit.

'Tom, no!' Shelley shrieked. '*Please!*'

'Leave him,' Martin Broadbank said. As if he had the slightest idea what was happening.

Tom lumbered through the drawing-room, as unresponsive as an amateur stage ghost on the battlements. Above his left shoulder, Shelley thought she could discern a dusty something, like a floating bruise.

There was such a silence in the room that when the car started up outside it was like an explosion in the night.

XV

Bunny

Vanessa being glued to Eddie Murphy – for the second time around – left the Weasel time to do a bit of thinking. He wondered, was tonight going to be the big turning-point for Tom, going out into the big world and that? And, nah, he couldn't see it at all.

Weasel contemplated this sitting-room with the big telly and the tasteful Laura Ashley drapes and the furniture which must have cost a bomb but wasn't what you could call an investment on account of it was all repro – imitation Chippendale and Sherrington and geezers of that order, tomorrow's junk.

Shelley doing her best, given that she wasn't allowed to have anything in the house that wasn't showroom-fresh, in case there was anything, like, *attached* to it.

Weasel had heard it said that kids that grew up where everything they came into contact with was sterilized and disinfected – these kids was *more likely* to pick up bugs and that when they went out, because their bodies hadn't built up any kind of natural immunity.

Well, God knows, it didn't start out like that for Tom, not in any respect, growing up in Bermondsey: pies and chips from the shop every night on account of his old lady being on shifts down the biscuit factory and his dad staggering home about eleven, stinking of oil from the docks and fags and beer from the boozer, and all their furniture secondhand, including the beds and the old telly, when they eventually got one.

Those days, Tom was a healthy kid and seemed happy – especially the night his old man come home with the guitar.

Weasel chuckled. The size of the bastard!

Those days – Elvis, Tommy Steele – all the kids wanted guitars. Those who got one, it was usually some four-quid Spanish effort and they'd attach a bit of old lamp-flex to the back to make like it was electric.

Christmases and birthdays had been and gone and Tom'd given up hope. Youngest of seven, all his clobber hand-me-downs, he'd been stringing rubber bands across shoebox lids with a carpenter's wooden rule shoved in the end for the fingerboard – amazingly he could get *tunes* out of this.

Then this night – Tom'd be about twelve, thirteen – in comes his old man, only half as pissed as usual, with this thing wrapped in tarpaulin that he couldn't hardly get through the back door. Tom's in bed (Weasel got this story years later from Tom's brother Norman) and the old man sends for him.

'Give us your hexpert hadvice on this, son,' he says, affecting a posh voice like he often done when he come home from the boozer. 'Hacquired it down the Eagle. Geezer assures me it's a musical instrument but I reckon it's a bleedin' old Hoover wiv the wheels come orf.'

Well, Tom never slept that night, nor the night after most likely. For when the tarpaulin comes off, what is underneath is, like, the stuff of dreams.

A few years later, you'd see George Harrison, hiding behind this red semi-acoustic monster, the famous Gretsch Chet Atkins. Now, whether this was or it wasn't, it certainly looked a lot like it.

It was knocked-off, obviously, smash and grab most likely, and whoever nicked it'd been forced to piss off pretty smartish – you could tell this by the flaming great crack up the back – which was how come Tom's old man had picked it up for peanuts in the pub.

His ma done some screaming when she seen it. Ain't having that bleeding great thing in my house, where's it gonna go? You'll wake up one morning and I'll have slung it out for the dustmen, just you wait.

No chance. Tom sleeps with the guitar in his single bed,

arms around it like a big red Teddy bear. Nights and weekends, Tom and Weasel spends hours repairing the axe, using tools nicked from the woodwork room at school.

It was probably still up there in Tom's music room, with the original red enamel sprayed on after they'd finished rebuilding it and sanding it down and that.

But Weasel's chief memory connected with this guitar was the night he hid in the school until everybody'd gone home and then let Tom and the guitar into the deserted building. They'd got out the headmaster's big Ferrograph tape recorder, complete with input socket, into which they'd plugged the guitar and . . . wow! After months of playing acoustically – no hope *whatever* of buying an amp – Tom lets rip in a big way.

'Turn it down!' Weasel's hissing at him, but there's no stopping Tom now and he turns the bastard up, high as it'll go; he's playing some old Shadows number, 'Apache', over and over again, louder and louder. And when Weasel looks out the window – oh, *no* – the flaming schoolyard's filling up with sodding kids, dozens of the little bastards, all bopping away.

Only one way this was going to end, and it did – Weasel smuggling Tom and the guitar out of a back window and staying behind to take the rap when the coppers and the caretaker come crashing in. Corporal punishment being all the rage with headmasters in those days, Weasel – who stayed shtumm about Tom despite all the threats – got his arse flogged raw next day.

Now, Tom never spoke of this, but he never forgot it neither, and if Weasel had to point to one single reason why the Storeys had so readily provided a home and job for a scruffy little ex-con, this would be it, and . . .

Weasel's thoughts were stopped just then by the sudden silence.

Vanessa was sitting on this pouffe thing in front of the telly. She had the remote control in her hand and she'd stopped the video.

'Daddy's coming,' Vanessa said.

'Blimey, Princess, you got good ears.'

Which she hadn't. Among Down's kids, good ears was not

common. Weasel himself – and he *had* got good ears – couldn't hear a thing from outside, no car noise, nothing.

Vanessa jumped from the pouffe, dropping the remote control on the carpet.

'Where you off to, Princess?'

Vanessa didn't reply and ran out of the room. Weasel still couldn't hear a car.

He didn't like this. What he didn't like was the thought – always at the back of his mind – that the kid might in some way have inherited Tom's complaint.

See, Tom had six uncles and six brothers. Seventh son of a seventh son – the drawbacks of this had been well laid down in several old blues numbers. However, Vanessa was only the first daughter of a seventh son of a seventh son. Which ought to be OK, right?

'Princess!'

Weasel was half-way out the door when the phone rang on the table just inside the room, within arm's length.

Weasel snatched it up. 'Yeah?'

'Weasel?'

'Shelley?'

The tone of her voice had rocked Weasel like a heavy one from Frank Bruno.

'Weasel, I don't know what to do. There's been an awful scene and Tom . . . Tom's . . . he's walked out on me.'

'Jeez.'

'And he's . . . Weasel, he's taken the car.'

'Shit,' said Weasel.

'I don't know what to do.'

Her voice was definitely shaking.

'Where are you?'

'I'm still here. Hall Farm. You . . .'

'Tom's coming back here?'

Daddy's coming.

'I don't know, Weasel. He's in a state. He's had . . . Something's happened, you know what I'm saying?'

'Yeah, yeah . . . Somebody else there, right? Can't spell it

237

out. Listen, Shel, I reckon the best fing I can do is get the old van out, put Vanessa in and come and pick you up, yeah?'

'I don't know . . . I don't know.' Getting worked up; not like Shelley; something climactic going down.

'Ten minutes, Shel, I could be there . . .'

'But what if Tom . . . ? I mean, if nobody's there when he . . . ?'

'How bad's he?'

'Pret . . . Pretty bad. He hit somebody.'

'Shit. But, look, if I come and pick you up and he's on his way back, I'll run into him on the . . .'

Weasel went cold; his chest went tight.

'Oh, fuck,' he said.

Shelley was kind of hyperventilating. Cool, practical, businesslike Shelley Love. Flames crackling down the line between them, echoes of a long-ago impact neither of them had heard.

'Listen,' Weasel said. 'You fink I should wait here for him?'

'I don't know, I don't know. I don't know what's best. I don't want you out on the road with Tom careering about in that state. I don't want Vanessa . . .'

Vanessa.

Daddy's coming.

'Listen, I'll call you back,' Weasel said, doing his best to keep the shakes out of his voice. 'Five minutes.'

'OK, Weasel, the number's five, five, three . . . Weasel? *Weasel!*'

But the Weasel had hung up and was racing for the door.

Shelley stood in Martin Broadbank's panelled hall clutching the phone to her chest.

'Come and sit down,' Broadbank said. 'It'll be all right. These things . . .'

'What do *you* know,' Shelley said bitterly, 'about *these things*?'

Her eyes were wet. *Just let me get through this without anyone getting hurt,* she pleaded with the God she'd never quite accepted. *Hurt or . . . or worse. Get me through it. Then we'll sort something out.*

Realizing that what she was thinking of sorting out – perhaps her only hope for a future (*her* future, the hell with Tom) – was some sort of separation. Just for a while.

Or possibly a long while; she couldn't think about this now. *Listen, I didn't mean that – the hell with Tom. I'm just . . . Please . . .*

'I wouldn't claim to understand any of this.' Martin Broadbank gently took the phone from Shelley, dropped it on its rest. 'I realize there's a lot of background here. But I do think you need some help. I think whatever it is is becoming a bit too much for you to handle on your own.' He took her arm. 'Shelley, please, if you can't sit down, at least come through to the kitchen.'

In the long, low-beamed kitchen, under a row of small spotlights, Meryl was applying a cold compress to Stephen Case's nose.

Broadbank smirked. 'Rather rubbed him up the wrong way, I suspect, Steve.'

'Or perhaps it was you, Martin.' Case eyed Shelley meaningfully.

'Yes, well.' Martin guided Shelley to a wooden stool. 'Let's just accept the poor chap was feeling a little . . . sensitive.'

'As well he bloody well might!' Shelley was riled. 'Don't you think it would have been reasonable – not to say polite, not to say *ethical* – to explain that Tom was the real target for tonight, not me?'

'No, no, Shelley,' Broadbank protested. 'It was you *I* wanted to see.' He had the grace to blush slightly. 'That is, I'm very serious about the Love-Storey possibilities. But, yes, it was wrong of me – and I apologize – not to tell you properly about Steve.'

Case said, 'Mrs Storey, I *have* made several attempts to talk to your husband. We do have this project on the go, and we want to do it in consultation with Tom, not have it sprung on him. After all, this is a recording dating back to perhaps the most . . . difficult period of his life and we really do . . .'

'. . . want to capitalize on that,' said Shelley. 'I used to *work* for a record company, don't treat me like the little wife.'

'I'm sorry . . .' Case snatched the pad from his nose '. . . but capitalizing is really not what we're about. We think this is very important material.'

'Why?' Shelley said, glancing back towards the hall. *Ring, Weasel, please ring.*

'Yes,' said Broadbank. 'Why, Steve?'

Tom Storey's verbal acid attack had, it was true, taken him by surprise. But Martin had sprung back, Meryl noticed, with some typically suave and nifty footwork.

And Tom Storey had been right, Martin *was* after his wife. It was now Martin and Shelley against Case.

Case was burbling about the importance of the work of people like Tom Storey now that rock music, *classic* rock music, was an established art form, part of our national heritage. Rediscovering lost Tom Storey material was like finding a Turner in the attic, Case said earnestly.

Meryl made coffee and listened and absorbed. She, too, had recovered. It had been a frightening night, but she'd been scared for all the wrong reasons, because, for a few minutes, through the sheer power of his projection, she'd thought Tom Storey was a murderer and that she was in great danger.

When, in fact, behind the shambling façade was probably the most profound psychic sensibility she'd ever been privileged to encounter. Ten years of the spiritualist church, ten years of trivia from the Other Side about the missing fiver in Uncle Jim's sock drawer. Eighteen months of one-sided conversations with the Lady Bluefoot.

No wonder she'd been frightened. Tom Storey was the real thing.

Meryl's tremulous excitement percolated alongside the coffee as she listened to Stephen Case's explanations. And filled in the gaps for herself.

'All I can say is it's music which seems to enter a different spiritual dimension,' Case was saying.

He was a hungry-looking man, his hair pulled back into a pony-tail because it was thinning elsewhere. A man snatching at the last chance of being trendy, Meryl thought. Pathetic, but dangerous.

And what did he know about spiritual dimensions? Nothing, she decided. He was relaying someone else's words. He was just a front man.

'Listen to me.' Shelley Storey stood up, pushing back her stool. 'And if this gets any further, I'm going to come after you, Mr Case. December 1980. What happened that night caused Tom a lot of serious emotional damage. I've spent the best years of my life trying to hold that man together. Now, coming out here tonight, you'll never know what a hell of a step that was for him, and he did it because he thought he was helping me. And the way it's gone – and what he did to you was nothing to what *I'd* like to do to you – the way it's gone has probably put him right back to where we started. If you want to compound that, you go ahead with your seedy little schemes, but, by God . . .'

Martin was watching the fiery Shelley with admiration. He was standing where Meryl had seen the apparition of the gruesome man. Meryl shivered, but it wasn't only fear this time, so much as anticipation. There was a great secret here.

'Mrs Storey . . .' Case was backing away, holding up both hands. 'I really think you're too close to this. We all know what happened that night. *Obviously* it's damaged Tom. But let me put your mind at rest. We don't want to release these tapes as they stand.'

'What's all this about then?' Martin demanded.

'What we *want* is for Tom and the others to go back into the studio and complete it. Perhaps . . . to the Abbey? We own it now. It closed down not long after that session, you know. Nobody wanted to work there.'

'Hardly surprising,' Martin said.

'But don't you think, Mrs Storey, that it would be . . . cathartic for Tom? To go back? Maybe his only real chance to get things together?'

Shelley said immediately, 'I think it would be insanity to go back.' And clamped her lips and turned away from him, but towards Meryl who saw that her eyes weren't quite so certain.

She's close to breaking point, thought Meryl, who'd been given a taste tonight of what life with Tom Storey could be like. Shelley was a strong, practical woman, a pragmatist.

Which wasn't enough.

Meryl thought, *She's reaching the stage where she'll consider anything*.

Weasel ran through into the kitchen, shouting, 'Vanessa! Princess!'

No sign of her. No sign of anything; she hadn't even put the lights on. Weasel did, and he saw that the back door was ajar.

Daddy's coming.

But he wasn't here yet. No car noise, no lights through the window, except for two or three across in the village. It was late. Too late for lights, too late for traffic.

'Princess!' Weasel ran out into the night. 'Where you gone?'

He stumbled down to the yard, wishing he'd brought a torch, but he wasn't going back for one now.

'Vanessa! This ain't funny!'

In the yard he shut up and stood still, listening for movement. It was dead quiet. No trees and no bushes around the house meant no sounds of wildlife.

No moon. No light.

With both hands, Weasel pulled on his straggly hair. Why was she doing this to him?

'*Vanessa!*'

In the distance, Weasel heard a vehicle noise. He ran up the steps and across the lawn towards the front of the house. The lawn was washed by the lights from the sitting-room, like a floodlit bowling green.

As the sound increased, it was clear this was a car and it was travelling pretty fast. Weasel imagined Tom all frozen-faced and staring-eyed at the wheel, maybe realizing this was the first time he'd done any driving at night, since . . .

Was it? Was this the first time since?

Jesus.

Some trees alongside a bend in the road were lit up. Headlights. Two or three hundred yards away. The car would have to slow for the hairpin bend twenty yards before the house. Everybody knew this bend.

There was another shaft of light pointing the other way from the elbow of the road, as if a motorbike was parked by the driveway gate.

Weasel ran to the edge of the lawn, where it sloped down to the perimeter fence Sir Wilf didn't like, six-foot slats nearly as thick as railways sleepers running to the edge of the shared driveway – a nicely-clipped hedge on Sir Wilfrid's side.

From up here, Weasel could see over the fence to the road beyond, and Vanessa with a lamp standing in the middle of it.

What the f—?

'Vanessa, Jesus, what you *doing*? Ain't you got no bleeding sense?'

Never spoken to the kid like this before. She was Down's – you didn't.

And she was just standing there in the middle of the lane in her blue hostess frock, holding the lamp to guide Daddy home. Like a little lighthouse.

The big car cruising down the hill towards the bend wouldn't get her in its headlights until it'd come round the hairpin and by then . . .

'*Noooooo!*'

. . . she'd be in pieces, all over its windscreen.

Instinctively, Weasel arched his body, quivering, wanting desperately to hurl himself from the edge of the lawn to the top of the fence, vault over it. But his body knew it was too puny, too clapped out.

Sobbing, he ran down the other side of the lawn, scrambling frantically towards the main gate, waving his arms, screeching, 'Vanessa, Princess, get out of the bleeding way, *he ain't rational*!'

Headlights hit the fence.

As he reached the gates, Weasel tripped and fell headlong. It smashed all the breath out of him and he couldn't even shout at her again.

The car took the bend too fast, like they always did.

Vanessa's small, dumpy figure, as still as a little bunny frozen stiff in the headlights.

XVI

Plop, Plop, Plop

Dave Reilly couldn't sleep.

Wearing a ragged blue bathrobe, he sat in the armchair in his bedsit with the light on, the walls studio-white around him. The only colour in the room was coming out of a TV set on the plywood MFI chest of drawers opposite the chair. The TV screen was showing – standard small-hour fare – a naff, seventies rock video, blokes in tinsel jackets with blond bobbed hair; they looked like singing spaniels. Dave had the sound off.

The bedsit belonged to Bart, who also owned Muthah Mirth. Tomorrow he'd have to tell Bart he wouldn't be playing the next night, or the night after, or . . .

And Bart would throw him out of the bedsit in which he'd hoped to see out December.

On the TV, the video had changed. Marc Bolan, the electric pixie who crashed his car into a tree and died. Prof Levin used to talk about how he'd once worked with Marc. *Fey and wispy? Are you kidding? Naked ambition, from the start. My experience, David, fey and wispy is invariably a front.*

Prof Levin was a straight bloke. One of the few. Too experienced for ambition, too old for bullshit.

And Prof had said,

I mean, she's . . . alive and everything?

Dave's anxiety flared up like toothache. He'd heard nothing since faxing Moira's agent. He started wondering who he could possibly phone at this hour, for reassurance. What had happened that night that he *didn't* know about?

As if what he did know about wasn't bad enough.

Some stuff on this album . . . the death sequence. You must remember that.

You mean Aelwyn?

Dave had fled the studio that night just as the song had descended to the death of Aelwyn . . . *his* death. Maybe this was an earlier take.

Which was impossible; there hadn't been any earlier takes. Rehearsals, yes; recordings, no.

He felt starved, pulled the ancient, two-bar electric fire closer to the chair. The point was to record it live, the whole band playing, a fusion of minds and spirits. The aim: to let in the echoes from the stone. Russell Hornby, who really didn't believe in any of this shit, had said, 'This is the climax, guys, you need to build up to it, it shouldn't become blasé.' So they'd rehearsed, many times, the build-up: Aelwyn's flight from Abergavenney Castle, the pursuit across the frozen hills, six verses . . . and, even in rehearsal, kept coming out of the song before the seventh verse because Russell Hornby, efficient, shaven-headed Russell, advised it. And Russell . . .

. . . did not basically believe this shit.

Looking back, there were so many more things which didn't add up.

The candles, the dark brown candles – they never had solved the mystery of the candles. Too much had happened too quickly afterwards. And now it emerged that somebody – Russell – had conned them over the tapes. Well, with hindsight, this was understandable; no producer would like to watch his week's work going up in smoke. Inexcusable, but understandable.

And 'On a Bad Day', the worst thing Dave had ever done – was this abomination among the tapes which somebody called Stephen Case had so thoughtfully recovered?

A toxic cocktail, Moira had called the band. Moira, who didn't even know about 'On a Bad Day', the most toxic song ever recorded.

But Russell knew.

Dave's head sank into his hands. This was all too much to take.

I mean . . . she's alive and everything?

Prof talking about a woman . . . a woman dying . . . on the tape . . .

There was no woman dying. *Aelwyn* died. Nobody else. Tom's Debbie and John Lennon, but nobody else . . . nobody on the *tape*.

Got to do it.

Dave sprang to his feet, switched off the TV, pulled his canvas suitcase from under the bed. There was a zip compartment underneath for stuff you wanted to keep flat. Inside the compartment was an LP record, made maybe ten years ago and long deleted. His only copy; he'd carried it around, wherever he went, for . . .

He didn't know why the *hell* he'd carried it around.

Yes he did. It was for a purpose such as this. For an emergency.

Davey, love, we're no' safe together, we're too much.

And it would bloody well *have* to be an emergency because the only time he'd tried this before, there'd been a very frosty reception and two days of severe headaches. *I told you, we can't even see each other again.*

Dave took the album back to the armchair and the stuttering electric fire. How ironic that the picture on the front should so mirror his old fantasies (although it would be stretching credibility to think she might actually have done this for *him*).

He looked at the photograph for a long time, memorizing the details, the colours of the sky, the formation of the clouds, the corrugated patterns in the sand where it met the sea, the shape of the rocks in the distance. And then gradually . . .

. . . gradually, he let his gaze drift away from the picture to a point in space, in the middle distance. Regulating his breathing, allowing his eyelids to fall, but not quite all the way, so that there was a hazy, unfocused image of the blank TV screen on the chest of drawers and the white wall behind.

And then concentrating on the noise of the sporadic night traffic, a distant radio, merging these separate sounds, letting them come into the room and join the fractured metallic chatter of the electric fire until all of it dissipated into a kind of aural fog, fading into the fuzzed images of the furniture, everything becoming part of the same sensory mush and then there was

a long beach, a deep blue-grey sky

and a woman side-on to the camera and to the sea, but her head turned away so you couldn't see her face because of the black hair almost to her waist. She had on jeans and a skimpy T-shirt. Bare feet. Hands behind her back loosely clasped around the neck of an acoustic guitar trailing along behind her.

He made the woman walk, silently tracking her along the sand as if through a movie camera on a dolly.

In her wake, a word was elegantly scrawled in the sand, as if it had been spelled out by the trailing guitar. He didn't look at the word, lest his attention be diverted and the woman walk out of his vision.

He heard the slumberous sighing of the sea, the skimming of a late-summer breeze, the keening of seagulls overhead. And he altered their voices until the sounds of the gulls and the sea were mixed into the rhythm of her bare feet padding and slithering along the beach and the soft bump, bump, bump of the acoustic guitar over the firm, corrugated ridges in the warm sand.

And he sent a word to the spirits of the air, a simple, spherical sound, sent rolling like a small ball along the beach.

Moirrrrrraaaaaaaaa

Calling her gently, whispering to her to turn around. Sending her all his love, sweeping in on the tide.

Knowing, not caring, that he was in tears.

Moirrrrrraaaaaaaaa

But she wouldn't turn.

She just kept on walking, and him staggering behind, losing the rhythm of her even pace, the breeze awakening, turning against him and the bored, restless sea slapping petulantly at the sand.

please.

Moira, *please* . . .

She was moving away from the shore, into the softer sand,

and the breeze lifted it, made it swirl around her ankles, and the guitar was clinking on the pebbles, its strings quivering, discordant protests coming out of the soundbox, and no message any more except the remains of the word deeply inscribed into the harder sand, close to the shore, and the word was,

death

And as he read it, she stopped and turned slowly, but he couldn't see her face, only the cowl of smog around her head, the black, hideous bonnet.

An acrid smell of burning as Dave's eyes sprang open through a screen of tears to find the cardboard record sleeve had slid between his fingers, down behind the protective wire in front of the electric fire.

. . . *the woman dying . . . she's fading . . . the voice, the whole quality of the voice getting sort of brittle . . .*

There was a sizzling; a peeling, laminated corner had caught fire.

And then – yeah – she's saying, very feebly, help me, help me.

As Dave tore the album from the fire, threw it to the carpet, stamped on it, he had a sudden image of fourteen years ago: thirteen candles in a circle, Tom Storey deliberately tumbling one into a pile of lyrics sheets, Simon St John languidly stamping out the flames.

Dave bent over the singed and smoking album cover.

Of course, the writing in the sand read,

moira

*

Martin Broadbank, his face all furrows of concern, said, 'Who knows? I might be able to help. Or . . . or Meryl might be able to help.'

All the lights were on in the drawing-room at Hall Farm: four table lamps and a small chandelier. The watchful Meryl perhaps aware of a need to drive away the dark.

Stephen Case had gone, leaving his card for Shelley, in case *he* could help. Suddenly everybody wanted to help.

Shelley went to the window, parted a curtain to look out. There was an aura of light on the drive from the lantern over the door.

'Why doesn't he ring?'

'Your transport manager?'

Shelley smiled palely. 'He's just an old friend of Tom's, from way back. If anybody can handle Tom at a time like this, it's . . . him.'

Meryl said, 'This is the little . . . ?'

'The little hippie.' Shelley let the curtain fall. 'With the earring and the bandana. Eric Beasley. Known as Weasel. He was Tom's regular roadie.'

Why doesn't he ring? Twenty minutes. He said five.

'Tell me about this band.' Martin Broadbank threw a small log on the fire, jabbed hard with a poker to produce more flames, more light. 'I rather think Steve has been exercising an undue economy with the truth. I'm sorry I was a party to it.'

'Wasn't your fault,' Shelley said. 'Really.'

Broadbank straightened up. He'd taken off his jacket, looked solid and ordinary, just another rich businessman in his Cotswold retreat, no special qualities. Oh, the freedom of living with someone like that . . .

'Shelley, why don't I drive you home?'

'I should wait for Weasel. I need to know what I'm going into. And also . . .'

Ring, Weasel, for God's sake, ring . . .

'. . . and also, I think, the fewer cars on the road between here and Larkfield the better.'

Shelley thought of the baby she'd taught Tom to love.

Vanessa. It had taken a long time, Tom looking down fearfully at his Nemesis in the cot, the impossible baby, the baby who should have died in flames, the baby with no great future, who served only as a reminder.

Vanessa the wonder baby. It had taken a long time to convince Tom that Vanessa was a wonderful thing.

Weasel had said he was going to put her into the van and bring her over here. Weasel knowing instinctively that Vanessa should not be there tonight when Tom arrived home.

Nor on the road between here and Larkfield.

Shelley gripped the curtain to hold back the hot tears building behind her eyes.

The woman was smiling at Weasel out of the darkness.

He did recognize her, but his mind was too blown-out to figure where he'd seen her before.

Weasel backed away from the car, gulping in the hard, dark air to stop himself throwing up.

He stood in the road. There was no other traffic. The lights shone down from the house upon the broken fence, giant slats like railway sleepers. The car had smashed into the bottom of the fence and slammed a bunch of sleepers back, and two of them had, like, see-sawed and come flying at the windscreen.

The sleepers lay half across the car bonnet, glass all over them, the other halves inside the car.

Weasel hadn't heard any screams, only a sound like a house falling down. The engine was still chuntering away, exhaust smell on the air and another smell when you were closer – like a rusty smell.

It was probably blood. Realizing this, Weasel clutched his guts and Vanessa's omelette came up.

Wiping his mouth on his sleeve, he felt better. He should do something, call the cops, get the road sealed off. Anybody came round the bend – splat.

On its side in the road was Vanessa's lamp, one of those red plastic ones with a handle. It was still on. As Weasel picked it

251

up, he thought he heard a car droning in the distance. He should go towards it waving the lamp, warn them.

He needed help.

Thought somebody would've come by now. It was less than half a mile outside the village; even at this hour *some* bastard must've heard the crash.

The car noise had faded out. They must've turned off. Which was a pity; they could've helped him, gone for the cops. He couldn't risk going back to the house in case another car showed up while he was away.

No choice. Weasel ran back through the gates.

'Princess?'

She was still standing on the lawn where he'd left her, by the concrete birdbath. 'You gotta help me,' Weasel said.

She didn't move, didn't even look at him. Most likely, she was still in shock. He'd never forget her standing in the middle of the road, still as a bloody garden gnome, the car screeching and swerving to avoid her and then hitting the fence.

'You smell bad, Weasel,' Vanessa said.

'Yeah, I been sick, Princess. Listen, you gotta go back up the house and you gotta ring 999. You know how to do that?'

After a second or two, he thought she nodded.

'And they'll say: What service you want? And you say police and . . .'

Ambulance?

Too late for that.

'. . . you say police. And they'll ask you where you are and you tell 'em, you say Larkfield St Mary, near Stroud, and you tell 'em there's been a serious accident, you got that? A serious accident.'

Vanessa stared at him for a moment and he thought, Oh, *Gawd*, but then she turned suddenly and ran towards the house and left him there and didn't look back.

All he could do was hope she'd get it right. Weasel walked back out the gateway to the car. It had come to him, who she was, the woman who'd smiled at him. He should make sure. He had the light now.

Gawd.

He hadn't seen the man's face, hadn't tried to. Seen his neck, that was enough. What was left of it. The sleeper had crashed in through the windscreen, taken him under the chin, pinning his neck to the head-restraint. The rusty smell was strongest here; Weasel gagged again.

The engine had coughed its last. All quiet in the car, except for this dripping sound, like *plop, plop, plop*, Oh, Gawd help us. He let the lamp's beam fall through the windscreen just once.

Typical. Even in his last second, Sir Wilf had been scowling. Even with a hole in his neck you could put your fist through and the top of his spine on view through the mush, his face showed no horror, only, like . . . rage.

Weasel stepped back to the rear door on the passenger side, the only one he'd been able to open.

There'd been no padded head restraint on this side; maybe Lady Tulley had found it inconvenient, some people did. Where the restraint should have been, another wooden sleeper lay like a shelf across the back of the seat, in which Lady Tulley's body still sat.

Her head was tossed like a handbag or something on the back seat, and now he could see it properly, no, she wasn't smiling after all.

Wedged between Lady Tulley's head and the driver's seat was a mud-spattered wheel. They must've had a puncture on the way; no wonder Sir Wilf was scowling.

Part Three

I

Dreamer

The neat, square, grey tower most visitors thought was
Abergavenny Castle, this actually wasn't it at all. This
was in fact a nineteenth-century folly, once Lord Abergavenny's hunting lodge, now housing the town's museum; it
just *looked* like a castle, see.

Eddie Edwards explained this to the vicar as they walked
along a narrow path between two jutting stone walls – pinky-
grey, like ash, like the colours of the Abbey. It had taken less
than half an hour to drive here from Ystrad Ddu, even at Mr
Edwards's famously moderate speeds.

'This, now, *this* is the real castle,' Mr Edwards said. 'These
walls and those segments by there. Not boring you already, am
I? Only you've gone quiet.'

'Sorry,' the vicar said, in a distant sort of way. 'Not much
left of it, is there?'

'Ample, for our purposes,' Mr Edwards said, striding forth.
'Now, Vicar, you follow me round by here, and you'll see what
a sound defensive position this was.'

It had been his idea to come today. He knew the vicar didn't
want to, but the boy needed taking out of himself. Mr Edwards
was, quite frankly, fed up with seeing him mooning about the
place, looking preoccupied and generally out-of-sorts.

He led the vicar around the side of the high wall, where the
castle hill fell away to reveal a magnificent expanse of countryside, out across the river. On the other side of the castle was the
town itself where they'd parked, not a terribly important town
architecturally speaking, but pleasant and lively.

Which was more than you could say for the vicar.

Had he always been such a loner? On the way here, Mr

Edwards had asked him if he'd ever been married, thinking maybe the wife had died, leaving him bereft. The vicar had smiled, shaken his head, declined to elaborate.

Couldn't be a Nancy-boy, surely, now? Didn't *behave* like a Nancy-boy. Still, though, the languid way he moved, the slightly effete mannerisms, the way he'd toss back that lock of feathery, fair hair . . .

Well, hell. Mr Edwards blew out his lips. What on earth did it matter if he was? Not like there was a surfeit of mild-mannered, sensitive fellows around these parts.

He separated his hands, as if measuring. 'Now, what we have to imagine here, see, Vicar, is the scene in the mid-twelfth century.'

The sun, making a speculative foray from behind a clump of clouds, had lit the vicar's pale hair, giving him a halo. And why not, indeed?

'There would've been a keep, like that new tower, same sort of shape and in fact on that very same mound. But all the rest of the buildings inside the walls would've been little more than wooden sheds, with maybe thatched roofs. Protection, it was about, see, not grandiose architectural statements.'

He opened out a white leaflet to a simple plan of the castle ruins. 'Now.' Pointing to a one-time three-storey section with a tree grown up in the middle. 'That's the south-west tower, OK? So therefore . . .' marching along the inside of the perimeter wall '. . . the great hall would have been just about . . .'

Mr Edwards stopped, beamed.

'Here.'

There was grass and a workman's hut, and a lower area where a kind of cellar had been. The vicar seemed relieved somehow that there was not more to see.

The last time Eddie Edwards had been here he'd still been an education adviser, planning another of those inter-school projects designed to take history out of the classroom.

How time did go by.

'So, Vicar, we'll imagine the centuries rolling back, and here we are in 1175.'

'Eddie.' The vicar was leaning against one of the castle walls. 'As I'm off duty today . . .'

He was wearing an old sheepskin jacket and patched jeans. Mr Edwards had to admit he did not look much like a vicar this morning.

'. . . Why don't you just call me Simon?'

'Well . . .' Simon? Simon? He was a married man! Mr Edwards took a couple of swift paces to the right. 'Well, as you like, Vicar. Now, this castle was built by the Norman invaders for the purpose of controlling the Welsh hereabouts, who had never quite adjusted to the idea of being conquered. And in 1175, the castle was still pretty new, and so was the owner. The Norman baron William de Braose.'

'Ah, yes.'

'Who, not to put too fine a point on it, Vic . . . Simon . . . was a bastard of the first order.'

'Quite.'

'Cruel, greedy, arrogant. If there'd been jackboots in 1175, rest assured he'd have had a pair or two made to size.'

'Bet he went from strength to strength in Norman Britain,' said Simon, flicking back his fair hair.

'Indeed. Now, before this, the castle was owned – and when I say owned, in those days, owning it was matter of getting up an army and evicting the current tenant – it was owned by a local Welsh chieftain, chap name of Seisyll, brother-in-law of the Prince of South Wales, so well connected, in his way. Now, this man Seisyll had taken it by force from the Norman in charge at the time whose name I forget, but he doesn't matter.'

Simon St John, Mr Edwards thought suddenly. Was St John perhaps a *Norman* name? Better be careful how he angled this story.

'Anyway, on agreeing to give *back* the castle, Seisyll was granted a royal pardon by the English king, Henry II.' Mr Edwards sniffed. 'Bloody good of him, give a man a royal pardon after you've pinched his lands, subjugated his . . . anyway, Seisyll moves out, William de Braose moves in, and they agree there will be a banquet at the castle, Normans and

Welsh together, to celebrate their new-found friendship. All this old ground for you, Simon?'

'No, we were told very little. The idea was that we . . .' The vicar stopped; a hunted look flitted across his smooth features. 'I'm sorry, I . . . It's very interesting, Eddie. Go on.'

What was all this about? *Duw*, there was more to this fellow than met the eye, all right. Mr Edwards walked to the centre of a grassy area, the high perimeter wall to his right.

'So a strong wooden building stood just about here – the great hall, enclosed by the high walls, looked down on by the keep. The banquet is prepared, the wild boar, the venison, whatever. And when Seisyll's party arrive, they have with them an entertainer, a harpist – Aelwyn.'

Mr Edwards paused for effect. Sun flashed through the branches of leafless trees.

'Aelwyn, now, he already was a well-known figure in the land, if not to the Normans. A bard, a chronicler, in poetry, of the times . . . and an individual, this is the important thing. Most bards, see, in those days were what you might call hacks. Earned their money glorifying the deeds of whichever land-grabbing scoundrel would become their patron. But nobody owned Aelwyn, it has been written . . . except the land itself.'

'What's that mean?' the vicar asked.

'Means he was a patriot in the truest sense, boy. He wanted the best for his country. He wanted peace. A land where the poet was king. Always a dream, in Wales, and in fact . . .'

Simon said, 'How do we know all this?'

'The answer to that,' said Mr Edwards, 'is that we don't. When I say it has been written, I don't mean in any authoritative chronicle. You'll find no mention of the man in Giraldus Cambrensis or Geoffrey of Monmouth.'

'So he's a legend, rather than a fact.'

'There is,' said Mr Edwards, 'a *poetic* truth in it. He is an archetype, if you like. The man of peace in a world of violence and double-dealing . . . and no more violent, no more corrupt region than the Welsh border in medieval times. I like to stand here and imagine that banquet, the wooden hall lit by huge candles and torches, perhaps snow flurries outside, the horses whinnying in the stables, the hounds baying, sensing treachery. And Aelwyn with his harp in a corner of the hall, nobody really listening to him as he plays.'

'And nobody wants to hear Aelwyn, the dreamer . . .'

Mr Edwards stopped, stared at Simon. 'What did you say?'

'I'm sorry, it was just a fragment of a song came into my head.'

'The words, man, say it again.'

'Nobody wants to hear Aelwyn the dreamer?'

Mr Edwards was astonished. 'A song, you say?'

The vicar looked very uncomfortable. As well he might. What deception was going on here?

'You knew then. You knew all along why they called him Aelwyn Breadwinner. Remember, when you asked me that? I do, Vicar, because I never got around to telling you. This song, now . . . *what* song?'

'I don't know, I . . .'

He was lying. A minister of God who swore and lied and showed little reverence and was quite possibly sexually deviant, and whose flippancy perhaps concealed some old sadness . . .

Mr Edwards was really quite thrilled.

'Look, Eddie . . .' Simon St John put a hand on his overcoated shoulder. He was still a clergyman, so Mr Edwards did not flinch. 'I'm sorry. I was a musician for many years before I went into the Church. I've an immense store of songs in my head, old and new, folk songs, all sorts. I wasn't bullshitting you, I really don't know much about Aelwyn, and I don't know why they called him Breadwinner.'

'Well.' Mr Edwards was mollified, but no less intrigued. 'I shall tell you. No big secret. Breadwinner was simply an English corruption of a Welsh word they could not easily pronounce. *Breuddwydiwr*. Dreamer. Aelwyn, the dreamer, see?'

'Yes. Jesus. You know, I don't somehow think the person who composed that song was remotely aware of this.'

Duw! Mr Edwards thought he'd better finish the story before he became as barmy as the vicar. There wasn't much more to tell anyway. His own theory was that Seisyll had brought Aelwyn along as a form of insurance, a witness, someone who would subsequently provide in poetry or song a record of this historic 'treaty' between the Welsh chieftain and the invader – evidence for posterity, in case the Normans should ever attempt to rewrite history.

And when Aelwyn was the only one to escape from the massacre . . . imagine how a report of *that* abomination would have sounded in verse!

Simon stood among the castle ruins and felt nothing.

It was a relief.

Mr Edwards's description of the massacre, over dinner, of Seisyll's party by de Braose's thugs was graphic and therefore speculative, fuelled by a sense of patriotic outrage. Simon couldn't figure it out. How could this Seisyll be so stupid as to walk unarmed into the stronghold of a man whose reputation as a devious bastard must surely have preceded him to Abergavenny?

Was Seisyll really the kind of guy who'd risk anything for a free dinner?

'The only real description of the massacre,' Mr Edwards was saying, 'was in the first account by Giraldus Cambrensis, which he was later impelled to revise for, ah, political reasons, exonerating de Braose from blame except for "allowing it to happen". Pah! And, of course, of the first, unexpurgated account there is now no trace.'

'Giraldus didn't quite have Aelwyn's guts and integrity then,' Simon was moved to remark. 'How is he supposed to have escaped, Eddie?'

Mr Edwards shrugged. 'Accounts differ. Word of mouth, see. One story suggests he was blind and was able to feel his way out through the hidden passages while the other poor buggers were cut down running for the exit. Problem with that is, castles were simple structures in those days, there wouldn't have *been* hidden passages. No, my feeling is that sitting, as he would have been, in some corner, playing his harp, perhaps on a platform, he would've had an overview of the proceedings. Perhaps observing de Braose's men nudging each other, or a glint of steel from someone's sleeve . . .'

'And by the time the heads were in the gravy, he was well away. Hmmm.' Simon strolled across the grass, watched the fields rolling away into the hills, crossed now by fast roads and power lines. The Abbey was in the other direction, so Aelwyn would have fled across what was now the town, eight, ten miles in search of sanctuary. A hell of a journey on foot, on a winter's night, with a trained hit-team on your tail. But at least Aelwyn knew the terrain.

Simon remembered Moira and Dave composing the Aelwyn song together in the studio one morning, trying out ideas on each other.

'*Aelwyn b . . . bom . . . bom . . . came down from the mountains.*'

'*Aelwyn . . . the poet . . . came . . .* '

'*Too obvious. What about Aelwyn, the dreamer?*'

'*OK . . . Aelwyn the dreamer came down from the mountains . . . his harp on his shoulder . . . Would he carry his harp on his shoulder, Davey, or would he have a horse?*'

'*His harp on his horse?*'

There'd been a good deal of giggling. Happy days.

And truly dreadful nights.

II

A Rebel and a Bastard

The man in the painting at the foot of the stairs had a hat with a plume, a white beard and a crafty smile.

'Now this one,' Martin Broadbank said, 'is my great, great, great, great, great grandfather, Ebenezer Broadbank.'

Vanessa looked at him solemnly.

'People say we look a lot like each other,' Martin said. 'Same nose. What do you think?'

Vanessa pouted, shook her head.

'You're quite right,' Martin said. 'Nothing like me. Anyway, this Ebenezer, he was a *terrible* man. He had four wives, all at the same time, all in different counties. One here in Gloucestershire, one up in Worcester, one in Oxford and one in, er, Hereford . . .'

Shelley watched him from the drawing-room and managed an almost-smile. A thin light drifted through the leaded windows.

It was not long after nine a.m. Shelley was wearing last night's backless cream dress and a cardigan borrowed from Meryl.

'Now this one . . . He was a *dreadful* character . . .'

Martin led Vanessa to the first landing, where they vanished from Shelley's sight. She thought she heard Vanessa giggle.

'Who are they really?'

'Who knows?' Meryl had a phone book on her knees. 'He picks them up in antique shops all over the place. Cavaliers are his favourites, he fancies himself as a bit of a cavalier.' Meryl opened the phone book. 'There's no harm in him, even if he causes it sometimes.'

She ran a fingernail down a page of numbers. 'I think I'll try the Corinium Court at Cirencester.'

It seemed Meryl very kindly had been phoning hotels since eight, to see if Tom had checked in anywhere. 'He needs his sleep,' Shelley had kept saying, pacing the kitchen. 'He knows he has to have plenty of sleep.'

She asked now, 'Is it old, this place?'

'Old-*ish*.'

'Don't bother,' Shelley said. 'He wouldn't stay at anywhere old.'

Meryl looked at her, head on one side. Shelley thought she was very striking, commanding somehow, but not in a sharp way; there was a natural composure, apparently undamaged by whatever had happened to her last night and the horrible business of the Tulleys.

Shelley had to keep erasing that from her thoughts. The police were dealing with it. They would have no reason to talk to her, nor to Vanessa. The Weasel had told the police Vanessa had been in bed and he himself had only left the house when he heard the smash.

An accident. A terrible accident on a very bad bend. Two fatalities; no other vehicles involved.

No Tom involved, thank God. And she hoped the police did not feel obliged to check out the Weasel on their computer.

Shelley had spent what remained of the night in a twin-bedded guest room at the farm. With Vanessa, whom Weasel had finally ferried to Hall Farm. Vanessa had clung to her for a long time, but said nothing.

Weasel had told Shelley he was pretty sure he'd seen Tom parked in the Volvo at the top of the hill while the police were sealing the road off. But when he'd run towards the car, Tom had driven away in a hurry.

Shelley had asked Weasel if Vanessa had seen . . . you know.

'Nah, she was in sort of a daze. Just, like, wandered out when I was on the blower to you. Figured Tom was on his way. Dunno where she got that from. Didn't make no sense.'

What Shelley mainly wasn't thinking about was the unspeakable possibility that Vanessa had in some way lured the Tulleys to their deaths. Standing in the middle of the road, Weasel had said, with a lamp. It was inexplicable. She'd never behaved so strangely before. But, then, they'd never left her before, not both of them.

'Mrs Storey,' Meryl said, 'I'm not understanding this about old places.'

The faint Cotswold roll in Meryl's voice was rather more apparent this morning. She also looked less dramatic than last night, in a roll-neck Fair Isle sweater, dusky pink cord jeans, trainers. She looked relaxed. It was clear, in the light of morning, that this was the woman of the house. And of its owner? Oh yes, Shelley thought. To a point.

'It's a sort of allergy,' she said.

Meryl closed the phone book. She was sitting on a hard chair, which placed her above Shelley. 'Mrs Storey,' she said, 'your husband's a very . . . receptive person, isn't he?'

'Shelley. Please call me Shelley.'

'And call him psychic, shall we?'

Shelley sighed in a kind of relief. 'Oh God, yes. Call him psychic if you must. He sees things. You know?'

'Oh yes. I know.' Meryl's eyes were bright. 'Must've been hard for you over the years, Shelley.'

'You can't imagine.' Shelley's eyes closed momentarily.

'Him seeing things and you not. And you not sure whether he was *really* seeing anything at all or whether it was only in his mind.'

'And what do you think?'

'What I think,' said Meryl, 'is that it's partly in the mind and partly not. Mind and spirit. It's a very powerful combination.'

'I wouldn't know.'

'If you don't mind me saying so, Shelley, I think he needs help.'

'Really,' Shelley said coldly.

'The old houses. He's afraid of what he might see in old houses, that right? Because of the extra layers.'

'I suppose so.' What right did this woman have to pry? 'More or less.'

'This is what I find strange. What brought this on? I imagine he hasn't always been like that?'

'No, I . . . There's a history.'

'Thought there might be,' Meryl said. 'You got time to tell me, while Martin's keeping the little girl occupied?'

'I don't . . .'

'I might be able to help.'

Everybody had been saying that. But how could they?

Round about nine, the phone awoke Dave Reilly from a murky sleep.

'Dave, it's Bart at Muthah's. You did collect the guitar, didn't you?'

'The Tak?' Dave's fogged eyes searched the room. 'No, I can't have.'

'Oh, you *did*.'

'I didn't, pal. It'd be here.' He did another thorough inventory of the contents of the bedsit – took maybe three seconds. 'I left it in your office, usual place, in the case, under the desk.'

'Oh, shit,' said Bart. 'They didn't take much else.'

'You're kidding.'

'It's insured, though, isn't it? Fire, theft?'

'Do me a favour.' Dave fumbled for his lighter and the packet of Silk Cut Extra Mild.

'I'm sorry, mate. I'll call the police. See, it wasn't even a break-in. Some bastard must have stayed inside after we closed.'

'Don't bother,' said Dave. They were so bloody careless at Muthah Mirth, complete amateurs. 'When did anybody ever get a stolen guitar back?'

'Can you borrow one for tonight?'

Dave said, 'I don't think I can make it anyway tonight. Something's come up.'

'Hey, now, we had a deal.'

'Yeah, we also had a deal related to overnight storage of that guitar.'

'It should have been bloody well insured, Dave.'

Dave said wearily, 'There are some things you can't insure against.'

'You're gonna let me down again?'

'Again?'

'Yes, Dave. Again.'

Shelley stood up. 'I think I'd like to go home now.'

There was so much more Meryl wanted to ask.

'You've both been very kind,' Shelley said, 'but we can't stay here. What if . . . when Tom comes home.'

'That little chap's at the house, surely? And . . . Well, Tom could be anywhere, couldn't he? Where were you from originally, London?'

'He wouldn't go back to London. He'll stay in the area, until he thinks it's safe.'

'Well,' said Meryl. 'You know your husband.'

But *does* she? Meryl wondered. I was the one shared his vision, not her.

In the vision everybody had been dead, except for Meryl and Tom. Within a short time, the Tulleys *were* dead. Horribly so.

In the early hours, while Martin was showing Shelley and Vanessa to their room, Meryl had taken the little man, Beasley, into the kitchen, got some coffee into him and, out of him, a harrowing description of the inside of the Tulleys' Daimler. When he'd told her, a bit hesitantly, that Lady Tulley had been decapitated, a long shiver had coursed through Meryl like a black waterfall.

It had left her hot and cold. Cold with fear, hot with anticipation.

She had to see him again. The appalling, awesome Tom Storey.

The shaving mirror was bored with Dave.

The shaving mirror had heard it all before, the same old questions.

Why can't I hold on to a guitar?

Why can't I hold down a relationship?

Why can't I write my own songs any more?

Why can't I direct my life?

Why do I have to shelter under other guys' tragedies?

Why can't I make any real money?

Why am I still living in a bloody bedsit?

Why do I keep letting people down?

Why me?

Why does it have to be like this?

The mirror was balanced on a glass shelf over the washbasin in the bedsit. Dave sat on a rickety stool and gazed into it through the smoke from his cigarette and said why, why, why, until it became almost a mantra, the mirror clouded with the smoke and his breath.

And after a while

because you're a useless twat, Dave, the mirror said in a familiar voice, grinding with irony. *You're physically wasted, emotionally stunted, spiritually sterile. Completely fuckin' useless.*

Meryl threw on a scarf and shouldered her black leather shopping bag.

'You're going *shopping*?' Martin was whispering at the door. 'At a time like this?'

A few yards away Vanessa was inspecting Martin's extensive landscaped gardens from the terrace. There was some frost on the ground.

'Life has to go on,' Meryl told him. 'Besides, you'll be all right on your own. That little girl seems to have taken quite a shine to you.'

Knowing he'd be wondering to what extent the little girl's stepmother felt the same way. Martin was a kind man in many respects but would be the last to reject any possible rewards for his altruism.

Meryl said, 'You know what I'd do, if I were you, Martin? I'd ring the police before they show up here. They'll be wanting to establish Sir Wilfrid and Angela's movements leading up to the accident. When they find out the Storeys and the Tulleys were *both* here . . .'

'You're quite right, of course,' said Martin. 'Nothing suspicious, but rather too coincidental. Be simple enough if Storey hadn't buggered off. Yes, you're right, good idea. I'll sort things out with the police. Give them a statement. Keep Shelley well out of it.'

'Of course you will, Martin. And perhaps you could also take Shelley and Vanessa home and stay with them a while. She'll need someone to repair that fence and everything.'

'I can't repair fences.'

No one better at it, Meryl thought, remembering last night, Stephen Case and the Tulleys.

'But you know the people who can,' she said. 'Why don't you make yourself useful?' A knowing smile. 'Will you be lunching out today, Martin?'

'Why, what have *you* got planned?'

'I was going to take my day off, after I've done the shopping. If that's all right with you?'

'Would it matter,' said Martin, good-humouredly, 'if it wasn't?'

He'd learned, where Meryl was concerned, never to push curiosity too far.

Meryl waved to Vanessa and moved swiftly across the frosty drive to her Peugeot, confidence and determination in every step.

*

The other thing people got wrong – these were the people who thought you were bound to be tranquil, serene and in control – was to equate possessing psychic faculties with being in a permanent state of spiritual grace.

There was nothing inherently spiritual about the other five senses, so why should the sixth be a stepping stone to sainthood?

The shaving mirror had heard this one, too.

The shaving mirror knew Dave had never wanted to be a saint anyway.

You are what you are, pal, the mirror said, a little more kindly. *You make of it what you make of it. Or that's what you think, until you realize all you are is what other people've made of you. You spend fuckin' years being what people want you to be. But sooner or later you've got to discover what you're supposed to be, yer know? This is the only way you're gonna live with yourself in the end.*

There were layers of white cloud in the mirror now, condensation upon condensation. Little white clouds which had floated in through the grimy bathroom window and settled in the mirror with the cigarette smoke.

A lot of the time what the mirror said was trite. The mirror was as likely to talk crap as the person looking into it.

And this was the other fallacy. That the messages coming from the mirror (the crystal, the cards, the tealeaves, the fat lady in a trance) were full of wisdom and insight.

Sometimes they sounded clever and evocative, like 'Subterranean Homesick Blues'. You were entertained, you were full of admiration. But were you *enlightened*?

Sometimes they were like *deathoak*, nearly an anagram of The Dakota, but not quite. Were you just too stupid to work out the significance of that spare T? Was it a cross? Think about it: the original crosses on which people were crucified often had no top pieces. In 'The Ballad of John and Yoko', Lennon was worried that the way things were going they were gonna crucify him.

Not both of them. Just him. Crucify *me*. John.

Dave shook his head. You put your mind to it, you could

make anything mean anything. Look at what they'd all done to
Nostradamus.

Ultimately, it was a waste of time. The cosmic joker would
lead you by the nose in ever-decreasing circles. Whatever the
system was, it wasn't a system you could beat. What it came
down to was: you were better off leaving it alone. If it would
leave *you* alone.

Somewhere in Dave's head, somewhere beyond reach, the
mirror was still rambling.

*. . . it's like the Beatles. It was great at first. We were big
novelties . . . all these educated gits prodding us with their fuckin'
intellects . . . 'So fresh, so unspoiled – listen to those delightful
rough, working-class accents.' And we're laughing up our fuckin'
sleeves and wheeling home the money in barrows. But you can only
go on like this for so long, this is the problem, Dave, and then it
becomes like an insult to yourself, to what you could be.*

'Yeh. Well, *I* never wanted to be a professional parody.
Never wanted a secondhand life. Wanted to be a . . . you ready
for this . . . *a creative person*. Figured I could channel it . . . *it*
. . . into art. Only it doesn't work like that, you probably know
that now. It doesn't co-operate. It took me a long time to find
that out, and now I can't cut it any more.'

Dave took hold of the mirror, like grabbing someone by the
lapels. 'Money. That's the only reason I ever got involved. I'm
just earning enough to get by. No big gigs, no festivals, no telly.
Just a crappy little stage act. Where's the harm?'

He heard raucous, contemptuous laughter.

'Of course, that was never a problem for you, was it? Bloody
millionaire at twenty-two. People tried to push you into stuff,
you told them to piss off, in public, and everybody loved you
for it. You were a "rebel". And when it came to it you could
waffle on about peace and love and nobody thought you were
sanctimonious and holier-than-thou or anything, because they
knew that underneath you were a rebel and a bastard, so *that*
was all right.'

He put the mirror back on the shelf but held on to it.
'Money. That's all. Not guilt. Not even about "On A Bad Day".

272

That was justified. Ill-timed, I agree. But justified. *Definitely* no guilt, John.'

No guilt. Sure.

The raucous laughter came again and he realized it was the phone. Startled, he let the mirror fall into the washbasin, where it didn't break. He ran both hands through his damp hair and breathed in long and raggedly.

The phone didn't stop.

He snatched it up. 'Found it, have you?'

'Nah.' A voice like a broken coffee-grinder. 'Me, I can't even remember what I was looking for. And when I find it I'll be too pissed to recognize it.'

'Oh.' Dave collapsed across the bed. 'Prof. I thought you were somebody else.'

'If only. David, I've been making a few inquiries. Woke some people up. Sod 'em, if *I* can't sleep, why should they? Anyway, it seems Russell Hornby, your erstwhile producer, is currently recording a band at the Manor in Oxford.'

'Why should I want to know that?'

'Seemed to me you might want to talk to him about certain tapes and how and why they came to be saved from the inferno.'

'Shit, Prof,' Dave said. 'You're determined to get me involved in this, aren't you?'

'And you aren't involved at all, are you? I mean, you were never there, you nor Tom nor whatsername, Moira . . .'

Moira.

I'm not ready to think about this. Talk to me about Russell Hornby, John Lennon, Aelwyn Breadwinner. Just don't mention Moira.

'You still there, David?'

Don't talk to me about long beaches, cold sea, messages in the sand. Don't talk to me about black bonnets.

'David!'

'Yeh,' he said.

'Pick me up at eleven.'

III

Can This Bastard
See My Aura?

G hosts.
　　The word itself. Whispering it was like creeping through a carpet of soft, damp leaves.

Meryl whispered it as she curved the Peugeot around the traffic island to find the Gloucester road out of Cirencester. It was a bright morning now and brisk rather than cold, for late November. The brightness and the sharp air made her feel comfortably alert, despite so little sleep.

Two and a half hours, to be precise. Meryl had lain down – in her own bedroom, not Martin's – and slept immediately, until it was light. She'd always been a good sleeper. Nothing kept her awake, least of all the Lady Bluefoot.

Least of all the ghosts.

Meryl Coleford, Miss Burns had demanded sternly. *What's this you've got?*

It would always be a paperback of ghost stories. At the school, the teachers had been vaguely disapproving, the other girls curious but always a mite fearful.

Not Meryl.

It's a wonder you can stay awake in class, all the sleepless nights you must have.

I never have sleepless nights, Miss. And I never have any nightmares.

At the church school, in the village where she lived now with Martin, every day had begun with a scripture lesson, and the only words in the Bible Meryl had found inspirational had been

Holy Ghost.

Religion, the way they taught it at school, was very boring. God and his angels were surely supernatural beings, but they might have been members of the parish council for all the charisma allotted to them by these sedate, matronly teachers. And when Meryl had asked the vicar himself how might she *see* God, where might she go to watch an angel and if she spent a whole night by herself in the church would she . . . the vicar had replied: Don't be silly.

She'd always remember that. *Don't be silly*.

But if nobody in the village had ever spotted God or even a solitary angel in the vicinity of the parish church, one or two had certainly seen ghosts of the dead, holy or otherwise. John Westbury, for instance, who was gardener at the Hall, could be persuaded of a summer evening to sit on his upturned barrow, light up his clay pipe and talk of the Lady Bluefoot, an apparition of such glamour and romance that God and the angels seemed, by comparison, terribly ordinary . . . and so distant, whereas She was *here*.

One day, Meryl had told herself, aged twelve, *I'm gonner live at the Hall and me and the Lady Bluefoot's gonner be best friends*.

Well, the Hall itself had been abandoned and become a picturesque ruin by the time Meryl was grown up, but the Hall Farm remained, and this, after all, was where Lord Rendall had lain when they brought his body from the fields and where his lady had seen him first. But although Meryl indeed lived here now and although she'd found a spiritualist church where the supernatural nature of God was not exactly played down, she'd become ever-so-slightly disillusioned. Yes, she *did* like to consider the Lady her best friend now, but it *had* all been rather one-sided, with no great mystical revelations and no . . . actual . . . manifestation.

Until last night.

The reality, the urgency of it, made Meryl grip the steering wheel tightly with both hands.

It had been a hard, harsh lesson. Revelation had come not with a soft and scented vaporous thing in blue shoes, but with the hideous vision of a man with a hole in his face who had shown to her the future – or, at least, the short-term future of Sir Wilfrid and Lady Tulley.

And the future of Stephen Case?

And of Martin and Shelley Storey?

In the white-hot exhilaration of having *seen*, Meryl had put to the back of her mind the sight of the other bloodied bodies around the table.

But as she drove, she thought, *Surely the future is not written in stone, else why should anyone be sent such a clear precognitive experience?*

Should she so eagerly have sent Martin off with Shelley Storey, in whose bloody breast his head had been buried, just to get him out of the way so she could pursue her own quest? Should she not have warned him, in the interests of his own survival, to forget Mrs Storey and her magnificent mammaries?

Meryl was in no doubt of the extent of her power over Martin; she was certainly of more lasting value to him than an hour or two with Shelley's nipples in his ears. He would listen to her. But she must be surer of her ground.

The way had been opened for her. She must follow it as far as it led.

Oh Lord, if only . . .

About eleven miles out of Cirencester, Meryl's heart lurched at the sight of a red and white flag against the light-brown of distant hills, a little man with a tall white hat and a frying pan.

She pulled into the forecourt of the Little Chef, past the garage, to a long, low building with a big sign:

TRAVELODGE.

There'd been a Little Chef on this road for years, but the motel part was new, had been open for barely three months. Meryl held her breath as she slid the Fiesta slowly towards a small group of parked cars and

Oh my Lord

one was a dusty, dark blue Volvo estate, obviously parked in a hurry, hopelessly askew and straddling a white dividing-line so you couldn't see whether it was outside apartment nine or apartment eleven.

Oh. This was almost uncanny. She'd *known*.

Meryl sat for several minutes, trembling at the sudden precision of her intuition. Had proximity to *him* brought this about? She felt suddenly quite nervous. He was a temperamental man, by all accounts. As well he might be with his peculiar talents.

Then, 'Come along, girl,' she said aloud. Switching off the engine and shouldering her door open, she gathered up her bag and her resolve and went to hammer on the door of number eleven.

At the Manor Studio in rural Oxfordshire, quite a few people recognized Prof Levin.

'Blimey, Prof,' an engineer said. 'Must be a fair while since you last showed your face here. Branson himself still around, was he?'

'Branson was just a kid,' said Prof. 'But it ain't changed, has it?'

'I'll see if I can find Russell for you,' the studio manager said. She didn't know Prof; too young. 'He's here somewhere. That's his car, if you'd like to go and have a worship.'

'Stone me.' Prof stared at the bronze monster under the trees. 'That's a . . . a whatsit.'

'Rolls-Royce Corniche,' Dave said. 'Makes you wonder.'

'I heard he was doing all right for himself. I didn't realize it was this much all right.'

'Whether it's made him happy,' the manager said drily, 'is debatable. Look, maybe he's not up yet. They were recording until about three this morning.'

'No hurry,' Prof said. 'We'll have a wander around, see what's new.'

The Manor was a real manor, a mellow fifteenth-century house in fifty acres at Shipton, a few miles outside Oxford. The studio was in the barn; the musicians slept in the house, in luxury rooms with round-the-clock service. There was a swimming-pool and a tennis court. The sun shone.

Dave had never been before. It made him feel nostalgic for all the albums he'd never made.

'The Abbey, it's not.' He was looking up at a brass chandelier and a mural depicting Richard Branson, founder of the studio, and Mike Oldfield and their mates, all in medieval costume. The romance of yesteryear – the early seventies, this would be.

'EMI own the place now,' Prof said. 'If there's a TMM connection, I don't know about it. But anybody can hire the Manor, if they've got the loot.'

On the way here, Dave driving, Prof had told him everything: about the box under the late Max Goff's bed, about the baking of the tapes and the chaos at Audico. Was that likely? Could mouldy recording tape do that? Was Prof going mad? Was Maurice of Audico losing his marbles? Did this tape, once listened to, ever go away?

You're talking about energies, Dave had said. Who can say?

And what about the woman's voice? What about the tape coming out of the oven, freezing cold? Was that kind of business inside Dave's experience?

Dave had nodded. Maybe. Hadn't elaborated.

Prof had laughed. He said that in tracking down Russell Hornby this morning one of the people he'd called up was Maurice at Audico and the last thing Maurice had said was: Listen, the other day, I was overwrought. I was talking out of the seat of my trousers. We'd had a break in, I was confused, I was angry. Disregard it. I'm sorry. Forget about it.

And Dave had smiled nervously. People did get deluded, he'd said, thinking – hoping – me too.

He and Prof walked out into the grounds, the house behind them, the lawn overhung by this huge and ancient tree, bare branches moving like a blurred photograph of juggling hands.

Dave's breathing became unsteady.

Prof noticed. 'Somebody walk over your grave?'

'Tom Storey wouldn't even have come here. Tom didn't like old places.'

'Why not?'

278

'Energies.'

'That's a useful word, David. What's it mean really?'

'Come on,' Dave said. 'Let's go back.'

Thinking, I'm cracking up. This is the Manor. This is a *different studio*.

The manager was waiting for them at the door to the kitchens. Russell, it seemed, was having breakfast.

'It's half-past bloody one,' Prof protested.

'He says – let me get this right – that you should have rung first, that he can't offer you any work. But if you won't go away, can he see you at the Crown in an hour?'

'That a pub?' Dave cast a worried glance at Prof.

'How far's the Crown?' Prof asked.

'Couple of miles.'

'OK,' said Prof. 'We'll do that. You didn't say I'd got Dave with me?'

'Who's Dave?'

'Good,' Prof said.

In the pub, waiting for Russell Hornby, Prof drinking draught Guinness and a single whisky, Dave looked deeply into his orange juice.

'That's a good question,' he said.

The pub was quiet. Prof had settled back with his drinks in a window seat and asked, 'What's it like, Dave, being you?'

'In fact,' Dave said, 'it's the first time anybody's ever asked me that. With the band, we knew instinctively where the others were at.'

'I don't mean the band. I mean you.'

It wasn't an old pub. The beams on the ceiling were painted shiny black or varnished. The chairs were vinyl-covered. There were gaming machines and a pool table. Dave had said that Tom Storey would probably be OK in here. Clearly not so sure about Prof, who'd thought, sod it, this encounter demands alcohol.

'You serious, Prof? You seriously want to know what it's like?'

'I'm too old to piss around with questions I don't expect an answer to.'

'What's it like being me?' Dave drank some orange juice. 'I should say it's a nightmare. But it's not a nightmare all the time. Or maybe it's no more of a nightmare than anybody's life, I wouldn't know. Until I was about twelve I thought everybody was like this.'

'Like what?'

'I had this quite promising thing going until very recently.' Dave unwrapped a packet of Silk Cut, looking gloomy. 'I started smoking again when I got in last night. Packed in for a whole week once. You don't mind secondary smoking, Prof?'

'More satisfying than secondary drinking.' Prof drained his whisky. 'What thing was this you had going?'

'Teacher. Actively left-wing, committed atheist. Good fun, really. She did a lot of living for the moment. We lived together for six months, for the moments.'

'I like it,' Prof said.

'It's funny, you get into a situation like that, it absorbs you so much that this other . . . aspect of you . . . can go into remission for weeks at a time. Like a good holiday. You're thinking, shit, life really is simple, why've I been messing about in the shallows all these years, not getting close to anyone?'

Prof watched Dave light up a cigarette, glancing from side to side, like a schoolboy behind the bike-sheds. Ludicrously, Dave still looked too young to be smoking.

'And then, Prof, she had to go and introduce me to her sister.'

'What, you fancied the sister?'

Dave laughed and choked on his own smoke. Nothing so easy as that, then. Prof waited.

'It was in a pub,' Dave said, 'pretty much like this one, near Southport. We had a table, like this one, except the place was more crowded. The sister comes in through the top door, spots us, waves and starts walking towards us. I couldn't tell you now what she looked like, how old she was, whether she was slim or curvaceous or what. All I could see was this black and red haze around her head. Shimmering. With, like, a light of its own. Only it's a dark light. And something inside her is feeding it, feeding the light.'

Prof felt chilled, as if a shadow had fallen across their table. He said tentatively, 'That's what they call an aura, right?'

'Who gives a shit what they call it, one like this is bad news. I've been seeing them on and off since I was a kid. Used to see pretty ones when I was young, light blues. One of my earliest memories, me ma on her birthday, with blue light coming off her.'

Why did you have to ask, Prof thought. Why'd you have to bloody well ask?

Dave was talking about his formative years. Nineteen sixty-seven, the Summer of Love. He'd been too young to know much about love, but, wow, all those psychedelic colours, the op-art mandalas . . . and the music. Wonderful, inspiring music. Years later before he understood most of it had been down to LSD and stuff. He'd thought it was a great psychic explosion, everybody realizing their true potential. Suddenly Dave Reilly was no longer a freak.

'It was more than drugs, David,' Prof said sadly. 'There was something in the air that ain't there any more.'

Maybe, Dave conceded. This had been when he first thought he could perhaps use his . . . *sensitivity* . . . to find new colours, go in search of the lost chord, all that stuff. By the time he was twenty-one he'd been in about four bands, each one weirder than the last. But, of course, punk rock had arrived then, and all that acid stuff was way out of line. Not that Dave was using anything – who needed it when your whole life was like an intermittent acid-trip? And he was still under the illusion he could make something of it ten years later, when he answered Epidemic's box-numbered small-ad in the *Melody Maker*.

'Ad? That was how it started? He placed an ad?'

Dave nodded. 'Straightforward as that. And when I finally got in to see him, Max Goff said' – Dave put on an Australian accent – '"How do I know you're the real McCoy, how do I know you're not shitting me?"'

Dave stubbed out his Silk Cut.

'So I looked at him, this big fat bastard smoking a cheroot, and his . . . light . . . was in two halves, one blue, one orangey-red, like the wires inside a plug. I'd never seen this before, I don't think it's in the rule-book. It was about ten a.m., he hadn't been up long, he was looking very pleased with himself. I looked at him, I didn't even think about it, I just said, "The girl sleeps on that side and the boy's on *that* side, right?" And then got up to leave before he could throw me out.'

Dave finished off his orange juice. 'Ten minutes later he was having a contract drawn up.'

'A small-ad in the *MM*,' Prof said. 'Blatant as that. Stone me.'

'Wanted: musicians of proven psychic ability. Box number. He had over fifty replies. The way it turned out, I was the only eventual member of the band who was one of those who actually answered the advert. He got the others by reputation, word of mouth. Starting with Tom, who was going through a fairly excitable phase, all kinds of tales circulating. Goff got him out of some sort of trouble, Tom being the original destroyer of hotel rooms. Threw a lot of people downstairs.'

'Those were the days,' Prof said absently. He was wondering, horrified, *Can this bastard see my aura?* Prof didn't like to think what colour his aura might be. He wished he was somewhere else.

Dave looked up with a sheepish grin. 'You're all right, Prof, it doesn't seem to work with mates, people I know well. At least . . . least, it never has. Up to now.'

Dave bit down on his lower lip. Some problem here.

'Never occurred to me,' Prof said gruffly. 'What happened about that girl? In the pub.'

Dave sighed. 'It's just a fleeting thing. You see somebody, usually for the first time, and it's like when you've been lying in the sun and you open your eyes. A black smudge. Then you rub your eyes and it's gone. Jan's sister. Yeh. I said to Jan that night, how long has Sara been ill? Jan says, what are you on about, she's not *ill*. I say, maybe she should go and have a check-up. Ooooh *God*. She was a card-carrying atheist. Beat me into a corner with psychology and logic.'

Prof said, 'I don't think I'm gonna ask you what happened to the sister.'

'Thanks,' Dave said.

'How often does this happen, David? How often do you see it?'

Dave sighed. 'I thought you'd have got the picture. When I was younger, I used to see auras in all the damn colours of the rainbow – OK, including the dark ones. On occasion. That is, sometimes I'd see them faintly discoloured, kind of going off, and I could say to whoever it was, are you feeling OK? And it – you know – it would sometimes be good advice, it would help them. They'd go to the doc or some natural healer or maybe just take a holiday or get a few early nights in. You do this – somebody tells you you don't look well, it makes you think about the way you're living. And the next time I'd see them their colour would be lighter. I still don't *like* all this, it was a bit of a bloody cross to bear, but the times you helped somebody made it bearable.'

Prof nodded at the window. A Rolls-Royce Corniche was pulling in, at once dominating the pub forecourt. 'Sorry,' Prof said. 'Go on.'

'But after the Abbey, it all changed,' Dave said. 'After Lennon, after Deborah, increasingly I stopped seeing variations. I just saw the darkest ones.'

'Oh my Christ,' said Prof.

'The ones where it's too late.'

Prof stared at him in horror. Is this real? *Can I believe any of this? Is this guy sick?*

'The Abbey changed everything. It wasn't obvious at first, it's happened over years, but that's when it began. I drove away from the Abbey, booked into a hotel for the night, near Cheltenham, came down to breakfast the following morning and there were four people in the room with, like, black bonnets on.'

'Shut up,' Prof said. 'For Christ's sake shut up.'

'There's a major hospital, you see, at Cheltenham, where . . .'

'David, this is the worst thing I've ever heard.'

Prof thought, *He looks so innocent, he looks so normal, so affable, he's hardly got a line on his face.*

'Now you know what an Angel of Death looks like,' Dave said, and smiled a truly sickly smile.

IV

End of Story

The door of chalet eleven was opened by a cleaner, a young woman with a plastic sack.

'I'm sorry, sir, I really am going as fast as I can . . . Oh.'

Meryl said, 'I'm looking for a gentleman.'

'I'm so sorry.' The cleaner looked flustered. 'I thought you was him back again. I said to him, I have to get this place cleaned by eleven. He says he don't want it cleaned, go away. Go away, he says.'

'Oh dear,' Meryl said.

Found him.

'And he's on his own, too, I know that, not as if . . . Anyway, he said he'd let me have ten minutes, but he's been back twice already. I'm not used to this, most people are gone by nine.'

Meryl smiled. 'He's been under a lot of pressure lately. You carry on, I'll see if I can head him off.'

The cleaner gratefully vanished back inside. Meryl heard a vacuum start up.

Now. Where?

On the other side of the Little Chef was a filling-station bordering the main road, open fields beyond it. A line of leafless poplars marked the perimeter. To Meryl as a child, the poplars would have looked like a fleet of witches' brooms lined up for a night mission. The older she got, the more she wished poplars *were* symbolic of supernatural transport. It was important to Meryl to be able to look out at the world and think, *There's more here than I can see.*

'You come here to hassle me, lady, you can piss off now,' Tom Storey said.

As soon as Russell Hornby had come through the door, Dave had taken himself off to the bar, to do what he'd said he wouldn't do again, which was to buy Prof Levin an alcoholic drink. He guessed Prof would appear sober for a long time before there was a problem. But when it happened, it would be a real problem.

When Russell strolled over to Prof's table and sat down, Dave felt Time's primitive gear-lever crunch jarringly into reverse.

Because Russell looked exactly the same. Spindly frame in denims, shaven head. *Let's become calm*, he used to say, wandering into their asylum.

Dave moved over to the table, facing Prof, behind Russell. He set down Prof's pint of Guinness. 'Afraid they're clean out of whisky chasers, Prof. What's yours, Russell?'

When Russell turned and saw him, the great gear lever lurched into neutral. There *had* been a change.

Not a pound of extra weight on him, not many more wrinkles. It was, if anything, Dave thought, his eyes. His eyes were so much older, had seen too much. And when they arrived on Dave, the eyes flared with . . . what? Extreme wariness?

'Thank you very much, David,' Prof said, glaring into his Guinness. 'I'll purchase my own flaming poison.'

Dave said, 'Still dry white, is it, Russell? Or are we into mineral water these days?'

'Dave Reilly,' Russell said quietly. 'What an excellent surprise.'

'Clearly.'

Russell said, 'What's this about?'

Prof said, 'Dave and me had something to ask you.'

Russell's lips twitched. 'And you couldn't have phoned?'

'We could have sent you a postcard.' Dave sat down. 'But we thought this would be cosier.'

'What's this band you're working with then, Russ?' Prof dredged Guinness froth out of his beard.

'Mice. Bunch of precocious brats.'

'Never heard of 'em.'

'Nobody's heard of anybody these days,' Russell said wearily, hardly moving his lips. 'Yeah, OK, dry white.'

'I'll get it.' Prof was up before Dave could move. Would return, of course, with a whisky for himself.

'But you're doing well,' Dave said. 'You're keeping busy. Nice car.'

'Sure.' Russell wasn't looking at him.

'Do much for TMM?'

'This and that.'

Russell gave him a sidelong glance. 'What is this, Dave?'

'It's a question. TMM, who, as you know, have acquired the Epidemic back-catalogue, have apparently discovered a missing gem.'

'Good for them.'

'Not in the archives, as such, but under the late Max Goff's bed, along with the whips and handcuffs and things.'

Russell's time-hardened eyes narrowed.

Dave said, 'This is the master of an album including, among other, possibly more intriguing items, the last known recorded works of the reclusive genius Tom Storey.'

Russell said, 'I've had nothing to do with this. Believe it.'

'Nothing to do with what?'

'Anything. Any of it.' Russell stood up suddenly. 'I'm sorry. I have no more time.'

A hand came down on his shoulder. 'Course you have, Russell,' Prof Levin said.

Tom Storey said, 'How I hate the fucking countryside.'

He was leaning against the dusty Volvo. He looked awful, still in last night's clothes, except for the tie. White stubble among the veins on his cheeks.

'Why do you live here, then?' Meryl asked him.

'I don't live in the countryside, as such,' Tom said. 'I live in a house. *Used* to live in a house. It's useless now.'

'I don't think so. The car went into the fence, that's all.

'It's destroyed,' Tom said. 'It's ruptured. The stupid old gits went frew the fence and they died there. They bust me wide open.' He turned his head away impatiently. 'What's the fucking use telling *you* this?'

'No . . . please.' Meryl reached out hesitantly and touched his arm. 'Give me time. Let me think about it.'

Tom shook his head. His moustache drooped. His yellow-white hair hung down like a lampshade. The sun had gone in; it was starting to feel like November again.

'In one respect,' Meryl said slowly, 'I should've thought the countryside'd be better for you. Not so many vibrations as the city, and slower.'

Tom said nothing. He'd come up behind her on the car park, big and menacing, but she could feel his nerves vibrating in the air. What she had to do now was persuade him, somehow, that she hadn't been sent here to bring him back.

'They say your house was built with all new materials. And no trees around it, just a fence. I'm truly thinking here, Mr Storey, I'm doing my best. If that fence marks the perimeter of the area you've had protected, then if something smashes that barrier . . .'

Tom's head turned slowly back towards her.

'And, if, in smashing that barrier, somebody died . . . ? Would that mean, their spirit . . . ?'

Tom said, 'You don't know nuffink.'

'I think I do.'

'You didn't know nuffink last night. You didn't see nuffink. You kept well shtumm, lady.'

'I'm sorry about that,' Meryl said. 'Nothing quite like that had ever happened to me before. I didn't know how to react. That's why I'm here. I've come to . . . apologize, I suppose.'

'Apology accepted,' Tom said. 'Now piss off and leave me alone.'

The chalet door, number eleven, was propped open and the

young woman came out with her vacuum cleaner and her black bin-sack. She gave Tom and Meryl a tiny smile and moved on to number nine.

'I'd really like to talk to you, Tom,' Meryl said. 'Can we go inside?'

'*I'm* going inside, you're leaving, and you're gonna forget you saw me, or else . . .' Tom raised his arms like a cartoon spook '. . . I'll make your nights miserable, I will.'

Meryl didn't move. She was quite unnerved but couldn't let him see that. She looked him steadily in the eyes. 'I believe you could, too. But I don't think you would.'

'Nah,' Tom said glumly. 'I'm frew wiv all that. Mug's game. Comes back on you. You wanna leave all that shit alone. You're too old.'

Meryl's spine stiffened.

'What I mean is,' Tom said hurriedly, 'is it's for kids.'

'I hope so.'

'Fuck it,' Tom said. 'I'm screwed. I ain't got a home no more. Let's go in, make some tea.'

'Look,' Russell said. 'I'm sorry. I got some clean tapes, scruffed them up a bit, changed the labels, gave them to Simon. I'm sorry, but it's very much against my religion, burning work-in-progress. Some bands are crazy, get stoned or blind pissed. Some of the old punk bands, they'd grab a reel, go outside and wind the tape twice around the bloody building, just for the hell of it. I'm paid to produce a record, end of the week I serve up the goods.'

Dave thought it was exactly the kind of explanation you would expect. If he'd been writing Russell's script this was what he'd have come up with. Which didn't *necessarily* mean it was a lie.

Prof said, 'What happened next? What did you do with the tapes?'

Russell relaxed, spread his arms behind his head, stretched, yawned; this one was easier. 'Turned them over to Max. He called me up, I told him what I'd done. He said to bring him the tapes, which I did. He took them off me, no explanation, told me to forget all about it. End of story.'

'Not so.' Prof leaned forward. 'As I understand it, Russell, Steve Case, of the TMM recording conglomerate, has plans to release this album. What do we know about this?'

'Nothing,' Russell said. 'Those tapes are a hopeless mish-mash. They don't make any sense. That album's ever released, it better not have my name on it, that's all I can say.'

'You're telling us you haven't heard from Case?'

Russell's eyes went wary again. 'I didn't say that.'

'Shit, Russell, we got to hire you by the hour to get some coherent facts?'

'I think you should hear this from Case, is all I'm saying.'

'Case and me are not speaking,' Prof said. 'We've had words.'

'OK,' Russell said. 'I'll be brief, because I really do have to get back to the Manor before the children wake up. Case called me last week and asked me if I'd be interested in completing my contract. After we'd gone through all the what-the-hell-is-this-about stuff, he said he thought it was potentially a brilliant album and he wanted the Philosopher's Stone to go back into the studio with me and finish it.'

There was silence. Russell leaned his chair back and smiled sweetly.

'Shiiiiit,' Dave breathed.

'I said, you must be joking,' Russell said. 'Do I look like a man who's desperate for money?'

'What did he say?'

'He said either you do it or you don't, but if you want to work with us again, you keep quiet about this. Which is what I was trying to do until you guys turned nasty.'

Dave drank some of Prof's whisky chaser and choked. 'Serves you fucking right,' Prof said.

'He wants us to go *back*? To the Abbey?'

'Well, there's a turn-up.' Prof snatched his glass back, swallowed the lot, began to laugh and then sing hoarsely,

290

'Fourteen years since you heard the news, your last chance to beat the Dakota Blues.'

'I'd be very grateful, guys,' Russell said, 'if you didn't go blabbing this around. It certainly can't be a short-term proposition, that place is derelict.'

'Yeah,' Prof said. 'I bet. Ever since Soup Kitchen, right?'

Russell, unsmiling, stood up. 'Right,' he said tightly. 'That's it. Thanks for the drink, guys.'

Sometimes Mrs Marina Edwards worried about Eddie.

Always so *enthusiastic*. She'd found, quite early in their life together, that the one thing you must never do was offer to help him with one of his hobbies. He'd assume you were actually *interested*. Tiring? Well. She felt exhausted just remembering the cycling phase, the quest for otters on a tributary of the Usk which went on for about eight miles, the search for the foundations of Owain Glyndwr's lost palace.

Nowadays, the words 'What's that you've got there?' seldom passed her lips. She sang in the choir, attended the WI, went shopping in Ross and Monmouth in her little Renault and left him to it, whatever it was.

But worried sometimes. You couldn't avoid that.

Especially when there were phone calls like this one while he was out.

'Where is he, then?'

'Went off with the vicar, I think, to Abergavenny. Said he wouldn't be back for lunch.'

'Shit.'

'I beg your pardon!'

'Look, I'm sorry, could you get him to ring me as soon as he comes in. At work or at home. But absolutely as soon as he gets back.'

'Well, who shall I say . . .'

'Sorry, yes, Ivor Speed. Dr Speed in Swansea. Tell him we're probably looking at a police matter.'

'Oh heavens,' said Marina.

V

Curse of the Witchy Woman

'**I** gave your name, by the way,' she said, 'as next of kin.'

She thought Malcolm Kaufmann might have looked less horrified on being told he'd been nominated for a charity bungee jump from the Forth Bridge.

'The Infirmary tell me you discharged yourself entirely against medical advice. And appearing to be still in shock. I cannot but agree.' Malcolm buzzed his secretary. 'A black coffee for Moira, please, Fiona.'

'What d'you have that thing for anyway? The kid works the whole time with an ear to the wall. Two sugars, Fiona, please! Jesus, would you mind if I stood up? I'm finding it a wee bit hard getting myself comfortable.'

'Moira . . .' In some anguish, Malcolm ran both hands through his light tan hair. 'Not only are you probably clinically insane, I don't think you're even my client any more.'

'Client?' She went and stood over by the filing cabinet. She was wearing this outsize, pastel blue fluffy sweater – mainstay of the *normal woman's wardrobe* – pulled down to near knee-level to hide the terrible mess she and the ambulance team had made of her jeans, getting them off. It was true that she was getting past the age when she could look like this and it would be rather fetching.

'Malcolm,' she said, in a small voice but precise. 'If it'd make you feel better, I'd gladly surrender ten per cent of the first-degree burns, but it would be quite nice if for just a few minutes you could see your way to assuming the role of mere friend.'

'I'm sorry.' Malcolm Kaufmann closed his desk diary, took the phone off the hook. 'Sit down. Or rather, do go on standing up, if that helps.' He pushed his chair back, smoothed his hair. 'Tell me ex-actly what happened.'

Where to begin? A wee lecture on metaphysics?

'Exactly,' she told him tiredly, 'is what I haven't precisely figured out. In plain, physical terms, a hotel kettle malfunctioned. I had hold of the flex at the time. I pulled the kettle on top of me. The lid came off. About a pint and a half of boiling water gushed over my milky-white thighs.'

Malcolm recoiled.

'Actually, I was wearing these jeans at the time. That probably made it worse. Whatever . . .' She wrinkled her nose. 'Blistering, and stuff. I won't give you details. Suffice to say . . .'

She tried for a grin; it didn't happen.

'. . . No intimate relations for wee Moira for *quite* some time.'

'You appear to have a charmed life,' Malcolm said soberly, 'in reverse. What did you do?'

'This is the Clydeview Private Hotel. What *could* I do? I ran to the *en suite*, which was about half a mile down the fucking corridor, gave myself a cold shower and screamed the place down.'

Malcolm was quiet for a surprising while.

'The Clydeview Private Hotel,' he said at last. 'We both know you could be earning enough to *buy* the Clydeview Private Hotel. What offends me the most is the thought that one day, perhaps not so far into the future, you will be generally regarded as a Tragic Case.'

Moira scowled, said she was awful sorry if anyone had seen her coming into his establishment in this condition, but when you discharged yourself in a hurry you were obliged to leave in the clothes they cut off you in the ambulance.

'Give Fiona your size,' Malcolm said at once. 'And I'll send her to Marks and Spencer. You can't go home like that.'

'I can't go home at all,' Moira said dismally. 'This is the real tragedy.'

*

Eddie Edwards had to sit down afterwards. He was feeling almost faint.

This was altogether beyond comprehension.

Ivor Speed had said to him that if they didn't put that piece of candle very rapidly into the hands of the police, both he and the University of Wales could be in very serious trouble.

Ivor Speed was not being humorous.

Eddie had asked him, his voice failing, 'Can you be sure of this?'

'Well, no, it's too early to say that. We may *never* be able to confirm it. But it's a strong and plausible possibility. Most candles today are made of this petroleum-based stuff or beeswax, if you can afford it. Old-fashioned tallow, now, that was bovine or sheep fat. Which we thought it was at first. Goes brown with age and oxidization, which partly explains the colour and the consistency. Although there were also traces of powdered charcoal here. And, er, possibly blood. We can't say for *sure* that it's human fat, but it's certainly consistent with the properties thereof. Where the hell did you find the dreadful thing?'

'Well, I . . . I'm not sure I should say,' Eddie stammered. 'I would need to talk to someone about it.'

'You need to talk to the police, boy, and fast.'

'Well, look . . . suppose it's hundreds of years old. That's not going to start a manhunt, is it?'

'Unlikely. It might look old, but it isn't. Probably. My chap reckons it's no more than a year or two or three since that stuff was wobbling about on somebody's midriff.'

'Oh, good God.'

'Get it to the police, Eddie. Look, I'll tell you what I'll do. There's a senior policeman I know in Gwent who isn't going to overreact and haul you into the station. Not in the short term. Not if I tell him about you. I'll ring him, OK?'

And the police would say: What made you think to send this candle for analysis?

Because it seemed so strange and old, so redolent of dark mystery, that's the only reason. Because, in forty years of being unable to pass a sign that says Museum, I have never seen its like before.

And because of the way the vicar reacted.

Was he going to tell the police that? No, he was not. He could not drop the vicar in it. But, by Christ, he was going to use this to get some answers out of that chap before the law was upon them.

Human fat? And recent? It was the 'recent' element which made the mind reel. The implications were clear. Much of Eddie Edwards's work as an adviser to schools had been angled on social history, especially for primary establishments and the less academically able streams at secondary level. Talk to youngsters about witchcraft and the like and you had their full attention, so yes, Eddie Edwards knew full well the significance of candles made with human grease.

But who? Who would burn a human body until the fatty tissue melted and collect it and mould it into a tube with a wick down the middle? And where would they acquire such a thing as a body without committing . . .

murder?

And *how had the candles been installed unnoticed*? The church was right in the centre of a very small, fairly remote community. Strangers going in and out were observed. Cars arriving late at night were noted. There were some very, very nosy people in this village, speaking as one of them and not ashamed to confess it. So how did whoever it was bring the candles into the church, unless it was someone with a right to be there?

And why? Why the little parish church of St Mary at Ystrad Ddu when, if they wanted to carry out some nauseous, heathen ceremony, there were so many comparatively isolated churches in this area . . . old, ruined churches, even.

Why not the Abbey?

He saw Marina watching him from the kitchen door, the question And What Have You Been Getting Into Now? written across her placid features.

'No problems, my love,' he said. 'Just a little something to sort out with the vicar.'

He couldn't but look embarrassed. Normally, the thought that he was with the vicar should be a comfort. In this case, perhaps quite the opposite.

'Listen to me,' Malcolm Kaufmann said. 'Don't talk. Don't throw anything at me. Just drink your coffee and listen.'

And Malcolm went on for a good while about her career as a singer and a songwriter; how it wasn't too late, how – with her distinctive presence . . . yes, *presence* – she might even wish to consider a little acting. The bottom line being that in whichever direction she wished to turn there were many and varied possibilities.

For a while.

'Until whichever goes first,' Moira said, 'my looks or my mind, right? Listen, do you know why I had to get out of the Infirmary? Because I was causing distress to the other sick folk on the casualty ward.'

Nurses waking her none too gently in the middle of the night, an old lady near-hysterical. *Make her stop. Tell her we don't want to hear about it. This is a hospital ward, tell her we don't want to hear about death!*

'Bad dreams,' Moira said. 'Another night like that and I wouldn't have extricated myself so easily. Be getting a discreet transfer to the divisional psychiatric unit.'

'Have you money?'

'A few grand in the Bank of Scotland, and a croft house I'm scared to go back to. See, I thought it was the island protecting me, Malcolm. I was wrong. It was the Duchess. I've been wrong about a lot.'

'Protecting you from what?' Malcolm was just this side of beating his head in exasperation. He was a showbiz agent, for God's sake. 'Is it this Dave Reilly?'

'Och, no.' This was getting neither of them anywhere. She was just grateful for the coffee and someone's filing cabinet to lean on. 'Let's just call it the Curse of the Witchy Woman.'

'I'm simply not buying it this time,' Malcolm said. 'Is this

296

anything to do with the TMM letter? Is that what's brought all this back?'

'Maybe. Partly. Maybe that's another symptom.'

'OK.' Malcolm picked up his phone, pressed the button to reclaim the line. 'Why don't you ring them now? Find out what they want?'

He held the phone out to her. She shrank away from it, shaking her head.

Malcolm didn't say anything; just sat there holding out the phone like some aborigine witch-doctor pointing the bone.

'I can't.'

'I would normally never think of applying a tin opener to someone else's can of worms,' Malcolm said. 'But if you don't phone them, I shall.'

The vicar of Ystrad Ddu choked back the sob which had become like an habitual cough. Pulled on his boots and his waterproof jacket.

Then, angrily, he flung the jacket off. He wanted to be cold. He wanted to be wet. He wanted to walk out there and die of exposure.

He strode out of the vicarage, leaving the front door unlocked, crossed the road to the church and followed, under a dishwater sky, the path curving around the churchyard to the great cleft rock.

Truth was, he'd wanted to sleep, but had been afraid to. Even in daylight. That was the truth.

Afraid of waking up again, sticky in the waxy darkness, throat full of grease and self-hatred, and the Bible on the floor. He could go to bed clutching the Bible and all it symbolized to his chest, and something inside him – so deep inside that it was now beyond his grasp – would oh-so-casually tip the good book physically and symbolically into the waiting darkness.

And release his devil.

Had he, therefore, answered the question which had brought

him here, made him apply for a post he didn't want in a place he'd never wanted to see again?

Is it in this place? Or is it inside me?

Swathes of rain swept up the valley as Simon veered from the winding path. He stood on a narrow ledge at the bottom of the cloven rock, the tree-strewn hill behind him sloping steeply to the churchyard.

He hesitated. A test beckoned. His breath quickened with anticipation and the promise of fear. Then he put his hands on the stone, started pulling himself up the side of the rock towards the cleft.

Simon was mindlessly angry. He hated his body, distrusted his soul.

He had no head for heights.

The rock was wet, slimed with moss and lichen.

Twice, he glared defiantly down between his legs, revelling in the awesome terror. The main part of the church roof was between his knees, about a hundred feet below. When he arrived here he'd been glad the church had no tower; vertigo would grab him in belfries, like having a coat thrown over his head and his arms seized and his body spun round and round.

Simon started to laugh aloud with the perverse joy of fear. This was what it had come to: if it wasn't perverse, it was without pleasure.

His intention had been to climb up until he could see the Holy Mountain, the Skirrid. To hold out his hands to it, draw in the emanations like a truth drug.

He'd have come directly up here first thing this morning if well-meaning Eddie Edwards hadn't turned up at eight-thirty, determined to haul him off to Abergavenny. Eddie was a force of nature. And, besides, *that* might have been divine intervention, he might have experienced a moment of revelation in the ruins of Abergavenny Castle, where Aelwyn had witnessed the unspeakable.

Aelwyn *Breuddwydiwr*. The dreamer. And not the only one, if Simon was expecting divine intervention.

He climbed on, carelessly. A piece of rock was torn off by

his left boot, and the boot took a savage, lunging step down towards the distant church slates, dragging his left hand from the rock, his right hand grabbing instinctively, just in time, at the outsprung root of a stunted rowan tree, while his mind was screaming for his body to be free of all this.

It left him hanging gloriously in space, intoxicated with the knowledge that certain death was simply a matter of relaxing his fingers.

I'm going to fucking do it, he decided. I'm really going to let go.

Far below him, a van crawled like a beetle up the village lane, and the church roof began to see-saw.

A blast of wind took him in the stomach. The tree root began to split. He saw his broken body supine amid broken slates across the spine of the roof.

His arm began to ache. He looked up. The rowan tree was growing out of the middle of the great cleft, clinging like him to the rock. But the tree had to go on clinging until some gale uprooted it, and he'd simply made the decision to let go, the mind committing the body to the air.

'Last chance!' He felt his face contort, his teeth bared like a wolf's. 'Tell me. *Is it the Abbey or is it me? Tell me, damn you!*'

The root snapped.

VI

Like a Dog Turd

Tom Storey started to laugh.

He was sprawled on the double bed, hands behind his head. Meryl sat upright on a padded stool alongside the fitted dressing-table unit, her hands in her lap. She didn't much like the laughter, but it was an improvement on his belligerence outside.

Tom said, 'When I was wiv Sile Copesake's band – sixtynine, seventy, this'd be – the motel was still quite a new fing in this country, not many around, you know? But Sile, he knew where to find 'em.'

Tom sank his chin into his chest. He'd taken off his jacket and his shirt to expose a grey vest with holes in it and a small, forlorn tattoo just below his right shoulder: *DEBS*, in a blue heart.

'See, in those days, hotels was still a bit prudish. Band shows up after a gig, one lady apiece, fine – they could be your wives or your regulars. Two ladies, difficult. *Free . . .* well . . .'

Meryl smiled. She was almost touched to think that this man thought he could shock her.

'Now Sile,' Tom said. 'Some nights, he'd want four.'

'Greedy,' Meryl said calmly.

'Yeah. Suppose it was, really. But you got to remember this was his heyday. He'd done his time, twenty years of it, seen kids he'd taught to play turning into superstars while he's still slogging round the clubs. Here he is, 1970, forty years old, blues is back, Sile's at the centre. He knows it ain't gonna last; he wants his share.'

'Sad, really.' Meryl was trying to remember who Sile Copesake had been.

'Yeah, it was. Sad. But the point I was making wiv motels is you got your own access from the car-park, no reception desk to pass, no stairs. The roadies could ferry the ladies in and out, nobody the wiser. Yeah.' Tom expelled a philosophical sigh. 'One fing you could say about Sile, he knew where to find the motels. Otherwise, he was a tit.'

Meryl said, 'And you? Did you use to have your four girls, Tom?'

'Me?' Tom smiled self-consciously. 'Nah. I used to like to talk a bit as well, those days. Maybe I was lonely. And when you talked to 'em . . . well, tell the truth, they wasn't all slags. Nah, one girl a night was enough. Wiv one girl, you could pretend.'

He looked strangely vulnerable. She tried to imagine him as a young man. Long, blond hair in the Viking warrior style and matching moustache. Meryl had never been a great follower of rock and roll. She realized she must be about the same age as Tom Storey, but you probably had to be a generation younger to have idolized him.

She supposed Viking was right, the rock musicians descending on some country town, raging through their concert. And then the orgying among the local girls.

But Tom Storey had only taken one girl into his chalet. He liked to pretend. Pretend she was his girlfriend? Pretend they were married? Pretend he had emotional security?

Meryl said gently, 'Pretend?'

'Piss off,' Tom said abruptly. He grinned cruelly. 'Look at me now, eh? Look at what's waiting outside me chalet nowadays. How far can you fall, eh?'

Meryl felt her face tighten and burn. The bastard. She felt a deep, savage need to hurt him back, emotionally and physically, but, other than the stool she was sitting on, there was nothing to throw at him. She sat very still, bit her lower lip. A heavy lorry rumbled past.

Tom had his legs apart; there was a small hole in the crotch of his trousers. Hardly what you'd call erotic. Poor Shelley, Meryl thought.

And then she said, without thinking, 'Who's the man with the hole in his face?'

She hadn't meant to say it. There was a raging silence. Then the light, functional, modern furniture in the room seemed to grow darker and heavier and more cumbersome, the atmosphere suddenly musty, the air stained brown. For long, long moments, it was an older room, from an older, poorer time.

And now Meryl finally *was* shocked. Tom Storey stared at her for shattered seconds, and then he began to weep.

All the way back to London, mainly motorway, Prof Levin kept on at Dave, wouldn't let him think, roaring over the grinding of big trucks, the hiss of air-brakes in the damp gloom of late November. 'What's your problem, David? You're the Angel of fucking Death. Get in there, man, go back, work it all out.'

Dave wouldn't think about it. He just drove, racing the retreating daylight to the end of the motorway. Resisting questioning Prof about the two words which had so rapidly relieved them of Russell Hornby's company: Soup Kitchen.

Prof, well pissed – several more drinks before Dave could prise him from the Crown – was still euphoric about getting the dirt out of Russell Hornby. Drink and euphoria, dangerous combination: it meant Prof was seeing the funny side.

'Maybe you need it, son, eh? Work with Storey again? Think that's possible? Think Case's gonna lure Storey out of his bunker? And Moira? Like that, wouldn't you? No, really? Think she's still got it, David, that special something?'

'I don't know what she's got,' Dave said soberly. He was thinking of the dark, smoky cowl, the hideous bonnet.

'And what about the other guy?'

'Do us a favour. Shut your gob, Prof.'

'And Soup Kitchen, and Barney Gwilliam. I'm getting old, David, I'm allowed to ramble. Hey, you know how they identified Graham Bond after the tube train got him? Thumb print. That was years ago; that don't matter. What's now is

Soup Kitchen. And Barney Gwilliam, a little pool of blood in studio ninety-seven.'

'For God's sake, Prof, what are you on . . .? Shit!'

The lorry driver had started blasting on his horn. Dave couldn't do anything about the situation; he was blocked on each side, the fast lane all Porsches and Jags and BMWs, an endless tin river. One small tug of his right hand would toss them into oblivion, a swift, blurred death, couple of burnt-out nobodies in a ten-year-old Fiat. The lorry was screaming, Do it! Do it!

'Barney Gwilliam, David. You ever hear about Barney Gwilliam?'

'I don't even know who he is.'

'What a short, selective memory you have, son. Barney Gwilliam was your engineer at the Abbey in December 1980.'

'Oh. Barney. I never knew his last name. Very quiet guy, got on with the job, didn't have a lot to say.'

'That was the boy. Brilliant. Drove a studio like a DC10. You're right. Didn't have a lot to say. But the manner of his passing, David, was truly . . . truly eloquent.'

Passing?

The big truck was screaming for space. In his mirror Dave saw that the figures 666 were part of its registration. The lorry bombarding him with bile from behind, Prof into a death trip in the passenger seat. And in the flat fields either side of the motorway, his mind constructed buildings: a fortress, massive, forbidding, many-windowed, all of them black; above it soared archways and buttresses of wind-worn, pink-grey stone; through the archways a woman walking, a woman with her head wrapped in black.

A blue sign said SERVICES 1M.

But he hadn't really seen her, had he? Not *really*. This was only his own projection, from a ten-year-old photo. A mind game. Contaminated by Prof's rambling about some death song on the album, a song that hadn't existed.

'Simon, yeah? Simon St John? Played cello and flute and

303

that. And bass. The only member of the band could read music, am I right?'

Sometimes, anyway, when you played mind games, they came back on you in a negative way, as if to teach you a lesson – don't mess with this stuff unless you're serious.

'Where's this Simon now, then, David?'

But he *had* been serious, desperately serious. Oh God. Oh Jesus. Not Moira.

'David, I'm tryin' a talk to you.'

'Last I heard he'd become a Christian,' Dave said. 'Like Cliff Richard.'

'He never! Dylan did that once. Never made a really good album since. They don't, do they, when they find God? Proves the old saying, don' it, 'bout the devil having all the best tunes?'

'That's all bollocks. It's only fanaticism makes bad music. The rule is, believe what you want but don't preach, it just sounds naff.'

'Used to call the blues *the devil's music*. Robert Johnson selling his soul at the crossroads at midnight, getting himself murdered. Graham Bond, remember him? The Aleister Crowley fixation? Poor bloody Bondy, flattened by a tube train. Late sixties, was that? Feels like yesterday. This is a sick, sick industry, David. Ambition fuelled by dope and sex and they all get cored, too young. Reach the point the only thing they got left to sell is their immortal fucking souls.'

A great black truck, transcontinental job, was coming up hard behind them in the middle lane, wanting to get past, too heavy to move into the fast lane.

'And the roll of the dead. Hendrix and Morrison and Brian Jones and Bolan and Joplin and Lennon and Kurt Cobain . . .'

Dave loosened his hands on the wheel. The wheel was wet.

'I'm getting off, Prof.'

'I think you better had,' Prof said soberly.

Moving from room to room in the big yellow house, Shelley kept looking over her shoulder.

It occurred to her that she was looking for Tom.

And not, to her shame, because she wanted to see him. It was the first time she'd been alone in this place and in some perverse way she was relishing the freedom. It was the kind of freedom which the mother of a dependent, handicapped child must feel when the child is taken temporarily into a home to give the parents a break.

Vanessa bustled around, making coffee. There was no question of needing relief from Vanessa. Shelley had never considered her to be handicapped, merely different.

Tom was the handicapped child – getting worse, as Weasel had noticed – and Shelley was breathing easier without him. It was an unnerving sensation.

She was also surprised to find she was not worried about him. He was, after all, a big strong man, an intelligent man, a man who was not mentally ill in any clinical sense. And if he'd been in an accident, the police would have known.

Martin had dealt with the police. Martin had driven her home, and the police were waiting, taking measurements and photographs around the demolished fence. The Tulleys' car had been removed, thank God, as had several pieces of timber from the fence. When a senior officer had asked to speak to the householder, Mr Storey, Martin had taken him on one side and Shelley had watched him talking smoothly and casually, the policeman nodding.

'I, er, said that Mr Storey was away from home at present,' Martin had explained afterwards. 'I'm afraid I implied – I hope you don't mind – a certain marital discord.'

And Shelley had erupted into laughter; this was when the terrifying sensation of freedom had first hit her, like a burst of wind in a flaccid sail.

'Call me when you need anything,' Martin had said as he slid into his white Jaguar. 'As soon as the police are finished, perhaps I could send my gardener to reorganize your poor fence. And we'll speak again, of course, about the Love-Storey displays.'

He was talking breezily, as if last evening had been a total, unsullied success. Shelley liked that, was somehow warmed by it.

Outside, the sun shone with unseasonal energy. She heard a policeman laugh lightly.

She was exhilarated and confused. It was as if, through their appalling deaths, Angela and Wilfrid Tulley had in some way opened up her own house to her – it was, after all, her house as much as Tom's fortress.

Shelley went to the kitchen stereo radio and tuned it, for the first time, to Classic FM, sprinkling Vivaldi into the room, like moist flower petals.

And then she began to cry, because this was all so very, very wrong.

Vanessa watched her solemnly.

Tom, very maudlin now, was saying what a good man he had been really, how he'd always worked hard, done his best for his family, could be harsh and forbidding, when he was sober, always generous when drunk. Like the night he'd brought home the big red, cracked Gretsch *Chet Atkins*, changed his son's life for good and all.

This was the old man, Tom's dad.

Bermondsey days. Tom's ma at the biscuit factory, the old man down the docks.

'He didn't know nuffink about rock and roll,' Tom said. 'But he sensed it was a way out the East End. Working down the docks'd made him restless, the way it done wiv a lot of blokes shifting gear from foreign ports. But he was trapped, my old man. Married to a good, steady breeder. My six older bruvvers was already grown-up, one had a kid. Here he was, a bleeding grandad.'

'And you were the seventh son,' Meryl said huskily. 'It's true then. It's really true.'

Tom laughed. He was still sprawled on the bed, and now Meryl was kneeling on the floor at the bedside, the acolyte at the feet of the great guru. This was ridiculous, and yet it wasn't.

Meryl had been introduced over the years to several spiritual teachers who'd been neat, sleekly attired and quietly spoken. And self-deluded. Or phoneys.

'Seventh son of a seventh son,' Tom said. 'What a load of old cobblers, eh?'

'Is it?'

What was so convincing about Tom was his attitude towards the psychic world. Resentment. Contempt, even. Something which he despised in himself.

'Is it really cobblers, Tom?'

'I wish,' Tom said ruefully. 'The old man, he hated it so bad, anyfink happened to him he'd go off and get pissed. Or he'd fight it off.'

'How would he do that?'

'Fight. Literally. He'd go and pick a bleeding fight. Anyfink he seen he couldn't hit, he'd need to take it out on somefing he *could* hit. Kind of reinforced his hold on reality. Wasn't hard to find a punch-up in dockland, those days. My old man done five terms for GBH, maybe six. He didn't come home nights, Ma never worried – he'd be safely banged up somewhere, poor, mad git.'

'When he came home . . .' Meryl said tremulously, 'from work, from the docks, did he smell of oil? Engine oil?'

'No,' Tom said.

'Oh.' Meryl was deflated. Nothing about this was simple, was it?

Tom said, 'When he came home from the garage was when he stank of oil. My uncle, ma's bruvver, had this little garage, doing up old bangers, motorbikes. The old man used to help him nights, when he was frew down the docks. Then they'd go and get pissed.'

Meryl caught her breath.

'One night – I'd've been fourteen, fifteen at the time – these geezers wander in suggesting a little extra business for the garage, respraying nicked motors, changing plates, all this. Now, one fing about my dad, he was honest, right? Yeah, yeah, he had his share of hookey gear, like anybody else, else I'd never've got the Gretsch, would I? And yeah, he got pissed and he lost his cool a lot. But crime with a capital C, no way, this was a straight garage. So he slings these geezers out. I mean slings, adjustable spanner round the ear job, you know?'

'Were you there, Tom?'

'Me? Nah. I was up my bedroom, as usual, pretending I was Muddy Waters. I knew about it, though, later that night. I woke up, hurting. Like toothache. Yeah. I knew about it.'

'About the men who came to the garage?'

'Nah. About the geezers waiting for him when he come out the boozer. The geezers wiv the hooks. Docker's hooks? They ever have fights wiv docker's hooks down at Gloucester quay? See, the hook, what you'd do is sharpen the point. Flick knives? Knuckle dusters? They was toys, next to the docker's hook.'

Meryl shuddered.

'He come home,' Tom said. 'He made it home. I heard Ma screaming. When I come downstairs he's standing in the kitchen door, swaying. The man wiv two mouths.'

'Oh my God.'

Tom shrugged. 'You wanted to hear it, darlin', I'm telling it you. The bastards'd laid his face open, shoved the hook in, thrust it up. Not much blood. Surprisingly little blood.'

Closing her eyes to shut out the pain in Tom's face, Meryl saw again the image of the man, like a brown column, swaying in her own kitchen doorway. She smelled again the thick odour of engine oil, and another, metallic smell, maybe blood. She felt nauseous.

'What'd happened,' Tom said, 'the hook'd gone up into his brain. Poor bastard couldn't even speak. Staggered home like a zombie. And we stood there, Ma and me, and we watched him collapse. Slowly. Like a tree. Nuffink we could do.'

Meryl felt a pressure behind her eyes.

'And he died there,' Tom said. 'On the living-room floor. The man wiv two mouths.'

'Thirty-odd years, Tom. Over thirty years and he's still . . .?'

'He ain't far away, ever. Give him a disturbed atmosphere, summink to latch on to, he's there, the poor old bleeder. See, lady, I . . . what you called?'

'Meryl.'

'See, Meryl, I don't know the science of this. It could be me what creates him, brings him into form. Like, the atmosphere, if it's disturbed, it works on me and what materializes – frew *me* – is the worst fing I ever saw. You know what I mean?'

'Yes,' she said. 'But he's more than that.'

Meryl, still kneeling on the motel carpet, looked at Tom, with his lank yellow-grey hair and the misshapen moustache emerging from his face like the stuffing from an old sofa. She saw a curiously heroic figure.

'He comes as a warning, Tom,' she said. 'He comes as a portent.'

'That's what you fink, is it?' Tom struggled up on his elbow, leaned against the padded headboard.

Meryl didn't move. 'He manifested, surely, to show us what was going to happen to Sir Wilfrid and Lady Tulley. Is that naïve of me?'

'You know,' Tom said, 'the first time I seen him, I must've been seventeen, and I done some serious praying.'

'To God?'

'I knelt down, 'side the bed, just like a bleeding seven-year-old, and I prayed to the Big Geezer never to let me see the old man again. Prayed wiv everyfink I'd got. And after that, it was only in dreams. He come to me in dreams. Well, you can cope with that. You wake up, bit of a sweat on, but that's all, no harm done. This was how it was, until . . .'

'Until your wife died.' Meryl was alarmed. She didn't know where this idea had come from. Martin had told her about Tom Storey's first wife, how she'd died, that was all.

Tom said, 'You're a witch, lady. You know that?'

'Nothing so exotic,' Meryl said, uncomfortable. One of her shoes had come off; her toes curled on the carpet. Her face was growing hot.

'We was doing an album,' Tom said. 'Four of us, all wiv the

309

same problem, seeing more'n we oughter see, knowing more than was good for us. But not understanding any of it.'

Meryl found her eyes drawn to his pathetic blue tattoo. What a strange, sad life he'd had.

'The others was kids. That age, you got no responsibility. It excites you a bit. It scares you sick, but when you're young you like being scared. On account of you fink one day you're gonna understand.'

'I know about the album, Tom. Stephen Case . . .'

'That ponce.'

'I didn't like him either. Tom, I need to ask you something. The vision? Those people lying dead at the dining table?'

Tom was watching her now, his eyes half-closed. 'I'm sorry. What I said earlier. I insulted you. I didn't mean to. I mean, I *did* mean to, but . . . anyway, I'm sorry. You're quite a sexy lady. When I seen you last night, all made up, the black clobber, I fought, you know, strewth.'

'I dress like that for my employer,' Meryl said primly. 'Tom, the vision. It wasn't only the Tulleys. It was Case. And your wife. And Martin. Dead. All dead.'

'Yeah.'

'Doesn't that scare you? After what happened to the Tulleys?'

'That was coincidence, the Tulleys. Nah. It don't scare me. Nuffink scares me no more. I seen it all before. The blood at the table, this is Aelwyn wosname, and the massacre. Picked it up at the Abbey, like a dog turd on your shoe. All illusion. Half of what you see, it's illusion. You learn that.'

'How can you talk of coincidence?'

'I'm tired,' Tom said. 'I'm knackered. Shagged out. I can't go home. I can't go back there again.'

'What about Shelley?'

'Shelley's got it together. Shelley don't need me.'

'And the little girl?'

'I don't know. I need to sleep. You gonna stay wiv me, while I get to sleep? Please?'

'Why should I stay if you're not scared?'

Meryl stood up, arms by her side.

'Fuck you, lady.' Tom clutched at one of her hands, his eyes wide open and glassy. 'Ain't you got no perception? I'm scared clean out of my perishing mind.'

The Holy Mountain, the Skirrid, was like a single wing. A cold sun made the serrated rims of ruptured clouds shine like metal. It spread a fan of light-rays around the peak.

Divine light. The scene shimmered.

He lay inside the cleft of rock above Ystrad Ddu, an enormous cradle lined with moss.

Above him, under the Skirrid, was a calm, still, bearded face. A face he knew.

Simon whispered, 'Jesus?'

When the root of the rowan tree had snapped, the arm of Jesus had reached out of the sky and grasped his wrist and held it firmly and pulled him back until his boots had found footholds in the rockface.

Divine intervention.

Jesus laughed.

Jesus wore a short leather jacket and jeans and hiking boots. Jesus had short grey hair starting high on his forehead above a deeply-lined face.

And an earring.

Jesus said, 'Close thing, Simon. Nobody tell you you need proper gear for rock-climbing? Ropes and spiky things to bang into crevices? Risky sport, mate.'

His face was so familiar from somewhere. He had a wide, friendly smile, although some of his teeth were chipped and discoloured. Jesus wouldn't have teeth like that.

'I followed you up here. Figured it was time we talked.'

He put a hand to help Simon to his feet.

'Sile Copesake,' he said. 'We haven't met.'

VII

December: Ain't It Always?

Motorway services. Dave felt like he'd driven a thousand miles without a break. His legs not too bothered about supporting him. Fuddled, he'd asked Prof on the way in here, 'Can we *talk* to Barney Gwilliam?' And Prof had asked him if he'd got a serviceable spade.

Now Prof brought coffee and doughnuts to the window table where Dave was sagging. 'I'm sorry,' he said. 'Sorry, sorry, sorry, OK?'

'Me too. I didn't know. Why'd he do it?'

'He didn't leave a note, David. We're into speculation. Listen, what I meant, I'm sorry about my behaviour, the things I said in the car. Angel of death. Sorry. Not funny.'

'Forget it.'

'Can't *forget* it. That's the whole flaming problem. I heard the Black Album just the once, can't forget it. It's lodged.' Prof tapped his head. 'Here. I'm stuck with it. Makes new doorways unto places you didn't know were there. I would really hate it to be released.'

Prof started fiddling in the breast pocket of his jacket. 'Here, let's get this thing out in the open.'

A folded paper tumbled out. Prof trapped it with a hand, smoothed it out, pushed it across to Dave. 'This was in the post for me this morning.'

It was a photocopy of a single-column clipping from an unidentified, undated newspaper.

STUDENT DOUBLE-DEATH PROBED
Detectives were last night investigating the deaths of two

Oxford students whose bodies were found in the flat they shared in the city.

The students, both aged 20, were . . .

Dave looked up at Prof. It meant nothing to him.

'Hang on,' Prof said, 'this is a better one.'

The second paper had two stories, expanding on the first, identifying the students as Mark Collier and Declan Smallwood. The room was in a mess, and it looked as if Smallwood had killed Collier by beating him over the head with a blunt instrument and then taken an overdose. They were described as 'very close friends'.

Prof said, 'Crime of passion was the implication. The papers didn't dwell on it. Gay domestic murders, who cares? Especially seven years ago. See this bit at the bottom . . .'

. . . shared an interest in music and had been working on an album of their songs.

'These boys,' Prof said, 'sound a bit like Simon and Garfunkel in the sixties. Bedsit dreamers. Called themselves Soup Kitchen. Final cutting, OK?'

Police found a bloodstained electric guitar near a student's battered body in a room lit by candles, an inquest was told today. Nearby lay the body of Mark Collier's killer, with

'Blunt instrument was dead right. Seems Smallwood beat the shit out of Collier with a secondhand Strat-copy and then topped himself. They reckoned he was so cut-up about what he'd done he lit the candles as a kind of ceremonial gesture before taking his pills. And the bottom line . . .'

Prof jabbed a finger at the final paragraph.

The students had returned to Oxford two days earlier after working on their music at a studio in Gwent, South Wales. Recording verdicts of murder and suicide, Coroner Paul Galloway said, 'There was an obsessional element in this relationship that may never be fully understood.'

313

Dave's whole body was now feeling as subdued as his legs. 'Russell was producing these kids? At the Abbey?'

'Guy I know sent me this stuff, music journalist. While I was waiting for you this morning, I called him back. Seems Soup Kitchen had signed to Epidemic, very hush hush at the time. The boys wanted somewhere atmospheric to record. They suggested the Manor, which was local for them, but they were told it was fully booked for months ahead. Then somebody says, Hey, what about the Abbey?'

'But it was closed down by then.'

'So they used a mobile. Maybe it impressed Smallwood and Collier that Epidemic were prepared to open up the Abbey just for them.'

Dave said, 'So this would be . . . how long after the Philosopher's Stone session?'

'Six, seven years. It didn't immediately close down because Tom Storey had a bad accident there, why should it? So the boys are taken up to the Abbey on two or three weekends, to get the feel of the place, get some demos down. The idea being they could go back and lay down the whole album during their Christmas holidays from the University.'

'Hang on . . .' Dave fumbled his cup into its saucer, spilling hot coffee over both hands. ''Strewth . . . This was December?'

'Ain't it always?' said Prof.

'What date?'

'They died on . . . the tenth. About then.'

'So they could've been in the studio on the night of the eighth?'

Prof shrugged.

'What about Barney?' Dave was mopping at his wrists with a napkin, trying to hold it steady.

'Barney died on the twenty-ninth, less than a week after joining the BBC, Cardiff-based. Two days before New Year's Eve, he sat himself in the studio, all alone, slashed his throat. And he'd been in that job less than a week and doing well. Whatever it was made him do it, he brought it with him.'

'Why the BBC? I mean, he was a top engineer. Be a major drop in pay, that, wouldn't it?'

'But maybe,' Prof said, 'a raise in peace of mind.' He pushed his coffee away. 'Or so he might have thought. I find this particularly heartbreaking, David, because here was a boy who lived for his work. To this guy, the studio – any studio – was home.'

'Let me get this right.' Dave sucked at his wrist where the coffee had burned it. 'Barney engineered this Soup Kitchen session at the Abbey.'

'I don't know that. I would've put it to Russell, but he didn't hang around, did he?'

Dave said, 'Maybe it's better you didn't. Maybe it's better he doesn't know we know about that. OK, let's assume he did engineer that session. Where does that get us?'

'Gets us to the central question of why he packed in and took a lower-paid job at the Beeb. Like I said, this is a boy who lived for his job. Juggling sounds, making music work. At the Beeb, half the time he'd be on speech programmes, routine stuff. Why's a man like Barney want to do this, unless . . .'

'Unless something happened to make him frightened of music. Scared to put a pair of cans over his ears because of what he might hear, scared to mess with a mixing deck because of the sounds his fingers might produce. That's what you're getting at?'

Prof said, 'You asked me to re-mix the Black Album, I'd be *shit* scared. Scared of what it might touch inside me. What it might bring out. It sticks like slime, some of that music. I tell you, the worst thing . . . I was never scared of death before. Scared of dying, how it might happen, sprawled in the gutter stinking of meths, whatever. But not death itself. Now . . .'

Dave shook his head. 'I really don't remember getting that far. I knew that was how it was going to end. I, me, Aelwyn, we were resigned to it, but I ran out on him. And Moira. We backed off.'

Thinking, No, *I* backed off, ran out on them all, Moira, Tom, Simon, everybody. And it was a long time before she came out of there.

'Ask her some time,' Prof said. 'Ask her about dying.'

Ice-crystals started to form around Dave's solar plexus. It was the second time Prof had spoken like this about Moira. He couldn't deal with it.

'So, OK,' Prof said, 'Barney quits. Maybe he's on the edge of a breakdown, who can say? He *was* the kind of guy who'd bottle things up. So he packs in, gets himself a nice, safe job at the BBC. But it doesn't go away. I know that it doesn't go away. It sets up home in dreams. What causes this? What did you let in? What did Soup Kitchen let in?'

'Sometimes,' Dave said, from the heart, 'I think it'd be better for everyone if I'd actually died that night.'

'Don't be a plonker.'

'No, think about it. Would Tom have gone rushing for the Land Rover? Would Mark Chapman have pulled the trigger?'

'You've got a wheel loose, son. You're coming off the track. Need to sort your head out. Anyway, like I said, I'd be shit scared. But I'd do it.'

'What you on about?'

'Remix the album. You go back, give Steve what he wants, take me with you as engineer.'

'You tired of life, Prof?'

'Yeah,' said Prof. 'I *am* tired of life. Tired of *this* life. Tired of hearing about guys who didn't make it. Tired of drinking coffee in dumps like this talking about poor sods with wonky auras. Tired of pretending not to be a piss artist. Tired of looking at your miserable face.'

The bedroom window faced a grassed-over courtyard. It had lace curtains and full-length drapes which Meryl didn't bother to draw.

She got undressed without preamble, laying her sweater and

trousers across a chair, unhooking her bra, tossing it on the chair too, but keeping her panties on. Plain pink ones.

She had heavy brown breasts, which dipped and wobbled as she got into bed. She hadn't even thought about the Lady Bluefoot for some hours.

'It's a waste of time,' Tom said gloomily, tossing his jeans out of the side of the bed. 'I can't do nuffink lately.'

'You can hold me.' Meryl unclipped her dark hair. She was excited, like the first time she went to the spiritualist church in Gloucester. I'm a psychic groupie, she thought.

Tom said, 'This ain't charity, is it?'

'Think of me as one of those bimbos after the concerts. A raddled old bimbo.'

'You ain't raddled. You're a sexy lady. And you done this before.'

'Not all that often,' Meryl said. 'Never with somebody like you.'

'Yeah. I can believe that.'

He put an arm around her, cupped a breast. Meryl was glad to feel the nipple begin to swell. Tom said miserably, 'I do love Shelley, you know. She done a lot for me. She gave up a hell of a lot.'

'She's a good woman,' Meryl said. 'But there are things she couldn't do. She couldn't make you free.'

'And you could? I don't fink so, lady.'

Meryl kissed his sad, grey-haired chest. 'Take me where you go,' she said. 'That's all I ask. Then we'll see.'

When Dave got back to the bedsit, around the corner from Muthah Mirth, there was a short note waiting for him on the inside of the door.

Please be out by eight tonight. Got to get place cleaned up for another artist. Don't forget your answering machine. Your phone calls amount to £7.30, leave money under telly.

Bart

Wherever he went he took his answering machine and an adaptor. The machine was still connected, its light flashing. Bart would have left a dismissive message on it, else why mention it?

He looked at his watch. The time was 6.45 p.m.

The calendar on the wall said that tomorrow it would be December.

A thin wind rattled the window panes.

He picked up the phone, called his mother in Hoylake. She was a long time coming to the phone and there was awkward silence when he asked if he could come up, stay for a few days while he got a few things sorted out, had a bit of a think.

'But, David, I thought you were in London until after Christmas.'

'Yeh, sorry, Ma, the schedule got changed.'

'Only it's Cecil.'

'Cecil?'

'Me friend. He's staying a few nights. He's got your room, I won't have talk.'

She'd never let anybody stay in his room before, was going to open it to the public when he was famous. He didn't think he would have wanted to stay with Cecil in the house even if the old guy hadn't got his room. Who wanted to be a wallflower, especially with your ma.

'I'm really sorry, David.'

'Don't worry about a thing. Have a good one. Christmas. I can make other arrangements.'

Like what? Sleep on Prof's sofa with the empties?

He began to pack up his things, none too carefully. Wouldn't exactly be a tight fit in the Fiat without the guitar. Tossing clothing into a case, he pressed the answer button on the machine.

The first message didn't waste time on pleasantries.

'Dave Reilly. Prof must've told you by now. It's Stephen Case at TMM. It's Wednesday, November thirtieth. If you'd like to discuss the album, I'll be in the office until seven. Or even eight, on a bad day. Cheers.'

The voice was affable, no implied threat.

Bombshell.

Dave stopped the machine, snatched up the phone, called Prof.

His voice shook. 'That song – "On a Bad Day". You told me it wasn't on the Black Album tape.'

'I dunno, David. How does it go?'

'You know how it goes. Just me and an acoustic guitar. Reference to Patience Strong.'

'I don't know *what* you're talking about. All the tracks on that tape were full-band stuff.'

'Well, how come Case knows about it if you don't?'

Prof didn't know the answer to that one either. In his consternation, Dave forgot to mention the sofa.

He didn't know Stephen Case. The message wasn't blackmail exactly. Might even be construed as a kindness. We have a tape which you might consider extremely embarrassing, in view of what happened soon after it was recorded. If we put out the Black Album, with only half a dozen tracks, we'd need all the extra material we could get. If that album was to be re-recorded, 'On a Bad Day' wouldn't *have* to be included.

This was what he was saying? Dave stared at the phone as if it might spring off its rest and smash him in the mouth.

You always liked Prof, trusted him. But suppose Prof is in on this, with Case. How else did Case track you down?

As if projected on the wall, he saw a soaring building. Fortress of a place. Dark. Forbidding.

Not the Dakota. The Abbey.

The four-wheel-drive Discovery bumping down the track, headlights on, trees and bushes springing up white and naked, Simon in the passenger seat, dazed.

The vehicle leaned alarmingly as Sile Copesake flung it around tight bends. Simon wasn't worried any more; the inevitability of all this was beyond resistance. Anyway, he hated driving; almost everybody was a better driver than he was, and this guy knew the terrain.

'During the war was when I first came here.' Sile had a soft voice, but not quite smooth – a Yorkshire undertow. 'Before you were born.'

He must be older than he looked.

'Evacuee,' Sile said. 'Imagine coming from Sheffield to a place like this. No smoke. No noise, no muck. You never wanted the war to end.'

Simon knew of Sile only by reputation. A grand old man, even in the seventies, which meant he'd have been in his forties at the time. A father figure in rock and blues, in the way of thirty-five-year-old fighter pilots in the war addressed as 'dad'. Used to lead a lot of bands involving musicians younger than him, the old master with apprentices. One of whom had been . . .

'You worked with Tom Storey? Look out . . .'

The headlights had picked up a couple of rabbits scooting for safety at the roadside.

'You really are still a townie, Simon,' Sile said, indulgently slowing down. 'Tom, yeah. Nineteen seventy-two. Got him on the rebound from a band called the Brain Police, named after an old Frank Zappa number. Tom was doing smack at the time. Needed a spot of straightening out.'

'That must have been a challenge.'

'Not really. Big softy, Tom. Wouldn't join the band unless he could bring his roadie. Little guy called Ferret.'

'Weasel,' Simon said.

'Was that it? Yeah. We said OK. It was the age of the guitar hero. Obvious Tom was going places. Everybody else was into power chords and lightning runs. Tom was unusually economical. Exquisite timing. Dropped in just the right notes at the right time, like rain from heaven. They used to say Hendrix, Clapton, Beck and young Storey, but it was really Storey and Peter Green. Melodic, lyrical. I tried to get Green when he dropped out of Fleetwood Mac, but it was no go.'

'They went the same way, though, in the end,' Simon said. 'Neurotic, reclusive.'

'Yeah, I often wonder if there were other attributes in

common. Talking to God and all that. You talk to God, don't you, Simon? Like a mate. Heard you exchanging a few words out there on the rock.'

It seemed like a long-ago dream. What could he have been doing, hanging from a tree-root, challenging the Almighty to give him a sign or let him die?

'I'm embarrassed,' Simon said.

'Times when we all need to blow,' Sile said. 'Just a little out of character, in view of the way they talk about you in the village. Very laid-back, the word is. Not fazed by anything. Maybe a little bit prissy. Must've been a picnic working with Tom Storey.'

'I think we kept each other on the rails,' Simon said. 'In a funny sort of way.'

He closed his eyes. This whole situation was strangely dreamlike, the coincidence unreal. Divine intervention. He thought, this man – and maybe God – saved my life.

In such circumstances, bewildered, lying deep in the cleft of rock in alignment with the Skirrid, what could he do but say, sure, I'll come with you. Wherever you're going.

Sile had stopped, switched off the engine. When Simon opened his eyes, both the headlights and sidelights were out. It was fully dark, no moon. He couldn't even see Sile Copesake.

He didn't move.

'You know where we are,' Sile said.

'I think so. Don't put the lights on yet. I may get scared and ask you to take me back.'

'If that's what you want.'

'Maybe you could tell me what this is all about. You followed me. You've been asking questions about me in the village. Does everybody know?'

'About the Philosopher's Stone? I doubt that.' Sile's voice was comforting, like talcum powder. 'What you should know, Simon – well, a lot of things you should know, but we've got plenty of time – is that I'm on the board of TMM these days.'

He let it lie a while. Through the windscreen, Simon saw big shadows looming like tall trees.

'Am I supposed to know where this is leading?'

Except that there was a breeze and trees moved in a breeze and these shadows didn't.

Yes, he knew where they were. Too late now for prayer. When God picked you up, he invariably swung you around and threw you in the deep end.

'I've never been back,' he said. 'A man called Eddie Edwards brought me half-way, but I couldn't go the distance. I saw the place and I chickened out.'

'So why did you come to Ystrad Ddu, Simon?'

He really did know the area, didn't he? A stranger would have pronounced it Istrad Doo. He'd been evacuated *here*? *Right here*?

'For my part,' Sile said. 'I've come to face up to my responsibilities. To you and the others. And to . . . this place.'

Simon had opened his mouth to speak. The breath seemed to evaporate in his throat as, with a muffled click, the headlights came on and the Abbey reared up around them, white on black, in all its jagged, soaring, Gothic glory.

from a distant phone box? Meryl, I've spent the entire day pacifying the police, entertaining Storey's charming but conversationally limited daughter, handling Shelley with kid gloves, or rather not handling her at all. And now I come home to a dark, silent house and a cold bed and you tell me you're out there "connecting" with this lunatic. Who's going to cook my breakfast in the morning, Lady fucking Bluefoot?'

Seconds later he let the phone slip from his ear. He couldn't believe it.

Meryl had hung up on him.

The police arrived informally, shortly before 8 p.m.

Eddie Edwards, watching from behind a curtain in the darkened front bedroom at his home, the Old Vicarage, was rather disappointed at first, when merely this elderly, grey Ford Sierra pulled up under his porch light and just one man emerged and with no great hurry.

He was tall but slumped. Walked with his neck bent, looking from a distance like an old-fashioned lamp-post.

'Coffee, I think, my love,' Eddie called to his wife, to get her out of the way, waiting for the ring before moving towards the door. Only one man; maybe it wasn't such a big deal after all.

'Mr Edwards?'

To his surprise, the policeman had a denser Welsh accent than you generally found in this part of the world, indicating origins considerably further west. He had a long, thin, pale face, like a half-moon.

'Oh, ah, Superintendent Gwyn Arthur Jones, sir, Gwent Police.' Sounded as if it was already well past his bedtime.

'*You're* not from these parts,' Eddie said brightly.

'Nor indeed, it seems, are you,' said Supt. Jones, adding hopefully, '*Siarad Cymreig?*'

'Lapsed, I'm afraid. Used to, see, but you get out of it, especially around here. Carmarthen, is it, you're from, Mr Jones? Come in, sit down.'

The policeman handed his overcoat to Eddie and bent his head to enter the sitting-room, which still had an air of Vicarage about it, thanks to Marina and a lot of chintz.

'From Pontmeurig, I come, sir, originally.'

'My God, there's an outpost. Must seem like the bright lights where you are now. Newport?'

'Abergavenny. Mind if I smoke? So many people in horror of the humble cigarette these days, I live in constant fear of an even more terrible backlash against my historic pipe.'

And his pipe did indeed look historic. Eddie spread his hands in happy acquiescence. Something less forbidding, somehow, about a pipe-smoker.

'Part of our great heritage, the pipe.' Superintendent Gwyn Arthur Jones bent over an old-fashioned chromium lighter with a flame like oxy-acetylene. 'Course, I haven't seen this candle yet, but I don't somehow think I'd care for one on my fiftieth birthday cake.'

'Not . . . not for a few years yet, surely,' Eddie said, thrown a little by the unobtrusive way this man changed gear.

'Week on Friday,' said Superintendent Jones mournfully. 'At least advancing age allows one to exhibit eccentricities. I could go quite over the top, see, on this business. Get the church sealed off, fill it up with little men in plastic suits, have my boys doing house-to-house. Make no mistake, Mr Edwards, we are talking Dead People here. Babies even, who knows until we hear from the lab.'

'Babies. Good God, man!'

'Newborn babies, it's been known.'

'You have reports on this kind of thing?'

'Like most men of limited intellect, I take the *News of the World*,' Gwyn Arthur Jones said drily. 'What I am getting at, Mr Edwards, is that other men might call out the troops but brought up in Pontmeurig one learns caution. Your vicar, now, what does he have to say?'

Eddie hesitated. 'He, er, he doesn't know yet, Superintendent. I haven't had a chance to see him. I did call, see, but he wasn't in. It's a busy job nowadays, for a vicar, with all these cutbacks. Four churches, he has, to look after.'

In fact, he'd been several times to the vicarage, banging furiously on the door, but not a sound, not a light.

'As cautious as myself, you are, obviously.' Gwyn Arthur Jones observing him shrewdly through a brackish smoke which reminded Eddie of autumn bonfires. 'So tell me all about it. No hurry. Do I smell coffee?'

It occurred to Eddie Edwards that at least you knew where you were with a handful of police cars with sirens and Alsatian dogs. With Gwyn Arthur Jones it was probably going to be less spectacular but rather more complicated.

Simon St John, sweating now, said, 'I don't know whether I can.'

Sile Copesake had bounded to the ground, like a man half his age, leaving the engine running for the lights. Now he was holding open the passenger door for Simon.

The Abbey sprouted all around them like a giant fungus stimulated by the light. Simon imagined it was sensing him. As if each broken arch had exposed nerve-endings.

'When I was a lad,' Sile said, 'I used to come here at night, alone, just to see if I dared.'

He put out a hand to help Simon down. Simon took it and held it but stayed where he was.

The hand was dry and firm. Simon held on to the hand, for what it might tell him. *Is he frightened now? Can he sense it too?*

The first time he'd shaken hands with Tom Storey, over fifteen years ago, there'd been a burning sensation all the way up to his shoulder, coloured lights in his head.

Nothing. He let Sile Copesake's hand go.

'OK, Simon?'

To Copesake, this would be just a ruined building, scary at one time, when he was a kid, because it was old and isolated and he knew what it had been. But now . . .

An incredibly obvious question occurred to Simon. It came very slowly, the way thoughts did in dreams, taking a long time to shake itself out of the mists.

He said, 'What are we doing here, Sile?'

Having intended to ask, what are *you* doing here? By this time only vaguely aware of clinging to a rock face in a deliberate position of extreme jeopardy and Sile Copesake materializing like an angel beamed from the Skirrid.

Simon stepped down from the Discovery feeling like someone getting out of bed after a long illness. Sometimes situations developed which seemed so charged with significance that your over-developed senses missed the obvious, the prosaic, the truth.

Sile had said:

What you should know is that I'm on the board of TMM these days.

Not that he'd been sent to save him, to extricate him from his madness. Just that he represented a major recording company.

'Let me show you something,' Sile, the recording company shareholder, said nonchalantly, walking towards the shadowy hulk of the Abbey.

What *is* this?

Very warily, Simon followed the wiry, leathery figure through the ruins, keeping away from the stone. Mustn't touch the stone; full of old blood, might bleed on *you*.

Sile had left the headlights on, with the engine obediently running, to light them along the path through the east transept or the south chapel or whatever the fuck it was, to the base of the tower. This was the other side from the courtyard where the cars had been parked during sessions.

'Mind the steps.' Rattle of keys.

'We're going in? How come you've got keys?'

'Because we own it, Simon. You could say we inherited it from the fat man.'

'But you knew it as a kid. You personally. You told me that.'

Stone steps led downwards. This side, you entered the building on a lower level.

Sile was just a voice talking easily in the darkness at the bottom of the steps.

'Been used for all kinds of enterprises, this place – hotel, outward-bound centre. And it was for sale again, summer 1980. And it was cheap. And Max Goff thought, what an amazing place for a studio. Everybody was doing it in those days, competing to offer the weirdest setting for big money bands to record in. Castles, disused railway stations. Bids going in for the pyramids, I shouldn't wonder.'

'And Max Goff,' Simon said slowly, 'being into New Age philosophy and psychic studies . . .' Did the guy think he didn't know all this?

'Cemented in blood,' Sile said. 'Soon as he heard that, he was fishing for his cheque book. He loved old places with an atmosphere. Yeah, I knew it as a kid, and it was a shock coming back in the seventies, seeing the state it was in. Poor old Abbot Richard wouldn't even recognize the location. It needed somebody like Goff to throw money at it.'

Simon still wouldn't go down the steps. A cold rain was flushing out his brain at last.

'It was only cheap, Sile,' he said, 'because it had a reputation. It was unlucky. Still collecting blood. You know about the young couple who fell out of the tower?'

Silence.

'*We* didn't know that,' Simon said. 'We were given all this holy ground, spiritual haven garbage. So when things started to go wrong, we naturally thought it must be us sinners.'

'Yeah.' Sile's voice was coming out of the well of darkness like some kind of Delphic oracle. 'It fucked you up, right? All four of you.'

'You have a nice line in understatement, Sile.' Wondering how much Copesake knew.

A lot, as it turned out.

'Tom Storey climbs into bed,' Sile said, 'and pulls the covers over his head. Moira Cairns melts back into the folk circuit. Reilly emerges as some screwed-up kind of alternative comic. And you take holy orders. That's drastic, Simon.'

'I think that part would have happened anyway,' Simon said cautiously. 'Sooner or later. Maybe, without the Abbey episode, it would have turned out less . . . fraught. I don't know.'

He heard Sile unlocking a big door with, presumably, a big key. A lot of echo, like entering a dungeon in some medieval epic.

Simon still didn't move. 'I don't think I want to go down.'

'But I think you have to,' Sile said. 'Else why did you come back? You came back because it fucked you up and you want to get unfucked, right?'

Simon went down one step.

'And you figured that now you were a priest of God you might have the wherewithal to straighten things out.'

Simon went down another step. 'How naïve we all are,' he said. The darkness held him like a stiff, black funeral coat.

'No, maybe you're right,' Sile said. 'Maybe you could reverse things. Which is what you're thinking you ought to have done first time round, am I right?'

'We were comparative youngsters.' Simon took another step into the dark. 'And we didn't know what we were up against. I didn't know until I left here. I thought I was handling it rather well.'

Two more steps and he was at the bottom. Standing where he'd stood in a thousand dense dreams, carrying on talking, but his nerves were singing.

'We destroyed the tapes, you know. I thought that would be an end of it. I still don't understand why it . . .' Realizing in a flush of panic that he was alone in the bottom of the well, stone walls close on either side, stone underfoot, stone overhead, all that blood, and . . .

'Sile? Where are you?'

Sile laughed. It came from inside. 'You're doing very well, Simon.'

'I can't see you.'

'Hold tight to the wall. Follow my voice.'

'I don't want to touch the fucking *wall*!'

Sound of another door opening.

'OK, Simon?'

'I want to get out.'

Turning to find darkness behind him now.

'No, you don't. Not really.' No echo to Sile Copesake's voice any more. Tight, muted. Inside the derelict abbey, and *no echo*.

'What are you *doing* to me?'

Sile said, 'I'm trying to help you. Come on. Here we go.'

Lights blasted at him, brutal lights beating down on him from all sides.

Simon rolled away, arm across his eyes, blinded, but more frightened by what he'd seen in the shattering atom of time before he'd shut out the glare.

'Sorry, mate, pressed the wrong switch.' Click, click, click. 'That's better.'

It had been a vision. A memory flash. His mind had done it.

But then . . . there should not be electricity in the Abbey. The Abbey was derelict.

There should not be electricity. There should not be concealed lighting in the low, vaulted ceiling.

There should not be a low, wide table with about five hundred switches. There should not be a bank of tape-decks, each with twenty-four level-meters. There should not be a sheet of industrial glass and beyond it, under the curved, white stone ceiling of the cellar where the monks had stored their wine, a piano and a drum kit with tubular bells and four glass booths with mikes and coils of wire across the floor and . . .

'Welcome back,' Sile Copesake said.

IX

Like Chicken Bones

Through the caravan window, he saw weak moonlight swirling like that Coffee-mate stuff in her thick glasses. She was different.

Again.

Something wrong. Well, yeah, her old man still missing. The way Weasel saw it, this was not necessarily a bad thing. Tom was out there finding himself. *He* wasn't a kid, *he* wasn't, like, handicapped.

Well, this *might* have been a good thing, Tom experiencing life in the Big World for the first time in years. Except for the business of Sir Wilf and Lady Wilf. If Tom, as Weasel strongly figured, had seen it happen, he might be in a bad way, emotionally. Or however.

Weasel had the caravan door open before she could knock.

'Princess?'

The kid stood there in the cold. Lemon-yellow shell-suit top, woolly beret.

Lights on in the house behind her, a car parked across the big turning circle – this Broadbank geezer, Shelley's 'customer', the man Weasel had seen conversing with the late Sir Wilf in his garden that day. Weasel was not too worried; there was clearly nothing deeper to this guy than wanting to get his leg over Shelley, which Shelley could handle.

Vanessa was saying nothing.

What was worrying, she had that same look she'd had last night standing in the middle of the road like a little rabbit waiting to be flattened.

'Princess, what you . . .?'

Weasel leapt down the steps, grabbed her by the shoulders.

What was this?

What it was, what was making her eyes swirl was the fact that they was pools of tears.

'Listen.' Weasel shook her just a little. Kindly. 'He's OK, your old man. He's having a break, like a holiday. Just a little holiday.'

Vanessa said, glasses so full of mist and night and steam and tears that Weasel couldn't see where her eyes were at, Vanessa said, 'He's going to die. He's going to die.'

He had insisted they leave the curtains drawn back, and Meryl caught the reflection of occasional headlights on the darkened windows of the chalets opposite.

Tom slept.

Although it was only early yet, exhaustion had claimed him soon after the gentle, sorrowful therapy (*think of it as therapy, Tom, you're no use to one another, you and Shelley, the way you are now. Just think of it as therapy*).

Even now, after the therapy, even now in sleep, his face was damp and worried.

He was the most awesomely tragic man she'd known. What she'd come to realize was that he wasn't scared so much for himself, as of what he might bring down on others. He didn't fear the Man with Two Mouths – his poor, murdered father – so much as what this gruesome revenant might be heralding.

I killed Debbie, Tom, lying flat on his back, no pillows, had said to the ceiling. *I killed Debbie in every sense. See, he was there that night, the old man. Seen him first as a monk, by the gate at the Abbey. Frows back his cowl-fing and there's this gaping hole in his mush, stupid old bleeder.*

Never speak ill of the dead, Meryl had been told as a child.

Come to warn me. Finks if he stands there and flashes his wound I'll get the message. Bleeding useless. 'Bout as much use as Hamlet's old feller. We fink the dead's gotta be wise. Big, big mistake. The dead's as confused – more confused – than what we are. Load of grief is all you get from the dead. Load of grief.

And he'd seen him again, the Man with Two Mouths, at Martin's dinner party. Come to warn his son of impending tragedy, this had been obvious to Meryl.

Yeah. Sir Wilf. Call that coincidence, Meryl? Busts frew me bleeding fence and dies? He's there now, Sir Wilf. Silly old git's polluted me energy field. Won't be long before some poor sod on his way home from the boozer'll be seeing him, standing at the roadside wiv his froat ripped out. "Scuse me, my man, but where exactly ham I?" And his lady wife, head underneath her arm, Anne Boleyn job. Soon as somebody sees 'em, it strengthens 'em, they get their energy from fear. People need to understand this. Fear feeds the dead.

Meryl had listened avidly, curled up against him, surrendering easily to the palpitating excitement. He was part of her destiny, this man, and together they were approaching something of universal magnificence. Afraid? Of course she was afraid. Oh God, she was afraid.

And wasn't it wonderful?

The Abbey. It all centred upon this Abbey. Earlier, Meryl had been to the garage shop for crisps and soft drinks. And a book of maps.

She'd sat on a bench near the cash-till and pored urgently over the map, following the road down to Gloucester and then Ross-on-Wye and then Monmouth. Monmouth to Abergavenny. And then . . .

A very rural area. Other abbeys were marked. Tintern, Llantony, Abbey Dore. Two hills outside Abergavenny, the Sugar Loaf and the Skirrid. Somewhere around there, had to be.

Altogether a journey of less than two hours. Perhaps ninety minutes.

So close, this place where part of Tom Storey's spirit was trapped.

All I can say, that man Stephen Case had told them at dinner, *is it's music which seems to enter a different spiritual dimension.*

Music Tom and his friends had made at the Abbey.

What we want is for Tom and the others to go back into the studio and complete it. Perhaps . . . to the Abbey? Don't you think it would be cathartic for Tom to go back?

And Shelley had said, *I think it would be insanity to go back.*

But what she meant, Meryl was sure, was, *I couldn't go back. I couldn't go with him. It would be too much. I've had enough. I could not take it.*

No, Meryl thought, looking down at the troubled face of the sleeping giant. But *I* could.

'See now, by here. Just stuck on the altar. Disgusting. Helen Harris it was found them. You want to speak to her?'

The candleholders were empty on the white-draped altar. Lit by overcoated Eddie's sputtering Tilley lamp, the little church looked more like a stone cowshed than ever.

Except for there being no cows. Cows were something Eddie could deal with. Policemen, *usually*, were also something he could handle.

Superintendent Gwyn Arthur Jones was something else. But if he wanted to talk to Helen Harris this would at least give Eddie a bit of a break; he could nip off to fetch the lady leaving Gwyn Arthur – oh, aye, it was *Gwyn Arthur* now, another dangerous sign – to sniff around, search for clues, whatever it was they did, these coppers.

What they did these days, it seemed, was to turn the spotlight on you psychologically.

'Go and fetch Helen now, shall I?'

'Not for the moment, Mr Edwards. It's you I'm more interested in.'

Oh *hell*.

'What I'm curious about, Eddie, see, is why you suddenly had the idea to send this candle away for analysis.'

Eddie cast around inside his hopeless old brain for something convincing. Had it all worked out a couple of hours ago. Now he just gave up.

'I'll be honest with you, Gwyn. I don't know. Just a feeling I had.'

Gwyn Arthur suddenly smiled broadly, which made Eddie feel extremely nervous. Going to pull out his handcuffs in a minute, this bugger.

'There you are, see!' The long, thin policeman expansive now, back to the altar, pipe in hand. 'You *can* do it!'

'What? Do what?'

· 'Tell it like it is, as they say in the American films. "Just a feeling." Magnificent. Why not indeed? Where would any of us be without these moments of "just a feeling"? Now all I need to know' – jabbing his pipe stem at Eddie's chest – 'is what lies *behind* this feeling.'

Oh bugger. Why do you keep letting yourself in for these situations? Why can't you *ever* keep your bloody old retired nose out of it?

'Black magic?' Gwyn Arthur sniffed. 'Rubbish, man! Dead babies? Nonsense! You know what this is all about.'

No, I don't, I bloody well don't! But the bloody vicar does. And where is the bugger now, when I need him?

'Gwyn,' he said, 'how can I explain a feeling?'

Bloody feeble *that* sounded. Never been more grateful in his life to hear, behind him, the rattling of the cast-iron ring handle and the door getting itself pushed open, a little awkwardly.

As you would expect from a woman in a powered wheelchair encumbered by a giant blue cycling cape.

'Good evening,' said Gwyn Arthur Jones, all proprietorial, the way these policemen could get during an investigation.

'Isabel,' said Eddie. 'What brings you out this cold night? Superintendent, this is Miss Isabel Pugh, who handles the church accounts and everybody else's for miles around.'

'Gwyn Arthur Jones,' said Gwyn Arthur pleasantly.

Isabel Pugh nodded briefly to him, looked around, and then suddenly spun her chair, forcing Eddie up against a pew end with the wheels trapping his legs.

'Eddie Edwards, what the hell is going on here? Funny

brown candles on the altar, and now it's a police matter. What is it we don't know?'

'Hey now . . .' Eddie put his hands on the chair's armrests. 'Ease up, now, girl.'

'And what,' said Gwyn Arthur, leaning down, 'have *you* heard about these "funny candles", Miss Pugh?'

He was, Eddie decided, about to become a touch exasperated, suspecting, perhaps, that somebody was, to put it crudely, pissing up his leg. Isabel, meanwhile, was explaining drily that if you didn't know about the candles you were either stone deaf or you weren't a resident of Ystrad Ddu.

'I see.' Gwyn Arthur straightened up. 'Very well. I shall leave you two to have a little chat and see what information you remember that you had forgotten, if that makes any sense. What I shall do, I think, is wander along to the vicarage to see if the Reverend Simon St John has returned.'

He smiled. A certain menace in that smile now, Eddie Edwards thought.

Isabel waited silently for a moment watching the church door after it had closed behind the policeman.

The Tilley lamp made a gassy sound. Eddie thought, as he had thought many times, what a tragedy it was, this lovely-looking girl imprisoned in metal and in Ystrad Ddu.

Satisfied that they were at last alone, she regarded him inquiringly.

He took a deep breath. In his experience Miss Isabel Pugh did not appreciate people fancy-dancing around a difficult subject.

'Human fat,' he said hoarsely. 'The bloody candles were made with human fat.'

'Shi-it.' Isabel sank back into her chair as if she'd been pushed. Oh, he'd surprised her all right, no question about that.

'Aye, that too, I shouldn't wonder. Shit.' And he told her about sending the candles away for analysis, knowing she'd ask the same questions as the copper and forestalling her by sighing heavily.

'It's the vicar, see.'

'Simon?'

'If that bugger doesn't know more than he's saying about those candles I'm an Englishman.'

Somehow, this time, she did not look quite so surprised, merely asking, 'Where is he?'

And so Eddie told her of all the times he'd been knocking on the vicarage door, the place in darkness. 'I thought we were friends,' he said. 'I thought he was about to confide in me. I . . .'

He took a chance.

'. . . I know there is something about the old Abbey.'

Isabel looked up at him, golden-streaked hair gleaming with speckles of rain in the lantern-light. All the aggression had evaporated from her voice.

'He came to see me, Eddie. He caught me by surprise, because he wanted to know about the Abbey, what happened to me there. Threw me at first, the vicar asking that. We were going to talk about it. We almost did, but . . .'

'Aye. I know how it is.' He didn't, in fact, know anybody to whom Isabel Pugh had spoken regarding the circumstances of her accident.

'And then,' she said, 'I thought about it when he'd gone and I decided that I did want to. I wanted to talk to him. He wasn't like a vicar at all, he was just like . . . like a chap. With problems. Most vicars, they never admit to having problems same as the rest of us. At first – you know the way I am – at first, I was trying to shock him.'

Isabel smiled. 'No shocking *him*. So the next night I rang him up. I wanted to talk, Eddie.' The smile had vanished. 'Wanted *desperately* to talk.'

He could understand her desperation, the way some local people regarded her. And her always so proud and self-sufficient. Would never look for sympathy among the natives of Ystrad Ddu.

'And he was a different man,' Isabel said. 'Spoke on the phone as if we had never met. Cold. Remote. So remote.'

338

Eddie saw the loneliness in her eyes. He felt so helpless, wished there was something meaningful he could do for her, say to her, this bright, clever girl condemned to Ystrad Ddu and memories of the bloody Abbey.

'I tell you one thing.' He put a hand on her blue-caped shoulder. 'That man is scared. He's more scared than you or I.'

'And I'm supposed to find that comforting?' Isabel said. 'Jesus, did you *have* to put them back?'

'What?'

'One of those reconstructions, is it?'

'What are you . . .'

And then he saw.

'Oh, my Christ!'

Stiff in the candleholders on the altar, shiny in the lamplight, and yellowish, like chicken bones.

Eddie Edwards closed his eyes, his heart feeling like it would burst through his overcoat.

'Eddie?'

Just the one eye struggled open to watch white light shivering on stone, the shadow of an occupied wheelchair painting the floor between the pews and the altar.

Clutching his chest, as if to restrain his bolting heart, Eddie dared to raise his gaze, and one was smoking – *smoking*!

As if it had just been blown out!

'Eddie?' Isabel Pugh reached up from her chair, grabbed his arm. 'Eddie!'

X

Monkscock

Several times, Shelley had been on the point of calling the police to report her husband missing.

It was all so terribly difficult. The police would hardly be doing their job if they didn't see it as a too-remarkable coincidence, a man disappearing the same night as a horrific death-crash outside his home, resulting in two visits on the same day to the same prestigious dwelling in a reputedly 'select' part of the Cotswolds.

She'd been glad when Martin Broadbank had arrived without telephoning first. If he'd phoned she'd have been obliged to put him off.

It had soon become obvious that he had something on his mind and was unsure how to tell her. When she'd put her dilemma to him, he'd looked immediately uncomfortable, so she knew it must concern Tom.

'Shelley, I don't know whether . . .' Martin fingered his coffee cup. He was sitting at the kitchen table, wearing a quilted body-warmer over his polo shirt. A gold identity bracelet on his left wrist said, *not quite gentry*. Which she rather liked. He was a rogue, of course; as a businessman, he'd conspired with Stephen Case to bring Tom to the dinner-table. But that had been done in all innocence; he was an *innocent* sort of rogue, the bastard.

'Oh hell,' Martin said abruptly. 'The fact is, Meryl called me. She says she's with Tom.'

'With Tom?' Shelley's heart leapt. And then confusion seized it. 'Where?'

'That's the problem. She wouldn't say. She said she was . . . helping him. Something about "spheres of existence . . ."'

Shelley sat down opposite him, hands flat on the table.

'Shelley, this is all getting a bit beyond me. I've never felt quite so . . .'

He looked up at her. Bemused was the least of it.

Meryl. The housekeeper. The woman dressed alluringly in black, the sort of housekeeper you might get from an escort agency. The woman who had passed out when Tom . . .

'There's an aspect of Meryl you should know about,' Martin said reluctantly. 'She's obsessed with . . .' He looked embarrassed '. . . I don't know, psychic nonsense. We're supposed to have a ghost and she talks to the thing all the time. I've always thought it was pretty harmless. I mean, it *has* been pretty damned harmless, until . . . oh God, this is ridiculous.'

'No it isn't,' Shelley said.

'Thanks.'

'Christ, I'm not saying it to make *you* feel better, Martin! I've had to live with it for over thirteen years, and it's not bloody ridiculous. If you say the woman's obsessed, that's . . . that's not harmless at all.'

Remembering now how kind Meryl had been, telephoning hotels and places to see if Tom had booked in. Oh yes, really bloody kind.

'Are you trying to tell me,' she said tightly, 'that your housekeeper is almost as psychologically disturbed as my husband? Are you telling me these two are shacked up together somewhere, smoothing each other's psyches? By God, you've set us all up, haven't you, Martin?'

'I'm sorry,' Martin said humbly. 'I had no idea, believe me. Meryl accused me of playing God, inviting you and Tom and Case and then sticking the Tulleys on the list just for the hell of it. It . . . seemed like an amusing thing to do.'

'Ha ha,' Shelley said bitterly.

'I mean, I was being perfectly genuine about the Love-Storey displays, all that.'

'Do you pay this woman? Meryl?'

'You make her sound like a prostitute. It isn't like that at all. It's just been a sort of comfortable arrangement, for us both.'

Shelley asked him, 'Have you *any* idea where they might have gone?'

He shook his head.

'Well, this is bloody marvellous,' Shelley said, defeated.

And then the back door opened, and Vanessa was standing there.

'Hullo,' Martin said cheerfully. 'How are you this evening?'

The poor child looked so forlorn. Her glasses were misted; it was a wonder she could see where she was going.

'Hey,' said Shelley brightly, 'where've you been, lady? I thought you were watching telly.'

Vanessa said nothing. Shelley became aware of Weasel in the shadows behind her. Weasel mumbled, 'Any news?'

Shelley glanced at Martin, who shrugged.

'Martin's had a call from his housekeeper. She's apparently located Tom and has whisked him off somewhere. For a spot of . . . shall we call it *counselling*?'

Weasel said, 'That . . . wossername? Morticia?'

Martin smiled. Shelley said, with half an eye on Vanessa, 'It's actually not that funny, Weasel. We don't know where they've gone. Also . . . Morticia is apparently fascinated by Tom in a . . . a non-physical sense, if you know what I mean. If she was only after his body, everything would be so much simpler.'

Vanessa was expressionless. Shelley was pretty sure she wouldn't have understood any of this.

'He'll be back tomorrow,' she told the child. 'By the time you get home from school he'll be back. With a present, he tells me. Go on. Go and watch telly. I'll bring you some supper through on a tray. With Vienetta to follow, how about that?'

It cut no ice with Vanessa tonight. But she went through to the drawing-room. 'She's such a good kid,' Shelley said sadly.

'Super kid,' Martin said.

'Yeah,' said Weasel dourly. 'Triffic. And she's in a real fucking state with all this shit.'

His face was thin and drawn, his hair a greasy pigtail in a rubber band.

'I don't believe this, Shel. Tom's gone off with this loony

slag, and you're sitting around like the fucking Government debating the bleeding issue.'

Shelley bridled. 'You got any better ideas, Weasel?'

'Yeah. Gimme a day off, lemme take the van. And I'll find him.' He stared defiantly at Shelley and then at Martin Broadbank. 'I done it before, ain't I? I come out of stir and I gone on the road and I found him.'

What could she say? It was true. Weasel's devotion to Tom was legendary. But . . .

'Yeah, I know,' Weasel said. 'It took me a few weeks. But I got here, di'n' I, in the end? And I'm smarter now. And I got better reason.'

He looked towards the door, where Vanessa had gone.

Shelley said wearily, 'Sure. Take the van.'

Simon stumbled back alone along the valley bottom with no light but the sliver of moon. He followed the single-track road, the sound of the thin river to his left and owls all around.

He'd refused a lift from Sile Copesake, could hardly bring himself to speak to the bastard.

It was cold, the tarmac shining with a breath of night frost, bare trees making stiff silhouettes along the hedge between the road and the river.

A set-up.

A record-company scam to lure Tom Storey out of hiding, bring him safe into the bosom of his old band. The target could only be Tom; where was the kudos – apart from the element of humour – in signing a neurotic clergyman, a half-crazed club comic and a now-obscure Scottish folk singer?

Poor bloody Storey. Simon had had a couple of Christmas cards from Shelley, trying to sound lively but the gloom seeping through.

We have the tapes, Sile had said.

God forbid!

Fascinating stuff. We could release it. Throw in a couple of spare cuts from the first album to make up the set. But I don't think you guys would be happy, somehow.

Sile Copesake, this sixty-year-old man in his element, wiry, athletic. Delightedly flicking switches, spinning tape, until some brittle acoustic guitar chords started to sidle edgily out of the speakers, underpinned by a hard, spiky bass.

And then the plaintive, razored, nasal voice of John Lennon . . .

> *Don't know what you got here*
> *But it sure ain't a song*
> *Sounds like Patience Strong*
> *On a bad day . . .*

Only it wasn't John Lennon; it was Dave Reilly, and Simon himself on bass, and he hadn't thought about it in years.

You can't put that out!

Never entered my head to, Simon. I'm very sorry, I didn't intend to play you that one, I was going to give you Aelwyn. Remember him?

Don't bother.

Sile had cut the sound.

Simon, listen, this is a good studio with a unique location. It was my baby. I brought Goff here in seventy-nine, he fell in love; didn't need persuading to buy the place. He'd got this new band that was going to put the Abbey on the map just like Mike Oldfield did with the Manor. Only better, because . . .

Because the band were destined to become part of the Abbey's bloody cement?

Sile had smiled.

If that was Goff's idea, it didn't exactly work, did it? After what happened, nobody wanted to work here. It was an unlucky studio. Unlucky for Epidemic and unlucky for the Abbey. Wasn't even making it as a tourist attraction. The curse of Aelwyn Breadwinner.

Sile had switched off the studio, leaving a couple of concealed lights on.

Goff was a New Age man. All ley-lines and healing powers. He didn't believe in negatives. This was holy ground, and it's ours now. TMM's. My baby again. I went out on a limb, persuaded the Board to refurbish it. Just like it was. State of the art, 1980. Same gear, most of it.

The vans that Eddie Edwards had seen. The vans which went to the Abbey and did not come back for hours.

It must have been done in a hell of a hurry.

So we're saying, come back. Finish what you began. Face the curse. What have you got to lose?

Sile Copesake's dry, Yorkshire rasp. So arrogant. How dare he?

You came back, already, Simon. You were drawn to this place. I was amazed when they told me. And delighted, of course. Gets you, this area, doesn't it? You have to come back.

Who told you?

People I know in the area, from way back. You've been carrying some bad luck and you came back to come to terms with something. I'm not going to ask you what that is, I'm just asking you to come back and play, for one week, maximum. Fit it in with your parish duties or take a holiday, it's up to you, but there's money in it, for what that matters.

When?

Soon as you like. The, er, eighth of December is next Thursday.

Piss off.

And Simon, clutching his head in his hands, blinded by images of crunched cars blazing in the night, dirty brown candles, a wheelchair crashing in pieces to the frozen earth, had raised his foot and slammed it flat against the plate glass door of one of the new shiny, new recording booths, watching it shatter around his ankle, the sound exquisitely trapped in the taut studio ambience.

Piss off.

When he walked into Ystrad Ddu he was thinking, why did you do that? This is why you came back: to face the demons, to cleanse yourself, to maybe cleanse the Abbey. To *find out why*.

But was this the way? He'd thought it was a summons from God, flashed down from the Skirrid, and it had turned out to be commercial enterprise, a sleazy record company's bid to turn over another million.

He thought of his latest despicable dream: hurling aside the stricken woman in her wheelchair to crawl towards the black-robed monk's cock. The rejection of the spiritual to quench the body's base cravings.

Celibacy. Crap.. A delusion.

Because you could never cage the mind.

He was sweating when he passed the chest-high, mud-splashed, moon-fingered Ystrad Ddu sign, primitively grateful to be back in Ystrad, where the cottage lights were coloured by curtains and the smells of woodsmoke and coalsmoke drifted out to claim him.

Welcome back, vicar.

The village never felt more hospitable than at night when it seemed to draw itself under the sheltering rock, and a beery haze formed around the Dragon Inn. This was the real heart of it, not the plain, towerless church. Everyone had been friendly enough the few times Simon had gone into the Dragon, as if they were saying: when you're here, you're part of us. But you take the road along the valley bottom at your own risk, Vicar.

Once again, he stood aghast at the thought that he, a feeble deviant with a public school gloss, was supposed to be this community's official spiritual adviser, God's sales-rep in Ystrad Ddu.

It was never quite funny.

Feeling too damned emotional to cry, Simon stumbled over the boundary inside which a narrow country lane became an even narrower village street, stone walls replacing the spiky, leafless hedgerows.

Under the first of Ystrad's three blueish streetlamps, metal gleamed. His path was blocked by something as uncompromising as a small tank.

'Fancy one of these, Vicar?' Isabel Pugh sat in her chair at the road's edge, holding something out towards him, like a carrot for a donkey.

It was stubby and brown and she held it very still.

It reminded him at once of the monk's cock, and he almost retched.

'Go on. Take it.'

He shrank away, but the wheelchair rolled inexorably towards him and her hand came up, and the smell reached him, butcher's shop ripe.

'Uuuurgh!'

Shrinking as the malformed, earwax-brown candle hit his cheek and slid down his front, leaving, he was convinced, a slimy trail like a black slug. In his head, the scraping of the wheelchair over the edge of the tower, the canteen-of-cutlery clash of metal on frozen earth and toppled stones.

'Please,' Simon whispered. The candle dropped, as if reluctant to leave him, to the glistening road and began to roll away, making a hard, wobbling sound.

'Please?' Isabel Pugh's face looked cold and angry under the streetlamp. 'You've got a bloody nerve, you have. Want to talk and then you want nothing to do with me, and these evil things sprouting on our altar.'

Simon threw his head back, wolflike, and screamed aloud at the shrivelled moon. 'Oh *God*!'

'You can come into the house,' Isabel Pugh snapped. 'Or not. As you please.'

With a whine of the motor, she turned her chair abruptly around and rattled over the cobbles to the cottage door.

XI

Flying

The stove doors were open, revealing orange coals and a single skeletal log in a nest of white-hot ash. The bottle of Southern Comfort was among the papers on the trestle table, down to its last quarter.

She nodded at the bottle. 'Finish it with me?'

'Your mother?'

'Whist drive,' Isabel said dismissively. 'Be away a couple of hours. Sit down, Vicar, warm yourself. Always wet and starved, you are, when you come here.'

'Vicar? What happened to Simon?'

'What indeed?' said Isabel, surveying him through narrowed eyes, her chained glasses magnifying a cluster of freckles on her nose. She'd pulled off her cyclist's cape to reveal a blue silk top, provocatively tied with a drawcord across her breasts.

It was as warm as ever in the living-room, but there were blueing goose-pimples on her arms. She was clearly very frightened and determined not to show it.

Making two of them.

'Eddie Edwards, he thinks he's gone bananas.' Words coming out in a breathless hurry. 'We had a senior policeman in the church. Funny bloke. He's still around. You go back home now, he'll nab you sure as . . .'

'Police?'

'Detective Superintendent somebody-or-other Jones. Waiting for you, he is. Crafty-looking devil. About the candles, Simon. He's here about the candles.'

To cover his reaction, Simon went swiftly into the kitchen, got himself a tumbler, brought it back, sat across the table from Isabel.

The candles? Police?

His wrist was still unsteady as he tilted the Southern Comfort bottle, spilling some.

'Human grease,' Isabel said suddenly, almost shrilly, and he swallowed half his drink and didn't even notice the sweetness of it. 'Can . . . Candles made from human fat.'

Stiffly upright in her wheelchair.

'But you knew that, didn't you?'

Fumbling her glasses straight, leaning forward and peering intently into his eyes.

Which were frozen in shock, the words *human fat* sitting on his senses. He couldn't speak.

'No,' she said. 'I don't think you knew that after all. Human fat. There's intriguing, isn't it?'

Simon blinked helplessly, feeling again the warm, slick, misshapen things, the grease on his fingers afterwards. Feeling an overwhelming desire for the hollow, solitary emptiness of prayer.

Isabel lowered her glasses, said more calmly, 'Eddie sent one away to a mate of his at Swansea University, who threatened to shop him to the police if he didn't report it. He tried to find you, to warn you, but you weren't there, weren't in. If you're going to be sick, Simon, the toilet's on the left through the kitchen. All us cripples have them to hand.'

It occurred to Simon to go to the lavatory and slip quietly away. To go where? Back to the new vicarage to sleep under blankets in the armchair with the Good Book across his knees?

Isabel smiled, with difficulty. 'You've got nowhere to run, Mister priest. You go home, you'd better have a good story because he didn't believe Eddie's, that copper. Or you could go to Eddie's house if you want to watch the poor old bugger crawling up the walls screaming, "No, no, it couldn't have happened," and "Oh, Lord, I'm going out of my mind."'

'I don't understand.'

'Oh, poor dab, he doesn't understand.' There was a quiver in the last word and she bit down on it. 'Well, let me try and explain it to you, best I can. When I arrived at the church tonight, there were these two ugly little brown candles in the holders on the altar . . .'

Simon shook his head, not wanting to believe this – that he didn't even have to *be* there any more for the candles to . . .

'. . . that Eddie swears blind were not there when he came in with this policeman about twenty minutes before. And one was, you know, *smoking*. As if it had quite recently been . . . blown . . . out.'

'No,' he said uselessly.

'And I . . .' She stopped, leaned back, coughed and swallowed. '. . . I have never seen a grown man in such a state of terror, squealing that we had to get them out of the way before the copper saw them. But too scared to go near the things, he was, so I had to . . . take them.'

Simon said, croaked, 'Where's the other?'

'Tossed one over the hedge,' she said rapidly. 'And the other, of course, at you.'

There were glaring tears of fear and disgust in her eyes. Her hands gripped the padded chair arms. 'I can't talk any more. Make like a bloody priest, Simon, for Christ's sake, comfort me.'

She dragged three Kleenex from a box on the table, mopped her eyes. Hesitantly, he went and knelt by her chair, picked up her left hand. It was soft and warm with sweat, but there were still goose-pimples among the fine down on her bare arms. Her body began to shake and she snatched her hand away from him and wailed.

'Is that it . . .?' Cheeks streaked with mascara. 'Simon, my legs might be written off, I might not be able to feel my fanny, except in my fevered imagination, but I'm not a bloody porcelain doll, I'm not fragile. And I don't care if you *are* a fucking queer; just hold me, can't you?'

But he was afraid to touch her, knowing this wasn't only the candles, that cheap, cosmic conjuring trick. He brought an arm awkwardly around the back of the chair, meaning to squeeze her shoulder, but she lifted her left arm and trapped his hand under it and against a breast.

'Simon.'

'Don't do this,' he said. 'I'm the fucking vicar.'

With her right hand, she clasped his fingers tightly over her breast.

'Simon, will you do something for me? Take me back to the Abbey.'

Where he knelt, the open stove was pumping heat into his back. It felt like the doors of hell had opened.

'You're joking.' His mouth was dry.

'I have these dreams. Recurring dreams. Listen, you must know this isn't bullshit. It took away my feelings, that place, that Abbey. It took away . . .'

She gulped at her drink, held on to the glass and, weighing her words, said,

'It took away a young, passionate girl, and threw out a crabby spinster. No, listen!'

'I don't want to.' He'd closed his eyes tight, as if that could seal off the sound of her voice. 'I don't want to know this.'

'I was flying, Simon, that night. Higher than I ever thought you could fly. I can feel it now, I can feel it in places where there isn't any feeling.'

Her breast swelling against his hand. Making him embarrassed, ashamed, confused. Excited. A little. Flesh was flesh.

'All night, when I was lying there under the rubble, I wasn't, see. I was flying. Not all the time, some of the time I was asleep, but other times I was awake and flying. Hallucination, they said. But I know I was flying, and the part of me that can fly, see . . . it's still there. I have recurring dreams. I go back there. Go back. For the healing.'

In his head, the scraping of the chair on the stone, the flurry of air, the clash of metal and stone, metal and stone, metal and . . .

'No, please . . .' Simon dragged his hand away from her breast, came violently to his feet, harsh tears like acid in his eyes. 'I won't take you there.'

Isabel was rocking in her wheelchair.

'Why not? WHY NOT, YOU BASTARD?'

And threw the chair into electric motion, crashing her useless legs into the trestles of the table, reversing, sending the chair whining across the carpet at Simon.

'WHY NOT, YOU CREEPY LITTLE QUEER?'

The wheelchair's footplate bit into his ankles and he was thrown across her, his arms around her neck, his face on hers, a mingling of desperate tears.

'All I knew was,' Tom said, 'if that session wasn't busted up, and fast, somebody was gonna die.'

After barely an hour's sleep he'd started talking, lying there on his back. I could be asleep, Meryl thought, and he'd still have to talk.

'You can't say how you know these fings, but I fink it was gonna be Moira. Would've been Dave, but Dave pissed off first, got the shakes, so Moira was in the frame. All down to this Aelwyn geezer. When he died, Dave was gonna die. How? Maybe he'd beat his head on the stone wall, who can say. Maybe one of us . . . don't bear finking about, none of it.'

And he was only thinking about it now, Meryl thought, because he was here, in this temporary place. He wouldn't let it pollute his home, threaten Shelley or Vanessa.

'Somebody had to be in the frame. Some bastard had to go. We'd done it all wrong, we'd screwed it, we was letting it dictate the terms.'

'It?' Meryl said softly. 'What was "it"?'

Tom's big hand roamed her midriff, fingertips like pumice-stone.

'Now you're asking, ain'tcher? Whatever it was, it wasn't gonna let go, and it got into me, right in, after that last break.'

'Break?'

'Guitar break, darlin'. I'm going over the top like bleeding John Wayne wiv a sub-machine-gun. Felt good. At the time. But afterwards . . . Warning signs everywhere. Monk shapes. Man wiv two mouths. Had to shake it. Take it out. Grabbed the Jeep. Forgot about Debs. *Forgot about my fucking wife.*'

Tom rolled away, lay on his stomach, lay on his anguish, face in the pillow.

'Hiding away,' he mumbled. 'No use. No relief. I need to nail it, nail it good.'

'Listen. Please. Will you just listen?'

Running his hands through his damp hair. A clock some-where chiming ten. Her mother would be back soon.

She held the Southern Comfort bottle upside down, shaking drops into her glass.

'Get some Scotch,' she said.

'Will you *listen*?' He'd told her, best he could, about Sile Copesake.

She put down the bottle.

'Sure.'

'You have to realize . . . the Abbey cannot cure you. There is no healing in the Abbey. The Abbey has become a bad, cruel place.'

'It's still got part of me.'

'And you won't get it back.'

'My youth. My energy. My virginity. All the best bits.'

'None of it. I promise you. Keep away. You can only lose what you have left.'

'Some loss.'

'Isabel, listen to me. You're part of its history now. The stones cemented in blood? You've heard that? Like attracts like. Blood attracts blood. Stay away.'

'But you're going back. They want you to go back.'

'Yes. Sure. I think I'm going back. If the others go back, I'll go back.'

'So how come, Mister Cleverdick Priest, if I go back I can only lose what I've got left, while you . . .'

'Because, you stupid cow, what *you* have left is good. You're a good person, Isabel. That's the difference. You're worthwhile. Me, what I've got left is really nothing worth saving. I'm soiled. I'm a piece of shit.'

'You're a prat is what you are.'

'OK, let me tell you about the candles.'

'Eddie said you'd know about them. What are you going to tell me? You've been followed here by evil satanists who're desecrating your church?'

'Sweetheart, evil satanists, I just throw holy water in their faces and kick their arses. Do you want to hear this? It isn't pretty. It isn't endearing.'

'Do you want to tell me?'

'Yes, if it'll get you off my back.'

'Get the Scotch then.'

The up side of being in a wheelchair was the curious power it gave you over intelligent, able-bodied people. The way it was now, with everybody so politically correct, concerned about facilities for the disabled, you almost had to be careful not to *abuse* the power.

Simon St John was the first person who'd called Isabel Pugh a stupid cow for precisely twenty-one years.

That she found endearing.

That and his longish fair hair, his rueful smile, his bizarre reputation for slagging people off at their own funerals. And the knowledge, gleaned from her mother, that in his attic, locked away like a weapon, he kept an electric bass guitar.

And not afraid to use it?

Maybe he was. Maybe that was precisely what he was afraid of.

Simon was telling her horror stories. Not pretty. Not endearing. Stories to convince her that he was a piece of shit. Stories which – but for one crazy, orgasmic night twenty-one year ago – she would have been rejecting out of hand. And him. Throwing him out, the pervert.

She poured herself more whisky. Bit of a risk. She pretended to be a heavy drinker (hard-drinking, hard-hitting, bitter, cynical cow) but in fact it tended to make her sick sooner than she'd care to admit.

She said, as conversationally as she could manage, 'And you don't know who he is, this monk?'

Teeth-grindingly determined not to let him know how much – whether she believed it or not – this was frightening her. And yes, all right, nauseating her too. Or maybe that was the whisky.

Simon said, 'There must have been hundreds of monks over the centuries. A large proportion of them were probably . . .'

'Gay.'

'Or whatever they called it then. Yes. Buggers,' he said, verbally scourging himself. 'Sodomites.'

'You mean he . . .'

'Don't even think about it. I've been trying not to think about it for fourteen years. Which is, I'm afraid, terribly difficult, because he . . .'

'Got you flying,' Isabel said, a horrid, blasphemous porno-video playing in her head, all darkness and sweat.

Get him out of here. Tell him your mother's due back.

'And 1980, this was?' She couldn't. She had to know. Wouldn't have slept much anyway, tonight.

'December. We were here from the first of December until . . . until the eighth. There's only one room on each floor, and I was sleeping in the fourth one, the room at the very top of the tower. That's the rebuilt tower, not the one where you . . .'

'On your own?'

'Yes. Until the second night. It was the second night he came.'

'Did you have girlfriends at all before then, Simon?'

'I suppose so.'

'Bisexual, eh? Fashionable in the seventies, it was, Bowie and all those guys. Before Aids.'

'I was never a designer-poof,' Simon said, affronted.

'Were you even one at all before then?' Isabel said, almost eagerly.

His eyes shut down. 'I don't know what you mean.'

Of course he knew what she meant. She was suddenly struck by the surrealism of the situation: a crippled slag and a gay vicar sharing a bottle of Scotch, reminiscing about their respective disabilities. Oh God, mustn't call it that, *now* who wasn't being politically correct?

She could never have been interested in a vicar in the old days. But then, in the old days, there surely never were vicars like Simon.

Or maybe there had *always* been vicars like Simon. Maybe, back in the twelfth century . . .

He was saying, 'You spend a lot of time looking for a psychological answer. It's just your own sick fantasies. This is holy ground, for God's sake. How can this be happening on holy ground? And then, as if to prove himself, he sent me things, little presents.'

Simon sat back in his chair, his hands open on his lap.

'I'd find myself sleeping like this, particularly in chairs. I've always preferred sleeping in chairs.' He smiled. 'Fear of bed, probably.'

'I hate bloody chairs,' Isabel said. 'As you can imagine.'

'When I woke up, quite often, there'd be something in my hand.'

Isabel raised an eyebrow.

'No, you slut,' Simon said. 'Not that. A wooden cup, once, smelling of wine, very vinegary. Half a loaf of the roughest bread you ever saw. A piece of rope. A knife with a wooden handle, bound with thin strips of leather.'

Isabel looked above her to the big hole in the ceiling, the chair-lift to her bedroom, her – you had to laugh – escape route. Otherwise, apart from minor aids, the room was as she had always known it, stiflingly conventional.

'And candles,' Simon said. 'Often candles.'

Couldn't get away from here fast enough, had the money now. Had only stayed because the best of her was at the Abbey.

'You know what I'm saying,' Simon said.

Isabel said, because she knew she ought to say it at some point. 'You're having me on, aren't you?'

Simon did his lopsided *if only* smile. 'All the items had a really pungent smell about them. Often it was the pong that woke me up. Diseased. Horrible. I'd wash my hands a hundred times, but there are some things you can't wash away.'

'Miracle man, aren't you?' Isabel was alarmed at the unstable, whinneying tone in her voice.

'And it all began at the Abbey. Dollops of tallow on the pillow in the morning. And, worst of all, on the sheets. You know . . . underneath. I didn't tell the others. I mean, God, it was fascinating at first. And I was . . . flying, if you like. Intensity . . . white hot . . .'

Shaking his head, too hard. Disgusted. But worried, perhaps, that he still wasn't quite disgusted enough.

'Also, I felt I had some degree of control. Even when – the most spectacular exhibition he put on – a whole circle of candles had appeared in the studio when we came back from supper, to record. I didn't count them. I should have counted them. Dave counted them, but he kept quiet because he didn't want to spook Tom, Tom being a bit . . . erratic.'

Isabel's senses were swimming. No, it was not pretty, it was not endearing.

But never had the wheelchair felt lighter beneath her. Never had she looked through the hole in the ceiling and seen a shaft of light going all the way to the night sky.

Simon was looking at her in dismay. 'There were thirteen. Thirteen candles.'

'So?'

'Do you know what I do now? When I go to sleep in the chair, I have the Bible on my knees. I take it to bed with me. I don't want dreams.'

'Dreams are all I have,' Isabel said.

'Dreams are a doorway.'

'Yesssss,' she said, excited.

'You really don't understand, do you? Or maybe you don't want to.'

'Simon, if the Abbey can send you bits and bobs and candles from the twelfth century, then it proves I've been right all this time. It's taken away the best of me . . . *and it can give it all back.*'

357

'No!' Beating his fist on the table. 'Whatever you got back you wouldn't want, believe me. Look – the candles. The candles it's been sending into the church. If they really are made from human grease, doesn't that tell you anything?'

She looked into his eyes. They were gentle eyes, full of pain. Whatever he'd been, he was a good man now. But he also had the knowledge and, with him, maybe, just maybe, she could fly again.

There was the jiggling sound of her mother's key in the door. For the sake of Simon's reputation more than hers, Isabel slid the bottle of whisky and their glasses along the table, behind her computer monitor.

'Listen.' Simon whispered urgently. 'The night the thirteen candles came was the night Tom Storey killed his wife. The night John Lennon was shot. It was a bad night. The eighth of December.'

'And seven years to the night,' Isabel said, as the door opened, 'since a young boy called Gareth and I took a dive from the south-west tower. But you knew that too, didn't you? It was what brought you to my door.'

She smiled sweetly at him. 'And I've always wanted to watch a record being made.'

'No way,' he said standing up. 'Just put it out of your mind.'

'Oh no,' Isabel Pugh said. 'I don't think so.'

XII

Heart of Nowhere

Until it was time to go to the airport, Stephen Case spent so much of the day on the phone he was sure his right ear must be bruised.

He spoke to Sile Copesake in Gwent and Sile said softly, 'Simon St John: it's a provisional yes.'

Dave Reilly called him, sounding hostile. The bottom line was maybe. Also, if he *did* confirm, he wanted Prof Levin as producer. Not engineer, *producer*. If that bastard Russell Hornby was anywhere within a hundred miles of the Abbey, the deal was off.

'I'll see what I can do,' Steve said. Prof getting involved, this had been the idea all along, hadn't it?

An hour later, Reilly's *maybe* was hardened by a call from Moira Cairns, who wouldn't say where she was. 'Mr Case, I'm prepared to come down and talk about it.' Lovely low Scottish burr, the voice had survived anyway.

'Of course, Ms Cairns,' Steve said expansively. 'Whatever you think best.'

The most curious call was from a woman called Meryl Coleford-Somers.

Meryl C. . .?

Hell, yes. Meryl. Mrs Whiplash.

Meryl said, 'He's an important man. You must treat him with care, you hear me?'

'Of course,' Steve said. 'It's what we're known for.'

Meryl said, 'And he won't sign anything. Not this time, he says.'

'Fine,' Steve said sensitively.

'He'll have a car there the whole time, and if the situation becomes in any way difficult, he reserves the right to leave, as and when.'

'I can accept that,' Steve said soothingly.

'I shall be driving him,' she said. 'I'll be with him.' And Steve wrote on his memo pad,

?? CALL BROADBANK!

And finally Simon St John. The vicar. Referred to him by Sile Copesake. Cautious, naturally. He wanted them all booked into a hotel for at least one night before they went near the Abbey. At which, Steve became equally cautious, especially when St John said he would arrange the hotel himself. What did he want, to talk them all out of it? The conversation became a little tense. Steve sensed that if he didn't agree, St John would cry off, leaving Steve with Sile Copesake to deal with.

He crossed his fingers, said OK. He took down directions to be passed on to Reilly and Cairns and, er, Meryl Coleford-Somers. Called up Sile to report this development, but Sile was out, and it was time anyway to summon TMM's chauffeured stretch Mercedes and have himself driven to Heathrow.

Steve remembered the heady days when, if you were meeting a rock star off the plane, you'd have to beat a path through a thousand schoolgirls. Now it was only the paparazzi, and they wouldn't recognize this guy from any of the flash financiers flying in. Big in America wasn't the same.

The British-born superstar said he'd kind of like to stay at the Ritz. He'd never stayed at the Ritz before. Last time he toured here, he wasn't quite big enough, and now he was, so he wanted to stay at the Ritz.

In the back of the Mercedes, *en route* to the Ritz, Steve said, 'We're really glad you could make it, Lee.'

A grin spread over Lee Gibson's swarthy pirate's face. He had a long, sharp nose and shoulder-length curly hair. He wore the kind of jacket of which Steve's was an imitation. Lee's was more creased.

'Yeah,' he said. 'Be interesting to see what the years've done to those neurotic assholes.'

Lee had been living in L.A. seven, eight years. There was a

time, Steve remembered, when it was considered suitable in America for British rock stars to maintain their British regional accents, especially if it was London or Liverpool. Not any more, apparently.

Lee also had a token Californian suntan, not enough of one to pose a melanoma risk, presumably. He gazed happily out of the Merc's middle window at all the grey-faced English people with tense expressions and umbrellas. Shot Steve another grin. 'What a shithole, huh?'

'Right,' Steve said.

'You fixed up about the mobile home? No way'm I gonna stay in that tower again. Fucking freezing, man.'

'It's ordered, Lee. Don't worry.'

'I never *worry*, man,' said Lee. 'All my worries are sub-contracted to the highest bidder.'

They both laughed, Steve through gritted teeth. Still unable to figure this out. Why should Lee Gibson, double-Grammy Award winner 1993, now among the top ten richest expatriate British rock musicians, have agreed to return to the country which failed to recognize his talent to reunite with a weird little band which had used him as a session-drummer?

It was certainly a coup for TMM and for Sile Copesake who'd organized it. It would sell a lot of albums. But it didn't make a lot of sense.

Surprising how sentimental people could be.

The sight of the guitar behind glass turned Moira's heart to marshmallow.

The guitar had a golden spruce top, rosewood body, an ebony fingerboard and mother of pearl around the soundhole.

It wasn't as big as some of the Dreadnoughts, maybe the old jumbo size, with a thin back. But it was the most expensive instrument in the store by several hundred pounds. And it shimmered with memories.

She had enough left for that and a new Ovation. Just about. If she was being really, *really* crazy.

There hadn't, in fact, been much left in the deposit account at the Bank of Scotland by the time Moira had come out of there. Knowing full well that if she went all the way back to Skye to fetch her regular Ovation she'd find some excuse to stay there, she'd drawn out a whole five grand, gone shopping for clothes. Cold weather clothes.

And for a guitar.

There'd been a nice secondhand Ovation Glen Campbell in the store, but she'd settled for a humbler model because it was the only Ovation they had new. Secondhand was always a risk. Like, maybe the last owner had sold it to buy smack. With a secondhand, it could sometimes take a couple of months to play out the bad stuff (drugs, or depression due to failure, broken relationship, money trouble). She didn't have a couple of months and the last thing she needed was to take any bad stuff with her to the Abbey.

To the Abbey. Black walls, death.

Jesus, I can't believe I'm doing this.

Malcolm had even been dialling the TMM number for her as she took the phone, like he was handing her a pistol to put in her mouth and helpfully cocking the hammer.

This guy Steve Case had sounded like your standard record company executive trash. Throwing out phrases like Aelwyn the Dreamer to prove they had the tapes. Her being distant, shooting hostile rays down the mouthpiece – as if any 1990s record company exec would be sensitive enough to notice.

But when he said, *We've remodelled the Abbey, we're going to reopen it*, she'd known at once what this was about and gone cold and still with the knowledge.

Got to go back.

The Duchess in the steam. The sad figures of lumbering Tom and Simon in his monk's robe and poor wee Davey fading away. So many years blocking it all out, avoiding the inevitable.

Oh, Lord . . .

And when it finally comes back, it comes back over the phone from London, courtesy of some smooth, laid-back creep with a coke spoon in his inside pocket.

Got to go back.
For the healing.

Who sang that? Van Morrison. Poor old Van, the eternal seeker after spiritual truth, redemption.

If it had come last year, a month ago . . . Christ, if it had come last week, she'd have hung up immediately. What did they think she was, a basket case?

OK, she'd said, very quietly. *I'll think about it. Call you back.*

And she had. Automatically, almost. With hardly a thought, except that she was no damn good to anybody, least of all herself, with the Duchess dead and the Abbey hanging over her.

And when she'd done it – called him back first thing this morning – it was like some cosmic flunkey was suddenly running in front of her removing all the barriers. Malcolm having the rest of her stuff taxied over from the Clydeview Private Hotel. A call back from Case's secretary to say the Reverend Simon St John had her booked into an inn a few miles from the Abbey. The *Reverend*! Jesus God, redemption took some strange, stony paths, didn't it just.

And now she was pointing at the mellow-looking guitar in the air-conditioned showcase – the only exhibit in the store behind protective glass; all the other guitars were on racks, so the punters could pull them down, try a few chords.

The young guy in charge said, 'You do know what that is, don't you?'

Looking down at her in his superior way, having no doubt cast her as a Mum pricing up Junior's first wee guitar for Christmas.

And, hell, it *was* a lot of money. These imports just got more and more pricey; no way you'd pay that much in the States, no way at all.

On the other hand, spending more money than she could afford would be a further statement of commitment, right? Leaving so abruptly, making no attempt to contact Simon or Tom, not even waiting for Davey to call back, all that was a demonstration of how insecure she still must be, underneath, about this thing. Having to act fast, get on the road, do some hard driving, before reason could prevail. *We're no' safe together . . . we're too much.* This, fourteen years ago, saying: We blew it, let's cut our losses, we're too inexperienced to handle this, let's get the hell out while we still can.

Thinking she could leave it all behind, that none of it was going with her, that by being somewhere else, doing other things with other people, she could shake it off. Like purging the body of a need for drugs. Only purging the spirit was just so much harder.

'Sure I know what it is,' she said to the store manager, almost snarling. 'It's an M38 Grand Auditorium. Now get the damn thing down before I change ma mind.'

Leaving him flushed and dumbfounded as she walked out of the store, nearly three and half grand lighter, a guitar case in each hand. Thinking, you lucky wee swine, if you don't sell more than a pair of castanets the next fortnight you'll still have earned your Christmas bonus.

Feeling better – *terrified*, but at least it had a focus – she headed south, eyes open.

Eyes open, right?

On her own now, but not naked.

Oh *God*.

At the pub, effortlessly hammering the locals at darts, Weasel had learned a good deal about this Meryl, who, being of farming – or, rather farm *labouring* – stock, had a whole bunch of relatives hereabouts.

Born out Bisley way into a big family, good-looker from an early age, never slow to exploit it. Big ideas. Too good for the local boys, except for the odd fumble behind the hedge, for the experience. Buggers off to Cheltenham, marries a businessman, Charles Somers, moves down to the West Country, but it don't last, couldn't be expected to, not with this lady.

Divorced, Meryl high-tails it back to Cheltenham, teaches

cookery for a few years at some snooty school. Succession of
blokes, then talk of her going all religious, but, like *weird*-
religious. Finally fetches up as 'cook-housekeeper' to that
Councillor Broadbank – talk about a slippery bastard.

So how would you feel – Weasel asking – if she'd pissed off
with your, er, best mate?

So much merry laughter at that one that the poor sodding
landlord must've been scared it'd bring half his beams down.

Next morning, Weasel stakes out this Hall Farm for an hour
or two, parking in the village half a mile away. Watches
Broadbank cruising off about ten then has a little nose around.
True enough, all quiet, no Meryl. The slippery bastard was on
the level this time.

Weasel motored over to the Love-Storey wholesale depot in
Stroud to borrow the phone. He rang Directory Enquiries and
got a number for Dave Reilly's old ma in Hoylake – it being
Dave who'd directed him to Tom when he come out of pokey,
so worth a shot.

Phone was answered by an unknown male, elderly. Maybe
Dave had got hisself a new daddy.

'David? Gone off with his girlfriend, pal.'

'Girlfriend? Who? Where's she hang out?'

'Scottish girl. She rang here for him, like you, yesterday.
We gave her his London number.'

'Which is?'

'Hang on. Rhoda, what's that number for your David?'

But when Weasel rang the London number some geezer,
gave his name as Adrian, said irritably that Dave Kite (Dave
Kite?) wasn't here no more, no idea where he'd gone, he'd had
to clear off in a hurry this morning so that he, Adrian, could
take up residence as was his right under the deal with Muthah
Mirth.

Scottish girl?

Couldn't be, could it?

Nah.

*

Dave, at the wheel of the grumbling old Fiat, was trying to remember coming across the Severn Bridge before. Didn't remember the mud flats, water like sheet-metal, or the crazy toll they made you pay to go into Wales. The fact that they let you out for nothing, if you were in any state to *get* yourself out . . . Was this an omen?

give yourself a break, Dave. Pretend there's no such things as omens, yeh?

'That's bloody rich. *You* believed in them. Least, she did, Yoko, which amounted to the same thing. And fate . . .'

don't fucking start, Reilly . . .

'. . . And how you could change the whole pattern of your life if you went off in some pre-arranged direction along a certain line of latitude, some crap like that. Is it right she used to put you on a plane for somewhere you'd never heard of, because it would be quote good for you unquote, and you never argued, you just went? "Directional Therapy", right?'

don't push it, Dave.

'All I'm saying is, how is that any more stupid than what I'm doing now? Moira Cairns leaves a message on me answer-phone and I leap up and pack me bags – yeh, yeh, I had to leave there anyway, but . . .'

did I say it was stupid? Listen, if there's only one woman you ever connected with, sooner or later you've gorra go for it. Even if you're wading into a river of shit with no wellies.

Curiously, the countryside seemed greener, better-wooded on the Welsh side of the bridge. And undulating; already there were hills, easy, rounded hills. He came off the motorway at Chepstow; should've waited for the Abergavenny exit, but he wanted to take it slowly.

On the basis that he couldn't believe he was here.

It was a bright, cold morning. December 4. Bright and cold and unreal. The further he drove into the green border country, the more detached he became, the deeper the feeling of unreality.

'Suppose she's not there.'

No reply.

'I said, suppose . . .'

He peered into the rear-view mirror. It was clear, no mist, just a reflection of the road from Chepstow to Monmouth. Ahead of him was the wide, wooded canyon of the Wye Valley. He drove around a bend and – *Christ!*

The abbey ruins were enormous. They filled the car windows, blocked out the forestry and the river and half the sky. He was thrown into panic, wanted to slam the Fiat into reverse, swing round in the road, race for the border.

wrong Abbey, Dave.

'What?'

'*Tintern. This is Tintern Abbey. A very famous national monument.*

'I . . .'

The ruins were massive, far too massive. And manicured, and spread out like an enormous medieval film set.

Unreal. There was no reality here. This abbey was a tourist attraction. There was scaffolding all over it; winter maintenance. This abbey was dead.

The road slid into the village of Tintern and Dave stopped the car, bowed his head over the steering wheel and took long, deep breaths. He sat back, leaned his head over the seat back.

What am I doing here?

Suppose the other Abbey – *that* Abbey – did not exist except in some maverick sphere of the imagination. Suppose he was driving in wild pursuit of an impossible dream. Suppose that he'd manufactured Moira's voice on his answering machine. That when he'd called Kaufmann's office and heard the secretary say, *I'm sorry, Moira's left, said to tell you she'll meet you at the Abbey, does that make any sense?* What she'd really said was, *I'm sorry, there's no one called Kaufmann here and I've never heard of a Moira, perhaps you have the wrong . . .*

He sat at the wheel several minutes with the engine running, shaking as violently as the gearstick, before forcing himself to go into a phone kiosk, feeling in his pocket for the out-of-date diary in which he'd written Kaufmann's and Stephen Case's numbers.

Trying to call Case, it was just like being in one of those blurred, inexact dreams; his fingers kept hitting the wrong buttons and he'd have to keep starting over.

He felt pitifully grateful when the crisp female voice answered 'TMM?' And almost a warm affection for the cool, offhand, 'Dave, glad you called. You need to know that Simon St John's booked you a room at a pub called . . . have you got a pen?'

He must have been looking strange because, when he left the phone box, clutching his diary, an elderly couple stared at him – he a retired colonel type with a tight, grey military moustache and she with knife-crease trousers, silk scarf and, around her fine, white coiffure . . . a very pronounced quivering nimbus of deepening purple and black.

No. No! No! No! The old couple staring at him and then turning and hurrying away, Dave laid his head against the cool, wet windscreen of his Fiat.

December again. Maybe, this time of year, tension thrust his psychic circuitry into overload, feeding his mind with misinformation. Maybe his eyes were going, he needed glasses. Maybe he had a brain tumour.

nobody said it was gonna be easy, Dave. Sometimes you just gorra take the rough with the rough.

'Bugger off,' Dave said.

The Castle Inn was on the old Hereford road, eight miles east of the Abbey, almost under the Skirrid. Despite its name, it was no older than the century, a bright, compact place; it felt OK.

Simon decided it would do.

Going directly to the Abbey would be beyond crazy; they needed to meet, talk things over, work out some kind of strategy. Maybe the closeness of the Skirrid would help.

His head felt like a spin-drier. Everything was happening at whirlwind speed, and yet it seemed as if time had been slowed, the machine pre-programmed to accommodate everything that needed to be arranged.

Sile Copesake had been on the phone at ten a.m. Calling from where? From the Abbey? He hadn't even thought to ask. Sile had told him, in essence, that the other members of the Philosopher's Stone had been contacted and were ready to record within the week. Sile had given him the number of a man called Stephen Case at TMM, who would be co-ordinating the operation.

Simon couldn't believe the way it was happening. In his admittedly limited experience, recording sessions usually took months to set up. He felt as if he was spiralling in a vortex. Which was exactly how it had happened last time, fourteen years ago. Whisked into Goff's magical new studio. The psychology: don't give them time to think too hard.

The other difference being that, then, they'd believed it was safe. Holy ground. Now they knew nowhere was safe, least of all the Abbey. This time, they were going to have to be prepared. Physically and spiritually.

Hence, the Castle Inn. He'd called Stephen Case, given him very detailed directions. Said he would be booking four rooms; no way could this band be plunged cold into the Abbey. To his slight surprise, Case had eventually said OK; he'd pass on the information.

Needing for there to be at least one technical difficulty, some small moral or ethical hitch, he'd called his bishop. And the Bishop had said, to his incredulous dismay, 'Simon, what an absolutely splendid idea, I had absolutely no idea you were a musician. I think it's awfully important for the Church to be involved in aspects of youth-culture, and . . . I say, let's tell the Press!'

Simon had talked him out of that one, at least. For the present.

When he got back to the vicarage after checking out the Castle Inn and its ambience he found an envelope behind the door. No stamp.

SIMON, it said.

And over the top of that,
PRIVATE. URGENT.
The note inside was handwritten.

> *I've been trying to get hold of you since last night. If you don't know already. I've had one of the brown candles analysed. It's believed to be made from animal fat, possibly human. I'm afraid I was forced to call in the police. Expect a visit from Supt. GA Jones. Try and see me before he sees you, for God's sake.*
>
> *Eddie*

Simon read the note twice.

'I really thought it was simply tallow,' he whispered, as if the policeman was already questioning him. 'Tallow, brown with age.'

He went to the study window to check the lane.

Nobody about, thank God. Quietly, he let himself out of the house and ran to his car.

'Thought I was leaving it behind, see, transferring to Gwent,' mused Gwyn Arthur to Eddie Edwards over pints of Welsh bitter in the Dragon.

'Filthy weather?'

'Not exactly that. Not *only* that. The things that happened in the West that you had problems explaining in a police report. I thought that here, being so close to the Border and barely an hour from Cardiff, it would all be so much less . . . do you know the word "numinous"?'

Eddie Edwards, never a man to throw his academic background in anyone's face, said he thought he probably did.

'Well, like that,' Gwyn Arthur said, cleaning out his pipe with his car key. 'Know why I sent myself on this job instead of one of my youngsters? Because I had a feeling, Eddie. A feeling.'

He craned his neck to see out of the window, where the pub's tiny car park went into a drastic slope towards the valley road. 'Where's that go to?'

'*Abaty Ystrad Ddu*,' said Eddie, 'to quote the bilingual sign which disappeared last year and was never replaced. Now, as far as the Welsh Office highways department is concerned, it goes to the heart of nowhere.'

Gwyn nodded. 'Feelings,' he said. 'Not much place for feelings any more in police work. If it isn't on the National Computer we don't want to know.'

'Like everything else, these days.'

'My day off, this is. Can't leave well alone, can I? Your vicar, now, think he knows all about those candles? Why is he avoiding me?'

'You think he might know something about it?'

'And the rest,' said Gwyn Arthur. 'And the rest.'

'And what do you think the rest is?'

'I think,' said Gwyn Arthur, 'that we shall probably see. And soon. The Heart of Nowhere, you said? Very good. I like that.'

Part Four

I

Old Love

O ut of the brown hedges, above the fields of sheep and
cows, a hill jutted like a cut thumb. It jolted Dave; it
was the first landmark he'd recognized since crossing
the Severn Bridge.

The Skirrid. The Holy Hill, said to have been split by an
earthquake or a bolt of lightning when the darkness fell over
Calvary. You never forgot the Skirrid.

Rusting, late-afternoon clouds were setting respectfully
around the summit of the hill. It did nothing to dispel the
dreamstate.

And at that moment, in this narrow, switchback lane, the
Fiat's engine began to die. Dave trod the accelerator flat to the
rubber mat, but the energy was draining away into a parched
kind of death-rattle.

He didn't say *shit* or anything like that. He didn't shake the
wheel or thump the dash. He felt curiously calm when the old
car finally gave up the ghost on the single-track country lane,
within pushing distance of a gated field-entrance.

Dave shrugged. He got out, let the handbrake off, walked the
car down a gentle gradient into the field entrance, applied the
handbrake, locked the car and left it there, his suitcase in the boot.

And walked off along the road.

He knew it must be getting cold, it was, after all, December,
but it didn't feel cold. He was wearing an old grey cotton jacket
over a polo-neck sweater.

The deserted lane led in almost a direct line towards the
Skirrid. It was as if some form of magnetism in the rock had
stilled the engine. Like he was destined to do this stretch on
foot. Like it was all meant.

Dave walked towards the mountain. It only looked like a mountain because it was on its own in the fields, the only mark on the sky, a solitary pilgrim in a wintry wasteland.

There ought to be a sense of sacred peace, but there wasn't. Close up, the hill looked crooked, crippled. There was a cindery projection, like a scab, a wound only partly-healed.

More than anything, the feeling the Skirrid was giving off was one of unrest. Dave remembered seeing it for the first time in 1980. Max Goff had sent each of them a guidebook to the area to prove what a safe and sanctified spot this was. The booklet told how local people had collected holy soil from the God-smitten hill. How tons of the stuff had been carried down and dumped in the foundations of churches, the way alleged splinters from the One True Cross had once been handed around.

There was supposed to have been a chapel up near the top dedicated to St Michael, God's senior bruiser, but there wasn't much left of it, apparently.

And it just didn't feel holy.

Maybe these legends were thrown up not so much by Christianity as ancient paganism. Other places, it was less exalted – you had a strange-looking chunk out of a hill, it was caused by some giant with big boots. Here, inside a wide circle of medieval castles and abbeys, it had to be an Act of God. Dismayed by developments in the Middle East, the Almighty decides to punch a hole in a small mountain in South Wales. Divine logic.

The nearness of the Skirrid made him think of the Abbey half a dozen miles the other side. And that led to thoughts of Moira Cairns and an image of a woman trailing a guitar along a beach, the word *deathoak* scrawled in the sand, and the hideous bonnet and an echo of Prof Levin asking, after hearing the Black Album, if she was still alive and everything.

And am I ever gonna see you again?
I doubt it
I doubt it.

Bloody song kept drifting into his head. He *hated* that song. That song was the worst thing he'd ever done.

can't take it back now, Dave.

'Shut up,' he screamed at the song locked in his brain. 'Shut the fuck up, will you?'

yeh, that was about the size of it. If you can't do better than that, shurrup. It was very hurtful.

He had to laugh. 'You're a bastard, John.'

famous for it. You read that one about me takin' the piss out of cripples in the street? In the Pool that'd be, or maybe it was Hamburg. Don't remember it meself, I was probably pissed.

'I didn't mean it, you know.'

on a Bad Day? Course you meant it.

'Well, all right. I did mean it. At the time.'

On a Bad Day. The words written down, for the first and last time, on the torn-off lid of a box of Maltesers. Hadn't eaten a Malteser from that day to this.

Chorus line,

> *And are we ever gonna see you*
> *Ever gonna see you again?*
> *I doubt it*
> *I doubt it.*

The words hung like a vapour trail in the sky around the half-obscured summit of the Skirrid. The way *deathoak* had shone like neon in the studio that night. The way the black aura throbbed in the air around . . . around half the bloody people he seemed to meet these days. If a tractor came past now, there'd be some old bloke in the saddle grinning through his terminal haze.

Oh God, why me. . .?

crackin' up, Dave?

'Sod off.' He carried on walking. By his reckoning, this Castle Inn of Simon's was less than a mile away. If he kept on walking, he was bound to get there sooner or later. Bound to get *somewhere*.

The atmosphere was heavy. Cold and sultry. Could you *have* cold and sultry? No birds sang. After a while he couldn't stand the silence.

'John?'

what?

'Tell me again. What am I doing here? Why've I come?'

well, principally, Dave, you've come because you're a stupid twat. Sorry, what d'you want me to say?

'Would the truth be stretching things?'

shit, you're sounding almost humble. Fucked if I know how to handle this. When I give you the truth, it's the last thing you ever want. I give you 'Woman' and 'Beautiful Boy' and stuff like that, you want 'Day in the Life' and 'Girl' and 'Norwegian Wood'. And then you wanna kill me. Everybody wants to kill me. Listen, you wanna know why you're doing this, I'll tell you, OK. Just don't throw it back at me, man. The reason you're doing this is Old Love. Old Love. It's like old gold, polishes up like new, only better. How's that?

'Yeh. Thanks.' Dave came to a fork in the road. The widest option curved away from the Skirrid, almost back the way he'd come. The hill was the only landmark he knew; he followed the straight route.

Sour clouds were massing now around the Skirrid, dense as mouldy cheese, hardened by dusk. There were only fields as far as he could see, which wasn't actually that far any more. No visible farmhouses; you wouldn't think this area could be so remote, would you?

After a few hundred yards, he became aware that the hedges were closer on either side, that the track he was following was no longer wide enough for a car and was gradually growing steeper.

The dusk closed around him. He had a feeling of walking towards the end of his life. He'd never felt as lonely.

but you still got me, Dave. You've always got me, son. For ever and ever.

'It's getting ridiculous,' Shelley said, not laughing. Looking in fact very worried, and Martin Broadbank was ashamed that he couldn't think of a damn thing to do about it.

Except for, perhaps, sitting next to her on that big, squashy sofa of hers, and putting a neighbourly arm around her shoulders.

At this moment, Martin was alone on the big sofa, Shelley standing in the centre of the rustic-brick-walled drawing-room. Although her crisp, white blouse was sufficiently unbuttoned to ensure that the option was never far from his thoughts, he had to concede that this perhaps wasn't the time to offer her his neighbourly arms.

The voluptuous Mrs Storey seemed, as usual, unaware of her effect on him. 'It must seem odd to you, Martin, that he's never been away from the house, even for one night, let alone two.'

'Well, Meryl . . .' He hesitated. 'She's a very capable woman. I'm sure she wouldn't let any harm come to him.'

Shelley's eyes sparked angrily. 'You mean apart from the harm she might personally inflict with her misguided spiritualist fervour?'

'But that's hardly . . .' Martin was mildly surprised that this seemed to be at the forefront of her concern rather than the probable impact of Meryl's undoubted sexual magnetism.

'Oh, Martin.' Shelley moved restlessly to the big picture window, overlooking the treeless, sloping lawns and two men in overalls repairing the fence. 'You've had rather a sheltered life, haven't you?'

He wanted to protest. He thought it unjust that he should be accused of naïvety on the sole basis of not being terribly intimidated by the dubious implications of what Meryl was wont to refer to as 'other spheres of existence'.

'Because I don't believe in this nonsense?'

'Because you don't realize the harm it can cause,' Shelley said simply.

'Shel?'

Shelley turned sharply from the window. The hairy little man, Weasel, was shuffling despondently in the doorway, shaking his head.

'Wasn't quick enough, Shel. Missed him. He was less than

379

five miles away all the time. In that new motel down the Gloucester road.'

'Of course.' Shelley punched her left palm. 'New.'

Martin was baffled.

'Checked out this morning,' Weasel said. 'About half-eleven.'

'Was he alone?'

'Er . . . Yeah. It was a double chalet, but he was on his own. When he checked out. So they said.'

'Perhaps Meryl booked another chalet then,' Martin said tentatively.

'What the hell does that matter?' Shelley snapped. 'The question is what we do next. Do you think there's any point at all in telling the police? I'm not bothered about any connections they might make with the Tulleys, that's irrelevant now.'

'I'm afraid,' said Martin gently, 'that the police don't organize searches for men who appear to have gone off with a woman. If you see what I mean.'

Shelley stiffened, glared at him and then sort of slumped. 'You're right, of course. But . . . I mean . . . what the *hell* does the stupid woman think she's *doing*?'

'She likes to think she can help,' Martin said, feeling foolish.

'Sunday tomorrer,' Weasel said. 'I'll make a few calls tonight, if I can use the blower.'

'What? Oh. Sure.'

'And I'll get on the road early. I'll pull out all the stops, Shel.'

'I know you will,' Shelley said, and silence fell. Martin felt the weight of something he couldn't understand.

In the corner of the drawing-room, the child, Vanessa, stood by a bookcase, still as a mannequin.

Her eyes, behind those extraordinary designer pebble glasses, were fixed on Weasel.

*

The mist and the darkness arrived together and very suddenly. As suddenly, it seemed, as stepping out of an artificially lit, windowless room and discovering it was night.

It had been day and now, he discovered, it was night. All of a sudden.

Dave didn't care.

Didn't give a toss.

What could happen to you on a holy mountain?

He could still see his feet in their puny moccasins. He could feel sharp stones under the rubber soles, indicating that this was not what you'd call a road any more and therefore what he should do, immediately, was turn back. Common sense demanded that he turn back.

'John?'

No answer.

'Come on, you bastard, don't piss about.'

There wasn't even a breeze to move the wintry silence. It was cold, though, on the Skirrid. Common sense suggested he turn around and find his way back to the car, because sooner or later another vehicle would pass that way – OK, probably driven by a person with an unpleasant black halo, but he didn't need to mention that.

But he carried on walking. Not *impelled* exactly. He just thought: Well, I might as well.

A kind of mystical apathy, he'd be thinking later.

Meanwhile, he found himself thinking of that poor bugger Aelwyn Breadwinner plodding through the night – and the snow; there seemed to have been snow – to hammer on the door of the Abbey. Sanctuary! Sanctuary!

He heard himself say, 'You sought sanctuary, didn't you?'

Silence. He hadn't thought about it; just heard himself say it: sanctuary. He stopped on the path, clutching frantically at an escaping thought disappearing like a firefly into the mist. No, don't chase it. Don't think. Carry on walking.

> *Aelwyn the dreamer*
> *Came down from the mountain*

Plodding feet in tempo with the song.

> *His harp on his shoulder*
> *His hopes for the future*

Keep going. Don't *think*.

> *Where William de Braose's*
> *Tables were groaning*
> *With wild boar and sweetmeats*
> *And liquor and . . .*

'Come on,' he yelled suddenly. 'You know what I'm saying. New York. You wanted to live in New York because you reckoned it was the only place – ha ha – where you could walk around without being bothered.'

Still silence. He let it lie, thinking hard. Then there was a scuffling in some bushes to his left; a bird or a rabbit. It seemed to kick-start the night; there was a fluttering in front of him and a beating of strong wings overhead.

'Come on!' Dave shouted against the noise. 'Think. The Dakota. The magic citadel. Protection. Sanctuary, right? The late Seventies this would be. You decided you wanted to become an American citizen. All-American ex-Beatle. But they wouldn't give you a green card for ages. The government was suspicious. You were a troublemaker. You gave press conferences in bed, you sat in a bag and mumbled subversion about giving peace a chance. You were a shit-stirrer and you had a big following. You were the very last kind of American citizen that the Reagan administration needed. You were under heavy surveillance, you . . .'

I lived there. It was my home.

'What?'

here's Yoko, here's me. It's our home.

The voice was in the mist. The mist laughed.

it was our city. Once, I – get this, Dave – we once gave a thousand dollars to a fund to provide New York cops with bulletproof vests. How unAmerican can you get?

'I didn't know that.'

*sanctuary. Good word. In England I couldn't go out the fuckin'
front door, man. Couldn't gerra bag of chips from the chippy,
nothing. And she says – this is Yoko – you'll be able to walk here,
she says. And it was right, y'know? It's like you've been psychologically crippled for years and somebody takes away your wheelchair
and says you don't need a wheelchair here. And nobody bothers you,
nobody wants a piece of you to take home and stick on the
mantelpiece. All the people, either they don't give a shit or they
respect your privacy and it's like, hi John, nice day. Not, can you
give us a spare pair of your underpants to auction for our new scout
hut or whatever. It's freedom. I'd forgotten what that was about.*

The path was getting narrower, he could feel the bank on
either side. The stones were sharper. The soles of his feet hurt.
He had an image of Christ *en route* to his execution, barefoot,
bloody great cross over his shoulder.

The way things are going, they're gonna cru . . .

The Romans and the Pharisees and the CIA and the FBI and
the Food and Drug Administration.

'What was it like? You remember Mark Chapman?'

Long, long silence.

He carried on tramping, pain in the soles of his feet, pains
in his calves now, he was seriously out of breath and out of
condition, and in this mist he'd never know when he got to the
summit anyway unless he was granted a Holy Vision.

*it's a funny thing, but I can't even recall what the little fucker
looked like. I* can vaguely *remember some young guy coming up to
me with a copy of the album, and I signed it and I remember him
being kind of shy, which was unusual – this is New York, man,
shyness is not a basic character flaw here. So I vaguely remember
him first time round. The* other *time . . . the last time? No.
Nothing. Maybe you got me on a bad day, Dave. On a Bad Day,
geddit?*

The mist laughed.

Dave felt terrible. Also cold, especially his hands. And
exhausted.

'I'm gonna have to stop.'

yeh, this is as far as you'll get.

He felt his feet beginning to slide back. Up to now he'd been drawn forward, like being on a slow escalator. But he knew that if he started to slip he'd lose contact, lose *meaningful* contact; it would be back to the insults and the banter. He fought for breath and threw his arms forward, as if there was an invisible rope out there he could grasp.

'Deathoak,' he managed. 'Is that just an anagram of The Dakota. With a spare T?'

There was no rope to grasp. The air was cold and still. His moccasins skidded on the wet stones and he fell and slid backwards, tearing his hands on the stones as he tried to stop the momentum.

Screaming, 'You got the green card. They let you st . . .' as the night and the clinging mist dragged him down the Skirrid.

'. . . they let you in. And then you . . .'

Must have been a gulley he hadn't noticed on his way up. It was as if someone had picked him up and flung him back and into space. He landed hard, was stunned.

And he knew he wasn't going back; he'd lost it.

Dave rolled over, was dizzy. Under his bleeding hands he felt cold grass; he rolled over again and buried his face in it. There was some kind of grassy slope. He closed his eyes and wrapped his arms around his head and rolled over and over down the cold, wet gradient, gathering mud and night and mist and feeling nothing until his hands and face were slashed and stinging and he realized he must have stopped and was in the middle of a vicious thorn bush or maybe had crashed a hedge-hogs' convention. He laughed.

Or maybe passed out. He didn't quite remember how he came to be rolling down the grass. Some time later he stood up.

He had to get out of here.

. . . could feel neither his fingers nor his toes in his worn-out boots, and the sweat froze on his face as he ran towards the distant light, a candle in a window slit . . . his ears always straining for . . . the clamour of men and horses . . . these murdering damned ewe-fuckers . . .

Then light flickered up ahead.

Sanctuary.

'Is it . . .?'

'By God, it is, too. You were right. How the hell did you
. . .?'

'Was just a feeling.'

'You're uncanny, you people. Seriously uncanny.'

They made him sit up.

'Take it gently, he might've broken something.'

'Jesus Christ, will you look at the state of his face?'

'Always looks worse than it is. Take it from an old soldier.'

Dave said, 'I didn't know you were ever a soldier, Prof.'

'National bloody service. Don't even talk about it. In fact
don't talk at all. Here, hang on to this. Bloody liability, you are,
Reilly.'

'What is it?'

'Think it's to put an umbrella on. In summer.'

'What's this place?'

'Nah, nah. Wrong question. You gotta say "Where am I?"
I'll pretend you said it. You're in what I believe is known as a
beer garden. The building you see there is the . . . what's it
called?'

'The Castle Inn.'

'Only we can't take you in looking like that. Maybe there's
some back stairs we can smuggle you up. By God, David, I'm
fucking glad to see you. Car abandoned by the roadside, three
degrees of frost forecast, we thought . . . I can't tell you what
we thought.'

Dave said, 'Who's that with you?'

The dark figure was edged with gold from the lights in the
inn. It was not in a long dress, but jeans and a dark sweater and
a black shawl around its head.

He whispered, 'Is it Moira?'

It *was* a black shawl, wasn't it?

II

Orphan

And you thought you were too old to fall in love.

Prof Levin had never met Moira until tonight. When he came down from Dave's room he found her ordering coffee in the Castle Inn's firelit lounge bar.

She was something to look at, even in her camouflage gear, jeans and trainers and a black anorak. She was a serious presence; you wouldn't forget anything about her, even after fourteen years.

And yet any pent-up love in Dave's eyes when he saw her had been smothered by something else. Pain. Fear even.

Why should Dave be afraid of Moira Cairns? *I was high on a woman*, he'd said, when Prof had asked him what substances he'd been absorbing the night they recorded the Black Album. What was he high on tonight, stumbling about like some wild man of the woods?

'Cream, Prof?' Moira set down a tray on a wrought-iron table near the shimmering coal fire.

'Lots,' Prof said.

On his way here, his headlights had found Dave's rusting Fiat wedged in a field gateway at the side of the road. Broken down, or what? It was another half-mile to the pub, where Prof had found no trace of Dave, only this dark-haired woman unloading her cases. He'd seen photos and album covers, he knew who she was, introduced himself.

They'd looked at each other and discovered a common concern for Reilly's mental condition.

He's out there, Moira had said thoughtfully. *And I don't think he's alone.*

What followed had been eerie. Moira had walked out to the

edge of the pub car park, where it met the beer garden, fields and woodland beyond it.

That's the Skirrid up there?

The what?

It's a holy hill, so-called. A lot of magnetic activity, Prof.

She'd sat down at one of the beer garden tables, in the dark and the cold, hands clasped on her knees, hooded head bowed, very still, Prof not knowing where to put himself, backing off to lean against the back wall of the pub. Until Dave had appeared, rolling and tumbling, as if she was reeling him in like a fish on a line.

Now Moira was hanging her anorak over the back of her chair, sitting down opposite him in front of the fire, setting up cups on saucers, all very cosy.

'How is he?'

She was wearing a washed-out grey sweatshirt, a chain around her neck with a silver Celtic cross.

'Confused is the word,' Prof said. 'He's taking a bath. Wants to look his best for you.'

Moira didn't smile. Dave and Moira, Prof wondered, was this a two-way thing? Fourteen years was a hell of a long time; she could have made contact if she'd wanted, could have let him find her. He thought, I wouldn't have bloody well let her get away from me so easily.

'How did you know,' he asked without much hope of a satisfactory answer, 'where he was and when he was coming back?'

Moira sugared her coffee. 'The four of us, the old Philosopher's Stone, were simultaneously converging on one spot, right? Which Simon St John chose, apparently. I got here just before dark. Not so dark I couldn't see the Skirrid rising up in the fields, but I could feel it anyway. It kind of draws you in. So when you showed me Davey's car, it was pretty obvious where he'd gone.'

'Magnetic activity, you said. What's that mean?'

Moira smiled. 'You're a technical guy, Prof. I can't give it to you in those terms. Holy hill makes more sense to me. Hill of dreams, hill of visions. You ever read Arthur Machen? No? He was a mystical kind of guy, wrote weird stories around the First World War period. This was Arthur's backyard, where he drew his inspiration.'

Her voice was low and husky, earthed by the not-quite-Glasgow accent.

'Whether this was intentional or not on his part,' she said, 'what Simon's done is given us a spiritual focus. We're all converging on the Skirrid, which is a sacred site with a lot of natural power. That's magnetism. You can measure it. Physically, scientifically. Give me a magnetometer, I could prove it to you. Maybe Simon thinks we need all the power we can get.'

'Before you face the Abbey?'

'We need time to regroup. In a different way maybe. Like – I have to tell you I'm a whole lot less certain about all this than I sound – fifteen or so years ago Max Goff was realizing that a rock band, or a folk band, or a string quartet, for that matter, was a very potent psychic unit, whether or not any of its members have, kind of heightened sensibilities.'

Moira paused to check he was picking up on this.

Prof said, 'And if they *have* got these . . . sensibilities?'

'Dynamite, potentially. A powder keg. Which is why – no matter what Davey tells you – we had to go our separate ways. Each of us was, like, carrying components of something combustible. If we stayed together, sooner or later . . . boom. You know?'

Prof said, 'I've heard the album.'

'Yeah. I know. Why else would I be telling you all this?'

'Pardon me, but how would *you* know I'd heard it?'

'I just did.'

'That's no answer.'

'It's the best you'll get off me, Prof,' said Moira tartly.

'OK, but how do you . . .' Prof had no idea where this was coming from, maybe the sodding Skirrid. 'How do you know my motives are pure?'

Moira grinned, dropped her left hand over his. 'You worked

with Davey on his solo album, right? He wrote to me about that. And when we came face to face outside of here, you were worried sick about him.'

'Only 'cause he's such a stupid git,' said Prof gruffly.

She put down her cup. 'I think I should go up and see him.'

'Room four,' Prof said.

Discreetly parked in his discreet Astra on the edge of the car park, Simon had watched and reasoned it out. Moira and the guy with a white beard and glasses, Prof Levin presumably, waiting for someone. And then Dave appearing out of the darkness, dishevelled, clothes wet with mud.

It was starting, the old madness. Nothing changed. Just like Dave to respond to the call of the Skirrid in knee-jerk fashion.

And Tom wasn't even here yet. From the moment of his arrival Tom was going to need careful handling. He'd look at this inn and see the oak beams and stuff, and probably panic because it was old and likely to resonate.

Simon would have had no problem putting them all up at the vicarage, somebody having to sleep on a sofa perhaps. But that would have been too close to the Abbey's own forcefield. Whereas, here, in this cosy old inn, there was an immense and ancient barrier between them and the Abbey. Breathing space.

He still wasn't sure how far he could *trust* the Skirrid, but it had been venerated for centuries, a circle of churches around it had been built on its holy soil, and it had borne a chapel dedicated to St Michael, the warrior.

Shelter. He would need to explain this to Tom.

A Peugeot car pulled in under the illuminated pub sign. A woman got out and looked around. She was tall, with dark hair, not remotely like the Shelley Storey Simon remembered from Epidemic. Couldn't be Tom, then. Simon looked away.

What he mustn't tell Tom, mustn't even *think* about when Tom was around . . . was the candles.

Human fat? Please, no. Human fat altered everything.

389

They wouldn't of course, be able to prove it. Such phenomena were invariably *beyond* physical proof. Therefore, the inquiry would, most likely, be dropped. In time.

So far he'd managed to avoid this Superintendent G. A. Jones. The man had not returned. Simon had phoned Eddie Edwards and expressed disbelief. Human fat? Ridiculous. Defies credibility. Let's bloody hope so, Eddie had said, jittery.

This was another of Simon's mistakes; he'd reacted badly to the candles in front of Eddie. He didn't have the resolve any more, didn't have the cool he'd displayed in December 1980 when the ring of candles had appeared in the studio. Of course, he hadn't known then about the human fat. But Tom must've sensed it. And when Tom had screamed,

they're black!

Tom had been right.

They were black. Very black. As black as . . .

the hair of the woman now tapping on his car window. The tall woman from the Peugeot.

He wound his window down.

'Is it Simon?' she asked hesitantly.

And, behind her, a familiar shambling figure was disentangling itself from the Peugeot.

Dave awoke and looked around in confusion. The furniture in the room was utterly strange.

A scuffed and hulking wardrobe barely fitted under the black ceiling beams. There was a chest and a chair and a dressing-table with no mirror. He stumbled to the window: metal kegs in a yard under a dirty bulb on a metal bracket.

He didn't *know* that view.

Didn't *know* this room. Didn't remember going to sleep in it. Didn't, in fact, remember going to sleep anywhere, only awakening. If you could call this being awake.

Tap, tap, tap.

He didn't know the white-panelled door on which someone was knocking.

Dave sat on the edge of the bed. This wasn't the bedsit, was it? This wasn't Muthah Mirth. Been evicted from there. Yeh. Right. Walked out on his contract. Let them down again. Unreliable. Drove across the Severn Bridge and accosted a woman with a black bonnet. Walked up a crooked mountain with John Lennon. Who wasn't really there, on account of being dead, but it was an interesting exchange of views he and John had had. Straightened out a few contentious points; couldn't remember what they were.

The only strong memory was coming down the mountain, and Moira Cairns waiting for him. But not *really*, obviously. She wasn't really there, any more than John Lennon was there, because – of course – she was dead too.

Nobody wore the black bonnet for very long.

Moira was dead.

Dave wept at this. It had kept him going for so long, the thought that one day, before they were too old to do anything about it, he might see Moira again.

But he'd known for a couple of days that it was too late, watching her on that long, long beach, writing *deathoak* in the sand with her guitar as she tramped towards the final horizon, her face terminally black-veiled.

Dead now, then. Dead as Lennon. No more real than the view over the yard lit by the dirty bulb.

It occurred to him, with no great sense of surprise, that he'd been committed. That this was what people politely called a Rest Home. What had happened, he'd escaped and run away up a mountain with a dead legend, but they'd laid a trap for him and he'd walked right into it, confused by the ghostly shape and the voice of the love of his life. And now they'd put him into another room he didn't know, and

he was naked.

He looked down at himself in horror. The bastards had taken away his clothes! And the dressing-table had no mirror; without a mirror he had no way of even confirming his own identity.

'Davey?'

Dave Kite. I'm Dave Kite. They hold benefits for me, with a trampoline full of Hendersons and Henry the Horse dancing the waltz.

Bang, bang, bang.

'Davey!'

He looked at the door. *Do they think I'm completely bloody bonkers?*

'Piss off! Either give me my clothes back or piss off!'

Silence.

There was another door and he pushed it open and went through. He saw a white lavatory and a wash-basin and a bath with a shower attachment hanging over it like the dirty bulb hung over the yard.

He saw a chair and on it were some clothes he vaguely recognized. He grabbed them – jockey shorts, jeans, a sweater and a jacket hung over the back – hugged them to his chest to make sure they were real. Buried his face in them, and breathed in the smell of earth, the smell of the grave.

Dave began frantically to pull on the clothes before they could disappear. While the banging on the white door continued, getting louder.

And the voice went on shouting, 'Davey?' with increasing urgency.

'Piss off!' he screamed.

Maybe he'd escape again; get out of the window.

'Simon,' Tom said, standing back to look at him under the Castle Inn sign. 'You bastard. You look exactly the bleeding same.'

Simon wished he could say the same for Tom, whose hair and moustache were almost white, whose face looked like crumpled chip-paper. The best he could have said was that Tom's shamble was the same.

Instead, he said, 'How's Shelley?'

Best to start off being as direct as possible. Shelley not being here was worrying him, and if there was something worrying you, Tom would catch it like a cold.

'Shelley's fine,' Tom said. 'I reckon.'

'So where is she?'

In Simon's view, Tom's biggest mistake had been not marrying Shelley first time around instead of getting himself ensnared by the sinewy charms of a TV disco dancer called Debbie Swann. That way, Debbie Swann would be alive and so, probably, would Shelley, who would never in a million years have left Tom alone at the Abbey.

But, then, who could say, really, how that night would have ended? The cards had been drawn from the pack. Black cards.

'Bit of a problem there,' Tom admitted. 'Me and Shelley. Temporary, I reckon. Strickly temporary. Sort itself out.' He glanced up anxiously at the inn's whitewashed walls. 'Place looks old.'

'It is old,' Simon agreed. 'But that's not a problem. I examined all our rooms. There's nothing much here. Except for anything we've brought with us.'

'Yeah,' Tom said. 'Sorry. I don't get out much. This is Meryl. She's, er . . .'

'His therapist,' said Meryl, rounding out the R. A country girl then, Simon thought, surprised, although there was no reason why he should be; Tom did, after all, live in the country.

'Yeah,' said Tom gratefully. 'Ferapist.'

'How do you do.' Simon reluctantly took the woman's hand. It wasn't in a glove, and her nails, which he expected to be long, sharp and thick with varnish, turned out to be short and practical. The handshake was firm.

'Wasn't for this lady,' Tom said, 'I wouldn't've come. Made me face up to responsibilities. Ferapy.'

Simon looked more closely at Meryl. Shrewd eyes. Not a bimbo. But anybody could be a therapist. Simon decided there was a history to this which would need to be uncovered before they went to the Abbey.

'Let's hope neither of you will have any regrets,' he said and could have chewed off his tongue. He patted Tom's arm. 'Go in, shall we? I think Dave and Moira are already here. And the producer, Ken Levin. Prof, as he's known. Are you all right about him?'

'Never worked wiv him, Si, but I used to know people who did. He's OK. Better than that wanker Hornby, anyway.'

'That's good.' Inside the pub lobby, Simon took off his overcoat and scarf, hung them over an arm. He opened the interior door for Meryl. 'After you. Sorry I was little short earlier on. I wasn't expecting . . . Well.'

Meryl smiled without looking at him and went through into the bar. But Tom didn't move.

'This a joke, Simon?'

'Sorry?'

'What the fuck is that?' Bloodshot eyes wide with shock.

'What the fuck is what?' said Simon.

'That white fing encircling your Gregory. It's a joke, right?'

'It's a dog collar,' said Simon.

It might have been a swastika armband, the way Tom was reacting. 'That's what bleeding vicars wear!'

'So I'm told,' Simon said, moving into the bar. 'You still not drinking, Tom? Coffee, is it?'

In the dimness of Room 4, second on the right along the low passage, his face looked like a Victorian portrait. Orphan boy, c.1886, Moira thought.

Someone had told her a year or two back that he was building up a small cult following as an alternative comedian with a particularly cynical line in impersonations of rock music icons. It had all sounded very worldly, a touch sophisticated, and not at all like his letters.

His face was quite startlingly unmarked by the years. Or so it seemed in this light. There were clear rings of pain around his eyes, but inside the eyes themselves was this credulous innocence. No cynicism, no sophistication. Only the innocence of long ago.

She was a different person, but he was alarmingly unchanged.

He stepped back a pace, gripping his arms, as if she was exuding cold. He stood by the bed. He kept glancing at her and then looking away and then glancing back. She thought there were tears in his eyes, but he blinked them away.

'You're exactly the same.' He nodded, swallowed. 'You're how I wanted to see you. You haven't changed.'

Yes I have, she wanted to scream at him. *I'm a totally different person. I've been around. I've been making my own living, sorting out my past, burying my mother. I'm mature, hard-boiled, hard-bitten. I've got scars all over me. Can you no' see the scars?*

Dave said. 'Thank you. You can go now.'

He smiled vaguely, turned and moved to the window, looking out of it and down. His shoulders shook, just once.

Moira said, 'Davey?'

He ignored her, began to mess with the window, unbolting the sash. Then something seemed to occur to him and he turned back to face her.

He said, 'On your way out, could you just send Lennon in one last time?'

Moira froze.

'Oh Jesus,' she said.

III

Supernatural Junkie

After an hour or so, Prof went up. He stood outside in the passage trying to see into the bedroom, but Moira wasn't opening the door wide enough.

'Thing is, they've started asking for you. Tom is getting restive.'

A lamp was burning low in the room behind her.

'Tell them . . . Can you no' tell them we're awful tired or something?'

She didn't look especially tired. She did look het-up, but controlling it, like a midwife at a bad birth. She had her sleeves pushed up over her elbows. There was a light sweat on her forehead.

Prof said, 'What would that sound like to you? See, I think I'm starting to get the hang of this, and the name of the game is, Don't Worry Tom.'

'Yeah, I remember the basic rules. Only Tom's so unpredictable, you have to keep changing them as you go along.'

Prof shuffled about. 'Is Dave OK? I mean, it's nearly two hours since he was gonna have a bath.'

'Yeah, well, all that happened, Prof, is he lay down afterwards and fell asleep, and when he awoke he was kind of disoriented. I think he'd . . . OD'd on whatever's coming off the Skirrid tonight.'

Prof was in no mood to go into this. 'I tell you, Moira, two hours, we've been here, we haven't even seen this Abbey yet, and already things are turning out rather weirder than I anticipated. Even considering the company.'

'Yeah,' Moira said. 'And it will get weirder, I have to say.'

396

'Tom's turned up with a woman looks like she's the madame of an expensive massage parlour.'

'Not Shelley?'

'Meryl,' Prof said. 'Her name's Meryl. And as for Simon . . . did you *know* he was a flaming church minister now?'

Moira's eyes widened briefly, then she gave a secretive kind of smile. 'Aw, hey,' she said softly, looking not at all displeased. 'You're kidding.'

'Says he can't stay too late tonight on account he's gotta be up early for Holy Communion at half-eight. Needs to let the wine breathe or whatever they do.'

'Hold on.' Moira's eyes narrowing warily. 'He's a *local* vicar?'

'Ustrad Dee? Am I pronouncing it right?'

Moira went quiet. From the room behind her came the low, even rhythm of an acoustic guitar – nail-strummed Martin, no mistaking it. Like a silken river.

Moira said slowly, 'You're telling me Simon St John has got himself made vicar of Ystrad Ddu? He's got the Abbey in his own backyard?'

'Well. Far's I can gather. Yeah.' The unlikeliness of this was occurring to Prof for the first time. Why would Simon want to spend his life in such stifling proximity to the ancient fun palace that spawned the Black Album?

'Oh hell,' Moira said. 'We are gonna have to talk about this. At some length.'

And then from inside the room came a chiming A-minor chord. And a tight and acid voice rang out, strident and angry in the darkness.

> *You die tonight,*
> *Who has the last laugh?*

The last word reverberated – *aff, aff, aff* – the full hard, bright vocal of, say, 'Come Together'. Prof clutched the door jamb; his legs felt weak.

Moira said, 'We'll talk later, OK?' And gently closed the door on him.

Shutting herself in with the howling ghost of John Lennon. Prof muttered, 'Get me out of here.'

In response to a peremptory phone call, Eddie Edwards went to meet Isabel Pugh in the church.

Girl's braver than me, he thought, weaving through the short, dark alley between the churchyard yews. Since the appearance of the candles he'd been far from happy in this place.

As he turned the iron handle, he could already hear her wheelchair's whine and the sound of the rubber on the stone floor.

By the light of the flickering candles, Isabel Pugh was riding up and down the short aisle, sending out waves of impatience and anxiety.

Eddie stood with his back to the door and waited.

Isabel was in her high-powered accountant's suit, no rug over her knees, a shortish grey skirt revealing her useless legs. The word was that she paid a woman from Nevill Hall Hospital to come over two nights a week to pummel those legs, with their wasted muscles; make them at least *look* as if they worked. Passive physiotherapy, it was called.

Well, it's her money; she's entitled to her bit of vanity, God knows she is.

'We have to help him,' she said, by way of greeting. 'You agree?'

'Help him?' Eddie said.

Or help you, more likely, he thought.

She was a bossy girl, liked her own way and was probably used to getting it – who could refuse to rush to the aid of a weeping woman in a wheelchair? She was also, of course, very attractive, no denying that.

But how much of an impact that would have on Simon St John was anybody's guess.

'How much do you know, Eddie?'

'Not enough.' He kept shooting sidelong glances at the candles to make sure they were still white.

'Do you know about his band?'

Eddie sighed. It was cold in the church. He sat down on the edge of a pew and pulled the too-long sleeves of his overcoat over his hands like mittens.

'Tell me about the band,' he said.

By nine-thirty, the bar of the Castle Inn was so full of noisy locals that nobody noticed the two strangers sliding in.

Simon was busy explaining to Tom and Meryl how he'd come to join the Church professionally. At the bar, ordering sandwiches, Prof had murmured to him about steering the conversation away from Dave and Moira and whatever was going on up there. If it came to it, he said, he'd have to imply they were making love. What *is* going on up there? Simon had asked, and Prof had wiped the air with open hands – nothing he'd want to talk about even if he understood.

'I'd always been drawn to the Church,' Simon was saying now, hunched over the fire, hands clasped. 'Always very impressed by the clergy as a boy. Other kids used to laugh at them, in their stupid robes, but they weren't having the same kind of . . . experiences as me.'

Prof saw Meryl pause with a prawn sandwich half-way to her lips. 'Experiences?' she said.

He thought, this woman's a supernatural junkie.

Simon said, 'Enough to make me less sure than my peers that religion was something you had to suffer until you grew up, like school dinners.'

'But there's religion,' Meryl said knowingly. 'And religion. Surely?'

Simon looked mildly annoyed, opened his mouth to reply, but another voice took up the space.

'Can we squeeze in, do you think?'

Steve Case was the only guy in the bar whose glass had olives in it. He stood it on their table, pulled out a stool and handed another over the table to his companion. 'Sorry to disrupt your evening. Prof. Er, Tom.'

'Stone me,' Tom said, ignoring Steve. 'If it ain't Sile bleeding Copesake.'

Prof looked up with a guarded interest. He'd met Sile Copesake once or twice but never worked with him, which was odd, seeing as both of them had been around the same scene for maybe thirty years.

'How are you, Tom?' Sile said.

He's in better nick than me, Prof thought, pulling in his belly. Sile hadn't got one, to speak of. His hair and his beard were both grey, both shaven close, so it was like he had designer stubble over half his head.

'And Prof Levin, right?' Sile wore a short leather jacket and jeans and looked fit enough to take the stage with a band half his age. As indeed, he often did.

'Sile.'

'Hope we're not intruding,' Steve Case said, planting himself next to Simon and the coal fire. 'But this seemed an opportune time to get together and sort a few things out before we go to the Abbey on Monday.'

Steve glanced over at Sile. It was clear to Prof that Steve was not in charge of this operation any more, if he ever had been.

Sile said in his soft Yorkshire rasp, 'We all need to be sure why we're here and that we're on the same side.'

Sile had his back to the fire, Prof on one side of him, Meryl on the other. 'And you are?'

'I'm with Tom,' Meryl said. 'I'm his . . .'

'Woman,' Tom said quickly before she could start tactfully implying he was undergoing therapy. Meryl looked surprised and quite thrilled.

'Right,' said Sile uncertainly. He must think Tom was weird, Prof thought. If the legends were to be believed, Sile was now screwing chicks a third his age.

Sile and Steve had more drinks brought over. Tom leaned back in his chair, didn't eat, didn't drink while Sile talked.

Sile talked about the Abbey, which he said he'd known since he was a kid evacuated to Wales during the war. Sile said the Abbey had always fascinated him, *moved* him. Did they know how it had been founded, by this monk running away from his past, all the bad things he'd done, and finding redemption?

Prof hadn't heard about that. It was supposed to matter? They were talking about a sodding recording studio.

Sile said he'd recommended the Abbey to Max Goff when Max was looking for somewhere remote and interesting where progressive bands could make adventurous albums. Max had believed that progresive rock music would return one day, more progressive than ever.

'I've got to tell you,' Sile said, 'I didn't know what he had in mind. I didn't know how he planned to use the Abbey or I'd've been less enthusiastic. I didn't know it was going to stir up demons.'

'Oh, please,' Simon said, looking pained. 'That wasn't *quite* how he explained it to us at the time.'

'I'm using the word loosely,' Sile said. 'Max Goff wouldn't have known a demon if it crawled up his trouser leg. He was a New Age guy. He believed in beautiful spirits.'

'Listen,' Tom said, 'There was a geezer called Aelwyn somefink, turned up outside the Abbey in eleven-whenever, pleading to be let in. Only when the monks got the door open the only way they could bring him in was on shovels.'

Sile nodded.

Tom said, 'Dave Reilly had this loony idea we could free this Aelwyn's soul wiv a song. It went wrong. Badly, badly, fucking wrong. None of us wanna talk about that, so if that's the direction you was heading, you better back off, Sile, OK?'

'OK, OK.' Sile made a cutting motion. 'All I want to say is, it's obvious that neither you guys nor the Abbey benefited a lot from that grim episode. The album's awesome, but it's unfinished and it's flawed.'

'How'd you get hold of them tapes?'

'Part of TMM's legacy from Epidemic. Prof'll tell you all about that. Prof was there when Steve found the tapes.'

Yeah, Prof thought. And maybe Prof was invited along to be a credible, trustworthy witness. Maybe Prof was set up.

He said, 'What you're really saying is you never exactly got your money's worth out of the Abbey after that business.'

'I wouldn't have chosen to put it precisely like that,' Sile said.

'Or after the other business. Soup Kitchen.'

A bubble of silence formed around their table.

'Wossat?' Tom demanded. 'What you on about?'

Prof deliberately didn't look at Sile, but he felt Sile looking at him. Daggers.

'Epidemic took another new band to the Abbey in '87.' Prof paused. Tom was also watching him intently now.

The name of the game is Don't Worry Tom.

'It didn't work out, though. Never made it to the shops either, that one, did it, Sile?'

'No,' Sile said coldly. His eyes were like stones. 'Tell me, where are the other two, Moira Cairns and Dave?'

'Very tired,' Prof said. 'Know what I mean?'

He was tired too and he knew that if he didn't get out of here, whether it was outside for a walk in the cold night or upstairs to bed, he was going to go over to the bar and order himself a drink. And then he'd have another drink and another and he'd end up slagging somebody off in a big way.

He looked at them all, from face to face, Case to Simon to Tom to Meryl. To Sile. He'd had enough of Case and now Copesake and all this bullshit. Time for some straight talking.

'Listen.' He rapped the table. 'Listen, what you're saying – let's get this right – is what this band, the Philosopher's Stone, did at the Abbey has, like, messed it up. The Abbey. As a studio. As an Abbey. Whatever. Or that's what people are saying. Left kind of a hex behind, a curse, whatever you want to call it. Is that the language we're talking, Sile? Is that really what we're saying? You believe in this hoodoo shit?'

Sile made no reply, just looked at him with an eyebrow raised, a very faint eyebrow, a smudge.

Prof said, 'Why don't you just come clean? TMM's been

landed with the Abbey, part of the Epidemic package, and you want to turn it into an earner again. Make it into the major studio it ought to've been first time around. Remove the stain.'

'Now just a minute . . .' Case was half-way out of his seat, but Sile waved him back.

Prof said, 'Mention the Abbey to anybody in the business now, all they can remember is it's where Tom had his personal tragedy. Release that album as it stands and it's so fucking scary nobody except a few young weirdos are gonna want to record there ever again, and you got a bloody great ruined white elephant on your books. How'm I doing so far?'

Sile was smiling faintly.

'But you bring the legendary Tom out of his hermit's cave, you take him back to where it all went wrong, and Tom straps on his axe and comes out like – what's that western with Lee Marvin as this old pissed-up gunfighter who makes a blazing comeback? Anyway, the result is not only a piece of history but a hot new album and everybody's laughing, right?'

He looked again from face to face. Case looked uncomfortable. Simon expressionless. Tom smiling kind of sardonically. Meryl distinctly disappointed because Meryl didn't want to hear about commercial ventures and business scams, what Meryl wanted was the supernatural.

'Sure.' Sile Copesake threw up his hands. 'Whatever you say, Prof, whatever you say.'

'What's that supposed to mean?'

'But for whatever reason,' Sile said, 'everybody turned up, didn't they? It must be *some* kind of magic place, don't you think?'

The sense of *déjà vu* was overpowering. For long, long minutes, December eighth, nineteen-eighty was no more than a membrane away.

Trying to unwrap Davey's subconscious was like that passing-the-parcel-game, or peeling an onion.

'Look,' she said – she was sitting next to him on the bed,

holding his hand – 'somehow, you made a connection. You linked into it. You had a vision. That doesny mean . . .'

'Yeh, but why?' His eyes were all glassy. He still wasn't fully out of it. 'Why did I get that vision? Why was I with him when he died? Why did I *become* him? You know I did, Moira. You know I did.'

And poor wee Davey began to sob again, sitting on the edge of the bed, slumped over the Martin guitar, his chin tucked into the rosewood valley of the soundbox.

Moira remembered his story in the fax, about the Liverpool blackout, how he'd wept over a Takamine in a music shop and the guy who ran the shop said he'd christened it now, he might as well buy it.

Now he'd christened the Martin, the M38 that cost an arm and a leg in Glasgow.

Helpless in the face of his total disorientation, his refusal to accept his surroundings or that she was here with him and real and alive, she'd returned to her own room and fetched the guitar, put it on his knees. He'd fumbled around for ages, like he'd never handled a guitar before.

And then he'd started to play this awful, bitter song about Patience Strong on a bad day, repeating the same lines over and over again.

> *If you die tonight*
> *Who has the last laugh?*
> *If that's your epitaph*
> *What can I say?*

A song she'd never heard before.

Dave lifted his head, wet-eyed. 'I'm sorry. I'm making a mess of your guitar. I told you I was a basket-case.'

'It's no' my guitar,' Moira said. 'It's your guitar. You had it stolen when you came North to find me that time, remember?'

'Huh?' He stared down, bewildered, at the instrument in his arms. 'That was an old Jumbo, this is . . .'

'An M38 Grand Auditorium,' Moira said. 'You don't really like it, do you?'

'It's . . .' He ran his hand over the golden spruce top then looked up at her. 'It's wonderful. It's bloody lovely. I haven't got a guitar. I had one, but it was stolen from Muthah . . .' He looked up at her. 'I don't understand.'

'You don't have to understand,' Moira said.

'They cost a fortune.'

Moira shrugged. 'Play "Dakota Blues",' she said.

'Moira?' His eyes full of a sorrowful longing, like one of Donald's Dobermanns. 'You are here, aren't you?'

She squeezed his hand. 'Aye, I am, Davey.'

'And you're OK?' he asked strangely. 'You're not . . . unwell?'

'Jesus, I'm fine. Play "Dakota Blues", huh.'

This was the only song of his she'd heard since the band split; she was figuring it might loosen something.

'I can't remember the chords.'

'Aw, come on, Davey, even *I* can remember the damn chords and I never played it. It's a basic twelve-bar blues format and then you come back down . . .'

But his fingers had already structured an E-chord and he was thumbing a bass line. He drew a breath and Moira held hers until what came out was not Lennon's voice but Dave's voice, a little nasal but definitely Dave's own voice.

> *Coolin' my heels*
> *In Strawberry Fields*
> *I can't find no peace there.*
>
> *The night is breathless*
> *Kirsty's restless*
> *She don't care.*
>
> *No hope of solace*
> *Or redemption*
> *In the air.*
>
> *Seven long years since I heard the news*
> *I'm still wakin' in the night*
> *With the . . .*

Dave's right hand slammed out a final ringing chord

. . . *DAKOTA BLUES*.

Moira said softly, 'Who was Kirsty?'

Dave laid the guitar on the bed behind him. 'Just this girl I took to New York in 1986. Two-day Winter Break. She was ten years younger than me, and we hadn't got a lot in common anyway. The second night we went to have a look at Strawberry Fields, the Lennon memorial area in Central Park, but she wasn't really interested. She wandered off and left me sitting there on a bench, and that was when I started writing the song.'

'So you saw the Dakota.'

'Can't miss it, can you?'

'And was it . . .?'

He nodded. 'A great, towering Gothic château with turrets and cupolas and . . .'

'A black flower?'

'Some sort of fountain, like a black metal flower. There's a line in the second verse about "metal petals".'

'I know.' Moira sighed. 'We've got so much to talk about and so little time.'

She saw the reproach in his eyes. His eyes said, *We've had fourteen years to talk about it. Where did you go?*

'This . . .' Moira hesitated. 'This question of redemption . . .'

'That's why we're here, isn't it?'

'Look at me,' she said. 'Do you know why you're here, Davey?'

He looked at her. He still seemed very young, though his hair was going grey.

'All kinds of reasons,' he said. 'Redemption's one – last chance of getting some, maybe that. Last hope of getting rid of the black bon . . . of seeing bad things on people.'

'What d'you mean?'

'I don't want to talk about that, do you mind? And there was an implied blackmail bit – they could release "On a Bad

Day", make me look like a scumbag. Well, that's no big deal. The main reason . . . Oh, what the hell, we're here, aren't we?'

He didn't look at her when he said this. The main reason was that *she* was going to be here. Moira felt like shit. She stood by his bedside and looked down at wee, sad-eyed Davey, wanted to love him and almost made it. She wished she hadn't bought him the Martin guitar; it seemed like such a cheap gesture now.

She sat down next to him, squeezed his hand really hard.

'We're gonna do it, Davey. We're going in there and we're gonna replay it. Our way this time.'

'But are we going to come out?'

'Hey, don't be ridiculous,' Moira said, tapping his hand against her knee, thinking, *Good question.*

Then there was another tapping behind her.

'Moira? Dave?'

A familiar, well-modulated voice the other side of the door. Moira was about to call out to him to come in when it occurred to her Simon might have Tom with him, and the sight of a wretched Dave and a tear-stained guitar could send the big guy prematurely into orbit.

'Stay there,' Moira said. 'Don't move. I'll be back.'

Simon. Jesus, it was good to see him. Pliable Simon. Willowy, amiable Simon.

And the dog-collar . . .

'It suits you. It really suits you.'

'It's not a fashion statement,' Simon said. He was alone, thank God.

'No, I mean it *suits* you,' Moira said. 'The whole priestly thing.'

'Wish I could agree with you,' Simon said ruefully, flicking back a lock of fair hair, just like he used to – except the hair was perhaps a little paler now. 'Listen, Moira, we need to do some urgent talking. Like, now. Where's Dave?'

'Dave's asleep,' Moira lied. 'Dave's . . . exhausted. What I

407

mean is, I don't think it would be good for Tom to see Dave right now.'

'You mean he's fucked up?'

'Let's just say we've a lot of stuff to unload before he's exposed to Tom.'

'But meanwhile,' Simon said, 'we're being pushed into a corner down there. We've got Steve Case and Sile Copesake from TMM trying to manhandle us into a situation that seems uncannily reminiscent of the last time, you know what I mean? *Fait accompli?* Out of our hands?'

'Terrific.'

'I'm sorry. I just didn't expect this. My idea was to book us in here for a couple of nights so we could really hammer this thing out between us before Monday. And *then* we could hang it on them. It didn't allow for the bastards turning up before we could even get our stuff unpacked. Anyway, I'm stalling. I just went to the loo, as it were.'

'What do you want me to do?'

'Just listen to what I've got in mind. If you think that's OK, I'll go back down and lay it on them.'

'OK,' Moira said. 'Lay it on me first. Like, the way I see it, we play by our rules this time or we're taking our ball home.'

The feeling of pushing Copesake and Case around, putting them on the spot, this was almost as good as a drink.

Well, somebody had to help these people. If they'd got in some shit last time, being produced by Russell Hornby couldn't have helped. It was all a question of which side you were on. Russell was a management man and therefore rich enough to own a Roller, whereas Prof was a musician's man and lucky to be allowed to produce his very first album at the age of sixty-four.

Copesake and Case. Pair of wankers. Stuff 'em.

And this was what Simon was doing.

Prof was starting to like this vicar. He was kind of suave.

Also he had the authority now that was invested in you by virtue of having God and the Skirrid on your side.

Simon had returned to his seat by the fire. It was getting towards last-orders time, although the way the local punters were not clustering around the bar suggested this was academic at the Castle Inn on a Saturday night.

'Here's the deal,' Simon said. 'It's not open to negotiation.'

Steve Case looked immediately hostile. Sile Copesake leaned back and sipped his pint of mild.

'We go in on Monday,' Simon said quietly. 'We go in for a week. At the end of that period we give you the new tapes, you give us the old tapes, the 1980 recordings, and you sign away all rights to them. Our management will be in touch about contracts, including Prof's, early next week.'

Management? Prof thought, what management?

'Hang on,' Steve Case said. 'How do we know . . .?'

'You don't,' Simon said. 'You trust us. We go in alone. We aren't disturbed. Nobody comes near. When it's over, we come out.'

'That's irregular,' Steve said. 'It's our premises.'

'That's the deal,' Simon said.

Sile Copesake unhurriedly finished his pint, set his tankard down on the table, wiped froth from his lips with the back of a hand.

'Fair enough,' he said.

For Prof – maybe for all of them – it was a strangely dispiriting moment of anti-climax. A dead moment.

IV

Whatever Gets You
Through the Night

'Well?' Moira asked playfully. 'Can you still respect me?'

She and Dave had slept together.

Dave said, 'You made me the second happiest man in the world.'

They were in Moira's car, the muddy old BMW, skirting Abergavenny under an ice-white sky.

'OK, I'll buy it,' she said after a while. 'Who's actually the happiest?'

'Whoever it was you were fantasizing about,' Dave said.

It was a cheap, throwaway line. He remembered using it once with Jan, who'd then presented him with a list including Harrison Ford, Michael Douglas and Richard Gere. At least, he said, you didn't say Rowan Atkinson. Oh, and Rowan Atkinson, Jan had said, but only when I opened my eyes.

All this was academic, anyway, because Dave and Moira had *slept* together only in the literal sense, entwined on Dave's bed, fully clothed. Innocent as children. A Martin guitar at their feet like a dog.

Now, away from there, it wasn't easy to believe this had happened. Or, rather, that *nothing* had happened.

Moira was driving; he was aching for her.

He studied her. Her black hair was almost down on her shoulders. It had been much longer before and tangly. There was a single vein of grey, which looked exotic. She wore no make-up. She'd changed her sweatshirt for an off-white jumper with a textured black sheep on the front.

Last night, eveything about last night, had been hermetically sealed against reality. The dream-medium had been congealing around him as the day wore on, from crossing the Severn Bridge.

A state of mind never remotely real enough for sex.

Moira said, 'You really want to know who I was thinking about. Who I dreamed about?'

They were on a dual-carriageway, hills either side alive with sheep and cows and horses, farms and cottages with smoking chimneys. No sign of the Skirrid.

They'd awoken early, cold. Moira had said, Let's get out of here before Tom's about. Things to discuss, not for Tom's ears. By half-past nine they'd driven fifty miles in a big circle and eaten greasily in a transport café.

It was there that Dave, scalding his hand pouring tea from a chromium pot with a loose lid, had asked her why. Fourteen years. All those letters, all those cards. The fruitless pilgrimage. Fourteen years. Fourteen *years*.

Why?

'There's no easy answer, Davey. If there was an easy answer I'd give it you.'

'It might have been presumptuous,' Dave said, 'it might have been wishful-thinking, it might have been the arrogance of youth, but I kind of had hopes for us.'

'Wouldn't have worked. Would've been disastrous.'

'That's what you said on the night – *that* night. I didn't understand it then, I don't understand it now.'

'We were carrying too much baggage, Davey.'

'I accept that. But you can jettison excess baggage, can't you? We just needed a breathing space.'

'Did you manage to jettison *your* excess baggage, Davey?'

'That's not fair.'

'Did you?'

'No. It gets heavier and bulkier all the time. But I do think we could have helped one another.'

'Or killed one another.'

'You don't mean that.'

411

Moira had said, 'Something killed my mother.' But declined to explain.

'Tom Storey,' Weasel said. 'Yeah, that Tom Storey.'

Sunday morning, and he was getting impatient. Gone through his list of mates; most of the people he was calling now could barely remember him, who he was, whose amps he used to carry out of the van into major gigs – the Albert Hall, once.

It was all so long ago. Reminders was called for. Luckily Tom Storey was still a magic name to most of them.

Vanessa was with him in Shelley's office, back of the house. It was the effect on the Princess that was getting to him most, always such a *happy* kid, would skip around singing to herself, saying hello to miserable gits like the late Sir Wilf. Even when Vanessa looked solemn, you knew she was happy inside.

Today, Vanessa was not happy inside or outside.

'Nah, see, I'll be straight wiv yer,' Weasel said down the blower. 'My instinct says somefink's going down at TMM, and this Meryl's – nah, it don't *matter* who she is, some tart – this Meryl's been set up to, like, lure Tom into . . . Nah . . . he ain't. He's, like, dead innocent. A big innocent.'

Funny thing. Since Tom had disappeared, Weasel was seeing much more of the big guy in Vanessa. This had never been obvious before, whose daughter she was – well, like, obviously, the ways their faces was arranged, these kids. But Tom, the times he was at peace with the world, had a kind face, too.

'He's stubborn, don't get me wrong. Like a big mule. But, like, if you know how to handle him, he'll follow you around. Listen, Steve Case, there's a guy called Steve Case. Where's he at now . . .? Yeah . . . Gotta be. Too much coincidence.'

Weasel had on the phone a geezer worked in maintenance in the TMM building. See, the thing about most of these people in what you might think of as humble positions with record companies was that they was generally all into the music. So you mentioned the name Tom Storey to, say, a caretaker of a certain age, and you had his full attention. Like telling a pensioner you'd been to bed with Vera Lynn. It was a magic name, on account of Tom's playing had given a lot of people a lot of pleasure and he was like an icon, and even on a Sunday morning . . .

'Sorry, wossa name again?' Weasel scrabbled on Shelley's desk for paper. 'Yeah, right, gimme that again . . .'

What he had now was the home number of a secretarial assistant in admin at TMM who used to work – this was especially good – at Epidemic. In the old days, Tom – Weasel too – used to spend a lot of time around the Epidemic offices, chatting up the ladies and that. How the big guy'd met Shelley, in fact. Tom had actually known Shelley a year or two before Debs, and afterwards, Shelley was the obvious shoulder – well, breast – to cry on while he was fixing up to make his miserable solo album, *Second Storey*, the one everybody tried to forget about . . .

'Hello? Yeah, that Barbara Walker? Oh. Yeah, if you could. Beasley. Eric Beasley. Nah, she prob'ly don't know me . . .'

He smiled at Vanessa, who was sitting in the window seat, hugging a cushion. 'I'll find him, Princess, 'fit's the last fing . . . Hello, Barbara Walker? My name's Eric B . . . Well, yeah . . . yeah, it is. Weasel, yeah! It's not . . . Ginger? Nah! Ginger Hodge! Fuck me! I never even knew your name was Barbara. That was your daughter, was it? Blimey, little Ginger Hodge.'

Now this – this was a stroke of luck. Ginger Hodge'd been office junior at Epidemic, all starry-eyed. Ginger Hodge was the kid Weasel had once driven – and her mate, nothing like *that* – up the M1 to Brum to catch Tom Petty and the Heartbreakers . . . '77 was that, or was it later? Time went by so fast. Little Ginger Hodge with a teenage daughter.

Weasel was on the phone with Ginger Hodge best part of an hour. Vanessa came and went twice and was back again by the time Weasel hung up, head full of enough info to keep him going all day, thinking and reasoning.

'How's it going, Weasel?' Shelley asked tiredly, head around the door, hair uncombed. This was a first; never seen her before without the full gloss. Shelley had been *natural* gloss – what she was about, health foods, vitamins.

The shit people took from Tom. Bastard. No excuse this time.

Weasel did some rapid thinking. Anything he told her she was going to pass on to this Broadbank, who might be OK, but might not, living with Morticia, ducking and diving in the business world, the local council . . .

'Hard going, Shel,' Weasel said heavily.

Shelley said, 'I just don't subscribe to your theory that Meryl has to be somehow in this with Case. I think she's just . . . fallen for Tom.'

Her face looking pinched, quite middle-aged, you had to admit it. Weasel felt desperately sorry.

'I mean, not in the way that women *used* to, Weasel, and that was never a major problem. But it's clear from what Martin says that she's hungry for some, I don't know, other-worldly experience. Women think they've got problems if somebody's after their husband's body, but when it's his . . . I don't even know what to call it. "Mind" doesn't even get close.'

He wanted to tell her what he'd learned: how, just lately, Sile Copesake had been spending hours locked in an office with Steve Case. Sile Copesake, whose band Tom had joined in a screwed-up state on the rebound from the Brain Police after his prediction about Carlos their manager's accident what put the slave-driving bastard in Stoke Mandeville. Sile Copesake, who would know all about Tom's extra-sensory wotsit, who was now a big-cheese on the TMM board of directors.

He wanted to tell her this and a lot more he'd got from little Ginger Hodge, sweet kid, delighted to help, promising to find out more and call him back Monday.

But, in the end, Weasel kept shtumm. He told himself that this was to spare Shelley unnecessary grief.

What he wanted, though, what he needed, was to find Tom

himself. And the big guy better come up with some good answers else Weasel was gonna butt him in the balls.

Bastard.

It was an important, much-valued part of clerical tradition for the vicar to hang around outside the church door after morning service for the purpose of shaking hands with each and every member of the congregation.

'Mrs Watkins, how are you? And how's Ted's knee?'

The vicar was also required to update his mental file on each of them.

'Get your car fixed in the end, Mr Willey?'

Simon had returned far later than he'd intended last night. Tom and Meryl had gone to bed, perhaps to conduct an impromptu therapy session. Simon had stayed behind in the emptying bar, having a final coffee and talking to Prof. Hearing about Barney Gwilliam and Soup Kitchen. And Dave.

At least he didn't have Dave's particular problem.

Ah, good morning, Mr Ellis. Tell me, is that your aura or is that chimney of yours smoking again?

So here he was, all smiling and jolly at the church door, while chewing himself up inside, anxious to get away, get back to the Castle Inn. One day to organize themselves. It wasn't enough, but it was all they had.

'Mrs Jarman,' he said warmly to the last parishioner, a nice, sparky-eyed old lady leaning over her Zimmer frame to shake his hand with both of hers, as if he was a healing force. 'God bless you for coming. Fantastic to see you on your feet again.'

'Seeing me on mine, now,' another voice said caustically, 'that really *would* be a sight for sore bloody eyes.'

Ah. He'd wondered where she'd gone. She'd been all too noticeable during the service, chair parked behind the pews. Isabel Pugh, chartered accountant of this parish, looking businesslike and deceptively demure in a charcoal-grey, tailored two-piece suit.

Now everyone had left, even Eddie Edwards, and the two of

them were alone together outside the little grey cowshed church, and Isabel, her head about two and half feet below his, was looking very much like an immovable object under the hard, white sky.

'Where were you last night?' Asked rather mildly, for her.

'Bugger,' said Simon, 'I clean forgot that I was supposed to be reporting to you, every hour, on the hour.'

Isabel's shiny hair was freshly and stylishly highlighted with gold. He wondered where she had it done; or did the hairdresser come to her? He found himself wanting to touch it. Silly.

'My information,' she said casually, 'is that you were out the other side of Pandy, at the Castle Inn.'

'Really.' God, she must be running an intelligence network from that chair.

'And your friends.' Her eyes glowed amber. He read them like traffic lights. Caution. 'Quite a little party, according to my information.'

'Don't tell me,' Simon said. 'You do the Castle Inn's accounts, right?' Two confirmatory dimples appeared, distressingly appealing, in Isabel's creamy cheeks.

It was another side of her. He was more comfortable with the embittered cripple, selfish and aggressive and determined to shock. Perhaps *that* was the act, because being pitied was so demeaning.

'I'd like to meet them,' Isabel said. 'You get so fed up with the same old miserable faces.'

'Isabel,' Simon said delicately, 'you don't know what miserable faces are like until you've met these people. Besides . . .'

'I thought about just turning up last night. It didn't seem polite, though.'

'How would you . . .?'

'I've got a van,' Isabel said. 'Wheel on, wheel off. Hand controls. It's behind the house. Don't get it out much. Hate the thing. Like driving your own ambulance. Or your own hearse. It would have embarrassed you, anyway, me creaking in. Especially if there was one of them you're sweet on. A bloke, I mean.'

'There isn't,' Simon said. 'You evil-minded bitch. Anyway, the warning remains. Any involvement here would be seriously detrimental to your well-being.'

'Well-being! Simon, when you're a fallen woman, in every sense, the only way is up.'

'Wrong,' Simon said. 'And you've got to start believing me. Vicars don't lie.'

Isabel said, 'You make me so mad that if I could feel my foot I'd stamp it.'

'Can I push you home?' Simon smiled sweetly. 'Save electricity?'

'Nobody pushes me anywhere, Vicar.'

His smile vanished as he thought of hurling her from the top of the tower and crawling towards the black monk, exposed. The aching, slavering desire he'd felt in his dream replaced now by a dark disgust, lodged like an old, cold brick in his chest.

'Look,' he almost shouted, virtually unaware of what he was going to say until it was out. 'You're good with other people's money. How would you like to manage a rock band?'

Moira changed down to second gear for the steep hill into the village. Dave remembered this place, especially the overhanging rock with the V-shaped fissure, the December sky sombre above it; darkness at the break of noon, again.

'John Lennon,' she said. 'That was who I kept dreaming about. Once, I awoke convinced he was in the room with us.'

They'd driven around in another circle, this time a smaller one. A sign had said *Ystrad Ddu 5*. They'd looked at one another and then nodded simultaneously, reluctantly, neither of them happy about it. Moira had said she didn't want to go there for the first time with the whole bunch of them tomorrow. Sure, sometimes there was safety in numbers; but sometimes, also, this was an illusion.

And there were going to be no illusions this time.

'*I* didn't bring him with me, Davey.'

'Bring who?'

Moira sighed. 'John Lennon.'

'Sorry.' Dave cupped his hands over his face. He decided to tell her everything.

Meryl and Tom came down to a late breakfast and were surprised to find themselves alone in a tiny, panelled dining-room, seated beneath a pastel-hued watercolour painting of serene ruins under an azure sky.

'Shit,' said Tom. 'Find another table, quick.'

'This is the only one laid,' Meryl pointed out.

Tom stabbed a calloused forefinger at the picture. 'You know what that is? It's a fucking omen.'

'Is that the Abbey? It looks quite pleasant.'

'I've heard of artistic bleeding licence,' said Tom. 'But this is a joke.'

'Perhaps it's a good omen, have you thought of that? It looks so pretty.' Meryl smiled at the pink-cheeked waitress. 'I think I'll just have a boiled egg. What are you having, Tom?'

'Coffee. Black.'

'Too much caffeine . . .' Meryl began, and then stopped. He was married to a health-food dealer; he'd know all about caffeine.

Besides, she was coming to realize how unwise it was to lecture Tom about anything. He was a good man, but he was also a difficult man.

Meryl thought about the devious but essentially bland Martin Broadbank and wondered if he'd made the inevitable move on Shelley Storey yet. In a way she hoped he had. Hoped, too, that Shelley had accepted it. Meryl liked everyone to be happy.

She thought about Stephen Case and his impassive colleague. How they'd reduced what she now thought of as the Abbey Experience to a matter of money and image. Both of them closer to Martin's viewpoint than to Tom's. But at least Martin got some sort of pleasure out of it, was not so grim and humourless.

She looked at the picture of the Abbey. It was really very

pleasant. Of course, that was summer. It would be bleaker now. The week ahead would be a testing time, but Meryl was prepared to be tested. Meryl was *begging* to be tested.

'You didn't actually stay in the Abbey last time, did you?'

'I commuted,' Tom said. 'No place for a pregnant woman.' She saw his eyes cloud.

'I wonder what the bedrooms are like,' she said brightly.

'I'll let you know.'

'Probably be a draughty old place. I hope the beds are aired.'

'Wouldn't wanna catch a cold. Goes to my sinuses.'

'We'll take some hot-water bottles.'

Tom said, 'Hang on. We?'

Meryl stared at him.

Tom said, 'You're staying here, darlin'. You do know that?'

Meryl stiffened.

'You was there last night when we discussed the terms. The band goes in alone. No Case, no Sile.'

'But . . .'

'And no you,' said Tom.

Meryl grabbed a handful of tablecloth. She was dumbfounded. Shattered. Speechless.

Who was it who'd rescued him from the motor lodge? Who'd persuaded him that it was in his best interests to come here? Who'd *brought* him here?

Who had *shared his vision*?

Meryl felt her eyes bulge and burn. 'This is ridiculous.'

'No, it ain't. It's common sense. This is a mopping-up operation. We got enough of our own shit to wade frew. It ain't your problem. Be bloody thankful.'

Meryl blinked back tears of rage and frustration, pushed back her chair. 'Excuse me.' She didn't even look at the girl bringing her egg from the kitchen.

Dave said, 'I was disgusted with him. I mean thousands – *millions* – of people were feeling really pissed off about it. It was just a bloody awful album.'

'It had a couple of good tracks,' Moira said. '"Starting Over", "Woman".'

'Patience Strong,' Dave said. 'Not as bloody *good* as Patience Strong. Made Patience Strong read like bloody Coleridge.'

Moira had parked on the edge of Ystrad Ddu, at the end of the straggly dozen or so grey stone houses, past the sagging, untidy pub. She wanted to hear this before they got too close to the Abbey.

It so happened that Dave had bought his copy of the album a couple of days before arriving for the session in December 1980.

Double Fantasy. John Lennon's album. Also Yoko's. Seven songs each – one of his, one of hers, one of his, etc. Well, everybody expected Yoko's songs to be not exactly balm to the ears and nobody was disappointed. But when Lennon's own compositions turned out to be largely dreary, sentimental and witless – that was it.

'What I couldn't help remembering,' Dave said, 'was how he used to slag McCartney off for being trite and bubblegum. After the split, this was. Do you remember "How Do You Sleep?" on *Imagine*? Really vicious. A public denunciation.'

Moira nodded. 'Made me wonder what had gone on between them.'

'Yet here he is, a few years later, living the life of a contented househusband in his New York fortress, baking bread, composing sweet little songs about his second wife and his second kid. Talk about hypocrisy.'

'Be careful,' Moira said. 'That was why Mark Chapman reckoned he was compelled to shoot him. Because he was the King of the Phoneys. A full-blown hypocrite, as defined in *The Catcher in the Rye*, Chapman's bible. All adults are phoneys, but some are phonier than others. You ever read that book?'

'Afterwards. After Chapman came out with all this crap about doing the deed to draw public attention to what a great novel it was. I was surprised, actually, it's a good read.'

'Yeah, but it's hardly an incitement to murder. It's like Charles Manson going on about having telepathic communication with the Beatles. Claiming the Tate killings were inspired by McCartney's song "Helter Skelter" then it turns out Manson didn't know what the hell the words meant. That a helter-skelter was a kiddies' fairground ride in Britain – he didn't know that. It makes me angry, the way so many of the worse things that happen are down to misinterpretation and simple ignorance.'

She leaned back into the head-restraint, stretched her legs. 'But Chapman killed him, Davey. Not you. Chapman took a plane over from Hawaii and bought himself a Saturday Night Special. You just felt cross with the guy. And then you had a bad experience which somehow got hooked up with his, and you hate yourself because you didn't follow through and find out where they were, call up the studio where he was recording and say, "Could you please give Mr Lennon an urgent message. I think something really terrible could be about to happen to him."'

Moira put a hand on his knee. 'Davey, you didn't *know* this was Lennon. You didn't even know it was New York. And with the really malevolent vibes buzzing around the Abbey on that occasion I'm pretty damn sure that if you'd rolled around on the grass all night you'd never have got the insight you needed to alter history.'

Dave put his hand over her hand. 'That's not the worst of it. The worst of it's that song. "On A Bad Day." You remember the afternoon of the eighth?'

'Yeah, I . . .'

Drove into Abergavenny to do a little shopping, then went along to Tom's hotel to pick him up, have a chat with Debbie. Stayed an hour or so, had afternoon tea with them in the restaurant. When we got back to the Abbey . . .

'. . . You were messing about in the studio with Simon and Lee Gibson and Russell.'

'Yeh. We recorded a song. It wasn't for the album, it was just a fun thing. Bit of a pastiche of "How Do You Sleep". Russell had played a couple of tracks from *Double Fantasy* and I asked him to take it off, then I sat down and started fooling about with a guitar and the song just came into me head. It was just there.'

Dave began to sing, in Lennon's voice,

> *Don't know what you got here*
> *But it sure ain't a song*
> *Sounds like Patience Strong*
> *On a bad day.*
>
> *If you die tonight*
> *Who has the last laugh?*
> *If that's your epitaph*
> *What can I say?*
>
> *Am I ever gonna see you again*
> *I doubt it*
> *Are we ever gonna hear you again?*
> *I doubt it*
> *I doubt it.*

Oh God. Moira closed her eyes. 'You wrote that the very afternoon before . . .?'

'And recorded it. In the Abbey.'

'Oh my,' Moira said hoarsely.

Dave took her hand from his knee. 'You don't want to touch me.'

'Don't be silly.'

'Mark Chapman's never been the quietest, most retiring of lifers,' Dave said bitterly. 'He's always going on about how he might *not* have shot Lennon. Earlier the same day he went along to the Dakota and asked John for his autograph on a copy of *Double Fantasy* and then went away again and thought about *not killing him*.'

'He's bonkers, Davey. He's a headcase.'

'Also, he kept on about hearing voices in his head. The Little People he called them.'

'Davey, every fruitcake killer claims to hear voices. The Yorkshire Ripper, all these psychos . . .'

'And while he's thinking about it, agonizing over whether to go through with it, a song echoing all his *Catcher in the Rye* sentiments is being laid down with a lot of malice a forethought . . .'

'Davey, you can't *possibly* think . . .'

'. . . at the Abbey.'

Moira sat up quickly and switched on the engine. 'That's it. I'm no' gonny listen to any more of this nonsense.'

She jammed the BMW into gear, let out the clutch and swung into the lane, which very soon began to narrow, tall trees meeting overhead. In summer this would be a tunnel of green.

'Where are we going?'

'You *know* where we're going, Davey. We're gonna have a wee stroll around the ruins and get our act together.'

'I can't,' Dave said. 'I just can't do it.'

'Tomorrow you're gonna have to. OK . . . OK.'

She slowed down to a crawl and began to look for a place to turn the car around.

Jesus, she thought. *Last time we were here we were young and innocent, most of us anyway. We had youth and energy and our patron was dear old Max Goff, good vibes merchant and New Age entrepreneur.*

This time we've got a bunch of cynical bastards pulling the strings, a legacy of death and disaster and we're all screwed up to hell.

She had a headache. On the way back to the Castle, she stopped at a garage, bought a double-pack of Anadin and two hundred Silk Cut.

Whatever gets you through the night . . .

V

Cortège

Weasel didn't remember a time when he'd ever been so badly pissed off: upset, angry, worried, humiliated, the lot, all at once.

Shelley had looked tired and glum and Vanessa didn't hardly say a word to him when he took her to Stroud, as usual on a Monday.

Vanessa's convent school was outside Stroud, and Weasel had to go into town Monday mornings to pick up supplies from the main Love-Storey distribution plant which was in this old mill-type building back of the shop.

Weasel in his brown overall with the Love-Storey logo and the Princess in her brown convent blazer, jumper and skirt, they looked like a team. Weasel liked that; him and the kid, they'd often joke about it on the way.

No jokes today.

'You want me to take you up to the convent, or is Alexandra's dad picking you up?'

Alexandra was this kid looked after Vanessa at school, her special friend. Most Mondays, Weasel would just take Vanessa as far as the shop and she'd go the final couple of miles with her mate, whose dad came through the town.

'What's it gonna be then?'

Vanessa still didn't reply, just looked moodily out the window, like she might spot Tom by the hedgerow thumbing a lift.

'You want me to take you all the way?'

Vanessa shook her head without looking at him.

Jeez. Tom was gonna pay for this and no mistake when Weasel got hold of the bleeder.

He parked the van up the side street by the shop and watched the kid trot off with her school bag without waving or looking back.

What was pissing him off most was that whenever this bastard place, the Abbey, come up on the horizon Weasel would be conveniently out of the picture – the first time it was the hepatitis do – and, but for that, Debbie would still be alive and he and Tom would have been on the road still, gigging.

On the minus side, there'd have been no Shelley, and Debbie – God rest her wotsit – hadn't been exactly of the same calibre. Debbie liked the high life and foreign holidays; not the kind of woman to hold Tom together when he was into one of his funny turns. Also, not the kind to devote the necessary attention to a Down's kiddie. With Debbie, no doubt about it, Vanessa would not be the smart madam she was, who could read books and went to a proper school. Vanessa might even have wound up in a home.

So maybe . . .

Anyway, not Weasel's job to question the situation, philosophize.

Weasel's job was to find the big guy and Morticia before the Bad Shadow merged with Tom's shadow.

He always saw it as a Bad Shadow, the thing following Tom. Like the dirty rainbow, the visible sob. No question, Tom Storey had been born the wrong side of the tracks – the black tracks most people couldn't see at all.

'What we got then?' Weasel said to Wendy in the old mill warehouse.

'Not a lot, Weasel. Usual for Cirencester, trial batch of spinach quiches and Cheze flans for Broadbanks in Chelt'nam and a special order for Safeway's in Ross, directions on box. And that's it. Welcome to the Recession.'

'Brill,' said Weasel. 'I won't have no job at all, it goes on like this. They'll be hiring a geezer wiv a moped.'

No, actually, this was not bad. It would leave him free to pursue his inquiries. He was expecting a call from little Ginger Hodge at TMM this afternoon.

Also . . . Ross? Ross-on-Wye? Weasel hadn't done a delivery that far west for quite some time. Ross was actually just over the Gloucestershire border, in Herefordshire, right? So Abergavenny would be . . . what, half an hour or so from there?

And maybe three-quarters of an hour from the Abbey.

Because, when you thought about it, that was the direction it was all pointing. Shelley had said Case was after Tom going back into the studio. Shelley was dead against it. But if Morticia was in with Case and Morticia had gone off with Tom . . .

Worth a butcher's.

A long time, anyway, since he done any sightseeing, places of historic interest, all that shit.

Normally, Prof would have been dashing into the dining-room waving his *Daily Telegraph*. Look at this, look at this!

But this week's motto was Don't Worry Tom. Also, by the looks of things, Don't Worry Dave was about to come into vogue.

So Prof folded his *Telegraph* under his arm and endeavoured to look controlled and smiling as he sauntered in for breakfast – their second and final breakfast at the Castle Inn.

Nervous as a kitten, Prof had been up at six, mooching round the car park, up the lane, taking guarded glances at the Skirrid. This idea of Simon's, having the Holy Mountain between them and the Abbey: could he credit that?

There was more than a glistening of frost on the ground. Going to be a cold one. Prof had been wearing a furry Russian hat, Christmas present last year from his cousin's daughter in Warsaw, who was well into Western rock and deeply impressed that Prof was at the centre of it, on joint-rolling terms with Famous Names.

He'd stood on the edge of the beer garden, facing the Skirrid, which was quite clear this morning despite a bit of mist. It wasn't really very high, and if it had been a few miles further west you probably wouldn't have noticed it at all.

Prof had had a quick look around to make sure nobody was

watching and then spread out his arms like some of the fey and mystical musicians, back in the early seventies, used to do every morning, paying their respects to the sun before venturing into the studio. Prof had closed his eyes and done it to the Skirrid.

Nothing happened.

'Daft sod,' he'd muttered, then gone back to the inn and bought the *Telegraph*, a good, solid, no nonsense read. The Skirrid. Bollocks. Dave might have thrown a wobbly that first night, been shell-shocked ever since, but Prof hadn't felt a sodding thing coming off the Skirrid.

It was the *Daily Telegraph* which had blown his mind. Bottom of page five. Two paragraphs.

The dining-room was empty, not even the little waitress around. This being way out of season, nobody was staying here apart from the band, and the Castle had adapted quickly to the little eccentricities of guests like Tom Storey who breakfasted at twelve a.m.

It was only half-nine. Prof sat down, turned to page five and read the two paragraphs again. The words hadn't altered.

'Strewth,' he said.

'Morning, Prof.'

'Oh!' Prof mashed the paper between his hands.

'Not you as well,' Moira said.

She was wearing a short woollen dress and looked very fetching. And she was alone.

'Where's Dave?'

'We're no' connected at the waist, Prof,' Moira said, a little extra Scottish today. 'If he doesny show in the next half hour I'll go up and tap lightly on his door.'

'Moira, would you . . .?' In the absence of Simon, who'd spent the night at his vicarage, Moira had to be the most balanced of them. 'Would you take a look at this?'

He folded, halved and quartered the *Telegraph*, handed it to her. Moira stood with one hand on the back of his chair and read where he'd pointed.

It didn't take her long. She sat down opposite him and laid the paper on the table, upturned to the small headline

RECORD PRODUCER
FOUND DEAD

Moira bit her upper lip. 'You saw him . . . when? Couple of days ago? I mean, how was he?' She was white.

Prof breathed out heavily. 'I have to say he was not happy to see us.'

'Dave says Stephen Case asked him if he was interested in going back to the Abbey to produce us.'

'And Russell said he wasn't that strapped for cash, or words to that effect. Least, that's what he told us he said.'

'You got the feeling Russell was nervous about going back?'

'He was certainly tense. He didn't want to talk to us at all, I had to lean on him a bit.'

'But suicidal?' One hand squeezing the other.

Prof blew out his lips. 'What's a suicidal guy look like?'

The young waitress came in then to take their orders and Prof and Moira looked at each other and said 'coffee' simultaneously. When she'd gone, Moira leaned across the table. 'Prof, I . . . Did Dave mention seeing anything . . . around Russell?'

'What d'you mean?' And then he understood, closed his eyes, rubbed his face with his hands. 'I hate this.' Talking through his hands. 'It gives me the creeps so bad.' He lowered his hands. 'No. He didn't. If he'd seen anything, he would have said it, the mood he was in that day. Maybe it's only sick people, how should I know?'

'I'm sorry to even mention it. And you're thinking, I've got to go in there and do the job Russell was supposed to've done. Listen, you no' under contract, Prof. You can still back out.'

Both Prof's hands were trembling. 'I was feeling really good about it yesterday, what with nailing Case and Copesake in the bar. I'd got it nicely under control, all the other stuff. I thought, this is just another record-industry scam. They love rumours and deaths and is Elvis alive and living in Ipswich. I'd even forgotten my own nightmares – two full, uninterrupted nights' sleep in a row and you think, What am I getting so worked up about? It's like Maurice at Audico. You put one working day between you and the weirdness and you're eager to put the whole thing down to imagination.'

Moira said, 'Who's Maurice?'

Prof stuck his head back into his hands and moaned.

Moira read the *Telegraph* report again. 'It says No Suspicious Circumstances. That's police-speak for suicide. But what else could it be? I've never been to the Manor, is this tree a feature?'

'Huh?'

'Be no leaves on it either, this time of year. I was just thinking of everybody waking up and looking out their windows and there's poor Russell dangling there. It's horrible, Prof. I never really liked the guy, especially the way he conned us over the tapes and wouldn't lift a finger to stop Tom driving off in the Land Rover. But it's such a lonely death. And yet there's, I don't know, an element of exhibitionism to it. Kind of, screw you, take a good look, this is what you drove me to.'

'I hate it,' Prof groaned. 'I hate it. I'd rather be producing Van Morrison.'

Then he went quiet.

The coffee came. Moira thanked the kid, poured.

Prof said, 'Tree.'

'Sorry?'

'We were walking along the lawn at the Manor – this was before we saw Russell, he wasn't up yet – and there's this tree. Dave said it was like – the way its branches were – like a juggling man. Then he went kind of shaky, and I said, what's wrong, goose on your grave? Something like that.'

'What did Dave say?'

'He just started going on about how Tom wouldn't come to a place like this on account of it being old.'

'Right.'

'Is this the same tree?'

Moira said, 'Are there many trees at the Manor?'

'Dozens. It's in, like, parkland.'

'Then let's assume it's a different tree, huh, Prof?'

Prof said, 'Barney Gwilliam and now Russell. Both topped themselves.'

'Look. Don't think twice about it. Go. Finish your coffee, get your bags, we'll settle the bill. We'll self-produce, too. Don't worry about a thing.'

'It'll sound – no offence, but it'll sound like crap.'

'Not your problem, Prof. Really. And we'll tell Tom your old mother's been taken sick.'

'Bollocks,' said Prof. 'Bollocks to all that. I'm too old to matter, anyway.'

If he kept saying that all the way to the Abbey he might even convince himself.

Cirencester turned out to be a mistake on the part of Wendy in the warehouse. They didn't need their soya sausage shelves topping up until Thursday at least, so Weasel didn't even have to open the back of the van in Circencester.

This meant he didn't find out what he was carrying until he was outside Broadbank's superstore on the less salubrious side of Cheltenham.

Well, how was he to know? There was a thick partition between the cab and the storage area, with only a six-inch-square glass pane which he hadn't got round to cleaning yet this year.

'Princess,' he said. 'You'll get me bleeding fired.'

She was crouching like a little puppy between two big cardboard boxes, for warmth probably, this van being partly refrigerated.

'As well as catching your death,' said Weasel, holding out his hand to help her out of there. Jeez, no wonder she'd been quiet on the way into Stroud. Playing her cards close to her chest, crafty little sod. And they said these kids was simple.

'Your dad, is it? Fought I knew where your dad was and wasn't saying, right?'

Vanessa gave him the full, solemn, I'm-only-a-handicapped-child-who-can't-be-held-responsible look.

'Yeah, you're breaking my heart,' Weasel said. 'Come on. In the cab. You'll get expelled from that convent, you will. Ninety-seven Hail Marys, if you're very lucky.'

Little bleeder. What was he gonna do now? He cast an eye over the cars in the employees' section, wondering if Broadbank himself was in residence this morning. He maybe wouldn't be averse to taking her back. Give him another shot at Shelley. But, nah. Nothing big or posh enough out there for Broadbank.

'What we gonna do wiv you then?'

Vanessa was offering no suggestions. He didn't want to take her to Ross. Certainly not to the Abbey. But if he whizzed her home now, by the time he got back to Ross it'd be too late to go and check out the Abbey. In daylight, anyway.

'Right.' Lap of the gods job. 'What we'll do is we'll go to a phone box and we'll ring Shelley. See how she wants to handle it.'

'No!'

'Now, listen, Princess, I ain't got time for this.'

'Noooooooooo!' Vanessa stood at the back of the van and screamed at him, which wasn't like her at all.

Then she turned and ran away.

Weasel went after her across the loading bay and into the car park. Vanessa screamed as she ran, and a few people coming out of the supermarket with their trolleys started to take notice.

'Shit,' Weasel muttered. All this talk of child-abuse, it wouldn't be long before somebody would get the idea she was escaping from this sinister-looking old hippie who'd been trying to lure her into his cab. Besides which, she was faster than him.

'All right!' Weasel shouted. 'You win, Princess, you win!'

Vanessa stopped.

'You can come wiv me and I won't ring Shelley. She'll fink you're at school anyway. You can come wiv me to Ross, but you gotta be a good girl and wear your seatbelt.'

Vanessa grinned and walked back towards the van.

'These kids,' Weasel said to a couple of old ladies who'd been directing heavy-duty suspicion his way. 'Don't get their own way, they show you up summink rotten.'

It's like a bleeding conspiracy, he thought. Looks like the Abbey's out of the question.

He'd think about that when they got to Ross.

'I'm not staying here,' Meryl said. 'And that's final.'

Tom shrugged. 'Up to you. You're a free person. Go home. Go back to old Broadarse, you want to.'

Prof thought Meryl was setting up to strangle him.

They were loading their gear into three cars: Simon's Astra, Moira's BMW and Dave's Fiat. Prof would be travelling with Dave, Tom with Simon, Moira with a couple of guitars.

'I'm telling you,' Tom said. 'Not only are we having no passengers, but there's probably no room to spare there anyway. Simon?'

'I think Tom probably *is* right,' Simon told Meryl. 'They've been refurbishing the place as fast as they can, but there's a possibility we'll have to share rooms.'

'*She'll* be sleeping with a man, then.' Meryl nodded towards Moira.

'Can't be ruled out,' Moira said, more than a little curtly. Prof didn't think she was too fond of Meryl and he could see why. He, too, could see a great deal of sense in not having a woman around who seemed to think that what you might call *non-material* matters were just a big adventure, an exciting voyage of discovery.

'If I do go back to the Cotswolds,' Meryl said dangerously, 'Shelley's going to know exactly where you are.'

'Only if you tell her, darlin'.' Tom reared menacingly, like one of those giant dinosaurs, a *Tyrannosaurus rex*. He was probably going to snap her in half.

'Look.' The ever-diplomatic Simon hastily put himself between them. 'I've got an idea. My house is only about a mile from the Abbey. Why don't you stay there? There's always a guest room prepared and I'll arrange for my housekeeper to pop round and show you where everything is. It's quite modern. If you were to stay there, perhaps you could pop in sometime when we're not recording, make sure Tom's OK. Or he could come over to you, if he's in need of . . . therapy. How would that be?'

Might as well take it, lady, Prof thought. It's the best offer you're going to get. He'd been secretly rather hoping *he'd* have to sleep elsewhere. Wondering where the late Russell Hornby had slept. And the late Barney Gwilliam.

The mist had descended around them like ice-cold candy-floss. Prof gazed over to where the holy, crooked mountain was, nothing of it visible now. For the first time it occurred to him that the protective magnetic field around the Skirrid might be the reason he'd had two consecutive nights of restful, dreamless sleep.

Pah. Such crap you got to thinking when the mist came down in the afternoon.

As they climbed into the cars, he heard Meryl saying rather sulkily that she'd follow behind as far as Ystrad Ddu and see what the place was like, not specifying whether she meant the village or the vicarage.

It took no more than twenty minutes to get to Ystrad Ddu, despite the mist being dense around them the whole way.

Four cars in slow procession, like a funeral cortège, minus the hearse.

'OK, David?'

'Fine.' Dave's eyes were fixed on the car in front, Moira's.

Sure he was fine. They all were.

Even though he couldn't see much of it, Prof sensed a roughening of the landscape. They were moving towards the Black Mountains of North Gwent, which were hardly mountains in comparison with Snowdonia or even the Brecon Beacons but appreciably harder than the placid pastures they'd left behind on the Hereford border.

They stopped in the village, and Simon went with Meryl and Tom into a plain detached house opposite an undistinguished little church. After about twenty minutes, Tom and Simon emerged and Simon nodded briefly to the others.

So that was that sorted out. Prof felt sorry for Meryl, but more sorry for himself.

A hundred yards or so from the edge of the village the road had shrunk to not much more than a lorry's width. The mist was rolling around them like wadding, leaving a dusting of fine rain on the windscreen.

'You remember this road, David?'

Dave smiled, said nothing. He glanced at the rear-view mirror and Prof, hunched in the front passenger seat, looked round, momentarily imagining there was a third person with them, in the back. He had a sensation like a caterpillar crawling along the back of his neck.

The cold mist was a muffling stillness around the car creating a silence Prof needed to break.

'Could've been a nicer day, David.'

'It's perfect,' Dave said. 'Wouldn't want you to get the wrong impression.'

'Be prepared, eh?'

'Anxious is the word. Be anxious. You'll find it makes you anxious anyway.'

'Right little bloody ray of sunshine *you* are,' said Prof. 'Who are you anxious about?'

Dave didn't reply, but he didn't stop looking at the car in front, containing Moira and a couple of guitars in cases on the back seat, one of them leaning forward, as if it was whispering something in Moira's ear.

Prof's next breath locked in his throat.

It wasn't a guitar; it was another woman.

Wasn't it? Wasn't that another woman, very thin and sharp-featured?

Prof gripped both his knees and squeezed.

Let me out.

Too late now. The cortège was no longer moving and when

he looked out and up, he saw two lines of enormous, still, grey-robed people hanging over them out of the quivering mist, with their arms linked above their heads.

Not people. Stone arches.

'Whatever happens, Prof,' Dave said, 'do try and remember it was your idea to come here.'

VI

Ferret

Three o'clock, almost. Couple of hours' daylight.

Decisions, decisions.

'What we gonna do then?'

'Fetch Daddy,' Vanessa said without any hesitation. Big-eyed and dead certain.

Having unloaded all his cargo, Weasel had filled the van up with petrol at a service station near the main roundabout at Wilton, outside Ross.

'Just like that, eh?'

The kid had to be feeling isolated. Confused. Messed up. Look at the things that had happened to her since she last saw her old man. Beginning with the crash, two dead neighbours. No, not *quite* beginning with that – even before then, Vanessa knew something was going down. All that *Daddy's coming* stuff. How many times had she said that, like a mantra, like it was information *being fed to her*?

Begging the question: how much like her old man was she? Being the first daughter of a seventh son of a seventh son didn't signify any miracle powers that Weasel knew of. But this was *no ordinary kid*. She seemed to handle things the doctors and the books and these counselling geezers said was impossible for a Down's child. Annoyed the hell out of Shelley, what the experts said. Shelley was a fine woman who wasn't into playing it by the book, who'd making a point of reading the book and then chucking it away.

Weasel decided he'd play it Shelley's way and chuck away the book.

He swivelled in his driving seat to face the kid. She was

sitting, all demure in her brown skirt and jumper, blazer neatly folded on her knee.

'Princess,' Weasel said, 'where *is* your Daddy?'

'You know, silly,' Vanessa said.

'I don't. I told you I don't. Cross my heart.'

'You *do*,' Vanessa insisted, contemplating him real seriously through those milk-bottle specs.

'Is he wiv Morticia – I mean Meryl. Is he wiv Meryl?'

Vanessa shook her head.

Not good so far. According to Shel, even Meryl had said Tom was with her. Had said she was 'connecting' with him.

'Is he wiv Mr Case? You met Mr Case, didn't you? Nah, shit, you didn't.' This was a useless idea. Maybe he'd take her back, call in a phone-box first and ring Shelley.

Weasel started up the engine. 'We'll find him, Princess. I swear we're gonna find him.'

Just not today. Weasel pulled out into the traffic heading for the M50.

'M . . .' Vanessa said, '. . . oira.'

Weasel hit the brakes, horns blasting him from all sides. He pulled up against the double-whites, set the hazard lights going.

'D'you say Moira?'

Vanessa looked blank.

'Simon,' Weasel said.

At least the kid didn't shake her head nor nothing.

'Dave.'

Vanessa smiled. Why'd she do that? She didn't know any Daves in the village, he was pretty sure of that. And the school was all girls.

Weasel said, 'Er . . . Elsie.'

Vanessa shook her head.

'Doris.'

Vanessa looked at him like he was stupid.

'Ruth.'

Vanessa turned away in disgust.

And then he said, like it was just another name:

437

'Abbey?'

Vanessa pushed her school blazer from her knees to the floor of the van, screaming and squirming like she had a bad stomach ache.

Actually, Prof's first reactions to the Abbey included a fair bit of relief.

What, if he admitted it, had been bugging him more than anything was the thought that the place would immediately reflect his worst dreams.

Yes, *those* dreams.

The one in particular involving a distressed young woman running through a skeleton of arches, open to the night sky, running hard and fast, her lungs ready to burst with the agony of trying . . . trying to fly. And when she failed, when she came to the final arch and a big blank wall, she flung herself at it, sobbing and clawing at the stone. And falling all around her, like black rain, was a derisive, discordant chanting – Gregorian gone sour.

In the dream, the arches had been great, soaring hoops of stone, like dinosaur ribs. Whereas these, when you got close, had a squat and rotting feel in the clinging mist. Not pleasant, but not awesome either. No wonder the place didn't get many visitors.

A considerable relief, all the same.

'Home from home, Prof?' said Dave, standing in the bit of a courtyard where the cars were parked. He had his white scarf wound around his neck and was clutching a guitar case to his chest as if it was a huge hot-water bottle.

'I've been in worse places, David. I did National Service, son, never forget that.'

'Where were you? Aden? Malaya?'

'Aldershot,' said Prof. 'Piss-awful place.'

He wished the mist would lift, so he could get a feel of the landscape and the setting, but he supposed it would simply get darker.

'Give it a couple of days,' Dave said. 'You'll grow to love it here.'

'You seem chirpy.'

'Hysteria,' said Dave. 'Wait till you see the stairs.'

Two towers were visible from the courtyard, one beyond it and half-ruined. The other, sprouting from a corner of the yard, had obviously been shortened and partly rebuilt; it had wider slits and a long, Gothic window under the conical, slated roof.

It was Simon, in an old sheepskin jacket and jeans, who led the way into the tower. Like Dave, he was exuding false confidence. It was more convincing from Simon, but it was still false.

First, they went down some steps into a kind of shallow well, with a big oak door at the bottom. There was a massive great keyhole but the door was unlocked and led into a short passage with two more doors, one closed, the other ajar with a couple of steep steps visible in the salty light from above.

'Studio's through that end door, Prof. Best if we unload our gear first, then you can start to familiarize yourself with the equipment. I don't think you'll have any problems. It's comparatively primitive gear, 24-track, exactly the same as it was in 'eighty.'

'The arthriticky old fingers should be able to cope with that,' said Prof. 'Gordon Bennett! How's anybody supposed to get a suitcase up there?'

He was going to be hard-pressed to get *himself* up there, the width and steepness of these steps.

'Take it easy.' Simon jammed the door wide. 'Let me take your case.'

'I'm not *that* old yet, son.' It was a very tight spiral with a low, curving stone roof, real corkscrew. 'How many steps?'

'About fifty, but you'll only need to make it up a dozen or so. You're on the first floor.'

'How many bloody floors are there?'

'Five, I think, one room on each. It was a hotel for some years, back in the sixties. Good gimmick at first, but I don't suppose anybody stayed here more than once. Keep going; it's steep, but it's not *that* easy to fall down a spiral staircase.'

'Take your word for it. Shit, me calf muscles are playing up already. This it? This alcove?'

A slit window with cobwebbed glass in it marked the first floor, which amounted to a small door in a recess guaranteed to crick Tom Storey's neck every time. The door was ajar; Prof battered it open with his suitcase.

'Won't be throwing too many parties in here.'

Somebody had tried to brighten it up with a coat of yellow emulsion, but Prof's room was essentially very dreary, largely due to the small, recessed, metal-framed window being too high in the far wall to show you anything but clouds and fog. The bed had four rickety posts but no curtains. There was a chair. A wooden partition with a door concealed a washbasin and a newish lavatory.

'Good job it's us and not bloody Pink Floyd is all I can say. The other rooms any better?'

'Marginally,' Simon said, head bowed in the doorway. 'But we wanted to save your legs.'

'What for?' Prof dumped himself on the bed. 'Sorry, shouldn't moan.'

Oaths and clumping on the stairs told them the other three were moving in, full of phoney banter.

'. . . stupid can you get, putting a frock on?'

'Just when you think you've forgotten . . .'

'. . . what a shithole this is . . .'

'Yours is the penthouse suite, Tom.'

'Like fuck it is.'

'Is that a rat?'

'Where? Oh, you bastard, Davey!'

Prof grinned. 'Sounds like a Sunday school outing.'

'Mmm,' said Simon. 'Let's just pray the accommodation is the worst of it.'

'You do a lot of praying, Simon?'

'Most of the time,' Simon said. At first Prof thought his expression was deadpan, then realized there was not a lot of pain about it. 'I'd like us to pray together tonight, if that doesn't offend you.'

'No, no,' Prof said vaguely, 'not at all.' Strewth, he thought.

Laying a small pile of books on the altar, Eddie Edwards said, 'I have been thinking about the Abbey.'

'I've thought of bugger all else in twenty years,' Isabel Pugh said without rancour.

It was getting very much colder now; she wore a woollen beret and a thick woollen cape that hung over the arms of the chair. Even inside the church, Eddie's breath was turning to steam. No heating, see. No heating, no lights; they were going to have to find somewhere more congenial to meet. But where else could you go in a village like this without being overheard and being thought quite mad?

Or not.

'Funny, isn't it?' Eddie said. 'Everyone here knows about those candles and Superintendent Gwyn Arthur Jones and his "discreet" inquiries about satanism. Yet, is there a big fuss about it? Oh, we must protect our children against this evil? Not a bloody word. They were *laughing* about it in the Dragon last night, Len Hughes doing an impression of Gwyn Arthur and his mouldy old pipe.'

'People have different ways of coping in the country,' Isabel said. 'You just haven't been here long enough to understand the psychology of it.'

'I'm getting wiser.' Picking up the books from the altar, Eddie sat on a front pew, arranged his overcoat over his knees as a table for them. 'But the villagers are an open book compared with Simon. Unless . . .' He gave her a shrewd look '. . . you know him better than me.'

Isabel said, 'What's your opinion, Eddie? If a man has an obsession, sexual, with a twelfth-century monk, is he a good bet for a husband?' She laughed, really laughed, finding a tissue up her sleeve to wipe her eyes. 'My luck all over, that is.'

'Yes,' Eddie said. 'I've been giving it a lot of thought, what you were telling me, about the candles – and the monk.'

'Just never tell Simon I told you, that's all.'

'Never,' Eddie promised. 'Let me tell you about my researches. Spent most of the day, I have, in Abergavenny museum and then Hereford Library.' He lifted the topmost book from his knees. 'Giraldus now, if you read between his lines . . .'

'Skip the boring bits,' said Isabel. 'Skip the sources and the dates. Just give me the dirt.'

'A hard, snappy woman you are, Isabel.'

'A cold woman I am.'

'Ah, no,' Eddie said. 'Not cold. Never that.'

'Well, you're too old for me anyway,' Isabel said, not unkindly. 'I'm sorry. Go on. Your researches.'

'I'm not going to bore you. You want the dirt, I'll give you the dirt. Richard Walden, founder of the Abbey. The facts, rarely spoken of. A pederast. Expelled from his monastery for giving it to choirboys. Or monastic novices, as they were known then. Corrupted half the youth of South Herefordshire.'

'There's novel.'

'Aye, and does a man like that change his spots just because he's had a holy vision?'

'Well, in theory he does,' said Isabel. 'Isn't that what holy visions are supposed to do?'

'Humbug.'

'You've got a point.' Isabel nodded. 'Not much light left in here. Shall I put a match to a candle or two?'

'I don't think so, really. You don't know where they've been. My God, I've been thinking and thinking about that. My most charitable conclusion being that the poor boy is very seriously confused.'

'No. I think he's telling the truth. I do.' Isabel's broad face shone with a most unlikely faith.

'Candles from the Middle Ages? I can't deal with that. It's even more lunatic than the idea of a satanic cabal in Ystrad, melting down bodies.'

442

'But the monk . . .?'

'The monk, yes. The obsession with the monk, certainly. It's not nice, not in my old-fashioned view, but it's not unlikely. Nobody likes to think of their vicar as a shirt-lifter; however, a lot of them are, that is an established fact. And it stretches credibility not at all to imagine that Simon knows all about Richard's unsavoury activities and is perhaps using that to make sense of his own . . . base desires. Here is a flawed human being, he is saying, just like me. But look, he went on to found a great abbey!'

'But can we *help* him?'

'That's what you asked me the other night. That's why I spent all day deep in my researches. Can we help him?' Eddie sighed. 'Buggered if I know.'

Isabel was jiggling up and down in her chair with frustration.

'But he's in there now, Eddie! He's gone to the Abbey, with the others. Last time he was there he reckons this . . . monk – Abbot Richard, if you like – transmitted thirteen of these filthy candles and arranged them around the studio. And then it all went wrong for them and there was that terrible car crash. All I'm saying is, we can't just sit around and wait for something *else* to happen.'

But wasn't that the pity of it. All she *could* do was sit around.

'Isabel, why's he doing this? Why did they have to go back, these people, this band?'

'Because they're all as barmy as him, presumably,' she said glumly, and then her hands tightened on the chair arms. 'No! Because they want to get their lives back, rescue their sanity, that's why they've gone back. You might not be able to understand that. But you know something? After twenty-one years like the last twenty-one, I think I bloody can.'

She set her chair in motion.

'Hang on.' Eddie stood up. 'Twenty-one years. And fourteen years since the other business?'

The chair squeaked to a halt. 'So?'

'Multiples of seven, that's all. Did anything happen at the Abbey in – let's see – nineteen eighty-seven?'

'Not that I can think.'

'Ah well, another one bites the dust.'

'Another what?'

'Theory. Puzzle. I don't know. You had your terrible fall twenty-one years ago, this other incident was fourteen years ago, and December 1994 makes it another multiple of seven. Were the dates the same? Forgive me, I ramble too much.'

The chair rolled back to where he sat. Isabel said, 'Look at me, Eddie.'

He never objected to that. He liked the way her eyebrows were just slightly irregular and that twist to her lips which could be either petulant or humorous and sometimes, intriguingly, both. He only wished it was light enough in here to see her better.

'Go ahead, then,' he said. 'Make your point.'

'My accident was on the tenth, OK? The car crash was in the early hours of the ninth. No anniversaries here, but close enough. Don't think I haven't thought about that. And don't ever dismiss anything as too far-fetched. It can be a fatal mistake.'

Eddie smiled. This was quite the reverse of the way Marina spoke to him at home.

'Aelwyn,' he said suddenly. 'Aelwyn Breuddwydiwr.'

'Who? Oh . . . *him*.'

Eddie put an arm around the back of the chair and gave one of her shoulders an affectionate squeeze. 'Just another one of my far-fetched ideas. Leave this with me.'

Weasel had two ten-pence pieces and pushed them both in. This was a drag; 10p bought you sod-all time these days. About time Love-Storey equipped him with a mobile. He called the shop.

'Hello, yes.'

'That you Shelley?'

'*Tom . . .?*'

'Nah, nah, it's Weasel. I'm sorry.'

444

'God, for one moment . . . What's wrong, Weasel? Oh, listen, a woman rang for you . . .'

The money counting itself down on the meter, 18p, 17p, 16p . . .

'Shel . . .'

'From London. I'm sure I recognized the voice, but she wouldn't leave a message, just a number. It could be about Tom, so could you call her back and then . . .?'

14p, 13p, 12p . . .

'Shel, listen, I got Vanessa wiv me . . .'

'Vanessa's at school. I'm picking her up in . . .'

'Nah, she ain't. She stowed away in the van.'

'She did *what*?'

10p, 9p . . .

'Hid in the van. Listen. It's Tom. I fink we found him.'

'Where are you?'

'I can't explain about this, I just got to check somefink out and then I'll get back to you, OK?'

5p, 4p, 3p . . .

'Weasel, what the hell . . .?'

'The money's running out, I got no time to explain, I'll call you . . .'

'Weasel, where are you? Bring Vanessa back at . . .'

'. . . later,' Weasel said into the dead phone. He ran back across the road to the dark green van parked outside the Dragon Hotel in Ystrad Ddu.

'Least she won't worry now, Princess. Gives us more time to play wiv.'

He was dead chuffed. They'd cracked it. Him and the kid between them, what a team!

Rolling into Ystrad-wotsit – and what a bleak and lonely spot this was in a mist – who should they see, who should be the *very first person* they seen . . . but bleeding Morticia, weird as life, striding across the road with a shopping bag.

Into the pub she goes; turns out it's a kind of village store, provisions and that. Weasel's treading on the brakes – you stay

there, Princess, don't move – and off into the boozer after her.
Inside, there's no sign of Morticia, maybe she went to the khasi,
but the two geezers standing at the bar just *reek* of the recording
industry. One has a little pony-tail and one of these shapeless
jackets that cost a bomb, the other's got long hair and shades
and looks kind of familiar.

'Looking for Tom,' Weasel says, dead casual. 'Tom Storey.'

'Who are *you*?' asks pony-tail, like Weasel is a piece of shit
that just dropped off somebody's shoe.

'Weasel. Tom's roadie. Everybody knows me. Got his gear
in the van.'

'What makes you think he's here?'

'Well, blimey, they ain't gonna send me here if he ain't. You
wiv Tom, are you?'

'Stephen Case,' pony-tail says coolly. 'TMM. Wait over
there, would you?'

Bingo. And Morticia here too. Knew it, bleeding *knew* it,
Morticia and this slimy git are hand in glove. Say no more.

Geezer keeps him waiting five, six minutes; when he comes
back at least he's a bit more pleasant.

'You say you've a van outside, Mr, er . . .'

'Weasel.'

'OK, Weasel, why don't you go and sit in it and someone
will be along to take you to Tom. He'll go with you, OK?'

'Spot on. Fanks a lot.'

Weasel buys a few items at the bar, comes out to the van
grinning like a frog, glad he didn't ring Shelley again earlier.
Next time he'll have something to say worth hearing.

'Spot of afternoon tea.'

Back in the van, Weasel, all smiles, produced a bag of
goodies – tuna sandwiches, crisps, Coke – he'd bought in the
pub. Bit of a sweetener.

'Do's a favour, Princess. Hop in the back again, would you?
Just for fifteen, twenty minutes, yeah?'

Be warm enough in the back now all the produce was

unloaded and the cooler turned off. What he wasn't going to have was the kid involved in any aggro which might result when he turned up at the Abbey or wherever they was headed.

'Not long now. Next face you see when those back doors opens'll be your dad's. Promise.'

Vanessa went along with it. Weasel closed the doors on the kid with a cheery thumbs-up sign and went back to the cab to wait, munching an apple, thinking how he was going to handle this.

How to tell the big guy he'd been scammed, set up, lured back into the studio on false pretences. Maybe save that for later. The fact that Weasel was not sure what the false pretences had actually been – or why – would kind of take the meat out of the sandwich.

Maybe he should just get Tom on his own, whizz him round the back of the van, tell him, I brung somefing for you, special delivery. And let the Princess do the rest.

In other words, play it by ear.

Presently, a farmer-looking geezer in a long coat, flat cap, appeared across the road. Walked over, tapped on the passenger door and Weasel let him in.

'Mr Weasel?'

'S'me. Where we going?'

'The Abbey, of course. Where did you think?' Bit of a Welsh accent.

'Oh, right.' Quite eager to see the place at last.

Weasel motored down this lane, narrow and getting narrower, trees meeting overhead, branches scratching the paintwork. Who in their right minds would live in the country?

'Right, now, what I want you to do, Mr Weasel . . . slow down . . . past the next telegraph pole you'll see a little track. Now. By here. This is it.'

'Shit, I can't get down there.'

'You'll be fine. Gets wider after a bit.'

'Bloody rough. Ain't got four-wheel drive, you know.'

Bet the poor kid's getting shaken up something rotten back there.

'This it, guv'nor? Don't look like no Abbey to me.'

'This is the Grange. The old Abbey farm.'

'Right.'

'Go round the back, you'll see a barn, double doors wide open. Drive in.'

'I ain't stopping long, mate. Can't I leave it outside?'

'As you please.'

Weasel pulled up outside this old, grey house, major dilapidation, few slates missing from the roof. Typical run-down Welsh farm, outbuildings collapsing all around. He wasn't going to drive into no barn where the roof might come down around him.

The geezer had the door open, and as soon as Weasel applied the handbrake he was hopping down and there was another guy sliding into the passenger seat. A guy with close-shaven grey hair and a tight beard like iron filings.

'Ferret. How are you, lad?'

'Jeez.'

It was only sodding Sile Copesake, godfather of the bleeding blues.

'Sile,' he said.

'So what's this all about, Ferret?'

'Weasel,' Weasel mumbled.

'Summat on your mind, Ferret? Everywhere I go, people keep telling me they've been getting calls from a little bastard in Gloucestershire running up his boss's phone bill.'

Shit. People couldn't keep nothing under their hats any more.

'You should've come directly to me, Ferret. I'd've cleared the whole thing up for you. As it is . . .'

'Look, Sile,' Weasel said. 'This is nuffink personal. I work for the Storeys, they been good to me. I don't wanna see 'em damaged, yeah? Tom's my gaffer. Always has been, always will be.'

'How touching,' said Sile. 'Tell me, Ferret . . .'

'It's Weasel!'

'All nasty little scurrying creatures are much the same to

me,' said Sile. He tutted. 'Forgotten what I was going to say now; you always have this effect on people?'

'Situation is,' Weasel said, sticking to his story without much hope. 'I got a whole pile of Tom's gear in the van. His favourite Telecaster. He can't work wivout his 'Caster, can he?'

Sile smiled. 'Where'd you get that idea?'

'Stands to reason, dunnit?'

'Does it?'

'Lemme speak to him.' This was not going at all how he'd planned. Something distinctly iffy about this whole set-up. Crummy farmhouse, middle of nowhere. Time for straight talk.

'Just get Tom out, willyer, I ain't got all night.'

Sile smiled. 'That's exactly what you have got, Weasel, and a very long night it's going to be.'

'You freatening me?' Weasel felt his fists bunching. He might be little but he'd always been able to handle himself. Never took no shit in stir.

'Threatening?' Sile looked amazed. 'Why should I have to threaten you?'

You know summink? Weasel thought but didn't say. *I never liked you much.*

He glared resentfully into Copesake's eyes, which were dry and dead, like cinders.

Never rated you neither. You was strictly mediocre as a guitarist, as a singer. Like, derivative. You only got there on the backs of all the real talent you got in your bands. You was a fixer, a wheeler-dealer. Too smart to have the blues. And you always worked with young guys. Young guys you could push around.

'Balls.' Sile grinned suddenly and his eyes lit up in the darkness of the cab, like somebody'd put bellows behind the cinders, and he pushed Weasel very hard in the chest and Weasel fell back against the driver's door.

'Never pushed anyone in my life,' Sile said.

Weasel gasped. Bastard had knocked all the breath out of him. Had he said all that out loud? Nah. Not a bleeding word.

'Never pushed nobody, eh?' he found himself gasping. 'What about . . .'bout Carlos Ferrers?'

'Yeah, OK,' Sile said, leaning back against the window, dead relaxed, like he'd never moved. Must be bloody fit, say that much, for a geezer wouldn't see sixty again. 'I'll give you that one, Ferret.'

'What . . . what you was always good at, Sile. Persuading people to split wiv their mates, sign up wiv you. Get 'em while they're weak, doing dope. Dope you bunged 'em, yeah? Prob'ly that's what got you up the ladder in . . . TMM. Yeah? And . . .'

It occurred to Weasel then that Sile hadn't contradicted him when he'd accused him of pushing old slave-driving Carlos down the stairs at the Croydon Lido or wherever it was. He'd said, *I'll give you that one.*

Cocky bastard. 'I tell you, one day, Copesake . . .' Weasel so mad his mouth was full of spit or bile or some shit '. . . you're gonna land yourself . . .'

'What *are* you going on about, lad?'

Weasel sat up. It seemed darker in the cab, except for where Sile was. There was like a hazy, whitish glow around Sile. It certainly wasn't from his smile, not with the state of Sile's teeth. You'd think he'd have had them capped, all the bread he was raking in.

Weasel's lips felt wet.

'I said, yeah,' Sile said. 'Yeah to everything. Except the bit about having no talent. I resent that. I resent that very much. That's the reason you're dying, Ferret.'

Weasel smelled a rich, rusty smell. It brought a memory he couldn't place. He sat upright with difficulty, wiped some spit off his chin. Bloody thick spit.

'Carlos tripped,' Sile said. 'Good as tripped, any road. Carlos drank too much tequila. Tom was in a shocking state that night, figuring he'd not only predicted it, he'd made it happen. Tom was crying on old Sile's shoulder. Pitiful. Like you, Ferret.'

Weasel held up his hands. Blood dripped from his fingers. He touched his lips; it was thick all over his mouth, like curry sauce.

'What you done? What you done to me, Copesake?'

'Just a bit of a push,' Sile said. 'Like this.'

Sile jerked forward, sending Weasel rocking back against the door again, and this time Weasel couldn't get himself up. He coughed, and a massive red gob splatted all over the dash.

'No wonder they wear leather aprons in abattoirs,' Sile said, looking bored now, leaning back as far as he could go, folding up his knife.

He shook his head sadly. 'Nobody's gonna think twice about it, when they find you in the van on some scrappy bit of derelict land in Wolverhampton or somewhere. You've got too much form, Ferret. Ex-con, dubious associates.'

Weasel, heaving feebly, saw that Sile was wearing thin leather gloves.

'Well, I must be off. Wish I could stay with you until you died, Ferret, lad, but I could do with a piss.'

Sound of the door handle, and then all that remained of Sile was a dent in the passenger seat. Weasel couldn't move. He tried to breathe and his mouth, his throat, his lungs were all flooded and all he could do was make stupid slurping sounds.

Lying back, he could see through the windscreen, hills and trees and some action in the sky, a last squeeze of sunlight, seeping through the mist like orange juice.

Weasel made a noise like

urrrrr

And a whole tomato hit the screen, bright red, red as the Gretsch Chet Atkins Tom's old feller'd brought back from the boozer all those years ago.

All those years. Weasel's eyes filling up.

Blown it good this time. Too clever for your own good. Sod-all use to Tom and Shelley and . . .

Princess!

Rage and agony exploded in Weasel's head and his whole body shuddered as he clutched in desperation at the steering wheel – *Princess, Princess! No! Please!* – tried hopelessly to haul himself up, no breath in his lungs, only holes and blood drowning him inside and out, big helpings of blood everywhere, over the seats, the dash, the vinyl roof.

Lifeblood dripping down the dirty little square of glass through which solemn eyes peered, big eyes behind spectacles thick as bottle-bottoms.

VII

Gin Trap

Seeing the drummer in the studio smoking a joint – that was quite a shock.

Not the joint, the drummer. As Moira had never thought for one minute that any of them were here for the music, the need for a drummer had never occurred to her.

The appearance of this particular guy showed how heavily TMM must be committed to this crazy project. And that was worrying.

'Oh, wow,' the drummer said. 'If it ain't the exquisite but criminally underrated Ms Cairns.'

'Oh shit,' Moira said under her breath, pausing in the doorway to take this in. 'Lee Gibson.'

The band had never had a full-time percussionist on the simple basis that Max Goff hadn't been able to find one with reputed psychic abilities. Drummers weren't like that.

Lee Gibson certainly hadn't been. What Moira most remembered about Lee were sneers and resentment. Resentment when it became clear that he was never going to be a full member of the band, for reasons he couldn't, at first, get his head around. Sneers when he did get his head around them.

Seeing him here, Tuesday morning, just before nine-thirty, setting up his kit like in the old days, this was downright *bizarre*. Especially when you considered who Lee *was* nowadays.

'You're looking like you just saw a ghost.' Lee flicked at a cymbal. 'Not that that would faze you too much, as I recall.'

Looking down the studio from the mixing desk, you'd think the drummer was the most important guy here. He was the only one didn't have a booth; the drums were out there on the studio floor, at the farthest end, near the rear door. In this studio, they seemed to take up nearly a quarter of the floor space.

'You do still see ghosts, I take it,' Lee said.

For a millionaire superstar, he didn't look that much different. Back in 'eighty, when most guys were having regular haircuts, Lee Gibson, ten years too young to have been one, was looking like a hippie. He'd always suited long hair, anyway, with that hook-nosed pirate's face. Now there was designer stubble; Lee's face had grown into that.

'You're looking good, though,' Lee said, like this was a major surprise, like he'd expected she'd be some kind of wizened crone by now.

Moira came in and shut the door. This early, she thought she'd have had the place to herself. Last night the whole band and Prof had gone out to the paddock behind the Abbey where TMM had set up a couple of Portakabins and a caravan, with two cooks and two technical guys working shifts. When the studio had been launched fifteen years ago, all this was inside the building, extending into the outhouses and barns. But those buildings were in a pretty bad state now, Case said, and needed major refurbishment.

The band had stayed in the Portakabin-canteen for several hours until close to midnight, putting off a return to the Abbey. In the end it was OK, not a bad night, if a wee bit cold in the third-floor tower room. She'd awoken a couple of times, sensing waves of need from Dave in the room below and choosing to ignore them.

No complications at this stage, OK.

The return of Lee Gibson, now *the* Lee Gibson. What kind of complication was this?

'How'd you get here, Lee?'

'By limo, I suppose. Didn't really notice. Spent the night in the village inn. Amazingly primitive. Rocks in the bed, appalling food. First place I stayed in three years where nobody recognized me.'

'Hell, Lee, nobody recognized you?' Moira whispered.

'What kind of morons *are* these people? Or maybe you just forgot to hang your gold discs over the bed again.'

'You're just a goddamn jealous bitch, Cairns,' said Lee. 'No, I won't be going back there tonight. I'm in a mobile home. Down by the river, in the trees. Quite comfy. Little office in there too, and a PA. Called . . . er . . . Michelle. Works nights.'

'All mod cons, then,' Moira said dryly.

'Yeah. All mod cons.'

Lee grinned. He'd be in his early thirties now. Over in the States, where he was pretty enormous, few people would even remember him as a drummer. Lee had switched pretty quickly to guitar: thrash metal and then grunge, strategic career move.

No. Him being here made no sense; it was unreal.

'OK.' Moira walked purposefully across the studio and sat on the edge of an amplifier. 'I'll admit it. I don't understand why you're doing this.'

''Cause I'm sentimental, babe,' Lee said. 'I have attachments to my roots.'

'Which is why you've cultivated that truly awful Californian accent, huh?'

Lee scowled. He could only take so much of this. It was more like the old Lee. Or actually, the extremely young Lee; he couldn't have been more than nineteen when he'd done that session. So could he just have come back on a whim, to relish the irony, the reversal of fortunes?

That didn't make enough sense, either.

'You figuring to put a couple of your own songs in this time?' Moira said casually.

'Shit, no.' Lee offered her a hit from his joint; she shook her head. 'I'm just the session drummer.'

He wore white jeans and a black shirt open to a hairy chest and a half-moon medallion. He was loving this.

'How's Tom?' he asked.

'As a guitarist or as a human being?'

'As a neurotic bastard,' said Lee. 'Shit, that cat was really unstable. What happened, his wife, all that – you didn't have to be frigging psychic to see that coming a mile off. Still . . . I can understand all that stuff better these days.'

'What stuff?'

'This psychic shit. Some gigs, you really feel you're wielding like cosmic power. Jim Morrison said that. Used to see himself as a shaman. That's a guy who connects with the spirit world.'

'Yeah I know what a shaman is. The rock audience is like a tribe and the musician's the medicine man.'

'Heavy shit,' Lee said. 'Up there on stage at a big gig or a festival I can feel where Morrison was coming from.'

'Except you were closer to being a real shaman in the old days,' Moira said. 'Tribal shamans used to bang drums to summon and dismiss the spirits, not stand there just growling out pretentious crap.'

'Yeah?'

'Yeah. Like this.' Moira stamped suddenly on the bass-drum pedal.

Bam!

'Leave those drums alone,' Lee snapped, not joking.

'Aw, come on, Lee, spill it.' Moira stepped away, lifting her hands. 'What the hell are you really doing here?'

'Well, it's not a frigging holiday.' Lee sat down on his stool, threw a pair of drumsticks in the air, watched them drop to the newly laid grey carpet, didn't pick them up. 'Pound of flesh situation, if you must know.'

'I'm sorry, I'm very ignorant, but are you with TMM or what?'

Lee stared at her, clearly amazed that somebody purporting to be a musician didn't know which record company he was signed to.

'You remember when I first went out to the States. I was drummer with Captain Blood, right?'

'Sure,' Moira said. Captain Blood. That was the second-division British blues band which acquired American personnel and came to sound even less like the original than Fleetwood Mac. Until, pretty soon, there was nothing left of it that was British except the name. And Lee Gibson, presumably.

'See, it was Sile Copesake let me go. Fixed it for me, actually. After Frankie Lomax OD'd.'

'You were in Sile's band?'

'Who wasn't? The guy was good to me, what can I say? Got me the Blood job. Backed me on the solo career when Blood split. Rest is history.'

'You mean Sile's calling in the favour,' Moira said.

'That's about it,' Lee was sounding suddenly English again. Maybe L.A.-speak was hard to sustain in Britain in December.

It made business sense. An album with Tom Storey on it, *plus* Lee Gibson, would be guaranteed to recoup expenses. But what if it was lousy? People who hadn't played together for getting on for fifteen years – about four generations in rock music – thrown into a studio, no rehearsals? Was this not a major gamble during a recession?

Maybe. Maybe not. What it certainly was, Moira realized, was a well-calculated replay of December 1980. The studio layout was exactly the same; even the same amps, you'd swear: two Voxes, a Fender Twin and a McCarthy Dual. And on a stand in the booth nearest the mixing desk was an orange-coloured basic Fender Telecaster, the only guitar Tom Storey ever used in the studio.

How did they know which was Tom's old booth? How did they know about the original amps? How did they know – peering into the second booth – that Dave liked to perch on a packing-case type McCarthy amp, even playing acoustic?

Russell? Had Russell told them all this? Before he . . .

She said to Lee, 'Hey, d'you hear about Russell Hornby?'

'Yeah.' Lee finished off his joint, holding it between clawed thumb and index finger in the time-honoured, waste-not-want-not fashion. Stylishly blew out some fragrant smoke. 'Aaaaah. Russell, yeah. Stupid bastard. Why'd he do a thing like that?'

Moira shook her head. She might as well have asked him if he knew Russell had got married again or bought himself an English setter. 'What's it like outside?'

'Filthy,' Lee said. 'Anyway, I don't get this whole business either. You were having a bad time before, you couldn't get out fast enough, you destroyed the frigging tapes. So what the hell are *you* doing back here? You all suddenly desperate for cash? That's the case, I'll *give* you some to get us all the hell out of this museum.'

It was a simple enough question. Why were they here?

And yet this was the one big question which, whenever the four of them were together, nobody seemed to ask.

'Straightforward enough, I suppose,' Moira said. 'We came here to make an album and we never finished it. It's taken us fourteen years to realize that this is one of those albums that's just got to be finished.'

'Or else?'

'Yeah,' Moira said.

Vanessa rubbed at the glass panel and peered through into the cab.

She just didn't know *what* was wrong with Weasel.

His eyes were still open, so he couldn't be asleep. He couldn't be dead either. Dead people's eyes were always closed; she'd seen a dead person once, Granny Love, Shelley's mummy. She looked like a doll, but Shelley had said she was very peaceful.

Weasel wasn't peaceful. For ages and ages, Weasel had been looking very angry through the dried soup.

Vanessa knew he wasn't angry at her. Weasel was *never* angry at her. He called her Princess, like Princess Diana, who used to live near their house but didn't any more.

She supposed she must have fallen asleep in the back of the van. Again! She'd fallen asleep the first time, after eating up all the food and then she'd woken up very cold and felt a bit sick and wanted to go to the toilet.

It had been dark by then. Vanessa had climbed out of the back door of the van and gone round to the front and pulled open the door to ask Weasel where the toilet was. But Weasel felt funny and wet and didn't smell very nice.

458

The van was in a big long shed with straw all over the place. There were cracks of light where the doors were. The doors had only been pulled to, and she opened them easily and it was very dark outside, but she was never frightened of the dark, not like Daddy.

It was a sort of farm, like Rudkins's farm up the lane, only Rudkins had chickens and horses and dogs everywhere and there were no animals here at all. Round the back of the house, Vanessa found a little shed with a creaky door and a string to put the light on, which was just a horrible bulb with dead flies all over it. There was a *very dirty lavatory* that she refused to touch with her bottom but had to use anyway because she just couldn't wait. It was a nuisance.

There'd been a light on in the house but Vanessa didn't like to knock because the Bad Man who'd had a fight with Weasel was probably inside and he might want to fight *her*.

So Vanessa had gone back to the van and didn't know what to do, so she prayed to her Guardian Angel, using the prayer she'd been taught at the convent.

O most faithful companion appointed by God to be my guide and protector and forever at my side . . . What thanks can I offer you for your faithfulness and love? You watch over me in sleep. You console me when I'm sad. You lift me up when I fall . . .

She didn't say it very loud, and then she lay down with her schoolbag as a pillow and her blazer and some dirty old sacks over her. The smell had reminded her of Weasel and she'd sat up again and put her hands together.

And please watch over Weasel, too, and make him better.

As she lay down again, she felt a bit worried about this. Perhaps her Guardian Angel wasn't allowed to watch over Weasel as well. Perhaps she ought to pray to Weasel's Guardian Angel. But was she allowed to do that?

She must have fallen asleep thinking about this, perhaps for hours and hours. Now she was awake again and she was hungry and thirsty.

She knocked on the glass. 'Weasel!'

There were holes in the barn roof and light coming down, grey and misty. She could see Weasel quite clearly. He hadn't moved. He didn't look *too* angry any more. Just sad.

If anybody should be angry, it should be her.

Weasel had said he was going to find Daddy.

What he'd said was, the next time those doors open, Daddy'll be there.

But the doors had never opened except when she'd opened them herself.

It was no way to treat a Princess.

She pushed the van doors open and scrambled down and peeped between the big barn doors to make sure the Bad Man wasn't there.

Outside it was very foggy and very cold. Colder than the back of the van. Vanessa couldn't even see the house. She felt very miserable. The ground was all muddy and dirty and full of puddles with coloured circles in them, which was oil. She hated going to the dirty old lavatory again. When she pulled the chain it made a horrible noise, like the noises Weasel had made when the Bad Man had gone and there was vegetable soup all over the windscreen.

Crouching over the dirty lavatory, desperate not to touch it because of the germs, Vanessa started to say another prayer to her Guardian Angel and then felt ashamed. He wouldn't want to talk to her in here!

Vanessa began to cry.

She didn't want to go back to the van. She didn't want to see poor Weasel again. She wanted to go home. She was very, very cold.

Outside the lavatory, it was so foggy and grey and her glasses were so misted up with tears that Vanessa almost bumped into the man.

Although not really. The man came out of the mist. You couldn't bump into him. He was one of *those* men.

'Grandad,' Vanessa said, relieved.

*

'I don't know, Eddie,' the museum curator said, 'you were bad enough when you were at work, all your awkward questions, but since you retired you've been a complete pain. How *can* I explain it? The massacre was 1175, no argument.'

'I don't need for you to *explain* it! All I want is for you to *confirm* it, see!'

Eddie realized he was yelling down the phone and lowered his voice. 'I just don't want any mistakes, see, Elwyn.' He consulted his notes. 'Can we go over it one more time?'

'Five minutes,' the museum curator said, 'then I've got a pensioners' club from Hirwaun to show around.'

'OK.' Eddie spelled it out, tracing his notes with his finger.

De Braose massacre of Seisyll's people . . . 1175.
Foundation work begins on Abaty Ystrad Ddu . . . 1177.

'But that doesn't mean there was nothing there at all, Eddie.'

'No, all it means is there was no massive great stone edifice. It means the Abbey was probably a bunch of huts. Or even bloody *tents*. See, these little anomalies have been at the back of my mind for years, without me realizing the significance.'

'There *is* no significance. This must've been how many of these ancient Abbeys began. Just this fellow Walden and a handful of followers and a lot of faith. They throw up a few wooden huts and then go out and raise the money, or apply to Rome or something. There is no great significance.'

'Not if you discredit the Aelwyn story, no. Which, on the surface, is what this appears to do. If there was no Abbey there, how could Aelwyn Breuddwydiwr come charging out of the snow with a bunch of armed men on his tail and bang like hell on the great oak door? You don't *have* great oak doors on sheds.'

'I'm still not following this, Eddie, and the pensioners from Hirwaun are filing in.'

'You don't have to, Elwyn. This is my problem. Thank you, boy.'

Eddie put down the phone, flushed with triumph. Then picked it up again and called Isabel Pugh.

'You're an accountant,' he said. 'Get out your calculator and do a sum for me. Never could trust my long-division.'

Lee's mobile home, movie-set size, movie-star luxury, was installed behind the Portakabin canteen. The only drawback, as Lee had pointed out, was having to share it with an office run by a TMM employee called Michelle. She was twenty-two and gorgeous. She had a lot of time for Lee Gibson. He conceded to Dave and Moira, showing them around, that this was not a *major* drawback.

Lee said he was fed up of waiting and was going to have a lie down for half an hour on his luxurious movie star's bed.

Moira and Dave walked back to the Abbey. They'd breakfasted at the canteen around eleven; hung around to wait for Simon and Tom and Prof, none of whom had shown yet.

'You envy him, Davey?' Moira said, as they strolled back to the Abbey, wraiths in the mist.

'Who, Lee? I think he envies me,' Dave said. 'I only wish he had cause.'

'It's no' the time.' Moira said. 'And definitely no' the place. Davey, why'd you keep looking at me?'

'Just checking you're not an illusion.'

'Don't lie, huh?' Moira said.

'I'm not l—'

'You're playing with the ends of your scarf. Always a bad sign.'

Through the mist they could see the great stone hoops of the Abbey's nave. It was like a giant gin-trap, Dave thought. All you had to do was tread on the bait, and the Abbey would have you. He felt an urge to pull Moira back, to prevent her going any further. Don't take her, he called silently to the Abbey. Please don't take her.

'Have you seen something, Davey?'

'No.'

'Then what's wrong?'

'Nothing. Honestly. Everything's fine. Well, fine as it could be under the . . . I . . .'

'What?'

'I like your anorak,' Dave said.

Moira glanced sideways at him. 'C & A's. No big deal.'

'I haven't seen it before, have I?'

Moira stopped and stared at him, the mist billowing around her like a toga. 'Davey, what the hell's so significant about my damned anorak? Listen, I'm no' moving another inch until you tell me what this is all about.'

Dave pushed a hand through his hair. The anorak was black. It had a hood. He was wondering if she'd been wearing it the other night at the Castle Inn when she and Prof had found him. When he'd seen something black around her face.

'Sorry,' he said. 'It's nothing. I'm just making small talk. When I get this close to the Abbey I talk about the first thing that comes into me head. Just until we get inside. Nerves, that's all.'

And he didn't need to look at her to know she didn't believe a word.

The Abbey arched above them. The tower, with its pointed roof, jutted out of the ruins like a bird of prey on a crag.

They went directly to the back entrance of the studio, hearing voices from inside. 'Maybe we can make a start late afternoon.' Moira squeezed his arm below the elbow. 'Have a wee warm-up session, hang a few ideas together.'

There was a crash of cymbals from within. 'Oh dear,' she said. 'He just hates people messing with his drums.'

'. . . all we need,' they heard Tom shouting.

'Just send out for coffee,' Simon said. 'Lots of . . .'

He broke off as Dave pushed the door open, dread welling up.

'. . . the hell's this?'

It was like some tragic, classical group-sculpture. Tom Storey stood in the middle of the studio floor, just beyond Lee's drumkit. Simon crouched to one side, his arms open like a goalkeeper's. Tom was holding up a smaller figure in a dressing-gown who seemed to have collapsed into the drums, hurling over two hi-hats, a snare and a pair of deep bongos.

Simon's hands slid supportively under the dressing-gowned arms. 'Steady, Prof.'

'Oh . . . *no*.' Dave dropped to his knees, helped Simon lay the sagging body on to the grey carpet.

'Prof is pissed,' Tom said bluntly.

'I don't believe this.' Dave looked down into Prof's filmed-over eyes. 'Two days at the Castle he doesn't touch a drop. In fact, before we left yesterday, he said, there's not gonna be any booze in there, is there? I don't want any booze.'

'Must've brought some wiv him, all the same.'

Dave shook his head. Prof grabbed a cymbal stand to haul himself upright and pulled it over on top of him with a wild clashing of metal. Dave saw Simon wince at the sound.

'Don' worry Tom.' Prof giggled feebly. 'Thasser name of the game. "Don' . . . worry . . . Tom."'

Moira turned away, closed her eyes, clenched both fists by her sides, breathed out viciously.

'This *fucking* place.'

VIII

Dream Made Flesh

No lights shone from the ugly yellow house on the hill. No smoke stained the morose sky above its chimneys. In the winter dusk it stood tasteless and unloved in its neat, shaven, treeless grounds.

When Martin rang the bell, it tinkled forlornly from room to abandoned room.

And yet she was in.

And called out, 'Round the back, would you, please?'

As if she were afraid to answer the front door because the people who entered through front doors were the official people. *Police, Mrs Storey. Could we come in?*

She already had the back door open. The kitchen was a dim cave behind her, and she offered no greeting. She'd clearly lost weight. Her face was gaunt, her brass-bell hair dull and tarnished.

This was a horrible place. Martin wanted to take her away, back to his house which, even without Meryl, was relatively warm and bright, but he knew she wouldn't leave, not even for half an hour.

In case the phone should ring. In case someone should return.

'I'm afraid this is all my fault.' He followed her in. 'I'm so terribly sorry.'

'I've picked up the phone about four times,' Shelley said listlessly. 'To call the police, you know?'

'It's a possibility we have to consider.'

'Yes.'

Inside it was too gloomy to decode the expression on her

face. The only gleamings came from the chrome covers on the Aga. He moved towards her across the kitchen.

'Don't touch me,' Shelley said emptily. 'Please don't touch me now.'

'I was going to put some lights on.'

'I don't want lights either.'

'Shelley . . .' He couldn't think what to say, how to cross the gulf. Through the window he could see lights in Larkfield village. It was as if there was a power failure up here.

'I was thinking I've got nothing left,' Shelley said. 'But perhaps I've always had nothing. Vanessa wasn't mine. Tom was never really mine; he just lived here in the house built to his own peculiar specifications. A fortress, not a home. Even Weasel, with his awful, jagged smile, Weasel was Tom's, like a one-man dog.'

'You've . . .'

He stopped. The crass old Martin would have said, You've still got your ideas, your flair, your acumen, your *business*.

The business in recession. The business built on Tom's money.

'I'm irrelevant,' she said. 'That's why I haven't called the police. So they find Vanessa and she's with her father. Who are you? What's your angle? I'm her stepmother. *Was* her stepmother.'

He knew she didn't want lights because she was crying silently, because her face was streaked. Because, right now, she wasn't good for the Love-Storey corporate image. And he was a potentially important client. And never likely to be anything more important than that.

He had, it was true, been feeling rather sorry for *himself*. Deserted by a housekeeper who, in his view, had been rather better than a wife – cooks, caters to all your needs, is watchful and intelligent and makes no emotional demands.

Perhaps emotional demands were what Meryl had gone in search of. Him too. Perhaps.

'What I can't understand,' he said. 'If Weasel was so anxious to call you from a phone box when he did . . .'

'Yes, I've thought about all that. He lives for Tom, but he still sees me as his employer and he's in my van. Details like that matter to Weasel.'

'What about Tom? You're his wife.'

'Tom's out of control, can't you get inside that yet? Tom responds to influences the rest of us can't bring ourselves to believe in. And when they take over, Tom can't do anything about it. He doesn't *want* to be ruled by them, which is why he had this house built. But he was never happy here either, and when he was pushed outside again he realized that. The other night, coming to your house, that was the first time Tom had left this place since it was built.'

'I just had no idea what I was doing.'

'I persuaded him to go. I *fought* to get him out. And now I have to accept the consequences. The whole rocky edifice is crumbling away and it's my fault, not yours at all. He used to play his guitar in the night, like a wolf baying in a trap, and I wasn't hearing it. Not really.'

'I heard. That is, I heard . . . about it.'

'But he was afraid to leave, you see,' Shelley said.

'Because there were things he knew he'd have to face up to out there? Look, this is no reflection on you whatsoever, but maybe Meryl *can* bring him round.'

'If they want each other, they can have each other.'

'I don't think it's like that,' Martin said. 'In fact, I'm sure it's not. You know what Tom was like with her at the dinner. Oblivious.'

'I know what he was like *after* the dinner. I know that something happened between them that made her very keen to find him. Weasel thinks she's in this with Case, to lure Tom out and get him back into the studio.'

'That's nonsense,' Martin said gently. 'I can tell you for a fact that they'd never met before that dinner party. And while I wouldn't trust Steve an inch, I do trust Meryl.'

'I'm sure you do,' Shelley said. 'At least to the point where – as she would say – the spheres collide. And then she goes completely off her head. Sod this, I'm going to call the police.

It's been a whole day now. Over a day. I can't stand it any longer.'

'That has to be your decision,' Martin said.

'Except there'll be publicity,' Shelley said despairingly. 'I used to work in publicity at Epidemic. I know what'll happen. A missing thirteen-year-old girl? A nationwide police hunt? And Tom Storey? There'll be reporters outside the gate, TV crews. Dirty washing on the line.'

'Would that be necessary?'

'You can't find a missing person without telling people to look out for her, can you?'

'God,' Martin said. 'This is a mess, isn't it? Where *are* they all?'

'It's like a black hole, isn't it?' Shelley said, parched-voiced. 'One after the other. Tom and Meryl and Weasel and Vanessa. As if something's sucking them in. As if they're *all* out of control. That's silly, isn't it?'

'You can't stay here on your own. Is there a spare bedroom. A settee I could doss down on?'

'I suppose you don't want to go home to a cold house and no supper.'

'No,' he admitted. 'I don't. I could always go to a restaurant. I could go to a hotel. But I'd be worrying about you.'

Suddenly Shelley switched on several spotlights. They all seemed to be pointing at Martin and he threw a hand across his eyes.

'Wouldn't do any good, would it?' Shelley said. 'The full glare of publicity. It's only when I'm on my own that I almost call the police. Also, I think if you went away now I'd be scared you'd disappear too. And then I really would go insane because there'd be nobody else who even knows what's been happening, let alone why.'

When his eyes adjusted he saw she was sitting at the kitchen table, both hands inside her hair.

Black hole?

Simon had sent them off through the dusk mist to the canteen. Tom and Dave and Moira. Moira hadn't wanted to go. Simon had said, Please, I've had some experience with this. I *am* a minister.

Bullshit, and she knew it, he could tell.

He had Prof in a rock and swivel chair behind the mixing desk. The chair had arms so he couldn't fall out. Simon figured that being in his usual work environment would help. He'd got about two pints of coffee down Prof; mustn't, on any account, let him sleep. Simon switched on all the studio lights. The desk was lit up like New York at night.

'Prof. Talk to me.'

As soon as the others had gone, he'd been up to Prof's room and searched for bottles. Nothing, and nowhere to hide any. He'd taken the liberty of going through Prof's suitcase; he'd had the top off the toilet cistern; he'd even climbed on a chair to reach the high window in case there was a plastic carrier bag hanging outside.

Clear.

And then he'd found the pot.

It was rolled on its side under the bed. A flagon, like a Chianti bottle, with a handle at the neck.

Bluish glazed pottery. Stamford ware. A baluster jar.

It stank of wine.

It stank like Prof's white beard, rusted brown around his mouth. Simon bent to sniff the beard and they both recoiled at once.

'Geddoff. What you doing? Bloody poofter.'

'Prof. Where did you get the wine?'

If you wanted to get discreetly pissed, you'd stick to spirits; you'd hardly try to smuggle in a case of red wine, would you?

And the baluster jar. It hadn't been there when he'd shown Prof the room, he was sure of it.

'Prof!'

'What!'

'The wine. Tell me where you got the wine.'

469

Prof struggled upright, the chair rocking. It would probably make him sick eventually. Simon had a plastic bucket standing by.

'Where?'

Prof grinned. 'Room service.'

And gradually, like the contents of Prof's stomach into the bucket, it all came out.

Prof waking up, he doesn't know when but it's some time in the night. And he's thirsty. Just plain thirsty, right? Thirsty as in needing liquid. Water, lemonade, nice cup of hot tea.

The big jar is on the floor at the side of the bed. No, he wasn't aware of it before, which he would have been, 'course he would. Couldn't have been there when he went to bed, else he'd have knocked it over, wouldn't he? 'Course he would.

It's heavy, this pot. Prof's thirst is roaring. He pulls it on to the bed, lifts it up to his mouth.

Beaujolais nouveau it ain't.

That's what he's thinking. *Beaujolais nouveau it ain't.* That's all he remembers thinking until he wakes up again with the same raging thirst. Which, considering how bloody cold it is in here, is not exactly normal, is it?

Feels around by the side of the bed and there it is again.

Full.

In which case he couldn't have had more than a sip last time, could he?

Prof heaves the big jar on to his chest, tips it towards his mouth.

Remembers nothing else until . . . well it must be morning. But no more than first light, surely. Headache? Not that he remembers. No, feeling OK, really. Except for the thirst.

*

'What did it taste like?' Simon asked.

'Wonderful,' Prof said, rolling his eyes. 'Didn't seem like the same stuff. Before, it was kind of weak and sour. You got any more?'

'No.'

'Came up from the cellar, right? The wine cellar.'

'This is the wine cellar. Hence the vaulted ceiling. This is where they stored the wine in casks. Imported wine from Bordeaux. Decanted into baluster jars. This *was* the wine cellar. Now it's a studio. Remember?'

'No more wine?'

'No more wine for you.'

'Shit.' Prof giggled.

Simon looked down at Prof. Stupid, stupid, stupid. Why had nobody told him this guy had a drink problem?

Like Simon had had a sex problem.

Whatever was in here, it always homed in on weaknesses.

He took the plastic bucket upstairs to the little, cold bathroom which shared the first floor with Prof's room. He half-filled the bucket with chilled spring water from the bath and brought it back, with a sponge.

'Blown it, din' I?' Prof mumbled as Simon mopped his face and his beard. 'Fucked up again.'

'It was useful, Prof. It was a warning not to relax, not for one moment.'

'Time is it?'

'Fivish.'

'Morning?'

'Afternoon, Prof. Evening.'

'Oh shit, we're losing time. We were gonna record . . .'

'Looks like we won't be recording tonight.'

He thought, Looks like it doesn't *want* us to record.

Yet.

When the child appeared on the vicarage doorstep, Meryl thought it was a visitation, a phantasm.

So silent. So still.

Meryl stood there with the door open, the dark air biting at her cheeks.

The porch light haloed the small figure.

Meryl's anger evaporated in the fragrant holiness of the moment.

This morning she'd driven to Abergavenny to buy more clothes. And toiletries, to supplement the frugal male contents of Simon's bathroom cabinet. Since her return, she'd been feeling increasingly resentful. Stalking the vicarage and doing things abruptly: washing her hair, switching the TV set on and off, walking up the street to the little village shop inside the pub on three separate occasions to buy items which were already on shelves in the larder. And making pot after pot of hot, placating tea.

Periodically, she'd go and stand at the big picture window and gaze out towards the wind-scoured hills stubbled with bare trees. Knowing that, sooner or later, tonight or tomorrow night, she would go to the Abbey.

She'd not yet even seen the Abbey, but she'd dreamed of it last night. In the dream, the Abbey had soared marble-white into a starry night sky. The Abbey was magnificently floodlit by its own inner incandescence.

Such a contrast to the hunched-up grey cottages of Ystrad Ddu crowding under their rocky canopy like old women under an umbrella.

The dream had been around her all day. This, she knew, was what had made her so restless. The dream meant that when at last she went to the Abbey, when she allowed herself to respond to its magnetic tug – a tug she experienced every time she left the house and walked into the lane, knowing where it ended – it must be at night, when the Abbey was at its most splendidly amorphous. And then, even if there was no soaring marble, it would still soar for her as it had in the dream.

Now the dream had come to the vicarage door in the form of a small, dumpy child with telescope glasses and the brown uniform – unmistakable, if creased and dusty – of a Gloucester-shire convent school.

Meryl couldn't breathe as she put out a hand, expecting it to slip through the brown blazer, through the child.

And the shock of the real, of the dream made flesh, made her cry out.

'Oh my lord! It *is* you. It's . . .' Frantically rummaging in her brain for the child's name.

'Vanessa,' the child said, in that voice that told you something was wrong with her. Not wrong, *different*. She had a different type of mind, a differently organized body.

For the first time, to Meryl, a Down's Syndrome child seemed as exotic as some extra-terrestrial being.

There was a great tumbling of Meryl's senses. Where had the child, Vanessa, come from? How did she get here? How and why had she come *here*?

When the miraculous occurred in your life, it was never the way you imagined it would be. Not the Lady Bluefoot but a hideous spirit with a torn face. Introduced not by a white-haired lady in veils but by a hulking, rough-spoken cockney guitarist with psychic agoraphobia.

The child looked up at Meryl.

The child said, 'I'm awfully cold.'

'Come in at once, my sweet,' Meryl said effusively. 'Come and get warm and I'll make you a lovely dinner.'

The child said, 'Can Grandad come in as well? And Weasel? They're awfully cold, too.'

IX

AA

WEDNESDAY, 7 DECEMBER

Several times in the night, Simon had gently lifted the Bible from his chest and placed it on his pillow. And then, in rubber-soled sandals, had crept down the spiralling stairs by the light of a pencil torch.

He'd placed himself in the smallest, topmost room. A cell with a slit, and more than fifty steep stairs to reach it: a penance, of sorts. It was also the room which the others were least likely to visit. So they wouldn't see the other little Bibles – one at each corner of the bed.

Moira's room was immediately below his, along with a bathroom. Then Dave, then Tom. Then another bathroom and also Prof Levin's room, which was Simon's destination.

Very quietly, shading the torch, he would ease open Prof's door and peer in. Prof would be on his back and snoring. Or on his side and not snoring. Or on his stomach with a pillow half over his head.

No smell of wine. Only the ancient aroma of stone and damp on the stairs.

No baluster jar tonight.

It never happened when you were prepared for it. Each time he returned to his bed and his Bibles and slept fitfully.

Now, in the minutes before dawn, Simon, in his oldest jeans and his sheepskin coat, let himself out of the tower by the rear studio entrance. Into the dark groundmist.

Under his arm he carried the glazed Stamford-ware baluster jar.

Under his sheepskin coat he was naked between the waist and the white band of his clerical collar.

There was a hard frost under his trainers as he crossed the grass to the other tower, the ruined one. The beam from his torch made a cold, white spot the size of a ping-pong ball on the ground and then the walls of the tower.

The lower stones in the walls were green with moss and peppery with lichen, the colours almost lurid in the thin, bright beam. The walls reared up on three sides. In the farthest right-hand corner was a black gouged area, as though masonry had been ripped away by a giant claw. Across this ruined, cavelike opening, to waist-height, were three iron bars, modern, and a half-toppled sign, which said in red: DANGER. KEEP OUT.

or you might wind up running an accounting business from an electric wheelchair.

Behind the bar, steps led up into the tower.

Stones lay in jagged piles on the grass at the bottom of the tower. Perhaps some of them had been winched from Isabel's legs and others from the smashed skull of Gareth Smith, dead with his trousers around his ankles.

Simon looked up into the thick air, still blue-black between Gothic arches like hands steepled in prayer.

Then he set down the baluster jar underneath the lower iron bar and climbed over the bar and into the well of darkness where the stairs were.

He tucked the jar under his arm and shone the torch on to the steps, greasy with moss and ice-trickles. It was just like the stairway in their restored tower, a spiral.

Simon began to climb.

As he climbed, he found himself imagining the young Isabel Pugh and Gareth Smith in December 1973. A cold night, but they wouldn't feel it. They'd be hot with excitement, sharpened, on Isabel's part at least, with a certain apprehension.

Thinking of Isabel in this context, Simon was surprised to discover he'd developed an almost painful erection.

He stopped. He put down the baluster jar on the step by his feet.

It was wrong. He would have to get rid of it. He pressed himself against the cold, curving wall, dripping with damp; he filled his lungs with brackish air full of the stench of decay. *Wrong, wrong, wrong.* And then he emptied his mind.

It didn't work. On the wall above his head came a sudden, irritable flaring of amber light. Somewhere out there a bird squawked, as though the light had awakened it before it was ready. Simon snatched up the jar and clambered up three more steps, until a deepset slit-window came in sight, about a foot over his head. He climbed another step to reach it and stood looking out, gulping in fresh, dawn air.

Here, just above the level of the mist, the sun was trying to squeeze through, leaving long, livid bruises in the cloud-mass.

'It isn't wrong, is it?' Simon said aloud. And shouted out, 'It isn't fucking wrong at all!'

He pulled away from the window and staggered up the remaining steps until the stone walls, and the dead weight of the Abbey, fell away and the purple and orange clouds were all around him, parting like long hills for a sudden bright river of coppery sunlight.

Simon pulled himself up to the stone platform, over which there must once have been a roof. Below him, the countryside was still dark, buried in black mist.

But he was above it, in the light.

Simon put down the jar and stood up on the top of the tower.

He touched his crotch. He was still hard. He thought of Isabel and moaned.

In the east, above the trees, was silhouetted the point of the Skirrid, the keel of an upturned boat. Above it, the sun swelling behind the clouds. It was as if the Skirrid was helping to nudge the sun into view.

The swelling from Simon's groin rose into his solar plexus and then upwards into his chest, expanding there and flooding light into his arms, down to the tips of his fingers.

He held up his hands, and it was as though his fingers were alight. The brightness throbbed in his chest; he could feel it filtering between his ribs, pushing at his skin like the sun at the clouds.

And when the pale orange ball finally rolled free from the clouds, a great sob erupted from Simon. For several minutes he stood there and hung his head, rocking from side to side, tears bleeding from his half-closed eyes.

Without thinking, he took off his sheepskin coat and stood, naked to the waist in the icy morning.

Bent down and picked up the jar. It felt so much heavier up here in the light. Despite its glaze, it would not reflect the sun.

'Figures,' Simon said.

A sour old smell drifted out of the jar. An old, old smell. Baluster jars, sometimes made in Stamford, Lincolnshire, were commonly used in the twelfth and thirteenth centuries to serve wine imported in casks from Bordeaux and Gascony.

Inside the Abbey, the jar had looked new. To Prof Levin, the wine had seemed fresh.

Up here, in the dawn – the *first* light, unsullied by mist, not yet darkened by the Abbey – the baluster jar had become a valuable antique.

Simon lifted it above his head like a trophy.

'Richard!'

In the dawn, the unsoiled time, there were no shadows around him on the tower, only light.

'Can you hear me, you bastard?'

The clouds were edged with copper wire. Down there, in the Abbey and its grounds, none of this would be visible.

'Parting of the ways,' Simon shouted. 'Official.'

He hefted the jar, the valuable antique, one last time and hurled it at the sun.

For almost a second, or so it seemed, the jar was a black stain on the bright morning. And then it dropped into the mist.

He didn't hear it shatter among the fallen masonry which had lain on Isabel Pugh. Perhaps the mist of ages reabsorbed it.

Simon turned away from the sun and the Skirrid and looked back into the black hole.

'God help me now,' he said, and lowered himself back into the darkness.

For some reason – and this had never happened before – Moira walked into the studio and threw her arms around Simon.

'What happened?'

Simon grinned.

'Hey.' Moira stepped back and surveyed him shrewdly for about ten seconds. 'You suddenly realized you're in love or something? Do I know him?'

'Yes,' said Simon. 'Maybe. And no, you bloody well don't know him.'

'Well, I'm pleased for you, Si. Now maybe you could explain what this is about.'

'Wait till the others get here.'

'Could be after lunch.'

'It won't be.'

And he was right. Within ten minutes, they were all standing around under the heavy white vaulted ceiling looking slightly bemused but not hostile. One of the guys from the mobile canteen had turned up with a trolley full of teas and coffees in styrofoam cups. Moira noticed Tom had had a shave and Davey wasn't wearing his scarf.

This was bizarre. The biggest bunch of paranoids in the music business and everybody looking *almost* relaxed.

Prof arrived last. Everybody cheered.

'Bastards,' Prof muttered and then grinned.

'Somefink's lifted from somebody,' Tom said. 'Somebody's lighter.'

'And we have to use it while we've got it,' said Simon, who'd gone round to everybody's door by nine a.m., waking them all up, summoning them to the studio.

Last night, they'd gone to bed in a state of major communal depression, Moira feeling no better than any of them, because

the Abbey had taken Round One. All Simon had said was, It
wasn't Prof's fault, OK? And didn't need to elaborate. They'd
put Prof to bed and assembled in the studio and tried to make
like a real band, and disaster was not the word.

They'd started with an old country rocker of Tom's, 'Take
Me to the River', so basic and simple it almost worked first time
– Simon on bass, Dave on rhythm and Moira backing vocals to
Tom's gruff bark. Half-way through, even Lee Gibson – who
nowadays, apparently, only went behind the kit for spotlighted
drum solos during his own gigs – started beaming, enjoying
himself.

> *Take me to the river* (Tom sang)
> *That's where I wanna be*
> *Take me to the river*
> *Where it reaches the sea.*
> *Sit me on a landin' stage*
> *Down by the waterside*
> *And let me watch my troubles*
> *Floating out on the tide.*

It broke down on Tom's solo. Or rather, Tom broke down.

Tom's solo on 'Take Me to the River' was legendary. So
fluid, Moira remembered some critic writing that trying to
separate out the individual notes was about as easy as lifting
single waves intact from the sea.

Or single tears.

'Poor little bleeder,' Tom had wailed, the words shockingly
amplified. 'It ain't right. It ain't right.'

Afterwards he couldn't remember what this was about. Dave
kept repeating the words to him, Tom shaking his head. 'How
should I know?' But too depressed to carry on. Lee Gibson
gritting his teeth and throwing his drumsticks in the air. Moira
calling the canteen on the intercom. Coffee. Black. Lots.

In a bid to cheer them up, Dave had climbed back on to his
favourite McCarthy amp, sat up there like a garden gnome with
the M38 on his knee, and performed his version of Dylan's 'Girl
from the North Country'. Even though the North Country in

Dave's song was Hartlepool and there were some good jokes, he'd had to stop because he was sounding so uncannily like Dylan he even scared himself. He'd felt driven suddenly, he said, by something he didn't understand.

'We're all scared to death, aren't we?' Moira had said. 'We're never gonna be able to let ourselves go. We're all terrified this time around of what we're gonna let in.'

'Hardly without good reason,' Dave said. 'You've got to admit that.'

'Yeah, but it's no good, Davey. We walk out of this one unfinished, we're never gonna live . . .'

With ourselves, she'd been going to say, but the sentence stopped itself.

Stopped *itself*.

Moira had felt herself go pale and turned away and suggested they call it a night.

Now, Wednesday morning, 7 December, she'd come into the studio to find a circle of seats between the drumkit and the mixing desk: stools, the producer's swivelling rocking-chair and the McCarthy packing-case amplifier.

They were all here, bar Lee. This wasn't his problem, Simon said. And anyway he'd still be in the sack with Michelle from TMM.

'This a summit meeting, Simon?' Tom said.

'Not quite.' Simon waved him to a stool, Prof to his chair, Dave to his amp.

'Last night,' he said, 'Prof got pissed, through no fault of his own, on red wine probably imported from Bordeaux in the 1170s.'

Prof opened his mouth.

'Don't say anything,' Simon said. 'Accept it.'

'Shit,' said Tom.

'Prof's an alcoholic,' Simon said.

'Now, look . . .' Prof was half-way out of his chair.

'Siddown,' said Simon. 'That's just one problem. We've all

got problems. But since Prof's was the first to show, I think it's time he attended a support group.'

'No way,' said Prof. 'Who the hell d'you think . . .?'

'And this is it.' Simon stood up, walked over to the mixing desk and produced from behind it a large plastic Pepsi Cola bottle. He removed the top and began carefully to lay a trail of water from the bottle around the outside of the circle of seats.

'Courtesy of the parish of Ystrad Ddu,' he said. The water soaked in, leaving a dark, circular stain on the pale grey carpet.

'Is that necessary, Simon?' Prof asked.

'Bet your ass on it.' Simon stepped inside the circle through the remaining gap and then, with a final sprinkle, closed it from the inside. He sat on his stool, next to Moira's, with the empty plastic bottle in his hands.

'OK?' The studio seemed a more intimate place, as if the walls were crowding in to listen. Moira was surprised to see Simon taking the initiative; he'd always been such a diffident guy. But, then, he *was* the only one of them formally recognized as being able to splash holy water around with impunity.

Until now, the atmosphere had seemed so much lighter this morning. It wasn't really; that was an illusion. The reality was last night.

But something had happened to Simon overnight to make him think it was worth carrying on. And he was sharing it while it lasted. Because they were a band.

Simon bowed his head over his hands, still holding the plastic Pepsi bottle. 'I'm not going to use any elaborate language. I'm not even going to address God, in case there are any of us for whom that kind of terminology doesn't mean a lot. Whatever message we're sending out here, you can all send it in whichever direction you want. Outwards, inwards, wherever.'

'I think we're all gonna be pointing in vaguely the same direction,' Moira said.

'Thanks.' Simon glanced briefly towards the huge, white-washed stone arches in the ceiling. 'OK. We've got problems. We've all had problems for a long time, and now we've come together to admit we can't handle them alone.'

'Right,' Tom said.

'We've come back to the place where we were all severely tested, and some of us failed the test pretty badly.'

'Some us didn't even finish the paper,' Dave muttered.

'We need help,' Simon said and was silent.

Moira heard a popping sound and saw small bubbles appear in the carpet where the holy water had fallen.

'Ignore it,' Simon whispered, flashing her the Don't Worry Tom look.

Moira nodded. She could see where he was coming from. To get through a session here they needed to balance an awareness of reality with enough illusion to enable them to function. Like crossing a narrow, rickety bridge across a deep, deep canyon. To make it to the other side, you needed confidence and fear in equal measures. Maybe that was the definition of courage.

'You know . . .' Simon smiled at Prof. 'I reckon you *have* been to AA meetings in the past.'

'Bollocks,' Prof said.

'We're meeting you more than half-way, Prof. Tell me, how does that intro go? You know . . . when you go to an AA meeting, you have to introduce yourselves and everybody states their name and one simple fact.'

'Yeah,' Prof said. 'I believe I've heard of that. Maybe saw it in a film once.'

'Go on then.'

'Sod it.' Prof sighed and then intoned, 'My name is Kenneth and I am an alcoholic.'

'Terrific,' Simon said. 'Now I'll have a go.'

He closed his eyes for a moment, smiled to himself, and then he said, 'My name is Simon. I am a pervert and a necromancer and, by continuing to practise as a priest, I am committing the grossest, most unforgivable blasphemy and endangering the immortal souls of all the poor bastards who, through me, seek God's blessing.'

There was a long silence.

'That's a tough one to follow, Simon,' Dave said. 'But I'll give it a whirl.'

X

Organism

Eddie Edwards had been staking out the place since just after eight, walking Zap up and down the street in the sharp air until the poor dog was dizzy, had to be. But it was nearly ten by the time Mrs Pugh left the house. Vicarage-cleaning day, too – the woman was giving herself an easy time of it in Simon's absence.

Soon as she was round the corner out of sight, Eddie was hauling Zap up the path and hammering on the door. His old plastic briefcase was under his arm, the handle snapped off years ago.

'Heavens,' Isabel said, 'I don't know which of you's tongue is hanging out furthest. Seen you go past that window fifteen times. Mug or a cup?'

'Mug, please, my dear.' Eddie unpacked his case on the accounting table. 'Sit now, Zap.'

'Always wanted a dog,' Isabel said sadly, pouring coffee. 'But you try taking a puppy for a walk in a wheelchair, and Mother couldn't be bothered. You're all red-faced and frozen, Eddie. Think it's going to snow?'

'Too cold for it,' Eddie said, hanging his overcoat over the back of a dining-chair, approaching the open stove with arms wide as if he wanted to hug it to death. 'Or maybe it's just me that's profoundly cold. Starting to frighten me, this business. Feels like a great claw is poised over us all.'

'Not all of us,' Isabel said. 'Only Simon.'

'Aye, and anyone who consorts with him.'

'Consorts, now, is it? I should be so lucky.'

Eddie accepted a mug of coffee, warming his hands on it. 'Getting fond of the boy, aren't you?' He added tentatively, 'I'm not sure that's good.'

483

Isabel wore her business suit and a lot of make-up. She looked glamorous, dangerous and terribly vulnerable.

'Not good?' she said aggressively. 'Bloody suicidal it is.' She smiled, couching the euphoric Zap's head in her lap. 'But what can you do?'

Simon said, 'He *talks* to you?'

'Well, you know.' Dave, embarrassed, shifted about on his amplifier. 'I mean, mostly it's insults. He gets impatient with me. I can understand that.' Dave shook his head, like a dog shaking off water. 'Maybe I just do such good impressions I can even fool myself.'

'If it's a guilt-trip,' Prof said, 'it's misplaced.'

'It's not misplaced,' Dave said quietly. 'We all know what we're capable of, and when we fall short we fall very *badly* short and it's a slippery slope. It's like Simon. He's bisexual. Well, fine. Fine for a normal person; no kind of sex is perverted, long as it's consenting adults or consenting sheep. But when the psychic element intrudes and you've got dead monks on your back, as it were, *that's* perverted, Simon's right. Perverted, blasphemous, the whole bit, and it's all too easy for people like us to slide into that kind of pit. Especially in this business.'

'Which I got out of,' Simon said. 'Not realizing that taking holy orders only increases the risk. For a priest, the temptations are truly enormous, black pits opening up all over the place. I won't go into details. Well, you know . . . a lot of priests crash spectacularly. Sometimes you think maybe a monastery – a hard-line Trappist outfit or something – is the only refuge. Complete seclusion.'

'Seclusion don't work,' said Tom. 'Seclusion's a real bummer. You start feeding on your own guts.'

'Seclusion's scary,' Moira agreed. 'Small things set you off – things you wouldn't normally notice.'

Dave turned to her. 'What happened with your mother?'

'She died. Just died. She had a stroke.'

'How old was she?'

'No age,' Moira said. 'No damned age at all.' She blew her nose. 'I let her down, Davey. I was so smug and hard and self-sufficient. She was looking out for me all this time, and I couldny see it.'

'Looking out for you?'

'We had a link. You all know about the comb, right?'

She looked across at Prof. 'I know the song you did,' he said. 'About the girl who's given this mystical comb and becomes, like, a princess, glamorous.'

'Was a real comb,' Moira said. She told him about being reunited with her mother at the age of twelve, being sent along a whole new life-path. 'The comb was this kind of symbolic link between us. It was very old. Celtic. A family heirloom.'

'*Was?*' Dave said.

'I buried it with her. Maybe that was stupid. Donald – he was ma mammy's minder, kind of – he thought it was insane. Thing is, I'm no' gonna have a kid of my own to pass it on to. I mean, like, I wouldn't, anyway, burden a kid with this hassle.'

'I got a terrific kid,' Tom said. 'And yeah, she's got somefink. She's starting to *see*, you know? I try not to fink too hard about it, and she don't say much. Never has, to me. We look at one anovver, and we know. She's close. Too close, you know? Soon's I woke up this morning, I could feel her reaching out. Bad news, getting close to me. It was starting to destroy Shelley.'

The morning was a dark one, as usual, because of the mist. Three red pilot lights winked on the mixing desk and the aluminium decks of the recording machines.

'There's this geezer fancies Shelley,' Tom said. 'Business-man. Got hisself a chain of supermarkets. But not a bad guy, really. Normal, yeah? Maybe Shelley should go wiv him, that's what I been thinking. Maybe it's the last chance she'll get to have a normal life.'

Simon said, 'And Meryl?'

'She works for the guy. She's a bit of a loony – finks it's a game.' Dave groaned. 'But she's strong. She ain't easily fazed.

Don't misunderstand. Ain't much between us, like. Convenience. Anyway, I was finking maybe if Shel goes off with this geezer, Vanessa'd have a better chance. Then, when she's grown-up, she can come and find me if she wants to. Maybe I'll give her a family heirloom.'

Tom smiled sadly.

'She's got Down's Syndrome, right?' Moira said.

Tom nodded. 'That's the complication. Down's Syndrome and psychic, I don't know what kind of combination that is.'

'Probably nobody knows,' said Simon.

It was all so much less mystical in the morning. It had become a slight problem.

'What *are* we going to do about you?' Meryl asked, as Vanessa helped herself to muesli with extra raisins. 'Take you into Abergavenny for some new clothes, for starters.'

It would be as well to get out of the house. Simon had said the woman came every Wednesday to give it a thorough clean, top to bottom.

And going shopping was always a good practical move; it was relaxing and it gave you breathing space. Immediately after breakfast, Meryl put Vanessa into the Peugeot and they set off along roads which were becoming familiar, through countryside Meryl was developing quite a feel for.

As soon as they were out of the valley, the mist thinning, she started to look out for the Skirrid.

She'd been dipping into Simon's books, starting with the local guides – Meryl always liked to know *precisely* where she was – and following up interesting items in a couple of border folklore volumes.

Always coming back to the Skirrid.

This hill made marvellous connections for Meryl. A link between Christianity and . . . and *Britain*. That was what was always so wrong with the religion she'd been taught in school. It was all so remote, so *foreign*. Meryl had wanted someone to assure her that *this – this England, this Wales – this* was the holy land, just as much as the Middle East, where the Muslims and the Jews were forever at each other's throats.

But where was it, this holy mountain?

'Where's the Skirrid, Vanessa, do you know?'

Vanessa didn't reply. She sat calmly in the passenger seat in her crumpled school blazer. Meryl had wanted to press it, but Vanessa wouldn't let her. She knew her own mind, this child, that was for certain. Seemed to know her limitations. And her potential?

Only child of the seventh son of a seventh son. It must mean something.

But whatever went on inside her head, she was still a problem. When, last night, she'd asked if Grandad could come in too, because he was cold, Meryl had looked up in great apprehension, half-expecting to see a lofty, cloudy entity with a pitifully damaged face looming out of the mist. And knowing, full of shivers . . . *that she could never close a door on Grandad*.

She'd seen nothing, thank the Lord. And felt nothing.

But Weasel? Vanessa had wanted Weasel to come in as well. The little man with the long, greasy hair and the ruined smile, Shelley's driver. How did he come into this? Why would he be with Vanessa and the Man with Two Mouths, unless . . .

Oh lord.

Where's Weasel. Weasel's not . . .

No! No!

The child dragging at her arm when she'd picked up the phone to ring Shelley. Hysteria in the air.

And not another word out of her that made any sense.

Meryl, feeling suddenly overburdened, realized she'd been staring through the windscreen at the Skirrid for about ten minutes. Only it was from a different angle than in the picture in the guidebook. From here, she could see two humps, a big one and a little one which was fuzzed around the edges as if there'd been quarrying. Meryl had read about people taking 'holy earth' from the Skirrid and bringing it down, using it on their gardens and in the foundations of buildings.

'Yes,' she said. 'Why not? Indeed, why not? Maybe you'll speak to the Skirrid.'

Eddie laid out his papers on the gate-leg dining-table.

'Let's take it from the beginning,' he said.

'But when is the beginning?' Isabel put her glasses on her nose. 'What's this?'

'That's a photocopy of what Giraldus has to say. Which isn't much, and you have to be careful with Giraldus, as is always the case with these medieval historians. They wrote to please. They had to. Write up the wrong history and your head would end up on a spike. See, this line . . .'

Eddie pointed.

> *William de Braose was not the instigator of the atrocity which I have preferred to pass over in silence. He was not the author of it, and, indeed, he played no part in it at all. If he was responsible in any way, it was because he did nothing to stop it.*

'Talk about a whitewash,' Eddie said. 'Well, we know this now, of course. We know that Giraldus was dependent on the goodwill of de Braose and actually changed his story from the first edition to the second. There is no question that de Braose ordered the massacre and was, if not a participant, at least a cheering spectator. Now. Giraldus also goes on, in a subsequent chapter, to record that de Braose was one of a number of barons who gave large donations towards the building of the new abbey at Ystrad Ddu. This . . . *this* I am inclined to believe.'

'So what's new about that?' Isabel said. 'People have always thrown money at the church, trying to buy their way into heaven.'

'Hmmm.' Eddie tapped the paper. 'I think Giraldus is trying to tell us something here, that's what I think. Let's go back. Richard Walden, now, despoiler of novices and altar boys. What we have here is not just a man who cannot control his urges but a man who will use his position, his status, to gratify those urges.'

'Again, what's new?'

'Try and follow my reasoning, girl. Not a humble man, see, wasn't Richard, before his alleged vision. No great humility afterwards, either, if he's going around soliciting large grants from wealthy Norman barons. This . . .' Eddie shook the photocopied works of Giraldus Cambrensis '. . . this is not the kind of man to whom holy visions are granted.'

'What about St Paul? He was no angel.'

'What?' Eddie rose up spluttering. 'Where is it recorded that St Paul introduced his member to defenceless choirboys?' Then, remembering who he was talking to, sat down again. 'Sorry, my dear. Get carried away, I do.'

'Don't feel you have to spare my feelings, Eddie. Everybody within a fifteen-mile radius of Ystrad knows I'm not a virgin . . . by about three seconds . . .'

Eddie felt himself blush. Isabel patted his hand. 'I hope you're not suggesting Simon . . .'

'Good *God* no! No, what I am saying, see . . . Here's the Abbey, a great religious house founded by a malignant pederast and lavishly financed out of the ill-gotten fortunes of brutal marcher lords. Suppose they were all friends or associates of de Braose. Suppose de Braose was repaying a favour.'

'And suppose,' said Isabel, wagging a finger and rocking her chair in sudden excitement, 'that Richard Walden's vision, if it happened at all, was not what you'd call a *holy* vision. The candles, I'm thinking of, the horrible brown candles made from . . . you know.'

'You're saying the man was a devil worshipper?'

'You've as good as said it yourself Eddie. You've been talking all around it. For days.'

'Yes,' said Eddie, going very still. 'I believe I have. It just didn't seem a scholarly conclusion.'

'Well, stuff that. What's scholarly matter if it feels right?'

'You know what you're saying, don't you?'

'I don't know,' Isabel said, looking worried. 'What am I saying?'

'That the Abbey is a satanic abbey, founded upon evil, built upon black soil.'

'No skin off my nose,' said Isabel.

'And if you believe that these candles were . . . sent . . . to Simon, then it's difficult to imagine he has not come to the same conclusion.'

'I suppose he must.'

'So what are we saying now?'

'I think . . . I *know* he's a good man.'

Eddie sighed. 'I thought that too. But if, knowing what we think he knows, he has gone back to that place, to live there for a week, in that tower, surrounded by the decaying legacy of evil. And no safer in decay, mind.'

'Less safe,' Isabel said. 'I speak from experience.'

'Yes. Er . . .' He hesitated. 'I never liked to ask, Isabel, but what *is* the problem exactly, with your . . .'

'Lower half? They could never agree, you know what doctors are like. At first it was spinal shock due to severely compressed nerves. I'm lucky. I still have control of my bowels and water-works. Well . . . let's say they came back. Nothing else, though. Crushed nerves, if they don't spring back into shape within a couple of years, you've had it. Twenty-one years? Well . . .'

Isabel failed to smile.

'You must hate the very thought of that place.'

'My own fault. Everybody says so. The Abbey's a holy place, not to be desecrated.'

'Hmmm,' Eddie said, reminded of something important. 'Tell me . . . did you do that sum on your calculator?'

There was a large shovel of coal on the hearth. Isabel wheeled herself over, lifted it with one hand and tipped the coal into the stove.

'Strong wrists, you must have, girl.'

'We compensate, us cripples. Yes, I did the sums. Multiples of seven. Interesting. So very interesting I've arranged to go with Mother tonight to the W.I. cheese and wine. A few faces will no doubt change colour when I roll over the threshold, but it might be worth the aggro if I can jog some memories.'

'Yes indeed,' Eddie said. 'I never thought of that. But it won't be easy, getting them to open up.'

Isabel smiled grimly. 'You'd probably find this quite difficult to believe, but I can be a terrible bully.'

'I would find it almost impossible to believe,' said Eddie, remembering her ramming him up against a pew end with her wheelchair. 'But my poor shins might just accept it.'

Moira passed the paper to Prof who read it, raised his eyebrows, and passed it to Simon. Blue Basildon Bond on which was inscribed:

BREADWINNER

and

DEATHOAK

Simon looked up. 'Could she have got this from you?'

'It's possible,' Moira said. 'Anything's possible. But even if she did . . . Look at the timing. How would you feel if it was your mother and all she left you when she died was a wee note with two words on it you never wanted to hear again and not even a goodbye on the end?'

'Point taken,' Simon said. 'I'm sorry, Moira.'

'And then there's the other thing, since we're all being so up-front. If I'm walking funny, it's due to getting my thighs badly blistered by boiling water.'

She passed Dave a meaningful glance and a rueful little smile. Prof noticed Dave looked shattered.

'What happened, I pulled a hotel kettle off the dresser after seeing something I didn't want to see. In the steam.'

'Your mother?' Dave guessed. 'The Duchess? Why the *hell* didn't you tell me?'

'You can all believe what you like,' Moira said. 'But something was seeping through, like damp through a wall. And you all were getting it, and *she* was absorbing my share. And I'm ashamed of that. I just didn't think. I thought all we had to do was stay away from each other and it would all gradually fade into history. And the Duchess would say to me, You have some damage to repair. And here she is, dead, and still saying it.'

Tom said, 'Who was that poet, wrote about how your mum and dad fuck you up?'

'Larkin,' Simon said.

'They fuck you up even more when they're dead,' Tom said sagely.

'Yeah, but Tom,' Moira said, 'I just don't see the Duchess wanting to put me in hospital with burns.'

Simon folded the blue paper, passed it back to Moira. 'You think there was something else seeping through?'

'What I think is, you guys have been getting lots of bad stuff over the years. Simon, you and the objects and the . . . I don't want to go into the sexual stuff . . . Tom and the spooks from his record collection and all kinds of paranoia – not to mention Debbie and the wee girl having Down's Syndrome. And Dave seeing black auras everywhere and John Lennon at his shoulder. But me . . .'

Moira shook her head as if, Prof thought, she couldn't believe she'd been so blind.

'. . . Me, I had the Duchess to protect me . . . and the Duchess didn't say a word about it, except *You have some damage to repair*. Until it . . . filled her up . . . blew out her brain . . . Jesus, I don't know what I'm saying, this might be the purest nonsense.'

Yeah, Prof thought. It might all be. But it ain't. Too much of it. And nothing explainable in physical human terms, *nothing*.

'Pardon me,' he said. 'But might all this have begun in earnest when certain old tapes went into the ovens at Audico and ended a beautiful friendship between Maurice Rubens and myself?'

Simon opened his hands. Who knew?

'This is implying human intercession,' Dave said.

'The Abbey uses people,' Simon said. 'Sometimes they submit to it, invite it even, and sometimes they don't even know. We walked into it with our eyes wide open and still couldn't see it. When Sile Copesake brought me down here last week, he said it was this place that had fucked me up and I'd come back to get unfucked.'

492

'Well if you're all gonna get unfucked before the week's out . . .' Prof looked pointedly at his watch. 'You better make a start. Mind if I leave the circle? Too much coffee.'

Lee Gibson arrived then, so all of them left the circle. 'We a band again?' Simon asked.

'Better find out.' Tom picked up the Telecaster, played, unplugged, what sounded like the opening riff from 'Hooked', a heavy rock number about a dockland pub-fight from his solo flop, *Second Storey*. He winced. 'Load of bollocks.'

'How are we this morning, Tom?' Lee said cheerfully.

'Shagged out,' said Tom. 'Plug me in, Prof.'

It was Simon who'd swung it, Prof was sure of this.

Simon, the willowy ex-public-schoolboy who'd confessed to being every kind of psychological misfit, had emerged as the leader. Simon had gathered energy and inspiration from somewhere and he was spreading it around like it was in danger of evaporating. Simon the bass player laying down the rhythm track and then re-emerging as Simon, the Classical One, viola solos that gave you the shivers, especially on a sonorous instrumental number, 'The Valley', which Prof had never heard before.

Also, Simon seemed to have a way with Tom – big mulish guy, you thought, but there was a formidable intellect in there which the big man kept tamped down under this thick layer of gruff cockney.

He was a bloody natural, was Tom, *the* most instinctive musician Prof had ever seen work. Made you realize how many of the other so-called guitar heroes were just brilliant technicians, without depth. Artisans.

What it was with Tom, he had no ego, no urge to be centre stage; he just wanted to fold himself into the backcloth. This was why his solo album hadn't worked, *couldn't* work: Tom simply had no desire to project. He'd pick up his Telecaster – any Telecaster would do, no modification necessary – and stand around waiting for something to do.

'Help me out here, Tom,' Simon would say, and Tom would build the musical equivalents of a suspension bridge or a skyscraper or a complex railway system.

At one point, they all gathered around Tom's booth and Tom was shaking his head a lot and Simon talked to him a while and then Tom said, 'Yeah, all right.' And he hit the riff to 'Hooked', only slower.

'We do this one live?' Simon said to Prof, who by now was recognizing that all he was here for was to organize whatever they wanted and get the levels right. Live takes, everybody playing together, seemed to suit their peculiar chemistry.

'Whatever,' Prof said.

Half an hour later, they were ready. By this time he'd realized that 'Hooked' on the *Second Storey* album had just been a speeded-up desensitized reworking of the Black Album track called 'The Man With Two Mouths'. This was a return to the original, even slower. Prof didn't know what the song was about, except some kind of underworld violence in London, but Tom's downbeat croak was oddly moving and afterwards the big guitarist stayed in his booth, back turned as if he was embarrassed. And the lights dimmed strangely.

Moira didn't play on this one; she sat with Prof behind the glass and smoked a cigarette. 'Wonderful, huh?' she said. 'I wouldn't waste time on another take, Prof, you'll no' get it like that again.'

Prof nodded, didn't question it. Questioned nothing, all afternoon, all night.

They did Dave's 'Dakota Blues'. For the first time, Dave sounded comfortable in his own voice, and Tom produced a spontaneous solo of such aching, bittersweet simplicity that Prof could've wept. Later, Moira introduced a little song she said she'd composed in the car on the way here, a whimsical number about a New Age traveller who joins a band of gypsies. Just Moira on guitar and Simon on violin. Prof recorded a rhythm track but figured he'd probably dump it. Simplicity was best, if you had the quality.

Between midday and midnight they laid down four very serviceable tracks, which was amazing, especially when you considered the state of these people only last night.

They were a band again, all right. They were – astonishingly – like a band which had been together on a nightly gigging basis for about ten years. They communicated without words. And they pulled Lee Gibson along with them. Lee, making a bomb in the States with his best-avoided heavy-metal crap, had been a bit cocky at first, until Tom Storey put him into perspective. He was a good drummer, actually, and enough of a real musician to recognize when he was in the Presence.

So Prof was getting stuff which would be a joy to mix at some future date . . . well away from the Abbey.

It *was* a good studio, though, he couldn't deny that. The low, vaulted ceiling, the stone walls. There was an ambience here you could use, or not.

And Simon decided he wanted to use it.

At ten minutes past midnight on the morning of Thursday 8 December, Simon announced he had a number which, he said, he'd intended for the Black Album in 1980, but it didn't work out, wouldn't come right.

'You don't wanna call it a night?' Prof said. 'Rather than go for something you aren't sure of.'

'No,' said Simon.

'Only, in my experience, if you go out while you're winning, it gives you a bit of encouragement. You come in fresh tomorrow, ready to hit it. Yeah?'

'If it's OK by everybody else, I'd like to go for it now,' Simon said. 'It's important to me. Something I want to say to somebody.' There were nods and shrugs.

'OK.' Prof mooched wearily back to his sanctum. Looked like this session was shaping up for the dawn shift. He was too old for this.

'And we can try a live take,' Simon said. 'Except I'll put the bass on later.'

'Yeah, yeah.'

This one was going to be a mainly instrumental, impression-istic piece called 'Holy Light', partly improvised, wordless vocals from Moira with elements of Gregorian chant.

Simon told Prof it was his attempt to convey what it must have been like for the founder of the Abbey, a monk called Richard Walden, weighed down by old sin and shame – so a heavy intro with cello and bass, both laid down by Simon, and then Tom would gradually introduce colours and Moira would do the white light.

'You remember this one?' Simon said to Moira.

'I remember how I blew it. It was supposed to be light and joyful and kind of inspirational, and it just made me depressed. I remember going out and wandering round in the dark and smoking several cigarettes, coming back, trying again . . . just couldn't sustain the mood. You really want to try this one again, Simon?'

'Yes,' said Simon solidly, like he was making a solemn vow in front of witnesses. 'And don't worry about sustaining the mood. The mood's changed. Lee, if you want to call it a night, we can do the bass and drums tomorrow. I'd like to work over that with you, but I'm not sure how it's going to go.'

'Yeah,' Lee said. 'I could do with a good coffee'

Dave looked up. 'Won't she be asleep?'

Lee stood up and stretched. 'Only for the first couple of minutes.'

He left by the back door. Bitter cold air came through in a rush and made the cymbals hiss.

Dave said, 'What's this about, Si?'

Simon was bringing his cello out of its case. 'It's about correcting history.'

Moira had been standing under two mikes, and when she fell to her knees and then rolled over on the grey carpet, both hands over her face, Prof started to get seriously alarmed.

OK, he'd engineered some pretty wild sessions in his time, hadn't everybody? Whole bands on acid. Occupational hazard.

But this was the Abbey. Simon had said to him that if there was one lesson to learn at the Abbey it was never to allow yourself to relax.

Prof tore off his cans. He couldn't bear to hear this any more. *whatdoIdo, whatdoIdo?*

He turned his back on the glass panel between the control room and the studio floor and watched the metal spools turning, getting it all down for posterity, for some poor bastard in a listening-studio to hear and dream and wake up screaming, *We can't release this!*

And the spools went on turning, the tape slithering past the heads.

gottastopit, gottastopit, gottastopit

He didn't need cans to hear it. The panel was only glass. He was surprised it hadn't shattered.

They'd all come out of their booths. Simon wanting the studio ambience. Wanting to fill the entire space until the music was absorbed by the stones in the walls and the vaulted ceiling which supported the tower's mass, so that it would be like the whole structure was held up by the music.

Simon's bid to establish control.

And Prof was frightened as he watched . . .

. . . Simon, stripped to the waist, droplets of sweat actually flying from his body as his bow slashed at the cello's strings and his face stretched in agony like something painted by Goya, the bow in ribbons, strands of it flying free.

Tom Storey, steady, legs apart, pacing him with long, loping, measured chords, potent as the strokes of a cut-throat razor.

While Dave had put down his golden-hued Martin guitar and rushed to where Moira lay, cradling her head in his lap, tears from both of them on Moira's cheeks.

Prof watched Moira's breast heaving. The sounds coming out of her before she fell had been the sick, soured Gregorian chant of his recurring dream.

Which had not been audible on the Black Album tape, he'd swear it, and yet . . .

. . . had been introduced into his subconscious mind *by* the tape.

He knew that Moira, in *her* mind, had been running in terror along the ruined nave, under the Abbey's gaunt, black ribcage guarding its diseased lungs, the ground quaking as the Abbey breathed.

Alive. They were inside an ancient, living, sentient organism. He gould see a fire burning in the deepest woodland, yellow and pink, below an ancient, lumpen tree with twisted, swollen branches and chattering twigs, the tree reaching out its branch-arms like a deformed man. Rough nails projected from the tree's midriffs, thick and glistening reddened strings looped around them and the rich, succulent smell of roasting meat.

Someone must have opened the door and let in the night mist, swirling now around the silent drums and cymbals.

The mist formed against the glass screen, full of stricken Goya faces

        (as Simon sweated over the cello, sawing savagely at the quivering strings)

                and then collected out on the studio floor, above where Moira lay weeping with her head in Dave's lap, Dave crying, too, and maybe it was the mingling, evaporating tears which turned the mist into a little cloud of throbbing blackness which settled around her face like a soft helmet.

And, oh, God, God, God, God, how he wanted a drink . . .

Prof scuttling around the control room, hands over his ears, the Abbey alive all around him, walls expanding and contracting, the sick, stone organism pulsing with soured, curdled energy, Prof's brain swollen inside his skull, the bones straining and cracking.

Stopitstopitstopit*stopitstopit*STOPITSTOPITSTOPITSTOP
ITSTOP

'It's over.'

    'Go away. I never want to see any of you bastards again.'

    'It's over, Prof.'

'You can take the tape. You can take it out on the bloody hill and burn it now. I'm not Russell, I'm not gonna con you. See, there it is, still turning. Rip it off, take it away, soak it in petrol . . .'

Their faces above him, with lights, like a surgical team over an operating table.

'It was necessary, Prof,' Moira said.

Prof sat up. 'How can anything like that *ever* be necessary? What happened to you, why'd you pass out, why was the black . . .?'

'I was seeing, Prof. Simon was showing us. Making a point.' She shook herself. 'Whole thing was very exhausting.'

Simon was kneeling by Prof's chair. 'That piece wouldn't work the first time, because I was trying to make it into the kind of vision which it wasn't. This abbey was never dedicated to the Light. It used to be in the middle of a forest, now it just gathers mist.'

'A black abbey?' Prof croaked.

'A black abbot, and he's still around, the essence of him. That was to let him know that we knew. That *I* knew. Me particularly, because he had me. Nearly.'

Simon stood up, his back to the tape deck. The needles on several of the twenty-four illuminated level-meters were still moving as if the tape was recording the ambient sounds from the studio floor.

Simon said loudly, 'If you're listening, Richard, I just want to say it's nearly over. You're fucked, man.'

Prof, feeling like a very old producer, sat up in his chair and swallowed bile

as the black needles on more than half the level-meters whipped over to the red area and stoped there for all of three seconds, as though they were recording a spasm of rage.

XI

Bart Simpson

THURSDAY, 8 DECEMBER

The first of the screams pierced the skin of Moira's sleep like a syringe.

Sometimes this happened. Like being a radio, picking up distress signals you couldn't do a thing about, maybe ships out there in the Atlantic. Best to shut them out, roll over, bury your head in the pillow, pull the bedclothes over.

Metaphorically speaking. Because burrowing in the bed would only seal you off from the sounds in the room – a ticking clock, gargling water-pipes, birdsong. The distress calls, coming from some inner space would, in fact, be that much louder.

But still you did it, instinctively, sometimes – like now – bending the pillow around your head. 'Go 'way, huh, lemme get some sleep, didny get to bed till gone four.'

And this time – the pillow around her head, the sheets and blankets over the pillow, the eiderdown on top of everything – it worked, thank God, the screams dwindling to feeble twitters. 'Fine, I can handle that, just let me have a few more . . .'

'. . . minutes.'

Moira struggled frantically through the jungle of bedclothes, breaking surface with a gasp.

The scream was real.

It had stopped, but its memory hung around like a kick in the stomach.

This had been a long, tremulous scream, beginning in mere pain and rising to an agony of high-pitched terror.

Moira sat up for a moment, pulling hair out of her eyes. The scream did not recur. A dark mauveness hazed from the high, uncurtained window. She groped on the floor for her watch. It was 7.30 a.m.

She slid her legs to the floor, calf-muscles aching. She was wearing the Bart Simpson nightshirt. It was up around her waist, revealing that one of the blisters on her thighs had burst in the night. She pulled a tissue from the box on the floor and dabbed away the yellowy matter, then sat on the edge of the bed, gathering her emotions, not ready yet to take on the scream. How did she *feel* about this – the climax of last night's session, Simon's shout of defiance?

Simon.

The scream.

The scream, a real scream, had come from above. There was only one room between hers and the roof.

Moira was up and running for the door.

Eddie fumbled his way to the phone with shaving foam over half his face.

'I'll see you in the church in twenty minutes,' she snapped before he could even remember his own exchange and number . . .

'Heaven's sake, Isabel, you know what time it is?'

'You want to hear this or not?'

'What about my breakfast?'

Isabel hung up, the bossy bitch.

Vanessa was missing, her single bed empty.

Meryl panicked at once . . .

Flinging on her dressing-gown, she raced downstairs. The only open door was the one to the living-room, but the room was empty.

'Vanessa!'

She ran to the front door to find it still locked and barred.

She dashed through to the kitchen; it too was empty, the back door firmly fastened. Meryl hugged her breasts, convinced the child had disappeared as mysteriously as she had arrived.

She was not natural. She was like a spirit, a fairy, a *changeling*.

Oh, don't be so stupid, Meryl! Stop. Think.

She went back into the hall and opened the front door, stepping out into the bitter air, clutching her dressing-gown to her throat.

Nothing. No one.

She hurried back into the living-room. Through the picture-window, sheep grazed contentedly on the damp and misted hills. She was furious with them: did they have no aspirations beyond the food chain?

Trembling with anxiety and cold, she made herself sit down next to the fireplace, where the cinders of last night's coal fire lay brown and dead. It was a mean little grate, far removed from the deep inglenooks at Martin's place. Meryl felt horribly lonely remembering the roaring fires of Hall Farm, the long, velvet curtains, the unseen, perfumed essence of the Lady Bluefoot.

Oh my lady, if only you were here with me.

But she wasn't. She was the house ghost of Hall Farm. Nice ghosts were like good wine and didn't travel.

Meryl stood up. She needed help. Quickly.

The village?

Although naturally, she believed, gregarious, she hadn't made herself known to any of the villagers here. This was on Simon's advice. He'd thought it best for her to keep a low profile. As, indeed, he told her, did most of the locals.

Except, that was, for a man called Eddie Edwards. If this man ever showed his face at the vicarage, she should clam up at once, Simon had decreed. She should have nothing whatsoever to do with Mr Eddie Edwards . . . or, even more important, with a certain Superintendent Gwyn Arthur Jones. If *he* were ever to turn up, she could say she was the vicar's aunt (aunt indeed, how old did he think she was?), looking after the place while the vicar took a short holiday with friends in Oxford or somewhere.

What a tangled web. After her years with Martin, Meryl was tired of tangled webs.

Martin! She'd telephone Martin, at once, before he left for work. It was the fair and honest thing to do, having promised Vanessa only that she would not involve Shelley.

Now. Phone. Office.

This was the room across the hall from which she'd borrowed books. And there, on a plain mahogany desk, sat the phone, and also . . .

'Vanessa!'

Wearing the pretty cotton nightdress Meryl had bought her in Abergavenny, the child was sitting calmly on a leather-frame blotter, gazing out of the window, across the street towards the disappointing village church. She didn't even turn around at Meryl's cry.

'You nearly gave me a heart attack. How long have you been in here?' Beginning to be angry with Vanessa; you could get more sense out of the sheep on the hills.

Anger, however, would get her nowhere. With a sigh, Meryl took off her navy-blue dressing-gown, put it around the girl's shoulders.

'Let me help you. Please.'

Vanessa carried on looking out of the window. She'd said so little to Meryl all the time she'd been here. Had eaten just enough food, with no great relish – not much of a compliment to Meryl's flair for whipping up mouth-watering sundaes.

She *had* said a small thank-you for the new clothes and left most of them on in the shop . . . while clinging determinedly to her school blazer, which she insisted on wearing whenever she went out, especially yesterday afternoon, shivering on the slopes of the Skirrid.

And yet she seemed content to be *here*. As if she was waiting for something to happen.

Why do you have to wear your dirty blazer? Why not your new quilted jacket?

So my guardian angel will know me, Vanessa had replied scornfully, like a good Catholic.

Meryl said now, 'I'm going to phone Shelley. Just to put her mind at rest. She must be terribly worried about you.'

The changeling turned round fast enough at that. 'No!'

'Why not? You tell me why not, or I'm going to phone her right now!'

What else could she do? Yesterday, within sight of the summit of the Skirrid, she'd knelt in the grass, holding Vanessa's hand, and prayed for guidance, the first time she'd done such a thing since childhood. She'd felt there *was* guidance to be had here, but no clear direction was signposted. She interpreted this as an indication that she should do nothing for the present. Stay where she was, learn patience.

She'd turned round to find Vanessa white-faced and shaking, her gaze fixed on the smaller of the two humps, almost below them now. Meryl had felt flecks of light snow on her face, but could see nothing.

Meryl said sharply, 'Do you hear me, miss?'

Vanessa shrugged, looked back out of the window, stiffened and instantly became animated. She turned, picked up the phone and, smiling, held it out towards Meryl.

'Why, thank you,' Meryl said, surprised.

But while she was reaching out for the receiver, Vanessa suddenly snatched it back, jumped down from the desk and dodged past Meryl out of the room, still clutching the receiver, dragging the phone to the floor and the wire from the wall.

Meryl shrieked and pursued the phone as it bumped along the carpet but, by the time she'd gathered it up, Vanessa was out of the front door and rushing across the road into the path of an electric wheelchair containing a young woman who looked as if she would be only too pleased to run the child down.

As Moira turned the spiral, wooden sandals clip-clopping on the stone steps, there was another sharp scream of rage and pain,

and she stopped, afraid, for the scream had an animal quality.
A howling.

In the Abbey, it was unwise ever to relax.

In the Abbey, God help you, it was not necessarily in your
best interests to heed a scream.

It was freezing on the uneven stone stairs. She'd stopped
alongside a slit window with old glass in it, opaque with grime.
Knowing that even if she could see out, there would only be
mist upon mist. As Simon had said last night, vapours gathered
here, always had, always would.

She moved on, went up seven more steps, bare toes numb
with cold, poking out of the open sandals.

Until, at last, she stood at the very summit of the spiral,
outside the recess concealing Simon's bedroom door, above her
a rough beamed ceiling. Above that, presumably, the tower's
conical roof.

She looked down at herself. Bart Simpson wore an evil grin.
In this situation, Bart Simpson would not be scared. Bart
Simpson was the devil incarnate.

What we gonna do, Bart?

'Piss off, kid, what would you know.'

Just to hear her own voice.

And then, 'Nooooooo!' A hideous, twisted yelp.

'Simon!'

'Don't come in! Whoever you are, for God's sake go away!'

'Simon, it's me. Moira.'

'Go away! Leave me alone!'

She heard his cough, and it turned into a dreadful gasping
retch. Simon puking his guts up. As if poisoned. She was
thinking about Prof and the medieval red wine in the twelfth-
century baluster jar which materialized in the night on the floor
by the bed.

She moved into the door recess, stood very still with her ear
to the door – wooden, white-painted, peeling, rotting at the
bottom with the damp. Moira breathed in and out twice to calm
herself. Some hope.

'Simon, listen to me. Are you . . . ?'

Bloated, strangled noises, the creaking of the bed. She rattled the handle. 'No!' he screeched. 'Jesus Christ, you bitch, will you *go away!*'

'I will not!'

'*Pleeeeeeeease!*'

She backed off and shouted for help, a desperate cry down a well. But a spiral stairway was not a well, there were only five steps to the next corkscrew twist and two thick, ancient ceilings between her and anything else human.

And then Simon, stifling a scream, produced such an agonized, pitiful squeal, like a kitten, that Moira leapt back up and threw herself at the door.

'It's locked!' he wailed. 'You can't.'

But it wasn't, of course. When she twisted the handle, the door almost creaked off its rusting hinges and Moira fell forwards into the room, landing on her knees at the foot of the bed. The curtains drawn across the window recess.

Simon lay half-sprawled across it, on his back, naked, one leg straight on the bed, the other buckled on the floor, both hands over his genitals.

'Moira . . . please . . . go . . . You . . . don't want to see this.'

His face puckered in misery, pain and shame under a hard film of sweat. Simon St John, classically trained, the laid-back one.

'Arrogance.' The word thrust through teeth so tightly gritted they seemed likely to splinter.

'Huh?' She moved hesitantly to the bed, prised a hand from his groin and held it tightly. 'Nobody's gonna hurt you, Simon.'

'You'd think a fucking vicar would know . . . uhhhh . . . the futility of arrogance.'

'You did what you thought was best,' Moira whispered. 'You made a stand.' He's gonna die, she thought in horror. He's gonna die here in this filthy attic.

She saw that his shoulders and upper back were on the bed,

his lower back and his ass held in space by the other leg bent crablike on the floor.

'Oh, dear God, Simon, love, you better turn over on your stomach.'

'I can't move. Whichever way I . . . move it's . . . bloody . . . ag—'

'Hold on.' She knelt down, pushed her hands under the middle of his back, through the rivers of sweat. This was like one of those awful funny stories that firemen told, unless it ended in death and then it maybe wasn't quite so funny.

When she tipped him over, his serrated shriek made her reel back into the wall.

He lay spreadeagled on the bed, weeping, impaled.

'Jesus God,' Moira said. 'What is it?'

'You know what . . . Christ, it hurts when I breathe. I can't breathe.'

'Simon, we have to get a doctor. Do you understand?'

'No! Pull . . . pull the bastard out. Can you do that? Can you bring yourself . . . uhhhh.' His hands clawed, nails piercing the mattress.

'I don't . . . I don't know how deep it goes, Simon.'

'Feels like it's half-way to my . . . throat. Oh *Jes* . . . *Listen*, a doctor would tell the cops, and we'd all be out of here so fast, questions, questions, questions.'

'That's such a bad thing, to get out?'

'Don't be f . . . foolish . . . We've got to finish it.'

Sure. And what if this finishes you first?

Oh God, calm yourself, hen. Have to think about this. There could be internal bleeding.

'What's it made of?'

'If it's like the others it's a . . . a kind of tallow. Fat. Lard.'

It looked hard as bone. Dark brown, near-black. Thick and knobbly, like an old, rustic walking-stick, and God knows how long.

How could something penetrate your mind so deep it could make you do this to yourself?

She climbed up on to the bed, balanced there on the mattress in her Bart Simpson nightwear, a foot either side of him. She thought, I can't. I just can't. I'm bound to be sick or something.

'Please.'

She touched the end of the candle, protruding about three inches. It felt just so disgusting.

'How did you, I mean, get it in?'

Simon squirmed.

'Listen to me. Just listen. I've never . . . seen an object appear. I don't think anybody has. Matthew Manning, Uri Geller, all these people it's happened to, they've never . . . uhhhh . . . seen it. It . . . must've started while I was asleep. What I'm saying . . .'

She looked at the repellent brown smears on her fingertips.

'It grew . . . formed . . . *inside*?'

Simon grunted, tried to nod.

What are we dealing with here?

And, oh God, ma poor mammy . . .

And she felt so angry. As angry as Simon had been in the studio, 'correcting history'.

'Simon,' she said, 'I want you to grab a big wedge of the pillowcase in your teeth and bite down on it hard as you can. Do it. OK.'

She wiped her sweating hands on Bart Simpson. It didn't wipe away his evil grin.

Moira said, 'I'm not gonna dress this up, Simon. It is gonna hurt like every kind of hell, and if there's a lot of blood I don't care what questions we have to answer, you're away to hospital, right.'

'Yes,' he said and took the pillow in his mouth.

XII

Darker Underneath

Meryl thought Simon St John must be terribly paranoid or something because, as far as she was concerned, Eddie Edwards was a delightful little man.

'I shouldn't really, see,' he said, fingers poised over Meryl's fruitcake. 'But it looks so good and I've had no breakfast. And, anyway, if our calculations are anything to go by, tonight looks like the first night of the end of the bloody world.'

'Eddie . . .' The woman in the wheelchir, Isabel, gave him a menacing glare. She looked to Meryl as if she could be quite an awkward customer, but there was only so much trouble someone could cause, surely, from a wheelchair.

'No need to crush my shins again,' said Eddie. 'I take your point, but this lady might be able to help us.'

Meryl watched Vanessa carrying over a fluffy pouffe thing to perch on next to Isabel's chair in the vicarage living-room. The girl kept looking at the woman in the wheelchair, big-eyed, even allowing for the glasses.

Why was Vanessa so drawn to this woman? What had the child felt, catching sight of the wheelchair from the study window? What connection had she made to make her go berserk like that? Meryl would have given anything to know, because there was no doubt, from Isabel's impatience when Vanessa had run out in front of her chair, that the two had never met before.

'Why we have to be so secretive about it,' Eddie said, dipping his fruitcake into his tea, 'I really cannot imagine. Not at this stage of the game.'

'It isn't a game, Eddie,' Isabel reminded him.

'Figure of speech, girl. I know this is no game, by God I do.'

509

Isabel had clearly been anxious at first to get away from the handicapped kid clinging to the chair. But then Eddie had come along the street. Eddie who expressed instant curiosity about the strange woman and the little girl at the vicarage and what their connection was with Simon.

Eddie who, on learning Vanessa was the child born out of the holocaust in the hills in 1980, had been only too happy to accept Meryl's offer of tea at the vicarage and to exchange information.

But suspicious Isabel was still resistant. 'We shouldn't go shouting it about, we could get . . .'

'In trouble? That's not like you, girl. Who's going to cause trouble for us? Is Abbot Richard Walden going to sue if we brand him a child-molester, a Satanist, a murderer?'

'No, but some of what I discovered last night at the W.I. is not so far in the past.' Isabel swung her chair abruptly around to point at Meryl. 'And I don't understand. This is not Tom Storey's wife, so what's she doing with his kid?'

It was not yet nine a.m.

'If you have the time,' Meryl said, 'I'll tell you the whole story.'

There *was* some blood. It came out in a sickening, greasy trickle, with the candle, which proved to be almost a foot long and lumpily irregular in shape. Moira tore off a length of bedsheet, wrapped the sticky cylinder in it, took it out of the room and laid it, with a final shiver of revulsion, at the top of the stairs.

It troubled her in another way, this candle. Its wick seemed to be of a vegetable nature – possibly a rush or a reed. And although the candle was many times longer than the ones she remembered, the colour and the rudimentary moulding were horribly similar.

This had to be settled.

On his bed, Simon was sobbing with relief. Simon was breaking his heart into the pillow. When, grimacing with pain, he rolled over, there was blood and water and shit and mucus where he'd lain.

'I still think we should get a doctor,' Moira said. 'You could have internal haemorrhaging, anything.'

'There are all kinds of little capillaries and blood vessels and things in the anus. Looks worse than it is, I'm sure.' Simon rolled over on his back, pulling the eiderdown up to his stomach. 'Certainly feels worse.'

'Oh, yeah? How can you be sure you're no' seriously damaged up there?'

'Because if it was as bad as it feels I'd be bloody dead, and if Dave doesn't recoil when he sees me, I'll assume there's nothing imminent in that direction. Oh . . . *God!*' Simon beat a fist on the bed. 'I wouldn't turn the other cheek on that bastard Walden, if I ever . . .'

'Simon, this is a spirit. An essence. A vapour. This is the Abbey.'

'It's a battle,' Simon said. 'There's personal malevolence here. Last night – this morning – I told him he was finished. You remember? I said: You're fucked, Richard. *Not me, old boy,* he's saying. *Not me, exactly.* Richard Walden, Satan, the Abbey, I don't care what you call it, it's personal. It's something set in motion years ago.'

Moira thought he should have some rest. She also thought this was as good a time as any to raise the question which worried her the most: *whose side had Simon been on?*

'The candle,' she said. 'I was hardly going to examine it thoroughly, but that thing looked dreadfully familiar. Mmmm?'

'Yes,' he said wearily. 'I thought it might.'

'I'm thinking back to a circle of thirteen of them.'

'Yes.'

'I'm thinking about how you were so cool, assuring Tom it was probably a practical joke.'

'I *was* very cool in those days. Cool and self-assured. And fascinated by something that was dark and mysterious and . . . and somehow powerfully religious, too.'

'How long's it been going on? How long you been able to do

it? Can you lift your legs?' She was easing the soiled sheet from underneath him.

'Thanks. I can't remember a time when it *didn't* go on. Strange little objects used to appear in my cot, they tell me. But nothing remotely as spectacular as . . .' He turned on his side, face creased in discomfort '. . . Richard's little gifts. I didn't . . . you see, I didn't think it was evil at first. You don't, when there's . . . love.'

'Love?'

'OK, eroticism. There's no more . . . powerfully corrupting combination than . . . religion and sex. I was hooked. From the beginning. When Goff first set us up for this, I read everything I could find on the Abbey, and I discovered Richard, the pederast monk who rediscovered his soul. I mean, don't get me wrong, I've never been into choirboys, in any sense.'

'Well, that's one wee mercy.'

'But Walden was very, very powerful and so very, very glamorous. He'd had a holy vision, a direct link with God, and now . . . now he had a direct link with me. I suppose that made me the conduit.'

'We were all conduits in different ways.'

'And the candles were a really dramatic demonstration of it, of what we had. Him and me. I mean, even after what happened that night, it took me a long time to work it out. And then there was the matter of getting free of it . . . on every level. First, there was Max Goff to pay off.'

'Oh, Simon . . .' His face was dirty with dried sweat and stained with pain, like a casualty of some old war. 'You never liked Goff. Even physically, he didn't have . . .'

'What he did have was the tapes. Which Russell gave him. After we burned blanks with a few first-takes stuck on the front, in case we checked. He refused to destroy them, but I . . . persuaded him to bury them, as it were. I believed . . . I was *given* to believe . . . that those tapes would have been . . . used . . . if I hadn't had . . . been helped. That is . . . what convinced me . . . Goff crying out, *Oh Richard!* when . . .'

He rolled over, weeping into the already saturated pillow. 'I was used. I let myself be used. I *enjoyed* being used. I'm just shit, Moira.'

'That's the pain talking.'

'Don't fucking patr— Oh, I'm sorry. I'm *sorry*. I'm never going to be able to repay you for this.' He tried to sit up and his eyes filled with agonized tears. He fell back. 'What you did for me . . . I can't repay that, ever. And all I do is rant at you.'

'Simon,' Moira said, 'if something shoved twelve inches of stiff candle up me, I'd be ranting from now till Hogmanay and then I'd get drunk and rant some more.'

He grinned momentarily. 'I must smell bloody awful. I've just got to get myself down to the bathroom, but I don't think I can even make it to the bloody basin.'

'Patience, Vicar. I'll fill a bowl of water, see what I can do.'

'You've done enough for me, Moira. Far too much. No wonder Dave . . . I'm sorry. Not my business.'

'After everything you just told me? Dave . . . He's a nice guy, always was. As guilt-ridden as any of us. But Dave and me? I don't think so any more. Could've been, once. Or maybe not, I can't say. I feel so sorry for the guy. And I feel sorry for Tom, you . . . even myself, just a wee bit. But that's no' the same thing.'

Simon stared at the blackened beams in the ceiling. 'I've been virtually celibate since that time with Goff. Going into the church . . . that was a fairly obvious step. That I should study theology. I was a good vicar, you know?'

'I'm sure you were.'

'Not here. I've not been very good here up to now.'

'Why *did* you come back? Or is that obvious, too?'

'I had to know.'

'Whether you could resist him?'

'Yes. Because I'd been celibate. The first time I'd been what you might naïvely call a free spirit. And therefore – you know – open to enslavement. Emotionally, sexually. And I thought I had a purity now. Arrogance, you see? I told you I'd been arrogant. And sooner or later, anyway, I was always going to have to find out the truth. About which of us had been the bad influence. About the nature of his . . . conversion. But as soon as I got here, I realized how ambivalent all this can become. We're only human, Moira. There are no absolutes for us.'

'However,' Moira said. 'I think the nature of his conversion is now pretty obvious. When you publicly rejected him – it – the position was made painfully clear.'

'Like I said, it's a battle. This time yesterday I was convinced I'd broken through. That was the first time I defied him. On top of the other tower, above the mist line.'

'I could tell. It galvanized us all day. You brought the band together.'

'And look at me now.' He closed his eyes. 'That's what arrogance does for you.'

'Wasn't arrogance. You've no arrogance in you. What happened was, something liberated you. Or someone. A realization maybe. A dawning?'

Simon opened his eyes and looked into hers. 'A woman. Can you believe that?'

'Oh, aye. I always could.'

'A crippled woman, in a wheelchair. A woman from the village who lost the use of her legs when she fell from the tower I was standing on yesterday. While making love with her boyfriend. He was killed. It was a long a time ago. Twenty-one years ago.'

'Well, well,' Moira said.

'Every seven years,' Simon said. 'Every seven years, the Abbey takes a life.'

'On December 8th, 1959, there was a terrible storm. Mother talks about it still. Apparently, we were almost flooded out next day.'

Isabel paused for a sip of tea.

'Anyway, a man called called Reg Welsby was farming up at Stoney Ridge, back of the forestry. He had some sheep and they'd got loose in the Abbey grounds and he went over there to get them back in and was struck by lightning.'

514

'Dead?' Meryl asked.

'Instantaneous. They found him lying on a flat stone half-way up the nave, which was odd – not exactly the tallest target in a vast open space, was he? But you don't question lightning, do you? It strikes where it strikes.'

'Act of God,' Eddie said.

'*I* bet,' said Isabel. 'Want to hear the rest?'

Eddie shuddered. 'I don't *want* to.'

But Meryl did. She sat rapt, chilled, but so horribly thrilled by the idea of cyclical deaths in this ancient ruin that she knew she had to see the Abbey before the day was out.

'Let's see . . .' Isabel counted on her fingers. '1966. When the Abbey was an outward-bound hostel for maladjusted boys from Birmingham, and two of them became even more malad-justed and there was a very nasty fight in one of the sheds, with hatchets, apparently. One of them died in hospital from his injuries.'

'December?' Eddie asked.

'Almost certainly. I can't get the exact dates, unless we go to the local paper offices and look it up in their files.'

'No time,' Eddie said. 'What else?'

'Oh, there was a death in 1952 . . . heart attack, I think, but I couldn't get much because old Mrs Collis was there last night and it was her *brother*, see. *Well*, it was getting fraught enough by then, me wheeling myself around with a bit of Cheddar on a stick and a glass of Château Pontrillas '93, asking discreet questions of different women and forgetting there's no such thing as discreet at the Women's Institute.'

'A tenacious girl, you are,' Eddie said admiringly.

'Anyway, at just about ten o'clock, I was asked to *leave*, would you believe? The first cripple in history to be ejected from the W.I. . . . and for gossiping! What's the W.I. *for*, except to manufacture gossip?'

Meryl laughed, feeling really comfortable with other people for the first time since she and the Lady Bluefoot had last prepared Martin's dinner at Hall Farm.

'What it is, see,' Isabel said, 'the older ones, who've seen it happen a few times, they know about the Abbey in their hearts of hearts. But will they talk about it? No way. Not lucky. Tempting fate. Fate, see. It has to be fate. Anything people can't explain, it's fate. This seven-year business . . . I doubt if anybody's really worked that out before.'

'Hard to believe,' Eddie said.

'No. It's not. Very stoical, country people, very unquestioning. I tell you what I've noticed, though – and I never questioned it either until I started talking to Simon and you. But when it's happened and it's *not* a local person who's dead, there's an enormous feeling of relief, a lightening of the atmosphere in Ystrad Ddu.'

Vanessa was looking up at her from her fluffy pouffe. Isabel put a hand on the girl's head.

'When Vanessa's mother died in that crash, I won't say there was rejoicing. But a sense of relief you could feel.'

Vanessa smiled.

'She knows me,' Isabel said. 'We've never met before, but we both nearly died at the Abbey, see. And we both came out . . . damaged.'

Meryl was stunned. She stumbled to her feet. She had to go out of the room to absorb this. 'More tea. I'll make more tea.'

She stood filling the kettle at the sink, watching the water tumble from the tap until the kettle overflowed and the water ran over her wrists. After a period of bewilderment, anger and incomprehension, a feeling of *being left out*, she seemed suddenly to be at the centre of everything that was blessed and magical. She turned off the tap, emptied some water from the kettle, put it on to boil and drifted numbly back into the living-room to hear Isabel saying,

'. . . one more, though, I got, before I was kicked out.'

'Good girl.' Eddie leaned forward eagerly in his chair.

'Nineteen forty-five, this is. Just after the war. Two boys, cousins, from . . . Leeds, I think it was, or Sheffield . . . had been evacuated to the Grange Farm to stay with a Mrs Price, whose husband had died leaving her with the farm to manage and no sons – this is when it *was* a farm, with stock, not like now. The boys would be in their teens and most of their family were killed in the bombing. Sheffield, it must have been. Anyway, the boys stayed on, and one died.'

'How?'

'I had to leave before I could find out. An accident, I think. I do know the other one came to inherit the farm and owns it still, though he's hardly ever here, hence the rundown state of the place. He lives in London now. His name's Copeley . . . Copesake . . . ?'

Meryl said sharply, 'Say that again, the name.'

'Copesake?'

'I've heard it somewhere, recently. Oh my Lord, where was it?' Meryl grabbed her head from either side. 'It's hardly a common name, is it?'

'Don't think too hard,' Eddie said. 'It'll come to you.'

'And that's about it,' Isabel said. 'Didn't I do well?'

'I don't know what to say, my love. A wonder, you are. What we have to decide now is what to do with it. Should we tell our friend Gwyn Arthur, do you think?'

'That copper?' Isabel was aghast.

'Don't dismiss Gwyn Arthur. He has a most unusual mind.'

'Yes, well, we have enough of those, Eddie. What we also have is a situation where there are people we . . . care about, in a place where all the statistics show they could come to real harm within the next twenty-four hours.'

'We should go over there now and tell them, you think?'

Isabel looked at him scornfully. 'You really think they don't *know*? Why else have they come?'

'Or we could go and . . . be with them,' Meryl said tremulously.

'And what,' Eddie demanded, 'do you mean by that?'

Meryl hugged herself. 'I don't know. I don't *know*.'

Moira found Dave and Tom in the studio working on the Aelwyn arrangement.

'We're doing this tonight?'

Dave said, 'You ever feel you haven't got a choice?' He was tuning his Martin with a new self-adhesive chromatic tuner you could stick on the pick-guard and watch the flashing lights. 'I can't keep this instrument, you know.'

'I thought we'd dealt with all that,' Moira said.

'It's too good for me.'

'It isn't.'

''Tis.'

''Tisn't . . . aw, Davey!'

Dave smiled. 'How are your . . . legs, this morning?'

'Shapely as ever, if horribly disfigured.'

'Bollocks,' said Dave. 'Where's Simon?'

'He's gonna stay in his room a while. He's a wee bit knackered, to be honest.'

'Not surprised,' said Tom. 'The boy done good. Last night, yeah?'

'Yeah, I was . . . kind of proud of him,' Moira said.

'It's the right attitude,' said Tom. 'You gotta go in fighting. Me, I'm shit scared, as ever, but it don't pay to show it. He showed us all up for bleeding wimps. Don't you fink?'

'Well,' Moira said guardedly. 'Maybe. But I think whether we go for Aelwyn tonight, that should be a general agreement. A vote.'

Dave looked up from his tuning. 'You mean you'd vote against?'

'I don't know, Davey. It's kind of your big number, how do *you* feel?'

Dave laid the guitar gently on the carpet. 'Like I said, I don't think we have a choice. Aelwyn brought it to a head last time. This time we're on our own. Nobody like . . . well, like Debbie. You know what I mean.'

'No need to tread eggshells, Dave,' said Tom. 'I can talk about it. You mean it's, like, us and them, and no . . .'

'Innocent bystanders,' Dave said. 'But Aelwyn's at the core of it.'

'Aye,' Moira said. 'I guess that's right.'

'I don't think I understood him last time. What he represented. I mean, I know I didn't.'

'And you do now?'

'No. But . . . I dunno, I think it can *come* to you. Like
Simon last night, with Holy Light. A complete reworking,
right? He reworked it *in the light of his experience*. And in the
end it wasn't holy light at all, quite the reverse. And now we
know. And you know what I think?'

Dave walked into the centre of the studio. 'I think this place
is probably the oldest recording studio in the world. Cemented
in blood? You remember they said that about the stones?'

He moved over to a painted stone wall. 'Whitewash. But it's
darker underneath. Last night, Simon brought the truth out of
the stones.'

And the bloody stones didn't like that one bit, Moira
thought.

Tom said, 'We used to fink this was holy ground, right.
Back in 'eighty. We was trusting. We fought we was protected.
We was bleeding stupid. And now we know.'

But do you? Moira thought. Do you really?

'I was pretty fazed, gotta admit,' Tom said, 'when I seen
Simon in his dog-collar the first time. But he's learned fings,
ain't he? He was just this classical geezer, before, the one who
knew what all the notes was called and what you could do wiv a
treble clef. But he was really firing from the hip last night. And
he hit the target, dead centre.'

'Aye,' said Moira, feeling the deepest trepidation, 'didn't he
just.'

Part Five

I

Spirit

It takes a while to find it in the dark, even with a hand-lamp, for so much has changed.

For instance, the line of the wood has altered, so the tree is no longer on the edge – there are fourteen years' worth of untrimmed bushes to get through now.

Once, apparently, when the Abbey was a hotel, everything up to the woods was lawn. And then, when it was a hostel for antisocial kids, it was a playing field.

When Max Goff created a studio here, he let the grass grow a little, turning it into something approaching a meadow, on the basis that prestige bands liked to think they were out in the wilds but it wasn't so wild that a stroll after lunch would destroy your Calvin Klein jeans.

But the tree's still here. The same tree, with the same view through the lower branches to the lights in the Abbey. Not so many lights now, because some of the rooms are still closed, due to the effects of damp and cold, the ravages of fourteen years.

It was a mild night last time, but Dave was cold because he was wearing only jeans and a T-shirt. Tonight he has on a sweater and his white scarf and he reckons he feels about the same. Cold. There have been snow flurries on the hills.

It was a mild night in New York too, on 8 December 1980. Mild for New Yorkers, anyway; it must have felt pretty cold to Mark David Chapman who came all the way from sunny Hawaii, bringing darkness. Yeh, his middle name is Dave; put that down on the charge sheet, too.

This tree – there's something different about it. Same branches, same angles. But something's changed.

Dave doesn't know much about nature.

The reason he's come out here now, at close to six p.m., is that he doesn't plan to return. No matter what happens tonight, what horrors manifest, he is not going to run out on Simon and Tom and Moira. He will not see this tree again.

Moira.

Things really haven't worked out, have they?

He remembers last month, being at Ma's bungalow in Hoylake, writing the letter which will turn out to be his first ever fax. Remembers wondering if it was still love, if it had ever been love or was maybe just a subconscious plea for empathy.

No, he decides. It was love.

He doesn't ask himself if it's *still* love. He can't bear to give himself a formal reply, for the record. It will only make him think of lonely shores and white sand, of wind and spray.

And black bonnets.

He looks up at the tree. This tree is not the same.

Damn it, Reilly, why can't you even admit to yourself why you came out here? You came here to be alone and to consider what to do. Maybe seek some advice (you out here, John?).

Dave shuts his eyes and lets go of his thoughts.

And nothing happens, inside or outside.

He's not here. He was never here. You've been inventing conversations with John Lennon for so long that sometimes you just know what he's going to say before you can get around to writing him a script.

Dave touches the tree. What kind of tree are you, anyway, apart from not being an oak?

This is the eighth of December. It's fourteen – twice seven – years since John Lennon was shot and Debbie died. He remembers – the most vibrantly shocking memory of his life – Tom staggering from the wreckage, the sudden explosion, the swollen black thing that was Debbie being thrown out of Tom's arms as his sleeves ignited.

Which left Tom wearing an aura of flames like St Elmo's fire on the mast of a sailing ship. And this was the last bright aura Dave ever saw. After that, all black.

He looks up at the tree. Ash? Beech? Horse-chestnut? Sycamore?

They've come back to the Abbey, the four of them, with their eyes open and their senses attuned and all that crap. They've come back because something from the Abbey has remained, like a virus, inside each of them. Because every time Dave sees a polluted black haze around somebody's rinsed coiffure or silky, shampooed tresses, he thinks, *This is what the Abbey left.*

But right now only one sullied aura concerns him.

Go over it again. Ask the question.

This is the eighth day of the month of December on a seventh year. He remembers Prof's news cuttings about Soup Kitchen in 1987. Simon has told him about this girl in the village and her accident in '73.

Now Dave has worked out something probably no one else knows. For what it's worth.

Before walking out here he went into the little TMM admin office next to Lee Gibson's luxury quarters. The woman in charge, Michelle, was not there (Lee likes to relax before a session) but her calculator was.

On the calculator, Dave brought up the figure 1994.

From it he subtracted 1175.

This gave him 819.

He stood looking down at this figure for a long time. It was an awkward-looking number, which was good. Nineteen itself was a number you couldn't do a thing with – there was a name for the ones you couldn't divide by any other number without getting a bunch of digits on the wrong side of the decimal point; 819 looked like it ought to be one of them.

What the hell. Just to reassure himself, because all the odds were against it anyway, Dave took a deep breath and divided 819 by seven.

No.

It came to 117.

Exactly. No decimal point.

No!
Dave felt nearly sick and did the calculation again.

It doesn't mean anything, he tells himself now. It doesn't mean that the seven-year cycle of death began with Aelwyn in 1175, or that Aelwyn was even part of it. It certainly doesn't mean that at least 117 people have died at the Abbey. It's a numerical coincidence.

Isn't it.

And it can't *possibly* mean that someone is destined to die here tonight.

Can it.

Even if one of those here is someone whose lustrous black hair – now with its single vein of white – has been seen on two separate occasions, by Liverpool's very own Angel of Death, to be softly framed by the hideous bonnet.

A night wind is drifting in from the Black Mountains in the west. It fumbles irritably among the bushes on the edge of the wood.

The wind is saying, *Don't piss about, ask the question?*

There are two lights high up in the tower, one just below the other. Simon's room. Moira's room.

The lowest of the two lights goes out.

In his head, Dave asks the question.

Behind the question is the knowledge that, for every single person he has told about the bonnet since the Black Album session, it has been too late.

Dave asks the question aloud.

'Should I tell her?'

Nothing comes to him. After nothing has continued to come to him for a couple of minutes, he tries to manufacture a reply from his dead buddy, John Lennon.

How the fuck should I know? What's it to me?

That the best you can come up with?

Is that the best you can come up with?

Maybe this is the one night Lennon is incommunicado. Maybe he goes to Strawberry Fields in Central Park to watch the annual influx of pilgrims, listen to the tuneless chorus of 'Give Peace a Chance'.

Dave feels frightened and very, very depressed. He doesn't know where to turn. He flashes his lamp up into the leafless branches of the tree which gave him sanctuary precisely fourteen years ago tonight.

The glistening smoothness of the wood tells him at once what kind of tree it is and what's different about it.

It's an elm tree, and it's dead now.

They sit clustered like witches around the small vicarage hearth, a built-up coal fire pumping big yellow flames under the brass cowl, and Meryl asks, 'Do you believe in the power of the Spirit?'

'I don't really know what you mean.' Isabel is restless, irritable. Never has she felt so helpless. 'If you've got the power, I've got the spirit,' she adds morosely.

The little girl, Vanessa, is next to Isabel on the sofa. They must look like three of the strangest witches of all time.

'Look into the fire,' Meryl says. She has switched off the light. Unearthly, she looks, with that burnished gleam to her long face. Woman's bloody daft. 'Look at the power there. We created it and we're containing it. It could burn this place down and us with it, but we're *using* it to warm us.'

'And how's that supposed to help Simon?'

Isabel has telephoned to the Abbey, twice – oh yes, they have a phone number again – using her most authoritative, clipped, accountant's voice. A sugary female tells her that Mr St John is in session in the studio all day and cannot be disturbed.

But it's urgent.

She's sorry; she has her instructions.

They could, of course, go along there and demand to be let in. An old man, a cripple, a mentally handicapped kid and a loony.

They could storm the gates.

Oh yes, there are gates now. The track terminates at big metal gates. Eddie has been and rattled them, demanding his rights of access to an ancient monument.

Sorry, a big, leathered man from a security firm told him. Closed for structural repairs. Eddie stumping off, mumbling about complaining to his MP.

There is another way, of course, he's told them. But it's a narrow little path, not much more than a sheep track. And totally impossible, Eddie is afraid, for a wheelchair. Especially as, with the security arrangements, they would have to go at night. *Oh yes*, Meryl said, and Isabel glowered.

'There's so much power around us.' Now Meryl clasps her hands together, shaking them like a cocktail. 'If only we knew how to use it. This was a very blessed landscape once, with the Skirrid and all the churches built on holy soil. Once upon a time, we'd have known how to direct it.'

Isabel is unimpressed. 'Prefer a flame-thrower, I would.'

Meryl smiles at her. 'I'm sorry we got off on the wrong foot. I can tell how you feel about Simon.'

'Unfortunately,' Isabel says, 'it's only from the waist up. And he doesn't like women anyway.'

'I wouldn't have said that.'

'What would you know?'

'Perhaps a bit more about men than you, my dear.'

There was no answer to that. She looks as if she knows a *lot* more about men than Isabel.

'Is it always like this,' Meryl asks, 'in December of the seventh year? A tension in the air in this village?'

'Not so's you'd notice. I'm trying to remember what it was like in '87. I don't remember anything happening then, that's the problem.' She sighs. 'What if all this is nonsense and we are all overreacting?'

'It's very far from nonsense. And you know it. And this child knows it.'

Vanessa has her hands folded on the lap. She looks up, blinking behind her enormous glasses.

'Where's the soil?' she demands.

Isabel looks blank. 'The soil?'

'It's in the shed,' Meryl says. 'In a couple of plastic binsacks.'

'What soil?'

'Vanessa and I bought a spade in Abergavenny and went up on the Skirrid to collect some of the holy earth. You know . . . where it was shaken up by the earthquake on the first Good Friday.'

'Personally, no. You can't climb many mountains in a wheelchair.'

'It's not a mountain really. It's just a funny-shaped hill. But strange.'

'Everything's strange to you, isn't it?' Isabel said disparagingly. 'I bet you go to fortune-tellers and seances and stuff like that.'

Meryl stiffened. 'Certainly not.'

'I'm sorry,' Isabel said. 'Just a whingeing cripple, I am, and a sour old maid. All I've ever done is sit in this chair and moan.'

'And build up the most lucrative business in the village, according to Eddie,' said Meryl. 'Don't sell yourself short. You *have* got the spirit.'

'I don't even know what I want to do.'

'But you know what you want,' Meryl says. 'That's a start.'

A woman dying.

Waxen face, *dwindling tendrils of mist from parted lips, eyelids fluttering as feeble as a moth in winter.*

Hunched over his mixing desk, lights low, Prof remembers this as clearly as if he were hearing the music now. Not actually hearing the music again – he can't even remember the basic melody – but seeing the images it conveyed.

He's thinking, Am I a bit psychic too, or was the music really *that* powerful?

Music he has to re-record tonight, and Prof is . . . well, nervous is not the word. He's seen and learned and experienced too much in the past weeks or so. At the age of sixty-four, his mind has been blown apart.

And he's supposed to know how to piece it together again?

Far more sensible, Prof thinks, to have a few drinks and let all these experiences and revelations sink into the general mush.

Now *that's* a first – first time that drink has seemed like the *sensible* option.

So far – last night, anyway – it's been quite a satisfying experience, producing this album. That last piece of Simon's, recorded out on the studio floor, with the ambience of the stone very definitely captured, that was dynamite. *Will* be dynamite when Prof has mixed it, with the bass and drums on. These tracks were supposed to have been recorded today, but Simon hasn't shown his face in the studio all day, like last night really took it out of him. Lee Gibson keeps sticking his head around the door to see if he's wanted yet, getting increasingly pissed off, muttering about temperamental half-assed wankers.

Lee isn't used to this, being kept waiting. Not for the first time, Prof wonders how the hell they persuaded a heavy-earner like Lee to fly over from the States, for *this*.

He saw Steve Case briefly this afternoon over at the canteen. This is as far as Steve comes, he won't set foot in the studio – 'A deal is a deal, Prof. How's it going, am I allowed to ask?'

'Not bad,' Prof told him. 'Had a few false starts and, er, minor setbacks, but it's shaping up OK. We're having a go at the number which should give us half of side two.'

'Aelwyn.'

'Yeah. The heavy one. The one that fucks people up, Steve.'

'Do *I* look fucked up, Prof?'

'I can't believe you heard it. I can't believe you heard the same music as me.'

'You're a sound engineer, Prof. You're *supposed* to hear these little . . . resonances.'

Resonances.

A woman dying.

There's only one woman here.

'Is . . . is Mr Beasley there?'

'No, he's not. Who's that?'

'Doesn't matter, honest. I'll call back.'

'No. Don't go. Please don't hang up. I know your voice, don't I, from somewhere?'

'Yes, you do. That's Shelley, isn't it? It's Barbara Walker. Ginger Hodge as was.'

'For heaven's sake, it is, too.'

'Oh look, I'm sorry, it's just I promised Weasel, and I didn't want to sound like I was going behind your back.'

'God, Ginger, if there's anything you can tell me. I'm . . . I'm just going out of my mind, if you want the truth.'

'What's . . . ?'

'It's Vanessa. She went off with Weasel and they've just . . . disappeared. Vanished. One mysterious phone call and then nothing. She's got Down's Syndrome, Ginger. She's got very poor eyesight, there was talk of a heart-murmur . . . I can't sleep, I can't . . .'

'Oh, Shelley. You haven't told the police or anything?'

'Not yet. Weasel's devoted to her, I mean he wouldn't . . .'

'No, he wouldn't, I can tell you that. Oh, I wish I'd called earlier. I didn't want to ring from the office, in case . . . I mean, they're not nice people at TMM. It's not like Epidemic was.'

'Ginger, I'll do anything.'

'Well, look, there's a lot of stuff I'm not sure about, so I don't want to say too much. But I do know where Tom is. At least, I'm pretty sure.'

When Shelley puts the phone down, she's appalled, hot with anxiety and absolutely furious at herself.

Why on *earth* didn't she realize?

Yet it seems so terrifyingly bizarre and so utterly unlikely that Tom, of all of them, should have acquiesced . . . agreed to return to the place which has given him the worst moments of his life.

Unless . . . *that woman* . . . that insane woman . . .

Shelley stands trembling in the hall, Martin Broadbank watching from the bottom of the stairs. He's been here all day, running his business from her office, breaking off to calm her when she goes into her headless chicken routine.

It's seven-thirty p.m. Shelley contemplates a journey.

531

II

Unhappy Ghosts

*A*elwyn.

It's been a long haul, my friend.

Eddie sits in his armchair, his papers on a coffee table. Marina is watching the television; such a placid woman, doesn't know what he'd do without her.

The TV screen might as well be blank for all it affects his concentration. If there's one thing Eddie can do it's focus.

Aelwyn.

In this mood, Eddie doesn't care who he bothers at home. The eminent professor of Welsh Literature at Aberystwyth he called an hour ago was not what you'd call cordial. How did Eddie get hold of his phone number? Who the hell was he anyway? If he wanted this kind of information, why didn't he drive over to the National Library like anyone else?

Eddie had to throw a few heavy names at him, Department of Education high-ups who didn't know Eddie Edwards from Adam, but this professor wouldn't find that out tonight.

'All I want is top-of-the-head stuff, I'm not after a biography,' Eddie said. Always so difficult to find out what these academic bastards really *think*. Everything has to be a considered, annotated response, with appendices and a bloody index. Takes him ages, like pulling bloody teeth, but he gets there in the end. And if Professor Vyrnwy Pritchard should ever discover that Edward Edwards never made it to chief education adviser and has in fact been safely retired for many a year . . . good.

Aelwyn.

This man, like many of these bardic figures, is an enigma.

Perhaps the greatest enigma of his profession during the medieval period.

In those days, bards were hacks, see.

If you were a medieval chieftain who wanted your mighty victories commemorated in peotry and song so that other chieftains would be less inclined to chance their arm against you, what you did was to hire yourself a bard.

The bard would sit around in your castle for a few weeks, getting well pissed up on your wine, and at the end of this period would produce some bloody awful piece of illiterate doggerel full of lurid verses about you slicing people's arms off with your mighty broadsword.

Aelwyn was different.

Aelwyn was not inspired by bloodstained battle-axes and intrepid acts of vengeance by the valiant Welsh against the brutal Normans.

Aelwyn's work was dedicated to the promotion of what, in twelfth-century Britain, was a deeply unfashionable commodity: peace. Hence the name applied to him, *Breuddwydiwr*. For most of the Middle Ages, the notion of peace was strictly for the dreamers.

Nothing remains of the man's apparently prodigious output: he was part of an oral tradition; if he committed anything to parchment, it has not survived. More out of legend, is Aelwyn, than recorded history, as Eddie has suspected. How could anyone survive, the historians ask, in such violent times when his message was one of conciliation and mutual understanding? When he stood up for the common people against the warlords? When the only chiefs and princes he was prepared to exalt in his verses were those who did not abuse either their power or the local peasantry?

So, as men such as this were thin on the ground in the strife-torn border country of the twelfth century, how did Aelwyn survive?

The answer – according, again, to legend rather than history – is in the personality and attitude of the bard. He hardly fitted the image of what might today be called a wimp. Aelwyn, it seems, was a tough customer, with an abrasive tongue, who would travel on foot with a harp over his shoulder but a sword at his belt.

Aelwyn could hold his own. Aelwyn took no shit.

And he had a following. There were few villages in Gwent and Powys and Hereford where Aelwyn was not welcomed with rejoicing, where food and ale and a bed would not be prepared for him.

Man of the people, see.

But in the eyes of the Norman, de Braose, and his kind, a very dangerous man. A rabble-rouser.

It was entirely typical of de Braose that he should invite the famous pacifist to his castle to witness the signing of the treaty with Seisyll and the border Welsh. Reasonable, too, that Aelwyn should fall for it – well, Seisyll did, didn't he?

Eddie leans back in his chair and closes his eyes.

He sees Aelwyn fleeing the carnage at the dinner-table. A shout goes up that a witness, the worst possible witness, has escaped.

But Eddie can't hear it. He's convinced now that it never came, that shout.

Consider the situation. How did they know? When did they find out? If Aelwyn had slipped away unseen it would not have been until later, when the bodies were disentangled, that his absence was noted. If he had actually been *seen* escaping, they would have caught up with him in minutes. Men on horseback? And him on foot?

He certainly would never have made it to the Abbey.

And yet the story says he did. That he stumbled towards the lights and the smoke of what, at that time, could have been no more than a grouping of huts, perhaps with a stockade around it.

Sanctuary, sanctuary.

Eddie stands up. 'Off to the Dragon for a pint, my love.'

'Bring some toilet rolls from the shop then, would you. Save my legs tomorrow.'

Zap wags his tail. 'No, no, not tonight, boy, I'm sorry.'

Eddie sets off, along the dark and freezing street, from the old vicarage to the new vicarage. In his overcoat pocket, two heavy torches. But he's far from sure about the wisdom of this.

For on such a night . . .

No. On *this* night.

Lee hurls a drumstick at the wall.

'What's *up* with these bastards?'

Prof is alone in the studio with the transatlantic megastar. It's the opportunity he's been waiting for.

'Lee,' he says. 'What the fuck are you doing here?'

The reason they're alone is that the band have had five attempts at 'The Ballad of Aelwyn Breadwinner'; each time one or other of them has walked out of his or her booth shaking his or her head. It's not working. Is this cold feet or what? So they've gone through the ruins and across the grass to the canteen to try and work it out.

When Prof asks the question, Lee looks at first kind of hunted and then kind of hostile.

'You don't need this hassle,' Prof reasons. 'You don't need the money. You're not, with all respect, a guy renowned for being kind and sentimental. And what've you got to be senti-mental *about*? By all accounts, they put you through the mill last time and the bloody album never even got released! Need I go on?'

'Well . . .' Lee hesitates, one hand pushing back his curly pirate's locks. 'It's partly contractual, obviously.'

Prof carries a stool over to the drums. 'If you don't mind me saying so, Lee, that's crap. Nobody has a contract like that.'

'Part loyalty, too, man,' Lee says uncomfortably. 'I got a lot of help from Sile Copesake. Sile found me the breaks. Shit, you know this business. One day, Sile says, I know you prefer drums, but don't neglect the guitar, yeah? Well, I used to play a bit, nothing virtuoso, just the chords. But I was surprised how well it came along after he'd said that. Then he says, like, there's this band could use a drummer. And so I go in as drummer and after a year or so I'm fronting the band. You know how it is.'

'He's got a piece of you, hasn't he?'

'Shit, Prof, this is not something I talk about, all right?'

'Because you're shit scared of him. He put you where you are, he can take you down again. But it's more than that. We've all heard stories about Sile Copesake. Not a nice man, basically. And he scares you, Lee. Not least becaue you can't think *why*.'

'Why what?'

'Why he's got to have you here. On drums. Nothing else. Not even back-up vocals. What's that gonna do for album sales? Lee Gibson: drums, sod all. Point is, it's just like last time, when you were just a session man. Everything just like last time.'

'Not exactly everything, Prof. You weren't here last time.'

'Nor I was. Russell Hornby was producing, and young Barney Gwilliam was turning the knobs. You hear about Barney, Lee? You hear about Russell?'

'Yeah. Unfortunate.' Lee's playing nervously with his other drumstick, pushing it through his fingers. 'It happens, in this game. It's not unusual.'

'OK, then,' Prof says conversationally. 'Let's start with Barney. Terrific sound engineer. Very sensitive boy. Barney could pick up on the nuances, know what I mean? Very thin-skinned. That boy could *feel* the music. No surprise, then, that when he came out of that session, hearing all that dark, *resonant* stuff over and over again through his cans, he was polluted.' Prof taps his head. 'Up here.'

'You don't know *what* kind of other problems he had, man.' Lee twirling a bit on his stool, eyes flicking from side to side.

'You and Russell, on the other hand, were not so sensitive. You both thought all this picking up vibes stuff was total crap. You had *thick* skins. And anyway, on drums, you were beating it out of you as it was coming in.'

'Like the shamans,' Lee says suddenly.

'What?'

536

'One of them, Dave or Moira . . . was saying shamans used to use drums to drive spirits away.'

'Yeah,' Prof says. 'That makes sense. Out, spirits, out! Bom! Bom! Maybe it explains why you were the one who *didn't* do away with himself rather than come back.'

A bulb blows in one of the spotlamps, the way bulbs seem to at the Abbey, and Lee springs up from his stool with a cry of alarm. 'Fuck's sake, man, you're supposed to be the producer. You're supposed to make us feel relaxed!'

Prof smiles. 'I was actually set up to be the engineer, working under Russell. Even for that I had to be conditioned. They sent another thick-skinned bastard, Steve Case, to kind of . . . initiate me.'

Lee moves towards the door. 'I need a coffee.'

'Siddown. You'll need a cof*fin*, you don't take some of this on board. I'm trying to help you, son.'

'You're trying to screw me up, man.'

'If that's what it takes,' Prof says. 'Listen, they set me up to "discover" the tapes and get them processed – baked, you know? Case pretended he didn't know about baking tapes and I bought it. Stupid. The idea was I'd listen to them. And not forget. Never forget. Not waking, not sleeping. Now you go and ask Case if *he's* heard those tapes right the way through, 'specially the stuff that begins with Aelwyn. No *way*. I should've realized earlier. He didn't know what I was on about when I was begging him not to release the album. And I thought that was an act.'

'Shit,' says Lee. 'What *is* it *about* those tapes?'

'I don't know, mate. That's why I'm here, God help me. I'm just giving you a friendly warning. Because you might not be a Little Innocent, but you could be playing way out of your league. And you might just be considered expendable, know what I mean?' Prof stands up and strolls back towards the control room door. He turns once and taps his nose. 'Word to the wise, eh?'

Lee swallows. 'Can I go for that coffee now?'

'Yeah. Or two coffees. Or make it three. And a bun. And a work-out with Michelle. You get what I'm saying?'

'Don't come back for a couple of hours?'

'Good boy,' says Prof.

'It's me, isn't it?' Dave lights up a Silk Cut. 'I can't get to it. Just haven't got the balls.'

All this Don't Worry Tom stuff. It was never Tom. Tom just carried the can. Tom might have driven away in too much of a hurry afterwards but at least he didn't run out on the session, which Dave is scared he's going to do again.

It's gone nine. The four of them are still in the canteen. It's a nice place, for a mobile unit. Tables with cloths on them, lamps in bottles, a cook and a waitress somewhere out of sight. All for them, the Philosopher's Stone, the cult band that never lasted long enough to become a cult.

Simon, particularly, is looking tired tonight, and pale. Dave thinks last night's reworking of the Richard Walden story must have taken more out of him that he's admitting. He wonders what *he's* going to feel like tomorrow. After Aelwyn.

'Davey,' Moira says. 'Think back. Last time, you seemed to forge an immediate link with Aelwyn. You *were* Aelwyn. You were scared. You were running like hell, all these guys after you, the clamour of men and horses, and then . . .'

'And then I lost it. Suddenly I wasn't scared any more. I'm thinking, this is wrong. But it wasn't wrong. I felt very confident, fairly relaxed. I had no thoughts of being pursued, no fear of death. And that was when it happened, the scene-shift.'

'I saw the candles light up,' Moira says. 'The black candles – OK, dark brown, but probably blacker inside than even Tom suspected – the black candles flared up by themselves, all together in a pile, higgledy piggledy.'

'I didn't see them.' Dave shakes his head. 'I must have been in New York by then. Maybe that was the point of transition. Like a cut in a film . . . fade out, a moment of black and then fade up . . . to what turned out to be the Dakota building. It was so out of context, it threw me completely. I had to get out.'

'And you were relaxed, presumably, because Lennon was relaxed,' Moira says. 'If I've got this right, he was coming home from a mixing session or something. Everything was fine, happier than he'd been in ages; he was working again after a long time of no inspiration; he doesn't seem to have had any kind of premonition, even though this little bastard had been hanging round him for a couple of days. OK, why were you getting this; where's the link?'

'Between Lennon and Aelwyn? Quite a few. Both singers and musicians, songwriters. And the peace thing. I've become quite a student of the Aelwyn myth. He wrote poems and he sang about peace, which didn't make him too popular with the establishment.'

'So we've got ourselves a rough parallel,' Moira says, 'with Lennon – as peace campaigner – and the American conservative establishment.'

'We know the FBI was watching him. We know he was expected to be a thorn in the side of the incoming Reagan regime. We know that Government agencies were determined to prevent him becoming an American citizen. And when he did get his green card, the people who were happiest were the ones the FBI saw as dangerous radicals.'

Dave opens out his hands. 'And yet he saw New York as a sanctuary. It was the one place he felt safe – ironically.'

'Like Aelwyn and the Abbey.' Moira helps herself to one of Dave's cigarettes. 'The place he thought he was safest was the place that killed him. And also . . . Have I said something?'

Simon is staring at her.

'Monks,' Tom says suddenly. 'I seen monks. Either side the gate. While you and Simon was out looking for Dave.'

'The monks killed him,' Simon says quietly, with certainty. 'Richard Walden knew de Braose wanted Aelwyn dead. When Aelwyn turned up in search of sanctuary he was invited in, and then . . .'

'Aaaaah!' Dave's chair crashes over as he leaps to his feet, backing away from the table. The ashtray in front of him is full of bright red, foaming blood.

'Davey!'

Moira's holding him. He smells her perfume, essence of long beaches, grey sea and wide sky. *Please don't let her die, please don't let her die . . .*

'It's OK, Davey, you've had a shock. You were right all along. There was nobody following Aelwyn. He was confident of sanctuary and he had a hell of story to tell. Come on, sit down.'

There's only ash in the ashtray. Only ash. Dave closes his eyes. When he opens them, Moira is exchanging meaningful glances with Simon. 'Sorry,' Dave says. 'Nothing. Trick of the light.'

'I can't explain this,' Simon says. 'I don't suppose we ever will. But maybe it all went wrong because the vision of Aelwyn was wrong. And the premonition Dave received was the closest parallel, in a . . . a contemporary event, to what *really* happened to Aelwyn. There's a theory, isn't there, that Mark Chapman did what he did under some kind of hypnotic suggestion planted by the CIA or some outfit like that.'

Dave says, 'I don't mean to sound apocalyptic or anything, but wherever Lennon is, maybe he's trying to get something across.'

He talks about the Liverpool power failure in the thirteenth minute of the thirteenth hour of the thirteenth day of December, in the thirteenth year since . . .

Simon's shaking his head. 'We could go on all night . . .'

'One more thing. You remember, "On a Bad Day", Simon?'

'Sure. I've wondered how much that was troubling you. All I can say is, don't lose any sleep, Dave. It was no more than a normal reaction. *Double Fantasy* really *was* a piece of crap.'

Dave stubs out his cigarette in the ashtray that didn't have blood in it. He has the feeling this has become Don't Worry Dave night.

'We can't prove the Aelwyn theory,' Moira says. 'But we can test it. Can you handle that, Dave? Think about it. Aelwyn's our baby. Whatever you want, we'll go with it. Excuse me.' Pushing her chair back. 'I'm away to the girls' room.'

When she's gone, Simon says quietly, 'OK, what's wrong, Dave? Is it Moira? That things haven't worked out how you hoped?'

Dave looks up. If only that was all it was.

He lights another cigarette, hands shaking, and he does what he should have done days ago. He tells Simon and Tom about the black bonnet. Moira's black bonnet.

Simon is silent for a long time. So long that Dave's worried Moira's going to come back from the loo before he can get a reaction. When she doesn't, he decides this is probably a set-up. She wanted Simon to get out of him whatever it was he was afraid to tell her.

Eventually, Simon says to him, 'Dave, can I put a theory to you? I mean, shoot me down in flames . . .'

'Go on.'

Simon talks for over ten minutes. Occasionally, Tom makes an observation. Moira has had time for a complete manicure. Afterwards, Dave says, 'I didn't know. I didn't know any of this.'

What Simon has told him is that after he ran out of the studio that night, whatever had begun did not end. For the rest of them it was only just starting to happen.

It began with the usual extraneous sounds – voices in the cans, whispers, vague ribbons of laughter. What some people call spirit-voices and Simon calls 'psychic fluff'.

Simon had already laid down his bass track and was now closeted with his cello and his viola, double-miked. Soon, it was as if the instruments were making their own sonorous responses to external stimuli, electrical impulses by-passing Simon's mental control, taking the music into ever deeper and darker places.

There was foreboding and trepidation . . . the rolling thunder of approaching death.

Prof could tell Dave about this, Simon said. About the impact it made on *him* nearly fourteen years later, on tape, the death sequence which began with Aelwyn.

Moira was at the core of it. There was a moment, Simon

says, when he was afraid Moira was actually going to die, and he couldn't do a thing about it; he felt like – who was it now, Merlin? – a prisoner in a lightless cavern at the bottom of a very deep pool.

In the end, it was Tom who may have saved her. Tom realizing where it was headed . . . that subtle forces had been invoked by the combination of the band and the night and the location – what Moira called the 'toxic cocktail' – and that it was going way too deep. 'I just let rip,' Tom said modestly, recalling his blazing, high-pitched electric shriek which Simon said Prof had described as being like a chainsaw, ripping the fabric of the music and the night and . . . and Moira – Prof had thought it was an attack on Moira. In fact, it *released* Moira; it was an attack on death.

'And I'm wondering,' Simon says now, 'if Moira's been carrying the memory of that around with her . . . you know, the closeness of death? You say you saw it around her on an old album cover . . . I don't know, maybe her mother's death, too? A premonition of that? She's full of self-recrimination over her mother, I know that much. She thinks her mother absorbed . . . what? The death that was coming to *her*?'

'Nuffink's ever what it seems, Dave,' Tom says. 'That's the only bleeding certainty in this life.'

On the way back to the studio, as if it's been arranged, they pass Lee Gibson. 'Just popping over for a coffee,' Lee says cheerily. 'Good luck, guys.'

'Give her one for me,' Dave says crudely. It's become an in-joke. None of them really knows whether Lee is sleeping with the admin assistant.

Dave is looking happier than Moira's seen him since they got here. She gives his hand a squeeze. He gives her a grin. They're going to do it. They're going to lay Aelwyn's unhappy ghost and a few of their own. After tonight, it's downhill all the way.

Moira glances up at the two shadowy towers, about twenty-five yards apart, the bitten-off top of the ruined one almost obscured by the frigid mist. The heavy truck with the hydraulic platform is still parked in the courtyard behind what is now the TMM tower; restoration will resume as soon as the band's out of here. So much to restore.

you have some damage to repair.

Tonight, Mammy. Tonight.

The cold bites. The tower house looms over them, a single, watchful light in one of the upper rooms.

The place observes her, she feels again, with an ancient knowledge. And a frightening edge of derision.

III

Bluefoot

Night and mist obscure the great rock overhanging the church as Eddie walks up the lane, worrying.

Always mist in this valley in winter. But it shouldn't be too bad, see, it's a reasonbly distinct path . . . for those who dare take it.

Eddie is still far from sure about going to the Abbey, is not sure *why* they're going, even if Meryl is. But he has to go with them; he's an old-fashioned man and would hate to think of women and children – well, one woman and one child – walking that path at night to emerge among the decaying stone teeth in the very mouth of Walden's abbey.

The other problem is: what are they going to do about Isabel? She isn't the type of person to sit demurely at home with her knitting, waiting for news. Isabel is a doer, a mover.

And Isabel in love is probably unstoppable.

There should be headlights on this machine, Isabel thinks. Why did nobody think to fit sodding headlights?

She has an elderly bicycle lamp on her lap; its glass has a crack across one corner and rattles. The lamp illuminates the road for no more than about five yards ahead, which is not *that* much of a problem because the electric wheelchair is grinding along so slowly that even a geriatric hedgehog wouldn't break sweat getting out of the way.

But the narrow road is empty. A hedgehog would at least be a bit of company. The verges and undergrowth are silent with frost. The wheelchair whines.

It's very, *very* cold. Isabel wears her woollen cape and

mittens and a white ski-hat with daft-looking brown reindeer on it. She's someone you see and feel sorry for, or so she hopes. For the first time in her life, this is what she hopes.

That's another first.

But the *first* first, the most dramatic first is that she's glided out of the front gate of the cottage . . . and turned *right*.

Never before has she done this in the chair; seems incredible, but it's true. Everything lies to the left: the church, the village hall, the school as used to be, the pub, the house of anyone she's ever wanted to visit. And, of course, the way out of the village. To the left lies civilization.

To the right: heartbreak, death, the Abbey.

And so never before, in the chair.

And, even before the advent of the chair, never alone.

And never in the dark. It was afternoon, quite a fine afternoon for the time of year, when she'd gone with Gareth and his little haversack containing, among other items, one of those blow-up airbeds you took to the seaside but which would lie equally well on a stone floor at the top of an old, ruined tower.

But she wouldn't have gone there in the dark, not even for Gareth who was two years older, a grown man, a man of the world.

Not that Isabel is particularly afraid of the dark, even now. No more so, anyway, than the average chairbound cripple wondering how she's going to kick an attacker in the balls with toes she hasn't been able to wriggle in over two decades.

What's more unnerving than the night is the slowness of the blasted chair. Keeps making her think the bloody batteries are about to give out. Thank God that this is a valley road, following the river, with no major humps and pitches.

And thank God that Meryl's not with her, with her talk of spirits and life beyond the grave.

Is he right, Isabel? Is this path impossible for a wheelchair?

I know which one he means. Used to. As a kid. Yes, he's right, damn it. I'll have to go the usual way, by the road.

But that's hopeless; they'll never let you in.

Deal with that problem when I come to it.

Well, take some of this. Please.

Oh that's daft . . . They're definitely not going to admit a crippled crank with a plastic binsack full of soil on her knees.

Take it anyway. We can't manage it all.

But the only thing on Isabel's knee, as the wheelchair moves through the night with all the speed and grace of an old badger on Valium, is the bike lamp with the cracked glass.

They don't exactly stroll in singing, with their arms around each other, but Prof has detected a distinct raising of spirits.

They've worked something out. Obviously.

Dave goes directly to his booth and thumbs a chord on the new Martin. 'Hey, listen to this!'

'Brilliant,' Tom says. 'I heard you was having lessons again.'

'What's wrong?' Prof adjusts one of Dave's mikes. 'You're gonna sit on the amp, as usual, I take it.'

'Yeh. No, nothing *wrong*. Listen. The bugger's in tune! Whenever I leave a guitar for five minutes in this studio, it's always way out of tune when I get back. Used to drive Russell spare. Now, listen to this . . . spot bloody on. After over an hour. Unprecedented! It's an omen. We'll get it right, now, I can feel it. I'm locked into it.'

'Don't go talking about omens,' Moira calls over. 'It's unlucky.'

Dave throws his plectrum at her. 'Only if you're superstitious.'

'Superstitious?' Tom crosses himself. 'Me?'

'By the way,' Dave says to him. 'I took that dead albatross out of your booth. It was starting to smell.'

'You bastard, I was teaching him to talk.'

Dave and Simon exchange grins.

Psychic humour, Prof thinks. Whatever next.

'Right, then,' he says. 'Aelwyn, The Ballad of. Go for it then, shall we?'

*

The mist's getting thicker, Eddie thinks, as crosses the road to the vicarage. But not *that* bloody thick.

'Ah. Mr Edwards.'

This is smoke, from a familiar pipe.

'If you're on your way to see your good friend, the vicar, I'm afraid he's not there.'

With that damn pipe and his long mac, Superintendent Gwyn Arthur Jones looks like nobody so much as Sherlock flaming Holmes.

'But perhaps you know that already, Eddie. Man like you. Nose to the ground.'

Eddie recovers some composure. 'Why is it, Gwyn, that you only come out at night, like a bloody vampire.'

'Hmmph.' The policeman looks affronted. 'No one's ever said that before. Pig, I get usually. And Filth. Anyone would think I was not welcome. Especially at the vicarage. What an extraordinary woman. And do you know . . .'

Gwyn Arthur throws his long shadow over Eddie under the second of the village's three lamp posts.

'. . . she's staying in his house but claims she doesn't know quite where he's gone. The vicar, this is. Oxford, she says. Or somewhere. Now, isn't that odd?'

'Gone to stay with friends, he has.'

'Oh *well*. Just the time for a holiday. December. Come and have a drink with me, Eddie.'

'Well, I would, see, only I've got to meet someone, isn't it?'

'Oh yes?' Into Eddie's face Gwyn Arthur blows enough smoke to evacuate a wasp's nest. 'Anyone I know?'

'Just a quick one then,' Eddie says miserably.

Oh God, oh God, not far now.

The trees either side of the road are now embracing overhead, the mesh of shadow-branches infilled by nightmist, making the road into a tunnel, but one with no light at the end.

There was a moon that night, in 1973. She's sure there was

a moon. Some sort of light, anyway. Or maybe it was just her, incandescent, in love.

If there's a moon tonight, she can't see it; the further she trundles down this road the worse the mist comes down. And the likelier it seems that the batteries will give out.

You can go back. You can still go back. To the fire and the telly and the chairlift to bed.

Big deal.

At least she'll be there before Meryl, who's relying on Eddie to take her. Rather him than me. See how *he* liked the saga of Lady Bluefoot and the fuzzy brown apparition with an extra hole in his face and the awful vision of slaughter around the dinner table.

Isabel sighs. Suddenly everybody's a visionary.

Except for me. Well, only the once. The night of flying.

Pinned down like a victim of the Blitz under tons of masonry. Pinned down all night, next to a poor boy whose eager, youthful loins have pumped their last.

Pinned down and feverish, but soothed by the body's natural morphine and some strange and ancient magic in the night.

The flying.

She didn't say a word about this to Meryl. In all these years, Simon St John has been the only person she's felt able to trust with her memories of ecstatic night-flight, escape from a broken body, freedom . . . sensations so cruelly crushed with the coming of the dawn and the police and the fire brigade and ambulance, the dawning of days, months, years of numbing misery and doctors shaking their stupid heads.

Only Simon understands – even if he's done his best to discourage it – her need to make just one meaningful return to the place where ecstasy and horror collided. To go back

for what she left behind?

Isabel stops the chair for a moment in the lane. Last chance to turn back.

She has her deepest and most terrible wish. She's returning to the Abbey, alone, in December of a seventh year.

I mean, talk about crazy. Talk about bloody fanciful, mystical bullshit, talk about . . .

talk about flying.

Isabel presses the green button, goes on.

He's on his own. Really on his own this time.

The hills are the same, more woodland maybe and harder, more bristly. Less scenic, less *picturesque* – what a strange, senseless word; Dave's suddenly mystified by the idea that a hard, frozen winter landscape could ever be considered pleasing to the eye.

The wildblown snow is there, the same harsh, grey spattering. And the track's the same, although you stay off it to avoid making footprints. And your feet, by God, are as cold as ever you remember.

But he isn't surprised to find Aelwyn is not the same and has a new voice.

Aelwyn Mark One was gentle and breathy, like the wimpy singers in all those acoustic bands of the early 70s. Sounding like a martyr before he was even over the wall of Abergavenny Castle . . . and running . . . crouching.

The new Aelwyn's singing isn't sweet, his notes soar only with pain. His song is free-form; it comes without rhyme or obvious meter. It struggles against the structure imposed by the tune. The song of the new Aelwyn makes no concessions.

The new Aelwyn is a man with dreams but no illusions. The new Aelwyn is a hard bastard in a hard land.

And I'm staying with him. I'm staying with him this time. Until the end.

'Let's try it again.' Prof's voice in the cans, sounding a bit dismayed.

'Left, he has. Twenty minutes ago.'

'*Left?*'

'Gone to the pub. Always goes to the pub on a Thursday, he does,' Eddie's wife tells Meryl. 'Who shall I say?'

'It's all right. I'll call him again.'

Meryl puts the phone down.

He's gone. He's gone alone. The old devil has lied to them. He's keeping it for himself. Doesn't want his style cramped by a handicapped child and a mad woman.

'And are you?' Meryl rushes out of the study to confront herself in a mirror in the hall. 'Are you mad?'

'Are you *mad*?'

In the glass she sees not the old smouldering allure in the mysterious, dark-eyed one who looks beyond the horizon, but plain, perplexed apprehension in the unpainted eyes of an ordinary middle-aged woman.

And she longs to be back with Martin, for whom the only unknown forces are market forces. With whom she can safely be a believer in Other Spheres, a confidante of ghosts, and it doesn't matter, because she's the only one, an exotic eccentric in a world of businessmen and socialites.

Out here, on the very edge of reality, you can entertain the silliest romantic fantasy and find someone desperate enough to believe you. And in no time at all you find yourself determined to make it happen.

Like taking a consignment of holy earth from the Skirrid to sanctify the Abbey.

And Meryl thinks, yes, possibly I am mad. Possibly I parted company with reality the minute that child appeared at the door with her strange, magnified eyes.

Or, *more* possibly, the night I slept with Tom Storey. The night I persuaded him, because it seemed so exciting, to return to confront his 'destiny'.

What have I *done*?

I haven't even tried to ring Shelley. I could be accused of kidnapping. Because I wanted it to be a mystery, I've never tried *too* hard to find out how Vanessa came to *be* here.

What have I turned *into*?

Slightly hysterically, Meryl hurtles back into the living-room, manufacturing a warm smile, to find Vanessa looking into the fire. Vanessa has a sorrowful fascination with fire.

'Vanessa.' Meryl kneels down on the carpet next to her. 'I want to talk to you.' The fire is burning low and red. 'Vanessa, who brought you here?'

'Weasel,' Vanessa says at once, turning to look at Meryl. 'In his van.'

'And where's the van now?'

'In the shed.'

'Where's the shed?'

'At the farm.'

'I see. Which farm is this?'

Vanessa looks blank.

'Is it near here?'

Vanessa just looks at Meryl, her mouth half-open.

'Where's Weasel then?'

'In the van.'

'But you said the van was at the farm.'

'Yes.'

'Vanessa . . .' Meryl hesitates. 'Why didn't you stay with Weasel?'

Vanessa thinks about this. 'He wouldn't talk to me.'

'Had you fallen out? Had an argument?'

Vanessa shakes her head.

'Then why wouldn't he talk to you?'

Vanessa looks mixed up. 'I think he was poorly.'

'Ill?'

Vanessa blinks hard behind her glasses.

'Vanessa, was Weasel ill?'

Oh no. There's a sick man somewhere in a van, been lying there for days. Or even . . .

'Vanessa, is Weasel . . . is he . . .?'

Vanessa stands up. Her convent school blazer is hanging, freshly-pressed now, from a coat hanger behind the door. Vanessa reaches up for it, takes it off the hanger, puts it on and methodically buttons it up.

'Can we go and find Daddy, now?'

*

She doesn't even remember the road any more. She's never been down it at night. Nobody from the village goes down this road at night, except for Dai Salmon, the poacher. And never in December, even him.

She wishes she weren't so alone. Perhaps Vanessa. Who already feels – because of the Abbey – like Isabel's little sister. The little miracle child, born like a phoenix from the flames.

Flames.

Shortly before they parted tonight, Isabel felt herself drawn towards Vanessa's magnified eyes and experienced the momentary illusion of gazing into the intense, gassy core of a furious fire.

Which, all right, was probably only a reflection in her specs of the fire in the vicarage hearth. She can only have imagined the rest, see, the muffled roaring.

debs, debsie, debs . . .

And the heat on a winter's night, the terrible sensuality of it. like the fl . . .

No! Why're you doing this to yourself, you daft bitch? Turn back while you can. Jesus Christ, you don't think for one minute you're going to wheel yourself in there and twenty-one years will drop away, and you and the gay vicar will fly away together?

She stops the chair. She feels so heartbroken and angry with herself she actually turns it around.

To find that the view to the rear is exactly the same as the view to the front: damp, filthy freezing mist and the imprints of hostile winter trees.

Oh Simon, what have we become? What has this place done to us?

There aren't many aspects of me, Isabel concludes in despair, that I don't hate and despise.

'Strewth,' Prof mutters, adjusting Dave's voice level as the meter hits the red again. He doesn't know what the *hell* to make of this.

Not exactly what he expected after the way they were when

they got back from the canteen: good mates, optimistic, ready to hit this thing head-on. Confident, at last, of what it was about.

Whatever's happening to Dave, he can tell Simon wasn't expecting it either. Simon was making a valiant attempt to follow it, contribute the odd fiddle-lick, but he's given up. Not as if there's even a tempo, as such, any more.

If Simon was in charge of last night's session, this is Dave's big moment. But it's not the same, no message here of the triumph of art over evil. Simon's a classically trained, string-quartet man; Dave's a self-taught guitarist who can't even sing in tune unless he's imitating somebody else.

God only knows who he's imitating here.

And Prof has no choice any more; he has to go with it.

This is the fourth take, each one more extreme than the last. Five minutes into Take Three you'd swear the bugger was singing in a *foreign language*. This was just before Prof stopped recording and went out on the studio floor to try and talk some sense.

'Look, Dave, come on, I'm gonna have problems mixing this. I'm all for *avant garde*, long as I understand it.'

Dave just grinning sheepishly, like even he doesn't know what it's about, and Simon saying, 'Let it go, eh, Prof. If it turns out to be a solo, where's the problem?'

OK, so this is a man of many voices; this is a guy who can give you a Simon that might fool Garfunkel. He *could* be faking it.

And as this strange, rough Aelwyn trecks bitterly through the snow, some bastard's turned the heating off, for authenticity.

Thanks.

Gwyn is buying.

Eddie, resigned to losing half an hour, says, 'I thought you fellows weren't supposed . . .'

'. . . To drink on duty. Everybody says that.' On the wonky, scuffed table Gwyn Arthur Jones deposits a whisky and dry

553

ginger for Eddie and a half of Welsh for himself. 'Uniform men, that is. And lower ranks.'

Gwyn Arthur drinks cautiously. 'Besides,' he says. 'I'm not on duty.'

'You mean anything I say will *not* be taken down?'

'It's what you don't say, Eddie, that will get you hanged.'

There are only half a dozen people in the bar tonight. Gwyn Arthur briefly eyes a scratched plastic container of cold meat pies and then seems to lose interest.

'That candle,' he says. 'Case closed.'

'Oh?' Eddie waits.

'Lack of evidence.'

'You mean the forensic boys couldn't turn up anything else?'

'No.' Gwyn Arthur finishes his beer, puts his glass down and stares sourly into the dregs. 'I mean we've lost the fucking candle.'

Only his desire not to prolong this session prevents a smile from creasing Eddie's features.

'Forensic have no valid explanation for the disappearance. We've suggested they fingerprint their own bell jars, or whatever such specimens are preserved in.'

'Somebody's taken it?'

'Let's just say it's gone. As if it had never existed. The lab asistant says she'll go to court to swear everything was locked up and still locked up the following morning, et cetera, et cetera. So. Don't suppose you've any others? No, don't tell me, I don't want to go through this again.'

'Go through what again?'

'Whatever it is you're going through, my friend.' Gwyn Arthur slowly raises his eyes. 'Like a cat on hot bricks, you are.'

'Nonsense,' Eddie says, squirming a little. *What's the time now? Oh hell . . .*

'If there's anything that inflames my curiosity beyond normal tolerance levels,' Gwyn says, 'it's the sight of a respectable citizen with something on his mind he desperately wants to unload but knows he daren't.'

'D . . . daren't?'

'Let me get you another drink,' Gwyn says. 'I can't recall seeing a man so obviously in need of something to calm his nerves . . .'

Gwyn Arthur stands, moves behind Eddie's chair and plants a firm and rather menacing hand on his shoulder.

'. . . and to lubricate his conscience, prior to unburdening himself at great length.'

The path is already slick with frost and every blade of grass is white and hoary. It seems so much colder than usual, for early December.

Or maybe it's just here, in this forgotten valley.

'Aren't you cold, in just that blazer?'

Meryl has tried in vain to persuade Vanessa to wear something warmer. How will her guardian angel recognize her anyway in the foggy dark? she asks the child, ludicrously.

Meryl has pulled on a thick, padded coat over her blouse and slacks and is still cold. She waves the vicarage torch in front of them and the beam bounces off a barrier of fog. In the village it was mist; out here it's fog.

'Is this the right path? Do *you* know?'

For the first couple of hundred yards she was carrying over her shoulder one of the black plastic sacks of Skirrid soil, but she's abandoned it now. It's just too heavy and cumbersome.

To leave the holy earth on the footpaths would have seemed such a pointed rejection of the legend that she took a couple of gloved handfuls of earth and filled the side-pockets of her coat before hiding the sack behind a tree.

Damn Eddie Edwards. Was there ever a man who could keep his word?

The child scurries ahead. Her only concession to the cold has been to put on the woollen gloves she allowed Meryl to buy for her in Abergavenny.

'Come back, Vanessa! Stay close to me. We could lose each other so easily in this fog.'

Vanessa glances back over her shoulder. Her enormous

glasses look like saucers in the torchlight. She turns away and hurries on. Seems to know where she's going, which is more than Meryl does.

The conditions don't worry her greatly; she's a country girl, she's been out in worse. And alone. And in the dark.

However, in her imagination, from the first she heard of it, the Abbey has existed in a kind of endless summer, in a night dense not with mist but with soft, scented spiritual promise. The very word . . . Although 'cathedral' has a soaring splendour, 'Abbey' is the most serene and beautiful word for a spiritual building. And although everything she's heard lately is suggestive of the brooding, the sinister and the soiled, she finds it hard to regard it in this way.

Meryl pats her pockets. What's a dry-cleaning bill against a great spiritual gesture?

She's examined the Ordnance Survey map and discovered the Skirrid lies almost due east of the Abbey. In the inside pocket of her coat is a compass.

She understands from books on Simon's shelves that a great archway stands at the extreme eastern end of the ruins. What she plans to do is build a little mound of holy earth directly under the arch so that when the morning sun rises over the Skirrid and penetrates the mist, its rays will find the mound and the holy light will find its way to the Abbey's sick, Satanic heart.

Before they leave, she and Vanessa will hold hands and call down the blessings of the Spirits and the great archangel whose chapel once crowned the holy mountain.

The simplicity of the intention warms her briefly. She decides to explain it to Vanessa, who's still hurrying on ahead.

'Vanessa . . . Vanessa!'

She never responds. She always goes her own way. A wilful child. Or disobedient, depending on how you evaluate your children.

It's all right, though; she can hear the patter of the child's feet in her sensible, brown school shoes.

All around her in the freezing fog, clammy as frogspawn, are the hunched shapes of frosted sheep. Sheep will sleep anywhere, in any conditions, their winter wool heavy with hoar.

It can't be very far; Eddie (damn him) said this was a shortcut. He said you would suddenly *be* there, surrounded by stones.

'Vanessa. Come on, now.'

The child's footsteps are softer, not so clumpy. Maybe the path's grassed over.

Meryl can actually see Vanessa's shoes – although not the rest of her – as they trip along in the glistening mist, such small, light graceful feet.

And they've stopped. The sound has softened into nothing.

'Vanessa, are you all right, my love?' Perhaps she's fallen.

Vanessa doesn't reply, but something tells Meryl to switch off her torch.

Which she does, without a thought.

Click.

And in the mist, the small shoes are glowing.

Glowing the most beautiful pastel shade of blue.

'Oh!'

Meryl's breathing is stilled. In this drab landscape, carelessly straddled by the coarse, promiscuous mist, something extraordinary is happening.

When it happens, it's never when or how you expect it.

There's a swish and rustle of silk and a light laugh which makes Meryl want to join in.

And then, like the opening of a flower, the raw country smells give way to a heady floral fragrance as if the mist itself is becoming refined and scented.

A few yards in front of Meryl, the blue shoes glow as softly as a child's nightlight.

Meryl's lips part and her gloved hands clasp her cheeks.

'Oh, my lady.'

IV

Crucifixion

Isabel spins the chair violently into the bushes as the car screams past, sliding on the bend.

This road isn't wide enough for two vehicles, even if one's only a wheelchair. It could have killed her.

Do you care?

Pulling twigs from her hair – she's lost the reindeer hat, damn it – she thinks, if it'd got me, I'd be on Eddie's list as yet another December casualty in the vicinity of the Abbey.

What an indignity!

The chair whinges in protest as she urges it back on the road. *Bloody right I care!*

There are lights ahead illuminating a sign:

NO ENTRY

in black on a metal gate which the car has almost crunched.

Isabel switches to manual, wheels herself closer. A slowly revolving searchlight, beyond the gate, burrows into the mist, and she sees the hook of a stone arch and feels an immediate chill under her cape, a cold hand cupping her heart.

The searchlight beam fades and retracts. The arch is gone.

But there's the sound of one hell of a row going on.

'I want to see Stephen Case,' he demands loudly. 'I want him out here now.'

The security man regards him with disinterest under the pulled-down brim of his imitation police hat.

'And who are you, sir, please?'

'My name's Broadbank, I'm a substantial TMM shareholder, and I want to bring my car through these gates *now*.'

'I'm sorry, that's impossible. There's an important session on. I've got my instructions.'

'And what's *your* name?' Martin knows night security men *never* give their names. He probably has a day-job, too, and a tax situation.

The man hesitates, decides to play safe. 'Look, all right, if you'll just stay there a minute, I'll see if Mr Case can come out.'

Martin turns to Shelley. 'I don't believe this set-up.'

'Well at least we know we've come to the right place.' Shelley's bell of blonde hair is tucked into her coat collar. She looks cold. Martin wants to put an arm around her but doesn't, because she also looks angry. 'Martin, I don't want to see Tom, I just want Vanessa. Understood?'

'Don't worry.'

But, unfortunately, when the security man returns, he's looking more sure of his ground. 'I'm afraid Mr Case is tied up just now, mate.'

Mate now, is it?

'Well, you can bloody well *un*tie him. You've got just one minute to bring him here, or I use my car phone to summon the police.'

'I doubt if you'd have a signal here, but you could give it a go.'

'We'll see about that. We'll bloody well . . .'

Shelley grips his arm: cool it.

As the security man turns away, she calls out, 'Excuse me. Don't go. Please. We're not trying to cause trouble. We're just looking for a little girl. Nearly fourteen, but she looks younger. It's Tom Storey's daughter. I'm . . . I'm Mrs Storey.'

The man returns to the fence, pushes back his cap.

'Please,' Shelley says. 'She has Down's Syndrome. You know? A . . . a mongol.'

This is a horrible, disparaging word, applied to someone like Vanessa, but Shelley doesn't have time for misinterpretation.

'We think she may have come here to find Tom. I don't think he knows.'

'My sister's youngster's got Down's Syndrome. They're great kids. Very trusting.'

'Yes. So you see the problem.'

'Only wish I could tell you we'd seen her, but we've not. I'm sorry.'

Martin says, 'What about a little chap, late forties, bit of a hippie type. Known as Weasel. No?'

'No. Unless he's one of the builders.'

Shelley shakes her head.

'But Mr Storey's definitely here.' He wants to be helpful now. 'You want me to get a message to him? About the kid?'

'Thank you,' Shelley says tightly. 'But I don't think we need worry him.'

This time Martin does put an arm around her, as she struggles for composure. They watch the security man walk away. The searchlight briefly brushes the ancient stonework again and then fades.

They walk slowly back to the car. For once, Martin can't think what to do. 'Did you believe him?'

'Yes.' Shelley coughs at the cold air, perhaps to choke a sob. 'I believed him. He hasn't seen her.' She raises her eyes to the invisible sky and sags in Martin's arms. 'Oh . . . my . . . God. *Nobody's* seen her.'

'That's not right.' A voice out of the swirling darkness. 'I've seen her.'

The levels are going up and down like an arse in a blue movie, only less rhythmically.

Prof finds it equally dispiriting. The sound comes at him from two speaker-racks set horizontally in wooden panelling either side of the control room window, and he wants to turn it down.

The glass is just a black rectangle, nothing visible on the studio floor, even though Prof's killed the control room lights, leaving only the coloured mosaic of the mixing desk. Usually, this is exciting, like piloting Concorde at night. His element, the night and the bones and muscles of music.

But music this ain't.

Dave Reilly's not even singing any more, he's talking, kind of, in a guttural mumble. Prof thinks it must be Welsh – that was Aelwyn's language, wasn't it? If it's English, there aren't many words he understands.

He can't see as far as Dave's booth. He imagines him sitting on his amplifier, the McCarthy Dual, the way he likes. He isn't using the amp; he's playing his Martin guitar, double-miked. If you can call that playing. As a rule, Dave uses a plectrum; now Prof pictures his fingers tearing at the strings, like a crow at a carcass in the road.

The noises coming out of that booth sound like the creature's not dead yet. Gonna be a total write-off. Sheer waste of tape.

A tiny red light moves across the studio, making trails in the darkness.

Cigarette.

Company.

Moira enters the control room, slides into the spare seat. 'Hi, Prof, mind if I . . .?'

'Please do.'

She puts down a coat and a bag; not a flying visit then. He hears her taking a long, ragged drag on the cigarette. She's on edge; is it any wonder? Maybe she's wondering what *he's* wondering: how long can this go on?

'What's happening?' Prof turns down the sound. Not only can't he understand it, he can't bear to listen to it. 'I mean, this is . . .'

'Not the kind of stuff you can put out on an album, huh?'

'Not if you want to work again, no. Shall I stop him?'

'I don't know what to say, Prof. It's not what I figured it was going to be either.'

'Maybe he's just getting something out of his system?'

'Somebody is,' Moira says tersely and pulls on the cigarette. Does she normally smoke? He doesn't think so.

Prof picks his jacket from the back of the chair, puts it on. 'You find it cold in here, Moira?'

'Yeah. Same out there.'

'Bastards economizing on the heating or what?'

'It's cold on those hills,' Moira says enigmatically.

Prof leans over to the radiator pipe. To his surprise, it's hot. Does she mean the cold is coming through *Dave*?

The idea gives Prof the jitters, even though he knows it isn't possible. 'What's going on, Moira? I mean, is he having some kind of extra-sensory experience? Are people gonna listen to this in fifteen years and go like, wow, that was really ahead of its time?'

'Nobody's gonna hear it in fifteen years' time. Nobody's gonna hear it tomorrow. We won't make the same mistake again, will we, Prof?'

'That's why you've come in? You think I'm gonna do a Russell?'

She touches his hand. 'I'm sorry. No, I don't.'

Dave's still ripping weird, wounded chords from the guitar; it shouldn't happen to a Martin. They can hear his breathing: irregular, snorting.

'I really don't like this,' Moira says. 'I'm scared to leave him in there and I'm scared to pull him out. He ran out himself on the session . . . last time. You know?'

'Yeah, and it's been preying on his mind ever since. Hang on, what's this?'

A long, deep sigh is issuing from the speakers like steam. '*deathhhhhhhhhhhh*'

'Turn it up!' Moira hisses urgently.

'*ooooooooooooooo OOOOO A K HHHHHHHHHHHHHHHHHH HHHHH. . .*'

In an instant of bizarre surrealism, Martin thinks he's looking at a strange, gliding dwarf, a male dwarf with a high voice and a silly Welsh accent.

'I don't want to interfere, but I hate to see you so anxious, see.'

Only when the searchlight swings round does Martin realize he's being addressed by a woman in a wheelchair. Questions like: Who the hell are you? Where did you spring from? are pre-empted by Shelley, who practically pounces on the chair.

'Calm down, come on,' the woman says. 'She's all right. She's fine.'

'Just one moment.' Martin gently eases Shelley's hand from an arm of the wheelchair. 'What's the name of the girl we're talking about?'

The woman in the chair inspects him candidly. 'Vanessa. Satisfied?'

Shelley lifts her head, eyes closed, and clenches both fists by her sides in relief.

Martin says, 'I'm terribly sorry, Mrs . . .'

'Isabel Pugh. Not Mrs.'

'I'm Martin Broadbank. Friend of the family. I'm very sorry I doubted you but things have been . . . well, pretty difficult actually. Where, er, where exactly is Vanessa now?' Looking around, half-expecting the child to have materialized from the mist.

Isabel Pugh hesitates, produces a wry expression. 'Ah, sod it,' she says. 'You should find her at the new vicarage in Ystrad Ddu. Directly opposite the church. You can be there in a couple of minutes.'

'Thank you.' Martin smiles. 'That sounds safe enough.'

'Well, yes.' Isabel Pugh looks to be in two minds about this. 'It should be. All the same, I should get over there pronto.'

'But she's being looked after?' Shelley stiffens.

'Yes, but I should . . . get her away.'

Martin looks at the Pugh woman with curiosity. She's wearing make-up, her hair well-groomed. She's pretty, soft-faced. She seems intelligent. She seems frightfully apprehensive.

'Just don't ask too many questions,' she says. 'You'll only regret it.'

*

563

The fog curls and eddies in strands around her.

Her.

Vanessa has talked of guardian angels; this is Meryl's. Now she knows.

And she's waited so long
to see her.

The crisp rustle of silk. Or taffeta. *Swishhhh*. Peremptory, a little haughty. The mist parts to let her through. Meryl was wrong. Ghosts *can* travel. If they sense a kinship with the living.

'We've been through so much together,' Meryl whispers. 'Please let me see your face.'

The frost gleams pale blue on the tumbled stones where she shimmers.

'See, Vanessa. See my friend.'

'*No*.' Vanessa backs way, the blue light cold in her glasses.

'Not long now.' Moira breathes out smoke. Her body is stiff with tension. 'You got an ashtray?'

'Just chuck it on the floor and stamp on it. What d'you mean, not long?'

'He said Deathoak. This is where it all ends. For Aelwyn, at least. Deathoak's the place of execution.'

'Deathoak's The Dakota,' Prof says. 'Or something. With a spare T.'

'Or a cross,' Moira says suddenly. 'Listen.'

There's a moment of silence, the needles on the meters quivering. Impenetrable darkness beyond the glass panel.

And then, bizarrely, Dave as Lennon comes scything from the speakers.

'. . . way things are go-win' . . .' A cackle of crazy laughter.

I'm out of here, Prof thinks, not moving. I'm going to engineer a couple of regular albums made by normal, vicious crack-heads and then I'm gonna retire.

'They'll crucify him,' Moira says breathlessly, fumbling in her bag. 'Oh, God, get him through this.' Prof hears the friction of a match, sees her face in the flaring, anxiety bringing a twitch to her cheek. She pulls her black anorak from the floor, drags it around her shoulders. She's shivering, Prof can feel the vibration of her.

Yeah. It's freezing, all right. He touches the heating pipe again. It's still very hot. This is all wrong; you'd think the water in there would be frozen solid.

'. . .'s going on, Moira? What's happening? Who's gonna crucify him?' His *teeth* chattering; he doesn't remember that happening since he was a little kid.

'The monks. The monks crucified him. Here. On a tree. Deathoak.'

'I don't get what you . . .'

'*Here*. Can't you feel it?'

The control room door opens.

'Whosat?' Prof yells, nerves leaping in the darkness.

'Bloody hell,' Simon shuts the door behind him. 'It's no warmer in here, is it?'

'Here?' Prof says to Moira. 'What d'you mean *here*?'

'You felt the walls?' Simon asks. 'The walls are like ice. Absolutely like ice. Where's it bloody well coming from?'

'Got to end soon,' Moira whispers. 'Got to.'

'Haven't heard a note out of Tom,' Prof says to Simon. 'He still down there?'

'Tom won't leave. In case he's needed.'

'Guy's a hero,' Moira says distantly, and then, 'Ssshh.' Leaning into the speakers. In a thick and sleepy voice, Dave's repeating one of the old verses, like the image is going around and around in his head.

> . . . *echoes of slaughter*
> *the wine turns . . . to water*
> *the water to . . . blood and*
> *the blood back . . . to water . . .*

In the pauses, he's hammering at the bass strings, staccato. 'Nails,' Moira says.

Dave sings the same verse again, cracks in his voice, beating the strings, no rhythm to it. Behind his voice, a swollen roaring, like the wind, like blood pounding in your ears.

'He's singing to himself,' Moira whispers. 'He's singing to himself while the nails are going in.'

They wanted her to go back with them, Mrs Storey and the kind-eyed man, Martin. He wanted to lift her into the car. They could get the chair in the boot, couldn't they?

The car is long and sleek and reassuring. One of those Jaguar XJ-somethings. These people seem so strong and sane. They could take her away. From the Abbey and the village and the valley. She has money; her mother has the W.I. She could settle on her own, somewhere cheerful and busy, even if it's only Abergavenny.

'No, thank you.' Isabel sighs. 'I'm waiting for my boyfriend.'

Just saying that makes her feel so emotional she has to turn the chair away. She gets an image of Simon, strands of pale hair falling around his sad, cynical eyes.

She knows Martin can sense her anxiety, wanting to ask her what she's doing here alone on a night like this. She wills him not to.

'Go on.' Isabel makes little shooing motions with her mittened hand. 'Go and get Vanessa, poor dab.'

'Thank you,' Shelley calls back from the car door, 'Thank you so much.'

As the Jaguar rolls away, Isabel returns to the barrier and the lights. The security man gives her a relieved smile. 'Thanks. I don't know where you came from, but thanks. Could have been a problem, that.' Women in wheelchairs are no threat. 'Anything I can do for you?'

'Well, I don't know, see.' Isabel trying to sound all Welsh and defenceless. 'Come up from the village, I have. Stupid, really.'

'Not wise, night like this.'

'Only, a friend of mine, she said Lee Gibson was here, see.'

Isabel wriggles about under her woolly cape. 'Seems daft, it does, to you, probably, but I've got nearly all his albums, see.'

Hoping to God she doesn't have to name any of them. Meryl, it was, who spotted Lee Gibson in the Dragon while buying a few things from the shop. All Meryl knew about him was what she'd read in the papers about his affair with some prominent Hollywood actress.

'You want to meet him, eh?'

'Do you really think . . .? Oh, all embarrassed, I am, now.'

There's not enough light, she knows, for him to see her dimples turning pink. But he smiles. 'Well, he's around. I've seen him in the canteen. He came out the studio an hour or so ago. I don't think he's gone back.'

The security man opens the gate and beckons her in.

'You stay here, by the lights, and I'll see if I can find him. You got an album or something for him to sign?'

Isabel nods and shrugs, indicating it's under the cape.

'Give me two minutes.'

'Terrible kind of you,' Isabel mumbles, as the guy strolls off, hands in pockets, in the direction of a low, prefabricated building with warm-looking lamps in its windows. When the door closes behind him, she presses the green button and steers the chair into the blackness beyond the intermittent searchlight. When he returns to find her gone, he'll simply think she's melted way, overcome by embarrassment.

Now.

Go.

Isabel, breathing faster, brings the bike lamp from under her cape and steers the chair away from the path, away from the prefabricated buildings and the artificial lights.

Across the turf, towards the ruins.

The ruins which ruined *her*.

Doing it, I am. I'm really doing it.

The nave of the Abbey church is a line of skeletal, frost-rimed, broken arches – less impressive than she remembers. She goes into it, determined not to stop or to think too hard until she reaches the end. Where the final arch connects to the two western towers. With Meryl, she's studied the plan of the Abbey layout in one of Simon's books.

She travels directly down the middle, the bike lamp shining up into the arcade of arches, enfolded in loose, drab drapes of mist.

The nave is floored with frosted grass, where pews and choir stalls once lined an aisle. Where the high rafters resounded to the gilded echoes of Gregorian chant.

She can almost hear it. She's becoming excited. Whatever Eddie and Simon have said about the monk, Walden, the power of the place can't be denied. The stonework glitters in the lamplight, the rime of frost tinted a delicate strawberry hue.

I'm back.

Rolling down the aisle, Isabel experiences an illusion of speed, as though the chair is feeding from natural electricity, the battery boosted, the wheels going round faster and faster. And the nave is a magic runway and, at the end, the chair will take off, retracting its wheels and soaring blissfully, to the pealing of bells, into the night sky, above the mist, above the pain and the misery, above . . .

The pealing bells become a jarring snarl of metal and Isabel is hurled out of heaven with her neck twisted round.

The chair has collided with a big stone, projecting a good two feet from the frozen grass.

The engine whines helplessly.

Isabel's head has been thrown back into the leather. Far above her, the arches seem to lean together as though about to collapse from the impact of a flimsy little electric wheelchair crashing into a big stone which the occupant hasn't seen, due to flashing her little lamp into the sky and fantasizing about . . . flying.

She knows the stone must also have smashed into a foot or an ankle. Guesses the skin is broken, probably bleeding – she's always slightly surprised to find that her unfeeling legs, which have to be bent like dolls' legs, still have actual blood running through them.

But the possibility of abrasions and whiplash injuries are

passed over as Isabel tries to reverse the chair and fails, slams her back into the leather, drags with her hands at the chair arms and screams,

'*YOU STUPID FUCKING BITCH!*'

And feels even more furious and even more helpless when, instead of the massive shriek of rage which will cause the stone to disintegrate, the words emerge like a batsqueak and are swallowed by the mist.

Isabel closes her eyes and breathes in and out a couple of times before attempting, calmly, to assess the situation.

This doesn't take very long.

For all the illusion of speed and vastness, the stone is not much more than half-way along the aisle, which itself can't be more than forty or fifty yards long.

The stone seems to be the stub of a broken pillar. Whether it was here originally or been recently dumped here it's a bloody stupid place to put a stone, like a bollard in the middle of a motorway.

Isabel has another go at reversing the chair, heaving her shoulders back. The motor dies in mid-whine.

Shit, shit, *shit*!

At the far end of the nave, where the mist is darkest, a yellow light glimmers dimly. It's probably in the south-west tower where the studio is. As distinct from the north-west tower where the lower part of Isabel's body died in orgasm.

Not much life left in the bicycle lamp, either. She gives it a shake and directs what's left of the beam at the point of impact to see what can be done, if anything, to extricate the chair.

When the bleary beam touches the spot, Isabel nearly faints with shock and, jerking her hand away, smashes the lamp against the stone and it goes out.

'*Simon!*' she wants to shriek, with such force that it will penetrate the stone walls and the inner soundproofing and bring him rushing from his studio.

But again, her voice is faint and feeble with fear.

It can't be. It can't be!

She shakes the lamp and hears the thin tinkle of the glass

and the bulb falling into her lap. She takes off her mittens and runs both shaking hands under her cape and down her thighs and the hands come out soaked from wrists to fingertips.

No!

Plunges the hands down again, exploring what she can't see, can't *feel* – her hands are like a doctor's hands probing someone else's broken body. There is no pain at all, except in her mind.

Which is still vividly filled with what it was shown by the lamp's last faltering beam: the jeans ripped way and the knees and shins sheeted with thick, dark blood, which wells and bubbles up through her fingers as she clasps the legs she hasn't felt, except in dreams, since December 1973.

Nails? Crucifixion?

This is not a recording studio, this is an asylum. The recording booth down there is a padded cell and the patient is displaying all the classic symptoms of advanced paranoid schizophrenia.

Two minutes, Prof assures himself for maybe the fourth time. Two minutes, and then I'm out of here.

His eyes flit along level-meters along the top of the panel lit-up like the windows of a distant train. Two needles keep rushing over to the red, the way you normally get only with sharp, hard chords, quickly muted.

Or hammer blows.

Don't even *imagine* . . .

While all the other needles are hard over on the red.

Which is – think about this, think technical – just about impossible. To get that, all twenty-four tracks would need to be recording simultaneously, and there's just one guy in one booth with one guitar, and it's . . .

'fucking *freezing in here!*'

'I know.' Moira hugging herself; Prof can feel her swaying from side to side. 'Come on, Davey . . .' She sniffs. She's crying. 'Please let go, darlin'. Please let *go*.'

'Can't stand this.' Prof covers his ears, but he can still see the illuminated meters; *pop, pop, pop,* go the little black needles.

He turns away, turns his back on the mixing desk – first time he's ever done *that* – and leans with both hands on the back wall.

'Uuuuuuuh . . .'

'Prof . . .' Simon spins round. 'You OK?'

It's . . . it's like the wall's been newly painted. It's slick and sticky and stinks: an acrid body-stench, bitter and metallic.

A scream falls from the speakers, a long scream like a trail of fire.

'Lights!' Moira's shrieking. '*Lights!*'

as Tom's shattering, squealing solo – *out, spirits, out* – explodes from the control-room speakers and out of the amplifier in the furthest booth, filling the stone vault with white-hot, blind fury . . .

and the lights go on . . .

(for one appalling second, to reveal the whitewashed walls bubbling butcher's red, and big globules dripping from the curved, vaulted ceiling like glistening scarlet stalactites.)

. . . and then go out, leaving whorls and firework-trails in the clouding air, and the wild blue flash . . .

'*DAVEY!!!!!*'

. . . would be just like another light-effect, if it weren't for the crackling and the extinguishing of all the lights on the panel and all the meters

and the new smell of cooking flesh.

In the absolute darkness, 'Nobody move,' Prof croaks. 'Simon, you there?'

'Yes. But Moira's . . . *Moira!*'

Prof stumbles to the door, leans out over the studio. 'Don't touch him, Moira. Whatever you do, don't *touch* him!'

It might be that all the power's gone, but take no chances, it could be a blip, could come racing back. Prof locates the master switch on the wall, hits it with the heel of his palm.

'OK,' he says. 'It's OK.'

Knowing full well that it isn't.

V

The Abbey's Children

It is not a word that Superintendent Gwyn Arthur Jones has encountered before.

He writes it down on a beermat.

TELEPORTATION

'Through time,' Eddie Edwards adds tentatively.

TIME, Gwyn writes, but he writes this word very slowly. It's the one he's having the most difficulty with.

They've been in the pub over an hour, and Eddie has given up all hope of taking Meryl and Vanessa the back way to the Abbey. And perhaps, he concludes, this is just as well.

Gwyn lays down his pen. 'I like to think I am, shall we say, more open-minded than the average copper.'

More's the pity, Eddie thinks. An average copper would long ago have given this up as a waste of his time.

'Inasmuch,' Gwyn says, 'as I was born and bred in a rural community and remain very much *of* that community and its belief-system. For instance, my father, a minister of the chapel, would never have dared deny the existence of the *cannwyl gorff*, the corpse candle, which floats through the air to herald a death. And, indeed, I myself have more than once encountered that which cannot be satisfactorily explained on a statement form. This is my position.'

Gwyn leans forward on the threadbare bench. 'And so – let me get this right – you are telling me that this man St John is capable of *teleporting – across time –* certain household wares of the twelfth century.'

'Gwyn,' Eddie says, 'I am not telling you he is doing this, nor even that it's happening to him. I am telling you what he *believes* is happening to him.'

'Or what he *says* he believes is happening to him.'

'No, I believe that he believes it.'

'And if I believe that you believe that he believes, et cetera.' Gwyn throws up his hands in impatience. 'Where does that leave any of us?'

Eddie feels stupid. 'Perhaps it solves your mystery of the disappearing candle.'

'Meaning that it has' – Gwyn spits out the unwieldy word in segments – 'de . . . material . . . ized. And has returned, presumably, to the twelfth century. Very good. But what about the non-vegetable constituent?'

'The fat.'

'The fat. Which, don't forget, was certified by experts as being – how can I put this delicately? – *not so long off the bone.* Certainly not eight centuries or more.'

'Right.' Eddie assembles his thoughts like a gambler rearranging the cards in his hand, not the best hand he's ever been dealt. 'Now, this is not from me, OK? This is from what I have read over the past few days in certain dubious publications discovered among the theological tomes in the vicar's library.'

'Go on.'

'If what we have is an object – say a candle – directly teleported, by some molecular process on the very fringe of physics, from, let us say, the year 1175, then, if that candle was only a few months old when it was, er, sent, then . . . Christ, Gwyn, do you think this is any easier for me, as a professional educator?'

'I think . . .' Gwyn Arthur closes his eyes '. . . that my humble police brain is becoming over-fatigued. I'd like to deal with something possibly more concrete. The arrival of the handicapped child. You're not, I trust, suggesting she has been . . .'

'Teleported, I think not. But there's something odd.'

'Indeed.' Gwyn Arthur finishes the half-pint which has lasted him for a good forty-five minutes, in spite of Eddie's repeated offers to buy him a replacement. It suggests to Eddie that the policeman's claim to be 'off duty' was somewhat relative.

'Let's move on.' Gwyn stands up, pipe between his teeth. He has the demeanour, Eddie thinks, of a policeman *teleported* directly from the 1930s or before.

'Why are you smiling, Eddie?'

'I wasn't. Not really.' Eddie stands up too.

'I want to go to the vicarage,' Gwyn says, 'and talk to this woman. God almighty, there may even be something there which falls within the general curtilage of what we might call *police business.*'

Moira's sitting on the drumstool, the Martin M38 in her arms, hugging it to her breast and rocking to and fro, eyes closed, making a keening sound.

Like a seagull, Prof thinks.

Nobody has spoken.

The only sound is the keening.

The last sound was the sound of pumping breath. Simon's mouth on Dave's then wrenched away, a gasp of air and back down, and Simon looking up, shaking his head, eyes glassy with tears, while Dave's own eyes are wide and clear and full of frozen terror.

Dave is dead.

Dead in a flash. A single blue flash dividing the black air like a razor.

They've all known this from the moment of the flash and Moira's trailing, curdled shriek of self-berating, God-cursing outrage.

First the outrage, now the remorse.

Prof stares in disbelief at the empty booth, at the space where Dave lay before Tom bent down and lifted the body into his arms and Simon ran ahead and opened the rear door for him. They have taken him – although no one has said so – to the Portakabin, the oasis of space which is *not Abbey.*

In the air, a mingling of rich and awful smells, the obscene reality of sudden death.

Dave is *dead*.

Dave Reilly, who agonized fourteen long years over the killing of John Lennon, has been blown away even more suddenly.

Gone.

The booth is empty.

The walls and the vaulted ceiling are perfectly white again, and, if a little damp, no longer icy to the touch.

Prof remembers the verse Dave sang towards the end.

> *Echoes of slaughter*
> *The wine turns to water*
> *the water to blood*
> *the blood back to water.*

And the blood on the walls (*cemented* in blood, who said that?) turned to water and the water seeped down to the socket into which was plugged the McCarthy Dual amplifier on which sat Dave Reilly, as was his wont.

As Prof suspected, the earth wire has been removed from the amplifier's plug. This is not uncommon in recording studios, where earthing sometimes causes a hum.

The McCarthy is built like a packing case, with metal corners and a metal handle where Dave was sitting.

With who knows how many volts surging through it, the McCarthy chassis is a killer.

And so everything is eminently explainable. At the inquest, the coroner will call for a new safety code for recording studios.

So neat. All ends tied. A large wreath from TMM and a small obituary in *Q* magazine.

The keening has died away. Moira looks up. Her eyes reflect the pain Prof feels, and also the glitter of cold rage, white surf on a distant shore.

Prof walks slowly across to the drums. 'And we're both thinking, why did we let this happen?'

Both of them knowing he isn't talking about studio safety, unearthed amplifier flex.

'The optimism when you came back just now . . . the really good atmosphere . . . the way Simon scored last night. Dave thought, I know he did, we all thought . . .'

'That we were winning,' Moira says.

'What's so ironic,' Prof says, 'is he was more worried about you than himself. He thought it was you who was . . . under the shadow. He kept seeing . . . well, you know what he kept seeing.'

Moira's black hair has fallen over her eyes. She doesn't brush it away. She goes on hugging the guitar, as if she's absorbing the last essence of Dave.

'The one person you're never gonna see it on,' she says very quietly, 'is yourself. There *was* a death hanging over us – fourteen years ago, the Abbey was due a death. Dave was in the frame, through Aelwyn, and then this Dakota business comes through and he gets the hell out and the death passes across the studio and starts to hover over me.'

Prof decides he's no longer frightened by this kind of talk, just angry. He glares at the walls of whitewashed stone. The Abbey. The fucking Abbey.

'I felt it,' he says. 'I felt that death. When I heard the tapes.'

'Yeah. It can be just so . . . alluring. Like sleep. As simple as that. All you want to do is drift away. Moments of extraordinary peace. Ecstasy, almost. That's death at its most insidious. And I was headed down that road . . . and then good old Tom comes in with *the* most brutal guitar break . . . just like tonight's.'

'Why didn't it work tonight?'

'Because the Abbey knew. It'd happened once and the Abbey digested the information. It was Dave . . .'

Moira stops to regain self-control.

'. . . Dave. Who said something like, this is the oldest recording studio in the world. And he was right. It stores emotions and hatred. And blood.'

'If . . . this death . . . was *passed* across to you, where did it go next? Did Tom . . .?'

'Sure.' The words overflowing from Moira now. 'Tom thought he could deal with it. But when we came back here with Dave after his Dakota stuff, there's Tom striding around the courtyard rambling about the ghosts he's seen and getting more and more worked up – and everybody thinks the poor guy's cracking up. But Tom thinks – and I can see this now, isn't hindsight wonderful? – Tom thinks, *I have to get out of here . . . I have to take the death away from the Abbey and then maybe it'll, like dissipate in the fresh air or something.*'

'Only it doesn't work like that.' Prof is thinking of Soup Kitchen, who took death all the way back to their rooms in Oxford.

'No. I remember Tom screaming at Russell for the keys to the Land Rover. And I'm saying, no, hang on, and Russell – Russell just walks away, because the bastard, God rest his sordid soul, knows the keys are in the Land Rover. Russell's become an agent of the Abbey. Those who co-operate with the Abbey find they come to no harm at all in the material world.'

'Right.' Prof is thinking of a Rolls-Royce Corniche parked outside the Manor. And then a body hanging from a tree. 'I wonder how it caught up with him.'

'Something in the night.'

To counter a shiver, Prof walks quickly over to the glass panel and peers through into the control room. The spool is still spinning, although the tape has wound itself through. He has to destroy that tape. He doesn't want *that* being played to any inquest.

Inquest.

'Poor Dave,' he says uselessly.

'Poor Davey, poor Debbie.'

'Jesus.' Prof realizes. 'Tom was carrying the . . . the death . . . when he . . . when they crashed.'

He looks across at the booth where an amplifier became an electric chair.

Execution.

Crucifixion.

'*Way things are go . . . win*"

'That it then, Moira? That it for another seven sodding, fucking years?'

'Correct,' another voice says, a flat voice, matter-of-fact, without emotion or concern.

Sile Copesake has come in the back way.

'You can all go home now,' he says, 'if you like.'

No lights on. No sound.

Martin hammers again on the vicarage door. It's a flimsy, modern door with a glass pane in it which he wants to put his fist through.

Shelley shakes the handle. 'Vanessa!'

'It's no good.' Martin thrusts his hands deep into the pockets of his Barbour jacket, stands back, looks towards the upper rooms.

No sign of life.

Shelley is back on the threshold of a breakdown. 'Why are they *doing* this to us? *Why?*'

'I don't think that woman was lying. She didn't seem the type. She seemed sincere. This *is* the right place, isn't it?'

'No,' Shelley snaps. 'That's why it says "vicarage" on the gate. Oh, this is a nightmare, Martin. It just goes on and on, like this damned mist.'

'OK, look. Let's go back to the Abbey and get Tom out. It's his daughter. Time he shared some of the burden, don't you think?' Martin takes Shelley's arm. 'Come on.'

As they emerge from the gate, a tall man and a short man are crossing the road towards them.

'Another thing that bothers me,' Martin says, 'is Meryl. Where is *Meryl?*'

Prof says coldly, 'We were just talking about you, Sile.'

Moira pushes back her hair. Her eyes are red and swollen.

Prof remembers how they had to pull her gently away from Dave; she was holding him like she's now holding his guitar.

'And Russell Hornby,' Prof says. 'And Debbie. And Barney Gwil . . .'

'Hush, Prof,' Moira says.

'They're getting a doctor from the village,' Sile says in his glass-paper drawl. 'Just a formality. And the police'll have to be told.'

He never changes. Leather jacket, close-cut hair, stubbly beard. And flat eyes, flat as slate. About the same age as Prof, but he looks fifty, always has. The Godfather of the British blues.

Moira says, 'Formality?'

'Another tragic recording industry accident. Were you close to him, lass?'

A question entirely without sympathy. Like you'd say, were you at University?

'Yes,' Moira says. 'We all were. We're a band.'

Sile pulls up a stool. 'Mixed up character, Dave.'

'Like Russell,' Prof says. 'Like Barney. Like Debbie.' Anger lodges in his throat. Is this a human being?

'Never mind,' Sile says philosophically, as if he's heard none of this. 'He's at peace now, eh?'

Moira says, very calmly. 'You're saying he wanted to die?'

Sile shrugs. 'Like I say, another tragic accident in the recording industry.' He slaps his knees, as if to say, well, that's that. 'Look, if the rest of you want to complete the session, you can come back in a week or two.'

'But it doesny matter to you, huh?'

'No.' Sile rises lithely to his feet. 'You're right. It doesn't matter any more.'

Prof can't believe it. He's washing his hands. He's saying, Look we all know what *really* happened. Just be thankful it's him and not either of you. Because the Abbey's not particularly selective.

Prof wants to kill him and half-rises; Sile's smile stops him.

A small smile, containing just sufficient pity to make it a very cruel smile. What it says is, we're about the same age, Prof, but I'm a very fit man and you're a clapped-out alky.

Sile nods, pleasantly enough, and walks away. There's a barely perceptible snigger in the air.

'No,' Moira whispers. 'Don't rise to it.'

'Fuck this, Moira.' Fury courses through Prof like the electricity that killed Dave. When Sile reaches the Gothic oak door, Prof calls out, 'As we're unlikely to work together in the future, and just to show I'm not like Russell, I'd like to say something.'

Sile stops. 'Make it quick, I'm easily bored by engineers.'

'It's about the blues.'

Moira says, 'Let it lie, huh, Prof, please?'

'I just want to say, Sile, that I'm one of a lot of people who've always known why you needed all those young guns you brought into the band over the years.'

'Not what you think,' Sile says. 'Goodnight.'

'That you're queer? Nothing so admirable, mate. Reason you needed those young guys was to provide the one commodity you hadn't got. You had the voice and the technique and the image and the confidence. But what you ain't never had . . .' Prof pauses ' . . . is the blues.'

Sile's face darkens. From across the room, fifteen feet away, Prof can see it happening, like a photo going into negative, and it makes him feel much better.

Moira sighs. 'Don't do this to us.'

'The blues,' Prof says, 'is, like, a very *heroic* form of self-pity. The blues is without arrogance. The blues is having the guts to accept what you are. Like, I lost my woman. I drink too much. Tom Storey, he's got the blues.'

'I know. I taught him.'

'Balls. You wouldn't know where to fucking begin, Sile. The only blues you had was the blues you bought.'

Prof turns away, bitter moisture in his eyes. There's the crash of the door. When he looks over his shoulder, Sile Copesake has gone.

'Oh God,' Moira says. 'I agree with everything. But that was a mistake, Prof.'

Prof kicks vaguely at the partition of the booth where Dave died. 'What we got to lose?'

'You just don't understand, do you?'

'Everybody keeps saying that. I don't know what it means. Dave's dead. Dave. Our mate. You heard what that cunt said – the Abbey's had its seven-year sacrifice and everybody's happy. We can all go home.'

'Sure we can. And in seven years' time we can make sure we're all safely abroad on a skiing holiday or locked up in our houses with the central heating up full. All of us knowing that Dave, *our mate*, is part of the filthy fabric of this place now. Just like Aelwyn.'

Prof looks back at the death-booth, as if he might see Dave's tortured shade strumming into eternity.

'Prof, it's no' gonna go away. You think your nightmares will end? You think Tom's gonna go back on the road, three nights at the Albert Hall and then Wembley Stadium?'

'Fuck it,' Prof says hoarsely. 'Fuck Copesake.'

'But *not here*. Not yet.'

'What is he? High priest? Caretaker?'

'Whatever he is, he's brimming with power, Prof. He's just, like, lit up with dark energy. I never saw anything like this. He's like the man who just sold his soul to the devil at the crossroads. Except it doesn't happen like that. It's gradual.'

'He told Simon he was here as a kid. Evacuated.'

'Yeah, yeah, he found his spiritual home early in life. Maybe he had a small, seductive, black vision like that Walden guy, he . . .'

'He persuaded Goff to buy it.'

'Sure. And he almost certainly persuaded him to put together a psychic band. The Philosopher's Stone is Sile's product. A manufactured sacrifice, like sheep bred for slaughter. We're the Abbey's children. What he just said was, there's only one way we get away from it.'

'Like Dave?'

Never mind, he's at peace now, eh?

'Except we don't. You think Dave's at peace? Like Aelwyn's at peace?'

'I'm out of my depth, Moira.'

'Too right. Copesake can walk in here and sneer at us and send us away, knowing that he . . . it, the Abbey . . . can get us back here just whenever it likes. Whenever it needs a life. And that goes for you, too.'

'He's only a bloke, Moira.'

'And the Abbey's only a heap of stones. What kind of shithead *are* you, Prof?'

'This is not real.' Prof hooks back a foot and sends it crashing through the glass door of Dave's booth. Reality.

Glass is still tinkling when the top door flies open and Simon bursts in, followed by Tom. They stop when they see Prof picking splinters from down his sock.

'Well done, Prof.' Simon sighs in deepest weariness. 'I did that, once. Maybe we should act like a traditional rock band and trash the whole place.'

There's a brief silence before, with all four fingers, Moira plucks a ringing A-chord from Dave's guitar.

'Right then.' She puts down the Martin and stands up. 'Let's do it. Let's do just that. Let's invoke the destructive spirit of the great Keith Moon.'

Prof is the first to realize she's serious. He takes a step back as Moira selects a straight mike-stand, chromium-plated, with an old-fashioned solid base. She lifts it, holds it briefly above her head and then swings it around like an Olympic throwing-hammer.

'Look, Moira.' Simon tries to grab the end of the stand. 'I know how you must feel. It's just the police are going to be in here soon. You know what that . . .'

Moira smiles briefly. And then, with all the force she can summon, she hurls the mike-stand at the five-foot-wide glass panel between the studio and the control room.

VI

Home at Last

Meryl calls out, 'Isn't she lovely, Vanessa? Isn't she graceful?'

Are they hand-in-hand? She can't quite tell.

A glimpse of blue, a swish of taffeta.

But Vanessa's dowdy brown school blazer is almost the same colour as the mist among the trees and the stones.

'Don't go without me.' Meryl begins to run. 'I'm coming. I'm coming.'

Blue is the only colour she can see and the only colour she *wants* to see. Blue is a delightful colour, whereas brown's the colour of old, varnished furniture in the dingy kitchens of days gone by and the colour of Tom Storey's sad old father, the Man with Two Mouths.

Meryl can do without brown.

Perhaps, when they get home, the Lady will dress Vanessa in blue.

Meryl runs gaily through the fog, the little blue light dancing ahead of her like a gas-flame.

'Pardon me, Eddie,' Gwyn says, 'but this is one for me.'

'Look, are you really a policeman?' The crinkle-haired man seems harassed. 'Because we don't have a great deal of time.'

'Jones, Gwyn Arthur, Detective Superintendent.' Gwyn opens his wallet, holds it up.

The man nods gratefully. He tells Gwyn about the missing child, Vanessa.

'Vanessa?' Eddie Edwards interrupts. 'Are you Vanessa's parents? But I thought . . .'

The crinkle-haired man explains that neither of them, in fact, is a parent of Vanessa, an admission which makes Gwyn Arthur begin to trust him. And the woman . . . the woman is close to coming apart.

'If I can just explain, see . . .' Eddie begins, but Gwyn plants a large hand on his shoulder and administers a painfully meaningful squeeze: Gwyn would like Eddie to keep his garrulous Valleys trap *shut*.

He smiles encouragingly at the couple. 'My immediate thought is to follow you to the Abbey in my car, and we'll ask one or two questions.' Turns to Eddie, enunciating, 'I should like to see the Abbey.'

'Fine,' Eddie says, 'Fine, but . . .'

'. . . while my good friend Mr Edwards remains here, on the offchance that the little girl should reappear. And if we get no joy at the Abbey, we can consider calling out the troops. How does that sound?'

Prof has never liked violence.

OK, he's angry, he's frustrated, he's frightened. Yeah, he wanted to kill Copesake, yeah, he wants Dave's death paid for.

But not like this.

With the glass panel gone, it's clear that the wall between the studio and the control room is no more than a partition, made of several layers of plywood under soundproof wadding.

From inside the control room, Simon is hacking at it with a microphone stand, the end unscrewed to expose an edge of raw metal. He's managed to dislodge two bolts attaching the partition to the curved stone ceiling.

'OK, Tom?'

On the studio side, Tom jumps up and gets his fingers in the space between the partition and the ceiling and hangs all his weight from it. Prof winces. If Tom slips he's going to wind up with huge gashes across the fingers of both hands.

This man is a guitarist.

This man is mad. Everybody here is totally bloody mad.

Prof turns away to avoid a storm of splinters as, with a creaking, splintering roar, the partition and Tom come down together. Tom lies half-stunned on his back on the studio floor with about a hundredweight of smashed-up panelling on top of him. He squirms from underneath as Simon steps through the gap.

'You OK, squire?'

'Never fucking better.' Sawdust in Tom's moustache and a cold fire in his eyes that scares Prof. Nobody smashing glass, tearing down fabric, actually screams out, *this is for Dave*. They don't speak any more than they have to; it's savage, systematic destruction, grown-up people – one of them a minister of the church – chopping and slashing and clawing. If they had paraffin would they torch the place?

The dust clears, like after an earthquake.

'OK,' Tom says. 'Give us a hand wiv the desk, Si.'

'Hey!' Prof is shocked. 'No!' He's spent half his life behind mixing desks. 'You can't smash the bloody desk.'

'Sorry, Prof,' Moira says. 'Si, just make sure the master switch is off, huh?' This is the Moira who didn't want him to cause trouble with Sile Copesake. Who wouldn't condone a little sarcasm.

'Off,' Simon confirms.

The two horizontal banks of speakers hang forlornly in space as Tom gets underneath to examine the plinth into which the desk is built. 'Interesting. It is definitely stone. Tell you what, Prof, maybe we can just shift the desk to one side. If you get that end . . . triffic.'

'I'm not . . .'

'Just bleeding do it, yeah?'

A hundred coloured wires are ripped and snapped.

The desk is dumped, upended in the corner by the tape-machines.

Simon looks into the gap. 'You're right. It's stone . . . and it's old. Moira, what can I say?' He smiles thinly. 'You must be psychic.'

'Just save your breath for the masonry. The cops show up,

we're screwed.' Moira leans over and starts brushing rubble and sawdust from the stone. 'Something on it. That Latin, Si?'

'It's not even lettering, I don't think. It's some sort of symbol, quite crudely carved. Can we . . .? Thanks. It's extremely old, probably as old as the Abbey. It's almost like . . .'

'Almost like a tomb,' Moira says.

It's Lee Gibson who discovers the child.

As a rule, Lee does not like to go outside here at night, except to walk (if there were cabs, he'd take a cab) the couple of hundred yards between the studio and his apartment. Two reasons: A: it's cold as hell and depressing; B: these are goddamn *religious ruins* and they are kind of eerie.

Except tonight it's even eerier, godammit, a whole *lot* eerier, inside his so-called luxury apartment behind the admin office.

Like, they really think he's gonna sit there with one thin wooden wall between him and the probably still-smoking remains of the late Dave Reilly? A stiff? They think he's gonna share a Portakabin with a fucking *stiff*?

When he gets back to L.A., he knows, he'll be dining out on this.

(*. . . Yeah, and the guy's sitting on his amp, mid-session, when – thanks to British weather and the standards of British workmanship since the buttholes went into Europe – all this water comes cascading down the fucking wall and the amp becomes like,* an electric chair, *and . . . whoooosh . . . about ten thousand volts turn this guy's ass into steak tartare.*)

But meantime, he's gonna keep his distance until the cops have been and Dave Reilly departs in a body bag. However, no way is he gonna saunter among the crumbling stones until the morgue wagon hits the trail. He also would rather not mingle with the bereaved. Which is how Lee and his flashlight have wound up on the edge of the wood behind the Abbey.

586

Now, in Wales (Lee is still telling the story to the guys back home) even the goddamn woods are eerie. What's good about life in California and neighbouring states is that trees know their place and mostly do not presume to grow weird, bloated branches blistered with frost. And in places where it's cold, the trees are the kind which are considerate enough not to shed their green bits.

Lee's wondering whether it would be *less* eerie if he switched off his flashlight, or whether that would be the fastest way to plunge into a ravine and break an arm, when the beam finds Eyes.

Eyes full of mist and ice.

And Lee damn near shits himself. (Like, I was a tad surprised, you know?) Until he realizes these are merely big, thick glasses on the nose of a little girl, who just stares at him, probably totally stunned at coming across *Lee Gibson* in a small wood in Wales.

'Scared the life outa me. What you doing out, night like this?' Kid's not what you'd call properly dressed for the conditions. School blazer, for chrissakes. 'You lost? You want me to call up your mom?'

The kid says not a word; maybe she's in shock like every other bastard around here tonight. Lee eventually extends a hand, the kid takes it and holds on, like she wasn't too sure he was real. Like, would *you* expect to find *Lee Gibson* in a Welsh wood at night and *on foot*?

'Where d'you live?'

No reply. Lee guides the kid back on to the track. 'Hey, you can talk to me, you know, I'm not gonna bite. Who's your mom?'

This is getting nowhere. Lee puts his flashlight on her, takes a better look. About twelve, not too tall – kind of dumpy, in fact. Mid-brown hair, not too much chin . . . Hey, man, something not totally one hundred per cent right here. This kid could be what d'you call it, used to be mongoloid? Maybe ran away from a home or some place like that. The cops will know what to do, when they get here. And, shit, the way things are going, Lee Gibson is not going to be able to avoid witnessing Reilly's Last Exit in the long, low van.

'Let's move, kid. Hey, you like rock music? I do that. I'm a rock star.'

The kid does not seem over-impressed. The kid finally speaks. The kid says her dad's a rock star, too. And Lee says, 'What?'

Couple of minutes later, they arrive back among the lights. No police cars yet. But at least there's one friendly face in the canteen.

'Hey, Sile,' Lee says. 'Look what I found. Kid reckons she's Tom Storey's daughter.'

Sile, sitting on his own behind a cup of black coffee, takes a good, long, serious look at the kid.

'What do you think?' Lee says, chuckling. 'Maybe there *is* a family resemblance.'

'Where d'you find her?'

'Down by the wood, across the grass. She was just wandering. Doesn't make much sense, though, does it? How would Storey's kid get here?'

'How indeed?' Sile says thoughtfully. 'Let's get you a drink, luv. What would you like?'

The kid just stands there in the school blazer. Not a movement.

'How about a hot chocolate? Then we'll take you to your daddy, eh?' Sile smiles, obviously likes kids. 'It's OK, Lee, you can push off now. I'll deal with this.'

'More like an altar than a tomb.' Simon stands back, rubbing dust and mould from his hands.

'That figures,' Moira says.

They've exposed the stone, or as much of it as they can get at. It's nearly three feet off the ground, which allowed the mixing desk to fit snugly on top of it. But, because the floor is higher in the control room than the studio, it probably goes down another foot or so.

The stone they can see, with the faded symbols on it Moira thought was lettering, forms a kind of thick shelf. Simon slips his finger under its lip. 'If it was cemented down, it isn't any more.'

'We can get it off?'

'*You* couldn't Moira, but Tom could.'

Tom's sweating. He looks, not happy, but somehow in better health than Moira's ever seen him. Tom Storey getting to grips with destiny. He gives the stone a tug, grins harshly. 'Piece of piss.'

'OK,' Moira says. 'Go for it.'

'Hold on.' Simon holds up a hand. 'I, er . . . this is a bit embarrassing.'

'Spit it out, Si,' Tom says. 'We ain't got all night.'

'I think, before we open it, bearing in mind what we know of the history of this place, I should say, um, a prayer.'

'Shit.' Tom sits on the stone shelf. 'I keep forgetting. Pray on, mate. Pray on.'

Silly child. Disobedient child. 'Where have you gone?'

Panting, Meryl stops and looks around.

Mist and mist and mist. Grey mist, greeny-brown mist and black mist where the trees are. No *blue* mist any more.

'Oh, my lady . . .'

Meryl's alone.

Has the Lady Bluefoot gone off with Vanessa? Was Vanessa, in fact, the one to whom the Lady was attracted? Was some secret bond established between the gentle, scented shade and the strange, other-worldly child during the night she spent at Hall Farm? Is she – not Meryl – the one whom the Lady has come all this way to be reunited with?

Meryl moans aloud with frustration and anguish.

In the fog, she's become a tragic figure, cold and alone and betrayed. The fog has shown her the unpalatable truth: that the whole of her adult life has been a saga of self-deception. All she ever wanted were links with the Spiritual – a strong mystical dimension, a sacred source of strength and inspiration.

And the source has repeatedly been sealed against her. While people for whom the whole business is clearly quit abhorrent – people like Tom Storey – are the chosen ones. Outside the presence of someone like Tom, or even Vanessa, Meryl is nothing. It's all so crushingly unfair.

She doesn't see how she can ever go back to Hall Farm now, to Martin's kitchen and Martin's bed. It would be meaningless. The Lady Bluefoot was nothing more than a tease, a sensory trick.

Meryl kneels on the frosty grass, buries her head in her coat-sleeve and weeps softly. She's left the Abbey behind; there are no signposts, no pathways. Even the child has deserted her. It's cold and dark, and the vile fog clings to her like old sins.

But then,

swish

to the right of her.
But this time Meryl refuses to raise her head from the darkness of her sleeve despite

swish

to the left of her, but it will only be old, dead leaves clustering damply together in the hedgerow. And even if it's more than this, it will be just another taunt. 'Go away,' Meryl sobs. 'You don't want me. You don't care about me. You never did care. You're cold. You're heartless. Go away.'

And

SWISHSHSHSHSHSHSHH

Directly above her.
And the scent, lightly floral,
softening the mist, which caresses the back of Meryl's neck, eases her head gently from the crook of her elbow, and Meryl looks up, the tiny hairs on her arms prickling. And she looks up, the goosebumps rising. And she looks up, in the most sacred terror, to where stands the Lady Bluefoot in her gown of light.

'There's not enough light,' Simon moans. 'Has nobody got a torch?'

'Move back,' Moira urges. 'If everybody moves back we might be able to . . .'

'Can't hold it much longer.' Tom grits his teeth. He's raised the stone about nine inches.

'It's no good.' Moira shakes her head. 'We've got to get the whole thing off.'

'Look, hang on . . .' Prof goes down the studio, comes back with one of the stools. Now he understands, he wants to help all he can. Feels so bad at thinking they'd gone apeshit, even Moira. 'Tom, if you can pull it back about three inches . . . that's it.'

Prof has wedged the aluminium stool in the gap, but the metal is already starting to bend. 'Sod it.' Simon moves round to where the stool is collapsing. 'We've probably done half a million quid's worth of damage, we can go the whole way. Tom, if you get that end . . .'

Together, they push the stone until they've got it standing up. 'What do you reckon?' Simon looks at Tom.

'Drop it,' Tom says, and they let go.

The huge, ancient stone stands alone for almost a second before it keels over and smacks down on to the stone of the studio floor with a force which makes the cymbals shiver and the stone itself divide into a spiderweb of cracks before fragmenting in a muffled medieval duststorm.

Only Prof sees this happen. The others are staring into the hole. 'What is it?' Simon says eventually.

Prof takes a look.

It's like a compost heap turned over after a winter of rotting. Except it's dry, and what seem like worms begin to disintegrate when Simon puts out a forefinger.

'Wood.' Moira says. 'It's the remains of the tree on which Aelwyn was crucified. The deathoak.'

Prof recoils at the smell, which he can't identify. 'How do you know that?'

Moira shrugs. 'I don't. And yet I do. You know?'

'How did you know it was under here? Under the desk?'

'Davey. I could hear it in the song that none of us could

591

understand. It was just like we were . . . on top of it. Aelwyn. The crucifixion. And what Davey said about the oldest recording studio in the world. And what *you* said about the tape and its effect on you and what happened at the factory where you had it baked.'

Moira brushes dust from her hair. Her face is streaked with sweat and dirt. 'We might have a few extra faculties between us, but we couldn't create music that would do all that. When Simon said, why don't we just trash the place, I just . . . It had to be the studio itself. It had to be the Abbey. That make sense to you, as an engineer?'

Prof shrugs. 'If a fluorescent light can put a powerful buzz on to quarter-inch magnetic tape, what's this place likely to do to two-inch with twenty-four tracks to mess with?' He glances down the hole, doesn't like it and glances away. 'What the hell have I been mixing on?'

Simon says, 'Maybe this – by or under this oak tree – is where Walden had his vision.'

'Not God,' Moira says. 'Not the angelic host.'

'I don't like to think what he saw, but he needed a sacrifice. And then along comes the famous Aelwyn the Dreamer, bard and peacemonger. He's on the run, he needs somewhere de Braose can't touch him. *Come in, come in,* says genial Richard. *Sit down, have a glass of French plonk, give us a song.*'

'And then,' says Moira, 'one of the monks gets on his horse and goes back to this guy de Braose and says, "Hey, guess who we've got!" I don't think we need to go into the rest.'

She bends over the hole, sifts gently about with her fingers, looks up. 'Guess what.'

'He's here?' Simon joins her. 'I wondered about that.'

'These fragments are bone. Look . . . You reckon you maybe chopped down the oak and built this stone thing around it and then put his body . . .?'

'No room for a body,' Simon says. 'How about just his head? Maybe they put his head on the stump and erected the tomb around it. You can't tell from this mush.'

A shadow falls across the hole.

It is Tom. He takes a resigned breath and looks down.

After a minute or two, he begins to shudder rigidly. Moira takes his hand, holds him back.

'What they did,' Tom says slowly, 'is dug the original foundations around the roots. Can you see the roots? No? They chop off the poor bleeder's head and they shove it into the roots. So that the roots is, like, enclosing his head. Like serpents. Representing . . . well, we all know what serpents represent. And then they wall him up. Encoiled in evil. His eyes open, staring up into darkness. For centuries.'

Tom steps back, his own eyes hot with pain.

'We got to get this poor sucker out,' Tom says.

Squatting in bracken, Meryl is covered in blue light.

She looks at her hands: they glow softly blue. When she opens her mouth, she breathes in blue air.

She looked up once – almost – but the light was too bright and her head is bowed again.

Has she been praying? Did she pray to the Lady Bluefoot and the Lady answered?

Diaphanous curtains of blue, the luminescence of a grotto, fall around her. Like the grotto at Lourdes, recreated here in the wintry hills of Gwent. Meryl's whole body is racked with long shivers of ecstasy, a body electric in a cloak of electric blue.

Can she look into the face of the Lady Bluefoot, who stands so tall and still not three yards away?

Can she?

Dare she?

Meryl covers her face with her hands. Blue light seeps through her fingers.

Slowly, reverently, she rises to her feet. The Lady, her silvery-blue hair loosely bunched in a net, turns imperiously and glides away, those tiny, blue-shod feet lost now in the folds of her long gown, which falls into powder and tints the mist.

Meryl follows, bathed in grace.

Where are they going? Back to the cold stones of the Abbey? She thinks not. They are going home. Back to Hall Farm, where poor Martin waits, in mourning for his housekeeper and his house-ghost.

We're coming, Martin, we're coming.

The Lady Bluefoot flickers in the mist and Meryl hurries behind. The lovely ghost makes her own tunnel of light, and it's so warm inside that Meryl sheds her coat and lets the mist take it. Cocooned in blue, she skips across the bracken and down into frosted pastures.

We're coming, Martin. We're coming back.

Meryl dances freely, at one with the winter night. She glides over furrows filled with fresh ice, through a hawthorn hedge without feeling it, between the boughs of sleeping trees.

And she's waiting.

The Lady Bluefoot has stopped and turned to face Meryl, opening her arms, her long sleeves a blur of light.

Oh, yes.

They're standing on level ground in a clearing; no trees, no stones. The Lady beckons and Meryl hesitates for a second.

This is the moment.

Can she?

Dare she?

A blue finger is crooked.

'Oh, *yes!*' Laughing with joy, Meryl runs into the clearing, a roaring in her ears, a squealing – she's never felt so happy – and her own arms open wide to embrace . . .

. . . the rigid, bony shoulders.

To kiss . . .

. . . the rotting, withered corpse-cheek.

There was no way he could have seen her. Even Superintendent Gwyn Arthur Jones, following close behind in his own car, will testify to this.

Well, sure, they were going fast, both of them – a child's life at stake.

'*Martin! No!*' Shelley screams, and rams her back into the seat, instinctively bracing herself for the impact, thinking this will add reverse momentum as Martin hits the brakes.

But Shelley never thought this was how it happens, that it could be quite so horrible, as the Jaguar breaks both the woman's legs and throws her spinning on to the bonnet, so that her face is suddenly in the windscreen, wide-eyed, wide-mouthed, lips torn back over teeth smashed by the glass.

Shelley cowers as the car howls and lurches to a stop, full of headlights from behind, to show the empty driver's seat, the blur of Martin hurling himself out, leaving his door wide open.

She sits there, almost relaxed, for what could be minutes but is probably only seconds, listens to the soporific, low hum of voices. And then she quietly lets herself out of the car and walks around the bonnet on legs like sponge.

The woman in the headlights is flimsily clad for such a night. Her pale silk blouse is torn and soaked with blood. Martin is kneeling over her, his head buried in a half-exposed breast.

The scene shimmers, dreamlike.

Martin's sobbing. There's blood all over the breast and over his face. He doesn't care; he presses his face into the breast. He's shaking, his arms tightly around her; she isn't. She's very calm and still.

Meryl smiles happily through the bubbling blood where she's bitten through her tongue.

VII

Stricken Angel

The words *C. F. Martin & Co* are indented in the side of the black guitar case Simon carries out of the bottom door of the studio.

Tom, Moira and Prof follow him out.

'Excuse me,' Prof says, 'but I'm not getting this. Where is he going?'

'He's going to the other tower, Prof.' Moira stops in the doorway and they watch Simon stroll, head down, across the frosted grass, the guitar case swinging from his right hand. 'The tower with no roof. He reckons you can climb to the top and when you emerge you're above the mist line when the sun comes up over the Skirrid. When the sun rises you're no longer the Abbey's, you're under the influence of . . . something else.'

'But that's hours off. He's gonna stay up there until daylight? Just him and the bones?'

'Hopefully, just him and the bones.'

She doesn't sound too sure.

'You're worried, aren't you, girl?'

'Maybe. Just give me a few minutes, huh?' Moira walks away from him into the mist. 'I need to think.'

The mist lit by blue.

Gwyn Arthur Jones stands up, a reassuring hand on Martin's shoulder, to find blue revolving lights behind him. What's going on? He's not sent for any troops. Has that bloody Eddie . . .?

Blue revolving beacons, the simultaneous slamming of car doors.

'OK, just stay where you are, please.'

Gwyn recognizes them both. PCs Burwarton and Griffiths.

'Radio for an ambulance, boy,' Gwyn says. 'Come on, don't piss about.'

'I beg your pardon, mate, *we* decide when to . . .'

Gwyn directs his torch beam at his own face.

'Oh, shit. Sorry, sir, I didn't recognize you, sir.' The boy looks confused. 'What's happening, sir? We were told a chap had electrocuted himself up at the Abbey.'

'Were you indeed? Well, now you're dealing with an RTA. Get an ambulance.'

'One's already on its way, sir. For the chap at the Ab—'

'That's a formality, Kelvyn? Is he dead?'

'So we understand.'

'In that case, when it comes, get this woman shipped to Nevill Hall. Not that there's any hope here either. You'll need a statement from this gentleman. Be kind to him; she dashed out in the road directly in front of him, as I'll be confirming when you take *my* statement. Later. Understood?'

'What about the Abbey, sir?'

'*I* shall deal with that. And I'll be taking the lady with me. Is all that clear, Kelvyn?'

'Yes, sir.'

'Splendid,' says Gwyn Arthur. 'Come away now, Mrs Storey, there's nothing you can do.'

In the corner of the ruins, where it seems a bite has been taken out of the tower, where there are fences for the protection of the public and a sign that warns you to keep out, a shadow detaches itself from the wall and stands amid the rubble in front of Simon.

'You feeling brave tonight, Simon?'

Simon stops. The plastic handle of the guitar case is sweaty in his hand.

'Piss off, Sile.'

'Nice language for a vicar.'

'If you don't get out of my way,' Simon says, keeping his

voice tight, 'the vicar's going to take this guitar case and ram it up your fucking balls.'

Sile sniffs. 'That's Reilly's case, isn't it? Why do you want to take Reilly's guitar for a walk? Some mystical ritual I don't know about?'

Simon makes no reply.

'What's in the case, Simon? Aelwyn's bits?'

Simon says, 'I'm going to count to five.'

Sile laughs. 'Which film was that in, lad?' He puts out an amused hand to pat Simon gently on the cheek. Simon reels back, but he isn't quick enough. He feels a bite of cold air on the left side of his face.

Sile chuckles. As he walks away, Simon hears the click of a knife blade snapped back into the handle. 'That should fetch him,' Sile says nonchalantly. 'Good luck, lad.'

Her long skirt skims over the ankle-deep frozen grass; it's like walking across a hairbrush.

The thought of a hairbrush leads to thoughts of a comb held in dead hands on a white-clad, dead breast six feet under Scotland. And from there to loneliness, emptiness, helplessness, depression.

It would never have worked out with Davey, would it? All these years knowing they were consecutive links on the Abbey's chain of death. Well, she knew it – all he could see, presumably, was his own death taunting him as a black halo around *her* head.

You can't win. Don't ever think you can interpret the signs and the portents; you're always going to be wrong in one tiny crucial detail.

Oh, *Davey*.

She inhales a sob, seeing again that vivid blue flash which lights up the whole booth. And thinking of another blue flash, glorious delphinium blue, in a seedy room in the Clydeview Private Hotel.

Deathoak, breadwinner – all the clues written in neon.

Clues which we cannot possibly be expected, and certainly can't be *meant*, to decipher . . . until it's too late.

Being 'psychic' is a *son-et-lumière* of superficial special effects, so glamorous, and then you realize that it's really just a sick joke. That it isn't going to help you or anybody. Except maybe materially, and sooner or later that has to be paid for.

The great shadow-arches of the black Abbey of Ystrad Ddu are gathering like locked horns over her head as she walks into what used to be the nave.

Taking a last look back towards the north-west tower, wedged in mist the colour of wet concrete; even if there was a light up there, the top of the tower would still be invisible in this.

Up there: Simon and Aelwyn and Dave. Dave's guitar case, fragments of Aelwyn's skull. All seriously symbolic.

And they could just as easily be false symbols. That one small, crucial element could be either wrong or missing. It's all anyone can think of to do, to take Aelwyn and Dave into the light, and it's really such a feeble gesture against a tradition of hard evil going back eight hundred years.

She feels helpless and hopeless. What the hell are *you* doing here, hen? You directed them to the deathoak and that's your part over, huh?

It would probably be the best thing for all of them if she gathered up her things and left.

And dwell on it for another seven years? And then?

This is when Moira literally stumbles upon the body in the wheelchair.

Tom and Prof wind up in a corner of the canteen without much hope between them, only a pot of tea.

Prof rubs his eyes. 'I used to be an engineer. A month ago, I was just an engineer.'

He looks around. 'All this. All this money, all these wages. Canteen staff, admin staff. And at the end of it, they haven't even got an album. Just a decent man dead, after fourteen years of torturing himself. Dead at the appropriate time, in the appropriate place. The smug, bloody Abbey getting its seven-year dues. This is all sick and sad and deeply crazy, Tom.'

'It's rock and roll,' Tom says.

'It's only rock and roll. What we always used to say.'

'Rock and roll ain't as powerful as it used to be. But it can still make you fink you're superhuman. All music can do that – your classical composers, your Beethoven and your Mozart, all those geezers reckoned they was close to summink your average punter couldn't reach in a couple of dozen lifetimes. The Messianic Freshold . . . the point where music makes you fink you got God worrying about his future.'

'And drugs,' Prof says. 'Drugs took a lot of people to the threshold of something.'

'Yeah, well, some people uses drugs to get 'em there – to the freshold – and some need the coke and the junk and stuff to *live* wiv it once they get there. And some can't live wiv it at all . . . like that geezer Cobain, topped himself. But this is it . . . real musicians don't harm nobody but themselves. It's the other bastards, the businessmen and the conmen and posers and the hangers-on and the outsiders who want in. The people who, for them, the music comes *second*.'

'Copesake,' Prof says.

'Copesake, yeah. And guys like Manson – wanted to be a rock star, reckons the music's telling him to kill . . . to take sacrifices, right? "Helter Skelter" – overnight, a song about sex, wiv fairground images and stuff, becomes evil. Musta scared McCartney, that – finks, Jesus what did I *put* in that song to inspire this nutter? And this geezer . . .'

Lee Gibson has come in.

'. . . Just another session-drummer, and now he's a superstar and he don't know why . . . except it come frew Sile. And he's hooked, even if he don't know it, and he'll keep coming back, and he'll get more and more eaten up and corrupt, and he'll spread it, like a disease.'

Prof shudders. 'You sound like you lost all faith in anything good. Like we can't do anything to stop it. Can we?'

'Not a lot,' Tom admits.

Prof says, 'What happened to all you need is love?'

'Evening gents.' Lee sits down. 'Rough night, eh? Where's the kid?'

'No kids here,' Prof says. 'This seem to you like a suitable place for kids?'

'No, the *kid*. Tom's kid.'

Tom's cup clatters into its saucer. 'What you on about?'

'Your kid. I found your kid wandering in the trees. She *said* she was your kid. Little . . . er . . . handicapped girl, with thick specs.'

Tom's out of his seat, skin as yellow-white as his hair. Lee's leaning back, making stay-cool gestures with both hands. 'Hey, it's OK man, she's in good hands. She was in here just five minutes ago.'

'Hands? Who's hands? Who brung her here?'

'He's looking for you, man.'

'Who?'

'Sile.'

Tom has Lee by the front of his suede shirt, hauling him out of his chair. *'Copesake's got my kid?'*

Lee, shakes him off, looks annoyed. 'Fuck you, man, what's wrong with that?'

There's actually frost in her hair. Her face is almost blue. Her eyes are almost closed. She's slumped in the chair under a dark-coloured cape, and the cloth is stiffening around her.

'Holy Christ,' Moira whispers.

She doesn't know what to do, how to handle this. She looks around; no one in sight, only the obscenely sentient stones of the Abbey.

No hands are visible; she doesn't know, anyway, where to find the pulse. She starts to rub the woman's cheeks, gently at first and then harder. When she steps back, the eyelids raise a fraction.

The woman mumbles. 'Not flying, am I?'

'Oh, Jesus, you're alive. Let's get you . . .'

She pushes at the chair; it won't move.

'Stuck,' the woman says. 'Legs smashed.'

The chair is wedged up against a stone.

'Hold on.' Moira gets behind the chair and tugs, hard as she can, and the chair suddenly jerks free and nearly has her over. 'OK, now, I'm gonna get you into the warm.'

That's a laugh.

'Police.'

'You took your time. Got any ID?'

Gwyn Arthur opens his wallet. The security man opens the gate. 'Just the two of you, is it?'

'That's right. Come on, Sergeant.'

Shelley stares at him. 'Oh. Right.'

'Saves explanations,' Gwyn Arthur tells her. 'Now, Mrs Storey. I take it you haven't been here before.'

'No.'

'Me neither. Don't like these places. Now, before we go any further, a few ground rules. The impression I get is that relations with your husband are not what they might be. If it turns out the little girl is with him, that's where my role in the affair ends. Custody battles are not the police's problem, and if she's his natural daughter, but not yours, you may have to . . .'

'I understand,' Shelley almost shouts. Thinking, come on, come *on*. 'If she's with Tom I'll save my anger until I've got over being relieved.'

The main source of any relief, Shelley is thinking, will be if Tom is not the victim of the accident, the electrocution. Oh please, please . . .

'Good girl.' Gwyn pats her arm. 'Very sensible. Now, I do have other enquiries to make. They're not your problem, but if you can bear with me. Now, what's the set-up here?'

'What are those lights.'

'Looks like caravans. Temporary buildings, anyway. Let's check that out first. And don't forget, I don't know what your

602

husband looks like, so as soon as you see him, ID him for me, would you?'

'Yes. Oh . . .'

As they reach the Portakabin, they see the door is wide open, warm light softening the mist, and the outline of a man in the entrance.

'This him?'

'No, this is the bastard who brought him here. Case. Stephen Case, works for the record company.'

'Mrs Storey!' Case's face registers first astonishment and then a kind of relief.

'Where is he?'

'Mrs Storey, we've got a problem . . .'

'Is he dead?'

'Dead?' Case nearly smiles. 'No, he's fine. I mean he's not *dead*, he's just gone berserk.'

Not the same place.

Not the same at all, by night.

Simon licks blood from the corner of his mouth. It's been running quite freely from the cut Sile Copesake made in his face, and it's all over his hands now from trying to wipe it away from his cheek, and over the guitar case. Blood all over him and Dave and Aelwyn.

What made him think – this is the stupidest thing – he would be above the mist-line?

He knows what fooled him into coming up here. It was the image of the other morning, the remembered exultation of a coppery dawn.

It's a different place before the dawn, if the dawn ever comes again. The mist, if anything, is even denser up here, like the sediment rising to the *top* of the bottle. The mist is soggy and clinging and soot-black and it clogs his thoughts and stifles his prayers.

'*Oh God . . . let me in.*'

Simon kneeling on frozen stone, hands clasped together in

the time-honoured fashion. Telling himself, think soft lights and white linen, stained glass and the scent of polish. Think *cathedral*.

A droplet of blood rolls down his lips. His tongue instinctively laps at it. The blood tastes salty and somehow nourishing. What did Sile mean, *that should fetch him*, slicing into his face?

As if he doesn't know.

He tries to imagine the sky above the mist, with stars and a sliver of moon, tries to summon *clarity*.

But close by his ear, something laughs. A grainy, lascivious laugh.

He stalks the misty ruins like an avenging angel.

Well . . .

If angels had stubble two days beyond the 'designer' stage. If angels wore T-shirts a couple of sizes too small, revealing their hairy navels and unsightly, sagging paunches . . .

If angels had accidentally killed their first wives and lived with fourteen years of guilt and remorse and become reclusive and suspicious . . .

. . . angels would maybe look like this.

'*Copesake* . . .' the angel bawls from inside the blackened medieval ribcage. '*I'm gonna tear your head off . . .*'

Superintendent Gwyn Arthur Jones is leaning under an archway, lighting his pipe. 'Over to you, I think, Mrs Storey.'

'Yes.' Shelley shakes her blonde hair free of her coat collar. She's thinking of the years of struggle, of convincing Tom it was an *accident*, that Vanessa is a delightful little girl, with a delicacy and a gentleness and a beauty of her own . . . and was *not* retribution, divine or any other kind. That it doesn't have to be like this for the rest of his life. That if he goes out into the world again, it isn't a foregone conclusion that someone's going to get hurt.

As she walks towards the stricken angel, she's thinking also of charming, kindly Martin Broadbank, who had it all, who thought he could go anywhere with impunity. Seeing the final picture of Martin also stricken, sobbing his heart out into a dying woman's breast.

Tom has his fist drawn back, as if to punch the stone in rage and anguish.

Shelley catches his arm. 'Save it, honey,' she says wearily.

'You're Isabel, aren't you?'

'And who are you?' She feels numb, as if, under cover of the mist, the paralysis has spread up her spine. In panic she turns her head, it does turn, and she sees a low white ceiling, like a crypt.

'I'm Moira. I'm a friend of Simon's.'

Isabel looks back, in sudden misery, into the beautiful woman's tired eyes.

Moira shakes her head and smiles. 'I'm no' *that* much of a friend.'

'I'm sorry.' Isabel sighs. 'I don't know where I am.' There's wreckage all around the chair, piles of smashed stones, glass and earth.

This Moira, too, has dust in her black hair. She says, 'This is the studio. I know it looks like a building site, but it was the only place I could get you into. That chair of yours is kind of knackered.'

'Me, too, I suppose. I haven't dared to look.' Isabel finds a weak laugh from somewhere. 'Not that it makes much difference. Just means I'll have to wear one of those rugs across my legs, like a tarpaulin, so people won't be frightened and disgusted.'

Moira picks up the studio phone. 'I'm gonna call the canteen, have some hot tea sent over. You've got nice legs. I bet Simon thinks you've got nice legs.'

Isabel says, 'I don't somehow think you are the kind who patronizes cripples, but I really don't have any illusions on that score. I get the feeling that Simon would have liked them better if they'd been hairy and muscular and ended in a jockstrap. Tell me honestly. Is it really a mess down there?'

'Down where? This bloody line's just ringing out. Something's been disconnected.' Moira sighs. 'Maybe we cut ourselves off taking the place apart.'

'My legs! They're totally paralysed, so I didn't feel any pain when I smashed into that stone, just the blood, gallons of it, all over my . . . my . . .'

Her hands, pulled from under her cape, are astonishingly clean. No sign of blood. Isabel wrenches the cape aside, starts to scream. 'I don't understand! Moira, what's happening to me? This is a dream! I'm flying again! Hold me down . . . Touch me for Christ's sake!'

'You're not dreaming.' Moira grips her hand. 'I don't know how much you know about this place . . .'

'More than is good for me.'

'I can tell. Listen, it wasny your blood. The blood came from the stone. The *sense* of blood. This place plays tricks with your mind. Did you feel your blood was draining away through your legs? Awful weak, ready to give up? You didn't want to fight any more? Is that how come you let yourself fall asleep in the freezing cold?'

Isabel slumps. 'Simon. Where is he?'

Moira is silent.

'*Where is he?*'

VIII

The Big Taunt

Tom and Shelley in shadow, holding on to each other. A few yards away, in the canteen doorway, Stephen Case and Prof Levin watching. Gwyn Arthur Jones is in the admin office, examining the body of Dave Reilly.

'She stowed away?' Tom's face looking like it's melting. 'She stowed away in Weasel's van – to find me? Well, where's Weasel, then?'

'Tom, we don't *know* where Weasel is. That's why we came.'

'We?'

'Martin and me. Martin Broadbank. You went off with his . . . with Meryl.' Shelley's voice tails off oddly, which makes Tom bend his head to her, with concern.

'Oh, Tom, she's dead. I'm sorry. Meryl's dead. She was knocked down by . . . by a car.'

'Where?'

'Few hundred yards down the road, I don't know how far.'

'*Meryl?* Meryl's dead?'

'I'm sorry. She just ran out. He . . . it was *Martin*. Martin hit her. I was in the car too. We hit her. Just now. She just appeared from nowhere, ran out in front of the car. It was . . .' Shelley bursts into tears. 'It was really horrible, she was . . .'

'She was a good woman. She meant well.'

'Yes.'

'This is wrong. This has got to end.'

'I'm sorry. He couldn't have avoided her.'

Tom says suddenly, 'I wanna know where Weasel is. This little guy is my oldest friend.'

'I know. I know, honey.'

'If Vanessa's here, Weasel's here, 'less Gibson's shitting us.'

'He wasn't.' Steve Case steps forward. He looks very unhappy. 'The child *was* here. Sile . . . Sile asked me to get her something to drink.'

Tom whirls on him. Case puts up his hands.

'She wouldn't have a drink. She kept trying to run out. I stopped her. I thought, with her being . . . you know . . . I thought maybe she should be . . . restrained. I took her to Lee's caravan.'

'She's not a mental patient!' Shelley screams at him. 'Don't you know *anything*?'

'I'm sorry. I mean, I'm sure it'll be all right. Sile said he'd take her to find you.'

'When was this?' Gwyn Arthur has returned, very silently.

'I don't know . . . half an hour ago, three-quarters. Not long before Tom and Prof arrived.'

'And when he said he'd take the little girl to her father, did he imply he knew where to find Mr Storey?'

'Well . . .' Case looks awkward. 'It's not . . . I mean, I suppose it's not as if Tom is a particularly difficult man to find.'

'Took us all of half a minute,' says Gwyn Arthur. 'Indicating he didn't search very hard. Right. Copesake. Where's he from?'

'He's my boss,' Steve protests feebly, 'I can't just . . .'

'Oh yes, you can, my friend,' Gwyn Arthur assures him grimly. 'And you will.'

'He . . . Well, he lives in London most of the time. But he has a farmhouse, the Grange. You go out of the gate here and it's the first turning on the left. Over an old cattle grid.'

'Good. And has he a car?'

'He's got a four-wheel-drive thing. He leaves it at the farm, comes over here on foot; it's only five minutes.'

'Excellent.'

'What are you going to do?'

'I'm going to keep poor Mr Reilly company for a minute or two, while I use your telephone. Meanwhile, perhaps you could be thinking of an answer to two particular questions. Firstly, why would Mr Copesake want to, let's say *go off*, with Mr

Storey's daughter? I'm sure, given time, you can think of a fairly sound reason for that.'

Gwyn Arthur beams savagely at each of them in turn.

'And the other question: where, precisely, is our good friend St John, vicar of Ystrad?'

It's brutally cold on the stone platform. Simon doesn't try to fight it. He hasn't brought a coat or anything to sit on; knows he must not fall asleep. He has no Bible, no cross, no symbol of his 'faith'.

This is not his first vigil between midnight and dawn. He once spent the entire period on his knees, like new knights were supposed to in the age of chivalry, praying for spiritual guidance.

That was the night before his ordination.

The arrangement was this: just one impure thought, one image of Richard Walden removing his coarse, brown robe, and the ordination would have been off.

Richard – he was sure of this now – played along. And when the first red line of dawn appeared in the window, Simon swore his famous oath of celibacy. For as long as he should remain a priest, there would be no sexual distractions.

This was a problem in waking hours, but not (because religious thought could be a more than adequate replacement) an insurmountable one. And when sex, in various forms, not all grotesque, visited his dreams, he began to surround his bed with Bibles, sometimes imagining a ring or a square of golden light connecting them.

It worked. After a fashion. But after some years, Simon began to realize it meant nothing. It was simply a smokescreen for himself. His parishioners automatically assumed he was gay and no one seemed to object as long as the choirboys remained unmolested. One day, in fact, the bishop made a pass at him.

It was his personal smokescreen. And behind the smoke-screen lay the Abbey. When the living of Ystrad Ddu became available, he made himself apply, desperately hoping (but not daring to pray) that he wouldn't get it.

From that day onwards, tonight's confrontation had been inevitable.

Simon can't feel his nose, is sure his lips are blue. Is gratified to think that, in these conditions, his penis has probably shrunk to the size of an acorn.

Mostly it is dead quiet. Occasionally, in case he should begin to think he's alone, there's a snigger close to his ear, the trickle of warm breath. He doesn't move, doesn't resist it.

But he doesn't respond either.

Tom says, 'Look, about Meryl . . .'

'I don't want to know, Tom.'

'It was just . . .'

'I don't want to *know*. And you are never to ask about Martin Broadbank.'

Tom looks hurt. In fact, nothing has happened between Shelley and Martin Broadbank and, one day, she'll probably tell him; just now she doesn't feel that strong, dependable, utterly trustworthy Shelley Love is the person she wants to be.

She also wants him to see the common ground between him and Martin. They both killed their women on the road from the Abbey, perhaps even at the same spot. He is not unique. It was not his fault – everybody knew what a mad bitch Debbie was in that Lotus, even when pregnant.

'So where *is* Simon?' They're standing in the grass, half-way between the Portakabin and the ruins. Shelley doesn't even want to begin thinking about poor Dave Reilly, lying dead back there.

'Ain't gonna tell him,' Tom says. 'And I'm sorry, darlin', but I ain't gonna tell you, case you feel obliged. It ain't important, not to the cops.'

'All right,' Shelley says. 'The other question.'

'Sile?'

'I don't know the man. I met him a couple of times when he came into Epidemic to see Max. But I don't *know* him. I can't *imagine* why he'd want to abduct a thirteen-year-old girl with Down's Syndrome. I can't imagine any *bad* reason.'

Tom says, his voice heavy with dread, 'I can.'

'Tom?'

'Let me fink about this.'

'In that case,' Shelley says, facing him up, 'you can bloody well think aloud.'

'It's probably not right.'

'*Tell me!*'

Tom puts his hands on her shoulders, gives her a condensed history of Sile and his connection with the Abbey. He tells her some things she doesn't know about the Abbey. He doesn't dress it up.

'This is ludicrous, Tom.' Shelley backing away into the mist, her voice risen most of an octave. 'I don't need this. Just now, I don't need it. I want some sense. I don't want . . .'

'All right. See that man over there we was wiv a minute ago? His name's Prof Levin. He's one of the best. You go and have a coffee wiv Prof, steady your nerves and by the time . . .'

'Don't *do* this to me!'

'You don't believe me. You never believed me. You humoured me for years and you went your own way, and you fought, he's gonna get straightened out one day, yeah?'

Tom keeps his hold on her shoulders. She can't really see his eyes, but she knows they're staring far into hers.

'Darlin', this is as straight as I get.'

'Right,' Gwyn Arthur tells Case and Prof. 'Things are moving. The two PCs up the road have been detailed to take a look at Grange Farm. There are others on their way.'

'Dreadful night, yeah?' Stephen Case says. He could be talking about the weather.

'Put your handkerchief away, Steve.' Prof snorts. 'Not your style.' Steve gives him that you'll-never-work-for-me-again look and Prof acknowledges it with one finger. Gwyn raises an eyebrow.

He nods towards the ruins. 'Mr and Mrs Storey seem to have a lot to talk about.'

'Leave 'em alone, eh?' Prof says.
'I think you're right, my friend.'

Tom has been talking rapidly at Shelley, and the thirteen
grotesque years of her marriage have been leaping up at her,
wiggling their flabby rubber hands like grinning cut-outs on a
children's ghost train.

Tom has been talking about seven-year cycles of death
maintained since the year 1175, and Shelley just wants to run
away and bury her head in some distant pillow.

'See, we was supposed to all piss off, shattered, after Dave
died. And the studio sealed off by the cops, who don't give a
shit what's underneath it. Another tragic accident in the music
business – we kept saying that. But, fanks to Moira, we *don't*
piss off, we take the place apart and we find the oak.'

Shelley just wants a quiet, dry place where she can have
long, unpublic hysterics. 'Yes,' she says tightly. 'Yes, OK.'

'Copesake knows. He's bound to know. Bound to've heard
us trashing the joint. And then this wanker Gibson turns up
with Vanessa, and she just stares at him, all big-eyed and solemn
– you know the way she does?'

'*Yes*,' Shelley sobs.

'And it's the big taunt.' Clutching her shoulders tightly.
'Telling him, *you blew it last time too.*'

'I don't unders—'

''Cause we passed that death, like passing the parcel, Dave
to Moira, to me, to . . . to Debbie. But at the end there was *life*.
Don't you see? Life out of death, out of the flames. Life!
Vanessa! Life born out of the Abbey. There was life where there
shoulda been only death!'

Under Tom's hands, Shelley's shoulders start to give way.

'The kid's a walking taunt,' Tom says quietly.

'He's going to kill her, isn't he?'

Tom won't answer.

'He's *got* to kill her. Hasn't he. *Hasn't he?*'

'Nobody's got to do anyfing,' Tom says lamely.

'But by all the laws of this warped logic, the laws of the Abbey, he has to do it. That's what you're saying.'

'You told me to fink aloud. That's what I done.'

'So tell the policeman.'

'You fink he's gonna believe that?'

'*Tell him!*'

Urgent footsteps on the brittle grass, *female* footsteps, make Shelley turn, frantically hoping against hope . . .

'Tom? Oh . . . Shelley. It is Shelley, isn't it?'

'Hello, Moira.'

Moira says, 'I'm sorry, Shelley, I need Tom.'

Tom says, 'What's wrong, Moira?'

Moira says, 'Please?'

Shelley screams, 'You've to tell the policeman!'

'What about Simon?'

'I've been learning things about that tower.'

'Tom, you've got to . . .'

Tom turns to Shelley, squeezes both her arms. 'Darlin' . . . *you* tell him. You tell the copper.'

'Where are you going? Tom!'

'Tell him.'

'*Tom!*'

IX

Blues

They think he's a stupid, garrulous old man, retired from work, retired from useful life.

Eddie Edwards, unwanted, has been discarded, like the small, tubby child excluded from the football team and anything exciting, like pinching apples from Morgan's orchard – aye, he remembers that, too. *You keep watch Eddie. You can be . . . the lookout.* As if anything ever happened for lookouts to look out for.

He has been home for a warming cup of tea and to apologize to Marina, who looks not in the least concerned – even she thinks he's too old to worry about any more; what's he going to do in the teeming metropolis of Ystrad Ddu, find himself another woman, a hot number in a tight skirt?

Nevertheless, he goes back on watch. He promised – hardly graciously, but he promised (. . . *while my good friend Mr Edwards remains here, on the offchance that the little girl should reappear.* Pah!).

He feels the most bitter when the police car whizzes past with its beacons spinning. And then the ambulance. An ambulance! And then the ambulance returns. But the police car does not. Gone to the Abbey!

So what action have the police been able to take? Who was in the ambulance? Not even anyone he can ask. The street is deserted, the pub closed now, the villagers locking their doors in some relief – relief that an ambulance has passed by on the night of the eighth of December on a seventh year, and neither they nor any of their loved ones are inside it.

Eddie prowls up and down between the church and the vicarage. Once or twice he goes into the church – half fearfully, he has to admit, after the business with the candles. What if the candles are alight upon the altar and the church is fetid with the stench of human grease?

And why is it always so much eerier when you are alone?

He doesn't think he'll go back to the church again; not the kind of place a child would hide.

What is he thinking about? He *knows* where Vanessa is. Or, at least, who she's with. And if bloody Gwyn had not been so keen to shut him up, he would know too.

So cold it is. Eddie wraps his overcoated arms around his chest and stamps his feet. This is a waste of bloody time. He marches up and down the street, past the Dragon, closed now for the night and back towards the church.

And it is then, above the church, in the mist, that he sees the small, moving light.

'Mrs Storey.'

Gwyn Arthur turns away from the gate, beckons her with his pipe. A uniformed policeman is on the other side of the gate, under the searchlight. He is expressionless.

'And *Mr* Storey – where is *he*?'

Something has happened. Something horribly serious. Shelley starts to babble: Tom was tired of hanging about doing nothing. He's gone to look for Vanessa. She doesn't know where he is, but he can't be far away.

'Pity. We rather need him. Mrs Storey, your firm's vans – what colour?'

'Green. Dark green.' Real dread seizes Shelley.

'I'd like you to come and look at one, if you don't mind.'

'Vanessa?' Her voice cracks.

'No sign, I'm afraid.'

She goes with them in the police car on a journey lasting no more than a couple of minutes, over rough road. When they stop, the headlights reveal a farmhouse of grey stone and peeling whitewash. Another policeman is waiting by an outbuilding whose double doors have been flung wide.

Gwyn Arthur says heavily, 'I wouldn't normally ask you to do this but, in the absence of your husband and in view of the urgency of the situation, I'd like you to take a look at a body.' Shelley slumps in her seat.

They park in front of the barn, the headlights illuminating most of the interior: rotting hay, a rusting motorcycle carcass and, in the middle of the barn, one of the two dark green Love-Storey vans.

Shelley's breath locks in her throat.

'It's not Vanessa,' Gwyn Arthur emphasizes.

Even before one of the uniformed policemen swings the van doors wide, Shelley starts to feel faint, knowing whose body this is going to be.

Eddie remembers thinking despondently, I shall soon be too old for this. Be too old before Zap is too old.

He meant too old to use the narrow, stony footpath which crawls stealthily behind the church to the great clefted rock of Ystrad Ddu. Too old I am, certainly, to attempt it at night, in a heavy mist.

But the small, wan light still taunts him, glimmering in and out of the murky canopy, like a candle behind filthy old lace curtains.

The light is somewhere up there, around the clefted rock.

Out of the question. Too old, too fat and only ever picked as the lookout, the one rewarded with the most withered-looking apples in the haul.

Anyway, perhaps it's only a couple of the village kids, up there for a dare.

Really?

On the night of the eighth of December of a seventh year, with ambulances racing past and police about? The night of the locked doors and the TV-volume turned up high?

The night on which only the retired idiot, Edward Edwards, is out on the street?

616

And a small, sad-faced handicapped child. And a woman with both legs paralysed.

Do you really have a choice?

Eddie pushes a leather-gloved hand into his overcoat pocket and flicks on his Maglite.

He swallows. He's afraid.

Who wouldn't be?

The path can best be picked up at the far end of the church-yard, under whitened yews. He shines his torch up the path; it looks impossibly steep, slick with frost and has a big puddle at the bottom, too wide to get round. Ice on the puddle has been broken, shards floating like dead fish in the brown water.

Someone came this way.

And I'm too . . .

Eddie wades miserably through the puddle, feeling the water seeping into his socks. He thinks of Marina hunched happily over a fat fire, reading Danielle Steel.

. . . old for this.

The first diversion in the track is marked by a thorn-bush, as they so often are in this area. One path down to the village, one upwards to the great cleft. Among the thorns, twin circles of ice reflect the Maglite's thrusting beam.

Eddie stops.

He takes off his leather gloves and inserts quivering fingers among the thorns.

Bringing out a pair of large, round spectacles, with very thick lenses.

He almost cries out.

Nothing worse than this. It makes for a rare and terrible moment when, like a cold blade entering your chest, it becomes shockingly apparent that your very worst fear is one hundred per cent justified.

The lenses are rimmed either with the juice of berries – too late in the year for that, obviously

– or with some other substance, still sticky.

*

617

He doesn't know what time it is. He has no watch. But the dawn must be hours away yet. So the vague luminescence, which allows him to see the jagged shapes of stones at the edge of the tower – the edge of his world – is more likely to be a moon of sorts, beyond the mist.

Which means the mist is thinning. Maybe.

Or maybe that his eyes have adjusted.

But this isn't the main subject for debate right now.

The knocking is.

The bumping, a throbbing from somewhere. It goes on, it gets louder. It's inside his head, but it's also . . . out there. Out *here*. Within the boundaries of his world.

Simon stands up.

The whispers and the sniggers, from earlier, were in the air; they had no substance, aural will-o'-the-wisps. But this is a sound he hears. He *feels* it, like the beating of his own heart.

The stone floor is maybe twenty-five feet across, the spiral stairs emerging about fifteen feet from where Simon was sitting, his back to the highest part of the wall, the part least likely to collapse and leave him

flying

like Isabel and her lover.

The mist winds around him, like a gauze bandage. The noise comes out of the mist, and Simon takes a couple of steps forward. And stops.

A black figure wobbles in front of him. Not a shadow. Quite solid. A small, dumpy figure, pear-shaped, throbbing and oscillating.

It's the guitar case.

Standing on end.

Like a small sarcophagus, a child's coffin, wobbling in the grey vapour. Was this how he left it? A black moulding of fleecy-lined reinforced leather-effect plastic, perhaps four feet tall, standing on end?

No, he laid it flat. It was not on end. And there was no noise inside it. No rapping. No rattling. No insistent *let-me-out* clamour.

He wants to reach out and simply push the case over. But guesses that if he does this, it will burst open with an awful gasping, farting sound, and the contents – the grit and the dirt, the pieces of Aelwyn's skull smudged with his brains – will be exposed to the mist and whatever wants to come and pick at them.

Leave it. That's what it wants. It wants him to push it over. It's a trick.

Simon?

I can't hear anything.

Come on, pal.

The guitar case sways. Its front swells and bulges out and then contracts. He can almost see the indented maker's name, C. F. Martin, warped and distended. Hears the plastic cracking.

The case is trying to breathe.

Come on, pal, it's hot in here.

'I can't hear you.'

Damn, he said that aloud. Never let them know. Never speak to them.

He puts a hand up to the handkerchief he's tied around his face to staunch the blood, where Sile slashed him. Still there.

A peal of convulsive, cackling laughter is funnelled through the tower, whorls of mist shivering like huge shoulders heaving with shared merriment, while the black guitar case rocks and wobbles in giddy glee.

You want to. You want to let me out.

He shakes his head, so weary.

You want to let it all out.

'Leave me alone. Piss off.'

Shit!

hahahahahahahahahahahahahahaha

He covers his ears with both hands, rocking his head.

HAHAHAHAHAHAHAHAHAHAHAHAHAHAHAHAHA

Simon cowers back into his corner of the tower. Never react, never scream at it, never curse . . . never leave yourself open to negative emotions.

Think beautiful thoughts.

Oh, don't be so f—

No!

No impurity. You did it once.

Just don't fall asleep. Stay cool. Stay *cold*.

Simon lies on his back, a finger jammed in each ear, staring up into where the sky used to be. It *is* getting lighter, surely, the mist above him no longer pea-soup thick, more like mush-room soup. It won't be long, it can't be long now, and when the morning comes he'll open the case and give up the spirits of Aelwyn and Dave to the light.

Please, God.

Eddie takes out his handkerchief, shakes it and wraps the glasses in it, placing the bundle in the inside pocket of his overcoat.

He knows whose glasses they are. But they can't be. Unless Meryl lost all sense of direction in the mist and ended up here.

This is his last hope; that theirs was the travelling light.

He wonders whether he should call out. *Meryl.*

But if it isn't her, if it's somebody else he'll feel . . . well, stupid.

Stupid. A better word, this is, than bloody terrified. Eddie shields his Maglite with a hand, pointing the beam down at the narrowing path from which stones bulge like sores and blisters.

The path does not curve into the great rock, but slightly above it. To get to the rock, you have to leave the path, which is risky enough by day, risky enough on a *nice* day.

Too risky for an old, retired man.

He takes the path curving around and above the cleft. Got to watch it here; there's no fence; one slip and you're down twenty feet to the rock; come off the rock and it's a hundred feet into the churchyard.

The cleft. He's often wondered how it was created. An entirely natural feature, obviously; would take two hundred men with stone chisels about fifty years to carve it out. No, volcanic activity, this is.

And yet it's known – not far and wide, exactly, but certainly hereabouts – as an observation point for the Skirrid, perfectly aligned with the cleft. Take half a dozen steps either way and the holy mountain disappears.

Not a problem on a misty night.

This, however, this steep, curving footpath, is the most perfect observation point for the cleft itself. Eddie directs his Maglite to the start of the channel, on the edge of the coniferous woods and follows it as it widens and deepens into an enormous V.

Wherein lies . . .

Jesus God!

Eddie rocks on the path, has to clutch at the bushes to prevent himself losing his footing.

About fifteen feet below him, in the deepest part of the cleft, lies a small body.

Eddie panics. He pockets his torch and comes down the path backwards, on all fours, his feet scrabbling for purchase on the path, sending small rocks and pebbles skittering into space, hearing them bounce from the great clefted rock of Ystrad Ddu. Not standing up until he reaches the wider area from which the rock can be reached.

Leaving the path behind, he hurries across the scrub with its spiky tufts of moorgrass hard with frost and hauls himself on to the rock, a bare and icy moonscape in the torchbeam. Not much breath left, but he must reach her before he stops because *if* he stops, if he allows himself even four seconds to fill and empty his lungs, it's going to take him for ever to get moving again.

An old man, he is. Too old for this. He feels his face suffused with blood but his actual head light as mist as he scrambles down into the cleft and slips, and his torch rolls out of his hand.

And someone else picks it up.

'Providence, eh?' A man says, in a friendly Northern voice.

He stands in Eddie's path, astride the cleft, and kicks him in the face when he tries to get up.

Simon's eyes jerk open.

Mustn't sleep!

How could he possibly have almost fallen asleep, with the bare stone beneath his head? And the only softness his hair and the handkerchief around his cheek – not stupid enough to lie down with an open, bloodied face exposed.

Simon prays.

Oh God, protect me from sleep. Keep me cold. Protect me from impure thoughts. Protect me from evil.

'Do you know what this is, Eddie?'

Eddie tries to reply. 'Urrr' is the best he can manage.

'Sacrificial rock,' Sile says. 'Goes back donkeys' years. Before the Abbey, oh aye, long before that. What they used to do is lie the sacrificial offering – animal, man or woman – in the bottom of the cleft, 'bout where we are now . . . where the little lass is lying, to be more exact . . . and then they'd cut its throat, and the blood'd run down the channel and drip off the edge. Anybody at the bottom who caught it in a bowl, it'd be considered lucky, I presume. I don't know really. But guess where the blood lands now.'

Sile laughs.

'Church roof,' he says. 'Now that's what you call subjugation. Bit like pissing on them, only more so. Church warden, aren't you, Eddie?'

'Urrr.'

'Thought you were. You'll have seen the candles, then. Anything can happen, in that church.'

Eddie can't move. After introducing himself, Sile Copesake has given Eddie what he calls 'a bit of a working over' to make sure he isn't overtaken by any latent pluck. This has involved stamping on Eddie's face until it feels like a punctured melon, and administering further sharp, disabling prods to his stomach and, with a leathery boot heel, to the area immediately below each of Eddie's knees. Sile and Eddie agree that Eddie's chances of rising unassisted are severely limited.

'The Skirrid, of course,' Sile says, 'all this "holy mountain" shit. Bit of a myth. Mind you, depends what they mean by "holy". They tried. But where is it now, the famous Chapel of St Michael the Archangel?'

Eddie retches. Bile bubbles from his lips and lies freezing on his chin. He's too old to withstand a beating.

'Oops,' Sile says.

Eddie is lying almost flat in the cleft. Looking out, he can see a couple of lights in the village, fuzzed by mist. His feet are pointed towards the opening, almost touching Vanessa's feet. She's lying the other way, still on her back, her head almost at the opening. If she could turn her head – which she probably can't – she would be able to look down on to the church roof a hundred feet below.

Or she'd be able to do that if she had her glasses.

A dark blotch above the bridge of her nose may account for the blood on the glasses. Eddie tried to speak to her before Sile beat him up; she didn't answer but tried – incredibly – to smile. He wonders how much she understands.

Not too much, he hopes.

'She'll not move,' Sile tells him. 'She's too cold and she can't see a foot in front of her without her glasses. Shame, really. Nice kid. What d'you say?'

'Wharreryergon' do?'

'Think about it,' Sile says.

Eddie won't let himself think too hard about it. He reckons it's going to be Vanessa, poor little kid, and then him. *You can be the lookout, Eddie, nothing ever happens to the lookout.* He wonders what Sile is waiting for.

Or perhaps the Seventh Cavalry will come charging out of the forestry, where no one goes from one month's end to another, even in the summer.

Eddie wheezes. He thinks several of his ribs are broken. He closes his eyes.

There's a couple of minutes of dead, frozen silence. And then a small voice, a voice that is, somehow, not quite right, as if the tongue is the wrong shape.

'Oh, most faithful companion, appointed by God to be my guide and protector and who is ever at my side, what thanks can I offer you for your faithfulness and love . . .?'

Sile says, 'Isn't that sweet? Isn't that just the sweetest thing you ever heard?'

Eddie says, with a lot of effort, 'Bas . . . ard.'

'Not really, Eddie. Just part of a tradition. An old, old tradition that's there for the joining. We don't all wear robes and goat's head masks. We don't even talk about Satan any more. Who the fuck's Satan, eh? You've got to believe in *yourself*, that's what it's about. I found meself here fifty years ago. At the Abbey. On the night me cousin died. Fell through the roof reslating the barn. I asked for it to happen after the old girl said she was going to leave us the farm. Just asked. Didn't have to disembowel a white cockerel. Went and asked.'

Eddie's mind churns with a memory of Isabel after the Women's Institute Cheese and Wine Evening.

. . . just after the war . . . two boys, cousins from Leeds or Sheffield . . . evacuated . . . Mrs Price, husband died leaving her with the farm to manage and no sons.

'Went to the Abbey and just asked for it to happen,' Sile says. 'Downhill all the way after that.'

. . . do know the other came to inherit the farm and owns it still . . . Copeley . . . Copestake . . .?

Eddie doesn't want to know any more. More to the point, he doesn't want Vanessa to know. Doesn't want the child to die knowing that there are people this bad in the world.

'Wharrayou waiting for?' he almost screams.

Sile's shadow shifts on the rock. Eddie still hasn't seen his face. He imagines it as slablike, featureless, except for the eyes, swirling like oil in a burner.

'It's a two-way street, mind you,' Sile says. 'You've got to do your bit. And you've got to get it right.'

'Wharrayou wait . . .?'

'Don't get impatient!' Sile kicks him playfully in the throat. Eddie retches and retches.

Sile explains, 'I'm waiting for your lad, Simon. He's a trier. He's gone up the north-west tower with a bag of old bones to try and work some magic of his own.'

Eddie can't get his breath.

'But he's got a weak spot,' Sile says. 'A soft spot. For a thing called Richard Walden. Here . . .'

Hands snatch Eddie up by the lapels. Breath comes in an agonizing gulp, like swallowing a plum.

'Don't die yet, Eddie. I'll have nobody to talk to. I was getting right bored with our little retarded friend.'

He lets Eddie's head fall, with a sickening crack, to the stone. 'Aye, an example to us all in this day, was Richard. And tonight's the night when Simon opens himself to Richard – or maybe Richard opens himself to Simon. And when it happens, there'll be such a mighty surge of energy between the Abbey and the Skirrid that you'll feel it yourself, Eddie, even you. Especially here. Satisfied?'

Sile stands up.

Vanessa says, in a small voice, 'Leave me not then, I entreat you, but still comfort me in adversity and obtain for me the great gift of final perseverance and the grace to die in the friendship of my creator and so enter into life everlasting.'

'Sorry kid,' Sile says. 'No can do.'

Eddie hears a click and then the sound of friction, a knife on rock. An array of small sparks twinkles in the stodgy air.

'Amen,' Vanessa says.

Eddie could break his heart.

And sleep takes Simon St John.

For a long time, he thinks he's still awake.

He thinks the sky has acquired a blush of mauve in the east, harbinger of dawn. He thinks the air has grown warmer. His face begins to sweat, and he reaches up and drags away the handkerchief exposing the deep slit Sile has laid in his cheek and causing the blood to flow again.

The opening of the cut opens his mind to mysterious images carried on silken wisps of night.

The first, however, is the least pleasant.

It is a picture – a faded, sepia photo or a gloomy Victorian Gothic painting – of himself all scrunched up in his pathetic, single bed, a brass-bound tome at each corner. His muscles are twisted and his throat constricted; he can't take in air, except in thin, straining breaths, and it hurts when he tries to move.

Simon lies on his back, weighed down; he can't turn over. He can't get out of this on his own. He reaches out with both hands in a mute plea; his hands pierce the fusty vapours, smelling of mould and mothballs

and emerge into an atmosphere soft with musky scents.

He begins to breathe in deep, fulfilling draughts of air like rough ale.

And into his reverie, the knocking comes again.

you ready, pal?

Yes. Now it *is* time, he thinks, to open the guitar case, to release the spirits like birds.

'Be right with you, Dave,' he mumbles.

He doesn't even need to get up. The guitar case comes to him. He sees its black bottle/coffin shape shouldering through the pink mist, waddling across the white, shining stone to where he lies.

The guitar case bows, like a penguin.

The click, clack of the fastenings.

A shadow over the purpling sky. It opens.

It's never really occurred to Simon before how similar a traditional guitar case is, in silhouette, to a black-cowled monk.

Simon laughs in delight. It's been a long, long time.

Warm breath on his face. Simon's back arches and luxuriates on the stone damp with his sweat.

A tongue laps at the thickening blood on his cheek. It occurs to Simon he must be naked.

Desire rolls over him like coils of smoke. His arms reach out and he clasps the black thing and pulls it on top of him, his loins arching upwards.

Prof Levin is the first to see the glow in the sky.

He doesn't know this country, it could be anywhere.

'Time is it?'

'Ten past two,' says one of the coppers. There are at least twenty of them here now, headed by a uniformed chief inspector, a veteran, it's been said, of hunts for missing children across countryside.

Shelley watches them, she and Tom almost holding each other up. Since hearing about Weasel, Tom has said very little.

'Can't be dawn then,' Prof says. 'Tom, here, take a look at this.'

One of the policemen says, 'That's a bloody fire, mate. That's a forest fire, that is, and if we can see it as clear as this in these conditions, it's going some. Gerry, better get on to the brigade.'

Prof says, 'A forest fire? In *December*?'

'Well if it's not a forest fire, I'm buggered if *I* know what it is.'

Moira clutches a policeman's arm. 'Where? Where do you reckon?'

'No more than a couple of miles, love.'

'Tom,' Moira shouts. 'Shelley. My car. Come on.'

She feels sick to her stomach; she's seen it before. Once.

Tom and Shelley don't move, grey-faced and terminally weary, like two people in a bus queue who can't understand that the service has been discontinued.

'I'm not leaving you,' Moira says.

She's got the engine going, full choke, before Tom and Shelley reach the car. If the gate's closed she's going to smash through it.

'What's happening?' Shelley says, sounding vaguely glad that something is.

'I don't know.' Once through the gates, Moira switches the headlights off. 'Just keep your eyes on that fire.'

In her head, the awful aroma of flaking flesh, the crumbling silhouette. *Debs, Debsie, Debs* . . .

Tom is in the passenger seat, Shelley in the back. She wants them where she can see them. Doesn't want them going with anyone else – two other cars are already following her. A fire in the hills, in December, too much of a coincidence.

'Whatever happens,' Moira instructs them, 'you must stay together.'

'I don't know what you mean,' Shelley says. 'Moira . . .'

The glow in the sky is orange and white; to Moira, on first sight, the gases seemed, just for a moment, to form the shape of a giant harp.

Tom says gruffly, 'Keep me away from the fire.'

In December?

Not even on a balmy August evening, it's being said, have so many people left their homes and crowded into the single street of Ystrad Ddu. Overcoats over pyjamas. People pointing, children squealing. Behind it all, a coarse roaring, like a giant blow-heater.

The Dragon has thrown open its doors again; the police clearly don't care. Cars clog the street; nobody gets out the other side. Moira stops the old BMW in the middle of the road and stands, bewildered, in the V of the open driver's door.

Lights in every house, curtains thrown back, people hanging out of windows. Water drips from roofs and guttering; the accumulation of humanity has raised the temperature – or, more likely, it's the heat from above.

A woman is to be seen roaming the crowds with a sheepdog on a lead shouting, 'Eddie? Has anybody seen Eddie?'

Confusingly, the scene recalls for Moira images from the fax Davey sent about the chaos in Liverpool when the power failed last December.

But there's power here. A terrible, savage, relentless energy. Above the village, a hissing wall of flame, the forest alight from end to end.

Voices floating in the mingled mist and smoke.

'. . . about evacuation? If it . . .'

No way. 'Won't spread down yere. Nothing to catch light on the rock, see. Go straight down the hill, it will, and the river'll keep it on . . .'

'. . . far's the Abbey, maybe.'

'. . . fireball. Honest to God. Ball of lightning. Freak thing, got to be.'

'. . . No, I didn't see it, but the wife's mother said it come rolling down off the Skirrid, so bright you couldn't look at it, see. Had to turn away.'

'How come *she* seen it, then, you had to turn away?'

'Fuck knows. Eyes in the back of her head, the wife's mother.'

A man in a Barbour jacket detaches himself from a knot of spectators, walks into the road and peers into Moira's BMW through a side window almost opaque with condensation. Shelley opens the car door. She can barely find the energy to shake her head in answer to the question swimming in Martin's eyes. She gets out. 'How were the police?'

'Put it this way, if it wasn't for our friend Jones, I think I'd be spending the night in a cell.' Martin doesn't sound as if he cares one way or the other. 'When they learned that Meryl and I were . . . linked, it became quite difficult.'

'How did they learn?'

'I told them.'

'As you would.'

'Don't make me out to be honest, Shelley. If I'd been totally honest, none of this would have . . .'

'Yes it would.' Shelley presses his arm. 'Nothing could stop it.'

Above the village, the fire rushes through the forest as if powered by giant bellows.

'Tom?'

Moira gets back into the car with Tom. He is staring straight ahead through the windscreen. He shows no interest in what's happening outside, might as well be stuck in a traffic jam on the M4.

'Anything?'

Tom looks down, rubs his eyes.

'Nuffink. Can't get . . . wevver it's the smoke or what. I don't like fire. I told you, keep me away from the fire, so you brung me here.'

'Let's try something. Come on.'

'Ain't moving. Don't like fire.'

'Tom, I know you don't like fire. Where we're going you won't see the fire.'

Moira takes his hand, leads him out of the car, along the street, past a couple of men at the roadside with pints of beer from the Dragon – festival time in Ystrad Ddu.

Tom doesn't once raise his gaze from the tarmac.

'Where we going?'

'To church.'

'Why?'

'Find some peace and quiet. Away from the fire. OK?'

Sometimes you have to treat Tom like a large kid. She leads him through the churchyard to the stone shed that passes for a church in this village. The door is unlocked.

Because the church is half under the rock, the light through the plain Gothic windows is only faintly blushed. They can't hear the roar from above which made the street sound like it was under a motorway.

'This place OK, do you think?'

Tom sniffs. 'See some action. I reckon it's OK.'

Moira digs a box of matches from the pocket of her long

skirt and approaches the two long, white candles on the altar. 'These OK?'

Tom nods. She lights both candles. Shadows rear. Tom sits on a wooden chair, head bowed, hands in his lap.

Moira waits.

The candle flames don't waver. Serene spears sending wisps of smoke towards the ceiling, which complete the illusion of a sacred shed – a minimum of crossbeams and then the roof slates, edged now with rosy light.

No wonder it's cold. Moira hugs herself, wishing she'd borrowed Isabel's woollen cape or something.

'Dad,' Tom says.

'Dad? Whose dad?'

come on then, Dad.

Keeps calling him 'dad' in that sarky voice.

'Get off my arm. Who are you?' Eddie splutters.

don't ask so may fuckin' questions.

'Not from round here, are you?'

that's true.

'Your friend's not saying much.'

he's new.

'In the fire brigade? Are you the fire brigade? What's going on?'

A hush has enfolded the street.

Nobody wants to breathe.

'Oh . . . my . . . Christ.' A lone, female voice.

The great clefted rock of Ystrad Ddu gleams like the metal apron in front of an open furnace.

Two figures on the very edge.

A buxom woman with blonde hair in a bell-shape rushes out into the middle of the road.

'*Noooooooooooooooooooooooooooooo*'

631

And then a third figure. Some people will swear later that they saw a third figure in the half-second before the blue lights and fire sirens.

Tom stands up slowly, carefully straightens the flat cushion on the wooden chair. His eyes have clouded. He beckons Moira to the altar.

She unwinds from a pew, shakes out her skirt. 'We gonna pray, Tom?'

'Too late,' Tom says glumly. Moira takes his hand; it's deathly cold, as if there's been no blood through it in hours. Something's over. He's not resisting any more; just standing there without expression, swaying like a big, rubber toy. Moira is reminded of Donald the gypsy, the last time she saw him, on the steps of the Duchess's caravan, soon to be stripped and sold.

The candle flames jerk sideways as the church door is thrust open. A policeman stands in the opening with another man – incongruously, Steve Case, straggly grey hair around his ears from a dismembered pony-tail.

The policeman nods towards Tom.

'This the dad?'

Case nods and steps inside the church. 'Tom . . .'

Tom says, 'Fuck's sake, geddout.'

'Look, sir,' the policeman says, 'I think we're going to need . . .'

There's a mass gasp from outside. A couple of seconds later, with a sound like a bomb in a crockery shop, the roof implodes.

Amazingly, when the dust starts to settle, the two altar candles are still alight.

'Stop!' A police-sounding shout. 'That's far enough. Nobody comes in.'

The policeman already inside, now crouching by a pew-end, says, 'Jesus,' and puts a hand over his mouth.

Moira pulls hair and dust from her eyes. At first she sees

only slates, dozens of them all over the pews and the stone floor, slates splintered into shards and arrows and needles.

And then she looks up.

'Holy shit,' she whispers.

Tom strolls to where the body hangs over a suspended crossbeam, so perfectly balanced it's actually swinging gently.

Tom stoops to peer into the face.

'Shit is right,' he says.

Most of the skin has been torn from one side of the face, slivers of slate projecting like stubble. The head is smashed and a grey ooze seeps into the eyes. The jaw is hanging off. Moira turns away as two or three discoloured teeth hit the stone floor with a ticking sound.

Over the noise of her own vomiting, she hears Tom say to the policeman, 'If he ain't got the blues by now . . .' on his way out.

And then the policeman starts to vomit. He's seen Steve Case up against a wall pulling from his left eye a two-inch sliver of slate. And something hanging out on a membrane and glistening looks very much like the eye itself.

Tom and Moira are out on to the road in time to see the firefighters reach Vanessa with their ladders.

She seems to be waiting for them quite calmly.

Shelley stands at the bottom of the ladder.

Moira says, 'You knew, huh?'

'Nah,' Tom says. He looks embarrassed.

Epilogue

S imon, spent in soft flesh, moist with a mingling of sweat and musk and mysterious tears, whispered, 'I don't understand.'

The sky was a deep, deep red, hung with curling rags of mist.

Another whisper, close and warm and full of wonder. 'Have you never heard of magic?'

He remembered the black, wobbling thing looming unsteadily across the stone parapet.

This?

The not-so-distant flames dancing in eyes close to his. Simon felt angry, deceived. 'I don't f . . . I don't understand.'

'Well, there's a bloody change. That's been the phrase on everybody's lips for days, except for yours. Oh, *Simon* understands. Simon understands *everything*.'

Simon closed his eyes. He didn't dare believe. About the rapture. That the rapture was no longer dark.

'You're not real.'

'I don't know which way to take that.'

Simon peered over the tower's edge. Far below, under the mist line, he could make out small patches of burning grass, like campfires. The fire had limped down from the hill, its wrath expended. It didn't quite reach the Abbey, but the warning was implicit.

He said, 'You're enjoying this, aren't you?'

'I'm flying,' Isabel said.

The dawn came again in a tight, bright line, like copper wire between two terminals.

Simon rose, shivering, and went to the guitar case, lying flat, just as it had been throughout the night.

He looked back at Isabel, also shivering now, inside Moira's black anorak in the south-eastern corner of the tower where they'd lain.

Lain.

He felt amazingly light-headed. He was trembling, but a grin was shuffling, half-embarrassed, across his face. To stop his hands from shaking, he picked up the guitar case and carried it across to the woman.

'If you don't tell me the truth,' he said carefully, 'I'm going to empty Aelwyn the Dreamer all over you.'

'Oh my God!' Isabel mock-cowered. 'All right. Tom. Tom, it was. Moira got Tom to carry me up. Over his shoulder, like a fireman. All those steps. All sixty-odd of them, poor dab. The cape was too big and cumbersome, so I borrowed Moira's coat.'

Isabel smiled, seemed about to say something flip and then went solemn. 'It was the only hope we had, Simon. Either of us. Tom wanted to stay with me, at least until we knew if you were . . . Anyway, I said, just leave me at the top and then get off down, quietly.'

He looked around the stone space. No wheelchair. Of course there wasn't. So how . . .?

'On my bum,' Isabel said. 'Very slowly. You were asleep. Moaning a lot. Disgusting.'

Simon said suddenly, 'Did you . . .? Look, did you lick the blood from my face?'

'What?'

'Where the cut is. Did you lick it off?'

Isabel bit her lip. 'No. I didn't do that.'

Simon went cold. He felt pressure in the palms of his hands. Who licked the blood? *Who had been drawn to the vapours of the blood?*

'Isabel,' he said in a hell of a rush. 'I had this dream. Seems a long time ago now. In the dream, I had to choose between you and Richard Walden. I pushed you off the tower. This was a dream.'

'You didn't push me off last night,' Isabel said simply.

'No. I didn't, did I? Why?'

'Thanks very much.'

'No, I mean . . . I mean, Christ, you were taking a hell of a risk because this is *his* place, and you knew that. At night, this is . . .'

The thoughts came frantically, elbowing each other out of the way. *This isn't how it happens. This is wrong. Something's terribly wrong. Trickery. Deception. It's not over. Not over* . . .

'Put that case down,' Isabel said, 'and come back and hold me.'

He sat down next to her. It was colder now, a hard December morning. She'd put most of her clothes back on. Still, as soon as he touched her, his jeans felt too tight again. It couldn't last. He kissed her. 'Don't start me off, Vicar,' Isabel said.

Simon held her, with desperation.

'I dragged myself across,' she said. 'On my bum. I leaned over you. Nearly passed out, you smelled so revolting. Like . . .' Isabel wrinkled her nose '. . . Well, shit, if you really want to know. And bad breath. And . . . body smells. All around you. All over you. It was like finding a dead body, and it's all decayed. I couldn't touch you. I didn't want to go near you. It was the most horrible moment of my life – that's saying something. I hated you.'

She stiffened slightly in his arms.

'Dragged myself to the edge of the tower and just leaned over, right over, desperate for some fresh air, and . . .'

Simon tensed at the image, felt the heat of her on his cheek.

'. . . came over dizzy. I *did* want to jump off. Thought about flying. All there was left to do. Dragged myself to the very edge. I thought, everything I ever want turns to shit.'

He said nothing. For years he'd felt that was all there was inside him. Shit. Rottenness.

'. . . going to let myself go. Just, you know, overbalance. And then something made me look up and . . . You ever tell this to anyone else, Simon . . .'

'Go on.'

'I saw the Skirrid. I didn't think you could see it from here, I mean, it was dark last time . . .'

'It was dark *this* time. And foggy.'

'. . . and it was white. All white. Like the Matterhorn or something. It was beautiful. Blazing white. For about . . . half a second? A quarter of a second? I mean, gone . . . but you went on seeing it. I can see it now. All white. And it reminded me.'

Isabel dug a hand into a pocket of Moira's anorak. 'Another dry cleaning bill.'

'What is it?'

'Soil. Still a few grains, see. Poor Meryl collected it in a binsack up on the Skirrid. She gave me a sackful to bring to the Abbey, but I felt stupid about it. The sack, that is. Wheeling myself in here with a sack. So what I did, I unscrewed part of the wheelchair frame and packed it with soil. Bloody thing went like an old lawnmower after that and . . . oh, I crashed it eventually, that's not the . . . Anyway, I unloaded as much of the soil as I could get into the coat pocket – that was another reason see, the cape didn't have pockets – and when the Skirrid lit up, I dragged myself back and spread the soil in a bit of a circle around you.'

Simon's eyes widened.

'And then I imagined the light . . . a circle of light around us.'

'Who told you to do that?'

She's a witch, he thought. Maybe all women are witches.

Isabel looked away. 'Sounds daft now.'

'I am out my depth,' Gwyn Arthur admitted. His pipe had gone out. There were too many people around.

Vanessa was on the vicarage sofa, between her father and his wife. She was wearing a nightie, a grey blanket around her shoulders. She looked about nine.

All right, fireball hit the hillside, igniting the woods. Fine so far.

Silas Copesake seeming oblivious of this? Well, yes, we are dealing here with a demented person, schizophrenic maybe. No problem with that.

But no way was Eddie Edward's official testimony going to contain references to a loose shadow around Copesake, like a dressing-gown (or a monk's robe), or to a hulking thing which appeared at first like a column of brown smoke rising from the smouldering woods, and began to glow only when it smiled.

Smiled *twice*. With two mouths.

Oh no. No indeed. None of that.

And what about the flames roaring up behind them and this little girl, Vanessa, calmly reciting a prayer to her guardian angel while Copesake was sharpening his sacrificial Swiss Army penknife to release her blood?

He needed the blood, see. The monk needed the blood.

Oh no. None of that.

And nothing about the column of brown smoke interceding, bending over her, the little girl lifted up as if on a cushion of murky, swirling air.

A moment of violence. Frenzied. *Like a street-fight, Gwyn, just like that . . .*

Before Copesake was over the edge.

All this time, Eddie lying there in the cradle of rock. Pretty badly beaten, couldn't get up, certain the flames would have him. And thinking, irrationally, about the glasses.

When the fireball, or whatever it was, hit the hillside, he'd struggled to a sitting position and taken the opportunity to give Vanessa her glasses, which he'd found earlier.

But they were the wrong glasses, see. They didn't fit. Too big. She gave them back, Gwyn. And then afterwards, when Copesake is over the edge, I'm being helped away by these two men. And one says – funny Northern accent – 'Hey, Dad, you found me glasses.' Just like that. And he takes them off me and puts them on. 'Blind as a fuckin' bat without me glasses.'

Gwyn Arthur Jones, detective superintendent, leading the inquiry into the death of Silas Copesake, blues singer, company director and probable murderer. Did he fall or was he pushed? And who the hell really cared?

Gwyn cared. And the reason he cared was that he was going

to have to compile reports for at least four inquests: Silas Copesake, Eric Beasley, the woman, Meryl, and the musician, David Reilly.

The way things were going, these reports were going to read like plots rejected as too far-fetched by the Brothers Grimm. Even the weather and atmospheric conditions made no sense: freak thunderbolts and ball-lightning, hints of seismic activity.

They say the Skirrid was cleft at the very moment of . . .

Oh, God, don't even *suggest* it.

'Not going to talk to me, is she?' Gwyn said to Tom Storey.

'Give her a day or so, mate,' Tom Storey said. 'Good night's sleep. Works wonders, dunnit?'

Gwyn pocketed his pipe and stood up. His best witness, a Down's Syndrome child. And yet, why did he think that when he'd gone, she'd be able to tell her dad *precisely* what had occurred?

He wandered into the vicarage garden. The air stank. Didn't they say fire was a purifying force? Didn't smell like it, but who could say?

Only Eddie Edwards, worst luck.

The other witness.

Eddie was at the hospital now, having his ribs strapped up. Gwyn hoped someone would have the sense to do the same to his mouth. Certainly, before Eddie made any formal statement, Gwyn was going to have to have a discreet word – indeed, make a few discreet threats. One way or another, Eddie's natural sense of drama would need to be severely curbed.

Gwyn's brain was still congested with the irrational discharge from the old chap when he'd stumbled into the churchyard.

Well, all right, could have been a couple of villagers. Gwyn had instructed his foot-soldiers to try and find them.

And they take an arm each, these two chaps, and they haul me out of the trench – me feeling like the pensioner who doesn't want to cross the road. What about the little girl? Who's going to bring her down? But they insist – dragging me away, they are. And now they've gone . . .

Gwyn remembered Eddie sitting on the churchyard wall,

looking around as though he might see the two men. And what did they look like, these two?

I . . . don't know. Didn't get a good look at them, see. One was doing all the talking. Merseyside, his accent, I think. Sure I know the voice . . . from somewhere. And the other . . . all I remember about him was he was wearing a white scarf . . .

At just after eight, there were footsteps on the spiral staircase and Moira arrived on the roof. She was alone.

A couple of hours ago, Prof Levin had stepped between the patches of smouldering grass and shouted up to see if they were OK. Simon had shouted back and waved. He thought he'd seen Prof grin through his white beard.

Now Moira said, 'You two get to go down in style. They're calling in one of the builders' guys to work that platform crane thing they were using to reroof the other tower.'

'I could carry her down the stairs,' Simon said.

'And break your back!' said Isabel. She laughed lightly. 'I won't be walking down either. But that's the way of things, isn't it? First you learn to fly, and then you think about learning to walk.'

'Where exactly are you paralysed *from*?' Moira asked curiously. 'If I'm not being intrusive.'

'Perhaps not quite as high up as I imagined,' Isabel said with a self-conscious little smile.

Moira looked at Simon. Expressionless. Kind of.

'But then,' Isabel said, 'they do say it's all in the head, isn't it?'

'And the heart,' Moira said. 'Don't forget the heart.'

Moira told them everything she knew, a lot of what she guessed and a few things she just hoped. She told them about Meryl, which distressed Isabel. She told them about Stephen Case, who was in hospital and would probably lose an eye. And Eddie, whose ribs were strapped up.

Simon said. 'How is he, you know . . . otherwise?'

'Pretty shaken up, I'm told. Nobody's been able to explain what happened. Just as well, huh?'

She told them about Vanessa, who was safe. And Sile, who was dead.

'I looked in Vanessa's eyes,' Isabel said. 'Last night, this was, the last time I saw her. I felt I could see flames.' She shook her head. 'Very, very strange.'

Simon thought about Isabel's circle of sacred soil and what had happened inside it. A little outpost of the holy mountain at the heart of the blackness. A tiny circle of love and redemption from which the evil had been banished.

And so had accumulated around Sile Copesake, like a cloud of flies around a turd.

And had they gone down together, Sile and Richard?

'You're going to have to get me out of here, Isabel,' Simon said. 'I've probably seen too much to be a vicar.'

People were clustering at the foot of the tower, an engine started up.

'They're bringing the crane,' Moira said. 'Let's do it, huh?'

Simon stood up. 'The guitar case?'

'We don't have much time.'

Moira picked up the Martin case and laid it at the edge of the tower. 'You got a prayer for an occasion like this, Si?'

'I'm not even a priest any more,' Simon said. 'I broke my vow of celibacy.'

Moira grinned. She snapped open the chromium hasps. 'In the movies, this is where a weird gust of wind comes out of nowhere and we see all this humble muck take off like a comet.'

She flung back the lid.

Nothing happened.

Moira and Simon started to laugh. Isabel looked at them and shook her head in pity.

'Come on, Aelwyn, you old bastard.' Simon could hear a

kind of hydraulic grinding as the guys down below positioned the platform-crane. 'You can do better than this.'

'Maybe he's shy,' Moira said. 'Anyhow, a Martin guitar needs its case. I'm gonna dump this stuff out and leave it up here, OK?'

She turned the case upside down, emptied out the mess of soil and bone and ancient wood-dust. 'Good luck, Aelwyn,' she said. Her voice softened. 'Davey.'

There was a clink.

Amid the human and vegetable debris lay something dull and metallic.

Simon picked it up.

It looked like a very old, mainly toothless dog comb. The early coppery sun shone through the gaps in the metal.

Simon and Isabel watched, more than a little perplexed, as Moira fell to her knees in the ancient dust and began to weep.

Overhead, many miles from the sea, a seagull keened.

Closing Credits

I t doesn't get any easier, does it?

I thought I was never going to sort this one out. In the end my wife, Carol, spent nearly three weeks working over the manuscript, editing, ironing out anomalies and helping to unscramble awful complexities of plot.

As I'm even more paranoid than Tom Storey, dozens of other people were consulted about the feasibility of various aspects of *December*. They include my editor at Pan Macmillan, Simon Spanton, who is reassuringly familiar with the area of operations, and my agent, Andrew Hewson, whose list of contacts makes Ed Victor look like a recluse.

The historical background is mainly accurate. There *was* a massacre, as described, at Abergavenny Castle in 1175. Thanks to Alun Lenny for putting me on the trail, to Barbara Erskine who covered some of the same ground in *Lady of Hay*, and to the team at Abergavenny Museum for filling in crucial details. The story of the harpist who was the only survivor is an elusive legend.

The most bizarre episode in the novel – the massive and inexplicable Liverpool power failure – is true in virtually every detail, right down to the strange times and dates. Thanks to Graham Nown for providing documentary proof.

The deeper mysteries of the recording studio were unlocked by the unfailingly-helpful Nyx Darke and Keith Skerret at the Manor in Oxfordshire, where the facilities are so good and the surroundings so congenial that producers rarely hang themselves. Tom Gittins of Ampex happily explained about baking tapes. Thanks also to Phil Barnwell, Neil Bond, Darren Broome and Mal Pope.

And to Bobbie Barnwell, lead singer of Ida Red, who talked about the psychology of being in a band.

Other problems were solved and details filled in by Ken Cannings, Jeremy and Sara Davies, Nigel Fullerton, Prof. John Harwood, Mike Kreciala, Trish Reynolds, Fred Slater and A. L. 'Socks' Sockett.

And they say writing is a lonely occupation . . .